Also by Dan Rafferty:

Death on the River Avon

And coming soon

Death in Bath

CW01648038

Reviews of Death on the River Avon:

5 Great read for a great city.*

I really enjoyed this book as it kept me guessing as to what was going to happen next and how the police were going to solve the problem and catch the killer, looking forward to the next one. WJ Alexander, Bath.

5 Accident or murder???*

Detective Inspector Dan Skelton, what a character! Intriguing storyline, I love a crime thriller and couldn't wait to find out what happened. Amazon customer.

5 What a fantastic book!*

This is an absolutely brilliant book! Once you start reading, you cannot stop until you finish it. George, Bristol.

4 A very good first book.*

A few proofreading typos in my first addition, but a very good first thriller by the author and looking forward to the next in 2024. The characters are relatable, and I pictured the scenes and locations easily. An enjoyable read. Brian, UK.

THE AVON ROGUE

First published 2025
This edition published 2025

danrafferty@btinternet.com

Published under licence by Brown Dog Books and
The Self-Publishing Partnership Ltd, 10b Greenway Farm,
Bath Rd, Wick, nr. Bath BS30 5RL, UK

www.selfpublishingpartnership.co.uk

ISBN printed book: 978-1-83952-961-0
ISBN ebook: 978-1-83952-962-7
Audiobook ISBN: 978-1-83952-978-8

Cover design by corshamprint.co.uk
Internal design by Richard Powell

Printed and bound in the UK

This book is printed on FSC® certified paper

MIX
Paper | Supporting responsible forestry
FSC® C013604
www.fsc.org

THE AVON ROGUE

DAN RAFFERTY

BROWN DOG BOOKS

This book is dedicated to my partner of forty-three years,
Ken Davies, an outstanding engineer and my rock

Contents

Chapter One

Detective Chief Inspector Dan Skelton was sitting at his desk on a Friday afternoon in June. It was almost 6 pm and he was feeling tired after a particularly busy week in which he was almost killed twice. On the first occasion, his colleague and friend Detective Sergeant Bill Alexander had saved his life by killing a terrorist, for which Skelton would always be grateful. On the second occasion, Skelton had managed to blind his attacker with a CO2 fire extinguisher. His attacker had raped and murdered two teenage girls and was just about to rape and kill a third victim until Skelton intervened.

Skelton had grown up in Scotland in a small town fifteen miles east of Glasgow. A highly intelligent kid, he did well at school and had the ability to make friends easily. He had always shown an interest in the law and especially in how the police were able to solve a crime. On leaving school, he went to Bath Spa University and studied criminology and three years later, he graduated with a 2.1 degree. He then joined the Metropolitan Police in London as a graduate recruit and after ten years in the force, had risen to the rank of detective chief inspector. Although perfectly happy with his lot in the Met, he yearned to be back in Bath, where he had studied, and a city that he adored.

He was just closing down his laptop when there was a knock on his door and in stepped Bill Alexander. 'A body has just been found in Alexandra Park. It looks like murder, sir.'

Skelton put his face on the desk and cupped his hands behind his head. He remained in that position for several seconds as Alexander stood in the doorway, waiting for instructions. Slowly, Skelton raised his head and leaned back in his chair, his hands still cupped behind his head and neck.

'Bill, I was just coming to get you. I thought we would pop over to the Poultney Arms for a few beers before heading home. If this is a murder, we can forget that drink and that will be the weekend screwed up as well!'

'I'm sorry, Dan, I had just put my jacket on before coming to get you, when the call came in. A young lad walking his dog discovered the body of a man in Alexandra Park a few minutes ago. Uniform are on their way, as is the CSI team, led by Bob Richards.'

Skelton stood up and stretched his arms. 'All right, Bill, let's take your car. With a bit of luck we might be able to have a glass or two later.'

Bath Police Station is situated on Manvers Street, right in the heart of this beautiful Georgian city, which dates back to Roman times. It is only a few minutes from both the train and the bus stations and the magnificent Bath Abbey. Bath is a world heritage city which attracts some six million visitors a year. In addition to all the visitors, there are two universities. Bath and Bath Spa, which bring in a combined 23,000 students. Consequently, the police are kept busy, although serious crimes such as rape and murder are hardly an everyday occurrence.

As usual, DS Alexander was driving, and Skelton was sitting in the front passenger seat. Skelton rarely drove. He would rather walk, which was always a bone of contention with Alexander, who until Skelton's arrival in Bath only three months previously would have been content to have driven everywhere. Walking had never scored highly on Alexander's to-do list, but Skelton had changed that. Skelton seemed obsessed in making sure that Alexander got as much exercise in the job as was possible. Alexander had to concede that in the three months since Skelton's arrival, he had lost two kilos in weight, something which Mrs Alexander had noticed and approved of!

Alexander was a fellow Scotsman, who in his youth had grown up in a tough neighbourhood in Glasgow. Alexander realised that if he was not careful, he could easily end up in jail, just like some of his friends. After an apprenticeship as a tool maker, he joined Strathclyde Police, eventually becoming a detective constable based in Maryhill. This was a very tough division and Alexander had had to learn how to fight dirty just to survive. He met his wife, Laura, when she had been seconded by the Ministry of Defence (naval construction) to work in Glasgow for twelve months. However, she had been born in Bath and had lived there all her life. She had no intention of living in Glasgow. Bill and Laura had visited Bath shortly after they had met and Alexander decided that he would have to move to Bath. This was a decision that he would never regret making.

They were driving up towards Bear Flat, an area of Bath renowned for its artists and poets. Indeed, four of the roads leading off from Bear Flat are known as the poets. These are called Longfellow, Chaucer, Milton and Keats.

Alexander turned left into Shakespeare Drive and accelerated up the steep hill which led to the entrance of Alexandra Park. The park provides stunning views across the whole of Georgian Bath due to its elevated position overlooking the city. A 'road closed' sign had been erected at the park entrance and a uniformed police officer was standing guard. Skelton recognised the young constable; it was Luke Meehan. Alexander pulled up. Skelton lowered the window, 'Are you manning the fort, Luke?'

Meehan smiled at Skelton and said, 'Yes, sir. Inspector Symonds said I was to charge every driver ten pounds for entry.' Skelton laughed.

'I tell you what, Luke, I will give it to him personally, but I don't think he will appreciate me shoving it up his arse!'

Meehan giggled as he moved the signpost from the entrance. 'Yes, sir, I think you best give him the tenner yourself otherwise I might end up directing traffic for the rest of my career!'

Skelton recalled the first few days at Bath Police Station. It had come as something of a shock to his colleagues and the men and woman under his command when he had informed them that he was gay and lived with his partner, Ken. Skelton certainly did not look gay and was not in any way effeminate, a trait that Skelton disapproved of. Perhaps the only clue to his sexuality was the way in which he dressed. All his suits were bespoke and were of the finest quality, as were all the clothes he wore. Hardly a day went by when he was not complimented on how well he was dressed. Whether on duty or off duty, he invariably looked more like a rich businessman or banker rather than a police officer.

Alexander slowly drove into the park and turned left. It was a single lane orbital track, which meant it was one-way traffic. There were several parked cars in the lay-bys, but the owners would not be allowed to leave until every car had been thoroughly searched. In the distance Skelton could see flashing blue lights, and as they got closer he saw four marked police cars and an ambulance, as well as two CSI vans. Inspector Graham Symonds was standing by a large bush with a clipboard in his hands. He would be in charge of the crime scene and would record the names of every officer or civilian that entered or left. He would also keep an inventory of every item that was removed from the scene as potential evidence. Skelton liked Symonds. He was a man who could keep a cool head in even the most trying circumstances.

Skelton got out of the car, just as Dr Challis was pulling up in his Land Rover Discovery behind him. Dr Challis was the Home Office pathologist that Avon and Somerset Constabulary consulted on suspicious deaths. Skelton approached Symonds and said, 'Can you book Bill and me in, as well as Dr Challis, please? Oh, and young Luke Meehan said I had to give you ten pounds entrance fee.'

Symonds smiled and looked at Skelton quizzically. 'I think we will waive the charge as I doubt it won't be worth the pain knowing where you would stick it, sir!'

Skelton laughed. 'Fair enough, Graham, you are getting to know me too well.'

Skelton and Alexander went and joined Dr Challis, who was getting into paper overalls to prevent contamination of the crime scene. Skelton asked Symonds, 'What have you got for us, Graham?'

Symonds looked at his clipboard and said, 'A young lad called Trevor Thomas was walking his dog at approximately 17.45 when the dog ran into this bush behind me. It started barking and even though it's a trained gun dog, it refused to come back despite Trevor blowing his whistle and calling its name. Trevor walked into the bush to find his dog barking at a man who was lying on the ground. He could see that the man was covered in blood and was not moving. He put the dog on its lead and called 999 for an ambulance and the control room alerted us. We were on the scene first and it was obvious to the officers that the man was dead. His throat has been cut but we haven't turned the body over, so there might be other injuries that we can't see. When the paramedic arrived, he confirmed the man deceased at 17.54 and estimated that he had died probably within the last hour. The injuries do not appear to have been self-inflicted and indeed no weapon was found with the body.'

Skelton absorbed the information that Symonds had provided. 'Where is young Trevor now, Graham?'

Symonds was speaking into his radio and when he had finished, he said, 'Trevor called his dad and he and his wife came over straight away. They are waiting in their vehicle, which is that green Range Rover parked just over there.'

Skelton looked over his shoulder and saw a man in the driver's seat. He guessed that Mrs Thomas was in the back of the vehicle with young Trevor and the dog. 'Send someone to let them know that I will be over to speak to them shortly. I better take a look at the scene so that I know exactly what we are dealing with here.' Alexander handed him a pair of paper overalls, which included a head cover. He quickly pulled them over his shoes and pulled the zip up. 'Right, let's go see what awaits us.'

Skelton was followed closely by Dr Challis and Alexander. Bob Richards, the head of forensic investigations, was standing near the body holding up a white plastic bag into which he was peering. On seeing Skelton approaching, he lowered the bag and said, 'Good evening, sir. This looks like a sex meeting gone horribly wrong if you ask me.'

Skelton lowered his face mask. 'What makes you think that, Bob?' Richards walked over to where Skelton and the others were standing and held open the plastic bag so that they could see what it contained. Richards said, 'I suspect that the victim brought this with him. All it contains is a beach towel, a tube of lube and some condoms. I've searched the body and there is nothing in his pockets. No phone, no ID, no credit cards, no wallet and no keys. It's my guess that the victim had arranged to meet someone here. I don't know if it was a robbery gone wrong or if he was lured here by the killer. Whatever it was, the guy was not expecting trouble that's for sure.'

Skelton thought for a moment and said, 'I think you are probably right, Bob, but it's too early to say for definite. It's possibly a robbery gone wrong given that the killer took all the victim's belongings. On the other hand, the killer may have wanted to remove the guy's phone to prevent us making any connection between him and the victim.'

Alexander coughed and asked, 'But why would the killer take all the victim's possessions but leave the plastic bag?' Skelton rubbed his nose and said, 'Well it could be one of two things. Maybe he was disturbed by the boy's dog and ran off, or perhaps he was deliberately leaving us a clue.'

It was Dr Challis who spoke next. 'But why would he leave a clue like that? It seems to me that he's done his best to make it difficult to identify the victim.'

Skelton shrugged his shoulders and said, 'Who knows?'

Skelton took a deep breath and looked at Richards. 'What's your view on the forensics so far, Bob?'

Richards placed the plastic bag gently on the ground. 'Well, we are of course conducting a fingertip search around the locus and when we remove the body, we will examine the site in minute detail. But interestingly, on looking closely at what footprints we have discovered so far, I can be pretty sure that the victim made some as we can easily match them to those distinct trainers he is wearing. The other footprints have made no distinctive marks, which could suggest that the killer had covered his shoes, suggesting that he is very much forensically aware.'

Skelton touched Dr Challis on the elbow and said, 'Would you take a look at the body, Doctor, and let us have your initial thoughts?'

Dr Challis carried his bag over to the body and carefully put it down. Skelton and Alexander watched and saw that there was a great deal of blood on the ground next to the victim's head. The victim's trousers and underpants were down to his ankles. He was lying on his stomach so it was not easy to get a clear view of the man's face, but Skelton reckoned he was in his mid-fifties. 'Come on, Bill, let's wait outside for the doctor to finish. Bob let me have a summary of your findings in the morning. We will have a team talk at nine, but if you find anything significant, call me straight away. As soon as the doctor is finished, take the victim's fingerprints and see if we can identify him from those. It's too early for anyone to have reported him missing. If the guy lived on his own that's going to mean that it will take even longer for someone to realise that he's gone missing.'

Skelton and Alexander had removed their forensic overalls and had been busy making arrangements for the rest of the murder squad to be called in. Officers had been detailed to conduct house to house enquiries. Others were busy interviewing potential witnesses who had been in the park. Cars were being searched before being allowed to leave the park. All CCTV cameras in and around the park were to be checked in the hope that they would pick up both the victim and his killer. DC Ross Turnbull was heading back to the police station to make a plea on social media for any information that could identify the victim and his killer.

Eventually Dr Challis emerged from the bushes and started taking off his forensic overalls. As he did so, he addressed the two detectives. 'Well, gentlemen, the victim was in his mid-fifties, I would say. It looks like a commando-style killing. He was stabbed in the heart from behind and his attacker was a good deal taller than the victim. I would say that the killer grabbed the victim by the jaw and covered his mouth using his left hand, brought the knife downwards over the victim's right shoulder and stabbed him with significant force to the heart. He then pulled out the knife, which would have caused a lot of blood to spurt from the wound and that would have undoubtedly sprayed onto the hand and arm of the attacker. He has then slit the victim's throat, causing even more blood spillage. The knife was probably quite long and had a serrated edge to it. He almost decapitated the poor fellow. There are no defensive wounds on his hands, which would indicate complete surprise. There are no indications of any sexual activity having taken place. It's my hunch that the victim had been expecting to engage in a homosexual encounter, hence the beach towel and the condoms. I think he had willingly dropped his trousers and underwear and was expecting that the killer was simply putting on a condom before engaging in sex. The absence of any defensive wounds confirms my conclusion. The killer would have been heavily bloodstained, so I would not be at all surprised if he changed his clothes before leaving the bushes. After all, as I understand it, the park was fairly busy and the site of a bloodstained man would have caused alarm and would almost certainly have been reported to the police.'

Skelton gave the command that the body be handed over to Bob Richard's team, who would carefully tape it for hairs, fibres and any possible DNA evidence before being taken away to the mortuary.

Skelton had made a note of Dr Challis's initial findings. He had not yet made up his mind if it was a robbery gone wrong or pre-meditated murder. However, his instincts were telling him that the victim had been lured there and the absence of defensive wounds suggested that the killer had surprised his victim, giving him no opportunity to defend himself. No witnesses had so far reported any screams or shouting, which again pointed to the victim having been taken completely by surprise. It was agreed that Dr Challis would conduct the autopsy at nine o'clock on Monday morning.

Skelton headed off in the direction of the green Range Rover and he could see the man at the wheel was talking on his phone. The man saw Skelton approaching and ended his call, opened the door and got out. He was aged about forty, tall and good looking. He was wearing a blue Polo long sleeved shirt and white Chino slacks and an expensive looking pair of brown brogue shoes. This was clearly a wealthy individual.

'Are you Mr Thomas?' Skelton asked politely. The man was closing the Range Rover door and was looking at Skelton intently.

'Yes, I am David Thomas and I'm Trevor's father, the boy who found the man's body.'

'Mr Thomas, I am Detective Chief Inspector Dan Skelton of Avon and Somerset Police.' Skelton held out his hand and the men shook hands. 'Mr Thomas, this must have been a terrible experience for young Trevor. How is he? Do you think he needs some counselling to help him cope?'

Mr Thomas folded his arms across his chest and looked Skelton up and down. 'No, Inspector, that will not be necessary. My wife there in the back sitting with Trevor is actually a doctor. She is a GP here in Bath and if Trevor needs any help my wife will be right there for him. But Trevor is a very resilient lad and I don't think this will give him any nightmares or whatever. I took him deer stalking when he was just ten years old and he killed a stag with his first shot. When the game keeper slit the stag's throat to drain the blood, Trevor was right by his side. He also comes game shooting with me, so he's seen plenty of dead things, Inspector.'

Skelton shook his head slightly, put his right hand on his jaw and said, 'Even so, Mr Thomas, this was the body of a man who we believe was murdered and had his throat cut. You will have to keep a close eye on him just in case he bottles it up.'

Thomas lowered his hands and smiled. 'Thank you, Inspector. My wife and I will certainly be keeping a close watch on him. I take it you want to have a word with him?'

Skelton rested his hand on the bonnet of the Range Rover and said, 'Yes, if I could have a few minutes with Trevor I would very much appreciate that. You and Dr Thomas are entitled to be present if you so wish. But Trevor is not a suspect and is not in any trouble, Mr Thomas.'

Thomas was staring closely into Skelton's eyes, smiled and said, 'I know the law well, Inspector. You see I am a lawyer but I don't practice criminal law. I specialise in commercial conveyancing and contract law. Let's ask Trevor what he wants to do.'

Thomas opened the rear door of the Range Rover and said, 'Amanda darling, this is Chief Inspector Dan Skelton. He would like to have a word with Trevor about what he found earlier.'

Dr Thomas slid out of her seat and got out. Skelton reckoned she too was around forty and about 5'10" tall. She was wearing a pretty summer dress and her hair was tied in a bun. Despite the seriousness of the situation, she was immensely calm and very self-assured. She held out her right hand and said in a very cultured voice, 'Inspector Skelton I'm sorry that we have had to meet in such tragic circumstances. Dr Amanda Thomas at your service.'

Skelton took the doctor's proffered hand and shook it warmly. 'Dr Thomas, it's an honour to meet you and I am sorry that we have had to detain you here, but I would just like a little chat with Trevor whilst it's still fresh in his mind. I won't take a formal statement this evening, but I will have to do that in the next day or two.'

Skelton heard the other rear door of the Range Rover closing shut and a second or two later young Trevor emerged around the bonnet. As he approached, Skelton guessed him to be about maybe fifteen years old. He had the good looks of his parents and was at least an inch taller than Skelton's 5'10". His skin was well tanned and his long blond hair would probably be due for a trim when the school holidays finished.

His father smiled at him and said, 'Trevor, come and meet Inspector Skelton. He needs to have a word about what you saw earlier.'

Trevor approached Skelton in a confident manner, his intense blue eyes emitting both intelligence and warmth. Skelton stepped forward, thrusting out his right hand and giving Trevor a very warm smile. 'Hi Trevor, I'm Dan Skelton. Sorry to meet you under these circumstances and I am very grateful for what you did back there.' Trevor gripped Skelton's hand very firmly but warmly and said, 'It's a pleasure to meet you, Mr Skelton. How can I help?'

The boy was incredibly mature for his age. He seemed more like a twenty-year-old. The boy was muscular and clearly attended the gym regularly and no doubt had a few hobbies. Skelton guessed that he probably played rugby, a game which was closer to his heart than football, which held no appeal for him whatsoever.

'Trevor, I need to spend a few minutes with you going over what you saw earlier. We can do it with your mum and dad present or we can go for a walk on our own if you would prefer that. Whatever you are most comfortable with suits me fine.'

Trevor smiled and said, 'Is it okay if we take the dog for a walk? His last walk kind of got cut short.'

Skelton who absolutely adored dogs suddenly remembered that Inspector Symonds had mentioned that the boy had a gundog. Skelton had three black Labradors which were all gundogs and which Skelton had trained himself to the highest possible standard. Skelton noticed the whistle hanging on a lanyard around the boy's neck.

'Yes of course you can bring the dog. What's its name?' The boy was already walking purposefully to the rear of the Range Rover.

'He's called Johnny and he's nearly two years old.' The boy opened the tailgate door and out jumped a black Labrador, tail wagging in greeting. The dog came running around to say hello to Dr and Mr Thomas and then went over to Skelton to sniff him out. The dog immediately scented Skelton's dogs on his clothes and Skelton wasted no time in getting down and gave the dog several hugs. The dog sensed that Skelton was a new friend and wagged his tail furiously.

Skelton was beaming with pleasure to see this young family enjoying the dog as part of the family, just as Skelton and his partner Ken regarded their dogs as their family. Skelton stood up from patting the dog and laughed. 'Well this is a pleasure for me. I have three black labs which I trained myself as gundogs.'

Mr Thomas was smiling at this news. 'Really? Where do you shoot, Mr Skelton?' Skelton rested against the wing of the Range Rover.

'Please just call me Dan. I have shot all over the country but my favourite shoots are in Devon, where you can almost guarantee some seriously high pheasants.'

Mr Thomas held out his hand and said, 'Dan, it's a pleasure to meet you and please call me David, and my wife is Amanda.'

The adults shook hands again, instantly recognising that a new friendship has just been created. Trevor had put Johnny on the sit command and the dog was happily sitting at his master's right-hand side, slightly behind his foot, waiting patiently for his next command.

Despite having found a dead body, Trevor seemed far from concerned about what he had seen, but Skelton needed to gently coax the boy to try and remember as much detail as possible. In a way, the murder scene itself was almost irrelevant so far as Trevor was concerned. Skelton's forensic team would go over that with a fine-tooth comb and Dr Challis had already told him how the man had been killed. What Skelton needed to tease from Trevor was what he had heard and seen before his dog had discovered the body.

Skelton had suggested that he, Trevor and of course Johnny, the Labrador, should head off in the opposite direction from the murder scene. Trevor asked his mum and dad to wait in the Range Rover. The parents immediately gave their consent and so Skelton led the way.

Alexandra Park is quite large and very popular with families and dog walkers. It regularly hosts concerts and is a big attraction on Guy Fawkes night when a huge fireworks display takes place. It has a tennis court and an outdoor lawn bowls green with six rinks. The park is always busy unless the weather is bad. Today was Friday and the weather had been hot and sunny, so the park would have been fairly busy. There are many trees in the park as well as substantial bushes which both dogs and young children love to explore.

'So, tell me, Trevor, how old are you and what school do you go to?' Trevor was watching Johnny as he carefully worked the bushes just ahead of him.

'I hope he doesn't find another body in that bloody bush!' Skelton had to laugh. This was a young man, not a boy, and his parents had done a wonderful job in bringing him up. 'Well, Trevor, I have three black labs and they have never yet found a man's body, so you with just Johnny are highly unlikely to ever find another one, but if you do, be sure to let me be the first to know!' They both laughed. 'So, are you going to tell me your age and school?'

Trevor gave a lop-sided grin. 'Actually, it's my birthday next Friday, I will be sixteen. We are having a party at the house. You can come if you like and bring the dogs. We've got plenty of room.'

Skelton smiled and said, 'Thank you, Trevor, that's very kind, but can we just concentrate at the moment on my questions as I've got a lot to do.'

Trevor stopped walking and looked at Skelton. 'Sorry, Dan. I guess I'm not concentrating as well as I should be. It's just that the last thing I expected to find today was a dead body.' 'Hey, are you okay buddy? If you want, we can go back and sit with your mum and dad?'

Trevor looked Skelton in the eyes and said, 'No it's okay. I will dine out on this for years to come. And to answer your question, I attend Beeching Cliff School.'

Skelton had guessed the answer. Beeching Cliff was an outstanding school with a high percentage of its pupils going on to university to study medicine, engineering, law and other such notable professions. Skelton had noted down Trevor's date of birth, address and mobile phone number as well as that of his parents.

Trevor said that he had entered the park at around 17.00, having walked the dog from home when he had left at close to 16.45. He had not seen anything unusual nor had heard any shouting or screaming. He was certain that he had not seen the deceased until Johnny had refused to leave the bush, which was most unusual and had caused him to go into the bush after him and discover the body.

'So, you don't remember seeing the dead man, before you found him in the bushes? Did you see anyone going into the bushes or coming out?'

Trevor thought for several seconds and said, 'Well no, I never saw anyone going into the bushes or coming out, but I did see a guy out jogging. I had sat down on the grass and was playing with Johnny, so I was not really paying much attention. But I remember looking up and I saw a young guy jogging towards us, but he sort of changed direction, and carried on down towards the exit.' Skelton noted this down.

'Which exit was he headed for? I can't remember what the Avenue is called but it's the one near the bowling green.' This was the entrance which Skelton and Alexander had used when they arrived earlier and is the only vehicular entrance or exit to the park.

'Can you describe the man to me, his age and build and what he was wearing?' Trevor put his whistle in his mouth and gave two sharp blows. Johnny, who had gone on a bit ahead, immediately came running back and Trevor called him to heel. The dog instinctively ran to Trevor's right side and walked behind him. Skelton admired their companionship and had never been so content in conducting a murder enquiry.

'Let's see, I would say the guy was in his early twenties, but he was wearing a hoodie, so I didn't see much of his face, but I don't think he had a beard. He was tall that's for sure, probably about six-four and well built. The guy must work out a lot judging by his body, and probably plays rugby. One thing I did notice before he sort of changed direction was that he seemed a bit out of breath. Maybe he had been out jogging too long and was a bit tired. And he had a backpack on his back.'

Skelton had noted all this down. 'Tell me what he was wearing, Trevor?'

'He was wearing a black top with a hood on it and black bottoms. He was in white trainers but I don't know which make. There are so many now but they didn't look like they were that expensive or new.'

Skelton and Trevor walked back to the Range Rover with Johnny dutifully following behind. Dr and Mr Thomas got out as they arrived. 'Well, Trevor has been a great help to me. You should be very proud of him. There is a good chance that he saw the killer and has given me an excellent description of the man. He is bound to show up on CCTV and when he does, we will circulate his image on social media and hopefully we will have his name in no time. I will need to take a formal statement from Trevor in a day or two depending on how busy we are with this enquiry. But I will phone and make an appointment in advance.'

They said their goodbyes and Skelton radioed that the green Range Rover was free to go.

Chapter Two

Alexander drove Skelton back to the police station and parked up. The detectives made their way to the CID office. There were about a dozen officers busy either on the phone or on their computers. Ross Turnbull had just put down the phone when he saw Skelton and Alexander enter the room.

'Sir, we got the jogger on CCTV. The bowling club apparently have him jogging towards the club and the Cooperative store on the corner of Shakespeare Avenue, have him coming towards them from the direction of the park. The film is on its way right now so it should be here in a few minutes.'

Skelton began taking off his suit jacket. 'That's great news, Ross, well done. Hopefully we will have this guy identified pronto and we can go and arrest him. With a bit of luck, we will have some good forensics that can nail the bastard. Talking of which, any sign of Bob Richards?'

Turnbull answered. 'He's gone to the mortuary with the body, so you won't see him for ages. He did, however, send us the victim's fingerprints and Peter Lowik is working on them now. Hopefully we will get a match any time now and we can discover who the poor guy was. Some poor woman is probably sitting at home now wondering where the blazes he is.'

Skelton was holding his jacket over his shoulder. 'Right, I will be in my office. As soon as Peter gets the result on the prints send him in. And as soon as the CCTV film arrives, I want to see it.'

Skelton was on the phone to his partner Ken, explaining what was happening and that it was unlikely that he would be home until the early hours of the morning. He was just putting down the phone when there was a knock on the door and Alexander led in Turnbull and Lowik.

'What news, men?' Lowik was an Australian and had been working for Avon and Somerset for over two years. Skelton liked and admired

Lowik for his dedication and professionalism. He also had a great sense of humour, which was a major asset when the pressure was on. Lowik sat on one of the two chairs opposite Skelton.

'Sir, I ran the prints through our system, the MOD, Interpol and every other system available to us. Nothing! This guy has never been fingerprinted in any country that we have access to. He is a John Doe at the moment. Our only chance now is if someone recognises him from his photograph from the CCTV. But the problem is that we have so far not been able to recognise him from any of the CCTV recordings, but we are still working on that. If we can't find him on the CCTV footage, then we might have to release a photograph of his face taken at the mortuary.'

Skelton stood up and walked across the room to the window. It was black outside and it was now 10.15 pm. 'Well that's a shame about the prints. It would have been helpful to have got a positive ID on the poor bugger. I don't really want to put out a face picture of him lying dead in the mortuary unless we really have to. I want you guys to go over the CCTV footage again and see if you can get an image of the victim. Make that a priority.' Skelton started towards the door. 'Right, let's go take a look at what we've got.'

DC Janet Griffin, another rising star in the police, was staring intently at the screen in front of her. Skelton got down on his knees so that he could get a good view. 'Right sir, we have two lots of footage taken this afternoon at about an hour before and an hour after the body was found. More work needs to be done to it to determine when both the victim and the killer entered the park. At the moment we have not been able to find the victim on the film.'

Skelton cleared his throat and said, 'Yes, so I understand. I have given instructions that the film is to be reviewed again just in case we missed him first time around. He may have been wearing a jacket over the shirt that we found him in. So as soon as we have looked at the jogger, get back to trying to identify the victim.'

The officers were standing at Griffin's desk, staring at the computer screen. The CCTV film was currently frozen. 'Run the film please, Janet.' The detectives watched intently as the images appeared on the screen. Suddenly a man dressed in black and wearing a hoodie as described by young Trevor appeared on the screen.

'Bingo, we've got him. You can't ID him with the hoodie up but get it on social media and someone will put a name to the face.' Peter Lowik was breathing heavily.

'Oh fuck, sir. He's one of us.'

Skelton was looking incredulous. 'What's that supposed to mean?'

'That is Police Constable Fergus Walsh, sir. I would know him anywhere. We were at the police training college together. He lives here in Bath and works out of Bristol. He cannot possibly be the murderer, sir. He is as clean as a whistle. He must have just happened to be jogging in the park at the time of the murder.'

Skelton got off his knees, stood up and stretched his arms. Seconds ago, he thought he had identified the prime suspect, only for Peter Lowik to tell him that the guy was a police officer. Of course, it was perfectly possible that he was the killer, but Lowik reckoned that the guy was one hundred percent trustworthy and just happened to be in the wrong place at the right time.

'Right, Peter, I am re-assigning objectives here. Janet, I want you to find the victim on the CCTV footage and as soon as you do, get it on to social media straight away.'

Griffin nodded her head and said, 'Right, sir, I am on it now.'

Skelton leaned on Griffin's desk and said, 'Peter, you know this guy Fergus Walsh, so you will be working with Bill and me on this. We are going to have to interview him right away. Given that he was in the park earlier he could not have been working, but of course he could be on night shift now. If he is not at work then he is either out socialising or at home. Let's go into my office and I want you to call him and we need to record the call just in case he is the killer. Remember, Peter, that just because he is a cop that does not automatically mean that he is innocent.'

Lowik looked slightly embarrassed and said, 'Yes I know that, sir, but I met him on my first day at the academy. He and I are good friends. It's just that I can't put Fergus down as a killer.'

Skelton was watching Lowik's face closely. 'Peter, we are both police officers and we must be professional at all times. I know that this guy is your friend but we have to treat him for the moment as a suspect. It will probably turn out that he just happened to have gone out for a run this afternoon. Unfortunately, it just happens to have been at the time when a guy gets killed. Our young witness describes very clearly that he saw a guy dressed in black wearing a hoodie running away from very close to where he found the body. He also says that when the guy saw him, he slightly changed direction. Another interesting observation that he made was that the jogger was slightly out of breath. Now that could easily be explained that he had been running for some time, or it could have been caused by the fact that the guy had just plunged a knife into a man's heart and cut his throat, almost decapitating him into the bargain.'

A few minutes later, Skelton was sitting on his chair in his office. The two chairs facing his desk were occupied by Alexander and Lowik. 'Right, Peter, make the call. you know what to say.'

Lowik had the phone set to record. He scrolled down his contacts list and pressed call. The phone rang twice and was answered. 'Hey Pete, what you up to?'

Lowik rocked slightly in the chair and said, 'Hi mate, where are you?'

Walsh replied, 'I'm just chilling out at home. You fancy going for a drink somewhere?'

Lowik looked over towards Skelton and Skelton said, 'Tell him.'

Lowik took a deep breath. 'Look, mate, this is an official call. A man was murdered in Alexandra Park this afternoon and we've got you on CCTV jogging out of the park. This is difficult for me, but you do appreciate that we need to treat you as a suspect.'

Skelton and Alexander heard the reply. 'Bloody hell, Pete, yes of course I went for a run this afternoon but I fucking never killed anyone.'

Lowik finished the call. It had been agreed that the three detectives would leave immediately and visit Walsh at his home address. Before leaving there was a knock at the door and Janet Griffin walked in holding a photograph.

'We've got a pic of the victim, sir. You were right. We missed him on the first review of the footage. He had been wearing a dark wind cheater over his shirt.'

Griffin handed the picture to Skelton, who studied it carefully before handing it to Alexander and Lowik. 'Good work, Janet. We will hold on to this as we're just off to interview the jogger. Have you put it on social media yet?' Griffin was heading back out the door. 'It's being done as we speak. Hopefully, we should get a response pretty quick, as it's a good quality image.'

Lowik had driven them to Walsh's house. It was a three-bed semi-detached on Entry Hill Drive in Coombe Down. These were expensive houses and the first thing that Skelton asked when Lowik gave him the address was, 'How can your mate afford a house up there, Peter?'

Lowik glanced to his left where Skelton was sitting in the front passenger seat. 'He lives with his mum, sir.'

Skelton then asked, 'What about his father?'

Lowik thought for a second. 'I asked him about his family when we first met. He told me that he's an only child and that his dad walked out when he was seventeen. Must have been tough on his mum. She's a lovely lady, cooks a real mean chicken curry. She works for a law firm in Bath. I think she is PA to the senior partner.'

As Lowik drove, Skelton digested this information. Not an uncommon thing for a husband to up sticks, being fed up with domestic responsibilities or maybe having met a younger woman. It was surprising just how many young adults ended up in trouble owing to the lack of a father to give them guidance and discipline. Skelton knew from personal experience that most of the young lads and girls that he had arrested came from broken homes, having been brought up by mothers on their own.

It was 10.30 pm when the car pulled up to the house. A blue Audi was parked outside. Lowik pointed to it and said, 'That's Fergus's pride and joy.'

The officers got out and Lowik led them to the door. He pressed the doorbell and it was almost immediately opened. Skelton was standing to the right of Lowik and Alexander was behind them. Skelton noted that Walsh was indeed a big guy, at least 6'4", and probably weighed about fifteen stone. Lowik spoke, 'Fergus, this is DCI Skelton and DS Alexander.'

Walsh nodded his head in the direction of Alexander and Skelton said, 'May we come in please, Fergus?'

Walsh stood aside and said, 'Sure, come on in and have a seat.'

They were seated in the sitting room. It was tastefully furnished. It consisted of two armchairs and a couch. A large flat screen TV was mounted on the wall and an expensive looking sound system was underneath it. A coffee table with some magazines stood in front of the couch. On the mantlepiece were numerous photographs. There was one of a bride and groom, presumably Walsh's mum and dad. There were numerous pictures of Walsh from being a baby to where, in pride of place, there was one of him in police uniform on graduation day. Walsh appeared quite calm but slightly nervous. There were no telltale signs of panic or discomfort that a trained detective can easily pick up on. Skelton had almost concluded that Walsh was innocent, but he could not discount the fact that the only person that young Trevor had seen was him running away from the murder scene. It was Skelton's job to prove him innocent or guilty.

Skelton began. 'Fergus, there are some procedures that we have to complete. We know that you were in Alexandra Park this afternoon as you have confirmed to Peter. What I need you to do is to tell us exactly what you did and who you saw whilst you were there. We need to eliminate you as a suspect and to do that, we will require to search your house and take away the clothes you were wearing, including your backpack and running shoes for forensic examination. Are you agreeable to us doing that?'

Walsh was seated on one of the armchairs, Lowik occupied the other and Skelton and Alexander had the couch. Walsh's hands rested on the arm rests and he appeared quite composed.

'Yes, sir, you have my full cooperation and I should tell you that we have a garage across the road and I will give you the key to that so that it can be searched as well.'

Skelton noted that Walsh was giving the clearest indication that they were unlikely to find anything in the house or garage that would implicate him in the murder. So either he was totally innocent or was confident that he had successfully removed anything that would forensically link him to the murder. Skelton glanced again at the picture of Walsh in his best uniform and could not help feeling that this young police officer had just been unfortunate to have taken a run past a crime scene on his day off from work.

Walsh explained that he regularly ran in Alexandra Park as he had often played there as a kid, and that he could run there without having to drive. He also worked out in the gym three times a week. Today he had spent the day on domestic chores such as doing the laundry and ironing his shirts for work, as well as cleaning the house. He had also done the weekly shop at Sainsbury's and had filled the car with petrol on the way back. At about 15.45 he had left the house in his running gear and had taken his backpack, in which he kept a set of waterproofs, a dry towel and a bottle of water.

He ran down Entry Hill, which took him on to the main thoroughfare, known as the Wellsway, and had turned right at the Cooperative store into Shakespeare Avenue. He entered the park and ran past the bowling green. He did five circuits of the park and would normally do six, but it had been a hot day and he decided that five was enough for the day. He had not seen anything unusual take place nor had he had any reason to be suspicious of anybody he had seen. On being shown the picture of the victim, he had stared at it for several seconds and had concluded that he thought the man had been sitting on a park bench and he probably passed by him a few times. He believed that he had passed the bench later but the man had gone. He did not see anyone with the man nor could he remember seeing the man anywhere else in the park.

He could also remember seeing the young lad with the black Labrador and readily admitted that he did slightly change direction when he saw him, explaining that he did not want to entice a playful chase with the Labrador, and it was at that precise time that he decided to end the run.

On getting home, he had taken off his clothes and thrown them in the washing machine but had not washed them, as they did not constitute a full load. He had then showered and had dinner and listened to some music. He had not watched the TV and so was unaware of the murder until Lowik's call.

Walsh handed over the soiled clothes, his running shoes and backpack and invited them to search the house and garage, which they did. As they emerged from the garage, Skelton said to Walsh, 'We need to search your car and I'm afraid I will have to ask you to give me your phone. You realise of course, that your phone will either incriminate you as a suspect, or it will confirm that you had nothing to do with the killing.'

Walsh pulled his phone from his trouser pocket and handed it to Skelton. 'Sir, you will need the code number to access the phone. It's 4418.'

Skelton made a note of the code number. Walsh excused himself and went into the house to get the car keys. He returned seconds later and gave the keys to Alexander. Alexander and Lowik searched the car and, as expected, it contained nothing of interest.

The officers bid goodnight to Walsh and got into the car, and as Lowik pulled away Alexander sitting in the back said, 'Well one thing's for sure. He's not the murderer. I'd bet my pension on that!'

Chapter Three

They were driving back to the police station when Skelton's phone rang. He glanced at the screen and said, 'Yes, Janet.'

It was Janet Griffin, hopefully with some news on the victim. 'Sir, I think we have got a positive ID on the victim. It would appear to be a one Stephen Cox, fifty-two years of age who lived in a small hamlet outside the town of Corsham in Wiltshire. He was due to have met his brother for a drink this evening but never showed up. His brother Harry began to get worried when he didn't arrive, and his calls to his phone were going straight to voice mail. So, he went to Stephen's house but he was not at home. He let himself in as he has a spare key, but the house was empty and his car is missing. Harry went back to the pub just in case Stephen had been delayed. A friend in the pub was on social media and saw our appeal for help. Harry called our number and he confirms that the picture is definitely that of his brother.'

Skelton gave the thumbs up sign to Alexander and Lowik. 'Janet, we are almost at the station now. Get the family support officer to meet us in my office. Call back Mr Cox and tell him to meet us outside his brother's house in about thirty minutes. Make sure you have the address and directions and notify Wiltshire of our presence. Ask them to put a guard on the house until tomorrow morning. Find out the make and registration plate of Stephen Cox's car and circulate it. My gut feeling is that it's parked somewhere close to Alexandra Park.'

The three detectives headed straight for Skelton's office to find PC Jim Broadbent waiting for them. He was the family liaison officer who would help and comfort the victim's family as best he could.

'Hi, Jim, thanks for hanging around for us. We all knew it would only be a matter of time before we got a positive ID. We best take two cars. Jim, you go with Peter and I will go with Bill. There is no point in taking a forensic team with us as I doubt if there will be anything worthwhile to find. Let's go, boys.'

Chapter Four

The hamlet that they were looking for, Broadstone, was located on the outskirts of Corsham and just before Gastard, a small village just a few miles from Melksham, a large market town. As he drove down the hill out of Corsham, Alexander slowed the car down and he saw the signpost indicating that they had arrived at their destination. 'Look Bill, there's a guy standing by that door. It must be the brother. Park across the road.' Alexander parked up and Lowik followed.

All four officers got out and Skelton led them towards the man standing by the front door of the house. Skelton had taken his warrant card from his inside jacket pocket and was holding it up so that the man could see it. 'Are you Harry Cox, sir?' The man looked worried and was nervously smoking a cigarette.

'Yes, I'm Harry Cox.'

Skelton held out his warrant card and said, 'I'm Detective Chief Inspector Skelton and this officer here is Jim Broadbent, our family liaison officer.' Skelton pointed to Broadbent, who nodded his head.

Harry Cox looked very similar to his brother but just a little older and slightly heavier. Cox's eyes darted from officer to officer and said, 'We best go inside and perhaps you can explain what's been going on. I've been worried sick all evening and nobody has explained to me what the hell's happened to our Stephen.'

The house was a small cottage, no doubt constructed for stone masons that worked in the Bath stone quarries in Corsham more than three centuries ago. The front door opened into a small kitchen, which led into a slightly larger sitting room looking out onto a reasonably sized garden. This would have been very useful for growing vegetables in times gone by. There were two small bedrooms upstairs and a family bathroom. It contained an old-fashioned bath with a shower head above the bath.

They were standing in the kitchen around the table, which had four chairs neatly arranged around it. 'Mr Cox, please take a seat.' Skelton pulled out a chair for him and one for himself. He indicated that Alexander and Broadbent should take the other two leaving Lowik to stand by the door. When they were all seated, Skelton gently cleared his throat and began. 'Mr Cox, I have here a photograph of a man that was taken this afternoon in Alexandra Park in Bath. I would like you to carefully look at this picture and tell me if it's your brother?'

Skelton carefully handed over the photograph and Cox stared at it and said, 'Yes that's my brother Steven, there is no doubt about that. But what was he doing in the park and where is he now? Is he all right or has there been an accident or something?' Cox was becoming quite emotional and agitated. Broadbent lent over and placed his hand on Cox's shoulder and squeezed it gently and then he took his hand and gently held it as Skelton continued.

'Mr Cox, I am afraid there is no easy way to say this. I am sorry to have to tell you that your brother was found dead this afternoon.' Cox burst out in tears and Broadbent was immediately ready with a handkerchief. Skelton waited until Cox had somewhat regained his composure.

'I have to tell you, Harry, that Stephen was murdered and his valuables were taken. We are not sure at the moment if this was a robbery gone wrong or if the killer had intended to kill your brother by luring him there. He was found in some bushes, so it was not a random attack, and there were no signs that Stephen had tried to run away or defend himself.'

Broadbent had stood up and found a glass in a cupboard and poured Cox a glass of water. Cox gratefully sipped the water whilst Broadbent continued to hold his hand and mumble support.

'Harry, please tell us about Stephen. Was he married, does he have kids and where did he work?' Cox had found some inner resolve. He knew that he needed to help the police in any way that he could so that they could find his brother's killer.

'No, Stephen never married and he never had kids either. You see Stephen was gay but he never had a partner as such. He had had a few boyfriends over the years but nothing serious. The thing is he likes younger guys. Not kids you understand. He just liked young hunky guys in their twenties. He used some dating app on his phone and I warned him several times to be careful. I mean what's a young guy going to see in a fifty-two-year-old, grey-haired man?'

Alarm bells were sounding in Skelton's brain. The missing phone was without doubt taken by the killer in order to prevent the police tracing him.

'Do you know if Stephen had arranged to meet someone today, or has he mentioned anyone recently that he's been seeing?'

Cox sipped some more water. 'No, he hasn't mentioned meeting anyone for quite a while. He got a nasty chest infection a couple of months back and it took six weeks to clear up. He was even off work for three weeks as he was that poorly. He certainly never mentioned anything about meeting anyone today. I know that he was off work today as he works shifts in the rubber factory in Melksham. Depending on his shifts, we always meet once a week in the Great Western pub in Corsham for a drink. It's only a ten-minute walk up the road for Stephen, and even less for me. We were supposed to meet at eight this evening, but of course he never showed up. I tried calling him, but it just went to voicemail. I got really worried and walked down here at about nine-thirty. The first thing I noticed was that his car was missing. I have a spare key to the house, so I let myself in and as you can see, he's not here and nothing has been disturbed.'

'Harry, is it all right if Peter there takes a look around just in case there is something that might give us a clue?' Cox looked up at Lowik and said, 'Go ahead, young man, and I hope you do find something.'

There was a knock on the door and Alexander got up to answer it. A minute later he was back. 'Uniform from Wiltshire have arrived. They will post a guard until ten in the morning, if you still think we need it?' Skelton thought for a minute. 'Let's see if Peter turns up anything, but it's my guess that the killer has never been in the house and I don't think that he had ever met Stephen until this afternoon. So, it's going to be a complete waste of time in turning it over to forensics.' He did not mention that it would also be a waste of money, a valuable resource that diminished in every new budget given to him by the chief constable.

Lowik had concluded his search and had found nothing of interest. Skelton had enquired whether or not Stephen owned a laptop and was informed that he did not.

As they were winding matters up, it had been agreed that Broadbent would collect Cox at 11.00 am in the morning and take him to the mortuary to formally identify the body. Skelton had picked up the spare keys to Stephen's car, which would make matters a lot easier when it was recovered.

Chapter Five

Alexander was driving Skelton back to Bath following the meeting with Harry Cox. It was just past midnight as they left Corsham and headed back towards Bath. 'So, Dan, what do you think of it so far?'

Skelton was deep in thought and it was several seconds before he spoke. 'Well, Bill, there are a few things which are troubling me that's for sure. First of all, our only known suspect is the only person seen near the murder scene by young Trevor and was seen running away from the direction from where the body was found. If it wasn't for the fact that he is a police officer, and has been so cooperative, we would probably have arrested him right away. However, everything he told us about him just being out for a run does stack up. Interestingly, he said that he never saw anyone acting suspiciously, which would suggest that he was not trying to steer us away from himself. That may be a smart move, as he knows that we will be checking every inch of CCTV footage from inside and outside the park. If he had said he had seen someone acting suspiciously, and we could not see him on CCTV, then we would have caught him lying. We are going to have to trace everyone that was in the park between three and six and hopefully someone may just have taken a pic that might identify the killer.'

Alexander indicated a left turn at the roundabout on to London Road, they would be back at the station inside ten minutes. 'What about motive, Dan?' Skelton shifted in the passenger seat and said, 'I don't buy Bob Richard's theory that it could have been a robbery gone wrong. I initially had an open mind, but when Dr Challis said that there were no defensive stab wounds, that changed my thinking. I think that Stephen was lured to the park by the killer who he must have met online. It has to be one of the dating apps like Gaydar, Tinder or Grinder. I think that over time, Stephen has been chatting to the killer online and had built up a degree of trust. It's perfectly possible that the relationship somewhat blossomed and Stephen made contact by phone.'

Alexander rubbed his jaw and asked, 'Why do you say that, Dan?'

Skelton cleared his throat, 'I think that the killer is a much younger man than Stephen, after all, his brother said that he liked younger hunky lads. The killer convinced Stephen that he wanted to meet up and have sex, hence the reason for Stephen turning up with a towel, condoms and some lube. So, Stephen gets quite excited and drives to Bath and goes into the park, where I think the killer was watching him. They talk on the phone and the killer directs him to sit on a bench near the bush where young Trevor found him. When he is sure that the coast is clear, he tells Stephen to go into the bush and get ready. Now Stephen thinks it's his lucky day and eagerly gets into the bushes and drops his trousers and pants in anticipation.'

Alexander was playing the scene in his mind. 'Then what happens?'

Skelton was also playing the scene over in his own mind. 'Up to this point, they have been talking on the phone. The killer ends the call and makes his way over to the bushes. He enters and sees Stephen waiting for him. He does not have to hide his face and what Stephen sees is a young, good-looking guy which gives him no cause for concern at all. The killer starts to pretend to drop his trousers and put on a condom. But, in fact he is reaching for the knife. In one quick move, he grabs Stephen by the mouth and brings the blade over his right shoulder and stabs him in the heart. He pulls the blade out of his chest and cuts his throat. The poor guy had no chance to defend himself and was dead in a matter of seconds.

'He carefully retrieves the knife, but he must be soaked in blood and can't be seen leaving the park like that, as someone would have called us. So, he cleans himself as best he can, changes his clothes and departs. He somehow blends perfectly into everyday park life and raises no suspicion at all.'

Alexander was parking the car at the police station. He switched off the engine and said, 'You mean just like a jogger, don't you?' Skelton opened the car door and got out, as did Alexander. Skelton closed the door and looked across the roof of the car at Alexander.

'Just like a jogger, Bill, and a pretty switched on jogger at that!'

Chapter Six

The next morning Skelton woke up at 7 am, went to the wardrobe and pulled on his dressing gown. The minute his feet hit the floor, Brenty-Boy gave a loud woof, to let him know he had heard him. He went downstairs to the kitchen where the dogs slept. Brenty-Boy was the oldest at nine, then came his son Josh aged seven and last of all Archie, who was two. The boys greeted him and he gave them all a big hug and let them out into the garden. He put enough water in the kettle for two mugs of tea and switched it on. He picked up the remote control for the TV and switched it on. The news was on. He made the tea and let the boys back into the kitchen and gave them each a Bonio biscuit. He took a mug of tea upstairs to Ken along with two digestive biscuits and went back downstairs.

He took out a KitKat from the fridge, sat at the breakfast bar and watched the news as he drank his tea and ate it. Eventually, the newsreader mentioned the murder in Alexandra Park and that the police were appealing for witnesses. A police news conference was being held at eleven that morning. Skelton had seen enough and went upstairs to shower and shave.

He quietly got dressed, picking out an immaculately ironed blue shirt and a blue pin stripped suit. He carefully put on his gold cufflinks and selected a dark blue tie. He expertly tied a Windsor knot and then took out a starched white handkerchief and carefully placed it in the breast pocket of his suit jacket. He said goodbye to Ken, went downstairs and picked up his iPad and put it in his satchel. He then gave the boys another cuddle, went out the front door and began walking into Bath.

It was another lovely bright morning and it already felt quite warm. Skelton always walked to work if he could. He loved walking in general and the walk into Bath each morning took twenty minutes. He used the time to plan his day as best he could.

The walk down Entry Hill led on to the Wellsway and then Bear Flat. He passed by the cooperative store where the CCTV had captured Walsh on film. He walked a few hundred metres to where there was another pedestrian entrance to Alexandra Park. Skelton stopped and studied it. There was no sign of any CCTV cameras, so the killer could have entered and left from here. He made a note in his mind and walked on. It was eight-thirty when he arrived at the police station. A blue Jaguar was just pulling into the parking space reserved for the superintendent. Skelton stopped and waited for Superintendent Paul Williams to get out of his car.

Williams had his briefcase in hand. Immaculately dressed in his uniform, he would be presiding over the news conference later this morning. 'Good morning, Dan, it's another beautiful day.'

Skelton smiled and said, 'Yes, sir, too bloody good to be working.' They both laughed.

Williams was Skelton's immediate superior, with Chief Superintendent Mike Sawyers in overall charge of the station. He liked both men and they in turn had a lot of respect for him. In the three months he had been at Bath, Skelton had already made a name for himself as a very competent detective and a good leader. Skelton knew that further promotion was his for the taking, but he was more than happy at being a detective chief inspector, which let him concentrate on catching villains rather than preparing budgets and attending innumerable meetings with the Home Office and other such government agencies, which further promotion would entail.

'We have a press conference at eleven this morning Dan. I know that you don't like speaking at them, so give me a full briefing at ten-fifteen and you can stand behind me and watch.'

Skelton nodded his head and said, 'Very good, sir. I will be at your office at ten-fifteen.'

Skelton climbed the stairs to his office, went in and hung his jacket on a wooden hanger. He switched on his computer and walked into the CID room and glanced at his watch, it was 8.35 am. Janet Griffin was sitting at her desk busy hammering away on her keyboard. Ross Turnbull was busy eating a bacon roll, as was DC Chris Spurrey, although Skelton suspected that Spurrey was on his second or third. The man was very tall and solidly built. He was the sort of officer that you could send into a pub fight and it would be all over in seconds.

'Morning, everyone.'

His officers looked up and Turnbull and Spurrey, who both had their mouths full, simply gave a thumbs up. Griffin said, 'Morning sir, it looks like a busy day ahead of us then.'

Skelton parked his bum on the edge of her desk and said, 'Yes, Janet, I think it will be nearly all hands down to the park today. I have to brief the super at ten-fifteen so I want a team talk at nine-thirty, so that we are all up to speed.' Griffin noted down the time and said, 'Right, sir, I will make sure that everybody is here by then.' Skelton stood up, thanked Griffin and headed back to his office.

He had only just sat down when there was a knock on the door and in walked Alexander carrying two bacon rolls. 'Morning, Dan, I thought you could use one of these.'

Skelton gave his friend a big smile and said, 'God bless you, Bill. I will make the tea.'

Chapter Seven

It was exactly 9.30 am when Skelton and Alexander entered the CID room. Every desk was occupied, with the occupant either on the phone or busy at their computer. Skelton noticed Bob Richards leaning over a desk in deep conversation with Ross Turnbull. Alexander called out, 'Right, listen up, everybody, kill the phones. The boss wants an update before he briefs the super in forty-five minutes, then we have a press conference at eleven.'

The officers on the phone quickly finished their calls and a few seconds later there was silence. Skelton cleared his throat and began. 'As you know, folks, a man was found murdered yesterday late afternoon by a young boy called Trevor Thomas. He had been walking his gundog called Johnny when it entered some bushes shortly after five, and started barking and refused to come out. Young Trevor entered the bushes and discovered the body. The victim's trousers and underpants were pulled down to his ankles, we believe in preparation for sex. He had been stabbed in the heart and his throat had been cut. He would have died almost immediately. There were no defensive wounds so he had been caught completely by surprise. We now know that the victim was Stephen Cox, aged fifty-two, who had travelled by car to Bath from Corsham, and we believe at this point in time that the purpose of his visit was to have sex. Stephen was gay but did not have a partner or regular boyfriend. His brother Harry believes that he used a dating app on his mobile phone to arrange to meet young men to have sex with. We do not yet know which app, or indeed apps, that he used as his mobile phone is missing. Obviously, we need to find that phone as it will undoubtedly help lead us to the killer. I suspect, however, that the killer removed the phone for that very reason. He also removed all of Stephen's belongings, in the hope that it would delay us in identifying him. However, we managed to get a good picture of Stephen from CCTV, which

Janet put out on social media yesterday evening, leading to a positive ID from his brother. Formal identification has not yet taken place, but Jim Broadbent is taking the brother to the mortuary this morning to carry out the formalities.

'Young Trevor noticed a jogger dressed in black and wearing a hoodie whilst playing with his dog shortly before finding the body. He said that he saw the man running from the direction of the bushes but could not say for certain that the man had been in the bushes. The man had been running directly towards him but suddenly changed direction. He believes that the man was out of breath, and it's perfectly possible that the reason for that was the fact that he had been jogging for some time on what was a hot afternoon. We obtained a picture of the jogger from CCTV situated at the bowling club in the park and from the Cooperative store on the corner of the Wellsway and Shakespeare Avenue. The jogger was instantly identified by Peter Lowik as being Police Constable Fergus Walsh who is based in Bristol but lives in Bath. We interviewed Walsh last night and he confirmed that he had indeed been out for a run in the park yesterday afternoon. He explained the reason for changing direction when he saw the boy and his dog was that he was tired and had decided to go home rather than do a final circuit of the park. We searched his home and garage, which revealed nothing unusual and we seized his running gear for forensic investigation. At this point in time, we believe that he may just have been in the wrong place at the right time. He claims not to have seen any suspicious activity in the park nor anyone looking suspicious.'

Skelton scanned the room and noticed that most detectives were busy taking notes. 'So far, our enquiries of people that were in the park when the body was discovered have not revealed anything suspicious. The super will be making an appeal on TV this morning for witnesses to come forward and for anyone that took photographs or videos to hand them in. Janet will be making a similar plea on social media. Today, I want us to go to the park and interview everyone that we see. There will be a heavy presence of uniformed officers to reassure the public. I want Ross, Peter and Chris to undertake a detailed search to locate every CCTV camera in and around the park and to obtain the relevant footage, which, to be on the safe side, will be between two-thirty and six. Uniform will be conducting house to house enquiries in the streets that surround the park. Bob, can we have an update please on forensics?'

Bob Richards stood up and said, 'Well, sir, as you rightly said, the killer removed all the victim's personal effects except for a plastic bag, which we assume he had brought along. This contained a beach towel, condoms and some lube. The only footprints that we have identified are those of the victim, but given the fact that the ground is bone dry at the moment, that is not surprising. We did identify a patch of ground next to the body which had been slightly disturbed and it's probably where the killer stood when he struck. There were also some drops of blood there, which may have come off the killer's hands or possibly even the knife. We have not found the knife, which Dr Challis believes to be quite long with a serrated edge to it. As you know, it is unusual for the killer not to dispose of the knife, so we will continue searching for it. If I could just ask you all to keep a lookout for it in and around the park. It's highly likely that the killer's DNA will be on it.'

Richards glanced at his notes and continued, 'We wrapped the body and had it removed to the mortuary. We have recovered some fibres which we suspect came from the killer's clothes but no hairs. There was no trace of any bodily fluids having come from the killer. We will be examining the clothes seized from Mr Walsh last night, but my personal opinion is that he will be in the clear. We recovered the deceased's car last night and that will be examined in detail today, but we found nothing of interest inside. I doubt if the killer has been in it.'

Richards sat back down. 'Thank you for that, Bob. We need to keep an open mind on the identity of the killer but just because we have no evidence that Fergus Walsh is the killer, he does still remain a person of interest to us.'

Peter Lowik rose to his feet, interrupting Skelton. 'Sir, I have known Fergus Walsh from our first day at police college. I cannot for a second believe that he would have any reason whatsoever to kill Mr Cox. Fergus is straight but does have some gay friends. Why on earth would he have wanted to lure that poor guy to the park and kill him? It does not make any sense whatsoever and personally, I think Fergus just happened to have been out running when the poor guy got killed.'

Lowik sat down. 'Peter, thank you for speaking up for your friend. But as I reminded you last night, we are police officers and we have a duty to perform, no matter where that may lead us. The fact that Walsh is a serving police officer should in no way impede our investigation. I will certainly be keeping an open mind on this and I expect every officer to do the same. The fact that Walsh was in the park at the time of the killing cannot be dismissed, but on the other hand, as you have just said, we have no motive that can link Walsh to the killing and no forensic evidence, which for the moment puts him in the clear. Any questions?'

Chris Spurrey stood up. 'What will we do for food today sir?' As usual, Spurrey's overriding concern was food.

Skelton shook his head, 'Don't worry, Chris, a mobile canteen is on its way and will be in the park.'

There were no more questions, so Skelton went back to his office and answered some emails before briefing Superintendent Williams and then attending the press conference.

Chapter Eight

Alexander drove Skelton to the park and they arrived shortly after 11.30. It was another warm day and although not as hot as the previous day, it was too warm to be wearing a jacket. Skelton and Alexander had taken their jackets off before getting into the car. Now they took them off the back seat and placed them neatly in the boot where they could not be seen. The last thing they needed was for someone to break into the car, tempted by what might be in the jackets. It had always amazed both detectives how stupid people can be when it came to protecting their property.

There was still police tape around the bushes where the body had been found and forensic officers could be seen carrying out a fingertip search of the grass, which surrounded the bushes. This would be both exhaustive and lengthy, but every cigarette butt, crisp packet, loose button or whatever would be bagged up and sent to the lab for analysis. Skelton studied the scene and thought back on the number of killings he had solved due to a cigarette butt being carelessly dropped by the murderer. The DNA would put the killer at the crime scene. Skelton was hoping for a similar lucky break but his instincts told him that the killer was forensically aware, and it was highly unlikely that he had left a clue to his identity.

'So, what's the plan, Dan?' Skelton focused his eyes on Alexander.

'Let's take a slow walk around the park, Bill. I want to look at all the entrances, to see what route the killer could have taken. I reckon that the killer had visual contact on Stephen and directed him to that particular bush, which he had already identified as the perfect murder spot. The bush is away from the footpath and so would provide some shelter from prying eyes. If the jogger was the killer, then his phone was probably hands free, otherwise he would have needed to stop running to make the call or calls to Stephen, directing him to that bush. Now if the killer was not the jogger, he should have been captured on CCTV and the boys are out now collecting every film they can get their hands on. It will be a slow process of elimination. We can safely discount the killer as being either a woman or a child, so that greatly reduces the pool of suspects. And according to Doc Challis, the killer was probably over six feet in height. That narrows the list of suspects significantly. We therefore need to identify and interview every male aged between the ages of, let's say, eighteen and forty, who was recorded as being in the park yesterday afternoon.'

Alexander was making a mental note of what Skelton had been saying and after Skelton had stopped speaking said, 'What if the killer knows the park well and all the CCTV sites? It's possible that he entered the park and kept well away from the CCTV cameras and simply lay somewhere where he could not be seen.'

Skelton smiled broadly. 'Well done, Bill, I was thinking the exact same thing this morning as I was walking to the office. If you take the road that runs parallel to the Wells Road, which I do most mornings, there is an entrance to the park there. I had a look this morning and there is no CCTV there and I didn't notice any nearby.' Skelton glanced at his watch. 'By the time we check out all the possible routes it should be around lunchtime. I don't fancy lunch in the mobile canteen, Bill, but I sure do fancy a pie and a couple of pints in the Bear.'

This was a popular pub on Bear Flat. Alexander looked sheepish.

'What's up, Bill?'

Alexander was pulling out his trouser pockets and they were empty. 'Sorry but I left my wallet in my jacket.'

Skelton thrust his hand in his own trouser pockets and from the right-hand side one, produced a large bundle of cash and from the other a handkerchief. 'Bill, you must never be ill-prepared when it comes to lunch, but even more importantly when it comes to having a pint. Lunch is on me.'

Alexander laughed and said, 'My wife told me never to go out without you, Dan. And she was bloody right today!'

Skelton put his arm around Alexander's shoulders and said quietly, 'Don't worry, Bill, I will find a more expensive place tomorrow for Sunday lunch, and that will be on you, sunshine.'

Alexander shook his head and said, 'I should have known better that you would come out best in this deal!'

Chapter Nine

The detectives looked like a couple of friends out for a gentle stroll around the park. As they reached a bench, Skelton gestured to Alexander that they should take a seat. As they sat down, Skelton took out his phone from his shirt pocket and said, 'Let's have a look on Google at the park. It will help us to gain a better understanding of its layout.' Skelton held the phone so that they could both see the park on the screen. There was in fact only one entrance and exit for vehicular traffic, which was on Shakespeare Avenue. This was the entrance that they had used this morning and yesterday afternoon. The map showed the surrounding roads, all named after poets and writers. There was Chaucer, Milton, Keats, Longfellow and Shakespeare. There were two other entrances which appeared on the map, for pedestrians only. One was off the road that Skelton had taken on his walk into the office earlier. Skelton was looking for the name of the road but could not see it listed. He made a mental note to check this out later.

The other entrance was adjacent to Greenway Lane and was opposite a pedestrian entrance to Beeching Cliff School. Greenway Lane has some magnificent large houses and these rarely come on to the property market. The houses offer some of the most stunning views in Bath as they look on to the truly stunning Lincoln Vale, a breathtaking National Trust site of meadows and woodland. Skelton suddenly remembered that young Trevor Thomas and his parents lived on Greenway Lane, so it was not surprising that Trevor brought his dog here as it was so convenient.

'Well, we know that Stephen parked his car on Chaucer Avenue and entered the park via the Shakespeare entrance and was captured on the CCTV at the bowling club. He had been wearing a dark windcheater over his blue shirt and that was why we missed him on the first review of the CCTV film. We don't know exactly what time he parked his car, as the parking is free there and so there was no parking ticket to check the time. But we do have him on the CCTV walking past the bowling club at 16.51 carrying a white plastic bag. We need to closely look at that afternoon's entire footage up until 18.00 hours. We know that it and the footage from the Cooperative store on Shakespeare Avenue shows the jogger leaving. But does it show the jogger entering the park? We need to analyse it carefully and identify all males that look tall and are aged between eighteen and forty.'

Alexander stood up and stretched his arms and scratched his nose. 'Well, if the killer came in past the bowling club, then he is certainly going to be on film. But if he used one of the pedestrian entrances, then we might have a problem. Do you want to give Ross a call and see what the team have discovered about CCTV coverage?'

Skelton already had his phone in his hand. He checked his address book and called Turnbull. He answered on the second ring. 'Hi, sir, how's it going?'

Skelton stood up and said, 'We are doing okay, Ross, but I'm interested to know what you guys have discovered about CCTV coverage.'

Skelton could hear vehicular traffic on the phone and guessed that Turnbull was on a main road somewhere. 'Well, there is good news and bad news, sir. The good news is that the pedestrian entrance at Greenway Lane opposite Beeching Cliff School does have CCTV. Chris has discovered that it's actually operated by the school for the protection of the kids. He is at the school now and the caretaker is being most helpful. We should have the tape back at the station this afternoon.'

Skelton was listening intently. 'Right, that's the good news, Ross, now give me the bad news.' Turnbull waited for a large lorry to pass so as not to drown out the conversation.

'The bad news is that the other pedestrian entrance does not have any CCTV. Apparently, it's been a bone of contention for a long time. The council which runs the park say they cannot afford to install and operate

CCTV at that site. So, if the killer came into the park and kept well away from the CCTV at the bowling club, then we are stuffed, sir.'

This was news that Skelton had been dreading. CCTV can be vital in helping to solve a crime. The biggest handicap to the police in recent years has been government cutbacks, not just to police budgets but to councils as well. This has led to many councils switching off CCTV cameras as they simply don't have the money to run them. The police have had to resort to asking volunteers to man CCTV cameras as they too don't have the money to employ operators.

'Any luck, Ross, with cameras elsewhere?'

Turnbull thought for a second and said, 'We've been to a fair number of houses already, sir, which are situated close to that entrance, but none of them have CCTV which covers the road and pavements.'

Skelton sat back down. 'Well, we can only hope that the bowling green camera will provide the evidence that we need, otherwise it's going to be down to forensics, and to be honest with you, Ross, I reckon that the killer will not have left us anything.' Skelton ended the call.

'Right, Bill, let's go and catch up with some of the troops and see if they have uncovered any eyewitnesses or, more importantly, someone with some photographs or videos from yesterday afternoon.'

Chapter Ten

Although it was a warm day, the park had not had as many visitors as it usually did on a Saturday morning. This was no doubt due to the fact that a murder had been committed the previous day and the killer had not been caught. Parents understandably were protective of their children, and Skelton reckoned that visitor numbers to the park would not increase until they had arrested the murderer. With such a lack of evidence, he was beginning to wonder just how long it would take to bring the killer to justice.

On speaking to several of his officers, none had so far come across any visitors today that had been in the park the previous day at the relevant time. Janet Griffin had called to say that whilst her plea on social media had created a very good response, so far no one had reported anything suspicious. Some videos and photographs had been sent in, but again none showed the victim or Fergus Walsh. Of course, they had already had half a dozen nutters claiming to be the killer. Unfortunately, these hoax calls had to be looked into in addition to those from the regular known hoax callers that frequently admitted to every crime committed in Bath and elsewhere in Somerset.

Skelton and Alexander were headed towards the bowling green. It was now 12.30 pm. Both detectives were deep in thought and it was Skelton that broke the silence. 'You know, Bill, the killer chose this park very carefully indeed. He must know it very well and knows exactly where all the CCTV cameras are located. The fact is that there really is only the one camera at the bowling club, which is located in the park itself. The only other camera is at the pedestrian entrance opposite the school. Chris is retrieving the film at the moment and is taking it back to the station to review it. So, until that's completed, we won't know what it will throw up, if anything.'

As they arrived at the entrance to the bowling club, a tall man aged around sixty with long grey hair was emerging from the gate entrance to the green. Skelton gave him a smile and said, 'Hello there, are you a member here?' As the man was wearing a blazer, white shirt and grey flannels he couldn't be anything other than a bowler, Skelton suddenly thought to himself.

The bowler returned the smile and said, 'Yes that's right, I'm Dan Kite, the captain.'

Skelton introduced himself and Alexander. 'I know that you had a visit from my officers yesterday with regard to your CCTV footage, and we would really appreciate some further cooperation, Mr Kite. As I am sure you know by now, the man was killed sometime between 16.45 and 17.30 yesterday afternoon. Do you by any chance know if there was anyone in the club around that time?' Skelton waited for a response.

'Yes, I was here yesterday afternoon playing a club competition. It was a pairs match, so there were four of us here. We started the game at four and finished it at about half past six. We heard the sirens and realised that something was going on in the park, so we came off the green and walked out the gate just here. If you go out on to the road and turn right you can see most of the park. We saw the police cars and then the paramedics arrived and we realised it must be something serious.'

Skelton thought for a second and was pleased that he had actually found a witness who was in the park at the time of the murder. 'Tell me, Mr Kite, did you seeing anyone acting suspiciously or see or hear anything that you thought was unusual?'

Kite closed his eyes and Skelton realised that the man was deep in thought. 'Well, when I arrived there were quite a lot of people in the park, especially kids. I didn't see anyone out of the ordinary that's for sure. Then at about five, our beer delivery turned up, so I broke away from the bowls match and went out to give the driver a hand. I did see a man sitting on a bench just about one hundred metres from that bush, which you lot taped off yesterday when you discovered the body.'

Skelton made a mental note to check the CCTV footage for the timing of the beer delivery, as it would give them a timeline for placing the man on the bench. 'This man you saw sitting on the bench, can you describe him to us?'

Kite closed his eyes again in order to faithfully recall what he could remember about the man. 'I think the guy was about mid-fifties, greyish hair. He was wearing a blue short-sleeve shirt, black trousers and a pair of white trainers. He had a dark jacket on the armrest of the bench.'

Skelton realised immediately that this was the victim, and he had to be careful in how he questioned the witness. 'Tell me, Mr Kite, was the man doing anything and did you see anyone else in the vicinity?'

Kite closed his eyes again. When he opened them, he had a look on his face which said he had remembered something important. 'Yes, he answered his phone and he seemed kind of excited. Like he had just got some good news. Then I saw a jogger run past behind him and then I came back in and continued playing the game.'

Both Skelton and Alexander had been taking notes. This was important evidence which could link the killer to the victim. 'Tell me about the jogger. Just take your time, Mr Kite, you are being very helpful to us and it's vital that you try and recall everything about him.'

Kite had closed his eyes again and Skelton's heart was pounding with excitement. Kite opened his eyes and said, 'Well he was young and fit that's for sure. But he was wearing a hoodie so I couldn't see his face or his hair. He was very tall, well over six feet and well built. I think he must go to the gym a lot as well as the jogging. He was dressed in black running gear and white trainers and he was carrying a backpack.'

'Mr Kite, are you sure about this? Did you by any chance see another jogger dressed differently?'

Kite did not close his eyes this time. 'No, I am certain I didn't see another jogger, but when we went out to see what all the fuss was about when you lot arrived, I did see a young lad down by the bushes and he had a black Labrador with him.'

Chapter Eleven

The detectives had thanked Mr Kite and retreated to the Bear pub for lunch. Skelton was outraged that the pub did not stock Fosters, his lager of choice, nor did they have any other lager which he could enjoy. The only lagers they stocked were very strong artisan brews and Skelton was not going to touch those. He settled for a pint of Guinness, which he would normally only drink in the winter. Alexander was not very keen on the beers either and settled for a pint of lemon and lime. They both ordered fish and chips and found a table.

The pub was clearly a focal point for the nouveau riche of the trendy Bear Flat area and was incredibly noisy, with lots of young children and their mothers. The mothers seemed oblivious to the noise that the children were creating and indeed, seemed to encourage it. Skelton had already decided that he would not be visiting the place again. Skelton took a deep gulp of his drink and looking at Alexander he asked, 'Well, Bill, what did you make of Mr Kite?'

Alexander took a sip of his drink and thought for a second. 'He seems to me to be a good reliable witness. He clearly has a good memory and you could see that he closed his eyes to try and recall every detail of what he had seen. We now know where the victim had been sitting and you've ordered forensics to check it out. It's also fairly certain that the killer directed him to those bushes by calling his phone, which of course the killer took with him.'

'Once we have had our lunch, Bill, let's go back to the park for an update from the troops and then head back to the office. Once all the CCTV footage has been reviewed, we will hopefully have some males that fit the criteria as a potential suspect and can post their images on social media, asking for them to identify themselves or for anyone else who knows their identity.'

Alexander took another sip from his drink and wished that he was having a proper pint of lager or cider. He too had decided that this was not his type of pub. 'The thing is, Dan, we keep coming back to the fact that it is perfectly possible to enter and leave that park and not be caught on CCTV. Walsh must know this and yet he was caught on the bowling club camera and on the camera mounted outside the Cooperative store on the corner of Shakespeare Avenue. So, either he was just out for an innocent run around the park or he wanted to pit his wits against us by purposely getting photographed. When we searched his house and garage there was nothing to incriminate him and he certainly didn't act like a guilty man to me. As you said yesterday and again this morning, we need to keep an open mind here. Maybe we might get lucky with forensics. I would guess that Bob and his team will have finished with the body and will give us a briefing this afternoon.'

They ate their meal in silence, finished their drinks and left the pub. They headed up Shakespeare Avenue, which is a steep hill, and both were sweating by the time they had reached the entrance to the park. As they walked towards the bowling green, Alexander touched Skelton on the shoulder and said, 'Look, that's the chief super's car.'

Skelton stopped walking and saw the blue BMW parked almost opposite the bowling club. Chief Superintendent Mike Sawyers was a very accomplished lawn bowls player, having won many tournaments both at local and county level. Skelton knew that he played at Bloomfield Bowling Club, one of four bowling clubs in Bath. He guessed that Alexandra Park must be hosting Bloomfield at home today. 'Let's pop in, Bill. We can update the boss and possibly even get a pint or two.'

Alexander opened the gate and Skelton went inside. It was only 2.15 pm and the game had not started, but there were a number of bowlers sitting outside enjoying a cold beer. Skelton noticed that quite a few of them had cans of Fosters and Skelton's mood improved immediately. Standing at the main entrance to the club house was Mike Sawyers. He had his back to them and was talking to another bowler. He was wearing his bowling gear and dressed in his club shirt and white shorts. Skelton climbed the stairs and tapped Sawyers on the shoulder.

'Dan, Bill, hello. How is it going, boys?'

Skelton gave him a big smile and said, 'Well it's bloody thirsty work, Mike.' He pointed to the almost empty pint glass that Sawyers was holding in his hand.

'Come away in, let me get you guys a drink. They only do cans here, but they are nice and cold.'

Skelton could see that they were not pint-sized cans so he made a quick decision. 'No, Mike, let me get these, poor Bill and I have been all over the park this morning and that climb up Shakespeare Avenue is a killer.'

Skelton ordered four cans of Fosters and a can of cider for Sawyers. Skelton and Alexander almost drained their glasses at the first gulp and had to top them up with the second can. The game was a friendly and not due to start until 2.30 pm. Sawyers led them to the back of the club house, which was deserted, and they sat down at a table.

'Well you guys better fill me in on this murder as I have been fielding questions about it since I got here.' Skelton took another glug of Fosters, the noisy pub they had just left now a distant memory.

'As you know, Mike, a young lad out walking his dog, discovered the body yesterday afternoon. We have the victim on CCTV from here but it's the only CCTV in the park. There is another one down at the entrance opposite Beeching Cliff School, but the only other pedestrian entrance has no camera, so if you stay clear of the bowling club, you can enter and leave the park and not be filmed. We also got pictures of someone we assumed was our prime suspect, a jogger dressed in black and wearing a hoodie. Now either by coincidence or design, he is seen entering the park shortly after the victim and is seen leaving again, when we know that the victim was dead.'

Skelton took another glug of Fosters and Alexander noticed that both their glasses were getting low, although Sawyers had not yet touched his. Alexander got up and headed to the bar. Sawyers lifted his glass and took a sip.

'Have you identified this jogger?' Skelton leaned forward, his arms resting on the table.

'Yes sir, we did, but it was not the result we were expecting. Peter Lowik took one look at the film and identified the jogger straight away. The guy is a serving police officer and by pure coincidence, he and Lowik started on the same day at the police college. His name is Fergus Walsh and he works out of Bristol. Lowik reckons the guy could never be the killer. I checked his record. He has been with Avon and Somerset Police for just over five years and has already received two commendations from the chief constable. He appears to be a very diligent officer but apparently lacks the capacity to be a detective. He is about to go on an advanced driving course, so it looks like he will probably end up being a traffic officer.

'Anyway, we went straight to his house and he was fully cooperative and showed no signs of distress or anxiety. He even told us to search his garage, which we did. He surrendered his jogging gear to us but it was clean and the killer's clothes would have been covered in blood. Nevertheless, we have sent it off to forensics, but it will no doubt come back negative. Walsh confirmed he had gone for a jog at the material time but had seen nothing suspicious.'

Alexander was back with two more cans. Sawyers was in deep thought. 'Fergus Walsh, I know that name from somewhere.'

Alexander sat down and said, 'Well if the guy is in the force you are bound to have come across his name in reports and appraisals, sir.'

Sawyers stood up. 'Yes, you are probably correct, Bill. Right, I've got to go out and play bowls. Enjoy your beers.' They shook hands and Sawyers went outside.

The detectives finished their beers and then popped into the loo before heading back to where Alexander had parked the car. As they walked towards the bush where the victim had been found, they noticed that the bench had been removed. It would have been taken to the lab for detailed forensic investigation. Suddenly, Skelton saw a black Labrador bounding towards him. It was Johnny, and he made a beeline for Skelton. Getting down on the grass, Skelton gave him a big hug and patted his head and massaged his ears.

'Johnny what are you up to?'

Skelton recognised young Trevor's voice and stood up. 'Hello, Trevor, enjoying your walk?'

Trevor broke into a beaming smile. 'Hey, Dan, I didn't know it was you,' he said, and stuck out his right hand, which Skelton warmly shook.

'Trevor, you didn't meet my colleague yesterday when we had our little chat. This is Bill Alexander. Bill, this is young Trevor, who with the help of Johnny here found the body.' Alexander gave the boy a big smile and shook his hand. 'Good to meet you, Trevor, and Dan told me how helpful you were yesterday.'

Trevor blushed and said, 'Oh it was nothing really. All I did was call 999. I'm just sorry that there was nothing I could do for the poor guy. You know my mum is a GP, and I have been taught first aid since I was about ten. When I saw all that blood I knew he was dead.'

Skelton placed his right hand on Trevor's shoulder and asked, 'Did you manage to get some sleep last night?'

Trevor looked a little bit guilty and said, 'Well actually my dad said it would help to have a couple of beers and talk. So that's what we did, but I had a bit of a headache this morning.'

Skelton and Alexander both laughed. Skelton ruffled Trevor's hair and said, 'You know something, Trevor? That's the same advice that both Bill and I would have given you. And judging by how you look it worked!'

Trevor laughed, then bent down and gave Johnny a hug.

'Well, we haven't found the killer yet, Trevor, but we still have some CCTV footage to look at, and we have appealed for help on social media. I don't suppose anything has jogged your memory about something you might have seen but omitted to tell me?'

Trevor had sat on the grass with Johnny lying beside him. Skelton and Alexander decided to sit beside them, to make Trevor feel more comfortable. Trevor was stroking Johnny's head and neck and the dog was loving it. 'Well to be honest, Dan, there is one odd sort of thing that I do remember, but it didn't seem relevant yesterday.'

Skelton was all ears and he knew that this could be vitally important. 'Go on, Trevor, tell us what it was.'

Trevor was gazing into the distance, trying to recall the scene as it happened. 'Well, it's funny really. We passed that bush earlier and I remember that Johnny ran inside it. He had only been in it a minute and I called him back and he came, right away. So, I don't think the dead man was there when Johnny first ran in, otherwise he would have barked and stayed there, just as he had done when he found the body. And I don't think there was anyone actually in the bush because Johnny is such a friendly dog he would have stayed there if there were any cuddles going.'

Skelton gave the dog another pat and said, 'That's very interesting, Trevor. What if there was someone in the bush who didn't want to be seen. Is it possible that they scared Johnny away?'

Trevor considered this for a second. 'No, I don't think so, and I certainly didn't hear any voices or noises. I think if someone had chased Johnny away, I would have known. You see, Johnny does not like being told off. If someone had scared him away, I would have known right away. But Johnny came out of that bush the first time perfectly relaxed.'

Skelton thanked Trevor and left him to continue his walk with his beloved dog. He and Alexander got into the car, and they headed back to the station.

All the detectives had been working hard that Saturday, and by 4.30 pm the review of all the CCTV footage so far recovered had been completed. The footage from the bowling club provided them with just eight suspects that fitted the criteria of the profile. These were males, all tall and aged between eighteen and forty. However, they were able to eliminate one right away owing to the fact, that he had a broken leg and was on crutches.

Skelton was certain that the killer had changed his clothes after killing the victim, and would have brought either a bag, or a backpack.

Of the remaining seven suspects, only two were carrying bags. Two others could probably be ruled out, as they were topless and were wearing just shorts. There was no place to hide a large knife there. It was decided that just five images would be released on social media, with a plea that they come forward, or for anyone to identify them so that the police could interview them.

The CCTV footage from the school was even more disappointing. The vast majority of visitors to the park had been kids with their mums and dogs. They only had one male adult that matched their profile and so he was added to the list to go on social media.

It was day two of the murder enquiry, and they seemed no further forward in catching the killer. What had got off to a flying start, with the victim and the then prime suspect caught on camera, had unravelled very quickly. Now they needed a break. Could forensics solve the case?

At 4.45 pm Bob Richards, head of Crime Scene Investigations, strode into the CID room. Skelton was sitting on Ross Turnbull's desk chatting with his detectives. On seeing Richards arrive, he stood up and asked, 'What news, Bob?'

It had been a really hot day and the heat and pressure had clearly got to him and he was sweating profusely. He took out a white handkerchief and wiped his brow and sat down on Janet Griffin's desk. He cleared his throat and began.

'Let's start with the park bench. The victim certainly sat on it. We got both his fingerprints and a fibre from his shirt. My guess is that he sat there waiting for instructions from the killer as to where he was to go. That would undoubtedly have been communicated by phone. We undertook a fingertip search of the crime scene but discovered neither the victim's phone nor the murder weapon. We have also failed to find the victim's wallet, credit cards, car keys or any other belongings. That's unusual as a killer will often drop something in his hurry to flee the scene.

'We think that the killer must have brought a bag of some description, into which he placed the murder weapon and the victim's personal effects. The killer must have been covered in blood, owing to the nature of the wounds on the deceased. He therefore must have changed his clothes before fleeing the scene. We did recover some black cotton clothing fibres from the body and from around the body. That's the only positive news that I can give you. So, if you can find those clothes, then we can solve the case. But one thing I would stress is this: the killer is in my opinion someone with a sound knowledge of forensics. He was able to carry out the killing without leaving his DNA and that's pretty hard to do. And the last thing I have to say is that we examined the clothing from the jogger. As we suspected, there was no hair or fibre match and no blood stains. So that puts PC Walsh in the clear.'

Skelton walked over to Richards and placed his hand on his shoulder and squeezed it. 'Well done, Bob, to you and your team. The killer might have got away with deleting his DNA from the crime scene, but the fact that you have retrieved some clothing fibres is a major breakthrough. What we need to do, as a matter of urgency, is find the clothes that the killer was wearing. If we manage to achieve that, we can all go out and get drunk!'

Chapter Twelve

It was Sunday morning, day three of the enquiry, and Skelton was walking into Bath. It was a cloudy morning but the forecast was for it to brighten up by midday. Skelton was dressed in a blue pinstripe double-breasted suit. He only ever wore double-breasted suits as he considered these far more stylish than a lounge suit. He was wearing a freshly ironed and starched pink shirt with a matching handkerchief in his breast pocket and his favourite pair of gold cufflinks, which his partner Ken had given him. Hardly ever a day went past without him being complimented on his sartorial excellence.

Most mornings he would take the direct route into the city, but today he took a different route and so at the bottom of Entry Hill, he turned right onto Greenwell Lane. This would put Beeching Cliff School on his left, way up on the hillside. The houses here were highly sought after but very rarely came on the market. They ranged from terraced houses, semi-detached and detached, the latter being the most expensive and sought after. They all offered excellent views across the stunningly glorious Lincoln Vale. He had no real reason to alter his usual route into work as both routes were probably equidistant.

As it was Sunday morning, Skelton had permitted himself a small lie-in. As a result, he would not arrive at his office until about 8.45, but there was no pressing need to be there early. Being a Sunday morning, the street was deserted except for the odd car going up or down the hill. Suddenly he saw a green Range Rover emerging from the driveway of a large, detached house and he remembered that Dr and Mr Thomson lived here. They had given him their address on Friday evening. Mr Thomson was driving and Dr Thomson was in the front passenger seat with Trevor in the back. No doubt Johnny was further back behind the dog guard. Thomson spotted

Skelton as he looked left and right. He lowered the front passenger door window and called out. 'Good morning, Dan, can I give you a lift?'

Skelton smiled and said, 'Good morning to you. No thanks, I much prefer to walk whenever I can. I'm sure that your good lady wife would approve.'

The Thomsons laughed. 'Yes, she certainly would. By the way, don't forget that we are having a party a week on Sunday, for Trevor's sixteenth birthday. Please do come along and bring your dogs, and of course your wife or partner.'

Skelton leaned on the driver's door and said, 'That's awfully kind of you but I am not married, but my civil partner's name is Ken.'

Dr Thomson looked mortified but before she could speak, young Trevor got in before her. 'Wow, a gay policeman. That's cool, Dan. My dad's brother, Uncle George, is gay and he's great fun.'

Dr Thomas leaned across her husband so that she was closer to Skelton. 'Dan, I had no idea that you are gay, and as Trevor has said, my husband's brother is also gay. He will be there on Sunday with his partner and he's also bringing some friends.'

It was duly agreed that Skelton would bring Ken and the three dogs to the party on Sunday.

Instead of going into the police station, Skelton headed towards Bog Island. This unusually named feature of Bath gained its name because there used be public toilets situated underground. The toilets, much to the annoyance of the local residents and the six million visitors to Bath every year, were closed down by the local authority and sold off. They were subsequently converted into a night club but the venture was not a success. Consequently, they have remained closed for years.

The local authority, in its infinite wisdom, decided that Bog Island should be the venue for the tourist coaches that bring thousands of visitors to the city every day. Here, dozens of coaches would drop off and pick up their passengers. Most passengers, many of them elderly, would endure fairly long journeys of more than two hours with most coaches not having any toilet facilities on board. Needless to say, many passengers require to use the toilet as soon as they arrive in Bath. However, with the Bog Island toilets closed, the desperate tourists are forced to use the toilets in the pubs situated on or near Bog Island. As the tourists are only in Bath for a relatively short period of time, they are usually only able to visit the world-famous Roman Baths. They don't have time to buy a drink in the pubs. Therefore, the poor landlords are left to pick up the huge bill for the extra water used by the tourists to flush the toilet and wash their hands.

Although there is an actual coach station in Bath, where the coaches can park up whilst the passengers go sightseeing, the local authority, again with a view to saving money, closed the coach station toilets as well. Consequently, Skelton often found himself being asked by tourists for directions to the nearest toilets. Unfortunately, there are no public toilets nearby and for elderly or partially disabled people the long walk must be a nightmare.

Skelton's trip to Bog Island this morning was for the purpose of buying the Sunday Telegraph newspaper. There is a newsagent there and Skelton enjoyed reading the newspapers, something that he shared in common with his father. Although he downloaded a digital copy of the Times newspaper to his iPad every day, he missed not being able to spread out the large newssheet, hence his desire for the Sunday Telegraph. He also preferred its sports section as it seemed to give better coverage to horse racing, his favourite sport.

Having bought the paper, he headed towards the office and passed two uniformed officers going out on foot patrol. The police station carpark still had a couple of TV vans parked there, waiting for news of the murder enquiry. On entering his office, he took off his jacket and switched on his laptop. He then put some water in the kettle, enough for two mugs of tea. He went through to the CID room where he found Alexander checking his emails.

'Good morning, Bill, the kettle's on. Why don't you come and join me for a mug of tea? I will have to give Williams a briefing later as he is holding a press conference at noon.'

Alexander stood up and said, 'I just happen to have a couple of KitKats in my drawer, Dan, to go with the tea.'

Alexander had arrived earlier than Skelton and had been at his desk since eight. He was able to report that the requests put out on social media had been a complete success. The seven male suspects had been identified and would be attending the police station this morning for interview. Whilst this news was welcome, the downside to it was that only one male had a criminal record and that was for a driving offence. Alexander had detailed Lowik and Turnbull to conduct the interviews as the suspects did not look viable as the actual killer. The time saved would allow Skelton and Alexander to take stock of the situation and plan the next course of action.

After briefing Superintendent Williams on the progress of their enquiries, Skelton returned to his office and dealt with all of the outstanding emails that had accumulated over the weekend. It was almost 1 pm before he was finished. His belly was rumbling and he wanted lunch. There was a tap on the door and Alexander opened it and stood in the doorway.

'I don't know about you Dan, but I could go some lunch!'

Skelton stood up and smiled. 'I was just thinking the same thing, Bill. I could go some roast beef and roast potatoes with plenty of veg. And I just happen to know a pub that does that rather well on a Sunday.'

Alexander returned the smile. 'Where did you have in mind?'

Skelton grabbed his jacket from the coat hanger. 'Let's take a walk over to the Pultney Arms, Bill, the walk will do you good.'

Alexander shook his head. 'I might have known that it would involve a walk. I am going to start charging for shoe leather. I just had a new pair of heels put on these shoes last week.'

Skelton slapped his friend on the back and said, 'Come on, Bill, stop moaning, and by the way, you owe me lunch, sunshine.'

Skelton did not quite hear the profanity that Alexander had muttered!

Later that afternoon, Skelton was going over the witness statements that Turnbull and Lowik had taken earlier from the seven suspects that had attended the station for interview. There was nothing that was remotely suspicious in their behaviour on the day of the murder. Two had, however, spotted the jogger dressed in black but none had noticed the victim. All seven had seen young Trevor and his dog. Skelton considered the statements for a few minutes and concluded that a man sitting quietly on a park bench was unlikely to have attracted much attention, but a man jogging and a boy playing with his dog would have stood out. It was just human nature to remember some things and to totally disregard others.

He could not get away from the fact that only Walsh, whilst no longer a suspect, featured heavily within the investigation. He could not, however, discount the possibility that the killer could have entered and left the park without being captured on CCTV. But of the witnesses so far interviewed, none could remember seeing a man acting in an unusual manner. A clever barrister would make out the same case for Walsh. He had been captured on CCTV and had been seen by several witnesses simply jogging around the park. No one had seen him going in or coming out of the bushes. He had readily made himself available for interview when contacted by Lowik. He also invited the police to search his house and had even informed them that he also had a garage, which he invited them to search as well. Finally, he had given them his running gear and backpack, which he said he had been wearing in the park. Both the Home Office pathologist and Bob Richards had concluded that the killer would have been covered in the victim's blood. There was no blood on Walsh's running gear or on the backpack. His phone was being examined by a forensic technician, and the fact that he had so far found nothing suspicious indicated that Walsh was truly innocent. His phone would reveal exactly where he had been before, during and after the killing. It would also reveal if he had in any way communicated with the victim either by phone or a gay dating website.

What possible motive could Walsh have to kill Mr Cox? Walsh was not gay, but according to Lowik, he did have gay friends. That indicated to Skelton that Walsh was highly unlikely to have killed Cox due to his sexuality. There was no evidence to suggest that they had ever met each other. So that discounted the theory that Walsh had held a grudge against Cox. As if the lack of evidence was not enough to rule Walsh out completely, there was the fact that he was a police officer with an unblemished record.

Skelton was beginning to feel exasperated. He had been optimistic at the start of the enquiry that it would be a relatively easy case to solve. Now he was forced to admit that there was not a shred of evidence to support a case against Walsh. The man, it seemed, had simply taken a jog around the park, which was something he did on a regular basis. This was not something unusual that merited further questioning. He had readily admitted that he had been in the park but had not seen the victim nor anyone acting suspiciously. He could easily have said differently to detract attention away from himself but had not done so. This would be a further point in Walsh's favour, underscored by his barrister. The simple fact that Skelton had to admit was that there was no evidence to even charge Walsh, never mind putting him before a judge and jury.

Skelton stood up and looked at his watch, it was nearly 5 pm. It was almost time to call it a day. He would soon be home and would prepare and cook Sunday dinner. They were having roast lamb, although Skelton was beginning to feel guilty about having two large meals. He would just have to do some extra walking, as would Bill Alexander!

He sauntered into the CID room, which was now deserted except for Lowik, who was just finishing a phone call. Skelton sat down on the desk directly across from Lowik. 'Peter, I want you tell me more about your friend Fergus Walsh, and please don't get defensive. I just want to get more of an understanding about the guy and what makes him tick.'

Lowik considered this for a moment and then leaned back in his chair. 'Well, as I told you on Friday, we first met on day one at the police college. He seemed a pleasant sort of guy but never said more about himself than he had to. Not the brightest star in the class when it came to coursework but he did pass all the essential tests. He loved the gym though, especially self-defence. As you know, he is a big bloke and I never saw anyone get the better of him. I remember once I had to play the baddie and he had to play the cop. I thought the only way I was going to beat him was to play dirty. But although he's a big bugger, he is also very quick. Before I knew it, he had me in a bear hug and I was crying out in pain. He had only gone and fractured three of my ribs.'

Skelton grimaced, he knew how painful fractured ribs could be, and they take at least six weeks to heal. 'What about relationships. Does he have a girlfriend?'

Lowik pondered the question for a moment. 'He has had several over the years I have known him, but you know what it's like working shifts. It is not easy to hold down a relationship. The last one was called Annie, but I think they broke up about a month ago. He is very close to his mum. She is a wonderful lady. I have met her quite a few times.'

Skelton recalled that Walsh lived with his mother. 'What about his father? You said something about him leaving them on their own.'

Lowik stood up, he was trying to remember what it was about the father. 'He never ever spoke about his father. He just said that the father left them when Fergus was still at school. I think that is why he is so close to his mum. He sort of had to grow up quick and become the man of the house. I guess he felt cheated that his father had walked out on them.'

Skelton thanked Lowik for his time and went back to his office. He switched off the laptop and pulled on his jacket. He reflected on what Lowik had said about Walsh and the forensic report from Bob Richards. As of now, as far as he was concerned, Walsh was no longer a suspect.

Chapter Thirteen

It was Monday morning, the sky was grey and overcast. Frequent showers were forecast for most of the day. It was 8.45 am when Alexander parked the car in the mortuary car park. He had picked up Skelton from his home and they spent the journey listening to classical music on the Classic FM radio station. Neither had spoken much during the journey. There had been no developments in the case despite a further appeal by Superintendent Williams for assistance from the public. They had listened to it on the eight o'clock news bulletin. The public mortuary is located next to the coroner's court, which is about a forty-minute drive from Bath.

The post-mortem examination was scheduled for nine and would be conducted by Dr Challis. The detectives were now suited and booted and had been shown into the large mortuary suite. There were at least twenty cadavers awaiting autopsy. Four mortuary technicians were already busy. Two were operating electric saws to open up the skulls so that the brains could be removed for examination. The other two technicians were busy opening up the bodies so that all the organs could be removed and examined for disease.

Dr Challis entered the suite and bid them a good morning. He was a man of few words but a highly competent forensic pathologist. As he worked on the victim's body, he spoke into a microphone which was mounted over his mouth. As expected, they did not expect to learn much from the autopsy, but tradition dictated that they needed to be there. Dr Challis concluded that death was due to a single stab wound to the heart, resulting in shock from loss of blood. The victim's throat had been slit, causing further loss of blood and the victim had made no attempt to defend himself. The deceased's lungs showed evidence of recent infection and were damaged as a result of smoking. Once he had dissected the lungs, Dr Challis reported evidence of carcinoma, which had spread to the liver.

With the autopsy completed, Dr Challis removed his face mask and said, 'This poor chap was already on borrowed time, gentlemen. He had lung cancer which, having spread to his liver, meant that there was no possible cure. He would no doubt have sought medical help but all that the doctors could do would have been to provide him with palliative care. In my opinion, he would have been dead in six months. Not that his killer would have known anything about that.'

Challis was removing his surgical gown and Skelton and Alexander were both doing likewise. 'As I said to you at the murder scene, this looked like a sexual encounter with the victim partially naked and ready to perform. He most definitely had his back to the killer and was not expecting anything untoward to happen. The killer simply walked up from behind and thrust the knife into Mr Cox's chest by reaching over his right shoulder. Mr Cox was only five-six and his killer was a good deal taller, probably over six feet. The killer had clasped his left hand over the victim's mouth, thus preventing any sound such as a scream or shout. He then slashed the victim's throat, stopping him from making another sound.'

Alexander was tying his shoelaces and asked, 'Is there anything else that you can tell us about the killer?'

Challis considered the question for a moment and said, 'I think the killer may have been in the military. The victim was very efficiently dispatched, as if by someone trained in close combat. Perhaps a commando or a special forces operative. I would not be surprised if the killer went to a lot of trouble and care to ensure that he would not be caught. We were talking earlier, and you said that anyone wanting to enter or leave the park could easily do so without being captured on CCTV. You admit yourselves that the police officer was your initial suspect. He uses the park regularly, so he could easily have avoided the CCTV, but he didn't. With respect gentlemen, I think you have been barking up the wrong tree. I believe you should be looking for a military man, with the experience to plan such an operation.'

It was almost noon before they got back to Bath. They had refused the offer of tea or coffee in the mortuary, so they headed straight to Skelton's office, which boasted a kettle and a fridge. Skelton fixed the tea, and they both sat down at Skelton's desk. Skelton was busy scrolling through his emails. There was nothing much of interest. Alexander excused himself and went off to the CID office. Next, Skelton checked the crime reports from the night shift. It had been a fairly quiet Sunday night, although someone had been glassed in a night club. The incident had been caught on CCTV and the assailant had been arrested. The victim had been rushed to hospital and had undergone surgery but the surgeon feared that the young man may lose the sight in one eye. This was a serious offence and needed the CID to handle the investigation.

Skelton went through to the CID room and saw Alexander working at his computer. 'Bill, there was a serious assault last night, and the poor guy might lose an eye. We've got a suspect in custody. It was all caught on CCTV so there is no need for you or me to get involved. Detail Turnbull and Spurrey to interview the suspect and to get witness statements. I want an update this afternoon.'

Alexander stood up and said, 'Very good, sir, I think they were headed for the canteen, so they can cut their lunch short.'

Skelton had been chewing over in his mind what Dr Challis had said about the killer and he needed to focus attention on that. There were lots of military bases in the area, so there would be a huge number of possible suspects to choose from. He decided to call a briefing with his team for 3 pm and assign them their tasks. With the benefit of hindsight, he should have considered the fact that the killer might have had professional training.

Skelton's phone rang. The caller ID said it was Chief Superintendent Alan Warwick, his old boss and friend from the Metropolitan Police in London.

'Good afternoon, Alan, how are you?' Skelton listened.

'Hi Dan, I am good thanks. I see that you have your hands full with a murder in a local park. Any luck in solving it yet?'

Skelton cleared his throat. 'No, nothing so far, Alan, but it's early days. We were at the PM this morning as it happens.'

'Dan, do you remember the name James Murray?'

Skelton leapt to his feet at the mention of the name. 'You mean that bastard who killed Joe Reilly and got away with it?'

Skelton waited for the answer. 'Yes, the one and the same. We just got very lucky this morning and acquired some really interesting intel on him. You won't believe this, but he is apparently buying a large house in Bath.'

Skelton almost dropped the phone. 'What the fuck is he doing coming to Bath? His manor is north London.'

'I think it might be worth your while coming up to London, Dan, for a briefing. As you know, we keep a very close eye on Murray, and he seems to have got very close to a guy he used to share a cell with in prison. The guy in question was convicted of a serious assault. As the evidence against him was overwhelming, he pleaded guilty and got a reduced sentence of four years.

'After his release, he went back to his home city of Bristol. His name is Ben Naylor, a large Black guy with links to organised crime in Bristol. The two of them have been spotted together here in London. The word is that Murray wants to take over Bristol and Naylor is his ticket to achieving that ambition. So, things might start to get a bit nasty down your way.'

When Skelton finished the call, he sat down at his desk and ran his hands through his hair. His mouth had become dry and he had completely lost his appetite. In Skelton's eyes, James Murray was public enemy number one. He was a seasoned villain of the highest order. He had been involved in serious crime since leaving school and had never earned an honest day's pay in his life. He had started his career doing house burglaries and that soon escalated into armed robberies. He was a ruthless bastard and never hesitated in using force whenever he needed to. Eventually, he came to the attention of the elite 'Flying Squad' of the Metropolitan Police. It was universally known as the 'Sweeney', coming from London cockney rhyming slang. (Flying squad rhyming with Sweeney Todd, the infamous barber and pie maker who killed his customers with a cut-throat razor, and turned them into pies.) Skelton had served on the squad for five years before moving over to the murder squad.

During his time in the Sweeney, he had made some very good friends, the best of whom was Joe Reilly. Joe was born and bred in London and his father had been an inspector in the Met. Whilst Joe was growing up, his father would regale him with stories about all the criminal gangs operating in London. From an early age, Joe knew that the only job he ever wanted to do was to become a police officer and, if possible, join the Sweeney.

Skelton and Reilly had become good friends, so much so in fact that Skelton was best man at Reilly's wedding to Sarah. A year later their only child was born and they had christened him Daniel. Skelton and his partner Ken were asked to be godparents. For more than six years, Skelton and Reilly were the best of friends.

It was only after Skelton had moved to the murder squad that the Sweeney had taken a particularly keen interest in Murray and his gang. Reilly was just a DC but was sure to rise in the ranks. He had already received three bravery commendations from the commissioner. Whilst Murray had been arrested several times on suspicion of armed robbery, the police found it virtually impossible to find witnesses to give evidence in court. Eventually, they managed to persuade a witness to give evidence and more or less guaranteed him protection. Murray and three other men were charged and went on trial at the Old Bailey. But the witness vanished and Murray and his consorts walked free. The police later learnt that the witness had been killed, although of course the body was never found.

Murray was gaining a reputation in the criminal world as an untouchable, and the Sweeney were keen to put an end to that. A small elite task force which included Joe Reilly was established just to go after Murray and his gang and bring them to justice. Progress was painfully slow. No one was prepared to talk to the police, as they knew that in doing so they risked a serious beating or worse.

After weeks of fruitless endeavour, the DI in charge decided to put Murray under constant surveillance in the hope that they might get lucky and catch him actually committing a crime. They knew that Murray was involved in drug dealing but had never been caught with any drugs.

One night, however, Reilly and another officer called Tom Bell were parked up near Murray's house. It was a large, detached house surrounded by a high fence. It was a lovely summer evening and Reilly and Bell were sitting in the car closely watching the house. At about midnight, they spotted a car, a dark Skoda which stopped at the entrance to Murray's house. The driver got out and pressed the intercom and spoke. The electric gates opened and the driver got back into the car and drove in. The gates closed.

Bell had called for a number plate check and was surprised to find that the car was registered to a known drug dealer who had served time in prison for supplying drugs. Reilly was desperate to know if Murray was actually taking delivery of a haul of drugs. If he was, then they would have a watertight case against him.

Reilly left Bell in the car and made his way over to the fence surrounding Murray's house. There were no CCTV cameras visible, so Reilly decided to take a risk. He jumped up and reached the top of the fence and hauled himself up. Slowly, he pulled himself up over the top and he dropped to the grass below. It was a large garden with numerous mature trees and several large bushes. Reilly knew from the plans that he had seen of the house that he was facing the side that contained the sitting room and Murray's bedroom. There were no lights showing on this side, so it was most likely that Murray was entertaining his visitor in the kitchen, which was around the other side of the house. Reilly was crouched down and slowly and quietly he made his way across the grass to reach the wall of the house.

When he had reached the edge of the house, he slowly peered around the corner and could see the Skoda. The kitchen lights were on, illuminating the path outside. Reilly needed to get over to the kitchen window to see what was going on inside. He had to be quick. He could not afford to risk being seen and certainly he must not allow himself to be caught. He got down on his hands and knees and made his way towards the kitchen window. Immediately below the window was a bench, which would be perfect for him to stand on in order to see inside.

He gingerly climbed up onto the bench and peered in. Murray was standing at the kitchen table with a glass of red wine in his hand. The visitor was seated and was opening a large black holdall that was sitting on the table. Reilly guessed that it was drugs that were in the bag. Bingo!

Then disaster struck. Reilly had not noticed in the gloom of the night that the bench was well past its sell-by date. Suddenly, the old wood gave way with a thunderous crash that would have been heard in the kitchen. Reilly had become stuck in the wooden frame and was desperately trying to free himself when Murray seized him. Reilly screamed as Murray plunged the knife into his chest. Bell heard the scream and realised that Reilly had been caught. He called for immediate backup and ran towards the gate shouting, 'Police, this is the police open the gate.'

The gate was not opened until the first police car arrived with its siren blaring and blue lights flashing. When they got in, Reilly was dead, killed by Murray. The holdall did indeed contain cocaine.

Murray was charged with murder and possession of class A drugs with intent to supply. The drug supplier was only charged with the second offence. At his trial, Murray admitted to stabbing the police officer to death, but his defence was that he thought the man was an intruder, and so had armed himself with a kitchen knife to defend himself and his property. He said at no time did the officer identify himself as a police officer, something which Bell had to agree with, as he had not heard Reilly identify himself. The judge ruled that Murray was perfectly entitled to defend himself and his property from an intruder, and had no way of knowing that the intruder was a police officer.

On being acquitted of the murder charge Murray had already admitted to the drug offence, and therefore was entitled to a reduction in the sentence. He got eight years and served only half before being freed on licence.

Skelton had to accept the fact that his friend had made a terrible mistake in entering the property in the first place. He, however, had no doubt whatsoever that Murray knew that Joe was a cop. The police had been watching him for a long time. Murray had murdered Joe and had got away with it. How Skelton wanted to right that wrong, but on leaving the Met, he thought that his chances of doing so had gone. Had fate suddenly given him another chance? How he would love to be able to tell Joe's widow and child that he had extracted revenge on Murray for killing Joe.

Skelton needed to tell Alexander about Murray, and he needed to go to London for a briefing. As there was a connection to Bristol, he also needed his friend Detective Inspector Patrick Rees to be in the loop. Rees worked in Bristol and knew all the local villains. He decided he would plan for himself, Rees and Alexander to visit London as soon as possible.

Chapter Fourteen

Following the autopsy that morning, Skelton had called for a team briefing and it was scheduled for 3.30 pm. Before that he made several phone calls, including one to DI Rees in Bristol. In view of the fact that Alan Warwick's call had serious implications for both Skelton and Rees, it was agreed that they and Bill Alexander would travel to London in the morning. Skelton and Alexander would board the train, which Rees would take from Bristol and which stopped at Bath Spa.

Next, he went and updated Superintendent Williams on the result of the autopsy and the phone call from Alan Warwick. Williams agreed that there was a distinct possibility that the killer had either been in the military or was still a serving officer. To that end, Skelton said that he would be calling a meeting of his officers later and the main thrust of the investigation would centre on identifying possible suspects from the military.

On reporting the telephone call from Alan Warwick, Williams had become quite agitated. He had readily agreed that the intelligence report was highly disturbing and needed immediate action. Williams was just about to depart on holiday, so he instructed Skelton to report on his meeting with Warwick directly to Chief Superintendent Mike Sawyers. Skelton wished Williams a good holiday and left.

When he entered the squad room, Skelton cast his eyes around and noticed that both Turnbull and Spurrey were absent. He reckoned that they must still be interviewing the suspect from the glassing in the night club. He caught Alexander's eye and walked towards him.

'Are Ross and Chris still with that prisoner, Bill?'

Alexander looked a little pensive. 'Yes sir. He was arrested by uniform officers and they brought him into the custody suite. As it looked like a GBH charge, uniform phoned CID and left a voicemail message but the officers on duty last night never got it. So, Ross and Chris have had to take the prisoner to his home so that it can be searched. Ross just called to say that they have just found a large stash of class A drugs and several thousand pounds in cash. It looks like it's going to tie them up for a day or two.'

Skelton gave Alexander a smile and said, 'That's a good result, Bill, and it might just be a golden opportunity for us. I noticed that the CRO report showed that he had no convictions. Has he ever come up on the radar for drug dealing?'

Alexander thought for a second. 'No, I don't recall ever having come across him before and Ross said the house address has never been tagged as a potential dealer. Are you happy to leave it with Ross and Chris or should we take it over?'

Skelton was always happy to delegate. After all, that is how an officer gains experience. But there comes a point when the experience of an older and more experienced officer needs to be brought into play.

'Bill, tell Ross to continue with the search and send a CIS team to lend a hand. Once the search is completed, stick him back in his cell. We can keep him in custody for seventy-two hours. That will give him plenty of time to consider his options.'

Alexander left the room to call Ross Turnbull, so Skelton began the briefing without him. 'As you may know, DS Alexander and I attended the autopsy on Mr Cox this morning. Dr Challis is of the view that the killer was most likely a trained soldier, possibly a commando or special forces. The victim had been killed in a very efficient and controlled manner, making it impossible to defend himself or to scream or shout for help. Dr Challis is also of the opinion that the killer was probably taller than six feet. This will help us to rule in or rule out possible suspects with a high degree of accuracy.'

Skelton paused for a moment and cast a glance around the room. He could see that his team were making notes. 'Now as you all know, we have many military bases situated around Bath, so I am certain that we will have quite a few suspects to check out. When DS Alexander comes back, he will put you into teams of two and assign you to a specific military base. You will be tasked with visiting the base and it will be your responsibility to identify any potential suspects. You are all detectives, so I am not going to lecture you on what to look out for. Now, Ross Turnbull and Chris Spurrey are temporally on another case for the next forty-eight hours. DS Alexander and I will be out all day tomorrow, so you folks are going to have a lot of work to do. Hopefully, in a few days' time, the whole team will once again be working as a complete unit. Any questions?'

There were none, so Skelton stepped aside from the lectern and Alexander proceeded to allot the teams of two and assign them a military base.

Chapter Fifteen

Detective Inspector Patrick Rees was stationed in the main police station in Bristol, although he lived in Bath with his wife, who was a practicing solicitor in Bristol. Luckily, she did not practice criminal law, so there was never a chance that Rees would find himself or one of his officers involved in a conflict of interest.

Rees and Skelton had been friends for years and it was actually Rees who had informed Skelton of a vacancy in the Avon and Somerset Constabulary. Rees boarded the intercity 125 train from Bristol Temple Meads departing at 10.00 am to London Paddington. Its first stop was Bath Spa, where Skelton and Alexander were standing on the station platform. As the train pulled into the station, Skelton could see Rees' face at the door of the carriage. It was a second-class carriage. With so much austerity restraints on budgets, senior police officers could no longer travel first-class.

The detectives made their way to the door of the train where Rees was positioned and climbed aboard. Rees had met Alexander a few times so they knew each other by first names. 'I know that we only have second-class tickets, but let's go up into first-class and see if our warrant cards can work some magic.'

It was Skelton who had made the suggestion and he led the way. The second-class carriages were fairly busy but there were only a handful of people in the first-class section.

Skelton chose a four-seater with a table. He preferred to face the direction of travel and let Alexander sit by the window whilst he took the aisle seat. Rees sat opposite Skelton. After exchanging pleasantries, Alexander said, 'Do you know that this will be the first time in over ten years that I've gone up to the big smoke!'

The expression 'the big smoke' came from the days when London was dependent on coal-fired power stations for supplying electricity. These monstrous constructions followed the banks of the Thames from which coal barges satisfied their appetite for vast volumes of coal, the smoke from which was discharged directly above the city on a 24/7 basis. Being built in a basin, London was often subject to periods of thick fog, known as 'pea soupers'. This combined with the relentless output of smoke from the power stations and domestic fires often produced a toxic mix known as 'smog' which was almost impenetrable and impossible to see through. The smog was highly dangerous to health and shortened the lives of many Londoners.

Following the introduction of the Clean Air Act, introduced by the government of the day, the air quality gradually improved as coal power stations were decommissioned and coal fires were banned in some parts of the capital. The improvement did not last long, however; as the number of motor vehicles increased, so did the pollution. The mayor of London had imposed a congestion charge in the hope that it would deter motorists from using their cars. It had been a partial success but with the introduction of online shopping the number of diesel vans have increased substantially. Now London, like most cities throughout the world, remains a centre for toxic air.

No government anywhere in the world seems to be making a serious effort to reduce toxic emissions. Consequently, millions of people are dying needlessly from heart and lung disease and other conditions as a direct result of inhaling harmful air. Whilst Skelton himself did not suffer from asthma, his partner Ken did, and this was one of the reasons they had moved to Bath. Although Bath itself was beginning to suffer from poor quality air, and the local authority had imposed a congestion charge in some parts of the city. Skelton had his doubts that the congestion charge would improve the quality of air. It seemed to him that this was merely a cash cow for the city, penalising the locals as well as visitors.

They had only been settled in their seats for a few minutes when the ticket inspector turned up. 'Tickets please, gentlemen.' Skelton removed the tickets from his jacket pocket as well as his warrant card and Rees and Alexander did likewise. Skelton gave the ticket inspector a smile and said, 'Good morning, I know that we are not supposed to be sitting here, but we are senior police officers, and we need somewhere to sit where we can't be overheard. Unfortunately, our budget does not allow us to travel first-class.'

The ticket inspector looked closely at Skelton's warrant card and said with a smile. 'You are a chief inspector, Mr Skelton, so you outrank me. Feel free to sit where you are and the tea trolly will be along in a minute!'

Skelton thanked the ticket inspector and after he was out of earshot said, 'Well so far, so good. I just hope that the same trick works on the return journey.'

After the tea trolly had arrived and departed, Skelton briefed the others on what he knew about Murray and how he had killed his best friend, Joe Reilly, and had got away with it. He went on to remind them of Chief Superintendent Alan Warwick's telephone call, informing him that Murray was buying a house in Bath. He then went on to say that Murray had become involved with a certain Ben Naylor, who was born and bred in Bristol. Looking at Rees, he asked, 'Now Patrick tell us what you know about this guy Naylor.'

Rees took a sip of his coffee and carefully placed the paper cup in front of him on the table. He was just about to start speaking, when he noticed a man coming along the corridor. He waited until the man had passed and was out of earshot. 'This guy, Ben Naylor, is a nasty piece of work, with a quick temper. He is a big powerful guy and was born and brought up in Bristol in a particularly rough part of the city. It's the usual story. He never knew his father and so was raised by his mother. He has three siblings all younger than him but their fathers also disappeared after they were born.

'With no father to lead by example and to enforce discipline, young Naylor became the father of the house, helping his mother as best he could to raise her three other children. He was a strong, big boy and it was not long before he realised that to get to the top of the food chain, in such a tough neighbourhood, you had to assert yourself, and that he duly did. By the age of fourteen he was in a gang and was the right-hand man to another thug called Mickey Chadwell. Soon they were involved in street robberies, stealing mobile phones, credit cards and whatever else they could get their dirty hands on. Soon they had progressed to drug dealing and pimping young girls, who themselves were from troubled backgrounds and vulnerable.'

Rees took another sip of coffee and went on. 'We managed to arrest quite a few of the gang members, but Chadwell and Naylor always managed to make sure that we had no evidence to convict them. We arrested them often enough, that's for sure. By the time they were in their early twenties, they were driving around in flash BMWs and sporting designer labels. Naylor had become the enforcer. If you owed a drug debt and couldn't pay it, Naylor would turn up on the doorstep. The sheer size of the guy was usually enough to frighten whoever it was that owed the debt to pay up. But, if you couldn't pay, then Naylor would knock the shit out of you.'

Skelton took a sip of tea and asked, 'How come Naylor got done for badly assaulting someone?'

Rees thought for a second and said. 'Well, the guy has a temper and is very protective of whichever girl he happens to be going out with. Three years ago, he took some bird up to London for the weekend. They went into a bar one night in the West End. Naylor reckoned that a guy at the bar had stared at his bird for too long and told him to fuck off. The other guy tried to reason with him but Naylor was either drunk or high on drugs. He attacks the guy and pounds his face to a pulp. By the time the bouncers had managed to pull him off, the poor guy was unconscious. Luckily it was all caught on CCTV. He was arrested and when he saw the CCTV the next morning, decided to plead guilty.

'He would have probably got six years in prison but because of his early guilty plea, the judge reduced the sentence to four years and he was released after serving just two.'

Alexander asked, 'I take it that it was while he was in prison that he met Murray?'

Rees finished his coffee and dropped the empty cup in the bin. 'Yes, according to the prison records, they got to know each other in the gym. They are both big guys and no doubt had a mutual admiration for each other's physique. They ended up sharing a cell for about three months and were released on licence about six weeks apart.'

Skelton finished the last of his tea and said, 'Did Naylor return to Bristol after being released?' Rees leaned back in the comfortable chair and stretched his arms. 'Yes, he did, and we have kept close tabs on him. He's had to live at the address given to the probation service. This is a flat owned by his half-sister called Lotta. The flat is not far from the Bristol Rovers football stadium and is worth about £350,000. The thing is, Lotta, has never had a well-paid job and is just nineteen. The flat was bought for cash and we are pretty sure that the cash came from Naylor. His two other half-sisters have similar flats close by, which they own, and which again were bought for cash. Naylor does not own a house or flat and we suspect that he chooses not to do so, in case we convict him of a serious crime and seize his property, under the Proceeds of Crime Act.'

Alexander was pondering this information and asked, 'What's he been up to since he was freed?'

Rees looked at Alexander and then Skelton. 'Good question. When he got out, he made no hesitation in teaming up with Chadwell, who has also been busy investing in property, none of course in his own name. We know of six flats that were bought using cash and the same law firm acted in all six transactions, as well as acting in the purchase of the flats owned by Naylor's siblings. We hope at some point in time to nail the lawyer for money laundering.'

Skelton looked out the window and saw that they were pulling into Reading Station. The next stop would be London Paddington. 'But what exactly has Naylor been up to? You haven't answered Bill's question.'

'Well, we thought we had him carefully monitored. He has to see his probation officer once a month, otherwise he goes back to prison for non-compliance with the conditions of his release. Chadwell has somehow managed to have acquired some sort of a share in a scrapyard business, just on the outskirts of Bristol. The guy who used to run it was a crook, and we suspect that more than a few dead bodies were disposed of in there. The owner was called Bobby Dyson but he seems to have vanished, although nobody has reported him missing. He was a widower and had no children, so maybe he has just gone away somewhere to retire. But I doubt it.'

Skelton considered this information for a minute as the train pulled out of the station. 'What have they been up to at the scrapyard?' Skelton asked.

'The yard seems to have become operations HQ. Members of the gang have been observed coming and going, including Naylor. We think that drugs are being taken there for distribution but we haven't had enough evidence to search the place yet. The scrapyard can only be accessed down a long narrow lane, so it's difficult to keep a close watch on it. The last thing we want to do is to let them know that we are aware that they are using the place. We might try flying a drone over it, but it's debatable if that will give us any useful intelligence. We have, however, recently recruited an informant. He is some way down the food chain in the organisation, but he might just be able to give us a lead.

'Naylor has been seen in various parts of the city where we know that Chadwell has business interests. Most likely collecting money owed. However, we had no idea that he had gone up to London until you called me. Hopefully this morning we will gain a better understanding of what he's been up to.'

Chapter Sixteen

The officers got off the train at Paddington and took a taxi to New Scotland Yard, the headquarters of the Metropolitan Police. Skelton led them into reception and they all produced their warrant cards for inspection by a retired police officer, who was now a civilian employee. They then had to pass through an airport-type X-Ray scanner, which could detect metal and explosives. Having signed in, they were given visitor's passes, which were on a lanyard. These they hung around their necks. They took the lift to the third floor, where they were told they would be met and taken to see Chief Superintendent Warwick.

The lift door opened on the third floor and Skelton stepped out, followed by the two other officers. A young fresh-faced police cadet was waiting to escort them. Skelton reckoned the lad was about seventeen and fresh out of school. He led them to a large meeting room, where tea, coffee and biscuits had been laid out for them. They each took a seat and waited for Warwick. Alexander had been quiet since getting into the taxi. He was too busy trying to identify which parts of the capital they were passing through. Skelton noticed this and every few minutes he would tell him where they were.

Now seated, Alexander said, 'The wife won't believe where I've been to today. Can we get a picture of me standing outside, with the New Scotland Yard sign behind me?'

Skelton chuckled, 'Yes Bill, we can certainly do that for you.'

The door opened and in walked Warwick dressed in a smart suit and freshly ironed shirt. All four were similarly dressed. It would have been hard to tell they were police officers if they walked into a pub together. They all stood up as Warwick entered the room. He had a big smile on his face and made a beeline for Skelton.

'Dan, great to see you again, it's been a few months now since you left us.'

Skelton held out his hand and said, 'Yes, time does fly, Alan, and it's sure good to see you as well.'

They shook hands warmly, both men smiling with pleasure.

'Alan let me introduce you to DI Patrick Rees, he's based in Bristol and knows all about Naylor.'

Warwick held out his hand, 'Good to meet you, Patrick. Dan often mentioned your name.'

Skelton then nodded his head towards Alexander and said, 'And this is Bill Alexander, my DS, and I have to say, the best one I have ever had.' Alexander blushed at the introduction.

'Hello Bill, I'm very pleased to meet you. It was you that saved Dan in that terrorist attack, wasn't it?'

Alexander shook hands and replied, 'Well, he was a wee bit wet behind the ears when he arrived in Bath, so I had to take him under my wing.'

They all laughed and Warwick said, 'Well we are all glad that you did, Bill, and I hope he did thank you.'

Skelton looked at the twinkle in Warwick's eye and said, 'Actually, Alan, I bought him a bottle of single malt whisky and the bugger had the nerve to blame me the next day for his sore head!'

They all laughed again, it was a good sign of unity and team spirit. After they had helped themselves to tea, coffee and biscuits, they sat down at the large table, which could seat fourteen. The room was large but had no windows. The room was functional, as it was meant to be. The lighting came from ceiling lights, which could be dimmed when necessary. Warwick had taken one of the chairs at the end of the table and Skelton sat opposite him. Alexander sat next to Skelton and Rees next to him.

Warwick opened the file before him and began the briefing. 'I am sure that Dan has briefed you on the killing of DC Joe Reilly and how his killer escaped justice. As you know, anyone killing a cop will be closely monitored right up until the day they die or become so ill they are unable to carry out another crime. James Murray was sentenced to eight years for possession with intent to supply class A drugs but was cleared of killing Joe. Every police officer, serving or retired, would give their right arm to see that bastard get his just desserts for that killing.

'When he was in prison we had eyes in there reporting his every move. He made numerous friends during the four years that he served, including Benjamin Naylor, with whom he shared a cell for three months. Both are big men and they like to keep themselves fit by going to the gym. The fitness is not intended to improve their health but to ensure that in a fight, they win.'

Warwick took a sip of his tea and then went back to his notes. 'We managed to bug their cell and got some interesting intel for a few days, but we think they sussed it. We are pretty sure that Murray had bribed a warder, who let it be known that they were being bugged. After which all we ever heard talk about was football and films.'

Skelton leaned across the desk and said, 'And what was the interesting stuff that you did hear?'

Warwick gave him a smile, before going on. 'The interesting stuff, as you call it, Dan, is this… Naylor had begun bragging about how much of Bristol was under the control of a guy called Mickey Chadwell. I take it you are all familiar with the name?'

The three officers nodded their heads in unison.

'He boasted that he and Chadwell were pretty rich, but that we would never be able to get our hands on their property, as it was not in their own names. It seems that both Chadwell and Naylor are a bit concerned that we have at last started to use our very extensive powers under the Proceeds of Crime Act. Criminals have, it would seem, cottoned on to the fact that after we have locked them up we will also seize all of their ill-gotten gains.

'Murray told Naylor that we had tried to seize his house in London where Joe was murdered but had been unsuccessful, thanks mainly to a clever lawyer and an accountant, who convinced the judge that his house had been bought from the proceeds of sound legal investments. Although, all the cash in the house that night was seized as Murray had pleaded guilty to the drugs offences.'

Skelton leaned back in his chair, glanced at his three colleges in turn and said, 'Come on, Alan, I know that you are saving the best bit for last.'

Warwick gave him a warm smile and said, 'Actually, Dan, I am, but let me continue with the intel we gained from bugging the cell.'

Skelton raised his arms in surrender, 'Please, Alan, do continue.'

'Before they realised that they were being bugged, Murray expressed an interest in working with Naylor. He went on to brag about how much of London was under his control and how difficult it was to expand territory without a turf war. Naylor was initially quite cold to the suggestion, pointing out that he and Mickey Chadwell went back a long way. But Murray convinced him that with his help, he could be an equal partner in both London and Bristol. But he would have to swear his loyalty to Murray and be prepared to go against Chadwell.'

There was silence in the room for a few seconds until Rees spoke. 'Shit, things could get very nasty in Bristol, but this is great intel, Alan. Do we have any idea when the shit is likely to hit the fan?'

Warwick shook his head and said, 'No not really, but my hunch is that it's likely to be sooner rather than later.' Rees made a note.

Warwick was sitting with his hands resting on top of the file. He looked across at Skelton and Alexander, and then turned his head to look at Rees. 'What I just told you was the sum of our intel from the prison. When Murray was released, we continued to keep a close eye on him and still do. Whilst he was locked up, his sidekick, a guy called Steve Driscoll, held the empire together as best he could. But a rival firm had successfully taken over the prostitution racket, which apparently had not gone down very well with Murray. When Murray got out, it seems his first priority was to get that part of the business back. The gangster that had taken it over is, or was, called Jimmy White, another career villain with loads of previous form.

'We got word one day, that a massive Black guy had been seen drinking with Murray in a pub that none of us could ever enter unless we were feeling suicidal! The informant said that the Black guy was not local and had a strange accent. We showed him a picture of Naylor and he said that it was definitely the guy in the pub.'

Warwick stood up and pushed back his chair and stretched. He then began slowly pacing the room. 'According to our man, Murray and the Black guy made a social visit to Jimmy White's pub over in Clerkenwell. The pub is called the Green Man and he's owned it a good few years. Word is that White invited them upstairs for a quite drink and chat. White never thought for a moment that he was in any danger in his own pub, not with half his gang drinking downstairs. There was no noise from upstairs or any raised voices. After only about ten minutes, Murray and the Black guy came downstairs smiling, like they had just had a friendly drink.'

Warwick ambled over to where he had been sitting and rested his hands on the table. 'When they came downstairs, Murray said hello to a couple of the punters that he knew and then they left the pub, still all smiles. What no one knew, was that they had gone upstairs and killed White and thrown his body out of the window. There was no sign of a struggle and no blood. It seems likely that they just simply broke his neck. A van was waiting downstairs, and his body loaded inside. Of course, the body has not been found and the CCTV film from the pub vanished. So, it looks like Murray and Naylor have formed a deadly partnership. I suspect that Murray now feels confident enough to start a turf war here in London and to take on Chadwell in Bristol.'

Warwick sat back down and watched Skelton's face closely. Skelton was slowly digesting this intel, understanding the magnitude of their problem. 'How did you discover that Murray was buying a house in Bath?'

Warwick chuckled and said, 'Just pure bloody good luck! Last Friday, one of my support staff had to go to a firm of solicitors to make a statement. The solicitors are based in Bristol and are marginally cheaper than the London law firms, but still charge an arm and a leg! He took the train, which as you know stops at Bath Spa. Anyway, he got up to go to the buffet bar, which is located in first-class. As he was walking down the compartment, he recognised Murray, who was sitting alone studying the sales particulars of a house. My guy strolled past and managed to see the name of the estate agent. On his way back from the buffet, he noticed that

Murray had left his seat, probably to go to the loo. The sales particulars were on the table, so he took a quick look and got the address of the property.'

Warwick dug into the file on the desk and pulled out four sets of the sales particulars and chucked a copy to each officer. 'When he got back to the office, he downloaded the particulars and then did a Land Registry Search. This revealed that the house is owned by a Mr and Mrs Dixon, who bought the house back in 1988 for £120,000 and are now selling it for £2.8 million. Not a bad little investment.'

Skelton was busy studying the particulars. It was a beautiful house. Detached with five bedrooms and almost an acre of garden. It overlooked the Vale, the most desirable view in Bath. 'And you think Murray is buying it?'

Warwick cleared his throat. 'Well, we can't be certain at the moment but we did call the estate agent on Monday morning, and he said that contracts had been exchanged but would not give the name of the buyer, owing to data protection rules. As you know, completion of the sale usually takes place thirty days after the exchange of contracts. So, if Murray is the buyer, he could be in Bath next month.'

Skelton stood up and began pacing the floor, just as Warwick had done earlier. 'If Murray is buying the property, then it means that things could start getting serious soon. We don't have a big problem with drugs in Bath and can generally keep a lid on it. But my guess is this, Murray will want to take control of the drug racket in Bath as well as the prostitution. He is not the kind of guy who will ask nicely for the current baron to stand aside. The guy running Bath now is called Jake Rattan. Known to his mates as Jake the Rat, and to his enemies as just the rat. He is a devious little turd with a bad temper and likes drugs almost as much as the punters he sells them to.'

Rees interrupted. 'Yes, you're right, Dan. He's from Bristol and I arrested him a few times. Drug dealing, assault and we are pretty sure he glassed a guy in a disco, but never managed to prove it. So far, he's managed to stay out of jail but it will be interesting to see what happens when Murray moves in.'

Skelton sat back down in his seat and said, 'Whilst drug dealing in Bath at the moment under Rattan is not a serious issue, I'm very concerned that if Murray takes over it could become a huge problem. We have not so far had the problem with the so called "county lines" where young kids from disadvantaged backgrounds are recruited to bring drugs into the city from further afield. We know that it's widespread in London and the northern cities, and I have no doubt that Murray would love to import it to Bath.'

Warwick glanced at his watch. It was 12.30. 'Well, that's about all I have for you guys. Now I've booked a table at my favourite Italian restaurant, and the Met is buying lunch.'

Skelton looked surprised and said, 'But I thought you guys were moaning about budget cuts?'

Warwick was wearing his poker player's face. 'Yes indeed, the cuts have been awful. We have lost hundreds of experienced officers and are having to make do with old kit. But since we have started to actively seize control of cash and property under the Proceeds of Crime Act, things have got slightly better. We managed to take quite a few million pounds last year from convicted criminals here in London. As I chair the committee that decides where the seized money goes, I make sure that some is set aside for entertaining visiting police officers. And, if I am not mistaken, you gentlemen fall into that particular category!'

They all laughed and headed off to lunch.

Chapter Seventeen

It was only a five-minute walk to the Italian restaurant. The traffic was terrible and Skelton could taste the pollution on his tongue. This was one aspect of London that he certainly did not miss. Warwick led them into the restaurant and he was greeted by the owner, Luigi. After Warwick and Luigi had finished exchanging pleasantries, they were shown to a table right at the back of the restaurant. It was situated in a private room, so they could speak freely without the fear of being overheard. 'Do you use this place often, Alan?' asked Rees.

Warwick was unfolding his napkin. 'Yes, we do actually, but don't worry the place is not bugged. I have a team search it regularly!'

They began with gin and tonics, large ones of course. For the starters, they managed to knock back a couple of bottles of pinot grigio. When the main courses had arrived, Warwick had chosen one of his favourite riojas, which everyone agreed was a terrific choice. They accounted for four bottles of that. When it came to the dessert, Warwick suggested that they order the cheese plate with a good assortment of cheeses from around the world. This of course, could only be consumed with the aid of a bottle of port!

The officers were in fine fettle, totally relaxed and enjoying telling stories about some of the funny things which had happened during their careers. Alan Warwick was an exceptionally good horse-racing pundit, who actually made more money from gambling than he did as a police officer. He was very shrewd and only backed a horse five or six times a year. He studied the form books with a passion. He noted which trainers were in form and those that were having a lean spell, similarly with jockeys. He looked to see what the horses' optimum trip was likely to be and which races they had been entered to run in.

Warwick did not have a betting account with the bookmakers, he was too far ahead of the game for that. Once a punter starts winning big money, the bookmaker will close down the account. The bookies only want punters that lose money, not win it! Warwick had devised a cunning way of waging big bets without the bookies realising it. On the day the horse that he was backing was due to run, his wife Marion was dispatched with lots of envelopes each containing £100.

Marion would enter the betting shop and fill out the betting slip, naming the horse, the meeting and time of the race. She would mark it as £100 to win and hand it over to the assistant, who would put it through the till and give her back the franked betting slip. This she would put back in the envelope and write on it the name and address of the bookie. She would repeat this exercise in dozens of different betting shops throughout the morning and early afternoon until all the betting money had been staked. The bookmakers did not realise that Warwick had actually made a very large gamble, which would have brought the odds on the horse down considerably.

Warwick was very selective about who he would give a tip to. Skelton was one of those who were lucky and privileged to receive Warwick's sage advice. Over the years, Skelton had received about thirty tips from his friend, all of which had won! This had enabled him and his partner Ken to partially finance extensions to their home, lay a driveway and buy some luxurious furnishings, not to mention some exotic holidays.

The cheese and biscuits had just been delivered, as had the port. Warwick was pouring himself a large glass and was about to pass it to his left where Skelton was sitting. 'Dan, did you ever tell these guys about that tip I gave you when you were in Cardiff?'

Skelton did not generally mention to his colleagues his love of horse racing, and certainly not any of Warwick's tips. If Warwick gave him a tip, he would only share it with Ken.

'No, Alan I don't think I have but I am happy to do so.'

Warwick picked up a piece of cheese and before popping it into his mouth said, 'Go on, Dan, I love hearing you tell it.' Alexander and Rees sat back and smiled waiting for Skelton to begin the story.

'I was attending a two-day course in Cardiff, run by the Home Office. I knew quite a few guys on the course, so on the first night we all went out to dinner. After the dinner, we went to a pub where, let's just say, I sank more than my fair share of Fosters. Afterwards, I staggered back to my hotel. It was an old-fashioned one, where you had to get the room key from reception. When I asked for my key, the receptionist said that there was a message for me and handed me the key and an envelope. I took the lift and went to my room and eventually managed to get the key in the lock. Mind you it was tricky, the lock kept moving!'

Warwick began giggling, as so did the others.

'Once safely inside the room, I took out the note from the envelope and sat on the bed. Well, I had to, as the room was sort of spinning! The note said, "Continue to meet with charming man tomorrow at 4.10 pm Newbury." I was somewhat flummoxed by this note. I had no recollection of this charming man and I had never been to Newbury in my life. Anyway, I stuck the note on the bedside cabinet and managed to get my clothes off without falling over too much!'

The tears of happiness were beginning to run down Warwick's face.

Skelton paused to take a piece of cheese and a biscuit before carrying on. 'In the morning, I woke up and the room had mercifully stopped spinning. As you guys know, I never suffer from hangovers, but I was a bit bleary eyed. Suddenly, I noticed the note on the cabinet and read it again. I was still mystified as to what the bloody thing meant. Then I saw the name on the bottom. A Warwick.

'The Times newspaper had been pushed under the room door, so I got up and pulled open the sport section. I found the race cards and there was a meeting at Newbury and a race running at 4.10 pm. I could not find "Charming Man" but there was a horse called Charmer running in it. Clearly Alan had sent me a coded message, just to be safe. The conference was due to finish at midday and in those days, we lived in Thames Ditton in Surrey. I reckoned that if I skipped lunch, I could easily drive back home and bet on the horse in my local bookies and watch the race live.'

Skelton could see that he had his audience in the palm of his hand. 'After breakfast, I went to the conference and when it ended, I made my excuses for not staying to lunch. Actually, I did have a very good excuse, as my father was arriving from Scotland to stay with us for two weeks. Ken was going to meet him coming off the coach and bring him home on the train. As I headed back to the hotel to get my car, I had to stop at both the bank and building society to get enough cash for the bet. I never use debit or credit cards when placing a bet. If you use real cash, you get a sense of reality in the risk you are taking.' The other officers nodded their heads in agreement.

'It was twelve-thirty when I pulled out of the hotel car park and I reckoned I would be home somewhere around three-thirty, so I had plenty of time, or at least I thought so. It was a very hot Friday afternoon and the traffic was atrocious. Just getting out of Cardiff took nearly an hour. When I reached the M4, I thought I was home and dry. But I had only been going about fifteen minutes when the traffic began slowing up and eventually I came to a halt. It turned out that there had been an accident in some road works. I sat there for what seemed an eternity. I kept glancing at my watch and as time marched on, the more desperate I become.'

Skelton took another sip of port, which drained the glass. 'Any more port left? This is thirsty work!'

Warwick passed him the port, and said, 'We are going to need another bottle of this.'

By coincidence, the waiter had just popped in to see if they had all they needed. He was quickly dispatched to bring back reinforcements!

'It was now three-thirty and I had just forty minutes left in which to get the bet on and to make matters worse, I had forgotten to bring my battery charger for my phone, which was now well and truly dead. I had no way of calling Ken to get him to place the bet for me. Then, suddenly, the traffic began moving, slowly at first but after a couple of miles I began to increase speed. I needed to get off that bloody motorway and find the nearest town or village that had a bookie. I was belting along now when at last I saw an exit off the motorway and flew up it. I saw a signpost indicating a town three miles away. I was on a roundabout and kept going until I saw another sign indicating another town two and half miles away. I decided to head for it. The time now was two minutes after four and I was sweating big time.'

Skelton took another mouthful of port and continued. 'I drove as fast as I possibly could and had to hit the brakes hard as I entered the village. I don't think you could even call it a village, it was probably just a hamlet. My heart was racing and my watch said four-oh-six. Looking in desperation, I saw that there was a church, then a pub, a baker's shop and a bookie. I leapt out the car and abandoned it on double yellow lines and raced to the shop. It was a one-man band, not one of the big betting shop chains. I looked up at the TV and saw that they were just about to load the horses into the stalls. I grabbed a betting slip and wrote. Four-ten Newbury Charmer a thousand pounds to win and hurried over to the counter which the bookie was standing behind. There was just one other man in the shop, and he was occupied watching the horses being loaded into the stalls.

'I handed the bookie the betting slip and grabbed the money out of my pocket. The bookie I would say was about fifty, grey haired and a little overweight. He had a bored expression on his face which quickly disappeared when he glanced at the betting slip and saw my one thousand quid on the counter. "Oh, I don't know if I can take this, mate." I must have had the look of a desperate man on my face. "Why the hell not?" I asked. "I can't lay it off, mate, the race is off in a minute." I thought, my god I have made all this bloody effort to get here and now the bookie was not for taking the bet. Now he was looking at his TV monitor and I saw that Charmer had gone out from five-to-one to six-to-one whilst the favourite had come in, to even money.'

Skelton took another glug of port, whilst his audience were waiting patiently for him to continue. 'Well, the bookie suddenly had a change of heart, here was I wanting to back what was basically an outsider, whilst the smart money was going on the favourite. He put the betting slip through the till and handed me it back. He took the thousand pounds and I went over to the TV to watch the race. It was only five furlongs, the minimum distance. Suddenly the gates of the stalls opened and the race was off. The bookie had thoughtfully turned up the volume so that all three of us in the shop could hear the commentary.'

Skelton took some more port and the others did likewise. 'As I said, it was a hot day and I had had a frantic journey to get the bet on, and added to that, this was the biggest stake I had ever made. I was sweating uncontrollably and was mopping my forehead with a handkerchief. With only half a furlong still to race, my horse hadn't even been mentioned and the favourite was way out in front. The bookie had come and joined me in watching the race and I glanced a look at his face and there was a smile forming on his lips. I was beginning to silently curse myself for betting such a large lump of cash and for Alan to have gone to such lengths to ensure that I got the tip.'

Skelton took another shot of port. 'Just when I was about to walk out the shop in disgust, the commentator said, "And Charmer is making a move from the back of the field and he's flying, but the favourite is staying on. No, he isn't, he's running out of steam and here comes Charmer. He's over the line and Charmer wins it." I yelled out YES!'

Skelton's audience roared with laughter and it was a couple of minutes before Skelton could finish the storey. Warwick wiped his face with his napkin and said, 'Go on Dan, tell them about the bookie.'

Skelton refilled his glass and took a drink. 'Now let's just say that the bookie was not best pleased. The other man in the shop, who had been watching the race, turned to me and said, "Think you must have had a few quid on that horse." I looked at the guy and gave him a wink and said, yes you could say I had a few quid on it.'

Skelton had to clear his throat. 'The bookie had retreated back behind his counter and I was standing next to it. I saw him getting down on his hands and knees and realised that he was opening the safe. Just then they announced that the jockeys had weighed-in and so I was certain of picking up my seven thousand pounds, which was my winnings of six thousand plus my stake money of a thousand. I looked down over the counter and saw the bookie busy counting the money into bundles of one hundred and then making them up to make a thousand. He was almost finished his task, when in walked a lady who happened to be his wife. She saw all the money on the floor and me standing at the counter, and immediately realised that they had lost a considerable bet.'

Skelton picked up another piece of cheese and popped it into his mouth and chewed. 'Just when the bookie thought that nothing more could go wrong, he realised that he did not have enough cash in the safe. So, he got out his wallet and emptied it. He was still short. So, he asked his wife to open her handbag. The look of fury on the woman's face was a sight to behold. Eventually, the bookie managed to scrape together the seven thousand quid and banged it on the counter. He looked at me through gritted teeth and said, "Just don't ever come fucking back!"'

Warwick roared with laughter and Skelton joined in. When they had at last stopped laughing, Skelton glanced at his watch, it was 3.45 pm. 'Bloody hell, is that the time. We need to get out of here.'

Chapter Eighteen

The next morning, Skelton got up at his usual time with no indication of a hangover whatsoever. Having showered and shaved he had a mug of tea along with a KitKat. He had let the dogs out for a run in the garden and they were now back on their beds happily munching on Bonios. At 7.30 am he left the house and began walking into Bath. It was very overcast and a trifle chilly so he walked a bit faster than usual. Instead of going straight to the police station, he popped into Marks & Spencer and picked up some square sausages, or Lorne sausages as they are also called. These sausages can usually only be bought in Scotland and the north of England but M&S had recently started selling them in Bath. He then bought a small white loaf of bread and paid for them at the checkout.

On entering his office, he put the sausages and bread in the fridge and took off his jacket. He wandered into the CID room and was not surprised to find that Alexander was not at his desk. Alexander, unlike Skelton, suffered badly from hangovers, particularly if he mixed his drinks, which he had done yesterday. He had had gin and tonic, followed by white wine, then red wine and finally port. Skelton was wondering if Alexander would make it into work today when in walked DC Peter Lowik. 'Good morning, sir. Did you have a good day in London yesterday?'

Skelton gave Lowik a smile and said, 'Good morning, Peter. Yes, it was a very worthwhile trip, that's for sure. Unfortunately, we were pressed into having lunch with my old boss, which whilst very pleasant did involve rather a lot of alcohol. For that reason, my money is on Bill turning up at some time this morning with a rather sore head.'

Lowik laughed. 'Yeah, Bill tends to suffer quite a bit after a drinking session. I just hope you kept him away from the bloody port though, that kills him.'

Skelton grimaced and said, 'Damn, I wish you had warned me, Peter. As well as the gin and tonics to get us started, we got through two bottles of white, four bottles of red and three bottles of port!'

Lowik threw his hands up in the air and cried, 'My god if he makes it in today, it will be a bloody miracle.'

Skelton could never understand why drink had such a bad effect on people the morning after, especially when he always felt perfectly okay.

Alexander did not make it into the office until almost eleven that morning. Since arriving, he had sat at his desk pretending to be looking at his computer, but his brain was barely capable of thought. Skelton popped his head around the door about ten minutes after his arrival and said, 'Good morning, Bill, you finally made it then.' Alexander raised his head and turned slowly to look at Skelton. His eyes were bloodshot and his face was a ghostly grey colour. He looked like he had just got out of bed.

'Aye, morning, Dan. Christ that was some bloody lunch yesterday, but I wish I never had that damn port. Whoever invented that stuff should be shot!'

Skelton smiled and said, 'Well, Bill, I don't recall anyone forcing you to drink it, but I will get you sorted out in a moment or two.'

Skelton went to the fridge and collected the square sausages and bread and headed to the canteen to cook them. Ten minutes later he placed a sausage sandwich which he had seasoned with salt, pepper and brown sauce on Alexander's desk along with a mug of tea. 'Go on, Bill, get stuck into that. It will either cure you or kill you.'

Alexander looked up and said, 'To tell you the truth, I don't care which one it is, so long as it puts me out of my misery.'

Skelton went back to his office and sat down to eat his sausage sandwich. He devoured it in seconds and wished he had made himself two instead of one. Having answered all his emails, he checked his watch and saw that it was almost midday. He had called for a briefing meeting with the team on the park murder for noon. He headed to the murder enquiry room and opened the door. He was surprised to see that Alexander had made it.

'How are you feeling, Bill?' Alexander had regained some colour but his eyes were still quite red.

'You were right about that sausage sandwich, Dan; I feel much better already.' Skelton gave him a slap on the shoulder and walked over to the lectern.

Skelton cleared his throat and began. 'Right, listen up everybody. It's been almost a week since Harry Cox was found murdered in Alexandra Park and to date we have made no arrests. As you all know, we initially believed that the prime suspect was the jogger dressed in black and wearing a hoodie, but he turned out to be an off-duty police officer, who just happened to have gone for a run around the park at about the time of the murder. Forensics have cleared him of any involvement. His phone was carefully examined and he had not been in contact with the victim either by phone or through a dating app. We believe that we have traced everyone that was in the park at the material time, but no one has reported seeing anyone acting suspiciously or having seen either the victim or the killer entering or leaving the bushes, where the killing took place.

'The only forensics that we do have are some black fibres found on the victim which could have come from the killer. At the moment, this is the only positive aspect of evidence that we have and so it's vitally important that if we do make an arrest, we must ensure that we recover all the suspect's dark clothing. Short of getting a confession, this will be our only opportunity to connect the killer to the victim.'

Skelton scanned the room and pointed at Janet Griffin, who was busy taking notes. 'Janet, can you give us an update please on the victim's phone?'

Griffin stood up and looked around the room at her fellow detectives. 'As you know, we have not found Mr Cox's phone despite an exhaustive search of the park and neighbourhood. We have, however, been able through his network provider to trace all the people bar one that he spoke to in the last six weeks of his life. Whether this be actually talking on the phone or texting. The only person that we have failed to trace called Mr Cox the evening before he was murdered and twice on the day of the murder.'

This information caused a few exchanges of words between some of the detectives. Skelton raised his hand for silence. 'Go on, Janet, please continue.'

Griffin leaned on the desk and looked around the room. She had their complete attention. 'We haven't been able to trace the owner of the phone who spoke to Mr Cox, as the phone is pay as you go. It's unregistered so tracing the owner is virtually impossible unless you actually find the phone on them. What we do know is this, the caller was in the park when they made the call on the eve of the killing and shortly before the murder was committed. It's my belief that the killer phoned Mr Cox the evening before the murder to arrange the meeting the following afternoon. Then fifteen minutes or so before the killing, the killer called to make sure that the victim was in the park. There was one final call, which again I suspect was the killer telling the victim to enter the bushes so that they could have sex.'

Skelton considered this scenario very carefully. 'Yes, Janet, I agree with you entirely. I suspect that the caller made the call on the Thursday evening to confirm the time and place of the rendezvous. I also suspect that this was probably the first time that they actually spoke in person. It seems to me that in all likelihood the killer had contacted the victim via a gay dating app. Mr Cox's brother confirmed that he did use such an app but does not know which one it was that he used. We have sent Mr Cox's email address to every gay dating website in the UK, asking them to see if they can confirm whether he was a registered member. Unfortunately, the response has been slow, but two websites have reported that they have no record of him. Chris Spurrey is chasing the other websites up and hopefully we will get a lead soon.'

Skelton rested his arms on the lectern and was just about to speak when Bill Alexander said. 'Sir, if the killer went to the park the evening before the killing, he might have been caught on CCTV at the bowling club.'

Skelton was pleased that Alexander had reached the same conclusion as himself. 'That's a good point, Bill. You and I will take a run up to the bowling club this afternoon and review it. In fact, we will bring in whatever footage has not so far been reviewed. Speaking of CCTV, as you all know it's perfectly possible to enter and leave the park without being captured on CCTV. We have reviewed the footage from the entrance of the school but that gave us no leads whatsoever. Ross, what about the victim's background?'

Ross Turnbull stood up and looked at his notebook and said, 'The victim was apparently very well liked by his family and friends and workmates. He had never been in trouble with the police, not even a speeding ticket. He certainly didn't seem to have any enemies. Out of everyone we spoke to, no one had a bad word to say about him. He played skittles on a Wednesday evening, provided his shift at the factory allowed. He met his brother once a week for a drink, and again this would depend on his shift arrangements. He had nearly twenty grand in the bank and we checked on his bank statements for any unusual activity. There was none, so we can rule out that he was being blackmailed.

'I also checked his bank statements to see if he was subscribing to a dating site or escorts but whatever app he used he didn't pay a subscription to it. His neighbours said that they had seen some young guys coming and going from his property, but no one remembers seeing any for several months. We also checked to see if he had left a note anywhere saying that he was meeting someone from a dating site, but nothing there either.'

Turnbull sat down. Skelton felt a distinct twinge of frustration. Five days into the investigation and they hadn't made a breakthrough. It's usually the first golden hour of an investigation that provides clues as to the identity of the killer. In this case, they thought they had found the killer on CCTV. The jogger in the park had been their prime suspect. But he was just an off-duty copper, out having a regular run around the park. There were no forensics on him and Peter Lowik spoke highly of him.

'On Monday, I reported that Dr Challis was of the opinion that the killer was most likely from a military background, possibly a commando or special forces. DS Alexander paired you up and assigned you to a military base. As you only had yesterday to get to work with the task of identifying possible suspects, I assume that you are not yet in a position to provide me with a list. Is that correct?'

Ross Turnbull stood up. 'Sir, Chris and I were tied up all day yesterday with that GBH case which in turn led to being also a serious drugs case. So, we haven't had a chance to do anything on the murder case.'

Skelton smiled and said, 'Yes, I know, Ross, that's completely understandable. To be honest, I was not expecting any of you to have had a proper opportunity to come up with a list of suspects. Now unless anyone has any questions, I want you all to prioritise working the military bases assigned to you. I don't expect to see any of you around here much over the next few days. Unless we get a breakthrough in the next twenty-four hours, the next briefing will take place on Friday morning at nine.'

Chapter Nineteen

After the team briefing, Skelton looked at his watch. It was 12.30 pm. The sausage sandwich had taken the edge off his appetite but he was thirsty. The big lunch from the day before needed some walking off and Alexander certainly needed some fresh air. Skelton loved a good walk at lunchtime and often took Alexander on convoluted walks around Bath. Whilst the pub of their choice was perhaps only a few minutes' walk from the police station, Skelton would lead them on a walk lasting perhaps fifteen or twenty minutes.

When Skelton first arrived in Bath as a police officer some three months previous, there were two pubs situated very close to the police station. There was the ale house on Bog Island and Lambrettas on North Parade. Both sold Foster's lager, Skelton's favourite drink, but both had recently stopped selling it. This annoyed Skelton very much and he had been forced to venture further afield. First, he tried the Royal Oak on Pultney Road, which did sell Fosters, but to him it lacked atmosphere.

The only other pubs which Skelton was aware of that sold Fosters in Bath was the Saracen's Head, which happened to be the oldest pub in Bath, and the Cat and Fiddle. Skelton decided that a pint or two in the Saracen's Head would be in order and a light lunch. He made his way to the CID room where he found Alexander coming off the phone.

'After that enormous lunch yesterday, I've decided that we should have a little light lunch. So, let's go for a nice little walk to clear your head and then we can have a couple of pints in the Saracen's Head.'

Alexander clasped his hands on his head and rested his elbows on the desk. 'In the name of the wee man, Dan. How can you even suggest going for a pint after that marathon session yesterday? When I got home yesterday I went straight to bed, much to my dear lady wife's dismay. You can bet that come the weekend there will be a list of jobs needing doing the length of your arm.'

Skelton felt sorry for his DS. 'Come on, Bill, the air will do you good and since I was partially responsible for getting you in that mess, the drinks are on me.'

This seemed to provide the encouragement that Alexander needed. He stood up and picked up his jacket. 'Peter, mind the shop until I get back and if I'm not back in an hour and a half, send a search party, but for god's sake don't tell my wife!'

The pub was only about a seven-minute walk away, far too short for Skelton. So, when they came out of the nick, they turned right and walked to the junction with North Parade. He turned right onto North Parade and they walked over the bridge over the river Avon. At the end of the road, they turned left onto Pultney Road. The weather had brightened up but it was still a little chilly. Both men were lost in their own thoughts and said very little. They walked past Bath Bowling Club on their left. This was the premier bowling club in Bath and boasted some very good players. As a boy, Skelton had played bowls and was good enough to win the Lanarkshire County Pairs Championship when he was just fourteen. He gave up bowling when he went to university but had always promised himself to play again when time permitted.

They passed the Bird Hotel and turned left. this would bring them onto Great Pultney Street, which was a magnificent Georgian Crescent. Skelton could imagine how coach and horses must have looked in a bygone age. The footpaths were quite crowded with workers popping out to lunch, plus the usual visitors and residents diligently going about their business. At the City Chambers, they crossed the street and then they turned right. If they carried on walking this would take them to the Saracen's Head. Suddenly Skelton said, 'Lets cross the road to the butchers, Bill. I want a couple of sirloin steaks for dinner tonight.'

Alexander glowered and said, 'I'm going to be lucky to get a cheese sandwich tonight after getting in such a state yesterday.'

They stopped at the butchers and Skelton studied the vast display of meats hanging in the window and laid out on the shelf. Skelton loved butcher shops and fish mongers and could quite easily gaze at them for ages. He went inside and emerged a few minutes later with two thinly sliced sirloin stakes, his and Ken's favourite cut. They were headed for the Saracen's Head when Skelton noticed the pub opposite the butchers. It was named Belushi's and he had not been inside it since his university days. He couldn't remember what it looked like inside or what beers it sold.

'Bill, have you been in there recently,' Skelton pointed in the direction of the pub. Alexander considered the question for a second. 'No, Dan, I haven't been in there in years. It used to be popular with the students but I don't know what the clientele is like nowadays.'

Skelton made up his mind. 'Let's have a look inside. You never know, they might sell Fosters.'

Skelton opened the door and walked in. The bar was straight ahead about fifteen metres away. There was a young couple sitting at the bar, sipping cocktails. The barman was standing behind the bar drinking from a mug, which Skelton guessed contained tea or coffee. When he saw the men approaching, he put it down and gave them a welcoming smile. Skelton studied the beer pumps and his face broke into a wide grin. 'Look, Bill, they sell Fosters here. This could easily become another watering hole for us.'

Apart from the young couple sipping cocktails at the bar, the pub was empty, which suited Skelton and Alexander as they could talk without being overheard. Skelton guessed the barman was about thirty-five and of a solid build. The guy looked fit and Skelton wondered if he had been in the army or one of the other armed forces. The barman smiled at them and said, 'Good afternoon, gentlemen, and what can I get you?'

Skelton returned the smile and replied, 'We will have a couple of pints of Fosters, please. Do you serve food at lunchtime, by any chance?'

The barman had picked up two empty Fosters glasses and was about to fill them up. 'Yes, we do food all day long and into the evening. The kitchen closes at 9.45. There are menus on the tables and you can order your food at the bar. I haven't seen you gentlemen in here before, are you visiting Bath today?'

Alexander answered the question. 'No actually, we both live and work in Bath. We like to get out of the office whenever we can for a spot of lunch, and this is pretty close to the office.' The barman placed the two-pint glasses in front of the officers and Skelton handed him a twenty-pound note.

The barman rang the till and asked, 'Oh where do you guy's work?'

Skelton smiled and said, 'Actually we are police officers. I am Detective Chief Inspector Dan Skelton, and this here is my colleague Detective Sergeant Bill Alexander. We work out of Manvers Street so this would be a convenient pub for us to use.'

The barman had a surprised look on his face at hearing that his new customers were police officers. 'Gosh, you don't look like police officers, but I'm delighted to meet you. My name is Joe and I run the place.'

The cops each took a mouthful of lager and replaced their glasses on the bar. 'Joe, it's good to meet you but we would appreciate it if you didn't broadcast the fact that we are cops, if you don't mind?' said Skelton.

Joe moved from behind the bar to where his new customers were standing and thrust his right hand out and shook hands with both men. 'Don't worry about that. I used to be in the marines, your secret is safe with me.'

'Well, Bill, apart from that superb lunch yesterday, what did you make of what Alan Warwick had to say?'

Alexander picked up his drink and took a long glug. He gently put the glass down on the table and looked at Skelton. 'Well, Dan, I never knew that you were such good friends with the young copper that was killed. It must have been tough on you, and it must seem very strange, knowing that Murray is moving to Bath. But you need to be very careful not to allow your personal emotions to cloud your judgement. Both Murray and

Naylor are very dangerous men and I certainly wouldn't fancy my chances against either of them in a fight. Tell me, does Murray know you?'

Skelton lifted his glass and took a long drink and carefully placed the half-empty glass back on the table. 'When I was in the Sweeney, I of course knew a fair bit about him, but I never actually worked on any of the cases he was thought to be involved in. When Joe was killed, I spent a lot of time with his widow, doing as much as I could to support her. Then when the case came to the Old Bailey, I would take her to the court every day. For over a week, I sat with her, holding her hand, as we both watched Murray sitting in the dock. The funny thing was that he rarely looked at us. He was more concerned with what the witnesses were saying and what his barrister was doing to get him off with the murder charge. When the judge ordered the jury to acquit him of murder, I will never forget the smile on his face. It was of utter contempt and I swore to myself that one day I would lock the bastard up for life or even kill him.'

Alexander was carefully watching Skelton as he spoke. 'So, Murray must know you?'

Skelton put both hands around the glass and said, 'To be honest, Bill, I'm not sure that he does. You see when I was in court with Joe's widow, I never gave evidence as I was not involved with the case. I was just in the public gallery, which of course was packed, owing to the fact that a policeman had been killed. In all probability, he may have assumed that I was a relative. I'm not sure if he will recognise me the next time we meet. I, however, will certainly recognise him, that's for sure.'

Chapter Twenty

Skelton was at his desk. He had spent the morning considering the list of possible suspects to the murder in Alexandra Park. Things were not looking good. Dr Challis had suggested that the killer might have served in the army or was serving in the army. His officers had worked diligently to provide a list of possible suspects but of the dozen names that they had come up with, all had perfect alibis. Skelton had the feeling that this was a crime that was going to be almost impossible to solve. He and his team would continue with their best endeavours to find the killer, but he was far from optimistic.

There was a knock on the door and in walked Alexander. Skelton smiled and said, 'Hi, Bill, take a seat. What can I do for you?'

Alexander rubbed his hand through his hair and sighed. He slowly sat down opposite Skelton and said, 'Sir, progress in this murder case has been non-existent. Apart from a few fibres on the victim, we have got absolutely nothing else to go on. We have eliminated every possible suspect, including our prime suspect, who happens to be a serving police officer. I think we have now run out of any further lines of enquiry.'

Skelton detected the frustration in Alexander's voice, and he shared that frustration, but as team leader he couldn't show it. He had to try and maintain morale in the team otherwise they would never solve the crime. Skelton leaned back in his chair and cupped his hands behind his head. He looked at Alexander straight into his eyes.

'Bill, we need to be patient. I agree that our enquiries have not progressed as I would have liked. The killer has left us few clues that's for sure. If I were a betting man, and I am, I reckon that the killer is pretty convinced that he's got away with this killing. Now if you were in his shoes, what would you do? Sit back and gloat and say right, I've pulled off the perfect crime and retire? Or having achieved what he thinks is the perfect crime, try to emulate it?'

Alexander stood up abruptly. 'Sir, do you think he will strike again?'

Skelton stood up and walked around to where Alexander was standing. He placed his right arm on Alexander's shoulder and said, 'Bill, that's what scares me. So, we need to remain focused on this. The killer is dammed smart that's for sure. He carefully chose his victim, but so far, we have found no positive motive for him to be murdered. The key to unlocking this mystery is to find a suspect with a motive. That's our job, Bill, and I'm bloody well determined that we will find a suspect with a motive. And when we do that, our killer will be going to jail for a very long time!'

Chapter Twenty-One

Skelton and his partner Ken were walking down Entry Hill, accompanied by their three black Labradors, Brenty-Boy, Josh and Archie, who were on their leads and walking perfectly to heel. They were headed to Trevor Thomas' birthday party. It was young Trevor and his black Labrador who had found the dead body in Alexandra Park.

Skelton remembered where the house was situated as he had seen the family drive out one Sunday morning as he walked to work. He and Alexander had also visited the house in order to take a witness statement from Trevor. Skelton had a birthday card in his left hand and a £50 gift voucher so that Trevor could chose a present of his choice.

Skelton had initially decided not to attend the birthday party, but changed his mind when he discovered that James Murray was moving to Bath from London. Murray had murdered Skelton's best friend but had got away with it on a legal technicality. By pure coincidence. Murray was buying a house next door to where the Thomas family lived. Both houses were very similar in design and Skelton guessed that the same builder was responsible for building them. They were both detached houses boasting six bedrooms, with generous sized rooms and each had about an acre of garden. Skelton was worried that Murray was moving to Bath, as he was sure that his agenda was to take over the drug racket in Bath and to become top dog in nearby Bristol. It was Skelton's mission to ensure that neither happened, but if it did, Skelton would do everything possible to ensure that Murray ended up in prison or dead.

As they approached the house, Skelton could see the estate agent's board on the next house along. It said, 'sold subject to contract'. Skelton reckoned that Murray would be moving into the house within the next two weeks. After that, it would only be a question of time before Murray would muscle in on the local drug racket. Skelton was acutely aware that

Murray would use as much force as was necessary to seize control. This could mean Jake the Rat, the current drugs baron, being warned off or more likely being seriously injured at best. Skelton had carefully considered whether or not to warn Mr and Mrs Thomas about their new neighbour, but decided that there was no point in worrying them.

Skelton rang the doorbell and it was almost immediately answered by Mr Thomas. 'Dan, great to see you and thank you for coming.' He looked down and saw the three black labs. 'Oh, great you've brought the dogs. Trevor will be delighted. And this must be your partner.' Skelton made the introductions, and they all went inside the house.

A large marque had been erected in the garden and long trellis tables were laden with food. The food looked delicious, and it was obvious that no expense had been spared. Opposite the food tables was a bar manned by three young men. Skelton noticed that draught beer and lager was available, but what brought a big smile to Skelton's face was the Fosters sign on the pump. His initial thoughts were that they would stay for an hour and make their excuses and go. But the sight of the delicious looking food and the barrel of Fosters quickly changed his mind. It was a Sunday afternoon, and he had the day off. He was going to enjoy himself!

Skelton got himself a pint of Fosters and a white wine spritzer for Ken. Ken was holding the dogs by their leads when suddenly young Trevor bounded up to them with Johnny the black lab by his side. Skelton made a high five and Trevor reciprocated.

'Dan, it's so great to see you and thank you for coming. My god what wonderful dogs you have. You can let them off their leads, the garden is dog proof.' Skelton's boys lost no time in getting to know Johnny and within minutes they were playing together in the large garden.

'Trevor, this is my partner, Ken. I have told him all about you finding that man's body and how well you coped in the circumstances.' Trevor and Ken shook hands and smiled.

'Have you caught the killer yet, Dan?'

Skelton took a mouthful of lager and said, 'To be honest, Trevor, progress has been very slow. We have eliminated every suspect that we had. The killer must have got into the park evading the CCTV cameras. So, he knew where they were sited, which makes me think he is a local man. But neither you nor any of the other people who were in the park saw anyone acting suspiciously.'

Trevor had a lager in his hand and lifted it up towards Skelton and said, 'But I saw that jogger and he looked suspicious to me!'

Skelton drained his glass. 'Actually, Trevor, the jogger was an off-duty police officer. We have interviewed him, and he is a regular jogger in the park. We also took possession of his jogging gear and forensic examination of his clothes confirmed that he could not possibly be the killer.'

Trevor took a sip of lager and asked, 'Blimey, if the killer has got away with this, is he likely to strike again?'

Skelton considered the question carefully. 'The thing is, Trevor, some killers that have got away with a murder might be content not to strike again. Why risk the chances of being caught when they think that they have committed the perfect crime? On the other hand, some killers have an insatiable appetite for killing and will go on to do so until they get caught. I am hoping and praying that this guy will be content with the kill in the park. But he might just be the type of guy who will go on killing until we catch him.'

Chapter Twenty-Two

The morning after the birthday party, Skelton was walking to work. It was a lovely sunny morning and Skelton was in good spirits. The birthday party had been a great success. He had sunk more than his fair share of the Fosters and the chicken curry had been totally amazing. He and Ken had cemented a firm friendship with the Thomas family, which he sensed would last a long time.

He arrived at the police station just before 8 am and on entering his office, took his suit jacket off and hung it up. Skelton had a fridge and a kettle in his office and his first task every morning was to fill the kettle and make some tea. He adored Twinings Breakfast Tea. He had two mugs before him, one for himself and one for Alexander. He finished making the tea when he heard a knock on the door and in walked Alexander.

'Good morning, sir. Did you have a good weekend?'

Skelton smiled at Alexander and said, 'Actually, Bill, it was very enjoyable. We went to young Trevor Thomas' birthday party yesterday afternoon and had a great time. The food and drink were splendid. We only meant to pop in for an hour in the afternoon, but we didn't leave until eight in the evening. That was when they ran out of Fosters!'

Alexander picked up his mug of tea and said, 'Christ, I don't know how you manage to put all that lager away without getting a hangover!'

Skelton smiled broadly and said, 'It's all in the genes, my boy!'

The officers sat down at Skelton's desk. Skelton booted up his computer and checked the crime reports from the weekend. It had been a remarkably quiet weekend. There had been a few assaults but nothing serious. He instructed Alexander to delegate the assaults to the CID team as there was nothing serious enough for Skelton and Alexander to get involved with.

'Bill, why don't you and I take a drive up to that house that Murray is buying. It's a Mr and Mrs Dixon that are selling it to Murray. I'd like to know when Murray is intending to move in. I want to be in a position to keep close tabs on the bastard when he gets here. If he so much as farts, I want to know about it. I never had the opportunity to nail him in London, but I am going to do my utmost to make sure I nail him here.'

Chapter Twenty-Three

It was two weeks after young Trevor's birthday party and Murray had moved into the house next door along with his girlfriend, who was named Penny Cole. A background check on her revealed that she had been a model. She had no criminal convictions but was suspected to have been a prostitute. It was unclear whether or not she had worked for Murray, but they had been together for the last six months. She was twenty-four years old and had been born and raised in south-east London. Her father had served several prison sentences and was currently in prison doing six years for GBH. She had the type of pedigree that appealed to Murray. She was almost six feet tall, with blond hair which covered her shoulders. She was dim-witted but beautiful, which suited Murray very well.

A few days after moving into the property, Murray had a visitor in the shape of Ben Naylor, the big Black guy with whom he had shared a cell in prison. He had also assisted Murray in killing Jimmy White in a pub in London. His body had never been found and although the police suspected them, there was not a shred of evidence against them. Murray had a clear plan. He had considerable influence in the East End of London, which included drugs and prostitution. He was earning very good money and his reputation was such that it would be a very brave or stupid person to try and muscle in on his patch. After all, he had killed a policeman and got away with it, and the criminal underworld knew that he and Naylor had murdered Jimmy White. Naylor was the enforcer for Mickey Chadwell in Bristol, but Murray had convinced Naylor that as a partnership they could take over Bristol. That would come in good time. First of all, he wanted to take over the drug racket in Bath and grow it.

Murray and Naylor were sitting down in the dining room. Each had a bottle of cider in their hand. Penny was in the kitchen making dinner. She was not a particularly good cook, so Murray preferred to dine out.

Tonight, however, he wanted to be at home, where he could speak freely without being overheard.

'Well, how did the move go, James?' asked Naylor. 'It was a piece of cake really. The removal men did a really good job. They packed up everything in London and brought it down here. All we had to do was to tell them where to put the furniture and stuff and they did. But this is a big house, so we are going to have to go out and do some serious shopping. Penny can't wait, so I am expecting some hefty credit card bills in the next few months.' They both laughed and sipped their cider.

Murray stood up and began pacing the room. 'I've got good money coming in from London but I bought this place with cash, which severely dented my savings. The house is in Penny's name, but she's leaving it to me in her will!' They both laughed out loud.

Murray took another drink from the cider bottle and said, 'I regard Bath as my new home and manor. Everything in London is going well but should I need to sort any crap out it's only an hour away on the train. I want to take over the drug trade here, which means having to sort out this guy called Jake Ratten, or Jake the Rat as he's known. Once that is sorted, you and I are going to take over Bristol, which means you ending your partnership with Mickey Chadwell and beginning your partnership with me, sunshine.'

Murray sat down and clinked bottles with Naylor. They both smiled. 'So, when do you want to make a move on the Rat?'

Murray stood up again and walked towards the window overlooking the garden. The lawn needed mowing and he would have to get a gardener in at least once a week. 'The thing is, Ben, I don't want to draw attention to myself with the police. If we waste the Rat the cops are going to want to know who had the balls to do it. Currently, no one in Bath would dare to make a move on him. So, they will conclude that either someone has moved into Bath, or it was Mickey Chadwell. This requires us to be exceptionally cunning. And I have a plan that will remove the Rat from the scene without arousing suspicion from the cops. All I need you to do, my friend, is to set up a meeting with the Rat, preferably at his place so that he feels safe and secure. After all, he will have his minders there and there will be only the two of us. What could possibly go wrong will be his immediate thought, but not quite his last!'

Chapter Twenty-Four

Skelton was on his way to see Superintendent Williams when he saw Inspector Bryan Stevens walking towards him. Stevens was in charge of the firearms unit of Avon and Somerset Constabulary, and was a legend in shooting circles. He joined the army straight from school and immediately impressed his training instructors with his incredible accuracy with any type of firearm that he was given. The instructors were in awe of this new recruit, not just by his shooting ability, but by his hard work ethic. In every training exercise he undertook Stevens would emerge top of the class.

It was no surprise that he volunteered to be a sniper. His instructors were in total agreement that he was the finest shot they had ever come across. He was soon representing the army in shooting competitions. In the twenty-five years he served in the army, he won every shooting competition that he entered. He served in many conflicts all over the world and retired with the rank of captain. Stevens had lost count of the number of enemy combatants that he had killed, and it certainly never caused him to lose any sleep.

Stevens had been born in Bath and on leaving the army returned to his roots. Still in his mid-forties, he applied to join the Avon and Somerset Constabulary. Within two years he had joined the firearms unit and his promotions were swift. After serving for ten years, he assumed command of the unit on the retirement of its commander. He was held in the highest esteem by his team and they adored him. A man of great charm and wit, he was a natural leader.

'Bryan, great to see you.' Skelton smiled and held out his right hand and the two men shook hands.

'Hello, Dan, always a pleasure to see you. It's a shame we never get to work together.'

Skelton smiled again and said, 'Bryan, as much as I would like to work with you, it's a comforting thought to know that the use of firearms in Somerset is rare. However, if I am ever in a situation where I need armed backup, I will feel very safe in the knowledge that we have probably the finest firearms unit in the country.'

Stevens chuckled and said, 'Thank you, Dan, for the compliment, and if I may say we have got a brilliant leader in you in charge of the CID.' The officers shook hands again and bade farewell to each other. Skelton headed for Williams' office.

He knocked on the door and heard Williams telling him to come in. Williams was in uniform and stood up to greet his visitor. 'Thanks for coming in, Dan, would you like a tea or coffee?'

Skelton had had his morning sausage sandwich and mug of tea just minutes previously. 'No, sir, thank you; I just finished my midmorning snack before coming to see you.'

Both officers were now seated and Williams began. 'Well, Murray has been here in Bath for a couple of weeks now. Has he been active in any way that we know of?'

Skelton cleared his throat and said, 'No, sir, he has been remarkably quiet. I don't think he is aware that we know of his arrival. I think he is just taking his time to get acquainted with the local scene. We do know that Ben Naylor visited him a few days after he moved in. Jake the Rat still seems to be in control of his little drugs empire, but we busted one of his dealers after he glassed a guy in a night club. He's in custody awaiting trial but I would bet that he pleads guilty to get a discount on his sentence.'

Williams leaned forward on his desk and said, 'I'm glad that nothing has happened so far, but I want you to keep a tight lid on this, as I am sure you will, given Murray's form.'

Skelton leaned forward and said, 'Sir, don't worry about that. Murray is and will be my chief priority. There is nothing I'd like better than to put him behind bars. I think this is going to be a waiting game and he seems to be taking his time to adjust to his new environment. But he is an out and out villain and will begin making moves here and in Bristol. There is no question about that. I speak to DI Rees in Bristol almost every day and it appears that Mickey Chadwell and Ben Naylor are still very much a team. However, with Naylor visiting Murray here in Bath, I reckon that Murray and Naylor will make a move on Chadwell sometime and fairly soon.'

Williams rested back in his chair and said, 'Okay, Dan, I have total confidence in you and I know that you are closely monitoring this situation, I just wish you the best of luck and I hope that you get Murray. But by all accounts, he's a shrewd bastard, after all he got away with killing a cop. By the way, speaking of killing, what's the state of play with that murder in Alexandra Park?'

Skelton cupped his hands behind his neck and grimaced. 'Sir, we've virtually run out of suspects for this murder. The killer left us with little clues except for some clothing fibres found on the deceased. In the first hour of the investigation, I was sure that we had the killer both on CCTV and an eyewitness maintained that the prime suspect acted in a suspicious way. But the guy turned out to be an off-duty police officer and forensics have cleared him completely.'

Williams stood up and walked to the window and looked out. It was raining and by the looks of the clouds, would continue to do so for some time. 'Tell me again this copper's name?'

Skelton stood up and joined Williams by the window. 'His name is Fergus Walsh, sir.'

Williams squeezed his chin in deep thought. It was several seconds before he spoke. 'I knew I knew that name! Several years ago, I can't remember exactly when, we had a missing persons case. A certain Fergus Walsh, living here in Bath, was reported missing by his wife. From memory, he was a chartered accountant and on the day he vanished was apparently working from home. His wife saw him in the morning and all was well. It was the summer holidays and their only child, who I think was also called Fergus, was in bed.

'Mrs Walsh went off to work and everything seemed perfectly normal. When she got home after work, the husband was nowhere to be seen. The son was not at home and she assumed that they had both gone out together. Shortly afterwards, the son turned up. He had been out playing football with his friends. She tried calling her husband's mobile phone but heard it ringing in the house. She began to get worried, looked around and found his wallet and credit cards on his bed side cabinet. His car was still parked outside. By about eight pm she called us to report him missing. We did the usual checks with the hospitals, but he wasn't there. Anyway, to cut a long story short, we never found any trace of him. He had totally vanished and there was nothing to indicate any evidence of foul play. We surmised that the guy had decided to walk out on his family and start a new life. The thing was, however, he had not taken any money or credit cards with him. The DCI concluded that being a chartered accountant, he would have known how to establish a new identity for himself.'

Skelton had listened intently to what Williams had said. He guessed that young Fergus Walsh had been reluctant to mention much about his father. He was probably deeply hurt by what he had done. Skelton was beginning to think that the murder in Alexandra Park was going to be the first murder case he would not solve.

Chapter Twenty-Five

It was shortly after 10.30 am when Skelton got up from his desk and headed for the toilet. He saw constable Dave Lake coming and called out to him. 'Hello, Dave, how are things with you today?' Lake was the elder statesman on the force and had an amazing ability to remember the names of just about every criminal he had ever come across. There was very little in the way of criminality that Lake was not aware of. He had for years supplied the CID team with numerous leads, resulting in many crimes being solved.

'Good morning, sir. All seems quiet at the moment in our beautiful city. Not much happening except for some burglaries and the odd assault. Do you think you will ever solve that murder in Alexandra Park?'

Skelton rubbed his chin and said, 'We have pretty much hit a brick wall on that one, I'm afraid to say. Tell me something, Dave, did you ever work on a missing person enquiry in the name of Fergus Walsh?'

Lake closed his eyes deep in thought and a few seconds later opened them. 'Yes, I remember the case well. It was a complete mystery to everyone. If I recall correctly, the man was a respected chartered accountant here in Bath. He was in his forties, married with a young son who was also called Fergus. Apparently, Mrs Walsh had breakfast with her husband and then left for work. Mr Walsh was working from home that day and the boy was also at home as it was the school holidays. Mrs Walsh said that the marriage was good and they had no money worries. She stated that her husband seemed to be his usual self when she left for work. She was confident that another woman was not involved and she had no idea why he had gone missing.'

Skelton let the information digest for a second. 'What enquiries were made, Dave?'

Lake adjusted his tie and thought for a second. 'Well of course from the outset, it was a purely missing person investigation as there was not a shred of evidence of foul play. The man had just vanished, leaving behind his wallet and credit cards, not to mention a very distressed wife. He even left his car parked outside and he had not even taken his phone with him. We undertook a pretty comprehensive search for him, but never found a body. CID interviewed his friends and work colleagues and every one of them was completely baffled by his disappearance.'

Skelton placed his right hand over his mouth for a second and asked, 'What about young Fergus? How old was he and how did he react to his father's disappearance?'

Lake thought for a second and said, 'To be honest, sir, I never met the boy as I never attended the house. But I seem to remember that he was about sixteen or seventeen. Wait a minute, the prime suspect you had for that murder in the park was called Fergus Walsh. Do you think there is some kind of connection?'

Skelton sighed. 'I can't for the life of me see any sort of connection. I mean he was just a schoolboy when his dad goes missing and just happened to be out jogging when our victim is murdered. He had no motive for killing him that we know of, and forensics cleared him of any involvement. Thanks for your time, Dave.'

Skelton went into the toilet and as he was washing his hands, made a mental note to dig out the missing person file on Fergus Walsh senior.

Chapter Twenty-Six

Jake Ratten was enjoying a bacon roll for his lunch with a mug of coffee. He was at home, which was a three-bedroom flat tastefully furnished and decorated. The money he earned from suppling drugs was sufficient for him to enjoy a good lifestyle. He owned an expensive BMW and frequently went on holiday to exotic locations. His current girlfriend was called Mandy Hughes. She was nineteen years of age and very pretty but not particularly bright. She, like Ratten, enjoyed recreational drugs, which certainly spiced up their sex life. They had met when she was working as a waitress in a fashionable restaurant in Bath. Ratten had asked her out straight away and she fell for his good looks and charm immediately. They were soon an item and Ratten told her to chuck her job in, which she did without giving notice. She guessed that Ratten was involved in drugs but the money and lifestyle were too good for her to ask awkward questions.

Ratten was only five foot seven but he worked out at the gym five days a week. He had a muscular build and a fiery temper. Ratten employed two minders who were both much bigger than him. He paid them well to protect him and to enforce any drug debts that had gone unpaid. The older of the two, Jason Andrews, was six foot four and had been in the army. He was twenty-eight and extremely aggressive. He had attacked one of his instructors, putting him in hospital for two weeks and putting Andrews in a military prison for two years, after which he was discharged from the army. Unable to get a job due to his record, he soon drifted into criminality. He was born in Twerton, a council estate in Bath. He soon came to the attention of Ratten and joined him as his number one minder.

His second minder was called Jeff Roberts and he was six feet tall and badly scarred on the forehead. This was the result of having been hit on the head with a machete two years previously in a fight. Despite the gash to his head, he was able to subdue his attacker by sticking a seven-inch knife into his belly. The guy almost bled to death but was saved by the paramedics called to the fight. Luckily for Roberts there was no CCTV footage of the fight and the guy that he had stabbed was not for helping the police. Roberts had met Ratten in a bar one evening and had soon become friends. It was not long before Roberts was on the Ratten payroll. Ratten now had two very aggressive minders and they would be very loyal to Ratten unless there was any change at the top.

The doorbell rang and Mandy got up to answer it. They were expecting both Andrews and Roberts as it was 1 pm, the time they had agreed to meet the night before. Mandy let them in, and the two men headed for the kitchen, where Ratten liked to hold court. Mandy excused herself and went to the bedroom for her daily call to her mum, which would last at least forty-five minutes. Ratten was sitting at the breakfast table and was holding the remains of the mug of coffee in his right hand. Radio 1 was providing the background music.

'Come in, lads, and take a seat. There's plenty of beers in the fridge, just help yourselves.' Andrews took a chair whilst Roberts went to the fridge and took out two cans of beer.

'Do you want a beer, Jake?'

Ratten stood up and began walking towards the dish washer. 'No thanks, Jeff, I just had a bacon sandwich and coffee.'

Roberts handed a beer to Andrews and sat down opposite him at the table. Ratten finished putting his mug and plate in the dishwasher and joined them.

Ratten never kept drugs in the flat except for the ones that he and Mandy used. Others down the food chain were entrusted to store the drugs. Andrews and Roberts were under strict orders that they were never to carry drugs when Ratten was with them. He was not going to jail for possession with intent to supply, that was for sure. He paid people to carry the risk, so that in the event of being caught by the police, it would be them not him that went to prison. He would of course ensure that they were well looked after, and a job would be waiting for them once they had served their time.

The purpose of today's little gathering was to go out and teach someone a lesson. Word had reached Ratten's ears that a guy by the name of Alex Steel was dealing drugs out in Twerton, a suburb of Bath. Twerton was a council estate with a history of drug dealing. Ratten should know, as he was the principal supplier of drugs. Steel had originally operated out of Bristol but had been warned off by Mickey Chadwell that if he continued to do so it would be dangerous to his health.

Steel knew that Jake the Rat ran the drugs scene in Bath, but he reckoned that the Rat was not nearly as dangerous as Mickey Chadwell. He had rented a semi-detached house in the centre of town. There was a pub nearby as well as a few shops. It was always busy during the day and early evening with people coming and going. Steel had brought his own couriers with him and was soon in business.

Steel was thirty-five years old and had turned to crime soon after leaving school. His father had served countless prison sentences for a variety of different offences. To Steel, crime was in his blood. So far, he had avoided going to prison but had several criminal convictions. It was down to his lawyer and the threats of violence he had made to witnesses that assured his liberty. He was very well built and knew how to use his fists. He was left-handed, or a 'south paw' in boxing terminology, and his upper cut could be savage.

His little business empire was steadily growing and the money was good. So far, the Rat had left him alone and everything was peaceful. He had a little network of dealers but no enforcer. Steel would take care of any enforcing himself. He had had to lean on one or two guys that had got behind with their payments. He had only needed to threaten them and they came up with the money. All in all, things were going really well.

Ratten had sat down at the table whilst Andrews and Roberts sipped on their beers. 'Right, lads, this guy Alex Steel who has invaded our patch needs teaching a lesson. I thought we had Twerton fairly secure, but the word is that Steel seems to be running quite a profitable operation down there. I've fixed it that at three o'clock this afternoon, he is expecting a new client to call at his house and pick up some coke. That new client is our young Billy. He will be here at two. As you know, Billy is only nineteen and is as thin as a rake. When Billy shows up on his doorstep, Steel will not be expecting any trouble. So, when Billy gets inside the house you two will be waiting outside for him to come out. When he does, you guys make your move and don't fuck it up. But, by all means, fuck him up!'

They all laughed and exchanged high fives.

Chapter Twenty-Seven

Young Billy was sitting in the back of the car, Roberts was driving and Andrews was in the front passenger seat. It was 2.50 pm when Roberts parked the car a short distance from the house where Steel lived. Billy was slightly nervous, but he knew that he would be well rewarded with both cash and drugs. All he had to do was knock on the door, go inside and hand over the cash and pick up the coke. When he had done that, he just had to keep the door open for a second or two, and Roberts and Andrews would do the rest. He was to wait in the car until it was all over.

It was almost 3 pm when Billy got out the car and walked towards the door of the house. His mouth was dry, and his hands were trembling slightly. He knocked on the door and waited. About thirty seconds later, Steel opened the door and saw the slim young guy standing before him. 'Come on in, Billy, I was expecting you.'

Billy did not speak but went inside. As soon as Billy was in, Andrews and Roberts got out the car. Both were carrying pickaxe handles behind their backs. They took up position on either side of the door and waited.

A couple of minutes later, the door opened, and they heard Billy say, 'Thanks, mate, I hope this stuff is as good as you say it is.'

Billy stepped onto the pavement and Roberts and Andrews made their move. Steel was taken completely by surprise and did not have time to put his hands up to protect himself. Andrews hit him hard under the chin and he fell backwards, hitting his head on the wall. Roberts closed the door. Steel was semi-conscious and in no fit state to defend himself. They each grabbed an arm and dragged him into the sitting room. Roberts was wearing a shoulder bag, from which he took out a roll of gaffer tape. Steel was trying to speak as Roberts applied the tape over his mouth. They did not want him to scream.

Andrews raised his pickaxe and said in a matter-of-fact voice, 'This is with the compliments of Mr Ratten, my friend. Once you have gotten out of the hospital, he says that you have to piss off back to Bristol. Fail to do so and you are a dead man.'

Steel tried to cover his head and face as best he could. When the first blow landed on his right shin, he would have screamed if he could have done, but the tape prevented this from happening. The two thugs were relentless, working as a team they each in turn delivered savage blows to his arms and legs. They finished off by hitting him on both sets of ribs. Mercifully, Steel had lost consciousness but was alive. He would be in hospital for a month and would walk permanently on crutches. His days of drug dealing were over.

Chapter Twenty-Eight

Alexander knocked on Skelton's door, it was almost 5 pm. 'Sir, paramedics were called to an address in Twerton earlier and they called us. They found a guy very badly beaten with his mouth taped shut. Uniform called for us to attend and Bob Richards and his team are on their way now. They managed to ID him as Alex Steel, a drug dealer originally from Bristol. He's on his way to the RUH now but is in no condition to talk to us.'

Skelton got up from his chair and picked up his suit jacket. 'I know that name. We got intel on him recently as dealing drugs on Jake Ratten's patch. My money is on the Rat as being behind this. You can bet your bottom dollar that Steel won't talk and there will be no witnesses. We might get lucky with forensics but don't hold your breath.'

Alexander drove them to the crime scene. A police constable was standing outside the house and Skelton recognised him as Luke Meehan. 'Hello, Luke, you always seem to get posted as the minder of the scene of crime.'

Meehan smiled and said, 'Well they have to put the good-looking copper in the photos, don't they.' The three officers laughed as Skelton and Alexander went inside.

Bob Richards, the head of forensics, greeted them. 'Good afternoon, gentlemen. Please don't come in any further in case you contaminate the crime scene.' Richards was in a paper boilersuit and was wearing a face mask. 'What have you got for us, Bob?' asked Skelton.

'Not a lot to be honest with you. Although the victim was savagely beaten there is very little blood. I suspect that whoever did this used a weapon or weapons on him to inflict blunt force injury. Might have been a baseball bat or something similar. I managed to see him before they took him to hospital, he was in a bad way. This makes me think that it was just a warning, probably from another drug dealer.'

It was obvious to Skelton that this was a crime that was highly unlikely to be solved. They might be lucky to get CCTV images of the offender or offenders, but a lack of witnesses and forensics would make it extremely difficult to get a conviction. The only consolation was that a drug dealer had been taken off the streets and was unlikely to ever get back on them. They would have to interview the victim in hospital, but that would be a waste of time.

Skelton and Alexander were back in the car. 'What do you think, sir? Was this the Rat's handywork or do you think that Murray was behind it?'

Skelton wiped his hand across his face and said, 'That's a good question, Bill. Gut feeling tells me that Murray would make a move against the Rat and not someone down the food chain. It doesn't matter who did it anyway, chances are we are not going to get a successful prosecution. The only good thing to come out of it is that we have got another turd off the street, and permanently.

'I think, Bill, we should pay the Rat a visit just to let him know that we are on to him. It will not solve the crime, but it will mark his card that we are on to him. Let's go now. You know where he lives don't you?'

'Yes, of course, sir, we should be there in about ten minutes.'

Alexander led them to the door of the flat. It was on the ground floor. The name J Ratten appeared next to the doorbell. He pushed the button and waited. After a few minutes the door was opened by Ratten. He looked at the two officers before him and immediately recognised Alexander.

'Well, if it's not DS Alexander. What can I do for you gentlemen?'

Skelton removed his warrant card from his jacket pocket and flashed it at Ratten. 'I am Detective Chief Inspector Skelton, and I am in charge of CID now. We want to come in and have a word with you.'

Ratten looked at the immaculately dressed police officer and immediately thought to himself that he looked more like a banker than a cop. 'Yes, come on in.' He stood aside and the officers stepped inside.

Ratten led them into the sitting room and invited them to sit down. 'This place must be costing you a fortune. How do you manage to afford it?' asked Skelton. Ratten's eyes glanced around the room. All the furniture was new and the whole flat had recently been redecorated. It had cost an arm and a leg, that was for sure. 'Oh, just some wise investments over the years and a clever accountant.' All three of them knew that he was lying. 'Can I get you gentlemen a drink? I usually have a gin and tonic around this time of the day.'

Skelton and Alexander were sitting next to each other on the large comfortable sofa. The Rat was standing in front of the tv. 'No thank you, this is not a social call,' said Skelton. 'Where were you this afternoon between one and four o'clock?'

The Rat sat down in one of the two armchairs and leaned back. 'I was here all day. I haven't been out the flat at all today.'

Skelton was studying the Rat closely. He had an arrogant confidence about him. He was damn sure that he would have an alibi. 'Can anyone vouch for that?'

The Rat smiled and said, 'Yes, Mandy my girlfriend can vouch for that. I was actually giving her one at about three o'clock this afternoon! She is in the bedroom. Do you want me to go and get her?'

Alexander glanced at Skelton. 'No that will not be necessary.'

Skelton stood up and walked across to the window, which looked out onto the street. It was busy with people going home from work. 'Do you know Alex Steel?'

The Rat placed his forefinger on his chin and thought for a moment. 'No, the name means nothing to me. Why do you ask?'

Skelton turned and faced the Rat. 'Mr Steel was savagely beaten up this afternoon and is now in the RUH, where he is likely to remain for some considerable time. We believe that he had started dealing down in Twerton and that pissed you off big time. What have you got to say about that?'

The Rat rested his arms on the arm rests and feigned shock. 'I have no idea what you are talking about. I'm not a drug dealer, Inspector. I do take the odd pill now and again as it beefs up our sex life, but that's all. I have never heard of this guy. I just hope you catch whoever it was that fucked him up.'

The two officers had been expecting such a reaction. The Rat was too clever to have dirtied his own hands in this. The most likely explanation was that he had sent his hired hands to administer the beating. The purpose of this visit was to warn him that the cops were onto him.

Skelton sat down and cleared his throat. 'Has James Murray been in touch yet?'

The Rat looked genuinely confused. 'Who? James Murray. I have never heard of him. Who is he?'

Skelton could tell that the Rat was being truthful. 'James Murray is a notorious gangster from London. He killed a police officer some years ago and got away with it on a technicality. The word is that he has teamed up with a certain Ben Naylor from Bristol. Murray recently bought a house in Bath, and we believe that he is going to take you down and then move into Bristol. That will mean a turf war with Mickey Chadwell.'

The Rat tried to hide his concern but couldn't. Skelton had rattled him, that was for sure. The arrogant attitude had all but gone.

The detectives left the flat, walked to the car and got in. 'Well, Bill, I think that little visit went better than planned. He had no idea that Murray is in Bath but when I mentioned Ben Naylor's name he almost flinched but managed to hold himself together. I reckon that the Rat is shitting himself now, which suits me fine. Not a bad way to round the day off. Let's go top it off with a pint!'

Chapter Twenty-Nine

Skelton had retrieved the file on the missing person enquiry and had it before him on his desk. Fergus Walsh was forty-seven-years-old when he had suddenly gone missing. Apparently a happily married man, he had been married to Nancy for twenty years at the time of his disappearance. A chartered accountant by profession and a partner in a local firm of accountants. He appeared to have been highly respected by all who knew him. He was the proud father of his son, Fergus, who was seventeen at the material time.

He had no criminal record and had never come to the attention of the police. He enjoyed a very good income and had been able to redeem his mortgage early. His bank and building society accounts had healthy balances and he enjoyed the benefit of a company car. His monthly outgoings were his council tax, utility bills and groceries. The family regularly dined out and were fortunate enough to be able to take three foreign holidays a year.

Since disappearing, he nor anyone else apart from his wife had accessed his bank or building society accounts. He had left behind his debit and credit cards as well as his house and car keys. A search of the house and garden had found no evidence of foul play. He had simply vanished without any explanation whatsoever.

Officers had canvassed the neighbours on the day he disappeared, but no one had seen him leave the house. It was a complete mystery and Skelton did not like mysteries.

All the hospitals in Somerset had been checked. He had never been admitted to any of them since leaving home. Every dead body that had been found in Somerset since his disappearance had been identified. Skelton closed the file and leaned back in his chair with his hands cupped behind his neck. He let out a long sigh and thought. He was totally baffled by the case, as had all the police officers been that had worked it. The one thing that Skelton thought he could be sure of was that Walsh was dead. Had he killed himself, or had he been murdered? Why had his body never been found? Either he or his killer had found the perfect hiding place which so far had not been discovered. What about a motive? There was nothing to indicate that Walsh had any reason to kill himself. He had never consulted his GP on mental health issues, and he was very much a liked man. The spouse or partner of a murder victim would usually be the prime suspect. His wife had been at work all day and his son was out playing football with his friends. Both had perfect alibis.

Skelton stood up and walked to the window. He glanced at his watch it was 12.50 pm. Time for lunch. He sighed again and thought to himself, Christ I've got two unsolved cases now. The victim in Alexandra Park and Fergus Walsh. Was there a connection? How could there be a bloody connection? It made no sense to him whatsoever. Skelton did his best thinking under a hot shower. He grimaced and thought his next was going to have to be bloody hot!

Chapter Thirty

Skelton went into the CID room and found Alexander on the phone, so he turned to see DC Ross Turnbull busy at his computer. All the other desks were empty. 'Hi, Ross, how is it going?'

Turnbull looked up and smiled. 'Actually, sir, we just got some CCTV film from a shop in Twerton, just across the road from where Alex Steel was beaten up. A white BMW pulls up a few minutes before 1500 hours and a young slim male gets out the rear driver's door. It's a bit grainy so it's going to be hard to identify him. A few minutes later the driver and passenger get out. I think the driver has got something behind his back, maybe a baseball bat but I can't tell. A few minutes later the kid gets back into the rear of the car. Eight minutes later he is joined by the driver and passenger. Again, the images are not very good and we didn't get the registration number. But my money is on them as the prime suspects.'

Skelton had his hands in his trouser pockets. 'That's a good start, Ross. Keep checking the other CCTV cameras and see if you can get the registration plate. The problem we have, Ross, is that even if we identify the occupants of the car, I doubt very much if the victim will give evidence. The guy must be in fear of his life, he knows that if he does give evidence, someone will finish him off.'

'You're probably right, sir. I guess the only positive take on this is that we got a drug dealer off the street and probably for life. Forensics found a load of drugs in the house. Are you going to charge him for dealing, sir?' Skelton took his hands out his pockets and leaned on Turnbull's computer screen. 'To be honest, Ross, I don't think it would be in the public interest to charge him. After all, they nearly killed him. I think his assailants inflicted more damage on him than we could ever do. As you say, he's off the streets for good, so let's leave it there.'

Alexander was off the phone and was putting on his jacket. 'Where are we having lunch today, sir?'

'Actually Bill, let's give the Saracen's Head a go today. I fancy a steak and ale pie today washed down with a couple of pints of Fosters.'

'Sounds good to me, sir. Lead on, McDuff!'

This was a Scottish saying and Skelton smiled and said, 'I'm leading!'

The officers left the station and turned right and then crossed the road to Bog Island. They continued walking past the City Chambers. It was a sunny day and the pavements were crowded with tourists, so progress was rather slow. They came to the Saracen's Head, the oldest pub in Bath, which was popular with tourists. They have in one alcove a bust of the famous playwright Charles Dickens, where it is said that he wrote The Pickwick Papers. On entering the pub, Skelton strolled up to the bar and was greeted by a young barman with a mop of brown hair. 'Yes, sir, and what can I get for you gentlemen today?'

Skelton smiled and said, 'Could we have two pints of Fosters, please, and can we order some food?'

'Yes, of course you can. Would you like to look at the menu or do you know what you're having?'

'I am having the steak and ale pie, what about you, Bill?'

'Make that two steak and ale pies, please.'

They took a table by the window and Skelton took the chair with his back to the window so that he had a good view of the pub. A few minutes later the young barman brought over the food. 'There you go, chaps; I hope that you enjoy it.'

Skelton thanked the young man and introduced himself. 'My name is Dan and this is Bill. What's your name?'

'Hello, Dan, hello, Bill, my name is Toby. It's good to meet you and if you need anything, just let me know.'

'You know something, Dan, I think you shook the Rat up yesterday when you mentioned that Ben Naylor was teaming up with Murray. There was the tiniest tremor on his face.'

'Yes, I noticed it as well, Bill. It's obvious that Murray has not yet made contact with the Rat, as he did not seem to recognise Murray's name. Murray will definitely make a move, that's for sure, but your guess is as good as mine as to when that might be. My gut instinct tells me that Murray will get Naylor to set the meeting up, as the Rat knows Naylor. The question is, how will the Rat respond? We know that he has muscle in the shape of his two minders, Andrews and Roberts, who I suspect were responsible for beating up Alex Steel the other day. Murray might have to bring in some extra muscle from London, which could mean bodies piling up on the street.'

Alexander sipped his pint. 'Christ, Dan, we could have a turf war on our hands in no time. Bath is not the kind of city where turf wars break out. You expect it in the big cities, like London, Manchester, Liverpool, Birmingham to name but a few. And if Murray makes a move into Bristol, then there will be a bloody war there as well. Do you think it's time we gave Murray a visit and marked his card for him, like we did with the Rat?'

Skelton drained his pint. 'Let me get us another couple of beers.'

Skelton walked to the bar and Toby saw him approach. 'Two more Fosters, Dan?'

'Yes please, Toby, and take a drink for yourself. Do you work here full time or just part time?'

'Actually, I am at university, so I just squeeze in a shift here whenever I can. I haven't seen you or Bill in here before. Are you new in town?'

'Bill and I work together. We are police officers working out of Manvers Street. We would appreciate it if you kept that under your hat if you don't mind.'

Young Toby promised that he would and Skelton picked up the two pints and headed back to Alexander.

'Well, Bill, I have been giving some careful consideration as to whether or not to visit Murray. Do we reveal our hand now and let him know that we know he's in town? Or do we just sit tight with our eyes wide open? It's a difficult call to make. After a lot of thought, I think you and I will go and visit Murray tomorrow morning. It might shake him up a bit as he probably thinks we have no idea of his presence in the city. It might also make him think twice about going after the Rat.'

Chapter Thirty-One

Alexander drove as usual, whilst Skelton sat in the front passenger seat. It was just after ten in the morning and the rain had stopped. It had been a very heavy shower but very welcome after weeks of dry weather. Gardeners and farmers would welcome the rain that was for sure. They parked the car outside Murray's front door and got out. They both pulled out their warrant cards and Skelton knocked on the door and waited. A couple of minutes later Murray answered.

'James Murray, I am Detective Chief Inspector Skelton, and this is Detective Sergeant Alexander of the Avon and Somerset Constabulary. Please may we come in?'

Murray's heart missed a beat as he looked at the warrant cards. He had not expected the police to have been aware of his presence in Bath this early. He was at a loss to understand how the cops had discovered where he lived. After all, he had only been in the city for just over two weeks and had been lying low. 'Yes, I am James Murray. Come on in and take a seat in the sitting room.'

A lot of the furniture looked new. Murray had been splashing the cash, that was clearly evident. Skelton had done a Land Registry Search and had discovered that the house was registered to a Penny Cole, which meant that she owned the property. Skelton had assigned DC Janet Griffin to undertake a detailed financial investigation into her finances. He also instructed her to carefully investigate the law firm that acted for her in the purchase of the property. He might not be able to seize the property from Murray, who he was certain had funded the purchase, but he might be able to seize it from Cole! Skelton smiled to himself as Murray led them into the sitting room.

'Please, take a seat and make yourself comfortable. Would you like a tea or coffee?'

'This is not a social visit, Mr Murray, so why don't you sit down and listen up.' Skelton's tone was severe and left Murray in no doubt as to who was in charge of this meeting. Murray sat down in the large armchair and he looked at Skelton and then to Alexander. He had a feeling that he had seen Skelton before but could not place where it had been. Cops did not usually make Murray nervous, but this cop was something else. His instincts told him that this cop was dangerous. Very dangerous.

'Right, I won't beat about the bush. You killed a good friend of mine and got away with it on a technicality. You went to prison for the drugs, met Ben Naylor and became friends. You and Naylor want to take over from Mickey Chadwell in Bristol, but first you want to establish yourself in Bath. That means taking out Jake the Rat. We know that this house is in the name of your girlfriend, but that's a mere technicality and I can still seize it, which I will certainly do.'

Murray's mind was racing, as was his heart. This cop was serious trouble. How the fuck did he know so much about him?

'We also know that you and Naylor killed Jimmy White in revenge for him moving onto your manor when you were in prison. We can't prove that murder at the moment, but we will try hard to do so.'

Murray could feel the beads of sweat running down his forehead. This cop had done his homework. How the fuck did he know that he moved to Bath? He was already talking about seizing the house. Could he do that? Was this cop going to end his plans to take over Bath and Bristol? Murray needed to keep calm.

'I was cleared of killing that copper and I've no idea what you're talking about us killing Jimmy White. I did my time in jail and I've moved on from that. I heard that Bath is a nice peaceful place to live. So, me and the girlfriend are just trying to be model citizens.'

Skelton stood up and walked over to Murray, who was still seated and holding onto the arm rests, trying to appear composed. 'When you killed Joe Reilly you made a very dangerous enemy and you are looking at him now. The first mistake you made was killing Joe and the second mistake was moving to Bath. I swear to god that I will do everything in my power to bring you down, be under no illusion about that. Don't get up, we will see ourselves out.'

The detectives left the house and got into the car. Alexander started the engine and said, 'Christ's sake, sir, you scared the shit out of him in there. You certainly rattled his cage that's for sure.'

'You know something, Bill, I rather enjoyed that little meeting. I think we gave Murray a lot to think about. And you're right, sunshine, we scared the bastard.'

Chapter Thirty-Two

Murray had recovered his composure and was on the phone to Naylor. He was very careful, however, about what he said in case Skelton had bugged the house or phone. From now on, business would only be discussed outside the house and certainly not on the phone. It had been agreed that they would meet up at 7 pm in the Saracen's Head. It was a big pub, and it would be easy to find a quiet spot where they could talk.

Murray was seated towards the rear of the pub; it was still fairly quiet. He was on his second pint and felt a lot more relaxed following the visit from the police earlier. Naylor walked in and they shook hands. Murray sent him to the bar to get the drinks and waited for him to return. He came back carrying two pints of lager and placed them on the table. They clinked glasses and Naylor sat down.

'You ever heard of a cop by the name of Skelton?'

Naylor thought for a second. 'Yeah, I know the name. He's in charge of the CID in Bath. He and another cop took out a terrorist a few months back. It was on the telly. He also solved the murders of two girls found dead in the river Avon. I hear that he's pretty sharp and I think he's Scottish.'

Murray sipped his drink. 'Yeh, he is Scottish all right, I should know. He and his sidekick paid me a visit at the house today. The bastard knew all about us serving time together, that we knocked off Jimmy and that the house is in Penny's name. This guy has got it in for me as it turns out, that cop that I killed was his mate.'

'Oh god, that's going to complicate things. But how the hell did he know that you had moved to Bath? Do you think the cops have been tailing you?'

'I don't think they tailed me but maybe my old house was bugged, or my phone was bugged. So, from now on we don't discuss business at the house or on the phone. In fact, we don't discuss it in the car either, just in case they have bugged the cars. I want you to take both our cars to that garage you have in Bristol and get them to go over them and see if they can find anything. Do it first thing in the morning.'

Naylor took a sip from his pint. 'Okay, James, consider it done. I will get your car back to you by mid-afternoon.'

'The cops tried to scare me off today, but that won't work. We've got plans for here and Bristol and I still have my manor in London. Skelton might know where I live and that I have plans for here and Bristol, but he can't stop me if we get ahead of him. Having warned me off today, he will expect us to keep our heads down. The last thing he will expect is for us to take down the Rat.'

Naylor leaned across the table and spoke softly. 'James, are you mad? If we take out the Rat now, the cops will be on top of us in a flash. I don't want to go back to prison for killing the Rat. I thought you just wanted to frighten the little shit and take over. You never mentioned to me that you were going to kill him. The cops know all about us. No, James, it's far too risky. We risk losing everything, for the sake of that little turd.'

Murray leaned closer to Naylor and looked him in the eye. He was very controlled and had a determined look on his face. 'Look, Ben, I have no intention of going back behind bars either. I have a plan to make Jake disappear forever. There will be no murder enquiry, I promise. And with Jake gone, Bath is ours. I want you to call the Rat and tell him I want to meet him alone at his flat. He can have his minders there, so he will feel completely safe. You just leave the rest to me. I want you to ensure that you have a cast-iron alibi for the night I make my visit. Then if something should go wrong, you are completely in the clear. Now just do it.'

Chapter Thirty-Three

Detectives Alexander, Turnbull and Lowik were sitting around the desk of the small conference room when Skelton walked in. 'Good morning, chaps. I called this meeting so that we can review the investigation into the murder of Stephen Cox, which took place in Alexandra Park. We had a prime suspect in the shape of Fergus Walsh, an off-duty cop. Forensics and his phone cleared him as being the killer. The pathologist suspects that the killer could be a soldier, maybe a commando given how he dispatched his victim. So far, every potential suspect from the armed forces has been eliminated from our enquiry. Now, I tasked Ross and Peter with checking the phone records of the victim with a view to identifying previous boyfriends. Can you guys tell us how you got on?'

Turnbull cleared his throat and began. 'Well, the victim kept all his bank records, phone bills, utility bills and whatever in well-ordered folders. It looks like he kept records for five years, then he disposed of them. We went through his bank and credit card folders in great detail. We were looking for unusual transactions such as large cash withdrawals or suspicious payments to third parties. We wondered if he was being blackmailed but we have ruled that out completely.

'We then concentrated on his phone records to see if we could trace former boyfriends. This was relatively easy to do by simply identifying patterns of activity with his phone and another phone. We came to the conclusion, that he had four boyfriends in the last five years. We traced all four of them. One is living here in Bath, so we interviewed him at his flat. He confirmed that he had met Stephen on Gaydar. He was about twenty-one at the time and is attracted to older guys. They dated for a couple of months but broke up. He is now in a happy relationship and has an alibi for the week of the murder. He was on holiday in Tenerife.

'The second suspect met Stephen on just three occasions. Again, this was on Gaydar. By mutual consent, they agreed that the relationship would not work. He too was away on holiday on the day of the murder. He went to Amsterdam.

'Now our third suspect, a guy named Colin Hart got us rather excited. He is in the army and was stationed in Warminster when Stephen was killed. Again, they met on Gaydar about two years ago. Colin was only nineteen when he met Stephen. The mutual attraction once again was that Colin likes older guys and Stephen liked younger guys. They were together, so to speak, for about six months, but Stephen found that with Colin always going away on training exercises or deployment the relationship was not going to work. On the day of the murder, Colin was on a training exercise in Bahrain.'

Skelton stood up and walked to the window and looked out. It was pouring with rain, and it looked like it was on for the day. 'What about the fourth suspect, Ross?'

Turnbull turned a page. 'The last guy we know Stephen was in contact with is Martin Day. They met on Gaydar about nine months before the killing. He lives in Chippenham, which is only a few miles from where Stephen lived. Martin works in a betting shop and is twenty-two years old. Martin says he was looking for a sugar daddy but Stephen was not up for this. Martin admits that Stephen reluctantly gave him fifty pounds each time they met. After their third meeting, Stephen ended the relationship. Martin was visiting his parents in Edinburgh on the day Stephen died. So, all four former boyfriends have been traced and eliminated as suspects.'

Skelton sat back down. Alexander stood up and stretched. It was nearly 12.30 pm and he was feeling hungry. 'Right, so we now know that the common denominator in this case is Gaydar. Can they tell us anything about any contact between the victim and a possible suspect?'

It was Peter Lowik's turn to address the audience. 'We had hoped that we could have obtained all the names of men that Stephen contacted but were sorely disappointed. It seems that a lot of people using this website create email addresses and often use burner phones. Tracing these people can be very difficult if not impossible. We did, however, manage to identify sixty-two Gaydar members who chatted to Stephen in the last six months before he died. We were able to conclude that whilst he chatted with these people, he never arranged to meet them.'

Alexander sat back down. 'What about the day of his death and the days before it?'

Lowik stretched his six foot frame. In his Aussie twang, he continued. 'This is the only really interesting thing we discovered. Three days before he died, he was in conversation with a guy using the profile, "Hunky Boy". There seems to have been mutual interest between the parties. Stephen as we know liked younger guys and his boyfriends liked older guys. This is exactly what we found here. The day before his death, Stephen gave Hunky Boy his mobile phone number and Hunky Boy gave him his. They spoke three times. Once on the day before the murder and twice on the day of it. Needless to say, Hunky Boy was using a burner phone and so it is totally untraceable, unless we are lucky enough to find it. But that's a hell of a long shot.'

Skelton placed the palm of his hands on the table and asked, 'What about the email address of Hunky Boy, can we trace that?'

Lowik ran his hands through his hair. 'No, sir, we tried that. This guy did not want to be found, which leads me and Ross to think that he must be the killer. He even deleted his Gaydar account just after the killing. We did manage to get the photo from Hunky Boy's profile and it's definitely not Walsh, sir. We also put it on social media. The guy whose photo it is contacted us straight away. We have eliminated him as a suspect as well.'

All eyes were on Skelton, waiting for him to speak. 'I always suspected that Stephen had arranged the meeting with the killer. I just couldn't work out exactly how they had made contact in the first place. Now we know that it was through Gaydar. What worries me, gentlemen, is that having so far not been caught, he may very well arrange to meet another potential victim and we have another murder on our hands. We need to set a trap for this guy and catch him. He must be feeling pretty confident as he knows that we have made no arrests and so therefore don't have any suspects. I don't think he will change a winning formula, and it's my hunch that he will use Gaydar again.

'Peter, you seem to have become pretty proficient in using Gaydar. I want you to dedicate your time to creating a false profile to lure the killer. Base it on the one that Stephen used. An older guy looking for a hunky younger guy. You will have to dig up a photo from somewhere and again it should resemble Stephen. I'm afraid you may have to man the site in the evenings, as I think the killer works during the day and so won't have access to Gaydar until after work. Any questions, Peter?'

'No, sir, I will get straight onto it after we finish here.'

'Let's concentrate on a motive for a moment. Why did the killer target Stephen? Does he hate older gay men, and if so, why? Could it be he was abused by an older man when he was younger? Is he now seeking revenge for what someone else did to him? That begs the question, why has he not gone after the man who abused him?'

Alexander cleared his throat. 'Maybe he has already and wants to punish more abusers.'

Skelton leaned forward in his chair and banged the table with his fist. 'That is a very good point, Bill. Our killer may have been abused when he was a youngster. When he got older and stronger, he may have confronted his abuser. Maybe he beat him up or worse, killed him. There are plenty of unsolved murders out there. He sets up a profile on Gaydar looking for older men that like youngsters. He starts chatting to Stephen, and comes to the conclusion that Stephen is an abuser. He decides to kill him as punishment for sexual abuse. So far, he has got away with it. I think it's just a question of time before he strikes again. I still think he is a local man, which means another body may end up on our doorstep.'

Chapter Thirty-Four

Skelton and Alexander walked out of the police station at 12.50 pm. The rain had stopped. As they walked down the steps, Skelton glanced to his right and saw a Black man coming out the public carpark next to the police station. He was carrying an expensive looking Gucci bag. Skelton recognised him almost immediately. The man was called Ali Hussain and was from south-east London. Skelton had not arrested him, but his squad had. He was a purveyor of drugs and had spent four years in prison. Now what was he doing in Bath?

Skelton grasped Alexander by the shoulder. 'Hold on a minute, Bill. Do you see that Black guy with the Gucci bag?'

Alexander searched the carpark and spotted the man. 'Yeah, I see him.'

'That guy's from London and delivers drugs. I reckon that either the Rat or Murray are about to receive a consignment of drugs. Let's follow him and see where he goes. This could be our lucky day, sunshine.'

The man exited the carpark and turned right along Manvers Street. The detectives followed behind at a casual pace. Hussain crossed the road and was walking towards Bog Island. Skelton was not sure if he was heading to a private address or was meeting his contact in a bar or restaurant. He would soon find out. The suspect walked past the ale house and glanced through the window but did not go in. He then turned left and had to dodge the hordes of tourists outside the abbey. The detectives followed, never taking their eyes off him. The man was walking in an assured manner and never once looked behind. The City Chambers were on the opposite side of the street and a wedding party were just leaving.

Skelton reckoned that the suspect was not going to a private address as this part of the city was mostly commercial premises. The guy stopped outside the old post office and was looking ahead of himself. The sign above the door said 'Belushi's', the door was open and he walked in.

Skelton said, 'Hold on for a minute. Let him get settled. There is only the one door, so he can't give us the slip.' They waited for five minutes. 'Come on, Bill, let's go and see who he is meeting. I doubt very much it will be the Rat or Murray, most likely a representative of either one of them.'

The bar is divided into two sections, one on the left and one on the right. He was not in this section, so he must be next door.

Joe the manager saw them approaching the bar. 'Good afternoon, gentlemen. I take it that you will both be having Fosters?'

They stopped at the bar and Skelton said, 'Yes please, Joe, we won't be eating today. How are you?' Joe was pouring the drinks. 'Oh, fine thanks, but a bit tired. We had a birthday party in here last night and the place was packed. We spent the morning tidying up.'

Alexander paid for the drinks and they both picked up a glass and Skelton headed for the other section of the bar. Hussain was sitting at a table by the window on his own. The Gucci bag was sitting on the bench seat beside him. He had a pint of cider on the table.

Unusually for Skelton, he took a chair with his back to the exit as he wanted to watch Hussain. Alexander sat opposite Skelton, so he would have his eyes on whoever came into this section of the bar. They pretended to make small talk and waited. After twenty minutes, Skelton was getting worried as Hussain was still sitting alone. Their drinks were almost empty, so Skelton went to the bar for two more pints. A young guy of muscular build was being served. He was carrying a Gucci bag identical to the one that Hussain had with him. Joe finished pouring a Guinness for him. The guy paid by debit card and made his way towards where Hussain was seated. Skelton missed the greetings.

When he returned with the pints, Hussain and his visitor were deep in conversation about football, a topic which bored Skelton. Skelton looked over towards the muscular white guy but did not recognise him. He mouthed to Alexander, 'Do you know him?'

Alexander shook his head. They had no legal grounds for searching the men, even though Skelton suspected drugs were involved. For the moment he was content to just sit and wait.

Hussain got up and went to the bar to get more drinks. The two detectives wished that they had ordered some food, but it was too late now. The suspect returned with the drinks and carried on talking about football. Skelton was considering his options. So far nothing suspicious had taken place that warranted them to search the suspects. He might get away with reasonable grounds for searching Hussain, as he had a conviction for possession with intent to supply. However, a clever barrister could claim that the search was discriminatory on the grounds of the man's colour. He had no grounds for searching the white guy, which again might cause a judge to direct the jury to find him innocent. If indeed, he had actually committed a crime. He was in a dilemma, which he hoped would soon be resolved. On the other hand, these might just be a couple of friends out for an afternoon drinks session.

Skelton was nursing his pint and Alexander did likewise. Both were curious as to what was inside the two Gucci bags. Skelton was particularly curious as to why the guys had matching bags. But he was not the fashion police and having matching bags was not a crime. Then the penny dropped. If these guys were to exchange bags, it would be very easy to do so and would probably go unnoticed. The perfect drug exchange. One guy delivers the drugs, and the other guy pays for them. Skelton could hardly contain the excitement that was building up inside him. If they exchanged the bags at the table, he would pounce. Chances were that these guys would not come quietly, in which case he and Alexander would have to batter them into submission.

The two suspects were finishing off their drinks and Skelton watched them carefully. They both stood up and each picked up their own bags and began walking out of the bar. Skelton nodded for Alexander to join him, they got up and began following the two suspects, who were by now just going out the door. The streets were still damp from the morning rain, but it was a lot brighter. There seemed to be even more tourists about, which made it tricky for the detectives to follow their suspects. They were having to dodge around tourists taking photos and people talking into their mobile phones.

'I reckon they are heading for Manvers Street carpark, where the exchange will take place. We are going to have to follow them, Bill, and nab them there. Call Ross and tell him to bring any other plain clothes officers with him and meet us at the entrance to the carpark. And tell them to behave as if they are just a bunch of workers gathered for a smoke.'

Alexander made the call. 'Ross is headed downstairs now with Spurrey and Lowik.'

The suspects were now at Bog Island and were heading towards Manvers Street. They seemed oblivious to the fact that they were being followed.

Skelton looked over towards the entrance and exit to the carpark and could see his men huddled in a group. They were laughing like a group of work colleagues finishing off a day's work. Perfect. 'Call Ross and tell him to get a traffic car to block off the exit as soon as he sees us entering.' Alexander made the call and Skelton could see Ross Turnbull answer his phone. 'We will follow them into the carpark. We know that Hussain has a car there, but his mate might also have a car there as well. If they split up, you follow the white guy, and I will take Hussain.' The suspects kept walking and turned left into the carpark. The net was tightening.

Skelton signalled Turnbull and his team to get behind him and follow, he pointed towards the suspects, indicating that they were the target. Turnbull gave the thumbs up sign, indicating that he understood. Skelton increased his steps, as he did not want to lose the suspects on the staircases down into the carpark. The police traffic car had parked across the exit of the carpark and its driver had got out to explain to the occupants of a car trying to leave that there would be a slight delay. The suspects were going down the stairs whilst the cops followed them. On the second floor, the suspects left the staircase and began walking towards the rows of parked cars. Hussain pressed the key fob and the lights on a BMW flashed on. As they got to the car, they exchanged bags. Bingo!

They opened the rear doors and threw the bags on the back seats. They closed the rear doors and were opening the front doors when Skelton shouted, 'Police! Freeze now.' Both suspects turned, looked and could see that there were five coppers after them. They jumped into the car and Hussain locked the doors and started the engine. Skelton had his baton in his right hand and began pounding it against the driver's window. It did not give and suddenly the BMW was off.

'Ross, call that car and registration plate in. Quick, everyone up the stairs, there should be a car up there blocking them in.' They raced up the stairs whilst the BMW manoeuvred its way out of the building. They could hear its engine revving as its occupants sought to escape.

Skelton had almost reached the exit to the carpark and could see the police car had blocked off the exit. But the entrance remained open, his heart pounded as he shouted to the uniformed officer to block the entrance. There were several cars waiting to leave so that would prevent the suspects from getting out the exit. Skelton had wanted the uniformed officer to move his car to block the entrance, but he misunderstood the order and was instead standing in the gap. The BMW had reached ground level and the driver could see that the exit was blocked and a police officer was guarding the entrance. The driver had only one option; to take out the copper.

Hussain gunned the engine and aimed the car at the entrance where the cop was standing with his right arm raised, giving the command to stop. The cop was brave but not stupid. As the car drove towards him, he dived out of its way, but he landed awkwardly, and his knee gave way. He was in no fit state to drive. As the BMW exited the carpark and turned right, it collided with a Mini waiting to enter. The damage to the Mini was quite extensive but the BMW was only lightly damaged. Skelton surveyed the scene. He quickly made his decision.

'Quick follow me.' He began running towards the police traffic car. 'Peter, look after him,' he said, pointing towards the injured cop. He opened the driver's door and got in. Alexander took the front passenger seat whilst Spurrey and Turnbull got in the back.

'Hell's teeth, sir, I never thought you could drive!'

Skelton started the engine. 'Just watch, Bill, but while you're at it, get on that radio and give control a running commentary. Tell them that I am a trained vehicle pursuit driver.' Skelton switched on the blue lights and siren and put his foot down. They were off.

They watched as the BMW turned right on to North Parade and Alexander informed control. Skelton went through a red light and gunned the engine. He was also driving a BMW, so the cars were equally matched, but were the drivers? Hussain went through a red and turned left onto Pulteney Road. Skelton was right behind him. They flew past Bath Bowls Club and had to break sharply at the roundabout. It looked like they were headed for London Road and when Hussain took the next left, this route was confirmed. They shot past the fire station on the right and Hussain was weaving in and out of traffic dangerously. Alexander was providing a blow-by-blow commentary so that other traffic cars could plan an interception.

The BMW went through another red as it turned right onto London Road. It was a 30 mph speed zone but they were doing 70. At the roundabout ahead, Hussain had three options. He could turn left, which would eventually lead him onto the motorway. He could take the second exit, but that was a very bendy stretch of road, or he could take the third exit. This was the bypass and was a dual carriageway. He opted for the third option, where he hoped he could outrun the cop car and lose it.

As soon as he hit the dual carriageway, Hussain put his foot to the floor and was soon doing 120, but the cop car was not far behind him. 'Shit, the bastards are still behind us. Sit tight. This could get a little bumpy.'

The white guy looked scared. He had been assured by the Rat that this was a regular arrangement that had worked perfectly well for months.

Now, with all the drugs and cash in the back of the car, he could be locked up for a very long time. He had only taken the job as he had a two-year old daughter, and he wanted the best of everything for her and her mother. Another roundabout was fast approaching and Hussain hit the brakes. He slowed down to 40 and flew across it, narrowly missing a Jeep. He knew that this road led to Chippenham and the motorway. But he wanted to avoid the motorway at all costs as the traffic cops would deploy a T-pack, whereby three traffic cars would surround him and force him to stop. His best option was country roads, where he might be able to shake off his pursuers, unless of course they deployed a chopper.

With Alexander keeping control up to date with their route, a plan was being hatched to deploy a stinger at the roundabout at Corsham. This was a bed of nails that would gradually deflate the BMW's tyres, forcing it to a halt. Hussain was on the road to Corsham, which was both winding and with a steep hill to climb. The road was also narrow, making it extremely dangerous to try and overtake. The cop car had little chance of overtaking and bringing Husain's car to a stop. Hussain hit the gas once again and the BMW responded by hitting 90. Skelton backed off slightly as he did not want to panic the driver and cause him to crash. At this speed the occupants of the BMW would in all probability be killed. That was not on Skelton's agenda.

Hussain was now on the steep climb up the hill towards Corsham. He could see a garage coming up on his right-hand side and there was a car parked opposite, on his side of the road. He would have to pull out to his right to pass the parked car. Then he saw the truck speeding down the hill towards him. He could see that it was a cement truck, if he hit that head on, they were both dead. All he could do was to hit the brakes and drive straight into the parked car. Hussain and his passenger began screaming seconds before the impact. There was a very loud bang then everything went black. The air bags had deployed as they had been designed to do. They had saved the occupants of the vehicle from certain death.

'Crash, crash, crash!' yelled Alexander into the radio. 'We need paramedics and the fire brigade.' Alexander was still relaying information to control as Skelton jumped out of the car. Spurrey and Turnbull were right behind him. People from the garage were running across the road to help. The windscreen had been smashed to pieces in the collision. This allowed Skelton to get his hand inside and open the driver's door. Hussain was out cold but breathing. The air bag had probably knocked him out. Skelton could not see the passenger due to the inflated air bags. Spurrey had managed to open the passenger door.

'Sir, this one is alive, but he's been knocked out. Should I try and lift him out?'

Skelton walked around the back of the car and called to Spurrey.

'No, we best leave them as they are, in case we injure them. The fire brigade will have to cut them out. Just check his airways are clear in case he chokes to death.'

Spurrey did as he was told and then searched the guy's pockets. He retrieved the man's phone, wallet and keys.

'This guy is called Andrew Osborne and lives in Bath. I think I've seen him hanging out with Jake Ratten.'

Turnbull had checked the driver, who was still out cold and had retrieved his wallet and phone. The credit cards confirmed that he was Ali Hussain. Skelton opened a rear door and pulled out the Gucci bags and placed them on the bonnet of the police car. He opened the first bag, which had been behind Hussain. It was full of cash. The other bag contained what appeared to be pure cocaine. This was one hell of a drugs bust. Another traffic car had arrived, as had a paramedic. Very soon two fire engines were on scene and the crews set about cutting the occupants from the wreck. The phone that Spurrey had taken from Osborne began to ring.

Skelton said, 'Give that to me,' and he looked at the screen. The caller ID said Jake Ratten.

'Yeah man?' Skelton listened intently as Ratten spoke.

'Did you get it, Andy?'

Skelton looked at Spurrey and spoke into the phone. He knew that he could not hide his soft Scottish accent, so there was no point in pretending to be Andy.

'Yes, Andy delivered the cash to Ali and picked up the coke. Unfortunately, Mr Ratten, they were involved in a car accident and are now on their way to the RUH. But don't worry, the drugs and cash are safe with me.'

Skelton listened. 'Who is this?'

'It's Detective Chief Inspector Skelton.'

The phone went dead.

Alexander joined them at the bonnet of the police car.

'That's been a great day's work, team. I want Chris and Ross to go in the ambulances. Handcuff them both as I don't want them running off. Those two are going to prison for a very long time. If we can get Osborne to talk, we might be able to put the Rat away as well. But even if we don't get the Rat, he's lost a hell of a lot of money and the drugs. So he is going to be very pissed off with us, for a long time.' Skelton exchanged high fives with his team. 'Come on, Bill, let's get this lot back to the station and have a few pints to celebrate.'

Chapter Thirty-Five

Skelton was sitting at his desk, finishing off a square sausage sandwich. He washed the last piece down with some tea. He had the file on Fergus Walsh, the missing father of PC Fergus Walsh, open in front of him. Included in the file were some bank and credit card statements. They were dated around the time of his disappearance and he assumed that they had already been carefully checked. An investigator will always check for any unusual activity in the bank and credit card accounts. Was there any evidence of blackmail? Had he made a substantial withdrawal of cash to fund his getaway? Skelton studied the credit card statements first, these covered the months of May, June and July. There was not much activity on them, just a handful of purchases totalling nearly £300 each month. The outstanding balance was cleared each month by direct debit.

He then turned his attention to the bank statement, which covered the same three months. On the credit side, there was only one credit each month, which was his salary. He had been a partner in a firm of chartered accountants; he had been well paid. Next, he looked at the monthly debits. There were no mortgage payments, so it appeared that the mortgage on the house had been redeemed, which left a healthy surplus in the bank account. He could see that a significant cheque was withdrawn but it did not identify the payee. He would need to look into this in case the cheque was to a third party.

There were monthly direct debits for council tax, the water, gas and electricity. There were numerous cash withdrawals from the ATM which totalled £1,000 each month. He used his debit card to pay for the shopping and petrol. On one of the statements, there appeared to be a quarterly standing order to the council for £75, but it did not detail what the payment was for. It seemed an insignificant amount and had obviously not drawn further investigation. He then picked up a photocopy of a Nationwide Building Society passbook. He quickly reconciled the large monthly cheque withdrawals from the bank as matching the cheque deposits to the building society. There was no financial suspicious activity whatsoever. Skelton sighed and leaned back in his chair. The man had clearly not intended to disappear, that was evident.

He picked up the Criminal Record Report. Walsh had never so much as received a speeding ticket. He then turned to the witness statements. Mrs Nancy Walsh had reported her husband as missing. It was a happy marriage and they had no financial problems. Mr Walsh had no health issues and had never consulted his GP with any mental health problems. They had a son, also called Fergus, and he was a seventeen-year-old schoolboy. It was the summer holidays when his father went missing. He had some lunch with his father at home before going out to play football at 2 pm. Mrs Walsh said that father and son got on well together. She stated that she had no idea where her husband had gone and further stated that she was certain that no other woman was involved. She also expressed that her husband was well liked and had no enemies. They both attended church every Sunday morning.

Skelton then read some more witness statements from friends and neighbours. These corroborated everything that Mrs Walsh had said. No one had any idea what could have become of Mr Walsh. There was also a witness statement from young Fergus Walsh's teacher. He said that Fergus was a model pupil and well liked by his classmates. He was well behaved and very respectful to the teachers. He liked playing both football and rugby.

He rose from his chair and picked up his mug and plate and went to the canteen to rinse them. He bumped into constable Dave Lake, who had served in Bath for many years and was only five years away from retiring. 'Hello, sir, that was a great drugs bust you made the other day. You surprised us all by your driving skills, we all thought you couldn't drive.'

Skelton chuckled, 'I prefer to walk, Dave, or let someone else drive, that way I can have the odd pint or two.'

Lake laughed, 'Yes we do know that you and Bill enjoy the lunchtime pint.'

'Dave, I've got a complete mystery on my hands. I have just spent the morning reading the file on Fergus Walsh, who went missing eight years ago. Since then, there have been no sightings of him, nor have we found his body. You worked the case back then. What are your thoughts on it?'

Lake rested against the wall and thought for a second. 'I remember the case very well. Nobody had a bad word to say about the guy and no one thought he was the sort that would top himself. The thing is, sir, if he was murdered or he killed himself, surely, we would have found his body by now?'

Skelton rubbed his chin. 'That's what I can't understand, Dave, but my money is on him having been murdered. Whoever did it must have found the perfect place to hide the body. But I'm fucked if I know where he is.'

Hussain and Osborne had been discharged the next day from hospital. Skelton and Alexander had interviewed them, but they were saying nothing. It was obvious that Osborne was scared of the Rat, even if they put him away behind bars. They did not have enough evidence to charge the Rat, but they were both happy that he had lost £250,000 in cash as well as the drugs. Murray was sitting tight for the moment, which had surprised Skelton. Maybe his little visit to Murray had had the desired effect. He certainly hoped so. DI Patrick Rees had been in touch from Bristol almost every day. He reported that both Mickey Chadwell and Ben Naylor were often seen together, so that partnership appeared intact. There was no evidence to suggest that Naylor was joining forces with Murray in Bath. Maybe their fears of a turf war in Bath and Bristol were unfounded.

Alexander knocked on the door and entered. Skelton was putting on his suit jacket. 'Good timing, Bill, I could go some fish and chips in the Saracen's Head. I saw a couple getting tucked into some the other day, and it looked delicious.'

Alexander smiled. 'You must have been reading my mind, I fancy some fish and chips today and a couple of pints. But I am putting a blindfold on you today in case you recognise another drug dealer and we end up going hungry again.'

Skelton laughed. 'All right, Bill, my eyes are shut tight. You lead the way, my friend.' Skelton closed his eyes and pretended to be blind, and Alexander led him by the arm.

They got to the Saracen's Head without incident and they walked in the door. Toby the barman was behind the bar and greeted them warmly. They ordered their food and drinks and returned to the same table that they had occupied on their previous visit. 'How did it go at court this morning, Bill.'

Alexander had attended Bath Magistrates Court that morning where Hussain and Osborne had appeared charged with conspiracy to supply drugs and money laundering. Hussain had also been charged with dangerous driving. 'A piece of cake, Dan. They were both remanded in custody and their case was sent to Bristol Crown Court for trial. My guess is that with the evidence we have against them, they will plead guilty so that they get twenty-five percent knocked off their sentence. But they will still get ten or twelve years each.'

They both lifted their pints and clinked glasses and smiled.

'Well, that was certainly a great result, Bill, but we aren't making much if any progress on the Stephen Cox case. I know Peter is up and running on the Gaydar website but so far nothing of interest has turned up. We have quite a dilemma here, Bill. If the killer is searching for another victim, he might not choose the profile that Peter is using, and some other poor soul ends up with his throat cut. On the other hand, the killer might have had enough and simply goes to ground. Neither scenario is good for us. I honestly don't know if we will solve this. I just wish we could get a lucky break. Talking of luck, I'm going next door to the bookies, William Haggas has a horse running this afternoon at Newmarket in a maiden's race. I think his horse will take some beating.'

Chapter Thirty-Six

James Murray had instructed Ben Naylor to set up the meeting with Jake Ratten. It had not been easy to arrange, as Ratten had been concerned by the visit from the police warning him that Murray was in town and was likely to make a move against him. However, Naylor managed to convince him that Murray would be on his own and that he could have his own minders with him, meaning it would be three against one. The meeting would take place at Ratten's flat, which meant that the Rat and his minders could have weapons should they need them. Murray would agree to being searched by Ratten's minders before getting close to him.

At precisely 8 pm, Murray approached the door of the flat. Naylor had picked him up from the house and dropped him off across the road from where the Rat lived. Naylor had then driven back to Bristol where he met his girlfriend. They had a table booked for nine at his favourite Indian restaurant where he was well known by the staff. The restaurant also had extensive CCTV cameras which would give him a perfect alibi should something sinister happen to the Rat.

Murray rang the bell. It was immediately answered by the Rat's minders, Jason Andrews and Jeff Roberts. 'Good evening, gentlemen, I see that you were expecting me.'

The minders closely looked him up and down before nodding that he should come inside. As Murray brushed past them, Andrews gruffly said, 'Just wait there. We need to search you properly before you go any further.'

Murray smiled. 'Go ahead, boys, but I am not carrying anything except my wallet and keys and a couple of pills for having a good time with.' The minders carefully patted Murray down. He was clean. They were content that should he decide to, they were man enough to cancel out the threat.

'Follow us through. Mr Ratten is waiting for you.'

The Rat was sitting in a large armchair, a gin and tonic was resting on a small table to his right. The three men entered the sitting room and the Rat got up to meet his visitor. Murray was slightly larger than him and was smartly dressed in a navy-blue blazer, trousers and a white shirt, which was open at the neck. The Rat was wearing blue jeans and a short-sleeved blue shirt with his initials on the breast pocket.

'Hello, I'm Jack Ratten. You must be James Murray.'

The Rat extended his right arm and Murray did likewise. They shook hands and Murray said, 'James Murray at your service. I have heard a lot about you. All good of course.'

The Rat laughed and said, 'Yes and I have heard quite a lot about you. Not many guys kill a cop and get away with it, that's for sure. Can I get you a drink?'

Murray smiled and said, 'Actually, a gin and tonic would go down rather well.'

The Rat nodded to Roberts to fix the drinks.

Murray was sitting opposite the Rat and the minders were seated on the sofa. 'Well, James, what brings you to Bath and what is it that you want from me?'

His tone was businesslike, almost formal. Murray took a sip from the glass. 'That's a lovely gin and tonic. You have trained your barman really well.'

They both smiled and raised their glasses in salute. 'Jake, this is just a social visit, so to speak. I know that you run Bath and I respect that, and I am only here to pay you my respects. As you probably know, I run a large manor in south-east London, which keeps me in a comfortable lifestyle. My reason for coming to Bath is simply to keep my head down in this beautiful city. Since I killed that cop in London, I am not very popular with the police, as I am sure you will understand. I thought that by moving here, I could semi-retire whilst my guys back in London minded the shop for me.'

The Rat had been listening intently. He knew that Murray was talking bullshit. That copper Skelton had warned him to expect trouble from

Murray, but so far his actions were very far from being hostile. In fact, Murray had put himself at great risk by coming here alone unarmed. Suddenly, the Rat was asking himself the question, 'Had Skelton tried to start a war, knowing that he could get either man killed?' The Rat was confused. Murray was not showing any signs of being dangerous. Could it be that Murray was actually a potential friend, rather than an enemy? The more he thought about it the more he became convinced that Skelton was the real enemy, not Murray. The Rat ordered Roberts to get more drinks and he began to relax.

Murray explained that he had bought a large-detached house in Bath with his girlfriend and that he found the city to be a wonderful place to live. He loved the bars and restaurants and the nightlife in general. He was hoping to settle down and have children, as the schools were so good. All that the Rat was hearing was a man who was not posing any threat whatsoever. In fact, he was warming to the man, so much so that he sent Andrews to fetch Mandy from the bedroom. After a few more drinks, they were all friends.

Mandy had sat on his knee and was enjoying a rum and coke. She had her arm on the back of her boyfriend's neck and was feeling good. Jake had told her earlier that the visitor could be trouble, but she was liking the man.

'Tell me, James, why did you choose to live in Bath? After all, London is such a big city compared to Bath.'

Murray took another sip from his glass and smiled. 'It's a long story really, but let's just say that the police in London are not great fans of mine. I accidently killed a copper, but I got away with it on a technicality. Ever since then, they have kept a very close eye on me. I visited Bath last year with a stag party and it blew me away. It's so quiet and peaceful here that I thought it would be a great place to lie low and enjoy life. I still have my business interests in London, and I can be back at the office within two hours.'

The Rat had been listening intently and Murray had answered Mandy's question honestly as far as he was concerned. He cleared his throat and asked, 'What's your girlfriend's name, James, and where is she this evening?'

Murray smiled and said, 'Her name is Penny, and she is quite a looker. She used to be a model until she met me. Now we are an item. She is at home this evening just watching television and taking it easy. We only moved to Bath recently and she has been very busy arranging the furniture and spending my money like there's no tomorrow!'

They all laughed. 'Tell you what, James, why don't the four of us go out together one evening next week for a meal and really get to know each other. Mandy and I would love to meet Penny, and maybe we could go on to a night club afterwards.'

Murray's face broke into a big smile and he said, 'That would be awesome. Yes, let's do it.'

The Rat's minders had gone into the kitchen as it had become obvious that Murray was not a threat. They were enjoying a beer and discussing a trip that they needed to make to Bristol the following day. Mandy had gone to the bathroom, leaving Jake chatting to James.

'I tell you what, Jake, your Mandy is stunning. You must have a wonderful sex life.'

Jake sat back in his chair and smiled. 'Yeah, you're right there, mate, I can't give her enough cock. She exhausts me every bloody night.' Both men laughed.

'I think I can help you out on that score, Jake.'

The Rat gave him a quizzical look and asked, 'How do you mean?'

Murray stood up and put his left hand into his trouser pocket and pulled out a purple pill. He held it between his thumb and forefinger and said, 'See this, Jake, it's super powered Viagra. I take one only once a week because it keeps you hard for two days. When I take it, Penny thinks I am the greatest stud in town. Here, my friend, take this now and in half an hour, Mandy will be screaming in utter pleasure.'

Jake looked closely at the pill. 'Are you sure about this? I mean I don't want you missing out on the action yourself.'

Murray placed his arm on the Rat's shoulder. 'Don't worry, Jake, I've got plenty more of those at home. You just get that down your neck and I will be off to leave you two love birds in peace.'

The Rat took the pill, popped it in his mouth, picked up his glass and washed it down.

Murray said his goodbyes and promised to call in a day or two to arrange their night out. As he shook hands with the Rat he said, 'You won't believe what that pill will do to you, my friend. Give Mandy one for me.'

The men embraced and Murray left.

Chapter Thirty-Seven

The next morning Mandy woke at 7 am and reached over to cuddle the Rat. She got no response. 'Jake honey, wake up.'

She shook him but there was still no response. She began to panic and started shaking him harder, but she suddenly realised that he was lifeless. She began to scream but there was no one in the flat to help. She picked up the phone by the side of the bed and called 999 and asked for an ambulance. The dispatcher asked if the patient was conscious and breathing and Mandy replied no. The dispatcher made it a priority one response and began giving Mandy instructions on CPR whilst the first responder made his way to the flat. It was several minutes before there was a loud knock on the door. Mandy stopped the compressions and raced to the door and let the first responder into the flat.

'Leave the door open, there will be an ambulance here in a couple of minutes.'

They raced to the bedroom and the first responder made an urgent assessment of the casualty. He was not breathing and his complexion was grey. 'Okay, Mandy, my name is Tom. I am going to try everything I can. Why don't you go and let my colleagues into the flat. They will be here in a minute.'

Mandy did as she was told whilst Tom got to work with the defibrillator. He injected the patient with adrenalin, hoping it would help re-start the heart. He was soon joined by the ambulance crew and all three worked on the Rat for twenty minutes, but at 7.30 am they declared life extinct.

As it was a sudden and unexplained death, Tom radioed control to confirm a dead on arrival and that the police should be notified. They left the Rat in his bed and went to the kitchen to wait for the police and comfort Mandy as best they could. They gently quizzed Mandy about Jake's health and whether he took any prescribed medications or drugs. Mandy told them that she and Jake sometimes took cocaine and smoked some weed but nothing else. She was asked whether Jake had taken any drugs the night before and she said no, as she had not seen Murray give Jake the Viagra tablet. A few minutes later a police constable arrived. It was Dave Lake and he had seen many dead bodies over the course of his police career. He introduced himself to Mandy and he already knew the ambulance staff. Tom told him what they knew about his medical history and said that Mandy was sure that no drugs had been taken. He then discovered that the deceased was Jake Ratten, the drug baron of Bath. Lake decided that this was not just a sudden and unexplained death but also suspicious. This was a case for the CID.

Skelton was just about to leave home for the police station when his mobile phone rang. It was Dave Lake. 'Good morning, Dave. What can I do for you today?'

'Good morning, sir, I am sorry to call you this early, but I thought you should know that I am at the scene of a sudden death. I am at Jake Ratten's flat and his girlfriend woke up to find him dead. There are no signs of any drugs in the flat and there are no signs of any obvious injury.'

Skelton let this information sink in. 'My god, I was not expecting this, Dave. Get Bob Richards and his team to treat the flat as a crime scene and stay there until Bill and I get there.'

Lake finished the call and radioed for the CSI team to attend. Meanwhile, Skelton called Alexander and asked him to collect him from the house. His daily walk into work was not going to happen today.

They arrived at the flat and the paramedics had departed the scene. There was blue and white police tape across the door, which was open. Inspector Graham Symonds was standing at the door along with Dave Lake. A crowd was gathering in the street hoping to see what had happened. Skelton and Alexander approached the door. 'Dave, move these people on, there is nothing for them to see. Graham, book us in please.'

The detectives were carrying paper overalls, which they put on before entering the flat. They made their way to the bedroom, where Bob Richards and his team were busy photographing the scene. The Rat was lying on his back, clearly dead. Richards looked up to see the detectives approach.

'Good morning, gentlemen. You obviously don't need to be introduced to the Rat, or what was the Rat.'

Skelton scanned the scene. There was nothing out of place and no signs of any drugs. He was naked and there were no marks of injury on the body.

'Has Dr Challis been yet, Bob?'

Dr Challis was the Home Office pathologist that the Avon and Somerset Police Force used to investigate suspicious deaths.

'He is on his way, sir, and should be here shortly. As you can see, there is no indication of the deceased having injected drugs and the girlfriend said they did not take any drugs last night. There is no sign of any injury, so at the moment it is a sudden unexplained death. However, it is suspicious in that he was a healthy young man with no medical history that would point towards a sudden death. This is one for Dr Challis to sort out.'

Skelton and Alexander had a look around the flat. There were some empty beer bottles in the trash can as well as some empty tonic water bottles. They had a look around the kitchen for drugs but found none. 'Come on, Bill, let's go talk to the girlfriend.'

She was not in the flat, so Skelton asked Inspector Symonds where she was. She had been taken next door to a neighbour, so they made their way there, having removed their boilersuits. Alexander rang the bell, and it was answered by a lady that Skelton guessed was about sixty years old. She was petite and had lovely blue eyes.

Skelton produced his warrant card and said, 'I am sorry to bother you, but we are police officers. I believe that you are looking after the young lady from next door. May we come in please?'

The lady stood aside and said, 'Yes do come in. The poor girl is in a terrible state. What a shock for her. They were such a lovely couple.'

'What is your name, please?' asked Skelton.

'I am Mrs Nisbet and I live here with my husband. He left for work at six-thirty this morning so he missed all the commotion. I will ring him later when Mandy's sister comes to pick her up. She is on her way from London and should be here in an hour or so. Come on into the kitchen, Mandy is having some sweet tea.'

They entered the kitchen to find Mandy softly crying with her head on the table resting on her arms. A pack of tissues was on the table beside her. She was clearly distressed. A police liaison officer would arrive in a few minutes to help comfort her in any way she could.

'Mandy, it's the police come to speak to you,' Mrs Nisbet said. Mandy looked up and dabbed her eyes with a tissue.

'Mandy, I am Detective Chief Inspector Skelton, and this here is Detective Sergeant Alexander. We are very sorry for your tragic loss this morning and please accept our condolences. We obviously need to investigate the reason why Jake died so suddenly and there will have to be a post-mortem examination. Has Jake been ill recently, or has he been using any drugs that you know of?'

Mandy blew her nose and spoke softly. 'No, Jake has been fine. We do both take recreational drugs but not last night. We had drinks last night but not a lot.'

Skelton indicated to Alexander to take a chair at the table and took one for himself. 'Did you go out last night for a drink or did you stay at home?'

Mandy dabbed her eyes with a fresh tissue. 'No, we had dinner at the flat and then some friends joined us for a drink. Well actually, one of the guys was a new friend, but we had a lovely time and Jake seemed perfectly fine.'

Alexander had his notebook out and asked, 'Who were these friends, Mandy?'

'Well two of the guys worked for Jake. Jason Andrews and Jeff Roberts. The other guy just moved to Bath recently, and he is called James Murray.'

Alexander shot a look at Skelton and Skelton made a grimace. 'Mandy, how did you come to meet James Murray?'

Mandy blew her nose and said, 'James recently moved to Bath and somehow got in touch with Jake on the phone. He came to the flat last night at about eight and left just after ten. He seems like a really nice bloke. In fact, we were going to make arrangements to go out to dinner with him and his girlfriend.'

Skelton gave Alexander a puzzled look. This was not in the script, thought Skelton. 'Mandy, this is very important. You must be honest with us. We need to discover how Jake died. Did Jake take any drugs last night?'

Mandy shook her head. 'No, we never took any drugs last night. Jake had a few gin and tonics, and I think he had a beer early on in the evening.'

Skelton stood up and walked over to the window then turned and faced Mandy. 'Are you quite sure that James Murray did not give Jake any pills or tablets to take?'

Mandy looked at the detective and said, 'No I never saw him give Jake anything and Jake certainly didn't say anything about drugs. After James left, Jason and Jeff finished their drinks and they left as well. I tided up and we went to bed. Jake said he was really tired and was sound asleep in minutes. When I woke up, I leaned across the bed to give him a cuddle and realised that he wasn't right.' Mandy began to sob loudly.

Mrs Nisbet entered the kitchen, followed by Marie Henderson, a police liaison officer. Marie would help console Mandy as best she could in the difficult weeks ahead.

They drove back to the station in silence. It was a short trip, although the traffic was quite heavy. At the station, Skelton made two mugs of tea. It was his favourite, Twinings Breakfast Tea. He added two and half sugars for himself and none for Alexander. He then poured the milk and stirred. He and Alexander sat down, and they sipped the tea.

'I don't buy this at all, Bill. If I was a betting man, and I am, I'd say that the Rat died of a drug overdose. I also think that Murray either spiked his drink or he somehow induced the Rat to take a pill. Whatever it was, we don't stand a snowball's chance in hell of proving that Murray killed him. This will be at least the third murder that the bastard has got away with.'

'But sir, we will have to wait for the results of the toxicology test before we can say that he died of an overdose. You never know, he might have had an undetected heart defect which killed him. It's not uncommon, as we both know, particularly if he was a drug user, which he was.'

Skelton leaned back in his chair deep in thought. 'No, Bill, you know I don't believe in coincidences. Murray pays a friendly visit to the Rat and the next morning he is dead in his own bed. Murray is a clever and cunning bastard. Had he taken the Rat out in a violent manner, he knows that we would have him down as the prime suspect. He could not run the risk of being caught on CCTV or by forensics. No, you know and I know and Murray knows he has got away with the perfect murder. I don't give a shit for the Rat, but I do care an awful lot for my friend Joe Reilly who Murray murdered. We have got to nail him, Bill, but how the blazes we do it is beyond me. We are going to need all our combined skills, and a lot of luck, but I will pursue him even if I have to play dirty.'

Chapter Thirty-Eight

Skelton checked his watch. It was 10.50 am and he had an appointment with Chief Superintendent Mike Sawyers, who was his overall boss at Manvers Street. They enjoyed a good working relationship and Sawyers had totally backed him from day one. He stood up and put on his suit jacket and did up the buttons. It was a bespoke double-breasted suit and a crisply ironed white handkerchief nestled in the breast pocket. He would usually enjoy a square sausage sandwich at 11 am with Alexander but Sawyers had called the meeting, so he would have to forsake his morning snack today.

He knocked on the door and Sawyers called him in. 'Good morning, Dan, how are you today? And please take a seat.'

Skelton began sitting down. 'I am good, sir, and I trust you are well?'

Sawyers smiled and said, 'Yes, I am fine thanks, and looking forward to Friday when me and Mrs Sawyers head off to Florida for a couple of weeks. Mind you, I will have to be careful not to overdo those huge steaks, or I won't be able to squeeze into this uniform.' They both laughed. 'Tell me, Dan, how are you getting on with that unsolved murder in the park, and what's the situation on the sudden death of Jake Ratten?'

Skelton leaned forward and placed his hands on the desk and cleared his throat. 'The Stephen Cox murder remains a mystery, unfortunately. We are pretty certain that he met his killer on Gaydar. We have set up a fictitious account and that is being monitored very closely. We have had lots of hits but they have come to nothing. As you know, our prime suspect, Fergus Walsh, a serving police officer, has been eliminated from our enquiries. We continue to look at serving armed forces personnel but to be honest, I think we might be barking up the wrong tree. We have also looked into his former boyfriends but drew a blank there as well. Unless we get lucky on Gaydar, this might remain an unsolved case.'

Sawyers had listened carefully but had made no comment. He fully realised that some murders remained unsolved. He could not criticise Skelton and his team; they were doing everything they could to get a result.

'What about Jake Ratten?'

Skelton took his hands off the desk and leaned back in his chair. 'The post-mortem could not determine the exact cause of death but the pathologist believes that he had died from poisoning by a substance or substances unknown. The toxicology results are not in yet, but I am certain that James Murray slipped the Rat a pill, pretending it to be something that would get him high or sexually excited. He murdered the Rat but there is no way on earth that I can prove it. There is no chance of him admitting to it, even if I was to beat the shit out of him. The only consolation is that a drug baron is no more. But what worries me most is that he has been replaced by another who is ten times more ruthless. Alexander and I will be paying him a visit. It will probably be a fruitless exercise, but I just want to mark his card again.'

Sawyers leaned across his desk. 'This guy worries me, Dan. I know that he killed a friend of yours and got away with it. Now it looks like he saunters into Bath and kills Jake Ratten and we can't do a thing about it. He is bloody dangerous that's for sure. What do you reckon his next move will be?'

Skelton placed both hands on his lips and then took them away. He sighed in frustration. 'Well, he has achieved his ambition to take control of the Bath drug scene with consummate ease. His key ambition is to seize control of Bristol. That will be impossible without bloodshed. Mickey Chadwell is ruthless, and he will defend his patch to the death. Likewise, Murray is even more ruthless than Chadwell. I think that whatever happens, one of them or both of them will end up dead. That I can live with, but I just hope that no innocent soul gets caught in the crossfire. The other thing to consider is will Ben Naylor stay loyal to Chadwell or will he change sides and back Murray? One thing for sure is this, all three men are very dangerous and I don't want another cop being killed. When we make a move on any of these guys, we only do so with armed backup.'

Sawyers stood up and walked to the window. It was a sunny morning and he looked down to the carpark where a police car was just leaving. He turned and faced Skelton. 'Dan, you and your team need to be very careful out there. We don't know where the action is going to kick off. It could be here, or it could be in Bristol. You best keep in close contact with DI Patrick Rees in Bristol. You need to know what Chadwell and Naylor are up to, and Rees needs to know what Murray is about. All I can do is to wish you all the very best of luck. Be sure to keep me posted on what is going on.'

Chapter Thirty-Nine

Alexander was driving as usual, whilst Skelton was seated in the passenger seat. It was two days after the Rat had been found dead. The toxicology results would not be in for a few weeks, but Dr Challis had reckoned that he had been poisoned. The stomach contents had been sent off for analysis along with blood. Whatever he had swallowed, he never expected it to kill him, that was for sure. Both Jason Andrews and Jeff Roberts, who had been with the Rat at the drinks party, confirmed that they never saw him take any tablets and that the relationship between him and Murray had been very cordial. If the Rat had taken any tablets, he must have done so himself. Murray had certainly not forced him, and he could not have slipped them into the Rat's drink, as he never had the opportunity.

The car pulled up outside Murray's house and the officers got out. Murray's door began opening and they could hear him speaking. Murray stepped outside and saw the police officers. 'Oh, it's you two again. What can I do for you this time?'

Penny Cole, Murray's girlfriend was standing on the step. She was wearing sunglasses and carrying an expensive looking handbag.

'Can we go inside and have a word?' asked Skelton.

'Yes, come on in but make it quick, we have a table booked for twelve-thirty.' All four went into the house and Murray led them into the sitting room. Skelton and Alexander sat on the sofa and the loving couple sat on the armchairs.

'You had a drink with Jake Ratten the other night. How did that come about?' asked Skelton.

'A mutual friend fixed it up. I wanted to pay him my respects and make friends. I was gutted to hear that he had passed away. He seemed in good fettle when I left him. Poor Mandy must be heart broken. They seemed like the perfect couple. What did he die from?'

Skelton looked at Murray with complete contempt. 'We both know that you slipped him something and you knew it would kill him. Of course, there are no witnesses, so I won't be able to prove it unfortunately.'

Murray tried to portray a look of all innocence, but it wasn't working. 'I never gave him anything, just ask Mandy and his two minders. We just had a pleasant drink together and were hoping to go out to dinner next week and then shit happens.'

Skelton stood up and walked closer to Murray. 'To be honest, Murray, I couldn't give a damn about the Rat though I would have loved to have put you away for killing him. I warned you the last time that we met that you are my worst enemy and I will eventually get you one way or another for having killed my best friend. Nothing will give me greater pleasure in taking you off the streets for life. We will be watching you like a hawk. The same goes for Chadwell and Naylor in Bristol.' Murray stood up, he was bigger than Skelton and more powerfully built. 'Yeah right, Inspector. If you don't mind, Penny and I are off for a celebratory lunch and you two are not invited.' It took all of Skelton's patience not to punch the bastard's face.

Back in the car, Alexander said, 'I don't know how we are ever going to get him, sir. He is a clever sod by a long way. He pulls off the perfect murder under our noses and laughs in our faces. God, I need a drink!'

Skelton placed his hand on Alexander's shoulder. 'Drive us back to the station, Bill, we will park up and stroll over to the pub and sort out a pint or two of Fosters.'

They left the car at the station and took a direct route to Belushi's bar. Normally Skelton would take them on a detour so that they got more exercise, but today his need for a pint and some lunch was too great. Joe was behind the bar, as was his assistant Tom. Joe greeted them. 'Good afternoon, gentlemen, I take it a couple of pints of Fosters will go down well?'

Skelton looked at the barmen and said, 'Do you know, if we weren't on duty today, we would stay in here all afternoon and get pissed. But never mind, two or three pints and a hamburger might just be what the doctor ordered.'

Tom poured the pints and took their food order. Tom was a young Australian and was studying for a degree at Bath University. The detectives went next door to the quiet lounge and were pleased to see that it was empty, unlike the main bar, which was occupied by about twenty people. They sat by the window and Skelton took a long sip from his pint.

'Do you know, Bill, of all the criminals I have come across, I have never actually hated any of them. But Murray is a different kettle of fish. He is pure evil and unfortunately, he has a very sharp brain. Okay, we put him away for dealing drugs, but he gets off for killing Joe Reilly. We think he killed Jimmy White the publican in London but again he gets away with it. Now he kills the Rat and he's out celebrating when he should be behind bars. I just wish we could get some luck, but the guy thinks outside the box, just like me. Go on, Bill, two more pints are urgently required.'

Alexander went off to the bar leaving Skelton in deep thought. Alexander was walking back to the table carrying two pints of Fosters when he saw Skelton bang his fist on the table and shouted, 'GOT IT!'

Alexander placed the beers on the table and asked, 'What have you got Dan?'

Skelton's face lit up, a big smile appearing on it. 'Sit down, my friend. Murray's girlfriend, Penny Cole, might be a looker but she is not the sharpest tool in the box. The house where they live is in her name, but we all know that the money came from Murray. Now if we could get to her and apply some pressure, she might be the chink in Murray's armour. I warned Murray that we could seize the house under the Proceeds of Crime Act, even if it was in Penny's name, and that shook him up. Now we could lean on Penny and say that unless she cooperates with us, we seize the house. It's obvious that she loves the finer things in life and if we can strike a deal that she keeps everything, in return for information, we might be able to hit Murray when and where he is not expecting it.'

Skelton had a smug look on his face. 'You know what, Dan, I think that's a plan and a half. There must be something in this Fosters that stimulates the grey matter. If I were you, boss, I'd get another couple in.'

Murray lost no time in contacting Jason Andrews and Jeff Roberts. They had worked for the Rat and had all his contacts. With the Rat gone, they were essentially unemployed, as they did not have the capital, or for that matter the brains, to run a drugs empire. The takeover was almost seamless, and soon the cash was rolling in. Murray conducted all his business dealings in pubs and restaurants, never at the house. He was concerned that Skelton may have bugged the house and telephones.

Ben Naylor, the guy with whom he had shared a cell and who was Mickey Chadwell's right-hand man, got in touch as soon as word that the Rat had died got out. They met in the Saracen's Head at midday and Murray had got the drinks in. 'Hi, Ben, thanks for coming. I thought you could manage a pint even though it's quite early.'

They exchanged high fives and Naylor sat opposite. 'How the hell did you do it?'

Murray sipped his beer and smiled. 'Let's just say that he took something he shouldn't have and never woke up.'

Naylor lifted his glass, 'I salute you, sir. I never thought you would take the Rat out this quick. When will you make a move on Mickey?'

Murray placed his palms on the table and said, 'The Rat was not expecting me. Mickey Chadwell is a different proposition. He has made lots of enemies, so he is always on his guard. Word will be getting back to him that I am in charge of Bath. You, my friend, will help spread the word. Tell him that Andrews and Roberts are working for me now. That is bound to upset him, and he might try to hit me in Bath. He is bound to feel safe in Bristol where he is king of the castle.'

Naylor took a sip of his beer. 'I don't think that Mickey will go after you. Not at the moment, anyhow. He was content to let Jake run Bath just so long as he did not stray anywhere near Bristol. But if you did venture near Bristol, that's another story. He's had at least four guys killed since I started working for him. He rarely just warns guys off. I seriously beat up a few guys and they got the message. Mind you, they were so fucked up, they could never work again.' They exchanged smiles. 'Those guys had made minor incursions and it got them punished big time. The guys we killed had started dealing on the outskirts of town, but Mickey heard about it and that was it, they were dead. We took over a scrap yard and disposed of the bodies in the bailer that crushes cars. The crushed cars go to the furnace and that's all the evidence gone.'

'Do you want another pint, Ben?'

'Yeah man, we are celebrating.' Murray returned with the pints.

It was 12.30 pm and Skelton had gone into the CID office where he found Alexander putting on his jacket. 'Good timing, Bill. Shall we try the Saracen's Head today. I could go some fish and chips.'

Alexander was putting his phone into his pocket. 'Do you know, the fish and chips in there are good. Count me in, sir.'

The detectives slowly made their way past the abbey, which was surrounded by tourists busy taking pictures. They bumped into Peter Lowik, who was carrying a packet of sandwiches and a can of Coke.

'Hi, Peter, having any luck on Gaydar?'

Lowik gave them a smile. 'You know what, my wife is getting twitchy with me. I keep telling her that I am using a gay website as part of an investigation into a murder, but she just raises her eyebrows.' They all laughed. 'To tell the truth, I have had a couple of interesting hits, but they never came to anything. I think the killer has gone to ground and might not surface anytime soon.'

'Peter, do you still see Fergus Walsh these days?' asked Skelton.

'Yeah, I had a few beers with him last Saturday.'

Skelton moved to his left to let a young lady pass. 'Did you discuss the case with him?'

Lowik frowned and said, 'Naturally we did. I mean he was our prime suspect until forensics ruled him out. He was keen to know what progress we were making. I told him we had ruled out former boyfriends, and a number of guys in the armed forces. I said we were pinning our hopes on Gaydar as we had run out of leads.'

Skelton thanked Lowik and he and Alexander set off to the pub.

It was Alex the landlord who was behind the bar, and he greeted them like long lost friends. 'Good afternoon, chaps. Good to see you. I take it you will be wanting a couple of pints? And what about food?'

Skelton smiled and said, 'Yes please, Alex, and two portions of fish and chips. We will take the usual seat by the window.' Alexander paid for the drinks and Skelton paid for the food. They took their seats.

'Bill, I need to go and wash my hands.'

Skelton made his way to the toilet when the toilet door opened and a huge Black guy came out. On seeing Skelton, he held the door open for him and smiled. Skelton returned the smile and went in. He could barely contain his excitement as he washed and dried his hands. He came out of the toilet and slowly walked over to the separate bar that contained a pool table. He glanced in and saw Ben Naylor facing him. He was seated at a table and a white guy had his back towards Skelton. He saw enough and went back to his own table.

'Guess who is sitting in the other bar, Bill.'

Alexander thought for a second and said, 'Well I bet it's not Jake Ratten, that's for sure.'

They both smiled. 'No, Bill, it's not the Rat but the guy who took over his enterprise and Ben Naylor.'

Alexander gripped his pint and said, 'Christ, they didn't waste any time, did they? Did they see you?'

'I met Naylor coming out the toilet, but he does not know me. I had a peak into the pool bar and Murray was sitting with his back to me. Our intel was spot on. It looks like these two are going into partnership. Will Murray go after Chadwell or will Chadwell take on Murray? We need a meeting with Patrick Rees. He lives in Bath, so a morning meeting for him is usually good. He can then go into Bristol when we are done. I will call him when we get back to the office.'

The fish and chips arrived, and Skelton got up and headed for the bar to get reinforcements.

Chapter Forty

Skelton got out of bed; it was 6.30 am. The second his feet touched the floor, Brenty-Boy, one of his three black Labradors, gave a loud woof. Brenty-Boy was the eldest at eight, followed by his son Josh, aged five and young Archie who was only two. He put on his dressing gown and went downstairs to the kitchen, where the boys slept. He was immediately welcomed by furious tail wagging and he got down on his knees and cuddled the boys. He then let them out into the garden to do their morning business. He put the kettle on to boil and switched on the television for the news. It seemed that just about every trade union in the country had called a strike. He quickly got bored and switched it off, made two mugs of tea and let the boys back in. He gave them each a Bonio biscuit and they went back to their beds. Ken would take them out for a walk at about 7.45 am.

Skelton got into the shower and turned the water on. He liked a hot shower, which for some reason stimulated his thinking powers. He had a lot on his mind this morning. There was the unsolved murder in the park. The killing of the Rat. The meeting this morning with Patrick Rees and the missing person case of Fergus Walsh senior. As he shampooed his hair, his mind turned to the missing person case. He was sure the guy was dead, probably murdered. He was missing something, he knew it. But what the blazes was it? He thought back to the bank statements. Was there a clue in there that he had missed? He turned the temperature up and he stood under the hot water. Suddenly, he remembered the quarterly direct debit for £75 to the council. What was this for? It had been dismissed by the detectives working the case as being irrelevant. Even he had given it little thought. Why was Walsh paying the council £300 per year. It was too cheap for a garage in Bath and besides, he owned one at the house. Skelton was intrigued. He had to find out what Walsh got for £300 a year.

He left the house and began walking into the city. It was a lovely sunny morning but a little fresh. As usual, Skelton was immaculately dressed and his freshly shined shoes enhanced his appearance. He carried a smart briefcase which contained some papers and his iPad. He was in a cheerful mood after his very hot shower. He would get Alexander to check with the council to see what Mr Walsh was getting for his money.

He popped into M&S to buy some square sausages and bread. He would treat his friends Patrick Rees and Alexander to an early morning snack to get the meeting off to a good start. He then went to the station where Dave Lake and Luke Meehan were just going out on patrol. They exchanged pleasantries and Skelton headed to his office. The meeting was due to start at 9 am so he checked his emails and crime reports from the night shift. Neither contained anything of real interest. He then went into the CID office, but it was empty except for Janet Griffin and Alexander. He bid them both a good morning and told Alexander that he was off to fry up some sausage sandwiches. This news was warmly welcomed by Alexander.

The meeting convened in Skelton's office. They were all friends, so it was very cordial, especially with the addition of the square sausages. They had been covered in a brown fruity sauce with a little salt and white pepper. Nothing was said until their plates had been cleared. 'I wish, Dan, I could get these every morning. They are the perfect start to the day.'

'I know, Patrick, I spoil Bill rotten.'

Alexander raised his hands in the air, 'Aye he does that all right.'

They all laughed before getting down to business. Skelton chaired the meeting. 'Right, we are pretty certain that Murray killed the Rat, but that's going to be virtually impossible to prove. Yesterday I saw Murray with Ben Naylor here in Bath. Our informants tell us that Murray has taken control of the Rat's enterprise and has recruited his henchmen Andrews and Roberts to work for him. Whilst I hate Murray with every fibre of my body, we have to take our hats off to him for his ingenuity. I mean, he has hardly set foot in Bath, yet he has killed the opposition and is now running the drugs racket. What we need to understand is this: will Murray be content to have control of Bath and leave Mickey Chadwell alone, or will he try and take him out? Our intel is that he will go for him, with the help of Ben Naylor, who you will remember he shared a cell with. On the other hand, will Chadwell see Murray as more of a threat than the Rat was and take him on?'

Rees cleared his throat. 'Ideally it would be fantastic if neither of them made a move on each other, but that would be like praying for a miracle and that is just not going to happen. Murray is hugely ambitious, and I don't think he will be happy until he takes over Bristol, which could see bodies pilling upon the street. But as you say, Dan, Chadwell will consider Murray as a big threat, much more so than the Rat ever was. It might be a question of who blinks first.'

Skelton stood up and stretched. 'I had a similar conversation with Bill. We need to get real intelligence from both camps. I think Murray has a chink in his armour in the shape of his girlfriend, Penny Cole. The house where they live is in her name, but Murray put the money up for it. If we can get to her and persuade her to give us Murray, we could strike a deal that she keeps the house and all the belongings.'

Skelton sat back down and as he did so, Alexander leaned on the desk and said, 'I think we are missing something here. Ben Naylor can't be in both camps for long. We think he did a deal with Murray to oust Chadwell, but Chadwell at some point is going to smell a rat. He might be happy at the moment to let Naylor visit Murray for old time's sake and to gather intelligence, but if he thinks that they are getting too close, he might take one or both of them out.'

Rees gently banged the desk. 'That is a very good point, Bill. However, provided no one else gets killed or injured we are in a win-win situation.'

'I agree with both of you. But unless we get someone inside one or both camps, we simply won't know who will deliver the first blow. I think we need to start grooming Penny Cole but it's not going to be easy. Bill, I want you to find out all that you can about her and her family. We need as much leverage as we can get. She is from London, so you might have to go up there and do some digging. I think she was on the game before Murray met her. See what form she has, if any, as well as the whole family. Talk to Janet Griffin, she has been looking into her finances. She may have already done most of the spade work.'

The meeting broke up just after 10 am and Rees headed off to Bristol. It was agreed that they would share any intel received, more or less on a daily basis. Alexander went off to talk to Janet Griffin and Skelton went to get the file on Fergus Walsh. He immediately pulled out the bank statements. These covered a period of just over six months. He highlighted the two direct debits for £75 to the council, which were paid on the first of the month. He assumed that these were quarterly payments and that a further two payments would have been made. What the devil was Fergus Walsh getting for £300 per year? He had discounted a garage, as Walsh had one at his home. Maybe a lock-up or workshop? He would have to visit Mrs Walsh and find out just exactly what Mr Walsh was getting from the council.

There was a knock on the door and in walked DC Chris Spurrey. 'Sir, there has been an attempted armed robbery at the petrol station on Frome Road. Uniform are on the scene, but the suspect got away empty handed. There should be good CCTV evidence. Do you want me and Peter to deal with it?'

Skelton stood up and reached for his jacket. 'No, Bill and I will handle this. I could do with getting out of the office.'

Alexander drove and Skelton was seated in the front passenger seat. It was a lovely day, and the traffic was light. They headed up the Wells Way and at the roundabout at the Red Lion turned left. They passed the huge Sainsbury's supermarket on their right and a few hundred metres later they were at the petrol station. There were several marked police cars parked up as well as the CSI van. Skelton spotted the three armed officers. The entrance was taped off and Dave Lake was standing guard. On seeing the detectives, he lifted the tape so that they could enter the garage. Alexander parked the car and they both got out. Sergeant Ian Perkins greeted them. He was in uniform and had his notebook in his right hand. Perkins had over twenty years on the force. He was a tough, no-nonsense bobby and was well liked by all his colleagues.

'Good morning, sir. Good morning, Bill. A guy in motorbike gear and a helmet produced what appears to have been a handgun and told the cashier to open the till and hand over the money. Fortunately, a colleague saw what was happening and pressed the alarm. The suspect panicked and ran out of the shop and got on his motorbike and drove off in the direction of the Wells Way. The garage was unusually quiet, so apart from the cashier and her colleague there were no other witnesses. The suspect was wearing gloves and was wearing a face mask as well as a helmet. The only description we have is that he seemed to be quite young about five foot six tall and had a local accent. He was dressed in black and both witnesses say that they doubt if they could recognise him again. Sorry, sir, that does not give you much to work on.'

Skelton asked, 'Did they get the number plate or is it on CCTV?'

Perkins shrugged his shoulders and said, 'No I am afraid the witnesses were too shaken up and they stayed behind the counter until we arrived. I have not checked the CCTV yet, but I reckon the bike will be on it.'

Skelton thanked Perkins and led Alexander into the shop. It was well stocked with supermarket goods. One of the armed officers was standing guard at the door of the office. Skelton gave him a smile and asked, 'Are the witnesses inside?'

The officer stood aside and said, 'Yes they are both in there, but they are a bit shocked, sir.'

Skelton brushed past and Alexander followed.

Skelton had his warrant card in his right hand and held it up for the witnesses to see. 'I am Detective Chief Inspector Skelton, and this is Detective Sergeant Alexander. I am so sorry that you had such a terrible experience. Are you hurt in anyway?'

The witnesses were both women and they both wore name tags. The one called Mary, who Skelton estimated to be about fifty said, 'No we were not hurt, just shaken up. I was on the till and June was standing by the door. She saw the gun and pressed the alarm. As soon as it went off the guy just ran.'

Skelton could see the CCTV cameras mounted on the wall behind the tills. 'I take it you have CCTV cameras outside at the pumps for people that fill up and don't pay?'

It was June's turn to speak. 'Yes, there are loads of cameras outside. I am sure that he will on the tapes.'

Skelton and Alexander studied the tapes. The suspect drove past the pumps and parked next to the ATM. Alexander wrote down the registration plate number and radioed it in. A check revealed that the bike had been stolen a week earlier. That was not helpful to the case at all. They closely watched as the suspect entered the shop.

'Look, Bill, he has a limp. Chances are that he fell off the bike.'

He went straight to where Mary was sat behind a plastic screen. He had both his gloved hands covering something that he was carrying. As he got to the screen, he opened his hands to reveal a handgun. It was impossible to say if it was real or a replica. His face was completely covered both by the helmet and a face mask. Mary begins to open the till and suddenly the suspect runs off. This must have been when June activated the alarm. Skelton thanked the witnesses and said that an officer would come and take statements.

'Shit, Bill, unless we get lucky and catch the suspect riding the bike, we are stuffed. We might get lucky and find the bike, but I reckon this was just a kid. Chances are that neither his prints nor his DNA are on record. He must be pretty desperate for money to stage an armed robbery. So, my guess is that he is hooked on drugs and either needs to buy or he owes money to the dealer. We are not having much luck with the cases that we are getting at the moment, that's for sure.' He checked his watch. It was

12.40 pm and time for lunch. 'Come on, Bill, let's get some lunch. Those sausage sandwiches seem like history.'

They walked out to the car and Alexander pressed the key fob. 'Wait a minute, sir, there is a really good pub just down the road from here. It's about a thirty second drive and it has a great reputation for its food.'

Skelton was all ears. 'What's it called, Bill?'

Alexander thought for a second. 'It's called the Cross Keys, I haven't been in it for years, but if it is half as good as I remember it, you will not be disappointed.'

They parked the car and Alexander led the way. As he entered the doorway, there was a door on the left and on the right. The one on the left had a sign saying 'The Eddie Cochran Lounge'. He pushed open the door and saw a couple sitting by the window having lunch. Skelton followed to the bar, and they were greeted by the landlord. He gave them a big cheery smile and said, 'Good afternoon, gentlemen, and what can I get you?'

Skelton's eyes darted to the beer pumps and saw that they sold Carlsberg lager, which was one of his favourites. 'Hello, I think we could force down a couple of pints of Carlsberg please. Do we need to book a table for lunch?'

The landlord smiled and said, 'At the weekends you do but I have a table free next door. I can strongly recommend the steak and ale pie if you are not vegetarians.'

Skelton and Alexander laughed. 'No, we have never been accused of that and probably never will. Each to their own I say. My name is Dan and this here is Bill. This is what I call a proper pub. Do you allow dogs in by any chance?'

The landlord was handing over the drinks. 'I will put that on a tab for you. Yes, we certainly allow dogs in here. At the weekends, there are nearly as many dogs as people. My name is Clive by the way.'

'Well Clive, I have three black labs and this place is in easy walking distance from the house, so you will be seeing much more of my face, that's for sure.'

The meals arrived and the portions were big. 'Bloody hell, Dan, one portion would have done the both of us.'

Skelton cut off a piece of the pie and put it in his mouth and began chewing. 'This is delicious, Bill. It reminds me of the steak pies we used to get in Scotland. I think we will start coming up here once a week. We will probably be on a diet the rest of the week!'

They sat in silence until their plates were clear. Clive came over to clear away the plates. 'Did you enjoy that?'

Skelton burped gently and said, 'That was excellent, Clive. We will be coming in once a week from now on. By the way, Bill and I are police officers, and we work in the CID in Manvers Street. We don't like to advertise the fact but thought we should let you know.'

Clive stood holding the empty plates. 'Were you guys at the garage earlier?'

'Yes, Bill and I attended an attempted armed robbery, but the suspect made off when the alarm was triggered.'

'I wondered what was going on when there were so many police cars over there. Can I get you anything else?'

Alexander looked up and said, 'Can you get me a bigger pair of trousers. I think I am going to burst these ones!'

Skelton roared with laughter.

They paid the bill and bid farewell to Clive. They were just getting into the car when Skelton saw him. A young guy was limping down the road towards the garage. He was wearing a grey track suit and he had his hands in the pockets. Skelton reckoned that he was about sixteen or seventeen and had short dark hair. It was not uncommon for criminals to revisit the scene of a crime.

'Bill, I think that young lad across the road is our suspect from this morning. I will go after him. You take the car and drive to the garage.'

Skelton waited for a car to pass before quickly walking across the road. The lad was limping badly and so his progress was slow. Skelton caught up with him and shouted, 'Police, stop now.'

The lad stopped and began turning around. Skelton could see that he was trying to get something out of his right-side pocket. Skelton was too quick for the guy and he grabbed his hand. The guy tried to resist but Skelton was far too strong for him. He squeezed the suspect's wrist with all his might and the gun fell to the ground. Skelton cuffed him just as Alexander arrived.

'Search him, Bill. What's your name, son, and where do you live?'

The boy looked scared. 'Sean Dempsy, but Dad threw me out the house last week, so I just sofa surf with my mates.'

Alexander concluded the search. 'He's only got a lighter and two-pound coins on him.'

Skelton put on a pair of gloves and bent down and picked up the gun. 'Is this gun real, Sean?'

'No, it only fires ball bearings.' Skelton checked the gun. The boy was telling the truth. 'Right, Sean, you are under arrest for carrying an imitation firearm and on suspicion of attempted armed robbery at the garage this morning.'

Skelton cautioned the prisoner and he and Alexander walked him to the car. They placed him on the back seat and closed the door. 'Looks like our luck has changed at last, Bill. I might just have a bet on the horses later.'

Chapter Forty-One

Mickey Chadwell and Ben Naylor were sitting in a bar in Bristol having a drink. It had just gone six and the bar was getting a bit busy, with workers stopping off for a drink before going home. 'Do you think James Murray killed the Rat, Ben?'

Naylor rubbed his chin and said, 'I don't know. The cops aren't saying much, just a suspicious death. For all we know he might have had a heart attack or something.'

Chadwell was staring closely at Naylor. 'No, I don't buy that. Murray moves into Bath and all of a sudden Jake Ratten the drug baron dies, and Murray takes over the firm. This guy killed a cop and got away with it. Now I think he has killed again and has a lot to gain from it. You did time with him. Why did he leave London for Bath? I don't understand that.'

Naylor sipped his drink and said, 'He told me that the cops were giving him a hard time in the big smoke. He killed a copper and got away with it. They want revenge and James was sure that they would fit him up somehow. You know what coppers are like. So, he bought a house in Bath with his girlfriend. I think he saw a business opportunity when the Rat died and took it.'

Chadwell had listened carefully. 'I am not buying this. How did Murray contact him? Did you arrange a meeting for him?'

Naylor raised his hands in the air. 'No, Mickey, I never did that. I went to see James after he moved in and he asked me who ran the drugs in Bath, so I told him. I couldn't see any harm in that. I told him that the Rat controlled the drugs in Bath but that you were the king in Bristol. I also told him that the Rat was under no illusion as to what would happen to him should he venture onto our patch.'

Chadwell thought for a few seconds and said, 'I don't like this at all. I think you should arrange a meeting with Murray and me. I want him to understand that should he dare make a move on Bristol he is a dead man.'

Meanwhile in Bath, Murray was taking stock of his recently acquired empire. He never had meetings at the house in case Skelton had bugged it. The Rat had lost his drug supplier, so Murray had to plug the gap. He sent Andrews up to London to meet with a supplier that Murray had used for years. Andrews had returned with £250,000 worth of pure cocaine. This was taken to a safe house where it would be cut and sorted into £30 wraps. These were distributed to the dealers who would sell it to their users or clients.

Word reached Murray that a user had racked up a £2,000 debt. The dealer had been assured on numerous occasions by the user that the debt would be settled. Now the user had done a runner with the debt outstanding. Murray instructed Andrews and Roberts to find him and teach him a lesson and to get the money. The user was called Arthur, but they did not have a surname for him. They knew that he was a lawyer and worked in Bath in a law firm. He was said to be aged about thirty. Andrews consulted the law directory and there were only two Arthurs practicing in Bath. They discounted the first one right away as being too old.

They took the dealer and drove him to the offices where the other Arthur worked. They parked up opposite the offices and waited. At just after six, a well-dressed man left the building. 'That's him there.' Andrews and Roberts got out the car and the dealer got out and walked away. Arthur was vaping and he did not hear the men approach. They both grabbed an arm and warned Arthur not to resist or there would be consequences. The man was terrified.

'What's this about?' Andrews spoke quietly into Arthur's ear.

'You owe us £2,000 for drugs and I don't think your legal partners would like to hear about it. Now you just come quietly with us and we will discuss this in a gentlemanly manner.'

Arthur had no choice but to comply.

They drove Arthur to a layby which was deserted and parked the car. Roberts was in the back with Arthur. He grabbed Arthur's testicles and squeezed very hard. Arthur shrieked in pain but there was no one around to hear him. 'That is just a tickler for what you will get if that £2,000 is not paid to your dealer by the day after tomorrow. We don't care how you get it. You can beg, steal or borrow, we don't mind whichever. You can run but you can't hide, we will find you. Now you can get out of the car and enjoy a walk home. It will help you think. Now fuck off!'

The debt was duly paid, and Arthur decided to give up drugs. He realised, with a shock, that it was bad for his health.

Chapter Forty-Two

DC Janet Griffin took a seat across from Skelton's desk. She had been tasked with looking into Murray and his girlfriend Penny Cole's finances. This had proved much harder than she had bargained for. 'Sir, we know that Murray sold his house in London for 1.2 million pounds. We were able to verify this with Land Registry. He used a firm of solicitors in London to do the conveyancing. The same firm of solicitors represented him at his trial for killing Joe Reilly. It has a reputation for acting on behalf of some of London's top gangsters.

'I got access to the Met police investigation into him when they tried to seize the house under the Proceeds of Crime Act. As well as owning the house, he had cash in the bank and investments worth 1.5 million. His lawyer and accountant worked hand in hand, to show that the money was the result of wise investments. He had bought several flats and rented them out. The Met could not find enough evidence to take it to court to try him in order to seize the assets.'

Skelton leaned back in his chair and raised his eyebrows. 'Well, I'm not surprised that you didn't get very far with Murray. What about the girlfriend?'

Griffin turned over a page of her notes. 'She was rather easy to investigate, sir. After leaving school, she had a few jobs working as a waitress. We have her PAYE records for the relevant times, but she was not making much money. Then she joined a modelling agency, which was in effect an escort agency. By all accounts, she was very attractive. I have some photographs here.' She handed the photographs over to Skelton. He studied them.

'I guess she started making decent money then?'

Griffin smiled and said, 'She was being paid a fairly decent salary, but I think she was making much more on the game. Everything would have been in cash. I have her bank statements here. She was paying in about eight thousand a month into her bank. She does this for about five months, then the cash deposits stop. This is when we think she met Murray.'

'How about the house here in Bath going into her name?'

'We were able to trace the transaction from the buyers who bought Murray's London home. His lawyers get the money and after deducting fees and disbursements, the money goes to an account in the British Virgin Islands. It's impossible to gain any information as to who controls that account. The next thing we know is that the solicitors for the sellers of the house in Bath receive the purchase price by a money transfer from an account in the British Virgin Islands. According to the Land Registry, the house is registered in the name of Penny Cole. Now Cole had no way of coming up with the money to buy the house herself. Murray must have provided the funds himself. What I can't understand is why he put it into her name?'

Skelton rocked back and forth in his chair and thought for a few seconds. 'Could be it's an insurance policy of sorts. If we take him down for drug dealing and money laundering, he will claim that he simply gifted the house to his lover. In which case, we would not be able to seize the house. But Murray would by law have to declare the gift in his tax return, as would Cole. I think that Murray has made a mistake here and doesn't realise that his little plan is not watertight. If we can get to young Penny and explain to her that we have grounds for seizing the house, she might be prepared to give us Murray. Well done, Janet, you have given me something to work with.'

Skelton followed Griffin out of his office into the CID room. Ross Turnbull was busy on his computer and Alexander and Spurrey were in deep conversation. 'Hi, guys, anything of interest happening?'

Alexander and Spurrey stopped speaking. 'No, sir, we were just discussing last night's football results. Chris had a bet on Aston Villa getting a draw away, but they conceded a goal in the last minute.'

Skelton smiled and said, 'Hard luck, Chris. You know more about football than I ever will. On the other hand, I know more about horse racing than you ever will. So, each to their own game.'

'Do you ever give tips, sir?'

Skelton smiled and said, 'Yes, I do occasionally, but if I do give you one, don't go blowing your salary on it. Only gamble what you can afford to lose and no more. The next time I see a horse I fancy I will give you the nod.'

Alexander gave a stretch and asked, 'Do you just bet on the flat horses, or do you do the jumps as well?'

'To be honest with you, I prefer national hunt racing. After all, being called Dan Skelton, how could I not?'

Skelton's namesake was an up-and-coming national hunt trainer. Skelton reckoned that he would be a champion trainer one day.

'Bill, I have a little job for you. That missing person case involving what was our prime suspect in the Alexandra Park murder, Fergus Walsh, intrigues me. I have his bank statements here and you will see that he was paying the council seventy-five pounds a quarter. It's not a lot of money, probably rent for something. I want you to get on to the council and find out exactly, what it was for.' He checked his watch, it was 12.45. 'Let's go and get some lunch. I fancy giving Belushi's a go today.'

Chapter Forty-Three

Skelton was on the phone to Patrick Rees. They talked almost every day about Chadwell and Murray. It seemed like it was business as usual in both Bristol and Bath. Arrests were being made every other day of drug dealers and users. The dealers were quickly replaced, usually by young men wanting to make big bucks. None of the arrested dealers would ever give the names of their suppliers. It was far too dangerous to do so. This meant that those in control of the drugs, namely Chadwell and Murray, would escape justice. Until such times as they got a lucky break, normal police operations would continue. It could be months if not years before they got either Chadwell or Murray. Skelton wanted Murray and would bide his time in getting him.

Alexander entered the office just as Skelton was finishing his call. It was 11 am and he was carrying two plates, each containing a square sausage sandwich. Skelton got up and switched on the kettle to make the tea. This was almost a daily ritual, time permitting. Skelton finished making the tea and they sat opposite each other at Skelton's desk. 'I've been in touch with the council, sir, about that seventy-five quid that Fergus Walsh was paying to the council each quarter. You will never guess what it was for?'

Skelton swallowed a piece of his sandwich and washed it down with some tea. 'Bill, if I could have guessed what it was for, I wouldn't have sent you to find out, would I?' Alexander raised his eyes and said, 'No I guess not. But anyway, it doesn't get us anywhere. He was renting an allotment not far from where he lived. He had it for about five years before vanishing.'

Skelton considered this new information. He recalled that his own father had rented two allotments. This had given Skelton a keen interest in gardening. In fact, he and Ken, his partner, were very enthusiastic gardeners. They both found it very relaxing as well as giving them enormous enjoyment.

'We should take a run out and have a look at it. Do you have any idea which allotment he rented?' Alexander finished off his sandwich. 'Well actually, the council sent me a plan. I have it here.' He dug into his jacket pocket and pulled out a sheet of paper. He handed it over and said, 'Look it's number seven on there.'

Alexander drove Skelton to the allotment. It was rather a dull day but still reasonably warm. They parked the car and got out. Alexander locked the car and they made their way through the gate. There were twenty plots of land on the allotment and there were a number of sheds. Some in pretty good condition whilst others were in a rather sorry state. Some of the plot holders were growing only vegetables, whilst others had a mixture of vegetables and flowers. They noticed an elderly gentleman pushing a wheelbarrow, which contained a load of weeds. He was heading towards the compost site and was making slow progress. Skelton estimated him to be well into his eighties. He was quite stooped and walked with a limp. The gate through which they entered formed part of a fence and there were two corresponding fences on the left and ahead, whilst on the right of the allotment was a high brick wall. There were several sheds situated close to the wall. Skelton noticed that someone had grown a large clematis which had climbed the wall.

'Let's have a word with the old chap. It looks like he's been here for donkey's years.'

They began walking towards him, taking their time, so as not to alarm him. He had not seen them, and he had not heard them despite wearing two hearing aids. He tipped out the contents of the wheelbarrow and slowly turned around. It was then that he saw the visitors. Skelton had withdrawn his warrant card and slowly approached the elderly man.

'Hello, sir, I am Detective Chief Inspector Skelton, and this is Detective Sergeant Alexander of Avon and Somerset Police. Would you mind us asking you a few questions about the allotment?'

The man was slightly built and looked tired from his exertions. 'What is it that you want to know? I've never had the police here before except when my shed got broken into a few years back. They never caught the culprit.'

'What is your name, sir, and how long have you been renting here?'

The old man dug out a pipe from his pocket and lit it. 'My name is Tom but everyone up here refers to me as Old Tom. I've been renting my two plots for over twenty years. You can't buy vegetables like mine in the supermarket, that's for sure. I come up here every day. I used to spend all day here, but I'm getting old, so I only do the mornings now.'

'You must have seen a lot of people come and go over the years?'

Tom pulled out his pipe and smiled. 'You can say that again. It's mostly men who take them on and to begin with they are full of enthusiasm. But usually after only one season they pack it in. It's a bit different these days with the cost-of-living crisis. Folk can't afford vegetables in the supermarket. So, there is now a waiting list for these plots. I will carry on here for as long as I can, but I'm eighty-six now. I might manage another two years if I'm lucky.'

'Do you ever recall a man by the name of Fergus Walsh, who had plot number seven here?'

Tom smiled and said, 'Yes of course I remember him well, and his boy, young Fergus. When Fergus first arrived, he would often bring his boy with him. He would only have been about twelve at the time. He hung around for a couple of years but became more interested in football and rugby. I've seen that a lot over the years. I was shocked when I read about Fergus going missing. And it's strange that he's never turned up. He was such a lovely man and so was the kid. In fact, young Fergus is in the police now. He pops in every now and again to say hello. He sometimes gives me a hand with the heavy digging.'

'Did Fergus ever seem depressed to you? Do you think he might have wanted to harm himself?'

Tom sucked deeply on his pipe and exhaled the smoke.

'Good god no. He was always very cheerful and I doubt if he had an enemy in the world.'

Skelton thanked Tom for his assistance and he and Alexander started walking back to the car. Skelton once again noticed the beautiful clematis, growing up the wall. He had never seen one with such vigorous growth. He guessed that Old Tom was keeping it well looked after with manure and compost.

Skelton turned back and said, 'That's a beautiful clematis Tom. Who grew that?'

'It is a beauty all right. I grew it for the wife a number of years back. She used to complain that I only grew veg and that the place had no colour. I don't grow flowers as a rule, so I asked a friend of mine what I should grow, and he said that.'

They had begun walking towards the massive wall of flowers. They were a mixture of blue and pink. Skelton said, 'That's a Prince Charles and Lady Diana and they are beautiful. And you've got sweet peas growing beside them. They really love fertile soil.'

Tom was taking out his pipe again. 'You are a gardener, Mr Skelton. Not many people can name the species of flowers. The thing is, when I planted them up, they did virtually nothing for years. Then, all of a sudden, they were off. I brought the wife up to see them and she was over the moon. It was at that point that I realised I was being selfish with my time. I was here seven days a week, morning and afternoon. I decided then and there, that from that day on, I would have every Wednesday afternoon off and take the wife out to lunch.'

Skelton was enjoying himself in the company of another gardener. 'You must put a lot of fertiliser on them to get them to grow like that. I have got quite a few in my garden but they are no way as vigorous as yours.'

Tom finished lighting his pipe. 'To be honest with you, I never thought they would come to anything. Then out of the blue, they were growing like crazy. Mind you, I still get the most pleasure out of my veg. Here come and see my cauliflowers, they are just over here.'

Tom led the way and the detectives followed. There were rows of cabbages, carrots, runner beans, potatoes, swede, strawberries and rhubarb. But what stood out the most were the large white cauliflowers, they were enormous. 'My god, Tom, those are the best I have ever seen. You certainly can't buy them like that in the supermarket. They are my favourite veg. Cauliflower and cheese sauce is a dish to die for.'

Tom got down on his knees and prized out two cauliflowers and gave one each to Skelton and Alexander. 'Here, have these on me. It's been great having you visit. If you are ever passing, just call in.'

They shook hands and said goodbye. As they walked to the car, Alexander said, 'Look at these. Like you, I love cauliflower and cheese sauce. So, we will be having this for Sunday lunch along with a roast and of course roast potatoes.'

Skelton gave Alexander a smile and said, 'For us, Bill, I boil an unsmoked gammon joint and make sauté potatoes. We have the cauliflower and cheese sauce which is just the perfect meal. Talking of all this food is making me hungry. Let's push the boat out, Bill. Take us to the Cross Keys and don't forget to loosen your belt before you sit down.'

Alexander laughed.

Chapter Forty-Four

The murder of Stephen Cox in Alexandra Park, two months ago, remained a mystery. No further suspects had come to light and their efforts to attract a possible suspect on Gaydar had been fruitless. Skelton had never once failed to solve a murder case and he was beginning to think that this was going to be his first. He and his team had tried their best, but they had to play the hand of cards they had been dealt. He was, of course frustrated, but he couldn't show his emotions. That would not do morale any good whatsoever. He checked the time. It was 10.50 am so he headed to the canteen where the cooks would be preparing square sausages for himself and Alexander. They had become such a hit in the canteen that they were now on the menu.

Suddenly the door burst open and in barged Alexander. 'Sir, a woman has been taken hostage in Twerton. A man apparently has a gun and is threatening to shoot her. It seems he is high on drugs or has mental health issues. The armed response unit is on its way and uniform are evacuating the neighbours. I have the address but nothing else to go on at the moment.'

'Let's go, Bill. This should make for an interesting situation.'

They arrived on scene within ten minutes. There were numerous police vehicles parked up and the road had been closed at both ends. Skelton saw Inspector Graham Symonds and Sergeant Ian Perkins standing behind a large police van, which they were using as cover.

Symonds saw Skelton approach and said, 'We wondered when the calvary would show up. I hope you didn't miss your morning sausages because of this.' Ian Perkins was smiling. Symonds always liked to rub up the CID whenever he could.

'Yes, we did miss our 11.00 am pick me up this morning. After all, when we heard that you were in charge of the crime scene, we knew that we had to get proper cops on the job without delay. Are we in time or have you already buggered it up?'

Perkins and Alexander could barely stop themselves from laughing. Symonds crossed his arms. He knew that Skelton had got the better of him. 'No, everything is hunky dory. I have carefully deployed my officers and have evacuated the neighbours. Bryan Stevens and his armed team arrived a few minutes ago and are taking up position.'

Skelton was relieved that Stevens was on duty. He was head of the firearms unit and had an excellent reputation within the force and further afield. 'What's the story, Graham?'

'It would appear to have just been a domestic row. It's a married couple by the name of George and Emily Fordyce. We have never been called to the premises before, but George has a record as long as your arm, mostly for violence and drugs. Just over half an hour ago a neighbour heard a lot of shouting coming from next door. It was not uncommon but this morning she said it was different. She said she could hear Emily crying but was too afraid to knock on the door and see if she was all right. The neighbour was just leaving her flat when Emily opened the door and ran into the corridor. Suddenly George appeared and he was carrying a handgun. He caught Emily at the top of the stairs and dragged her back to the flat. The neighbour called us and here we are. The neighbour reckons that George was high on drugs. So, my guess is that this will be a long drawn out job. Once he has come down from his high, we should be able to negotiate a release and we can all go home, whilst George goes off to prison for quite some time.'

'Have we made contact with him yet?'

'No not yet, sir, but Robin Oatley our chief negotiator will be here any time now. I think we should wait until he arrives.'

Skelton nodded his head. 'Yes, I agree. We leave it to Robin to handle the negotiations. We don't want to confuse him with more than one officer negotiating.'

Suddenly, an unmarked police car arrived. The driver stopped and got out. It was Robin Oatley. He was not very tall and had a beer belly of some considerable size. He was in his late forties and had served as a skilled negotiator for over ten years. Skelton was satisfied that he had a good team in place to deal with whatever situation arose. Oatley approached the police van and said, 'Well, good morning gentlemen. I believe that a lady is being held hostage by her husband and that he is armed with a gun and is possibly high on drugs. I might just have to try and keep him calm until the effects of the drugs wear off and I can reason with him. However, if he is suffering from a mental health issue, there is no way of knowing how he will react. We might have to rush the premises using force. But that will be your decision, sir.'

Skelton took his hands out of his trouser pockets and said, 'Thank you, Robin. Why don't you go and get yourself set up in the command vehicle. When you are ready, make the call. Keep me updated on the radio. I will join you once I have spoken to Bryan Stevens. Come on, Bill, you come with me.'

They made their way towards the other parked police vehicles, and they could see that several armed officers had taken up position behind the vehicles. They spotted Stevens and quickly made their way towards him. Stevens was on his radio, so they waited until he was finished.

'Good morning, sir, good morning, Bill. We have evacuated the building and the neighbouring properties. I have two men positioned outside the suspect's door on the landing. All seems quite at the moment. There had been some shouting from inside the flat when we arrived. It was a man's voice, and he was clearly agitated. They are in a first floor flat and if you look up there, those two windows just below that satellite dish is the flat in question. He has not come to the windows so far. It could be that the drugs have worn off and he has now calmed down. But you can never be sure what is going to happen. He might have more drugs with him, which could make him very volatile.'

'Thank you, Bryan. You have my authority to react in any way you see fit, provided you can justify your decision. Bill and I will go to the command vehicle and see how Robin is getting on. Good luck.'

On their way they passed two officers with video cameras, these were linked to the command vehicle and would give them a bird's eye view of the scene. They climbed into the vehicle and sat at the table where Robin Oatley was just finishing a call. 'I have established contact with George, he is in a mess. He is high on something and might also have been drinking. He wants us to "fuck off, or he will kill the wife". I told him that we were going nowhere and that we just wanted this to end peacefully. He wouldn't let me talk to Emily, but I could hear her crying. I suspect we could be here for a long time. I think you should mobilise the canteen, sir. Tea, coffee and bacon rolls do a lot for morale.'

It was a squalid one-bedroom flat situated on the end of a grubby council tenement. There was little furniture, and what it did contain had come from charity shops. Apart from the bedroom, there was a small kitchen and living room. This contained an old sofa and two armchairs. A small coffee table was in front of the sofa. On it were several empty vodka bottles and some empty drug wrappers that had contained coke. Emily was sitting hunched on the sofa and was quietly crying. George was sitting on the armchair facing the door. He had a glass of vodka in one hand and the other held the gun, which rested on his groin. He was talking to himself in an animated fashion. He was clearly out of it and in no condition to make reasonable decisions.

Emily had left him several times because of the violence, but always returned to him, as she clearly loved him. Life had not been easy, especially when George was serving time. He had always been a violent man and Emily enjoyed watching him fight. He never lost and had a fearful reputation. He was now forty years old, and some youngsters would try and take him on. George was, however, very strong and fast on his feet. He would use his fists and his feet, as well as any weapon that came to hand. He particularly liked to glass opponents in the face, leaving them scarred for life. He was proud to boast that he had never done an honest day's work in his life. He didn't care how he made some money. He was happy to steal, burgle, deal drugs, collect debt and had recently started selling guns on the black market.

The phone rang several times before George answered. 'Who is this? What do you want?' Oatley's voice came out of the speaker.

'George, it's Robin again. I am just checking that you and Emily are all right.'

George remembered the copper calling earlier. 'Look, we are fine. Just leave us alone and no one will get hurt.'

'George, you know we can't do that. You were seen with a gun, so we need you to come out so that we can sort this out. We need to make sure that Emily is safe. The flat is surrounded with armed police, George. We don't want to hurt you. All you need to do is put the gun down and open the door with your hands on your head. Armed officers are waiting to meet you and to bring you and Emily down to safety. You know it's the only thing to do, George. There is no alternative.'

There was silence for a few seconds then they heard Emily's voice. 'George, give yourself up. Please do it for me, I don't want you getting hurt or killed because of me. I will always be here for you. I promise.'

George was staring at Emily. 'Shut up you silly cow. I should have done away with you years ago. You can't cook and you're just a slag. God knows what I ever saw in you. Look, copper, unless you lot get the fuck out of here, I am going to shoot this cow and I will take as many coppers as I can with me.' He ended the call.

'This is not looking good, sir. We could try firing tear gas and stun grenades through the windows and then rush the room, but the chances are he will shoot Emily before we get him. I think we will have to play the long game. At some point, exhaustion will get the better of him and he will fall asleep. We need to drill a hole in the wall and get a tiny camera in there. That way, we will know when he is asleep.'

Skelton stood up and stretched. 'Yes, I agree, Robin. Get your boys to work in getting that camera in place. When we judge that he is in a deep sleep, Bryan's men break down the door and Taser him or shoot him, depending on how he reacts. I feel really sorry for Emily. Imagine being married to that piece of shit. The only good thing that might come out of this is that George goes to prison for a very long stretch. Bill, let's go and grab a bacon roll from the mobile canteen. Can we bring you one back, Robin?'

Oatley smiled and said, 'Yes please, with lots of ketchup and a black tea with two sugars.'

Oatley's technicians had gained entry to the neighbouring flat. They needed to silently drill a hole in the wall and insert the tiny camera. This would give them and the command team a view of George's flat. The technicians had practised this drill many times and were highly proficient in what they did. In only a few minutes, the camera was working, and the police could see inside the sitting room. The lens could rotate, giving the officers a panoramic view of what was taking place. Skelton and Alexander had re-joined Oatley in the command vehicle and all three had their eyes on the television monitor. Oatley had control of the joystick and was guiding it around the room. A woman was sitting on a sofa with her knees tucked under her chin. The man was sitting in an armchair. He had a glass with clear liquid in his left hand and his right hand was clutching something against his groin. It looked like a gun, but it was impossible to tell. No shots had been fired, which possibly indicated that it was a replica gun, but the officers had to treat the gun as being lethal.

The officers watched intently as the camera focused on George. A lead from the camera was being fed to Bryan Stevens, who was in charge of the firearms unit. He had two men deployed to the left and right of the door to the flat. The armchair that George was sitting in faced the window and not the door. This made it difficult for the officers as they could not see George if they entered the flat, as he was hidden by the back of the chair. George was facing his wife, which meant that he had the advantage of being able to shoot her before the officers could react to the situation. George drained his glass and put it on the table in front of him. It looked like he had finished off the three bottles of vodka that were sitting on the table.

Skelton cleared his throat and said, 'I think that with all that vodka inside him, he is going to doze off anytime soon. Let's hope that he falls into a deep sleep, and we can rush the flat before he realises what's happening. What do you make of the situation, Robin?'

Robin Oatley leaned back in his chair and thought for a second or two. 'Well, we have a guy here who has been consuming both drugs and alcohol. We know that he is a man of violence and is possibly suffering from mental health issues. I doubt if we can reason with him. In fact, he seems to get angrier each time I call him. I think you need to order the firearms officers to enter the flat when we think he is asleep. It will of course be a risk, but if he is confused, he might not have the opportunity to harm Emily before we can neutralise the risk.'

Skelton stood up and stretched. He clasped the back of his neck with his right hand and squeezed. 'I am going to brief Bryan. He has a lead to the camera and can see exactly what George is up to. If he does fall asleep, we leave him for twenty minutes then Bryan sends his men in. On the other hand, if he stays awake and starts threatening Emily again, we may have to change the plan. The next twenty minutes or so are going to be very interesting.'

Skelton left the command vehicle and made his way to Stevens. It had started to rain and Skelton could feel his hair getting wet. Stevens was sitting at a table next to a marked police car. On the table was a laptop and Stevens was busy watching it, but he turned around as Skelton approached.

'I was expecting you, sir. I agree that we let George fall asleep and then rush the flat. It does come with risk but I think the risk is mitigated by the fact that he will be confused and slow after consuming those drugs and alcohol. My guys will be inside that flat in seconds of me giving the command. Depending on how George reacts, he will be either tasered or shot. My guys will try and get in front of Emily before George can react. They are in full bulletproof gear, so they should be all right.'

Skelton patted Stevens on the shoulder. 'Very good, Bryan. It is your call. If he falls asleep, give him twenty minutes or more if you think it's necessary. Our primary concern here is to protect Emily and arrest George. Good luck to you and your men.'

He walked back to the command vehicle, now completely soaked from the heavy rain. He hoped that there was a towel in the vehicle so that he could dry himself.

Ten minutes after getting back to the command vehicle, Skelton watched the screen and noticed George's head slump forward onto his chest. A couple of minutes later they could almost hear him snoring. Five minutes later, they watched in silence as Emily got off the sofa. They had not expected her to make a move, as she seemed to have lost the will to save herself.

It was Alexander who broke the silence. 'Come on, Emily, just tip toe past him and get out the door and then leave the rest to us.'

The officers had their eyes glued to the screen. Emily had gently placed her feet on the floor and steadily stood up. She then very slowly began walking, but not towards the door and safety. Instead, she walked towards the kitchen and a few seconds later she was back in the sitting room, her hands behind her back.

'Come on, Emily, just keep on walking to the door and you will be safe, my darling,' whispered Oatley. Emily was walking towards George, who was in a deep sleep. Her movements were slow and deliberate. Then suddenly, she moved with lightning speed. She brought her hands from behind her back and the officers watched in horror as they saw the large kitchen knife that she now brandished in both hands. They heard Stevens give the command, 'Go, Go, Go.'

Emily brought the knife down with as much force as she could muster. The knife went deep into George's chest, piercing his heart with tremendous force. Suddenly the door bust open, and the two armed officers entered the flat. Emily had raised her hands above her head in complete submission.

'Armed police. Keep your arms raised and walk towards us.' Emily immediately obeyed the command. One officer handcuffed her whilst the other ran to attend George. He was an advanced paramedic but he quickly realised that George was beyond saving. The knife was embedded right up to the hilt in George's chest.

Skelton was the first to speak. 'I did not see that coming. Had she simply walked out the door she would have been safe and well. What a tragedy.'

It was Alexander who was next to speak. 'Sir, don't you go blaming yourself for this. None of us saw it coming. I think the poor lassie had taken all she could. A good barrister might get her off with murder and possibly even manslaughter if the jury sides with her. Given George's criminal record and his threats to shoot Emily, I think she might just get away with it.'

Chapter Forty-Five

Andy Cuthbertson left the house which he shared with two friends and closed the door behind him. It was just after 9 pm on this mild September evening and it was almost dark. After getting home from work earlier he had taken a shower and eaten his dinner. He spent some time watching television but there was nothing much of interest to him. He tried texting some mates to see if they wanted to go out but as it was over halfway through the month and the monthly salary another week away, they were all strapped for cash. Cuthbertson supplemented his income by dealing drugs to his friends, partially to help pay for his own drug habit. So this evening he had money in his pocket and he wanted to go out and have some fun. He had broken up with his girlfriend at the weekend, so he was footloose and fancy free.

Cuthbertson pressed the key fob and the lights on his car flashed. It was a Mini Cooper, his pride and joy. The car was just over a year old and he had got a good lease deal covering a three-year period. He intended to keep it for two years and then negotiate a new deal on a new car. The car was sporty, which suited Cuthbertson as he considered himself an ace one driver. He liked nothing better than to race the car around the narrow lanes that surrounded Bath. He decided to drive into the city centre and check out some bars. It was Wednesday and he was sure that some girl students would be out looking for fun. The two universities in Bath had begun the new term last week, and the girls would be exploring the city, looking for excitement. Cuthbertson was just over six feet tall with a good body, which he kept in shape by going to the gym twice a week. He was a handsome twenty-four-year-old and had no problem in pulling the birds.

He parked the car and checked his hair in the mirror and smiled to himself. He knew that he was a handsome devil and any young student would jump at the chance of going out with him. He had lost count of the students that he had picked up and taken away their virginity. He smiled again at the memories. He was wearing blue jeans and a tight white tee-shirt, which showed off his good physique. Over the tee-shirt he wore a navy-blue blazer. He was very smartly dressed for the evening, and he was on a mission to get a shag. Belushi's bar was a popular bar for students as it operated a discount scheme. He decided to head there and check it out.

He entered the bar and was pleased to see that it was pretty much full. There were lots of pretty girls and he noticed more than one glance and smile in his direction. He slowly made his way to the bar, smiling broadly as he did so. Although the bar was busy, the bar staff were great in serving the crowd efficiently. He ordered a pint of Thatchers Gold, a local cider which was very popular in Somerset. He glanced around and noticed a very pretty girl standing on her own at a table at the far end of the bar. He smiled at her and she smiled back. He decided not to waste any time on anyone else, she would be perfect for the night. He made his way over to where she was standing.

'Hello, are you all on your own tonight?'

The girl blushed. He reckoned she was about twenty-two and so unlikely to be a student, unless she was doing a masters degree. She had long blond hair which covered her shoulders. 'Yes, I am on my own tonight. I thought I would come into town and have a drink as my parents went on holiday this morning, leaving me all alone in the house.'

Cuthbertson smiled and said, 'So you live with your mum and dad then?'

The girl smiled and took a sip from her drink. 'Yes, I live with them as renting is so expensive these days. I am hoping to get a flat share in the new year with a couple of girlfriends.'

Cuthbertson took a mouthful of cider. 'My name is Andy. I hope you don't mind me chatting with you.'

The girl smiled. 'No of course not, and my name is Angela. But I have to tell you that I have a bus to catch later as I don't drive, and a taxi is too expensive.'

Andy placed his hand on her right shoulder. 'Don't worry about the bus, I can give you a lift home. I'd love to get to know you better. Where do you live?'

Angela smiled and allowed Andy to keep his hand on her shoulder. It felt good. 'That would be great, but I live in Radstock, so it might be a bit out of your way.'

Andy placed both hands on her shoulders. 'Nonsense, Angela, it's not that far away. We are just getting to know one another. Let me get you another drink and see if we can find a seat where we can have a chat.'

Andy got a glass of red wine for Angela and another pint for himself. Andy reckoned that as he was such a good driver the drink driving law did not apply to him. Nor for that matter taking a line of coke. He had been driving over the legal limit for years and had never been caught.

They made their way through to the other bar and noticed a couple getting up to leave. 'Do you mind if we take these seats if you're leaving?'

The man looked at Andy and winked. 'No go ahead, I think I just got lucky. I hope you two enjoy yourselves.'

The time seemed to fly. In no time at all they were kissing passionately and Andy was getting aroused. He was on his fourth pint and excused himself to go to the toilet. He knew that the bar had a zero tolerance on drugs, so he would have to be really careful. He went to a cubicle and closed the door behind him. He began to relieve himself whilst pulling the wrap of coke from his pocket. When he had finished urinating, he snorted the line of coke. He flushed the toilet and opened the door. There were four guys at the urinals all busy chatting to one another. Andy washed and dried his hands and went upstairs to re-join Angela.

It had been agreed that Andy would drive Angela home to Radstock and that he would stay the night. Angela worked in Radstock, and she needed to be at the hairdresser where she worked by 8.30 am. She also had to feed her mum's cat, as her parents were away on holiday.

Angela picked up her handbag and felt a little giddy from the wine she had consumed. Andy felt like he was on top of the world as a result of the cider and the line of coke that he had taken. They kissed passionately again before leaving the bar. As they got to the exit, a very handsome and smartly dressed bouncer wished them good night. Andy gave him a wink and said, 'Don't worry, mate, this is going to be a very good night.'

They both laughed as Andy took Angela's hand and led her to his car. As they approached the car, Andy pressed the key fob and the lights flashed. The street was deserted as he opened the passenger door for Angela to get in. He gently closed the door as Angela put on her seat belt. As he walked round to the driver's door, he could see a young couple walking towards him, arm in arm. It was definitely a night for romance. He sat down and closed the door and leaned across and kissed Angela on the lips. He put on his seat belt and started the engine. He indicated that he was pulling out and started to drive towards Radstock, which was about eight miles away.

He drove up the Wellsway. It was just after midnight. The traffic was light, so Andy disregarded the speed limit. All he wanted to do was get Angela out of her knickers as soon as possible. At the top of the Wellsway, he crossed over the roundabout and saw the road sign for Radstock and guessed that they would get there in about fifteen minutes. Both he and Angela were finding the drive exhilarating and she would giggle every now and then.

The stretch of road they were on was full of sharp bends. Andy saw the signpost, 'Collision Route'. He smiled to himself. He knew the road well and the cider and coke made him all the more relaxed. The car was now travelling at over seventy and there were no other cars on the road. They were in the countryside with very few houses around. On the left there were trees and fields but few houses. Andy glanced over to Angela and asked, 'Do you like my driving, baby?'

It was the last words she would ever hear. They had come to a sharp bend on the road and Andy had oversteered. Suddenly he lost control of the car, it mounted the pavement and crashed through some bushes. He stood on the brakes but as the car was already airborne this had no effect at all. The car hit the tree at over sixty miles an hour. The front passenger side of the Mini bore the full impact. Whilst the air bags instantly inflated, they could not save Angela. She was killed outright.

Andy was knocked out for a couple of minutes but amazingly was not injured apart from some bruising to his legs and a slight cut to his right thumb. As he came round, he began to panic. He leaned across his seat and pushed his hand through the air bag. He found her neck and checked for a pulse but there was none. He knew he was in serious trouble but there was nothing he could do for Angela. She was dead, so calling an ambulance wasn't going to help her, and besides the ambulance would radio the police and firefighters. The first thing the police would do would be to get him to provide a sample of breath for excess alcohol and then a tongue wipe for drugs. He would fail both, added to which there would be a charge of causing death by dangerous driving. That would mean a very long time behind bars.

He opened the door but it would not open fully, owing to the damage caused by the tree. He had difficulty in getting out of the car but after a struggle he managed. It was pitch black where the collision had happened. There were no streetlights. He made his way round to the back of the car. The taillights were still on and these gave him just enough light to make it to the road. He emerged from the bushes and lay flat on the ground. He looked and listened for traffic but there was none. He gingerly stood up and looked towards the wrecked Mini. It was impossible to see it from the road. He began the long walk back to Bath and home. He knew that the car would be found so he needed a plan. As he walked his mind raced. Then he hatched his plan. He pulled out his phone and called his brother in Bristol.

Chapter Forty-Six

Angela should have been at work the next morning. When she had not turned up by 9.30 am, her boss tried calling both her home telephone and mobile. There was no answer to either, both went to message mode. Angela had worked for Muriel McKay for two years and had been the perfect employee. The clients loved her and she was always cheerful and polite. For her not to turn up for work was completely out of character. Muriel spent the day fretting and she tried calling Angela at least a dozen times without joy. At three o'clock she decided to call the remaining clients for the day and cancel their appointments. She closed the shop and drove to Angela's home. She knew that her parents had just gone on holiday, so they wouldn't be at home.

Muriel got out the car and walked up the path to the front door and rang the bell. There was no answer. She tried the door, but it was locked. The window curtains were drawn, so she went round the back. A large ginger cat was sitting beside the cat flap. As Muriel approached, the cat got up and went through the cat flap and into the kitchen. Muriel looked through the kitchen window and she could see through to the sitting room. No one appeared to be at home. She was now convinced that something had happened to Angela. She would have to drive to the police station and report her missing.

Andy's two housemates worked for the same company and were away this week on a training course. This suited Andy down to the ground as they would be unable to help the police with their enquires. As he walked towards the house, he saw his brother's car. It was a Land Rover Discovery. Andy opened the front passenger door and climbed in.

'Are you all right, Andy?'

Andy ran his hands through his hair and sighed. 'I've fucked up big time, Charlie. I had a few drinks and did a line of coke. I picked up this bird in the pub and was giving her a lift home. I was going a bit fast on the road to Radstock and lost control on a bend. The girl is dead, so I need an alibi. I will report that the car was stolen last night and that I spent the night at your place. When you brought me back home this morning the car was gone. My housemates are away this week which is a stroke of luck. We will have to smash the glass on the back door and hide the spare keys for the car. The police will think that there was a break-in and that the thieves took the car.'

Charlie hit the steering wheel with his right fist. 'For Christ's sake, Andy, you really screwed up big time that's for sure. Its nearly six and people will be getting up soon. We better get in the house and sort this mess out and I need to go home and get ready for work. Call the police after I have gone and report the break-in and the theft of your car.'

They went around to the back of the house and found a brick, which Andy used to break a pane of glass in the door. He slid his hand in and found the key in the lock and unlocked the door. They went inside the kitchen but did not put the light on as it was now light enough to see. On the breakfast bar was a key holder and Andy picked up the spare keys and gave them to Charlie. 'You take these with you. We don't want the police finding them here.'

Charlie took the keys and put them in his pocket. They went into the sitting room where Andy explained the story that they would both tell the police. They sat together for twenty minutes rehearsing it. They would tell the police that Charlie had picked Andy up at the house at seven the previous evening and they had gone to Charlie's flat in Bristol. Charlie had made them a curry and boiled rice and they chilled out over a few beers. They had not left the flat and had gone to bed at 11 pm. They got up at six and Charlie drove them back to Andy's house and they immediately noticed that the car had gone. Andy had his house keys with him and had opened the front door. On entering the kitchen, they saw that the window on the back door had been smashed and the car keys had been taken. They even discussed the route that Charlie had taken so that the police could not find holes in the story.

Andy watched as Charlie drove away. He made a cup of tea and went upstairs to shower and shave. At 8 am he called the police and reported the break-in and the theft of his car. The police call handler explained that as it was just a domestic break-in and a car theft, a police officer would call round later. Andy called his boss and explained what had supposedly happened and said he would not be at work today as he needed to wait for the police to come to the house. Shortly after eleven, a police community support officer called on Andy and took a statement. She explained that it was unlikely that the thief or thieves had left any forensic evidence so a forensic officer would not be attending. She gave Andy a crime number for the insurance company and some leaflets about being a victim of crime. These provided some useful phone numbers should he need counselling. The police would be looking for the stolen car and there was a good chance of it being recovered, she assured him.

When the police officer left the house, Andy called Charlie and told him that the cop was in no way suspicious. The chances were that when they found the crashed car, they would conclude that the driver must have stolen the car and crashed it. The dead passenger was probably an accomplice. So far as Andy was concerned, they had nothing to worry about. He then phoned his insurance company and reported the theft of the car and gave them the crime number.

He then picked up the trainers that he had been wearing and went outside and put them in the rubbish bin. He had heard that the police could match footprints and so he was taking no chances.

The stretch of road where the collision occurred had very few houses and therefore few pedestrians. Passing vehicles would usually be travelling too fast to notice where the Mini had crashed through the bush and collided with the tree some twenty feet below. Angela had lain dead inside the car for three days before being discovered. A young man was driving his clapped-out car when suddenly the engine lost power. He switched on his hazard warning lights and called the RAC. He was told to get out of the car and wait for assistance to arrive. When he got out of the car, he stood on the pavement and casually glanced through the bushes. He thought he could see the rear of a car some way below. He gingerly made his way down and discovered the wreck of the Mini. The driver's seat was empty but when he got to the passenger seat, he found the dead girl. He threw up as he had never seen a dead body before. He managed to make his way back up to the road and called the police. Unlike the RAC, they arrived in minutes.

Chapter Forty-Seven

Inspector Dougie Wall was in charge of the Avon and Somerset traffic police. In cases of a fatal collision, Dougie would be called in as there would have to be an inquest and the traffic collision investigation team would carry out a detailed investigation, to try and determine how the collision occurred. When Wall arrived at the scene, his immediate concern was to find the driver of the car. The vehicle had clearly been travelling at high speed and so it was most likely that the driver had been badly injured. The driver's door was open, so it appeared that he had managed to exit the vehicle. Wall was concerned that the driver may be lying badly injured or had succumbed to his injuries. He radioed for backup and requested the canine unit to attend. Despite an exhaustive search of the area, no body was found.

Wall became even more concerned when he learnt that the car had been reported stolen three days earlier. This was a case for the CID and forensics. He called Detective Chief Inspector Skelton on his mobile phone. It was just after ten in the morning when Skelton's phone vibrated. He took it out of his shirt pocket and checked the caller's identity.

'Hello, Dougie, what can I do for you this morning?'

Wall was seated in his patrol car and he watched as Bob Richards, the head of forensics, alighted from his van.

'Sorry to bother you, sir, but we have a fatal collision here and the driver appears to have made off. It looks like the passenger, a young lady, has been dead for two or three days. Where the collision has happened it's very difficult to see the vehicle from the road. The car was reported stolen three days ago. I would appreciate it if you would come down and take a look.'

Skelton had listened intently to the call. It was not often he was called to a traffic collision. 'Give me the location, Dougie, and Bill Alexander and I will be with you as soon as possible.'

Wall gave the location and Skelton headed off to round up Alexander. Skelton knew the stretch of road in question and realised that it would be heavily congested with so many police cars in attendance. He ordered for a marked police car to take them to the location with the siren and lights on. When they arrived, Skelton got out the front passenger seat and was greeted by Inspector Wall.

'We've got a full turnout here, sir. The police surgeon is with the body now and Bob Richards and his team are on site. The owner of the vehicle is Andrew Cuthbertson and he reported it stolen three days ago. Apparently, his house was broken into and the car keys were taken. The deceased we have just discovered is Angela Dixon and her boss reported her missing on the same day as Cuthbertson reported his car stolen. There is no sign of the driver but a search team is combing the woodland in case he was injured and crawled away from the wreckage.'

'Thanks, Dougie. Bill and I will go down and take a look and then visit the girl's boss. We will also need to pay a visit to Mr Cuthbertson and find out about the break-in. Bill, you do a background check on Cuthbertson before we go and interview him.'

The detectives carefully made their way down to the wreckage of the Mini. 'Whoever was driving that car must have been travelling at a hell of a speed, sir. He has gone over those bushes back there and hit the tree. In my experience the tree always wins the contest. It looks like the front passenger side has borne the main impact of the crash.' They made their way towards the passenger door where they could see the police surgeon was examining the body. Dr Simpson heard them approach and turned to greet them. 'Good morning, gentlemen, I have examined the body. Rigor mortis has completely passed over so I would say that she has been dead at least forty-eight hours. It looks like she broke her neck on impact. There is some blood on her nose and lips but not a lot indicating that death was instantaneous. Bob Richards has retrieved her belongings, including her phone, but the battery is flat. I don't think that the post-mortem will tell us a great deal more, except for the presence of alcohol and drugs.'

Skelton looked the body over and asked, 'What about the driver, Doctor. Do you think he would have been injured?'

'Bob found a small amount of blood on the driver's air bag which indicates that he suffered some sort of injury but probably nothing serious.'

They all turned around at the sound of someone approaching. It was Bob Richards.

'There was very little blood inside the car, and we have had a good look on the ground. We can't find a trail of blood, so if you ask me, the driver was very lucky. We have, however, got some really good footprints. It looks like he was wearing trainers and I say he, as the feet are big, unlike a woman. We can match the blood DNA to the driver and also the trainers.' Skelton thanked the doctor and Bob Richards. 'Come on, Bill, get on the radio and find out the name and address of the girl's boss. We need to go and see her.'

The marked police car took them to the hairdressers where Angela had worked. It was Saturday lunchtime and as they approached the premises, they could see that two clients were seated having their hair cut by two ladies. Skelton opened the door and Alexander followed him in.

'Can I help you gentlemen?' asked Muriel McKay.

Skelton took out his warrant card and said, 'I am Detective Chief Inspector Skelton of Avon and Somerset Police and this is Detective Sergeant Alexander. Are you Mrs McKay by any chance?'

The woman appeared agitated and said, 'Yes that's right, I am Muriel McKay. Is this about Angela by any chance?'

Skelton was putting his warrant card back into his pocket. 'Yes, it is about Angela. Is there somewhere we can talk in private?'

Mrs McKay led them into the back shop where there was a table and four chairs. 'Please take a seat. Have you any news on Angela? Her mother called me yesterday. She is worried sick. She and her husband have been in

Spain since Wednesday, but they haven't been able to contact Angela, which is so unusual. I told them that I had reported her missing on Thursday. The poor woman nearly freaked out. Her husband called back later saying that they had managed to book a flight to Bristol, and it was due in this morning at 11 am.'

Skelton leaned across the table and said, 'Mrs McKay, I am terribly sorry to tell you that Angela was in a car accident and was killed. She is still to be formally identified, but we are pretty sure that it is her.'

Mrs McKay put her hands on her face. 'Oh my goodness, that's awful. Her parents will be heartbroken. She was their only child.'

Skelton cleared his throat. 'I understand that she was at work as usual on Wednesday. Did she say what she was going to do after she had finished working?'

Mrs McKay thought for a second. 'She told me that she was going to take the bus into Bath and go for a drink. Her best friend Lizzie Doyle was meant to go with her, but she tested positive for Covid and had to self-isolate.'

Alexander was making notes. 'Did she say if she was going to meet anyone else? Maybe a boyfriend or another girlfriend?'

'No, she doesn't have a boyfriend at the moment, but she was such a pretty girl.'

Alexander asked, 'Did she say exactly where she was going to go to in Bath?'

Mrs McKay thought for a second. 'Yes, it's that bar that's popular with the students. Let me think of its name. I know, it's called Belushi's on Green Street.'

They thanked Mrs McKay and made their way back to the car. 'Bill, get on the radio and ask for a family liaison officer to meet us at Angela's house. Her mum and dad should be arriving from Bristol airport anytime soon. We need to break the news to them.'

It had been a difficult meeting with Angela's parents. They had last spoken to Angela on the phone on the evening she had gone missing.

She had been in an excited mood as she was going into Bath for a drink, which is not something she did very often. They said she told them that she was going to take the bus into Bath and get the last bus home. They did not know anyone with a Mini Cooper and had never heard of Andy Cuthbertson.

They were now heading to Cuthbertson's home address. Alexander had done a background check on him. He had six points on his driving licence for speeding. A police community officer had supplied intel to the effect that she suspected him of dealing drugs, but there was no evidence to back this up.

They had been driven back to Bath in the marked police car. It had been a busy morning and they had not had time for a proper lunch, so had made do with a MacDonald's hamburger and chips. Skelton had checked the computer on the break-in and theft of Cuthbertson's car. The crime report did not indicate anything suspicious but the constable who compiled it lacked Skelton's years of experience. Skelton called Cuthbertson, who said he would be at home after he finished work. He arranged an appointment for 6 pm.

Alexander drove them into the quiet residential estate just off Rush Hill bang on six. They checked the house numbers and found Cuthbertson's house. It was a four-bedroom terraced house. Some of the houses were multi-occupied and therefore rented. This was an expensive neighbourhood. Alexander said that he had never dealt with a crime on this estate. This peaked Skelton's curiosity. The detectives got out the car and made their way to Cuthbertson's front door. Skelton knocked on the door and it was quickly answered by a tall handsome young man. The man appeared slightly anxious, but this was not uncommon when a senior police officer knocks on your door. Skelton and Alexander held out their warrant cards. 'Mr Cuthbertson, I am Detective Chief Inspector Skelton and this is Detective Sergeant Alexander. May we come in please?'

Skelton had made no mention on the phone of the fact that they had found the wrecked Mini Cooper. He wanted to see how Cuthbertson would react at the news. Both Skelton and Alexander appeared friendly and professional. So far as Cuthbertson was concerned, the cops were just investigating the break-in and the theft of his car.

Cuthbertson went over the story that he had concocted with his brother. He told them that his housemates were away on a training course and that his brother had picked him up on the Wednesday evening and driven them to Bristol, where his brother had made a curry. They chilled out over a few beers and went to bed. They had not left the flat until the next morning when his brother drove him home. He immediately noticed that his car was gone and went inside the house to discover the broken glass from the back door.

Skelton closely observed Cuthbertson's body language. He was not making a lot of eye contact. He had no marks on his face, but Skelton noticed the small sticking plaster on his thumb. 'I see that you have cut your thumb, Mr Cuthbertson?'

Cuthbertson looked at his thumb and said, 'Oh it's just a scratch. I cut it on the broken glass on the back door. Do you want to see it?'

Skelton smiled and said, 'That would be very helpful. Please lead the way. Skelton noticed that the man's legs appeared to be stiff.'

'You seem a bit stiff, sir! What have you been up to?'

Cuthbertson turned around and smiled. 'I overdid it at the gym the other day. I must be getting old.' He laughed. Having inspected the back door, they returned to the sitting room.

'Do you mind if we sit down, sir?'

'By all means, please take a seat.'

Cuthbertson sat down and placed his arms behind his neck and yawned. Skelton noticed it right away. A guilty suspect will often fain boredom or tiredness and this was not lost on Alexander either.

'We found your car this morning.'

Cuthbertson placed his arms on his legs. 'That's good, when can I get it back?' The guy was doing his best to put on a good show.

'Unfortunately, sir, it is a complete wreck and a young woman was killed. Do you know anything about that?'

Cuthbertson stood up. 'No of course I don't know anything about it. My house was broken into and my car keys were stolen. Whoever did it also stole my car. I was in Bristol that night with my brother. Just ask him.'

'Mr Cuthbertson, we are keeping an open mind on this and need to eliminate you as a suspect in what is a very serious crime. Would you be prepared to supply us with a DNA sample and your mobile phone? And we would like to take any trainers that you may have for examination.'

Cuthbertson erupted in anger. 'For fuck's sake, man, I am the victim here. They broke into my house and stole the car keys. The woman that got killed must have been one of the thieves. You should be out there looking for whoever it was that stole my car. I am not giving you any DNA. Not my phone, not my trainers. I am an innocent man. So, if you are finished here why don't you go away and leave me in peace.'

Skelton and Alexander stood up and Skelton looked Cuthbertson in the eyes. 'I hear what you say, sir. Unfortunately, I don't have enough evidence to arrest you. Well, not at the moment anyway. But rest assured my friend, we are going to start digging deep. Then, when we have found what we are looking for, we will be back and you will be heading to prison for a long time.'

The detectives got in the car and Alexander started the engine. 'I think you scared the shit out of him, sir, but in the best possible taste!'

Skelton turned and faced his friend. 'Do you want the good news or the bad news, Bill?'

Alexander thought for a second or two. 'The bad first then the good.'

'Okay, Bill, the bad news is that we are going to work on for a few hours. The good news is that we are going to have to go to Belushi's, but as we are working on a case, the beer and food is on the force.'

Alexander laughed. 'What a bugger, but you know we'll cope!'

Skelton smiled. It was always a pleasure to work with Alexander.

Alexander drove them back to the police station. They both went to the bathroom to freshen up. It was just after 7 pm when they left the station and headed for Belushi's bar. They sauntered to the bar and saw Joe and Tom behind the bar and a young guy that they didn't recognise. Joe greeted them.

'We don't usually see you guys in here on a Saturday. I expect you will be wanting a couple of pints of Fosters?'

'Yes please, Joe. It's been a long day. And who is the new boy?' he said, pointing to the young man with curly hair.

'This is your namesake, another Dan.'

Young Dan gave them a smile. '

Hello, Dan. As Joe said, I am another Dan, and this here is Bill.' Skelton and Alexander stretched their arms over the bar and shook hands with young Dan.

There were about a dozen people seated but only Skelton and Alexander were physically standing at the bar, which suited them very well. 'Joe, we are actually here on official business today. We need to see your CCTV footage from last Wednesday night. We are interested to learn whether or not a man and a woman were in here that night and whether or not they left together.'

Joe handed over the two pints and said, 'No problem, Dan. Do you want to review the tape here or take it back to the station?'

Skelton took a mouthful of lager and glanced at Alexander. 'As much as we would love to stay here, I think we will just order some food and have another round of drinks.' They ordered the food and took their drinks into the back room of the pub and found a seat.

'What happens if Cuthbertson did not meet her in here? I mean he could have picked her up somewhere else, possibly at the bus stop.'

Skelton considered the question for a minute. 'That would certainly complicate matters. I think we should review the CCTV footage back at the station and see what we get. Angela said that she was coming in here that night. It is of course possible that she went onto another bar. We just have to hope that Cuthbertson met her in here and gave her a lift in his car.'

Back at the station, the detectives went to the IT office where they would review the CCTV footage from the pub. They knew that Angela had said she was getting the bus into Bath. So that would place her at the bus station at about 8.30 pm, and it was a ten-minute walk from there to the pub. Alexander was operating the controls and he fast forwarded the tape to 8.40 pm and waited. A few minutes later, they had Angela at the bar ordering a glass of red wine. They watched as she moved along the bar to her right, where she placed her glass on a table. It was nearly half an hour before Cuthbertson showed up. Skelton and Alexander exchanged high fives. The final frames that they reviewed were of the exit of the bar. This clearly showed Cuthbertson walking hand in hand with Angela.

'Right, Bill, we have enough evidence to show that Cuthbertson left the pub with Angela. He lied to us about being with his brother in Bristol. We could go and arrest him now, but to be honest with you, it has been a long day and I am tired. It's Sunday tomorrow and I doubt if he will be expecting an early morning call from us. Why don't you pick me up at my house at seven and arrange for the custody van to join us. I am going home to have a large gin and tonic and some toasted cheese.'

The next morning Alexander picked up Skelton at seven. The custody van was already parked outside Skelton's house. They drove in convoy to Cuthbertson's house. Skelton got out the car and walked to the driver's door of the custody van and the driver got out. Sergeant Ian Perkins was the driver, and he was accompanied by PC Luke Meehan.

'Okay, Ian, you and Luke go round the back. Bill and I will knock him up. There may be two other occupants inside that live here but they are of no concern to us.'

Skelton hammered on the front door. It was answered a few minutes later by a young man wearing just boxer shorts. Skelton did not recognise him; he had his warrant card in his left hand.

'Police officers, sir. We are looking for Andrew Cuthbertson, is he in?'

The young man looked bleary eyed. 'He should be in his room. It's up the stairs and first on the left.'

He stood aside as Skelton and Alexander shoved past him and mounted the stairs. Skelton turned the door handle and opened the door. Cuthbertson was lying in bed and was wearing earphones and was oblivious to the presence of the police officers. Skelton shook Cuthbertson's leg and pulled off the earphones.

'Come on get up, you are under arrest.'

Cuthbertson was wearing only his underpants. 'What the fuck are you arresting me for? I haven't done anything. I want a lawyer. I know my rights.'

Skelton grabbed Cuthbertson's right arm and put the cuffs on it and pulled both arms behind Cuthbertson's back. 'You were driving your car and crashed it and killed an innocent young girl and we can prove it, sunshine.'

Cuthbertson went quiet. They placed him in the custody van and went back inside to search his room. They found £800 in cash and numerous wraps of cocaine. Skelton was putting the cash and cocaine into evidence bags. Alexander had been busy searching the wardrobe. 'There are no trainers in here, sir. Do you think he's gone and ditched them?'

Skelton finished sealing the evidence bag. 'Well, Bill, I don't think he is the smartest criminal we have come across. Let's go and have a look in the bin. I am pretty sure we will find them in there and that will make Bob Richards' day. If they match the footprints at the scene and his DNA matches the blood in the car, he is going to prison. We can also do him for conspiracy to supply drugs. Not a bad result for a Sunday morning. With a bit of luck, we can have Sunday lunch in the Saracen's Head, washed down with a few beers!'

Chapter Forty-Eight

Mickey Chadwell and Ben Naylor were sitting inside the office of the scrapyard which Chadwell had acquired on the demise of its previous owner. They were drinking tea and Chadwell was busy texting on his burner phone. The burner phone was untraceable by the police, so they couldn't bug it.

'Right, Ben, I want you to drive me up to London tomorrow. I've fixed up a meeting with an old pal of mine, called Harry Campbell. We've done business together for years. He owns a pub in Brixton, but that's just a cover for all his other business interests. He has some first-rate coke coming into the country next week. Provided the price is right, we will take it off his hands and make ourselves a handsome profit. Pick me up from the house at nine-thirty.'

Naylor stood up and stretched his arms in the air. 'No problem, Mickey. I need to fill the car up with petrol and have it valeted. Mind if I leave now?'

Chadwell stood up and picked up the two empty mugs. 'Go whenever you want, Ben. I will wash these mugs, then lock up and go for a drink on the way home.'

The drive up to London was uneventful and Naylor found a parking space a short walk from the pub where they were meeting Harry Campbell. They got out the car and Naylor locked it. Chadwell opened the door of the pub and went inside. It was just after midday, and there were no customers as yet. A woman in her late thirties was stacking a fridge with bottles. She turned around as she heard her first customers of the day approach. She gave them a smile and said, 'What can I get you?'

Chadwell returned the smile. 'I seem to remember that the Guinness is rather good in here. So, let's have two pints, please. Harry is expecting us, so could you let him know that Mickey Chadwell is here to see him.'

They took their drinks to a table by a window and sat down. A few minutes later, Harry Campbell limped down the stairs and made his way over to them. He was a heavy-set man and completely bald. He had broken his leg badly in a car accident many years ago, and it had left him with a pronounced limp, and he needed a stick to help him walk.

'Hi, Mickey, long time no see. How the devil are you?'

Chadwell got up and gave Campbell a hug. 'Hi, Harry, great to see you again. It's been a long time since my last visit, but the Guinness is still superb.' They both laughed. 'Harry, I want you to meet my associate, Ben Naylor.'

Naylor stood up and stretched out his right hand and said, 'Mickey has told me a lot about you. It's an honour to meet you, Harry.'

After exchanging pleasantries, they got down to business. The coke coming in from Amsterdam next week had a street value of £1.5 million. Campbell would accept £500k cash. Chadwell reckoned that if the coke was cut professionally, it would be worth £3m. Not a bad little profit! For security reasons, neither Campbell nor Chadwell would be present at the handover. If they got caught, they would be heading to prison for a very long time. They agreed the date and location for the handover of the cash and drugs. It would take place at a fruit wholesaler that Campbell owned.

Chadwell knew the location and had used it before. He would be sending two of his most trusted men with the cash. The deal was done, and the three men said their goodbyes.

Having driven back to Bristol, Naylor dropped Chadwell off at his home. He then drove around the block and called Murray. They arranged to meet at a Starbuck's coffee shop in Bath, 4.30 pm. Naylor parked his car and began walking to the coffee shop. He was feeling anxious and had every reason to be so. He was just about to pull off the biggest deal of his career but it would be very dangerous. People could get killed if it went wrong. Naylor walked into the shop and saw Murray sitting at a table. Naylor walked over and sat down. There were beads of sweat on his forehead. He picked up a paper napkin and wiped his brow.

'What's up, Ben, have you been running?'

Naylor smiled. 'No, I haven't been running, James. It's just that I have some very interesting news for you.'

When Naylor had finished telling Murray about the forthcoming drug deal, Murray sat in silence for a few minutes. Murray knew Harry Campbell but had never actually worked with him. He did, however, have a good reputation in the criminal world and the cops had never managed to convict him of a criminal offence.

'Who will Chadwell send to do the deal?'

Naylor sipped his coffee. 'He will send Steve Quinn and Frank Hughes. They have worked for him for years and know how to do their jobs. Both are very handy with their fists and will take some stopping.'

Murray closed his eyes and thought carefully. 'If we pull this off, Chadwell is going to be furious, and all hell will break loose. We need to protect you and make sure that we don't give Chadwell anything to make him suspicious of you. On the day of the deal, you are going to have to stay calm and relaxed. Do you have the address of the warehouse?'

'He said it was on the Brixton Road. Do you know it?'

Murray finished his coffee. 'I haven't been up there for a while. But I will take a run up there in the morning and see what it looks like. Then I need to go and see a friend of mine and pick up a couple of handguns. If we pull this off, Ben, we share fifty-fifty, equal partners.'

They exchanged high fives and began walking out the shop. They didn't notice Skelton, who was at the pedestrian crossing waiting for the lights to change. Skelton, however, very much noticed them. He would have a word with Patrick Rees, in the morning.

The next morning, Skelton was sitting at his desk. He had just completed the intel report on the sighting of Murray and Naylor. He picked up the phone and called Detective Inspector Patrick Rees in Bristol. Rees answered the call on the second ring.

'Good morning, Dan, and how are you?'

'Patrick, good morning to you. Do you have a moment?'

Rees stood up and said, 'Yes of course, Dan, fire away.'

Skelton leaned back in his chair. 'I was waiting to cross the road yesterday afternoon at about five when I saw James Murray and Ben Naylor come out of a coffee shop. They looked pleased with themselves. Has anything happened to Mickey Chadwell by any chance?'

Rees was silent for a second. 'No, not that I am aware of, but it sounds suspicious that those two are hanging out together. I just wonder if they are planning a hit on Chadwell sometime soon. They won't scare him off, that's for sure.'

Skelton stood up. 'I think if they do make a move on Chadwell, it will be in Bristol, so I just thought I would give you the heads up.'

Murray left his house and got into the car. Jason Andrews was driving, and Jeff Roberts was sitting in the back. Murray opened the front passenger door and got in. Murray had inherited the two thugs following the Rat's untimely death. They had proved their worth on several occasions. Both were ex-army and were well disciplined. The fact that they were both very capable shots was an added bonus. Murray had briefed them the previous evening after having met Ben Naylor. The car in which they were travelling had cloned number plates. They would not be using the satnav, as this would leave an audit trial for the police to discover. Murray knew the route they would be taking. He would give instructions for Andrews to follow. Eventually they arrived at the warehouse and parked up outside. Murray instructed them to don their face masks. This was nothing out of the ordinary following Covid, particularly in a food environment.

The purpose of today's visit to the warehouse was to give Andrews and Roberts an opportunity to familiarise themselves with the layout. They would need as much information from Ben Naylor as possible about the handover of the drugs and cash. It was due to take place a week today. Inside the warehouse, it was a hive of activity with lorry loads of fruit and vegetables being unloaded. They slowly made their way around the complex, stopping every now and again to inspect the produce. No one paid them any attention, which suited Murray just fine. It was not a large warehouse but big enough for their visit not to raise suspicion. Murray spotted the office block just ahead of him. His instincts told him that the exchange would take place inside the office. It would provide a good deal of privacy and would shield the illegal activity that would be taking place. All Mickey Chadwell's men had to do was to drive their vehicle up to the office door and take the cash inside. There, they would exchange the cash for the coke, and that was the deal done. Murray had other plans for the transaction, and it was all one sided.

Having seen enough, they left the warehouse and returned to the car. Murray gave the driver directions and ten minutes later, they pulled up outside some lock-up garages. They were looking for number twenty, and they quickly found it. The door was slightly open.

'Come on, boys, let's go inside and get you tooled up.'

Murray led them through the door, and they saw a small man sitting on a chair, reading a newspaper. He had a huge mop of hair and was smoking a fag.

'James, good to see you, come on in. Would one of you pull the door closed, please. We don't want prying eyes looking in.'

Roberts closed the door but the lights were on, so they were able to see. Herby Levine was a supplier of guns and had been plying his trade for years. He had somehow managed to evade detection by the police and as he was now in his sixties, was about to retire. He was doing this job as a favour to Murray, who had been a good customer over the years.

'Herby, it's great to see you and thanks for agreeing to my request at such short notice. This is Jason and Jeff; they were both in the army. It was they who suggested we try and get this particular model of handgun.'

Herby stood up and smiled. 'I must say that it is a first-class choice of weapon. The British forces have been using it for quite a few years now. The Glock 17 gen 4 pistol replaced its predecessor the Browning, which had a thirteen-round magazine capacity. The Glock is renowned for its high reliability and accuracy. The magazine holds nine millimetre bullets, which comes in handy, I can assure you.'

Levine took the suitcase from under the worktop and opened it. It contained two handguns and two boxes of ammunition. 'The serial numbers have been erased and they have never been used in a crime before. They are untraceable, gentlemen; I can assure you of that. The guys who owned them, are sadly no longer with us.'

Andrews and Roberts examined the guns. Murray asked, 'Are you guys happy with them?'

Andrews carefully returned his gun to the suitcase. 'Yes, James, these are perfect. We really need to give them a clean and test fire them, but they look good to me.'

Roberts returned his gun to the suitcase. Murray was pleased. 'Take them outside and put them in the boot. I just need to pay Herby and then we can head home.'

Chapter Forty-Nine

Skelton had called for a meeting with his CID colleagues at 10 am. They sat around a large table in a meeting room. Alexander was sitting next to him and around the table sat Ross Turnbull, Janet Griffin, Peter Lowik and Chris Spurrey. These were the detectives still working on the Stephen Cox murder in Alexandra Park several months previously.

'Well as you know, we have completely exhausted our supply of suspects in this case. Peter here has been trying to find a possible suspect on Gaydar but despite some early promising leads, the fountain has run dry. Bob Richards managed to get some fibres from the victim, which we think came from the killer, as well as some footprints. The killer left no DNA behind, which makes us think he is forensically aware. We have reviewed all the evidence and witness statements plus the CCTV footage. Unless any one of you disagrees, I propose closing the investigation down until such time as any new evidence emerges.'

Janet Griffin cleared her throat. 'I agree entirely, sir. We have diligently followed every line of enquiry with zero results. Perhaps if we leave it for a couple of months, we can come back and look at it again with fresh eyes.'

Peter Lowik spoke next. 'Sir, I have been on that Gaydar site now for two months and to be honest, I don't think I can take any more.'

Skelton looked over to Lowik and said, 'Yes, I know you have, Peter, and I am very grateful for your dedication. Let's wrap this up and we will meet again in two months, unless something pops up before then.'

He closed the meeting. 'Bill, you go to the canteen and get the sausage sandwiches and I will make the tea.'

They were sitting around Skelton's desk. Skelton was deep in thought and Alexander knew never to disturb him when he was like this. The two men had a superb working relationship, and each trusted the other implicitly. It was several minutes before Skelton found his voice. 'I had been meaning to go and visit the wife of Fergus Walsh, our missing person and father of PC Fergus Walsh. But I never got around to it. I know that she was interviewed when he went missing both as a witness and as a suspect. Perhaps we never asked her the right questions that could have thrown up a suspect. If I can arrange a meeting with her this evening, can you drive us to her house?'

Alexander finished his tea. 'Sounds like a bit of a long shot to me, sir. It's no bother to me to drive you there as the wife is going out this evening. I was banking on a Chinese takeaway.'

Skelton stood up. 'Actually, Bill, I fancy a Chinese tonight, so I will call Ken and tell him the good news.'

Skelton had called Nancy Walsh at her place of work. She was the PA to the senior partner of a local legal practice. She initially was surprised at the call, but Skelton assured her that it was just routine. On being asked if her son would be at home with her, she replied that he would be at work. That suited Skelton.

Alexander drove them to the house and it was just after six when he and Skelton got out the car. Mrs Walsh had been looking out of the window when the car arrived. She had the door open as the officers walked up the path. Skelton gave her a big smile.

'Hello, Mrs Walsh, I am DCI Skelton, and this is DS Alexander. Thank you so much for agreeing to see us this evening.'

Mrs Walsh returned the smile and said, 'Please do come in. Can I get you some tea or a beer or something? And please take a seat.'

'No, please don't trouble yourself, Mrs Walsh. When we are finished here, we will both be heading to our homes for dinner. I take it that Fergus is out this evening?' Skelton already knew the answer to the question, he had checked Fergus Walsh's work rota.

'No, Fergus is working this evening and being a Friday, he will probably be very busy. I doubt if he will be home before midnight.'

They exchanged small talk for a few minutes before Skelton got serious. 'Mrs Walsh, I need to ask you about your husband's relationship with your son.'

Mrs Walsh looked a little perplexed. 'What do you mean? My husband and son got on very well, as it happens. But of course, like all teenagers, Fergus had his moods. I would say that up until he was fourteen years old, he and his dad were very close. They would go to football and rugby matches together. Fergus also liked going to his dad's allotment, but of course he grew out of that. He preferred playing football and rugby, you see. He was just a typical teenage boy, although I have to say, there came a point when he didn't like to be in the house alone with his dad.'

Skelton was listening intently.

'I could never quite get to the bottom of it, Mr Skelton. It just seemed that they rowed about things. Probably just petty things. Maybe my husband would not allow Fergus to go out and play football, but Fergus would go out anyway. He was big for his age, and in fact with all the training that he did, he got bigger than his dad.'

Skelton paused for a second before asking, 'Was there ever any physical aggression between them?'

Mrs Walsh looked uncomfortable. She was clearly out of her comfort zone. 'They had a few shouting matches and I remember one day my husband raised his hand to Fergus but Fergus glared at him and said something like, "If you ever touch me again, I will kill you." But of course, he never meant that. It was just him having a tantrum and trying to sound big.'

'Mrs Walsh, how old was your son when your husband disappeared?'

'He was seventeen at the time and had passed his driving test about a month earlier. The weekend after he passed his test, we took him to Bristol and bought him a car. I think the car was called a Golf, but I can't be sure. You can ask Fergus, he will know.'

Skelton stood up. 'Your husband rented an allotment you said. Did your son go there much?'

'He did initially but rugby and football took priority. I think he got bored with the allotment.'

Skelton and Alexander thanked Mrs Walsh for her time and said goodbye. Alexander started the engine and drove off towards the Chinese Takeaway on Rush Hill. 'What did you make of that, Dan?'

Skelton put both hands on his head and said, 'I think young Fergus was being abused by his father. I also think that when he was big enough and old enough, he killed him. Fergus Walsh was our prime suspect in the murder of Stephen Cox, but we had no forensics but CCTV footage and eyewitnesses had put him close to the murder scene. We know that Stephen was attracted to young men. What if Walsh was out looking to extract revenge for being abused by his father? It would be the ideal motive for killing Steven.'

Alexander stopped the car. 'Bloody hell, Dan, it's beginning to make a lot of sense to me. But what did he do with his father's body and why have we never found it?'

Skelton looked across the car seat. 'I haven't figured that bit of the puzzle out yet. But I will, Bill. Now let's go get those takeaways, I am starving.'

The next morning being a Saturday, Skelton had the weekend off. He was looking forward to walking his dogs this morning. It was a chilly September morning, but the sun was up and the weather forecast was good. He slipped on a jacket and picked up the dogs' leads and whistle. They were trained gun dogs and it was Skelton who had trained them. Brenty-Boy was the oldest and the best gun dog that Skelton had ever encountered. He was a large black Labrador and his son Josh was the spitting image of him. It was often difficult to tell them apart. The youngest dog was called Archie and he was slightly smaller than the other two. His dogs adored Skelton and his partner Ken and they in turn adored the boys. Skelton opened the kitchen door and the boys jumped outside. They patiently waited for their master to close the door. Skelton did not need to put them on the lead, as they would walk perfectly to heel until given the command to leave heel.

They walked gently up Entry Hill Rise until they reached what was effectively countryside. He gave the command for the boys to go and they charged off, using their keen sense of smell. The boys were having a great time, but Skelton noticed that Brenty-Boy was limping slightly on his back right leg. He would have to keep an eye on it and perhaps take him to the vet and have it checked out. Labradors are prone to hip disease, which can be painful. If there was no improvement by Monday, he would ask Ken to take him to the vet. The dog was eight years old, so it was likely that he would need daily medication for the rest of his life.

The walk lasted almost an hour and Skelton felt relaxed and happy in the company of his boys. He could also forget all about work for the weekend, which would see him fully refreshed for whatever the new week would throw at him. On returning from the walk, he gave the boys a Bonio and when they finished those, he gave them each a bone. This would give them almost two hours of utter joy as they chewed on the marrow. He then cooked a full English breakfast, which he and Ken ate in the conservatory and washed down with mugs of tea. All in all, it was a very pleasant way to start the day. Having had breakfast, he went upstairs to shower and shave. He noticed the business card, which he had taken from the Cross Keys pub and remembered that the landlord, Clive, had said it was very popular on Sunday, so he picked up the phone and called the pub. He made a reservation for 1 pm the next day and was assured that he could bring his dogs. That would be a real treat for them as they were such social animals.

Ken and Skelton spent the entire afternoon working in the garden. They were both very keen gardeners, but Ken was the real expert. He instinctively knew what plants and trees grew best in a particular location. However, it was Skelton who really had green fingers and could grow almost anything. At 5 pm they finished working in the garden and Skelton poured them both a can of Fosters straight from the fridge. It was refreshingly cold. It went down a treat after a hard day's work in the garden. They decided to order an Indian takeaway and have a quiet night in watching television. The boys would curl up at their feet in utter contentment.

On Sunday morning, Skelton took the boys out for their morning walk and noticed that Brenty-Boy was still limping slightly. Ken would have to take him to the vet. Luckily the veterinary hospital was just up the road. After the walk, Skelton showered, shaved and dressed. Although it was Sunday, Skelton dressed very smartly in grey trousers, a blue shirt and navy-blue blazer. He chose a tie from the tie rack and made a perfect Windsor knot. Ken was also smartly dressed but chose not to wear a tie. It was 12.30 pm when they came downstairs. The boys were sleeping and one of them was snoring. What a life!

Skelton picked up their leads and whistle. Archie had opened an eye and saw Skelton with the leads in his hand. Suddenly, all three dogs were wide awake and wagging their tails furiously. They did not usually go for a walk at this time of the day. This was going to be a treat. As the walk to the Cross Keys pub entailed having to cross some busy roads, Skelton put them on the lead. Although they were perfectly trained, he did not like crossing the road without them being on the lead. They set off for the half-hour walk in pleasant sunshine.

Ken held the door open to the 'Eddie Cochrane Lounge' and Skelton walked the boys inside. He counted five dogs of differing colours and sizes and with the three that Skelton had brought in, there were now eight. This was definitely a dog friendly bar. A yellow Labrador came up to say hello and the boys were soon getting to know her. Clive the landlord was behind the bar.

'Hello, Dan, I see that you have brought your dogs with you. They look fantastic. Feel free to let them off their leads.'

Skelton smiled and said, 'Thanks, Clive, they are very well behaved, so you won't have any trouble. This is my partner, Ken. We have booked a table for lunch.'

Ken and Clive shook hands and Skelton patted the boys. They ordered their drinks and Clive told them that their table was ready. This was in the main bar, so Skelton led the dogs through to the main bar and saw another four dogs including a black Labrador. It came running up to greet them and Skelton gave it a cuddle. He let the boys off their leads, and they instantly began making new friends, both doggy and human. They sat down and Ken said, 'This is a great pub for the dogs. We must come here whenever we can.'

For the next two hours, they enjoyed a wonderful roast beef lunch followed by apple pie and custard. They had also got through two bottles of white wine. Neither drank red wine, as Ken always had some sort of allergic reaction to it, resulting in a terrible hangover. They had also got to know several fellow dog lovers.

'That was excellent, Dan. I couldn't eat another thing. I am going to have a lie down when we get home. I doubt very much if I could eat dinner tonight.'

Skelton smiled and said, 'Me neither, at least we have a half-hour walk home, which might burn off some of the calories. If Bill Alexander had his way, we would be having lunch here every day of the week. But he would soon be as big as the side of a barn.'

They both laughed.

Chapter Fifty

It was Monday morning and the alarm had woken Skelton. He rested for a few minutes before getting out of bed. The second his foot touched the floor, Brenty-Boy let out a loud woof. That dog had an amazing sense of hearing. He slipped on his slippers, put on his dressing gown and went downstairs. He let the boys out into the garden and put the kettle on to boil. He turned on the TV for the news but after only a few minutes gave up and switched it off. He could not bear politicians being interviewed. He let the boys back into the kitchen and noticed that Brenty-Boy was still limping. Ken would have to call the vet and make an appointment.

Skelton took a mug of tea up to Ken and one for himself. He took off his dressing gown and climbed into the shower. The water was hot, just the way he liked it. For some reason that Skelton could not explain, a hot shower always made him think deeply. It was like throwing a switch. Whatever was on his mind, he seemed to be able to rationalise it under the hot flowing water. He was thinking about the missing Fergus Walsh and his police officer son. He recalled visiting the allotment that Fergus Walsh had rented. What was it that Old Tom had said about the clematis growing up the wall? Something about planting it and it had done little for years. Then it began growing with vigour.

He poured some shampoo into his hand and began working it in to his scalp and hair. Then Ken had said something about it needing lots of fertiliser to grow like that. Skelton rinsed the shampoo and applied some conditioner. He turned the temp up a little and worked the conditioner into his hair. He began rinsing when he called out, 'That's it. That's where he hid the bloody body!'

He got out the shower and grabbed the towel. He dried himself and filled the sink with water. He quickly shaved and brushed his teeth. He went into the bedroom to dress. Ken was just getting out of bed.

'I've worked out where that missing man's body is buried. The son killed him and buried him under the clematis in the allotment.'

Ken rubbed his eyes. 'Are you sure, Dan?'

Skelton pulled on a fresh pair of boxer shorts. 'There is only one way to tell for certain and that is to dig it up. I am going to take a team up there this morning. Bob Richards will be in his element. Nothing excites him more than finding a dead body. I just hope he doesn't damage the clematis or Old Tom is going to be mighty upset. Can you phone the vet this morning and make an appointment for Brenty? He's still limping, so the sooner we get him some pain relief the better.'

Skelton finished dressing and having brushed his hair he sprayed it so that it would stay perfect for the rest of the day. He then opened the cupboard above the sink, which housed more than twenty different aftershaves. He selected the one due on today and sprayed it onto the back of his left hand. Then he used his right hand to spread it on his face and throat. He took a final look in the mirror and was pleased with the result. He was good to go. He went downstairs and said goodbye to the dogs and Ken. He was looking forward to his walk to the police station. This could be a big day.

He went to his office and took off his suit jacket and hung it up. He then went into the CID room and saw Alexander reading his computer screen. 'Good morning, Bill, I hope you had a good weekend, I certainly did.'

Alexander turned around. 'Good morning, sir. Yes, the wife and I went to see our daughter and her husband on Saturday and had a lovely dinner with them. We had Sunday lunch in a great little pub and the wife volunteered to drive us home. Needless to say, I took advantage and had a few sherbets.'

Alexander and Skelton were both Scotsmen. In Scotland, using the word sherbets meant that he had a few alcoholic drinks.

'Bill, go and see if you can find Bob Richards and bring him to my office. I am just going to see Graham Symonds as we are going to need a few of his men this morning.'

Ten minutes later the four officers were gathered in Skelton's office. Skelton was standing behind his chair looking serious. 'Right, gentlemen, let me tell you why I have asked you here this morning. We have on our books a missing person by the name of Fergus Walsh who disappeared about eight years ago. No trace of him has ever been found.'

Bob Richards raised his hand. 'Yes, Bob, go ahead.'

'That was the name of the prime suspect in that murder in Alexandra Park. Are they related?'

Skelton rested his hands on the back of the chair. 'Yes, Bob. They were father and son. I have a hunch that the father was abusing the boy and when he was big enough and old enough, he killed him. I also think that the boy, now a grown man and a police officer, killed Stephen Cox. It's my guess that he found Stephen's profile on Gaydar and noticed that he liked young guys. Not boys, you understand, but I suspect that Walsh interpreted him as a sexual predator, just like his father. As you know, we had no forensics on Walsh but Bob found some foreign fibres on Mr Cox's body. Unfortunately, we never found a match with Walsh but what if he disposed of the clothing he was wearing? He readily gave us the clothing that he said he had been wearing when the murder occurred. Being a copper, he is forensically educated, and he might simply have given us a spare set of clothing identical to the ones he wore at the murder scene.

'Bob, I want you and your team to conduct a dig underneath a very healthy clematis growing up a wall in the allotment that Walsh senior used to rent. Graham, I need you to put at least four officers to guard the entrance to the allotment and the suspected crime scene. I have checked with Bristol and young Fergus has a rest day today. If we do find a body, then we will have to find him and arrest him.'

The officers left the station together and Alexander got into his car and Skelton got in beside him. A convoy of police vehicles made its way to the allotment, Alexander parked up and Skelton climbed out of the car. He peered into the allotments. He quickly saw Old Tom, who was busy with a hoe. There was no one else present, which suited Skelton fine. Bob

Richards and his team joined Skelton. 'Hang on here for a minute, I need to have a word with Old Tom there. Bill, you come with me.'

The officers strode off in the direction of the old gardener. Tom saw them approach and rested his arms on the hoe.

'Good morning, Tom, how are you today?'

Skelton stretched out his right hand and shook hands with Tom. 'I am fine thanks apart from the usual aches and pains that you get at my age. What's with all those coppers at the gate? Is there something wrong, Dan?'

Skelton smiled and said, 'It's nothing for you to worry about, Tom. Me and my officers will shortly be getting into overalls and will be digging under your beautiful clematis. I have a feeling that Fergus Walsh might be buried underneath it.'

Tom's jaw dropped and he said, 'Bloody hell.'

Skelton went on. 'Can you remember when that plant started to grow vigorously?'

Tom took out his pipe and began lighting it. He thought for a few seconds and said, 'It was the spring after Fergus vanished. Up until then, I thought it was never going to grow.'

Skelton put his hand on the hoe and said, 'I'm afraid you will have to call it a day, my friend, and go home, but before you do, does young Fergus have anything in your shed?'

Tom puffed on his pipe. 'Yes, Fergus has a backpack in my shed. He has a key to it so that he can shelter if it rains. I've not looked inside it, so I don't know what's in it. Do you want to see it?'

Skelton gave Alexander a nod. 'Bill, go and get Bob Richards and tell him to get his overalls on. Come on Tom, you can show me that backpack.'

Bob Richards gingerly removed the backpack from the shed and photographed it. He carefully opened it and found the blood-soaked jogging gear. He photographed the entire contents of the backpack before placing the clothing and trainers into evidence bags.

'Christ, Dan, you are one hell of a detective,' said Alexander.

Skelton smiled and gently punched Alexander on the shoulder. 'No, Bill, I have always been a good gardener, and plants don't grow well without lots of manure, or even better a dead body!'

Richards and his team soon got to work digging slowly under the clematis. It was not long before they discovered bones. They needed to call in Dr Challis, the Home Office pathologist. Skelton was convinced that they had found Fergus Walsh senior. Now they just had to find his son and arrest him for his father's murder.

Chapter Fifty-One

Skelton and Alexander left the burial site and made their way to the car. Skelton called Peter Lowik. 'Peter, we need to get hold of Fergus Walsh. We have just found what we think is his father's body, but for god's sake don't tell him that. We are going to have to arrest him, but he is a big guy and a cop, so I don't want him to know that we are coming for him. Bill and I are headed back to the station. I want you to round up Chris Spurrey and Ross Turnbull and meet me in my office in fifteen minutes.'

'Christ almighty, sir, I was not expecting this. Do you know where he is?'

'Peter, I know that he is off work today. So, when I get back, I want you to call him and arrange a meeting. See if he will meet you for a drink. I'd like for you to arrange to see him in the Saracen's Head if that's possible?'

Lowik cleared his throat and said, 'I will try my best, sir.'

The team were in Skelton's office and the atmosphere was tense. Lowik was doing his best to compose himself but the thought of helping to arrest his mate was not hanging comfortably on him. Skelton sensed this. He was a natural leader; he had a duty to look after his team and protect them the best he could. Skelton stood up and walked over to where Lowik was sitting. He placed his hand on Lowik's right shoulder. 'Peter, I know this is going to be tough on you, given that Fergus is your friend. However, you are a professional police officer and it's your duty to uphold the law without fear or favour. Call Fergus now and see if he will meet you for a drink and lunch. Suggest to him that you go to the Saracen's Head as the food there is great. It's only just after midday, so the suggestion of lunch will seem natural. Make the call.'

Fergus Walsh had three rest days and was at home ironing his shirts. He took the call from Lowik and was delighted that his friend had called him out to lunch. Lowik had sounded in great form and seemed keen on meeting up. Walsh had been in the Saracen's Head a few times for a drink but had never eaten there. He remembered seeing people getting stuck into their food and the plates were always cleared. A good sign that the food was good. They had arranged to meet at 1.30 pm. Walsh was feeling hungry and was looking forward to exploring the food that the Saracen's Head had to offer.

Skelton briefed the team. All four officers would travel together in Alexander's car. The custody van would be driven by Ian Perkins with Luke Meehan riding shotgun. There is a loading bay outside the Saracen's Head where they would park up. Lowik would enter the pub on his own and engage Walsh in conversation. Skelton instructed him to relax as best he could. There is a front and back door to the pub. After Lowik had entered the pub, the other officers would make their entrance. Skelton and Alexander would enter by the front door whilst Spurrey and Turnbull would take the back door.

Alexander parked the car in the loading bay. They could not be seen from the pub, whilst Perkins parked behind.

'Right, Peter, in you go and good luck. But any sign of trouble, press the red button on your radio and we will be in in a flash'

Lowik cleared his throat and got out the rear door of the car. He saw Ian Perkins and Luke Meehan in the custody van and gave them a wave. He opened the front door of the pub. There was a bar on his left side and a bar on his right, but the latter did not serve drinks. Walsh was not at either bar. Lowik wondered if Walsh would show. He began walking to the left side of the bar towards the rear of the pub when he saw Walsh sitting at a table for two. Lowik's heart was thumping.

Walsh saw his friend and stood up. He called out, 'Peter, over here.'

Lowik smiled and began walking towards Walsh, who was now on his feet. 'Great to see you, Peter, what are you drinking?'

They shook hands and Lowik said, 'I will have a pint of Thatchers Gold please, mate.'

Walsh went to the bar and ordered the drink. He was quickly served by Alex, the general manager. He paid by debit card and returned to the table.

'This is a nice surprise, Peter. Are you not working today?'

Lowik took a long slow swig from his drink before answering the question. 'I have a rest day, mate. I have been doing lots of overtime and I just felt in the mood for a few beers and some lunch. I haven't seen you for a couple of weeks and thought we could catch up on the gossip.'

Spurrey and Turnbull got out the back of the car and proceeded to walk around to the back of the pub. It would take them just twenty seconds to do so. Skelton and Alexander climbed out and entered the front door. Alex saw them come in and said, 'Hi guys, can I get you a couple of pints?'

Skelton looked at him and said, 'Not today thanks, Alex, we are not staying.'

Skelton and Alexander scanned the bars, no sign of their quarry. They had to be in the back area. Skelton led the way with Alexander close behind. They saw Spurrey and Turnbull entering the back door and Lowik and Walsh sitting on their own. There were about half a dozen other diners tucking into their meals.

Walsh looked up and saw Skelton and Alexander, but was not worried by them. As he didn't have eyes in the back of his head he could not see Spurrey and Turnbull.

'Oh, look Peter, your DCI and DS have just walked in. This must be a favourite watering hole for you guys.'

Spurrey was behind him and grabbed him around both arms with lightning speed. Walsh began to wrestle from the vice like grip but Lowik had the hand cuffs out. He was quickly cuffed without incident.

Skelton moved closer. 'Fergus Walsh, I am arresting you for the murder of your father and that of Stephen Cox.' He proceeded to caution him. Walsh looked a beaten man.

He glared at Lowik. 'You bastard, I thought we were mates.'

Lowik was in his face. 'No, sunshine, you are not my mate. You are fucked big time.'

They led Walsh out of the bar through the front door. Ian Perkins and Luke Meehan were standing by the front of the custody van. When they saw the man in handcuffs, they quickly moved to the rear and opened the door for their prisoner. Skelton watched as the van drove off. He was immensely proud of his team and a smile began forming on his face. Alexander was watching him.

'That was a bloody good result, sir. You just solved two murders in one go. Not a bad start to the week.'

Skelton raised his right arm and exchanged high fives with the entire team. 'Bill, I am putting you in charge of the drinks party back at the station. You all have my permission to get well and truly drunk!'

Chapter Fifty-Two

Skelton spent the next few days preparing the necessary paperwork for the trial of Fergus Walsh. The case against him was watertight, he had no defence. Whilst he took great satisfaction at solving both murders, the meeting with Walsh's mother had been truly awful. The poor woman was heartbroken to learn that her beloved son had killed his father and her husband. Skelton doubted if the woman would ever recover from the shock. But Skelton had no time to dwell on that. He had a sense of foreboding that Murray was making plans to go after Chadwell. It did not concern him if Murray killed Chadwell or if Chadwell killed Murray. The world would be a safer place with both of them gone. What worried Skelton was the possibility that some innocent bystander could get hurt or even killed. He had set up surveillance on Murray in the hope that Murray would leave his girlfriend at home, so that Skelton could pay her a visit. But so far this had not happened. Mind you, it was early days. As soon as Murray went out on his own, Skelton would pounce.

It had only been a few days since Skelton had seen Murray and Ben Naylor together in Bath. It had been reported to him that Naylor had also visited Murray's house the day after. Skelton could not be sure of the significance of these meetings. These guys had spent time in prison together. Were they just friends or had they built up a partnership to oust Mickey Chadwell in Bristol?

Murray had been busy. He did not want any drugs or significant sums of cash in the house. He had already learnt that lesson and was determined not to repeat the mistake again. He had secured a small workshop in an industrial estate just off the Lower Bristol Road in Bath. It was very secure. The windows had heavy metal bars and the door was on rollers. It would require considerable effort to gain entry to the premises. The contents were very basic. There was a large metal desk and four chairs. There were also two sturdy metal cabinets with locks. The cabinet on the left contained drugs whilst the one on the right was where the cash was kept.

The industrial estate was a hive of activity. It contained lots of small businesses so there were lots of comings and goings. This suited Murray perfectly. No one would pay him or his minders any hint of suspicion. They were free to come and go as they pleased. Skelton was unaware that this was now the centre of Murray's criminal activities.

Meanwhile over in Bristol, Mickey Chadwell was chairing a meeting. He had called in Ben Naylor, along with Steve Quinn and Frank Hughes. Today was Monday and on Friday, Quinn and Hughes were to drive to London with £500,000 in cash and collect a consignment of pure coke. They were sitting in the office of the scrap yard which Chadwell now operated. It was of course a front for the drugs business and so far, the police had left them well alone. Chadwell rested his arms on the desk and then looked at the three men sat around the desk.

'Right the deal is all set to take place on Friday morning at eleven. Steve and Frank will take the cash to the warehouse. You have both been there, so you know the layout. You drive the car up to the office and take the cash inside. Harry Campbell's man will be wating for you. He is called Joe. You hand over the bag of money and he will give you the coke. You get back into the car and drive back here. It should be a piece of cake for you boys.'

Quinn and Hughes exchanged glances and Quinn said, 'Yeah leave it to us, Mickey, we should be back here about one. Then we get the boys to start cutting it, before you know it, we will have it out on the street and the money will be rolling in.'

Naylor smiled but it was a nervous smile. The meeting broke up and Naylor left the office and began driving to Bath. Once he was clear of the scrap yard, he pulled over and called Murray. They agreed to meet at the lock-up on the industrial estate.

Murray was putting on his shoes in the sitting room when Penny walked in. She was carrying a mug of tea. 'Are you going out, James?'

Murray stood up and smiled. 'Yes, I am meeting Ben in half an hour along with Jason and Jeff. He is going to brief us on this little job on Friday. It should only take about half an hour. After that I am going to take Ben out to lunch. Do you want to join us?'

Penny sat down. 'No, I am going to get my hair done this afternoon at two. So, I will take a taxi into town and see you back here about five. Good luck with the meeting and enjoy your lunch with Ben. I will have some salad before I leave. Shall we get an Indian takeaway this evening?'

Murray leaned over and kissed her on the cheek. 'That's a good idea. I could go a curry tonight and the football is on the telly. It will be good to have a night in.'

DC Richard Pearce was sitting in the unmarked police car that was parked in the street close to where Murray lived. He saw that Murray was alone, which meant that Penny was on her own in the house. He waited until Murray had driven off before making the call to Skelton. Ten minutes later, Skelton and Alexander were pulling up outside Murray's house.

Skelton rang the bell and Penny opened the door. She looked surprised to see the detectives. 'You have just missed James, he is going into town to have lunch.'

Skelton smiled and said, 'It's actually you that we have come to see. Can we come in?'

Penny stood aside. 'You know your way.'

They were seated in the sitting room. Penny was in an armchair whilst Skelton and Alexander were on the sofa. Both men looked serious. Skelton would do the talking. 'This is a nice little setup that you have here, Penny. The house is in your name but that doesn't mean that we can't seize it if James is involved in drugs. We can also seize any cash and bank accounts. We know all about you, Penny. You never earned enough money to buy this place. And you never declared the money you made on the game to the tax man. That is a serious offence, and you could go to prison for that, which would not best please James.'

Penny shifted in her seat. Skelton could tell that the news had come as a shock to her. Her mind was racing. The thought of losing the house and going to prison had unsettled her. She was looking frightened, just as Skelton had hoped.

'What is it you want from me?'

Skelton stood up and walked over to where she was seated. 'We know that James killed Jake Ratten and that he now controls the drugs in Bath. We need to know where he is operating from, we also need to know what he is doing with Ben Naylor. You give us that information and you get to keep the house and we can do a deal with the tax man so that you don't go to prison.'

Penny began to shake. She had made up her mind. Skelton returned to the sofa. Penny stood up and ran her hands through her hair. 'James has got some sort of a workshop on an industrial site just off Lower Bristol Road, but I have never been there. James spent time in prison with Ben and they are good friends. I know that they have some sort of a job on this Friday in London. They will not be going but they will be sending Jason and Jeff. I don't know any more than that. James is meeting Ben today for lunch.'

Skelton and Alexander stood up and exchanged glances. 'Penny, this is just between us. James will not hear about this arrangement between us. You can go on living just as you have been and from time to time, when James is not here, we will call in for a little chat.'

Chapter Fifty-Three

Murray, Naylor, Jason Andrews and Jeff Roberts were sat around the desk. Naylor had just given them the run down for the job on Friday. Murray was deep in thought. Jason and Jeff would be armed, unlike Chadwell's men, who would not. In all probability, the mere sight of the guns would be enough for Chadwell's men to hand over the money and drugs.

'Okay listen up. The meeting is scheduled for eleven Friday morning. I don't want to take any chances with traffic on Friday. So, Jason and Jeff drive up to London on Thursday and get a hotel near the warehouse. On Friday morning, you get in position. Ben has given you the details of the car they will be using. When that car enters the warehouse, you go in after it. Chances are that on seeing your shooters, they will hand over the money and drugs. But if not, you will have to shoot them. Do you understand?'

Jason and Jeff both nodded their heads in unison. The mission was on.

Skelton had called a meeting with his detectives following the visit to Penny. 'Bill and I had a quite little chat with James Murray's girlfriend this morning. We made it clear to her that unless she cooperates with us, she loses the house and goes to prison for tax evasion. That got her attention, I can assure you.' The officers all smiled. 'We got two useful pieces of information from her. The first is that Murray has acquired some sort of workshop or lock-up on an industrial estate off Lower Bristol Road. Now as you know, there are dozens of industrial estates down there, but Penny does not know which one it is. It is going to be like finding a needle in a haystack searching for it. The chances are that the owner or leaseholder has sub-let it to Murray. So, Land Registry searches will not help us to find it. I want Chris Spurrey and Peter Lowik to get down there and have a nose around, to see if they can find it. I think it will be a long shot, but we have to try.'

Spurrey nodded his head at Lowik.

'Penny also told us that Murray and Naylor have some sort of a job on in London on Friday but has no details of what it might be. However, Murray and Naylor will not be in attendance. We don't know where in London it is, but we do know that Jason Andrews and Jeff Roberts will be going. We will therefore spring a surprise for them. We know where they both live, so we will mount surveillance on them from six on Friday morning. Bill will sort out the details and assign you accordingly. Make sure you get their car details from the computer right away.'

Skelton was just finishing sending an email when Alexander knocked on his door and entered. 'Sir, it is just going on one and I could go for some lunch.'

Skelton closed down his laptop and sighed. 'It's been a busy morning and we never had a sausage sandwich, so I think a visit to the Saracen's Head is in order. I saw someone having a sirloin steak in there the other day and it looked fantastic.'

'Do you know, sir, that since you joined us here, I have never eaten so well. I used to just use the canteen. I saw that guy with the sirloin steak as well and the guy devoured it. I think two medium cooked sirloins is the order of the day. Let's go.'

It was a cloudy grey day but that did not stop the usual horde of tourists descending on the city. As they walked to the abbey, it seemed like they were in Japan as there were so many Japanese people taking photographs. Their progress was painfully slow but eventually they got to the pub. Skelton held the door open for Alexander and they both walked to the bar. Both Alex and Toby were behind the bar and Toby was busy pulling a pint of Guinness. Alex greeted them with a smile and said, 'Good afternoon, gentlemen.' He then whispered, 'You aren't going to be arresting any of my customers today, will you?'

Both Skelton and Alexander smiled. Skelton rested his elbows on the bar and said, 'No not today, Alex. But what we would both like is a couple of pints and two medium cooked sirloin steaks.'

Alex chuckled to himself. 'I wondered when you two would tackle our sirloin steaks. They are twenty-eight day aged and my chef cooks them to perfection. Oh, and just to let you know, this is my last week in here. A new general manager takes over on Friday. His name is Dale, and he is from Cardiff.'

Skelton stretched out to shake Alex's hand. 'Sorry to hear that you are leaving us. We must get to know Dale.'

Their usual seats by the window had just become free and Skelton took the stool with his back to the window. Both men took a long slurp from their glass and Alexander said, 'This job in London on Friday sounds interesting. It looks like Ben Naylor and Murray are definitely working together, but it's a shame they are not going to be physically involved in it. Any idea what it might be?'

Skelton took another sip from his glass. I suspect they are buying drugs. They always need a supply, so Murray is dispatching Andrews and Roberts to do the dirty work. With a bit of luck, we can follow them to London and let them buy the drugs and arrest them. Murray loses both the money and drugs and Andrews and Roberts go to jail. That will please me and piss Murray off big time!'

Alex brought over the sirloin steaks. 'There you go, gentlemen. I am sure you will enjoy them.'

'Bloody hell, Bill, these look absolutely delicious. Alex, could you bring us over another couple of pints, this looks like thirsty work.'

The men sat in silence, except for the odd burp. When they had cleared their plates, Skelton dabbed his mouth with the napkin and said, 'That, Bill, is the best sirloin steak I have ever tasted.'

Alexander let out another burp and said, 'Dan, I could not eat another thing, but I could go for another pint. Let me go and get the refills. I just hope I can stay awake this afternoon.'

Skelton stood up and began walking to the toilets. He went in and after washing and drying his hands, began walking back to his table but decided to look into the pool bar. Sitting in deep conversation were Murray and Naylor. He approached their table and Murray saw him.

'Well, if it's not Mr Skelton, and what can we do for you?' Naylor turned his head to see.

'I wonder what Mickey Chadwell will make of you two, meeting up yet again? I get the impression that you guys are not meeting up for old time's sake. I think you fancy your chances with Chadwell. Now Chadwell is not a man you upset unless you have just bought a funeral plan!'

Murray spread the palms of his hands on the table. 'Ben and I were just having some lunch and a beer. No harm in that, Inspector.'

Skelton possessed natural authority and he decided to exercise it here. He looked at them in the eye and said, 'You two think you are a pair of smart bastards. Now I don't give a shit if its Mickey Chadwell that gets you before I do but rest assured one of us will. I don't think Chadwell is going to be very pleased when he hears about this. Oh, and when we tell him about your little meeting in the coffee shop the other day, the shit is going to well and truly hit the fan!' Skelton gave them a big smile. 'Enjoy your lunch, it might be one of your last.'

Skelton walked back to his table and patted Alexander on the shoulder. 'I love this pub, Bill. We arrested Fergus Walsh in here the other day, and I have just totally pissed off Murray and Naylor. They seem to have lost their appetite and I can't wait for Friday.'

Chapter Fifty-Four

Chris Spurrey and Peter Lowik were in an unmarked police car and had just begun a slow drive around the industrial estate off Lower Bristol Road. The area was huge and just about every type of business you could think of was present. They passed paint shops, electricians, plumbers, car rentals and lockups. Some of the premises appeared to be unoccupied. They had the details of the cars owned by Murray and his known associates but there was no trace of any of them. After two hours, they gave up and went back to the station and reported to Skelton, who told them to make daily trips to the estate in case their luck changed. Murray and his men would have to show up sometime. This was going to be a waiting game.

On Thursday afternoon, Jason Andrews drove over to pick up Roberts from his flat. He was carrying a small overnight bag and wearing black jeans, a white top and a jacket with a hood. Andrews was a big guy and regularly worked out at the local gym. He was thirty years old and in good shape. Roberts was a little older at thirty-four and his hair was already turning grey. However, he was also in good shape and preferred running as opposed to the gym. Roberts opened the boot and put his bag in then got into the passenger seat.

They exchanged pleasantries and Andrews started to drive. 'I have found us a Travelodge which is about a mile away from the warehouse. I booked us a room each. When we get there, we can book in and then take the tube up to the West End. I haven't been in London for years. One place that I really love is China Town. I love a good Chinese.'

Roberts smiled and said, 'You seem to have a plan, Jason. You can count me in. I know a few good pubs in the West End so we can check them out as well. We can't go out and get drunk though. We are going to need our wits about us tomorrow morning. I know that James reckons on the job being a piece of cake, but you can't afford to take things for granted.'

The drive took just under two hours, and it was almost 5 pm when they booked into the Travelodge. They went to their rooms and placed their bags in the wardrobe. They met up at reception and walked across the road to the tube station. They were soon on their way to the West End.

On Friday morning, at just before 6, Chris Spurrey drove Peter Lowik to the flat owned by Jason Andrews. As Spurrey parked the car he said, 'There is no sign of his car. Do you think he has gone already?'

Lowik's eyes were scanning the street. 'Maybe he spent the night with Roberts. I will radio Janet and Ross and ask them to look out for the car.'

It soon became apparent that Roberts' car was parked outside his flat but there was no sign of Andrews' car.

It was a very slow tedious morning for the officers. They reckoned that Andrews and Roberts would have to leave Bath by 9 am to get to London for the job. When it got to ten, they realised that the mission had to be aborted. The officers drove back to the police station and headed for the canteen. Skelton had been kept updated throughout the morning. Skelton went to see Alexander and found him seated at his desk, filling in some forms.

'It looks like Murray has outsmarted us this morning. I think he must have sent Andrews and Roberts up to London yesterday. Any chance that we had of nicking those two buggers has gone and Murray has pulled off another deal right under our noses. I haven't got an appetite for lunch today, Bill. I will be in my office if you need me.'

Alexander looked up at his boss and said, 'Sir, you will get Murray one day. It's only a question of time.'

Chapter Fifty-Five

Steve Quinn was driving and Frank Hughes was in the front passenger seat. On the back seat was the holdall containing the cash to buy the drugs. It was just after 8.30 am when they joined the M4, which would take them to London. The traffic was running smoothly. So far everything was going to plan. All being well, they would be back in Bristol around 2 pm. The sun was shining but as it had rained during the night it reflected on the wet road surface. Quinn could cope with that. He knew the route to the warehouse well. He reckoned that they would arrive at their destination around 10.30 am so they would have to park up and wait. That was not a problem.

At the Travelodge, Jason Andrews and Jeff Roberts had set their alarms for 8 am. They had got up, showered and shaved. They had breakfast together and were content to read the newspapers they had requested from reception. Roberts was closely studying the sports section of the Telegraph. When they finished reading, it was 9.45. Almost time to go. Each man returned to his room and retrieved his overnight bag, inside of which was a handgun. Neither man expected to use it but were perfectly prepared to if required to do so. Andrews excused himself and went to the bathroom. He closed the cubicle door behind him and took out the wrap of coke. This would steady his nerves. When he had finished, he flushed the toilet and left.

Quinn and Hughes had an uneventful journey, and it was 10.40 when they reached the street where the warehouse was situated. Quinn found a parking space and parked the car. All was going to plan.

Andrews and Roberts checked out of the Travelodge at 10 am and got into the car. They were both carrying their overnight bags. They removed their guns and stuffed them into their coat pockets. Andrews could feel the coke working its magic and he felt good. The car was a blue BMW and they had cloned the plates. Once they were safely back in Bath, they would torch the car, thus destroying any forensic evidence against them. Roberts drove the car to the street where the warehouse was situated, parked up and waited. They watched the warehouse and could see lorries coming and going. At two minutes to eleven, they saw a red BMW enter. It was time to make their move. Roberts started the engine, pulled out and accelerated down the road. He slowly drove into the entrance and could see the red BMW parked outside the office. The car was empty, which meant that the occupants were now inside the office. They pulled on their balaclava masks, got out of the car and walked to the door.

Andrews drew his gun first, followed by Roberts. He turned the door handle and went inside. A man in his forties was sitting at the desk and had a suitcase in front of him. On seeing the two armed men he raised his hands. Steve Quinn was carrying a large bag whilst Frank Hughes was carrying nothing. Andrews brandished his gun and said, 'Just hand over the money and the coke and nobody will get hurt. None of you wants to die a brave man.'

Quinn put his bag next to the suitcase on the desk. 'Okay, it's all yours. Don't shoot.'

Roberts moved in closer. He pointed the gun at the man sitting at his desk and said, 'Get up, turn around and put your hands behind your back.' He had cable ties in his hand. 'You two do the same and be quick.'

Andrews covered him as he got to work. First, he applied the cable ties to each man's hands and pulled them tight. He then removed the gaffer tape from his pocket and taped their mouths shut. 'Now lie on the floor face down.' The men did as they were ordered. Andrews picked up the suitcase whilst Roberts took the bag. 'You guys just keep quiet and all will be fine.'

Roberts took the key from the door lock and opened the door. Andrews followed him out. Roberts closed the door and locked it with the key and placed it in his pocket. They put the guns back in their pockets and looked around. Nobody was about, so they got to the car and got in. They took off their balaclava masks and Roberts reversed the car out of the warehouse.

The job was done, and they were on their way back to Bath. Murray had been right – it had been a piece of cake.

Roberts drove the BMW to the lock-up on the industrial estate where Murray was waiting for them. The three men exchanged high fives; the mission had gone perfectly to plan. Murray was delighted with both Andrews and Roberts. He would be giving them both a hefty bonus.

Roberts drove the BMW to an abandoned farm and doused the interior in petrol and set it on fire.

Chapter Fifty-Six

Mickey Chadwell knew that something was wrong shortly after 11 am. Neither Quinn nor Hughes had called to say that everything had gone to plan. He tried calling Quinn's mobile phone whilst Naylor tried contacting Hughes' phone, but they were not answering. 'Something is not right here, Ben. I don't know if they have been arrested or if they have made off with the money? If it's the latter, I will find them and god help them when I do. I need to call Harry Campbell and see if he knows what's going on.' He made the call. 'Harry, what's going on? I can't get a hold of my men.'

Campbell was worried. 'Mickey my man should have called me by now and I can't get him to answer his phone. I am going to drive over there now and see what's going on. I will call you just as soon as I have any news. But this has never happened before. Leave it with me, Mickey.' He ended the call.

Campbell drove over to the warehouse and saw the red BMW parked outside the office. He got out the car, went to the office door and pulled down on the handle, but the door was locked. He tried knocking on the door but got no answer. He knew he could not break the door down; it was far too strong. He knew the manager would have a spare key, so he went looking for him. When he found him, they returned to the office and the door was unlocked. They freed the men, but they were certainly not going to call the police. Campbell called Chadwell. It was the most difficult call he had ever made. Chadwell reacted very badly to the news.

Ben Naylor was nervous but did his best not to show it. He and Murray had pulled off the perfect heist but there would be consequences for everyone involved. Chadwell would guess that it was an inside job. Fortunately, Chadwell would be suspicious of Quinn and Hughes. Had they got drunk and let slip that they were going to London to exchange the money for the drugs? Who would have the balls to stitch Chadwell up?

It was 3.30 pm when Quinn and Hughes returned from London. Chadwell and Naylor were waiting for them. Naylor had to put on a show. He knew that his life would depend upon it. Chadwell greeted them with, 'And what the fuck happened in London this morning? You don't look hurt, so you must just have handed over my money and coke like they were presents.'

Whilst Quinn and Hughes had not been badly hurt, their wrists were badly bruised from the cable ties. It was Quinn who spoke. 'Mickey, these two guys had shooters and had we tried to resist them, they would have shot us. Look at our wrists, they put cable ties on us, and they were pulled really tight. They put gaffer tape over our mouths so we couldn't call for help. Look, we are really sorry that you lost your cash and the coke but there was nothing we could have done. These guys meant business and would have killed us, that's for sure.'

Naylor stood up and made his way around the table to where Quinn was sitting. He hit Quinn square in the face, knocking him off his chair. Quinn's face was a mess, with his nose clearly broken and three teeth lying on the floor. 'You lying bastard, this was an inside job and you and this cunt here set it up.'

Naylor punched Hughes on the jaw and sent him flying off his chair. He landed on the floor out cold. Chadwell stood up and kicked Quinn in the ribs, breaking several of them. The poor man was in agony. 'Please, Mickey, you have got to believe us. We had nothing to do with this. I swear it on my baby's life.'

Chadwell was not buying it. Without question, it was an inside job. Ben was right about that. Chadwell had had enough. Quinn and Hughes had double crossed him, that was for sure. Now they would pay the price for their treachery. 'Ben get the cable ties, we need to teach these fuckers a lesson.'

Hughes was still out cold, but Quinn was awake. 'Please Mickey. This is not right. Somebody tipped those guys off, but it was not us. Come on, you know us for Christ's sake.'

Naylor returned with the cable ties and quickly attached them to their hapless victims' wrists and ankles. He then put the gaffer tape over their mouths. Naylor picked up Quinn whilst Chadwell got Hughes.

They dragged them outside into the scrap yard. There were six cars waiting to go into the car crusher. They put Quinn in an old Honda Civic whilst Hughes got put in a Skoda. Chadwell climbed into the crane whilst Naylor got into the cab of the crusher. Chadwell started the engine and swung the magnet of the crane over the roof of the Honda. He hoisted it up and into the giant jaws of the crusher and dropped it into them. Naylor had started the power to the jaws of the crusher and in less than five minutes the car was reduced to less than a quarter of its original size. They repeated the exercise with the Skoda. Both the crushed cars would be taken to the furnace on Monday and all evidence that either Quinn or Hughes existed would be gone forever.

Chapter Fifty-Seven

Detective Inspector Patrick Rees was sitting at his desk three days after Quinn and Hughes had met their end. He was studying the missing persons reports filed by their wives. He knew that both men had worked for Mickey Chadwell. Normally, a missing person investigation would be dealt with by a less senior officer, but Rees was intrigued that two of Chadwell's men were missing. According to the men's wives, they had said that they were going to London for the day but had never come back. All attempts to call their phones had failed. Rees picked up the phone and called Dan Skelton. Skelton saw the caller ID, picked up the phone and said, 'Good morning, Patrick, what can I do for you this fine morning?'

'Dan, I have just received two missing person reports this morning. The guys are a Steven Quinn and a Francis Hughes and both work for Mickey Chadwell. According to their wives, they went up to London last Friday but have not been heard from since then. I was just wondering if James Murray and Ben Naylor have got something to do with this?'

Skelton stood up and thought for a second. 'Well Patrick, we have had no reports of any trouble here in Bath but interestingly, we had some intel that Murray was involved in some sort of a job on Friday. Unfortunately, the two guys that we thought were working for Murray on the job gave us the slip. So we don't know where the job took place. We suspect that Murray had arranged a drug deal and had sent Jason Andrews and Jeff Roberts to London to carry it out. There have been no reports of any unidentified bodies turning up in London, so it's a mystery as to where Quinn and Hughes have got to.'

'Okay, Dan, I am going to go and visit Chadwell and see what he has to say. I will keep you posted.' Skelton put the phone down and walked to the CID room where Chris Spurrey and Janet Griffin were in deep conversation. Bill Alexander was just coming off the phone. The officers looked up as Skelton approached,

'Have there been any sightings of Jason Andrews and Jeff Roberts since Friday?'

Janet Griffin raised her right hand and said, 'Yes, sir. I was driving past Bog Island on Friday as I was leaving work and I saw the two of them going into the ale house. A couple of minutes later as I was sitting at the traffic lights, I saw Murray and he was walking in the direction of the ale house.'

Skelton sat down on a vacant seat and rested his hands on his knees. 'I just got some interesting news from Bristol this morning. Apparently two of Mickey Chadwell's men have gone missing. DI Rees is going to pay him a visit to see if he can shed any light on it. I just wonder if there is some kind of connection between the missing men and James Murray.'

Bill Alexander stood up and said, 'Do you think that job in London could have involved the missing men?'

Skelton leaned back in the chair and said, 'It is possible that Ben Naylor gave Murray the details of a planned operation involving Mickey Chadwell's boys, and Murray sent Jason Andrews and Jeff Roberts to intervene. Maybe they killed Chadwell's men. Their bodies have not been found so far. If Chadwell thinks Murray is in some way involved, then there will be trouble here in Bath, that's for sure.'

DI Patrick Rees and DS Rodger Fell drove to the scrap yard. The entrance road was very rough, which caused Fell to drive slowly. He parked the unmarked police car outside the gate and both officers got out. Fell locked the car and followed Rees. As they made their way into the scrap yard, Mickey Chadwell and Ben Naylor were coming out of the office. Chadwell was wiping his hands on a rag. Chadwell's heart missed a beat when he saw Rees. 'Well, if it's not Mr Rees and his sidekick Mr Fell. And what can I do for you this morning?'

Rees and Fell walked up closer to Chadwell and Naylor. 'I understand that you have lost a couple of your men,' said Rees.

Chadwell finished with the rag and put it in his trouser pocket. It was Naylor who next spoke. 'That's right, the last time we saw them was on Thursday. The two of them have been a bit unreliable of late and we reckon that they have moved on. Isn't that right, Mickey?'

Chadwell touched his nose with his right hand and said, 'Yeah that's right, Ben. I couldn't depend on them recently and I think they had enough of working in the yard. It would have been nice of them to tell me they weren't coming back.'

Rees took his hands out of his pockets and said, 'I don't buy that. I think you sent them up to London on Friday to buy some drugs but something bad happened. We think James Murray had a hand in this. What do you say about that, Mickey?'

Ben Naylor was sweating but was trying his best not to show it, but Rees was too sharp to miss it.

Chadwell cleared his throat and said, 'I don't know what you're talking about. I just run this little scrap yard. I don't have anything to do with drugs, Mr Rees.'

Rees pointed his index finger at Chadwell and said, 'You run the drug scene in Bristol, Mickey, we all know that. I think Steve Quinn and Frank Hughes fucked up last Friday and either James Murray or you had them killed.' The beads of sweat were now clear to see on Naylor's forehead. 'What's wrong, Ben, is it getting too hot for you?' Naylor wiped the sweat away but did not answer. 'Come on, Rodger, we will leave these two gentlemen alone for now. But be sure of this, we will be back. Oh, and by the way, Ben, do give my best wishes to James Murray when you next see him. I believe you guys are becoming inseparable these days.'

Chapter Fifty-Eight

When Rees and Fell had gone, Chadwell motioned for Naylor to join him in the office. 'What's this with you and Murray. Are you feeding him information on me? Who else would have known about the deal on Friday except for the four of us?'

Naylor was seated opposite Chadwell and had regained some of his composure after the chat with Rees. 'Look, Mickey, the cops are trying to confuse you so that they can spilt us up. But that is not going to happen. I have worked for you for years and you are like a brother to me. Yes, I do occasionally see James, but we did time together and became good mates. He knows that I would never do anything that would harm you, Mickey.'

Chadwell stood up and looked down on Naylor. 'You better be telling the truth, Ben. I don't want to kill you, but you know that I will do if you ever betray me.'

Naylor stood up and put his arms around Chadwell's shoulders and said, 'No, Mickey, I would never ever betray you, I swear it.'

Patrick Rees called Skelton and gave him the heads up on the meeting with Chadwell and Naylor. He ended the conversation by saying, 'I think Murray was behind whatever it was that happened in London on Friday. Chadwell has lost two men and will have to replace them. I also suspect he is running short of drugs and will need more real soon.'

Chadwell and Naylor loaded the bailed cars from the crusher onto a lorry and the driver drove it off to the furnace in Wales. There would be no trace of Quinn or Hughes ever again. They closed the scrap yard just after five and Chadwell went home. Naylor, however, drove to Bath, where he had arranged to meet Murray and collect his share of the cash. It had been agreed that Murray would keep all the drugs and when they had been sold, Naylor would get his share in cash. It was 6.30 pm when Naylor entered the Saracen's Head. He used the back door as he had parked his car in the Waitrose supermarket car park opposite. Murray was already seated at a table by the window. He had a large suitcase with him which contained Naylor's share of the booty.

Murray stood up to greet his friend. 'What are you drinking, Ben?'

Naylor thought for a second and said, 'Get me a pint of Thatchers Gold please.'

Murray returned to the table with the drinks. This section of the pub was empty except for them. The other section was pretty full, with people wanting a drink after work.

Murray smiled and clinked glasses with Naylor. 'Well, it all went to plan on Friday, my friend. When my guys showed up with the guns, your guys were as good as gold. My guys tied them up, so they never came to any real harm. Your money is in the suitcase. Enjoy it.'

Naylor took a sip of his pint and said, 'Actually, those two guys did come to harm. Mickey was very suspicious, and I thought he was going to blame me for what happened. So I had to shift the blame. Mickey bought my version and so we put Steve and Frank in the car crusher. We sent the bailed cars to the furnace in Wales this morning. The thing is the police called round this morning. They know that we are missing two men. They haven't a clue what has happened to them, and they won't find out either. But they know I have been seeing you and they told Mickey. He was not very happy, but I assured him of my loyalty, and I think he bought that as well.'

Murray considered the news that Naylor had just delivered. 'So, you guys are now two men short. What are you going to do about it?'

Naylor took another swig from his glass. 'That won't be a problem. Mickey will bring in a couple of guys that he uses from time to time. We will be back up to strength tomorrow.'

'Jason and Jeff did a really good job on Friday. I have ordered them each a brand new Nissan Juke as a reward. They will be ready in about six weeks. But you don't have to wait that long, Ben, for your reward. Your share is in that suitcase. Just be careful how you spend it. We don't want Skelton getting to hear about it.'

Naylor put his glass down and said, 'Rest assured, James. That money will be going to my lawyers first thing in the morning. For a percentage, they will launder it and I will be the proud owner of a nice flat here in Bath. I will rent it out for about two thousand a month, which is not a bad little earner.' They clinked glasses and smiled.

The officer who was keeping observation on Murray's house called Skelton when he saw Murray getting into the taxi to meet Naylor. This would mean that Penny was alone. Alexander drove Skelton to the house a few minutes after Murray had left. Skelton rang the doorbell and a few seconds later, Penny opened the door.

'Oh, it's you two. James is not here. He took a taxi into town not long ago.'

Skelton brushed past her and said, 'We know that James took a taxi but it's you we have come to see.' After Alexander had entered the house, she closed the door and followed the officers into the sitting room. Alexander had taken a seat on the sofa whilst Skelton was standing by the patio doors.

'Have a seat Penny, DS Alexander and I want a word with you.' Penny sat down in the armchair and crossed her legs. As usual, she was feeling uncomfortable in the presence of the police, especially Skelton.

Skelton turned around so that he could see Penny and said, 'Tell us about what Jason and Jeff got up to last Friday up in London.'

Penny uncrossed her legs and said, 'All I know is that James was very pleased with them. Mickey Chadwell sent two of his men up to London with a big bag of cash to buy drugs. When they were doing the deal, Jason and Jeff showed up with guns and forced them to hand over the money and the drugs. They tied them up and put gaffer tape over their mouths and that was it.'

Both Skelton and Alexander were listening intently then Alexander spoke. 'Did they just tie them up or did they shoot them?'

Penny stood up abruptly and said, 'Oh no, they never hurt them. They just tied them up so that they couldn't get away and that was it. James was really pleased that there were no dead bodies to get rid of. The boys came back to the workshop where James was waiting for them. All they had to do was get rid of the car that they used. They torched it on some abandoned farm, but I don't know where.'

Penny was being very cooperative. The thought of losing her home and going to prison was having the desired effect on her. 'Just one more thing, Penny. Have you discovered where the lock-up is located?' asked Skelton.

Penny ran her hands through her hair and said, 'No, James has not taken me there.'

Skelton and Alexander thanked Penny and left the house. Alexander unlocked the car and they got in. 'I think, Bill, that Murray and Naylor pulled off quite a stunt on Friday. I think Naylor persuaded Mickey Chadwell that Steve Quinn and Frank Hughes had betrayed them, and they killed them. I suspect that both of them ended up in the car crusher and that they went to a furnace. The chances of finding any forensics will be pretty slim.'

Alexander started the car and said, 'Shall we put a tail on Murray in the hope that he leads us to the lock-up?' '

'I was just thinking the same thing, Bill. No point in doing anything this evening but I will get Richard Pearce to begin tailing him in the morning. The thing is, though, he has had the drugs and money since Friday, chances are that he will have already disposed of them by now. Not only has Murray done Chadwell over but we probably won't be able to prove anything against him. So, we are stuffed as well, and I don't like that one little bit.'

Chapter Fifty-Nine

It took three days before Murray drove to the lock-up with Richard Pearce on his tail. Pearce carefully parked the car twenty metres away from its location and waited and watched as Murray got out of the car. Pearce began taking pictures as Murray walked to the door with the keys in his hand. He photographed Murray opening the door and going inside. He called Skelton with the location and address of the lock-up. Skelton instructed him to stay put until Murray locked up and left. Murray only stayed about ten minutes before locking up. Pearce followed him home and returned to the station, his mission accomplished.

It was 12.45 when Alexander knocked on Skelton's door and entered. 'Where do you fancy having lunch today, sir?'

Skelton checked his watch and said, 'Well since it's Friday, Bill, why don't we try the fish and chips in the Saracen's Head washed down with a couple of pints.'

Alexander smiled and said, 'That pub seems to be turning into our local. If it was good enough for Charles Dickens, it's certainly good enough for us. Lead on, MacDuff.'

They left the police station, turned right and began approaching Bog Island. Three luxury coaches were unloading passengers, making the place very crowded indeed. They had to almost fight their way through the hordes of visitors who by the sound of their accents, were mainly Americans. They eventually made it to the front door of the pub and were delighted to see that their favourite seats by the window were free. 'Bill, you go and grab the table and I will get the drinks and order the food.'

Toby finished serving the lady standing next to Skelton. 'Good afternoon, Dan, how's your day going?'

'Hello, Toby, its going fine thanks, but a couple of pints for Bill and me plus two portions of fish and chips, and I will be in heaven. Where is Alex today?'

Toby finished pouring the drinks and said, 'He's in the kitchen today, the chef burned his hand and had to go to the hospital, so Alex is cooking.'

Skelton began paying for the food and said, 'Sorry to hear about the chef. I hope his hand is all right?'

Toby rested his hands on the bar and said, 'Yes, he will be fine, its nothing serious. He should be back in tomorrow I think.'

Skelton thanked Toby and carried the drinks over to Alexander. 'Here you go, Bill, get that down your neck. Fish and chips might be slightly delayed as Alex is cooking.'

Alexander placed his glass on the table and asked, 'Now that we know where Murray has his lock-up, should we pay it a visit?'

Skelton was thinking. He took another sip from his glass before answering. 'I doubt if we will find anything there. Murray had plenty of time to get rid of the drugs and cash. I mean it was a week ago today that they got Chadwell's goodies. He would have got the drugs onto the streets pretty damn quick, and the cash will have been laundered by now. I think we might just take a trip down and see exactly where it is. You can bet that Murray is probably scheming another assault on Chadwell's empire. But the stakes are going up all the time. Ben Naylor won't be able to pull that stunt again otherwise he is a dead man.'

Toby was bringing over the fish and chips. Skelton saw the two large cod and chips and the mushy peas. 'Go on, Bill, best get another couple of pints in to wash that lot down.'

Alexander turned round to see Toby carrying the plates. 'Bloody hell, Dan, I am going to have to go on a diet.'

After they had finished their lunch, the two officers began to make their way back to the office. They were just turning right onto Bog Island when Skelton noticed a well-dressed young lady inserting her card into an ATM. As she keyed in her PIN, he noticed a young foreign looking man aged in his early twenties. He was looking nervous. As the young lady was retrieving her card, the machine began dispensing the cash. As quick as a flash, the young man made a grab for the cash. He had not anticipated Skelton being on to him. Just as he had grabbed the cash, Skelton grabbed him by the arms and wrestled him to the ground. Alexander was onto him too. The guy had no chance to escape and was very soon in handcuffs. Alexander radioed for the custody van and it arrived in minutes. Skelton reunited the lady with her cash. 'Come on, Bill, let's get back to the office. You can do the paperwork, sunshine.'

Alexander glowered and said, 'Thank you very much, sir. I should just about finish it before its time to go home.'

Skelton went to his office and replied to some emails that had arrived whilst he had been out to lunch. When he had finished, he sat back in his chair and began thinking about what had happened in the last week. He was certain that at some point Murray was going to take on Mickey Chadwell, but where and when were the two questions that he had no answers to. He was intrigued by the operation that Chadwell was operating from the scrap yard in Bristol. Suddenly there was a knock on the door and in walked Alexander.

'I have finished the paperwork on that guy we arrested at the ATM. He has five previous convictions for similar offences. It seems he has a drug habit that needs feeding. He will be appearing before the magistrates court tomorrow morning.'

'Well done, Bill. Take a seat.'

Alexander sat down and looked closely at Skelton. 'What's on your mind, sir?'

Skelton had his hands behind his neck. 'Tell me, Bill, when you were a boy, what did you do after school in the evenings?'

Alexander was a little surprised by the question and placed his hands on the desk and said, 'Me and a few mates would play football most days. Why do you ask?'

Skelton smiled and said, 'That's what my friends did, but not me. You see when I was a boy of about eight, I walked into a scrap yard which was just up the road from where we lived. It was owned by a man called Bobby Dunn. I asked if I could play in the cars. They were mostly wrecks. He told me I could but if I wanted to make some money he would give me a job after school and at weekends. He actually owned another scrap yard, which was situated down a lane not far from the main yard. He kept three guard dogs in the main yard and two in what was called the top yard.

'As you know, Bill, I love dogs and very soon it became my job to walk and feed the dogs. One Saturday afternoon I had fed the dogs in the main yard and was about to walk to the top yard when Bobby said he would give me a lift. He had just acquired a Ford Popular which he was going to keep for a while before scrapping it for spare parts. We drove along the main road then turned left onto the long lane that led to the top yard. He suddenly stopped the car and got out. He opened my door and told me to get into the driver's seat. So, I slid over a little anxious. Bobby pointed out the clutch, brake and accelerator pedals and told me to put the car in gear. Before I knew it, I was driving the car. We did this every day from thereon.'

Skelton leaned his arms on the desk as Alexander studied his features. 'By the age of ten, Bill, I was driving cranes and lorries and even a bulldozer. I had my own personal tractor and dumper truck. After school, I would be at Bobby Dunn's before doing my homework. I loved it there and learnt so much about life. In those days before we realised about what our actions were having on the environment, the men in the yard would strip about six cars every day for spare parts, which we would sell. We had an area in the main yard which we used to set the shells of the cars on fire. It was my job to set the cars on fire. Can you imagine a ten-year-old boy being paid to set cars on fire? We used to burn the cars to soften the metal. Then Bobby would use our big crane to drop a two-tonne weight on them to crush them. This made it easier to load onto a lorry and take them to another scrap yard that had a crusher, or bailer as they are called.

So, whilst my school friends were out playing football, I was setting fire to cars and getting paid for it. I had a marvellous childhood, Bill.'

Alexander stood up and said, 'You never mentioned this before, Dan. Why have you brought it up now?'

Skelton leaned back in his chair and said, 'I have been thinking about Mickey Chadwell and the scrap yard that he runs in Bristol. I reckon that it's the perfect place to dispose of dead bodies.'

Chapter Sixty

It was a Saturday afternoon in November and Tommy Burns had arranged to meet friends in Victoria Park. It was a dry overcast day and quite chilly. Tommy was seventeen years old and had decided that university was not for him. The thought of incurring a huge amount of debt for tuition fees did not appeal to him. Tommy was good with his hands and his uncle was a carpenter. His uncle had promised him an apprenticeship and Tommy was looking forward to finishing school and starting work.

Tommy was good-looking boy of average height and weight. He liked to go running after school but was not interested in competing. He just liked to run on his own with his earphones in, listening to music. He often ran around Victoria Park after school and would see many fellow joggers. As well as running, he liked going to the gym two or three times a week.

It would be Tommy's eighteenth birthday in a couple of weeks and his parents had promised him a car. He was an only child and was particularly close to both his mum and dad. His mum was a primary school teacher, and his dad was a postman. They lived in a terraced house, in Bath Hampton which was a few miles from Victoria Park. He took the bus and got off at the bus station in Bath. The city was very busy as Bath Rugby had a match starting at 6 pm. There were hordes of supporters on the streets, many of them waring the club colours. Although Tommy didn't have a girlfriend, he had recently met a girl called Susan Peat. She was also seventeen and was planning to go to university and become a nurse just like her mother. Susan was the eldest of three sisters and had the looks to be a model, if she wanted such a career.

Susan lived almost next door to Brian Driscoll, who was Tommy's best friend. Brian and Tommy had gone to school together and were like brothers. The previous week, Brian was leaving his house to meet Tommy at McDonald's, when he bumped into Susan and suggested that she should join them. Tommy had never met Susan before but on being introduced, he was smitten by her. She was a tall blonde girl with piercing blue eyes and was very mature for her age. She also had an infectious laugh. Susan liked the look of Tommy and she very much hoped that he would invite her out for a date.

Tommy was on his way to meet Brian and Susan in the park. None of them had much money as they were all still at school and their pocket money did not go very far. Victoria Park is a very large park and very popular with families, especially at the weekend. Tommy had the idea that he would spend a couple of hours wandering through the park with Brian and Susan and then they could all go to McDonald's. Tommy was planning to ask Susan out on her own. He thought he would take her to the pictures next Saturday afternoon. He would let her choose which film they would see. He hoped that Brian would understand. Although they were great friends, he could hardly ask him to join them on their first date. Brian did not have a girlfriend, but it was just a matter of time before he found one.

Tommy had arranged to meet them at the café in the park. They would not actually go inside the café, as they needed their money for McDonald's. As Tommy made his way to the café, he spotted Brian and Susan, who were deep in conversation. Susan was wearing a blue coat to keep out the cold and Brian had on a hoodie. The hood covered his head so only his face was exposed. The two of them were laughing loudly when Susan spotted Tommy. A great big smile appeared on her face, and she ran to meet him. Tommy put out his arms to greet her and kissed her on the forehead.

'Hi Tommy, great to see you. How have you been?'

Tommy was smiling broadly. 'I'm great thanks, and great to see you.'

Tommy turned to see Brian, who was waiting to exchange high fives. Tommy raised his hand and took the high fives and then the boys exchanged hugs. Tommy was having the time of his life. Here he was in a beautiful park with his best friend and his prospective girlfriend. He hoped that one day, if he worked hard enough and saved as much as he could, he would buy a flat in Bath. Perhaps he and Susan would get married and have kids. He knew one thing for certain, that whoever he married, Brian would be his best man at the wedding.

The three friends joined hands, Tommy had Susan's left hand and Brian held her right. They walked hand in hand without a care in the world. It was what being a teenager should be. Happiness and joy. Tommy was wishing that he had brought a coat. He was just wearing a pullover on top of his tee-shirt and the temperature was slowly falling. Maybe he could cuddle Susan to get warm. He smiled at the thought. They had been walking for about ten minutes and were approaching the band stand. Tommy noticed that there were four boys sitting there. He reckoned they were about fifteen or sixteen and they were all smoking. Suddenly, Tommy got a whiff of the smoke. It was weed. Tommy did not do drugs and neither did Brian or Susan, but they all knew the smell of weed.

Tommy pulled Susan's hand in the opposite direction and all three made the turn. They now had their backs to the four boys. Brian spoke. 'Listen, after we go to McDonald's, why don't we all go back to my place and watch a film? Dad will have some beers in the fridge and we can chill out. You can stay the night, Tommy. How about that?'

It was Susan who spoke first. 'Oh yes, that would be great. What do you say, Tommy?'

Tommy dropped Susan's hand so that he could give these sweet, beautiful people a hug. 'Count me in, that's for sure.' They all laughed.

It was Susan who noticed the boys first. 'Look, there's those boys from the band stand. They look pretty much out of their minds. Let's head to McDonald's.'

The three friends began to quicken their step, but the four boys were running towards them. The smallest of them, who was wearing a Liverpool FC shirt and blue jeans, seemed to be the leader. Whilst Tommy and Brian were bigger and older than the four boys, it was two against four should a fight break out. Tommy's heart began to pump harder; he was going to have to protect his friends as best he could.

The boy in the Liverpool shirt was about sixteen and was only about five foot six. He had red hair and was plainly looking for trouble. It was obvious now that he was the gang leader. Suddenly he pulled out a very large knife from under his shirt. Susan screamed.

'I want your mobile phones and whatever cash you have on you.' To Tommy, it sounded like the boy had a Bristol accent. Tommy got in front of Brian and Susan.

'Look we don't want any trouble. We are leaving now. Just leave us alone.'

The gang leader swayed slightly and said, 'Give me the fucking phones and the money, or I will do you.'

He waved the blade from left to right. His three mates stood behind him. They made no effort to stop him. This was a joint enterprise attack. In the eyes of the law, all four were equally guilty to whatever was about to happen.

Susan began to sob, she was frightened. Brian put his arm over her shoulder. 'It's all right, we will be out of here in a minute.' Tommy took his phone and the twenty-pound note that was his pocket money from his pocket. As he moved closer to the red headed boy, he gripped the phone and the money in his right hand. His mum and dad would buy him a new phone. It happened in a flash. For no apparent reason, the boy stuck the knife deep into Tommy's neck. Susan let out a blood curling scream and Brian rushed forward to try and take the knife away. But the boy was off his face from the cannabis. He came at Brian and lunged with the blade. It went deep into Brian's tummy. Tommy had fallen to the ground, blood was spurting from the deep wound. He would be dead in a few seconds. Brian fell to his knees. He was clutching the wound to his tummy and could feel the warm blood on his fingers.

Susan was now screaming at the top of her voice. The other boys suddenly realised the extent of the trouble they had caused. One of them grabbed the red head and said, 'Come on, we have to get the fuck out of here.'

They didn't bother to pick up Tommy's phone or the twenty-pound note. They simply ran away, leaving Tommy dead and Brian fighting for his life.

Luckily for Brian, two young medical students heard Susan's screams and ran to the scene. One of them was wearing a scarf and he took it off and used it to apply pressure to the wound. The other called the ambulance and police. It was obvious that Tommy was beyond help. Yet more lives ruined due to a teenager carrying a knife.

Chapter Sixty-One

Skelton was in the kitchen and was just pouring himself a can of Fosters when his phone rang. It was Inspector Graham Symonds. Skelton answered, 'Hello, Graham, I take it this is not a social call on a Saturday afternoon.'

'I am sorry to disturb you, sir, but there has been a murder in Victoria Park and another young lad is fighting for his life. Can you come down straight away please?'

Skelton had been looking forward to having an Indian takeaway that evening. That was no longer going to happen. 'Yes, Graham, let me call Bill Alexander. He can pick me up and take us to the park. We should be there in half an hour.'

Skelton called Alexander and then Ross Turnbull. Turnbull answered on the second ring. 'Ross, there has been a murder in Victoria Park. Get the murder squad mobilised, Bill and I will be there in half an hour.'

'Yes sir, consider it done.'

Alexander drove them as close as he could to the forensic tent which had been erected by the forensic team. Bob Richards the head of forensics was already clad in white overalls and was giving directions to his team. The body of Tommy was still in situ, albeit under the protection of the blue forensic tent. Inspector Graham Symonds was in charge of the crime scene, something which he did very well.

'Come on, Bill, let's see what they have got for us.'

They got out of the car and Alexander counted nine police vehicles and an ambulance. Skelton led the way, and they approached Symonds. 'Hello, Graham, what do we have here then?'

Symonds cleared his throat and added Skelton and Alexander's names to his sheet. 'Three young friends out for a stroll in the park, two boys and a girl. Four boys who had been on the band stand approached them and demanded their mobile phones and cash. A young boy named Tommy Burns was handing over his mobile when the boy in a Liverpool FC shirt stabbed him in the neck. His friend called Brian Driscoll was then stabbed in the stomach. He is in a serious condition but should live. The girl was unhurt but is in shock. She is in the ambulance over there if you want to see her. Her parents are with her. She's not been able to describe the other boys in the group.'

Skelton saw that the rest of the murder squad were gathered outside the back of the tent. 'Come with me, Bill.'

The officers made their way over to join the rest of the team. The team turned to face Skelton and Alexander. Skelton had his hands in his coat pockets to help keep out the cold. 'Right, we have a young man dead and his friend is in hospital. Janet, I want you to go to the hospital and get a statement from him as soon as he is stable. His name is Brian Driscoll. See if you can get a description of his attackers and radio it in as soon as you can.'

Janet Griffin took her leave. Skelton continued. 'We understand that there were four boys hanging around the band stand. Our two boys and the girl were confronted by them. The knife man, or should I say boy, was wearing a Liverpool FC top and had red hair. It's unlikely they got here by car. At the moment, we don't know if they are local or from outside Bath. I want you guys to get over to the train and bus stations and review the CCTV. Find out if they boarded a train or bus and find out where they were headed. The killer was likely covered in blood, so he may have dumped the Liverpool top. He should still be easy to spot as he has red hair and is aged about sixteen. Bill and I will wait here for the Home Office pathologist to arrive. Right, off you go and make sure you keep me posted.'

Skelton and Alexander made their way to the entrance of the tent. Bob Richards was standing at the entrance. He was holding two pairs of paper overalls. 'Here you go, chaps, put these on and we can go inside. I am afraid it's not a pretty scene in there. The poor boy must have bled out. There is blood everywhere. We have recovered a mobile phone and a twenty-pound note which we think belonged to the victim. Look, here comes Dr Challis.'

Dr Challis was the Home Office pathologist, and he would make an initial examination of the body and later conduct a post-mortem examination to determine the cause of death. Dr Challis was already in his overalls, and he made his way to join the police officers. He saw Skelton and said, 'I was on my way to see Bath Rugby play this evening when I got the call. Shall we have a look inside the tent and see what we have?'

The officers stood aside and let Dr Challis enter the tent. The tent was well lit from powerful lights. The first thing that Dr Challis did was to take several photographs of the body in situ. He then knelt down and examined the young man's body. 'It looks to me that he received just the one blow to his neck. There are no defensive wounds to his hands. So, he must have been taken by surprise.'

Dr Challis turned the body over and took a rectal temperature reading. 'I'd say he has been dead for about an hour but no doubt you have witnesses to confirm this. There are more blood stains over there, which must have come from his friend. That's all I have to say at the moment. I will do the post-mortem tomorrow at noon.' He then turned to Bob Richards and said, 'You can have the body, Bob, and when you're finished, send it to the mortuary.'

Skelton and Alexander left the tent. Skelton placed his arm on Alexander's shoulder and said, 'I hate bloody knives, Bill. We have a poor innocent boy killed and his friend badly injured. The poor girl who witnessed this will probably be scarred for life. Meanwhile, we will have to track down the killers and lock them up for life. That's four more lives ruined not to mention the victim's families. I am going to announce a knife amnesty in the hope that we can get some knives off the streets and hopefully prevent another tragedy from happening. Let's get out of these overalls and pop over to the ambulance and see the girl.'

The officers approached the ambulance and as they got closer, they could hear the sound of crying. A paramedic was standing outside. He watched the officers approach. Skelton had his warrant card in his hand and flashed it to the paramedic. 'DCI Skelton, and this is DS Alexander. Is the girl in any state to make a statement?'

The paramedic shook his head and said, 'No, I am sorry, she is in a terrible state of shock. We are going to have to take her to the hospital and have the doctors check her over and treat her. I am sorry that there was nothing we could do for the boy. He was already dead when we arrived. My colleagues treated his mate. He was lucky that two medical students got to him and provided first aid. We think he should recover physically but mentally, who can say?'

Alexander's radio went off. It was Chris Spurrey who was at the train station. Alexander finished the conversation and turned to Skelton. 'Sir, they have the suspects on CCTV. The red head boy ditched his Liverpool top and presumably the murder weapon as well. They boarded a train for Bristol about twenty minutes ago. British Transport Police and Bristol have been informed. There will be a reception committee waiting to greet them when their train arrives. Chris is organising transport to pick them up at Bristol. I guess we can head back to the station and wait for the prisoners to arrive and interview them.'

Skelton gently slapped Alexander on the back and said, 'Good work, Bill. Make sure you put out the word that the Liverpool FC top and the knife need to be found. They are both vital evidence. Let's head to the station, we have a long night ahead of us. Hopefully tomorrow we can give poor Tommy's parents the news that we have found his killers. I hope it gives them a little comfort.'

Chapter Sixty-two

A few days later, Skelton was reviewing the witness statements regarding the murder of Tommy Burns. The murder weapon had been found, as had the Liverpool FC football shirt that the killer had worn. The DNA evidence was excellent. Although the red head had stabbed the victim to death, his three mates were also charged with murder. They would all stand trial at Bristol Crown Court in due course. All four had been remanded into custody.

There was a knock on the door and in walked Alexander. 'Have you got a minute, sir?'

Skelton leaned back in his chair and said, 'Yes, of course, Bill, take a seat. What's on your mind?'

Alexander pulled the chair from under the desk and sat down. 'I know that you have been very busy with Tommy Burns' murder but there seems to be a mini crime wave taking place up on Bear Flat.' This was one of the more exclusive areas of Bath and was renowned for its artists and poets.

Skelton placed his hands on the desk and said, 'Tell me more, Bill.' Alexander had a sheath of papers in his hand, and he spread them on the desk in front of him. 'Over the last four or five days, we have had reports of people having their mobile phones and wallets stolen. The offences have occurred in residential streets, so no CCTV has as yet turned up. Witnesses have said that two young white males, aged in their late teens, have approached them and demanded their wallets and mobile phones. There have been six victims so far, four females and two elderly men. They describe the suspects as both being about six feet tall and of a solid build. Once they have committed the offence, they simply walk off. Uniform have searched the area after each report and have increased patrols. But so far, they have failed to identify any suspects. I was just wondering if we should put a couple of our folk onto it.'

Skelton stood up and walked over to the window and looked out. It was almost noon on this November day, but it was almost dark. Heavy rain was battering the window. 'I saw those crime reports and thought it was a bit of unusual activity. To be honest with you, I doubt very much if anything will be happening today, but when the weather clears up delegate Janet Griffin and Peter Lowik to cruise around and see if they can identify the suspects. I will come and get you just before one and we will have lunch in Belushi's today. We are going to need umbrellas, that's for sure.'

It was just after one when they left the station. The streets were almost deserted due to the heavy rain. It was also fairly windy, so the umbrellas were not quite keeping them dry. When they got to Belushi's, both officer's trousers were soaking wet. Alexander pushed open the door and held it open for Skelton. Joe, like the good general manager he was, had the heating on. It was a very inviting atmosphere. One thing that Skelton hated was a cold pub. Whenever he came across one, he would refuse to stay and have a drink. Joe was standing behind the bar and was busy on his computer. On seeing the officers approaching, he immediately swung into action. He pulled two Fosters glasses from the shelf and began pouring. 'Good afternoon, gentlemen, that weather reminds me of when I used to live in Edinburgh.'

Alexander laughed and said, 'It reminds me of when I lived in Glasgow, it was always raining up there. What are you having to eat, Dan?'

Skelton thought for a second and said, 'I fancy a hamburger today. This is the first time we have had lunch this week. We have been so busy working on that case.'

They took their drinks into the back room of the pub and sat down. Skelton had his back to the window so that he could see what was happening in the bar. Joe brought them their food and another couple of pints. Skelton shook the leg of his trousers and said, 'We should just be about dry by the time we finish this. With that murder enquiry keeping us busy, I've not had much time to think about James Murray and Ben Naylor. I wonder what they have been up to. I have spoken to Patrick Rees and there is not much happening in Bristol.' Alexander took a drink and said, 'Do you think Murray will be content in just running Bath? After all Mickey Chadwell is a very dangerous man.'

Skelton pushed his empty plate aside and used the napkin to wipe his lips. 'No, Murray has Ben Naylor in Chadwell's camp. He is there for a reason. I think Murray is just biding his time, waiting for the right opportunity to strike. My guess is that he will strike Chadwell at his scrap yard. There will be no witnesses and no CCTV.'

Alexander pushed his empty plate aside and said, 'But what if Chadwell decides to take Murray out in Bath? We know that he is good at hiding bodies. We have both been to Murray's house. He has no CCTV. Chadwell could hit him there and take the body back to the scrapyard and safely dispose of it.'

Skelton gulped down some more beer. 'That's a good point, Bill. It's easy to kill someone without leaving any blood behind.'

Alexander looked out of the window of the pub and said, 'I think that rain is on for the day. I will go and get us another couple of beers.' As he stood up, he saw two young men carrying drinks into the back room. They were both about six feet tall and solidly built. They took a seat and ignored Alexander, who was now heading towards the bar.

Joe saw him approaching and said, 'I take it you want two more?'

Alexander smiled and said, 'If it was up to me, we would be in here all afternoon. I hate getting soaked in the rain.'

Having paid for the drinks, Alexander was making his way slowly back to Skelton. As he got closer to where the two young men were seated, he noticed that one of them had two mobile phones and two wallets on the table in front of him. He had seen some young people with two mobile phones. One was usually for business and the other for personal use. But he had never seen anyone with two wallets except for thieves. He carried on walking back to Skelton and placed the drinks on the table and sat down.

He leaned closer to Skelton and quietly said, 'You see those two guys behind me, one of them has two mobile phones and two wallets. They might just be the guys behind those robberies on Bear Flat.'

Skelton lifted his glass and took a sip. He closely watched the two men. They certainly matched the descriptions given by the victims. 'Well, Bill, we have enough suspicion to search them. Let's go.'

They both stood up and began walking. Alexander positioned himself in the doorway blocking their exit, should they decide to run. Skelton took out his warrant card and held it in his left hand and approached the table.

'We are police officers and I would like to know why you have two wallets and two mobile phones in front of you.'

The guy who Skelton had been addressing laughed and said, 'One of the phones is mine and the other is his. The same with the wallets. So, if you don't mind, leave us alone to enjoy our drinks.'

Skelton leaned down and scooped up the wallets. 'I want both your names.'

Skelton could see the anxiety in their faces. Alexander left the doorway and placed his hands on the guy closest to him and said, 'Just sit tight, pal, and give the officer your name and address.'

Both the suspects remained silent. Skelton opened the first wallet and pulled out a driving licence. The photograph was that of a sixty-two-year-old man. He then opened the second wallet. He found a driving licence in it which belonged to a sixty-six-year-old. Skelton held out the driving licences and said, 'You two must have had amazing cosmetic surgery. You are both under arrest on suspicion of robbery and handling stolen goods.'

Skelton and Alexander handcuffed the two suspects and waited for the custody van to arrive. 'Bill, rather than get soaked walking back to the station, let's take a lift in the van. Let me go and explain to Joe what's happened. Thankfully there are no other customers in today.'

Chapter Sixty-Three

Murray closed the door of his house and began walking to his car, which was parked on the road. He noticed the young blond boy that lived next door. He had met his parents David and Amanda Thomas but had never actually spoken to the boy. He seemed to recall that his father had said his son's name was Trevor. The boy had a black Labrador with him that was walking off the lead behind him.

As the boy approached, he gave him a smile and said, 'Hello I am James and I live here. I have met your mum and dad and I think your name is Trevor.'

The boy returned the smile and said, 'Yes that's right, my name is Trevor, and this is my dog, Johnny.' The dog began wagging its tail at the mention of its name.

Murray got down and began patting the dog. 'What a lovely dog, he is obviously well trained.'

Trevor smiled again. 'Yes, Dad sent him away when he was a pup to a professional gundog trainer. He did a fantastic job on him and taught me how to work him. I go shooting with my dad, but I prefer to work Johnny rather than shoot. Do you shoot, James?'

Murray raised himself up and said, 'No actually, I don't shoot, Trevor. I was brought up in London and there is no shooting there. But now that I live in Bath, I might try some clay pigeon shooting. That could be fun.'

Trevor patted Johnny on his head and said, 'Just ask my dad, he will take you clay pigeon shooting. There are quite a few places around here. You should apply for a shotgun licence and maybe come shooting with me and my dad. We go down to Devon, it's great down there.'

Murray could hardly explain that having killed a police officer, he had absolutely no chance of being granted a shotgun licence. Murray patted the dog again. He was not really a dog person, but this well-trained gundog was a different kettle of fish.

'Trevor, tell your mum and dad that they must bring you around one evening for drinks. I take it you are allowed alcohol?'

Trevor grinned and said, 'My mum is a doctor and let me have a glass of wine with dinner when I was fifteen. I much prefer lager, so I have one of those with dinner most nights. I know that you have to handle alcohol in moderation, but it didn't stop me getting pissed on my birthday!'

They both laughed and Johnny joined in with wagging his tail in unison. Murray pressed the key fob and the doors unlocked. 'It was great meeting you, Trevor, and make sure that you bring your mum and dad around for drinks.'

Murray got into the car and drove to the workshop on the industrial estate. It was a Saturday morning, and the estate was not as busy as during the week. Jason Andrews and Jeff Roberts were already sitting at the table drinking tea. Murray walked in and acknowledged his men with a simple 'Morning' and picked up the electric kettle and filled it with water. 'Do you guys want some more tea?'

They both declined. Murray turned to Andrews and said, 'So why did you want to see me?'

Andrews cleared his throat and stood up. 'One of our dealers was warned off last night.'

Murray banged his hand hard on the table and said, 'Who warned him off and what the fuck have you two done about it?'

Andrews sat back down and said, 'We don't know who the guy was, but our guy is Ryan Riggins. He was working in Widcombe last night. Ryan is a good lad and was walking past the Ram pub when he was approached by a big guy with a beard. The guy with the beard told him that if he caught him dealing again in Bath, he would end up being fished out of the river. He said that only Mickey Chadwell's men could deal in Bath.'

Murray was silent for a second or two. 'That's odd. Ben Naylor has never mentioned that Chadwell was thinking of moving into the Bath scene. Has Ryan ever seen this guy with the beard before?'

Andrews got up to rinse his mug in the sink and said, 'Ryan said that he had seen the guy a couple of times before. He's not sure if he lives in Bath though.'

Murray sat down with his mug of tea. 'Okay, leave this with me. I will call Ben and arrange a meeting with him. I don't like this one little bit. I want you two to pick up Ryan and drive around the city this evening and see if he can pick out the guy with the beard. If he does, then you two grab him and bring him here. Make sure that you are tooled up.'

Andrews and Roberts stood up and went outside. They had travelled together in one of the new Nissan Jukes that Murray had given them. Murray called Naylor and arranged to meet him in McDonald's at 2 pm.

Murray arrived first and ordered two teas. He was not hungry as he had too much on his mind. He needed to find out from Naylor what Mickey Chadwell was up to. Naylor walked into McDonald's and saw Murray sitting by the window. He waved and walked over to the table and sat down. 'Hi, James, what can I do for you?'

Murray handed over one of the teas and said, What's Mickey up to here in Bath?'

Naylor was totally surprised by the question. 'I don't know what you mean, James. What's happened?'

Murray leaned across the table and spoke quietly. 'Last night one of my boys was warned off from dealing. He was told by a guy with a beard that if he was caught dealing again, then they would have to fish his body out of the river. He said that only Mickey Chadwell's crew could deal in Bath.'

Naylor was confused, it was obvious from his facial expression. 'I don't know anything about this, James. Mickey has never mentioned anything to me that he was planning to take over Bath. I was with him all day yesterday and he never said a thing about Bath. We have been busy arranging for more stocks and our dealers are really busy in Bristol. We had to take on a couple of guys to replace the two that we lost. One is called Stan Perry, he lives in Bristol and Ivor Thomson, who lives in Twerton. Funnily enough, Ivor has a beard.'

Murray was slightly confused. He was certain that Ben was telling the truth. Ben was Chadwell's right-hand man. If Chadwell was thinking of taking Murray on, he would have confided in Ben. This meeting had raised more questions than answers. Murray finished his tea.

'Ben, this is an odd situation. I've got my men out looking for this guy with the beard. We will have to find him and get some answers out of him. In the meantime, if Chadwell mentions anything to you about Bath, you let me know straight away.'

The meeting broke up and they left the restaurant in silence.

Chapter Sixty-Four

Chadwell was in his office at the scrap yard. He was on his own when the door opened and in walked Ivor Thomson. He had known Thomson for a few years, they had worked together off and on. Thomson and Stan Perry had replaced Steve Quinn and Frank Hughes, who had been killed. Thomson was a big man with a bushy brown beard. He had served seven years in the army and had seen action on a number of fronts. He had lost count of the number of enemy combatants that he had killed. He had taken a number of handguns as souvenirs and he was carrying one on him now.

Chadwell looked up and saw Thomson approaching. 'Come on in, Ivor, and take a seat. How did it go last night?'

Thomson sat down. 'It was a piece of cake, Mickey. I knew where to find Murray's dealer and I warned him off. The poor guy nearly pissed himself.' They both laughed.

Chadwell stood up and asked, 'You didn't mention this little secret of ours to Ben, did you?'

Thomson leaned back in his chair and said, 'No of course not, Mickey. You told me that this was a secret operation. As an ex-sergeant in the army, I know when to keep a secret. If Ben asks me about what I have been up to, I will deny everything.'

Chadwell placed one hand on Thomson's shoulder and said, 'Murray's men are going to be looking for you. That should keep them busy. They have lost a dealer, which will be affecting their revenue. I want you to keep off the streets of Bath for a week. Then when they think it's all safe and quiet, we launch phase two of the exercise. That will really piss them off.'

It was just after 7 pm, Roberts was driving, Andrews was in the back of the Nissan Juke and young Ryan Riggins was in the front passenger seat, so that he could get a clear view. They were looking for the man with the beard who had scared the life out of Riggins. The guy had pulled a gun on him and warned him that if he caught him dealing again, he was a dead man. Both Roberts and Andrews were carrying guns for their own protection. They weren't going looking for a guy with a gun unarmed.

Roberts turned to Riggins and asked, 'What time was it when this guy approached you?'

Riggins was looking ahead scanning both sides of the pavement. 'It was about this time last night. I was walking towards the Ram, and he came from the opposite direction. I am sure I have seen him before. He's a big guy with a beard, so he's not easy to forget.'

They turned into Widcombe high street and saw the doctor's surgery on the right and the Ram on the opposite side. Apart from a young couple enjoying a fag outside the Ram, the street was deserted.

Roberts found a parking space outside the pharmacy and parked the car. It would be too dangerous to drive around the streets of Bath. The police might wonder what they were up to and pull them over. They were carrying guns, which the police would regard as highly suspicious. It was going to be a waiting game. It was 7.30 when Riggins replacement showed up. He would walk up and down the high street hoping to deal some drugs and lure the man with the beard into a trap. In the course of an hour, the dealer had made four deals, but there was no sign of the man with a beard. At 8.30, they decided that the guy was not going to show up. They called it a night and agreed to meet up again the next night. Andrews passed Riggins £40 for his time.

For the next five nights, they repeated the exercise but with no luck. On Saturday morning Roberts and Andrews drove to the workshop just off the Lower Bristol Road. Murray's car was parked outside. They pushed open the door and saw Murray sitting at the table talking on his phone. When he saw them, he ended the call. 'Good morning, lads, and how did it go last night?'

Andrews was headed for the kettle to make some tea and began filling it with water. 'Another waste of time, James. I am beginning to wonder if this guy actually exists. Young Riggins gets to sit in a warm car for a few hours and gets paid for it. We saw lots of guys with beards but not the guy who supposedly threatened Ryan. I think we should call it a day. The one thing I will say is this, Ryan is not prepared to deal for us again.'

Murray listened intently and said, 'Do you know what I am thinking? I think this guy with the beard was some sort of vigilante. He happened to know that Ryan deals drugs and decided to frighten him. Just for good measure, he mentions Mickey Chadwell's name. Of course, we swallowed the bait hook, line and sinker. I met Ben Naylor last week and he said he knew nothing about Chadwell wanting to take us on. In addition to this, you guys have been out all week and Ryan's replacement has been able to go about his business unhindered. None of our other dealers have had a problem except with the cops. Okay, this is what we do. Let Ryan bugger off and do whatever he wants. What's the name of his replacement?'

Andrews brought over two mugs of tea and said, 'Billy Raeburn, is his name. He works in the ticket office at the train station. He likes coke, so he is effectively working for us for free.'

Murray sipped his tea. 'Right, give young Ryan a hundred quid and tell Billy that he is definitely on the books. As far as I am concerned, it's business as usual.'

Chapter Sixty-Five

Skelton and Alexander were sitting in Skelton's office enjoying a square sausage sandwich and a mug of tea. It had been a relatively quiet couple of weeks. There had been a few missing person enquiries which had been resolved amicably. As ever, there were sudden deaths to investigate. These were largely due to natural causes or drug overdoses. With a little bit of extra time on their hands, the officers had even re-opened a couple of cold cases. These were two murder cases that had remained unsolved. Despite their best efforts, it seemed that they would remain unsolved.

Billy Raeburn had finished work at five and had gone home to his parent's house. He was an only child. His father worked for the council and his mother was a housewife. They lived in a two-bed council flat in Fox Hill. Billy was twenty-five and had worked for the railway since leaving school. He had recently broken up with his girlfriend, who objected to him using drugs. He was not a heavy user but liked a line of coke a few times a week. He found the cost of buying the drugs was leaving him short of money. The dealer that he used said he could make good money dealing himself. Billy was of medium build and could not be described as being handsome. He was the sort of guy that blended perfectly into the background. Perfect for being a drug dealer. Initially, he dealt to his friends and acquaintances. Then in addition to this, he was assigned to Widcombe where there many people taking drugs. He soon had a regular clientele.

Billy went to his room and got changed out of his uniform. He pulled on a shirt and a pair of black jeans. He put on a heavy jumper as it was a cold night. He heard his father's voice, who was just home from work. Dinner would be ready shortly. It was a Monday night, so he already knew that they would be having lamb chops. Mum was a creature of habit. He knew precisely, what would be for dinner every night of the week. On Fridays they always got fish and chips from the local fish and chip shop.

All in all, Billy enjoyed living at home. He knew that he could never afford to buy a flat on his salary. The ten percent deposit that he needed would be very difficult to achieve unless he dealt more drugs. So far, he had not caught the attention of the police, but he knew that he had to be really careful. He had almost £800 under his pillow at the moment, and a stash of drugs. If he got arrested, he would certainly be going to prison.

After dinner, he put on his coat. It was late November and frost had been forecast for overnight. He decided to put on a scarf as well. His drugs beat covered Widcombe to Bath Train Station. Where the train station was situated, the river Avon flowed. This was a wide stretch of water, and the current was treacherous. Anyone falling into the river was as good as dead. He checked his burner phone. He had three texts from his usual clients. They lived locally so he would drop off their drugs before taking the bus into the city.

He got off the bus at the bus station and headed for the train station where he worked. He would walk past the train station and enter the carpark, which led to a bridge over the river Avon. He immediately felt the cold coming off the river. He walked across the bridge and Widcombe village was directly ahead of him. He had several regular customers or clients in Widcombe, and he knew he would sell quite a bit of weed tonight. He crossed the main road and turned left; he could see the Ram pub just ahead. One of his regulars was standing outside the Ram smoking a fag. They both waved to each other. When the deal was done, Billy walked along the high street and saw another client standing outside the florist shop. This guy wanted a line of coke. No problem. Having reached the end of the high street, Billy turned around and headed back towards the station.

When he got to the pedestrian crossing he pushed the button for the lights to change in his favour. Suddenly, he was aware of a large man with a beard standing next to him. The man tapped him on the shoulder and smiled. 'Can you sort me out with some coke, mate. I haven't used you before but the guy who is usually here who is called Ryan hasn't been around for a while.'

Billy looked at the guy. No one had told him to be suspicious of a big man with a beard. 'Yes, I can sort that out for you. I have three wraps left.'

The lights turned green and they began crossing the road. When they got to the bridge, the street was deserted. No pedestrians and virtually no traffic. Billy stopped on the bridge and pulled out the drugs. 'Here you go mate, that will cost you ninety quid.'

The big, bearded man smiled and said, 'Excellent, let me get my money out.' The man who was wearing a heavy overcoat put his hand into the right pocket and pulled out a gun. Billy froze in complete fear. He didn't hear the gun go off. He was already dead. Ivor Thomas picked up Billy's lifeless body and threw it over the bridge into the river Avon. There were no witnesses and the CCTV in the train station did not cover the bridge.

Thomson had driven into the city, but his car had cloned plates. The police would have their cameras, but they would be unable to trace his car. He would change the plates again, first thing in the morning. The route he had travelled had been carefully chosen. He had parked the car on the edge of Widcombe and remained in the car waiting for his victim. There was no way that he would walk into Widcombe high street, that was too dangerous owing to all the CCTV cameras. This was a well-planned mission, just as he had been taught when he had been a soldier. Mission accomplished.

Chapter Sixty-Six

It had gone midnight and Billy Raeburn had not returned home. His mother had tried calling his mobile, but it went through to message mode. By 2 am she began to get desperately worried. If Billy was going to stay out, he would always ring and let either his mum or dad know. This was completely out of character for Billy. Mrs Raeburn had no way of knowing that her son was dead and his body was in the river Avon.

Mrs Raeburn went to bed, but she could not sleep. She hoped that Billy would come home and get changed for work in the morning. He started work at eight so he would have to come home by seven, to shower and shave. Mr and Mrs Raeburn got up at seven, hoping to see Billy come in the door, but he never showed up. Mr Raeburn worked for the council and his office was just a short walk from the train station. He reasoned that his son had probably met a girl and had gone back to her place. Maybe he would go straight to work this morning without his uniform. Mr Raeburn would go to the station before going to work. He would have a few words to say to his son for upsetting his mother.

Mr Raeburn caught the bus and got off at the bus station. He walked through the entrance to the train station and headed for the ticket office where his son worked. He desperately looked to see if his son was there, but it was a young lady who was dispensing the train tickets. He recalled that Billy had said that she was called Ann. Mr Raeburn took his place in the queue and waited. When it was his turn, he said to Ann, 'Good morning, I am Billy's father. He never came home last night. Has he showed up for work this morning?'

Ann was clearly perplexed by this news. 'No, I'm sorry, we haven't seen Billy this morning and he hasn't called in. Have you checked with the hospital, in case there has been an accident or something?'

Mr Raeburn realised that this was a good idea, so he thanked Ann and went outside to the taxi rank. He took a cab to the RUH, the main hospital in Bath. Mr Raeburn explained who he was to the receptionist and gave her Billy's details. No one by that name had been admitted to the hospital. She even checked with the mortuary but thankfully that came back as a blank. He called his wife and updated her. Now he would have to go to the police station. Luckily it was situated across the road from his office in Manvers Street. At the police station, he completed a missing person form. He was assured by the police officer that his son was likely to turn up safe and well in a day or two. On leaving the police station, Mr Raeburn went to his office and told his boss what had happened and went home to be with his wife. All that they could do now was to hope and pray that Billy would turn up safe and well.

Ivor Thomson's first job this morning was to change the registration plates on his car. It was safely parked in his garage. He kept the door closed from prying eyes. It only took him ten minutes to finish the job. He opened the garage door and reversed the car out. He got out, closed the garage door and locked it. He began his journey to the scrap yard in Bristol and arrived just before nine. He went to the office and found Mickey Chadwell eating a bacon sandwich.

'Morning, Mickey, it looks like you are enjoying that.'

Chadwell finished chewing and asked, 'How did it go last night, Ivor?'

Thomson sat down with a smug smile on his face. 'To be honest, Mickey, It could not have gone any better, even if I say so myself. I shot the boy and threw him in the river. There were no witnesses and no CCTV. James Murray is now a man short and it might be a few days before they find the young man's body.'

Chadwell stood up and patted Thomson on the head. 'Well done, Ivor. Don't mention this to anyone, especially Ben.'

Jason Andrews and Jeff Roberts were seated in the workshop just off the Lower Bristol Road and were drinking tea. Roberts was checking his phone and said, 'Young Billy Raeburn never replied to the three text messages I sent him last night. That's not like Billy. I will send him another one now and see if he gets back to me. If he doesn't, then we will pop into the train station and have a word with him. He has probably run out of credit on his phone and can't reply.'

There was no word from Billy, so they decided they would go into Bath for lunch and drop in on Billy. He was bound to be needing some more drugs to sell.

Roberts drove and Andrews sat in the front seat. It was a cold day and they had the heater on to keep warm. They parked the car, walked to the train station and went into the ticket office, which was deserted except for a young lady behind the partition. Roberts went up to the booth and said, 'We are friends of Billy Raeburn. Is he around?'

Ann smiled and said, 'No, Billy didn't turn up for work today and his dad was here earlier looking for him. He never went home last night. His dad was going to check with the hospital in case something has happened to him.'

They left the ticket office and Andrews said, 'I don't like this one little bit. Billy was working Ryan Riggins old patch. That guy with the beard threatened to shoot Ryan and put him in the river. What if he has gone and done that with Billy? We best pass on lunch and go and see James. He will want to know about this, but we better call in on Billy's flat, just in case he has turned up.'

On discovering that Billy had not come home, they drove to James Murray's house. Murray let them in and all three sat down around the kitchen table. Andrews broke the news to Murray, who sat in silence for a few seconds. 'Well, there was nothing on the lunchtime news about a body being found. What if Billy has just done a runner? It's not the first time that one of my boys has made off with the drugs and my money. But I must say, it is worrying. I best meet up with Ben Naylor and see if he knows anything about this. It is possible that Mickey Chadwell is behind this, in which case it could mean war.'

Later that day, Murray and Naylor were seated in the Saracen's Head. They were both perched on stools at a table by the window. Just behind them was the Charles Dickens corner, where Dickens would come to write and enjoy a beer or two. Although the bar was quite busy, there was no one in earshot to hear what they were saying. Murray took a sip of his lager and said, 'One of my boys has gone missing, Ben. He was out working last night in Widcombe and never went home. He works in the ticket office of the train station in Bath but never showed up this morning for work. It could be he has just done a runner, but he has been very dependable. You know that my lad Ryan Riggins was threatened by a man with a beard a couple of weeks back. I am just worried that young Billy might have come to harm. Do you know anything about this?'

Naylor was listening intently to Murray. He took a sip from his cider and said, 'It's got nothing to do with us, James. If Mickey was behind it, I would have known for certain. We do have an enforcer with a beard, and he is called Ivor Thomson. We haven't given him any instructions to take out one of your guys. I reckon that your boy has just done a runner with your cash. It happens, you know. If he's been reported missing to the cops, they will find him once he starts using his debit or credit cards. He probably won't return to Bath as you would seriously hurt him. Forget it, James, it's not worth worrying about. Let me get us another drink.'

Chapter Sixty-Seven

It was just after 11 am when Skelton and Alexander emerged from the mortuary. The post-mortem examination confirmed that young Billy had been shot in the heart with a 9 mm bullet. Alexander unlocked the car and Skelton said, 'We best go and see Mr and Mrs Raeburn and break the news. We need to find out if Billy had any enemies that they know of. So far, we don't have a motive for the killing, which will make it more difficult to solve. I suspect that Billy was working for James Murray, so after we have been to see the Raeburns, we will swing by and have a word with Murray. I am going to call Bob Richards and tell him to close the pedestrian bridge at the back of the train station and carryout a fingertip search, to see if they can find the bullet casing. I am going to instruct the team to start canvassing for possible witnesses. We will have to launch an appeal for help from the public. I will leave that to Chief Superintendent Sawyers.'

They parked the car outside the flat where Mr and Mrs Raeburn lived. They knew that George Sewell, a police liaison officer, would be inside trying to give the grieving couple some comfort. Skelton knocked on the door and it was quickly opened by George Sewell. 'Good morning, George, can we come in?'

Sewell stood aside to let the officers in. Mr and Mrs Raeburn were sitting on the sofa holding hands. Mrs Raeburn's eyes were red.

Sewell went behind the sofa and place a hand on the necks of the couple. 'I am Detective Chief Inspector Skelton, and this is Detective Sergeant Alexander. We have just attended the post-mortem of your son and I am very sorry to have to tell you that he had been shot. If it's any comfort to you, he died instantly.'

Mrs Raeburn burst into tears and Sewell pulled some tissues from his pocket and placed them into her hands. Mr Raeburn looked up and said, 'Who would want to kill our Billy? He wouldn't harm a fly.'

Skelton nodded to Alexander to take a seat on one of the armchairs. Skelton sat down on the other one. 'We know that Billy was dealing drugs. Did anyone ever threaten him, or do you know if he had any enemies?'

Mr Raeburn stood up and tried to compose himself as best he could. He walked over to the mantelpiece and rested his right hand on it. Raeburn took a deep breath and said, 'Billy was not a big time dealer. He just did it to make some pocket money. He never mentioned anyone bothering him. I think he mainly dealt to his friends and guys he got to know.'

Skelton stood up and put his hand on Raeburn's shoulder. 'When you feel up to it, I want you to give George a list of all of Billy's friends and any girlfriends that he had. We are going to have to talk to them and see if they can shed any light on this. We will be making an appeal on the television later today and on social media as well. I can assure you that we will do our very best to find whoever it was that killed your son.'

After leaving Mr and Mrs Raeburn, they drove to the house of James Murray. Skelton rang the bell, Murray opened the door.

'Oh, it's you two again, you best come in. Penny is in the kitchen preparing lunch. We will go into the sitting room.' Skelton and Alexander took a seat on the sofa whilst Murray sat down on an armchair. 'Well, what can I do for you two today?'

Skelton sat forward on the sofa. 'Does the name Billy Raeburn mean anything to you?'

Murray's heart missed a beat. Billy had gone missing, and it was assumed that he had done a runner. 'No, I can't say I have heard that name before. Why, what's he done?'

Skelton waited a second and then said, 'We fished his body out of the river yesterday, but he hadn't drowned. Someone had shot him.'

Murray was genuinely shocked. He expected that young Billy would eventually turn up. There would of course be consequences for him, such as a good hiding. Murray stood up and walked over to the window and looked out. 'I am very sorry to hear that, Inspector, but it's got nothing to do with me.'

Skelton leaned back in the sofa and said, 'Billy was dealing drugs for you. We believe that Mickey Chadwell has decided to take over Bath, but not in a subtle fashion. He had Billy Raeburn killed to warn you off. We think it's just a question of time before he comes gunning for you.'

Murray was sweating but was doing his utmost to hide it. Murray turned and faced the detectives. Skelton could see the fear in his eyes. He had unnerved the man, just the way he had hoped for. 'Inspector, I don't know what you are talking about. I have never heard of this guy Billy, and I don't deal drugs any more. You know I went to prison for that in London, so I stopped doing drugs.'

Skelton stood up, as did Alexander. Skelton walked over to Murray and stared into his eyes. 'We both know that you are talking bollocks. Mickey Chadwell wants to run Bath. I honestly hope that he kills you, but I don't want any more innocent kids getting killed in this drugs war. I warned you once before that you are my worst enemy. If you and Chadwell want to kill each other, that's fine by me. I look forward to attending the post-mortems.'

The detectives went out to the car. They were just about to get in when they heard a voice call, 'Hey, Dan, how are you doing?'

They turned around to see young Trevor Thomas. Skelton smiled and said, 'Hello, Trevor, not at school today?'

'No, we got the day off. I am just going down the road to see a friend and chill out. What brings you up here?'

Skelton rested his hand on the roof of the car and said, 'We are just making some enquiries, Trevor. Nothing for you to worry about.'

They said goodbye and the detectives got in the car. Alexander looked across at Skelton and said, 'You certainly scarred the shit out of Murray. What do you think he will do?'

Skelton adjusted his tie and said, 'I honestly have no idea what he will do. If it was Mickey Chadwell that was responsible for young Billy's murder, I thought Ben Naylor would have warned Murray what was coming. I wonder if Chadwell no longer trusts Naylor. Patrick Rees warned Chadwell that Naylor and Murray were spending quite a bit of time together here in Bath. All I can say with some confidence is that the body count is going to increase.'

They drove back to the police station. As they were getting out of the car, Skelton said, 'I think we will skip lunch today. I am going to have to go and brief the chief super on what's going on. He will want to do an appeal on the TV. I need to see what Janet has put out on social media. Maybe we can have a couple of beers after work. I fancy getting a Chinese takeaway this evening.'

Murray was rattled. As soon as the cops had left, he called Ben Naylor. They agreed to meet in the Saracen's Head at six. Murray arrived early and took a seat below Dicken's corner. Naylor arrived a few minutes later and Murray got him a pint of cider. 'What's on your mind, James? Is something bothering you?'

Murray took a long slug from his glass of cider and put it down on the table. 'You are bloody right something is bothering me. Skelton and Alexander came to my house this morning. One of my lads went missing the other day. We thought he had simply done a runner. The cops fished him out of the river yesterday, he had been shot. The cops think Mickey Chadwell is behind it. What do you know about it, Ben?'

Naylor had listened in disbelief. 'That's rubbish, James. I am the number one enforcer for Mickey. If Mickey had ordered a hit, I would have been the guy to do it. We do have a couple of new guys, as you know, perfectly able to do a hit, but I would have known if Mickey had authorised it. This is very strange. You don't think the cops are trying to stir something up between you and Mickey? They would love nothing better than for you guys to go after one another.'

Murray drained his glass. 'Let me go and get another couple of pints, I need to think about this. It could be that someone else has moved in on my patch. If they have, then he's a dead man.'

Murray was being served by Dale, the new general manager. He paid for the drinks and was heading back to his table when the front door of the bar opened and in walked Skelton and Alexander. Murray almost dropped the drinks but managed to regain his composure. Skelton smiled and said, 'Well, I wasn't expecting to see you twice in one day.'

His eyes darted towards Dickens corner and he saw Ben Naylor sitting with an almost finished drink in front of him. 'I see that you and Ben are having one of your regular get togethers. Are you and Ben man enough to take on Mickey Chadwell?'

Murray ignored the question and said, 'You know that Ben and I are old friends. We are just having a friendly drink. I would buy you both a drink, but we are not friends.'

When Naylor left the scrap yard just after five, Chadwell activated the tracker which he had placed underneath Naylor's car. Since the London job when he had lost both the drugs and money, he had his suspicions that Naylor and Murray were somehow behind it, but he had no proof. The cops, however, had warned him that Naylor and Murray were regularly being seen together in Bath. Ivor Thomson was driving and Chadwell was sitting in the passenger seat with his laptop. They followed Naylor's car at a discreet distance. Chadwell could easily follow it on the laptop. 'It looks like he is heading for Bath, Ivor. I reckon he is on his way to see James Murray. He will have realised by now that one of his dealer's has gone missing. It's only a matter of time before the police find the body and that really will piss him off.'

Chadwell was carefully watching the screen when Thomson's phone rang. It was on hands free, so he took the call. It was Stan Perry. 'Yes, Stan, I am in the car with Mickey.'

They heard Perry's voice say, 'I've just had a news update on my phone. The police in Bath recovered a body from the river Avon last night and a post-mortem has revealed that the guy had been shot. I thought you guys would want to know.'

Thomson ended the call. Chadwell turned and looked at Thomson and said, 'Murray will have heard the news by now. He is going to be a worried man. He must be meeting Ben to see what he knows about it. I can see from the tracker that Ben is heading into Bath now. That will be a very interesting meeting.'

Chapter Sixty-Eight

The search of the pedestrian bridge over the river proved to be a waste of time. The spent bullet case could not be found. Chances were that it had fallen into the river and had been washed away. The train station manager had confirmed that the CCTV cameras only covered the car park and not the pedestrian bridge. Despite appeals on television and on social media, no witnesses had come forward.

Murray had convened a meeting with Andrews and Roberts in the workshop the morning after the cops had been to see him. Murray was clearly agitated. He had hardly slept that night, owing to the fact that someone had shot one of his men. Ben Naylor had told him that Mickey Chadwell had nothing to do with it. If Chadwell was not behind it, who the hell was?

'Right, listen up you two. As you know, Billy Raeburn went missing but turned up dead in the river having been shot. I met with Ben Naylor last night and he swears that Mickey Chadwell is not behind it. What's the word on the street, Jason?'

Roberts cleared his throat and said, 'Not a bloody thing, James. When young Billy went missing, we scoured the streets for him but found nothing. We checked with Ryan Riggins to see if the big guy with the beard had been in touch, but nothing. None of our dealers has heard a thing. We did wonder if a vigilante has decided to rid the streets of Bath of drug dealers. Me and Jeff both thought it must be Mickey Chadwell who was behind this.'

Murray stood up and stretched. He felt tired from the lack of sleep. 'I had a visit from the cops yesterday. They said that they thought that Chadwell was behind Billy's killing and that he would take me on. So, from now on until the cops catch the killer, I want you guys to accompany me wherever I go. I should be safe enough at the house. Make sure that you are tooled up.'

Andrews smiled and said, 'Don't worry, James. Since we heard that Billy had been shot we are both carrying guns.'

Skelton and Alexander were on their way to Bristol to see DI Patrick Rees. Skelton had briefed Rees on the phone about the murder and said that he wanted to interview Mickey Chadwell. It was a matter of courtesy that Rees should be part of the enquiry team. Alexander parked the car in the police station car park. Rees was waiting for them in reception.

'Morning, Dan, and good morning, Bill. We will travel in my car since I know the way. I called Chadwell earlier, he is expecting us. I wanted to make sure that he would be in his office when we arrive.'

Rees drove them to the scrap yard. He parked the car and they all got out. It had been agreed that Skelton would conduct the interview. They made their way to Chadwell's office and Rees knocked on the door before going in. Chadwell was sitting at his desk, he was wearing a shirt, tie and a blue blazer. He looked more like a businessman than the crook and killer that he actually was. Rees made the introductions and they all sat down.

Chadwell placed his hands on the desk and said, 'What is it that I can do for you gentlemen?'

Skelton carefully assessed the man sitting opposite him. He was a big powerful man and it looked like he regularly worked out at the gym. Skelton was ready with his questions. 'Mickey, we fished the body of a young man out of the river in Bath the other day. The lad worked for James Murray, and he was dealing drugs for him, but of course Murray denies this. The poor lad had been shot in the heart. It was a professional hit. Now the only guy on our radar that could have sanctioned such a hit, is you. What do you have to say about that?'

Chadwell leaned back in his chair and said, 'What James Murray gets up to in Bath, is of no concern to me. I simply run a small business dealing in scrap metal. I don't own a gun and none of my associates have guns. Why on earth would I have wanted to kill the young guy. He never did any harm to me. That James Murray is a cop killer. I think you should be asking him the questions not me. The kid probably ripped him off and he had him killed.'

This was not the answers that Skelton had been expecting. Yes, of course he knew that Chadwell would deny any involvement in the murder, but to suggest that Murray was behind it was a novel approach.

Skelton's hands were resting on the desk. He carefully studied Chadwell's body language. The man was super confident, he was not showing any of the classic signs of stress.

Skelton's eyes narrowed as he spoke. 'Mickey, we all know that you control the drugs and prostitution in Bristol, just like Murray does in Bath. I think that you had that young guy murdered in order to scare Murray off. The thing is, Murray does not scare easily. So, what happens next? Do you kill another one of his dealers, just to enforce the message, or does Murray decide to come after you?'

Chadwell wiped his mouth with his right hand and said, 'Come on, Inspector, you are clutching at straws here. I had nothing to do with that young guy being killed in Bath. You clearly don't have a clue what happened to him, so you decided to try and pin it on me. You have no evidence whatsoever and so if you are finished with your questions, I have a lunch appointment in twenty minutes and I don't want to be late.'

The detectives walked out the office in silence. Skelton's eyes surveyed the wrecked cars. He could see men salvaging spare parts, something that he did many years before at Bobby Dunn's scrap yard. How much he had enjoyed those days before going to university. They had been some of his happiest days. They climbed into the car, Rees slowly turned it around and they began their journey back into Bristol.

It was Alexander who broke the silence. 'This enquiry is going nowhere fast. Chadwell is very confident that's for sure, but Murray was clearly spooked yesterday. What happens next is anyone's guess.'

Chapter Sixty-Nine

Skelton was making no real progress with Billy Raeburn's murder. They had used the automated number plate cameras to identify every car that had been in the vicinity on the night of the murder. One car, a Land Rover Discovery, had cloned plates. The registration plates that it had been displaying belonged to a Jeep. They had interviewed the owner of the Jeep, who confirmed that his number plates had been stolen. Skelton knew that the owner of the Land Rover had probably used them to escape speeding fines or had filled up with fuel and had driven off without paying. On the other hand, the driver might have been the killer. They did not have a description of the killer, so there was not much point in trying to track down all the owners of Land Rover Discoveries in the West Country.

Chadwell was sitting in his office with Stan Perry and Ivor Thomson. He had sent Ben Naylor to the other side of Bristol to collect a drug debt. Chadwell had become increasingly suspicious of Naylor. James Murray and Naylor were spending a lot of time together and this worried him. He kept thinking back to the day when Steve Quinn and Frank Hughes had returned from London having lost the drugs and Chadwell's money. Quinn and Hughes had been loyal employees in the past. But Naylor immediately blamed them for the loss and they had killed the pair of them. It would have been easy for Naylor to have tipped Murray off about the deal and for Murray to send his men to intercept Quinn and Hughes. Neither Quinn nor Hughes were armed, so they would have been no match for the other guys who were carrying guns. It was all beginning to make sense and that was why Chadwell had not told Naylor that he had instructed Thomson to kill Murray's dealer. He wanted both Naylor and Murray to be totally in the dark.

Chadwell stood up and walked to the window to give himself a little time to think and make up his mind. He came back to the table and sat down. Thomson and Perry remained silent, they could see that Chadwell was deep in thought. Chadwell ran his right hand through his hair. He had come to a decision and it was a very painful decision. A pained expression appeared on his face. Then he spoke.

'I think Ben has betrayed me and has teamed up with James Murray. The two of them are seeing a lot of one another. Murray is a dangerous bastard. He killed a police officer and got away with it. Ben is also very dangerous and would kill someone at the drop of a hat. The time has come for Ben to disappear. He should be back here in a couple of hours. I want you guys to shoot him and put his body in one of those cars that are due to go into the crusher this afternoon. I don't want to be here, as I was very fond of Ben for a long time. But this is business. Call me when the job has been done. And make sure you kill him quickly, he is as strong as an ox and in a fight he has never lost. So be extremely careful.'

Ben Naylor arrived at the scrap yard at 2 pm. He noticed that Mickey's car had gone but Thomson and Perry's cars were still in the yard. He also noticed that the cars belonging to Mickey's genuine employees had gone. He went to the office and opened the door and found Thomson and Perry sitting at the desk reading newspapers. 'Where is everybody?' he asked.

Thomson looked up and said, 'Mickey had to go to a meeting and gave the boys the afternoon off. Would you like some tea?'

Naylor took a seat, and said, 'Yes, I'd love a mug of tea, I haven't had one since breakfast this morning.'

Thomson stood up and handed Naylor his newspaper. Naylor took the paper and immediately turned to the sports section. Thomson filled the kettle and switched it on. He turned around and saw that both Naylor and Perry were busy reading their papers. He took the Glock 17 pistol from his pocket and took off the safety catch. He was two feet from Naylor's head when he pulled the trigger. There was a deafening explosion and Naylor's brain landed on the newspaper. He died instantly.

Both Thomson and Perry put on boilersuits. Perry went out into the yard and found the wheelbarrow. He wheeled it into the office. The newspaper was covered in brains and blood. They worked as a team and placed Naylor's body in the wheelbarrow. He was a big heavy man, and they were both sweating from their exertions. They covered the body with an old sheet and wheeled Naylor's body out of the office and over to the wreck of a Ford Focus. They managed to get the body inside the wreck. Perry got up in the crane and started the engine. He lowered the grab and opened the jaws over the roof of the Ford Focus. He gently lifted the car and placed it into the car crusher where Thomson was waiting. In less than five minutes the car had been crushed. Tomorrow, it would be heading to the furnace in Wales.

Thomson and Perry went inside the office. They got to work clearing up the blood. They put the newspapers in the wood burner and took off their overalls. They, too, went into the wood burner. Thomson called Mickey and reported that the mission had been a complete success.

Chapter Seventy

Murray was at home drinking a cold beer. It was just after 7 pm and Penny was in the kitchen, preparing dinner. Murray was getting worried. He had texted Ben Naylor an hour earlier but had received no reply. Perhaps Ben was driving and was unable to use his phone, he thought. He was bound to text back as soon as he was able to do so.

Murray wanted to meet with Naylor. He had decided that the time had come for himself and Naylor to formalise their partnership. It would mean having to kill Mickey Chadwell. Naylor had said that Chadwell had taken on two very capable minders called Thomson and Perry. They would have to find a way of getting Chadwell on his own. The scrap yard would be the ideal place to do it. Naylor had told him that he had disposed of bodies in the car crusher. It would be the perfect place for Chadwell to disappear without a trace. That would leave Murray and Naylor to run Bristol as well as Bath. They would explain the position to Thomson and Perry and give them a pay rise to keep them happy. Murray almost smiled but he knew that what he and Naylor were proposing to do was dangerous. But Murray and Naylor were a great team, he knew it would all work out.

The next day was a Friday and Murray woke up at just before eight. Penny had brought him a cup of tea and he picked up his phone to check for messages and emails. He was surprised that Ben had not replied and so he sent him another text, suggesting that they meet up for lunch in Belushi's bar. He sent the text and got up and jumped into the shower. He had a shave and went to check his phone. There was still nothing from Ben. This was unusual but not something to be seriously worried about. There were all sorts of reasons why Ben was not responding. He might have lost or damaged his phone. His network might have gone down and could not get a signal.

Skelton was in his kitchen, waiting for the kettle to boil. He had just given his dogs a Bonio and they were happily chewing them on their beds. He had the local news on the TV. It was being reported that the police had made no arrests in the murder of Billy Raeburn. Having showered and shaved, Skelton got dressed. He put on a crisply ironed blue shirt and a dark pin-striped suit. He chose a silk tie from the vast collection in his wardrobe. He checked himself in the mirror and was happy with the result. It was a cold November morning, so he put on a scarf and heavy blue overcoat, to keep him warm. He said goodbye to Ken and gave the dogs a cuddle. Brenty-Boy was now on daily medication for the hip disease that the vet had diagnosed. As the condition worsened, he would gradually need regular injections to keep him as pain free as possible. The vet reckoned that at some point in the future, they would have to make the very sad decision of putting him to sleep. Skelton hated the idea, but the dog's happiness and welfare were paramount.

It was a cold foggy morning and Skelton walked faster than usual. He would have a hot mug of tea as soon as he got to the station. He walked down Entry Hill and passed Alexandra Park on his right. He eventually found himself at the bus station. He had to cross the road and waited for the lights to change. He noticed a green Land Rover Discovery had come to a halt on the red light and he glanced at the number plate. He looked closer and saw that something was not quite right. The plate seemed somewhat odd. He remembered that they had been unable to trace a Land Rover Discovery in the Billy Raeburn case. It had cloned plates. Skelton pulled out his warrant card and walked over to the driver's door. He knocked on the window and flashed his card. The driver was a big man and had a bushy beard.

The driver lowered the window and said, 'Yes, Officer, what can I do for you?'

Skelton returned the warrant card to his jacket pocket and said, 'Just a routine enquiry, sir, when the lights change just pull in around the corner and we will have you on your way in no time.' He took out his phone and called control for a vehicle number plate check. The car was registered to an Ivor Thomson in Twerton.

When the lights changed, Thomson drove around the corner and pulled in. Thomson was wearing a jacket and coat; the Glock 17 was in his coat pocket.

Skelton went to the driver's door and said, 'Can you turn the engine off please, and do you have any ID on you?' Thomson turned the engine off and undid his seatbelt and got out. He had his wallet in his hand, and he took out his driving licence and handed it to the officer. Skelton read the name on the licence. Ivor Thomson. Skelton held on to the driving licence and went to the front of the vehicle and bent over and inspected the registration plate. Something was not right. He could see that there was a second plate below the genuine plate. Thomson was beginning to get worried.

Skelton turned and said, 'It looks like you have another plate under this. Can you explain why?'

Thomson tried to remain cool. 'I had a slight bump, Officer, and the original plate got cracked, so I had a new one made and fitted it myself.'

Skelton had a gut instinct and he never ignored a gut instinct. It's what police officers relied upon. 'We need to go to the police station and sort this out. You can drive us there and we will have you on your way in no time.'

Thomson had not bargained for this. 'Look, Officer, I have a meeting in Bristol to go to. Could I not pop into the station later on today and sort this out?'

Skelton moved in closer. 'No. either you drive us there now, or I will call for backup and you will be arrested, and you will be delayed for hours. I suggest that we both get into the vehicle now.' Thomson realised that he had no choice but to comply. He would have to change his story and admit to using cloned plates. It was not the end of the world.

Thomson drove them into the car park of the police station on Manvers Street and parked. They both got out of the vehicle. 'If you follow me, Mr Thomson, into reception, take a seat and I will be back down in a jiffy.'

Skelton went upstairs to the CID office where he found Chris Spurrey working on his computer. Skelton still had Thomson's driving licence. 'Chris run this guy through the CRO system. I have him downstairs in reception.' Spurrey took the driving licence and began typing.

'Bloody hell, sir, this guy has got serious form. He got ten years for attempted murder and has three other convictions for assault. He was released from prison just over a year ago. What is he doing in reception?'

Just at that point, Bryan Stevens, the head of the firearms unit walked in. 'Good morning, sir, and good morning, Chris. It's a bit chilly out there today.'

Stevens was in uniform complete with body armour, and he had a pistol in its holster. Skelton said, 'I am glad you are here, Bryan. I have a guy in reception who I pulled in because of suspicious number plates. It turns out that he some serious form for violence. I haven't searched him yet but given his form, I want you two with me when I do, especially you, Bryan. Come on, follow me.'

Skelton led the way with Stevens right behind him and Spurrey brought up the rear. Thomson was sending a text message on his phone, when he looked up to see the two plain clothed police officers and an armed officer in uniform. He dropped the phone, jumped up and thrust his hand into his coat pocket and grabbed the gun. He was too late, Stevens had him covered.

'If you make a move, you are a dead man.'

Stevens had the pistol aimed directly at Thomson's chest. Thomson froze. He knew from experience that to try and pull the gun from his pocket would be futile. The police officer would shoot, and it would be all over in a flash and Thomson would be dead or very seriously wounded. 'Slowly take your hand out of your pocket and put your hands above your head.'

Thomson did as he was instructed. Skelton moved in and took the gun from Thomson's pocket. Spurrey got behind Thomson and put him in handcuffs.

Skelton said, 'Search him, Chris, in case he has any more surprises on him. Then take him to the custody suite and get him booked in. The preliminary charge is possession of a firearm without a certificate. Bryan, take charge of this gun and get it over to the lab. I think we just found the killer of young Billy Raeburn.'

Skelton went to his office and put some water in the kettle and switched it on. Alexander knocked on the door and entered. 'Good morning, sir,

anything happening this morning?' Skelton smiled and said, 'Actually, Bill, I just arrested a guy and he's in custody. He had a gun on him. It's the same calibre of the gun that was used to kill Billy Raeburn. I sent it to the lab and with any luck, we will get the results back later today. They always prioritise a murder case.'

Alexander had an incredulous look on his face. 'But we had no suspects in that case. How did you find this guy with the gun?'

Skelton patted Alexander on both his shoulders. 'Good old-fashioned detective work. I am a nosey bugger, Bill, and I spotted a suspicious number plate whilst walking into work this morning. I got him to drive me here and when we did a CRO check on him, I was even more suspicious. Luckily, Bryan Stevens turned up, otherwise I might have got shot. Remind me to take him out to lunch. He hardly ever drinks, so no point in going for a piss-up!'

Chapter Seventy-One

It was Friday lunchtime and Murray was seriously getting concerned about Ben Naylor. He decided to call Mickey Chadwell to find out what was going on. Murray checked his phone and found the contact number for Chadwell. He pressed the call button and waited. It was answered on the fourth ring.

'Mickey Chadwell speaking.'

Murray cleared his throat and said, 'Mickey, It's James Murray. How are you?'

Chadwell had been anticipating the call. 'Hello, James, I am good thanks. How about yourself?'

Murray tried to hide his nerves before replying. 'I am fine thanks, Mickey. I was just wondering if Ben is with you. I have been trying to contact him, but he is not answering his phone.'

Chadwell stood up and smiled. 'No Ben is not here. You see, we sort of terminated our relationship. I was getting rather concerned about the amount of time that you and he were spending together. There was also the fact that I lost a lot of money and drugs not long after you guys were getting cosily acquainted.'

Murray had beads of sweat running down his brow.

Murray was now very worried. Ben Naylor was the key to getting Mickey Chadwell out of the way and taking control of Bristol. 'Mickey what has happened to Ben. Is he all right?'

Chadwell sat back down. He would relish what he had to say next. 'Ben is not around any longer, so you can forget trying to contact him. He won't be answering the phone any more.' Murray felt as though he just been poleaxed. This was never in the script that he had composed with Ben. Chadwell continued, 'James, you are no longer welcome in Bath. If you should decide to stay on, it will prove very bad for your health. So, I want you to put your house on the market and move back to London. I will be taking over Bath and your presence will not be tolerated.'

Murray silently rose from his chair. His mind was trying desperately hard to compute the information that Chadwell had just relayed. He had just lost Ben, but it was not the end of the world. He believed that he still had Ivor Thomson and Stan Perry, two very capable men with guns. He had fought hard to take over Bath and he was not for surrendering it without a fight. There was no way that he was for leaving Bath. This meant war. He may have lost a battle in the demise of Ben, but when it came to war, Murray reigned supreme.

'Listen up, Mickey. I am not fucking going anywhere. Bath belongs to me and if you or any of your cronies set foot in it, you are dead men.' He slammed the phone down and made his way to the kitchen, where he fixed himself a stiff drink.

He took the rum and coke into the sitting room and switched on the television. He tuned into BBC1 and saw that the evening news was coming on. He sat down and watched the screen. Suddenly the police station in Manvers Street filled the screen. He turned up the volume and listened.

'At a press conference earlier this afternoon, the police announced that a man had been arrested and charged with the murder of Billy Raeburn and possession of a firearm. Detectives charged Ivor Thomson, a forty-two-year-old man from Twerton. He will appear before magistrates tomorrow morning.'

Murray took another sip from the glass and thought to himself. 'I might have lost Ben today, but Chadwell has just lost one of his two key men. I still have my two key men, so suddenly the advantage is with me. Maybe I should strike whilst I have that advantage.'

Chapter Seventy-Two

It was Monday morning and Skelton was reviewing the evidence in the Billy Raeburn case. He had a smug look on his face, he was delighted that he had arrested the killer on gut instinct. Had it not been for the cloned licence plates badly fitted to the Land Rover, Thomson would have probably escaped justice and the police would have had an unsolved murder on their hands. There was a knock on the door and in walked Alexander carrying a plate with two square sausage sandwiches. 'I thought you could go one of these, sir. Shall I put the kettle on?'

Skelton stood up and said, 'It's all right, Bill, I will make the tea. Take a seat. I was just reviewing the evidence in the Billy Raeburn case and the forensics are excellent. The gun that Thomson was carrying killed young Billy. The lab is still running tests to see if it can be linked to any other unsolved cases.'

The officers sat at Skelton's desk and ate their sandwiches in silence. Skelton took out a handkerchief and wiped his lips and finished his tea. 'I was thinking, Bill, that Mickey Chadwell has lost a key man in Ivor Thomson now that we have him in custody. I phoned Patrick Rees on Friday evening to tell him the news. He said that things were quite in Bristol and that Ben Naylor seems to be lying low. I wonder if Murry and Naylor will make a move soon on Chadwell. With Thomson out of the way, it would be a good opportunity for them to strike.'

Alexander stood up and began removing the plate and the two tea mugs. 'I never thought of that, sir. It would mean that Bristol would see the action and that would suit us very well. We don't want any collateral damage here. I would not be surprised if Murray gives Naylor the nod to kill Chadwell.'

Chadwell had called Stan Perry and told him to meet him at the yard. When Perry arrived, Chadwell was just finishing a call. He put his phone in his pocket and said, 'No wonder we could not get Ivor on the phone. The police arrested him for that boy's murder on Friday and he is in custody. That means we are now two men down both Ben and Ivor. James Murray called me on Friday night looking for Ben. I told him that Ben no longer existed and that he should get out of Bath, but that was before I knew what had happened to Ivor. He will have heard about Ivor's arrest and knows that we are now two men down. That stacks the odds in his favour. We need to be on alert, so I want you by my side until we can sort Murray out. We both carry guns from now on.'

Perry sat down and said, 'Do we just sit here and see what happens or do we go over to Bath and hit him at his house?'

Chadwell was in deep thought. Eventually he stood up and said, 'I am not sure what to do at the moment. If Ivor was still around it was my intention to kill Murray and get rid of his body in the usual way. But Murray will now be incredibly sensitive. I am sure that he and Ben were plotting to get me. He knows that I had Ben killed, so he will be very cautious of what he does next, but with Ivor now out of the equation he might come here and take us on.'

Murray was sitting at the kitchen table when his phone rang. It was Jason Andrews to say that he and Jeff Roberts were at the front door. Murray got up and went to the door and let them in. All three were now seated at the kitchen table with a small bottle of beer in front of them.

Murray cleared his throat and said, 'Right, this is what I know. Mickey Chadwell has killed Ben Naylor, which has ruined my plans. The idea was that Ben would kill Mickey, then Ben and I would form a new partnership. That clearly is not going to happen now. We also know that Mickey's other top man, Ivor Thomson, killed young Billy, but the police have arrested him and he is in custody awaiting trial for murder. That means that Mickey is now two men short but despite that, Mickey told me to leave town. I responded by telling him that if he or any of his men came to Bath, then they were dead.'

Murray took a sip of his beer and continued. 'I have been giving this situation a lot of thought. Mickey was scared that Ben was going to kill him, but Mickey had Ben killed. This means that the potential and immediate threat to Mickey has gone. With him being two men short, he is going to feel vulnerable, and I think it's highly unlikely that he will make a move against me. The odds are stacked against him, and I don't think he will gamble his chances. So, what do we do? The answer, gentlemen, is that we carry on as before. I lost the advantage with Ben having been removed. He was my eyes and ears. He would have warned me if Mickey was about to make a move. He also knew the layout of the scrapyard and we don't. That puts us at a disadvantage if we decided to take Mickey down there. I have therefore decided that we will remain at status quo. We will conduct business as usual in Bath and Mickey can run his business in Bristol.'

Chapter Seventy-Three

Mickey Chadwell had other ideas. He was going to take on Murry but on his own terms. First, he needed to find a replacement for Ivor Thomson and that was not going to be easy. He had one guy in mind. Dave Austin, who basically kept his dealers supplied with drugs. He was not of the same calibre as Thomson and was known to enjoy the odd line of coke. Physically speaking, he was of a much smaller build to Thomson but was more than capable with his fists. He had several criminal convictions but none for dealing drugs. He would have to rely on Stan Perry and himself when it came to dealing with James Murray. Chadwell called Dave Austin and told him to report to the yard at midday.

Detective Inspector Patrick Rees and DS Roger Fell were travelling in an unmarked police car in the Temple Meads area of Bristol. It was just after 11 am and they were on their way to speak to a witness in a robbery case. Rees was in the passenger seat and Fell was driving. 'I haven't seen Ben Naylor for a while, Roger. I wonder if he has gone away on holiday?'

They were stationary in a line of traffic when Fell noticed a blue BMW driving towards him. The driver was Dave Austin and Fell recognised him immediately. 'I haven't seen Naylor either but there is Dave Austin, who works for Chadwell. Should we pull him over and see what he knows about Naylor?'

Rees was looking through the windscreen and saw the BMW with Austin driving it. 'Yes, turn around Roger and follow him. I am curious to know where Ben Naylor is these days. He hasn't been seen in Bath with James Murray recently.'

They followed the BMW and were immediately behind it when it stopped at traffic lights. Rees unbuckled his seat belt and opened the door and got out. He sprinted to the driver's door and knocked on the window.

Austin recognised him and lowered the window. 'Hello, Mr Rees, what can I do for you?'

Rees lowered his head and said, 'Pull up down the road there. I want a quiet little chat with you.'

Rees made his way back to the car and got in. 'He is going to park up just down there. If I am not mistaken, he has some weed in the car. He might be carrying other drugs as well. This could be interesting.'

Austin parked the BMW. He was already sweating. He had about £3,000 worth of weed and coke in the boot. He was on his way to drop it off to a dealer before going to his meeting with Mickey Chadwell. He opened the door and got out. Hopefully the cops were only fishing for information, and he would be on his way. Rees got out the police car and approached Austin. Rees could see that the man was nervous. 'Open the boot, Dave, and let's see what you have got in there.'

Austin pushed the button on the boot and opened it. The smell of weed was pretty powerful. Rees picked up the brown package and looked inside. 'I reckon you have between two and three thousand pounds worth of drugs here, Dave. You could get three or four years in prison for possession and intent to supply.'

The beads of sweat were running down Austin's forehead and he wiped them away. Rees put his hand on Austin's shoulder and said, 'Get into the back of my car. We need to have a serious little chat.'

Austin got into the back seat and Rees got into the front passenger seat. Rees turned and faced Austin. 'Dave here has got rather a lot of drugs in the boot of his car, certainly more than for his own personal use.'

Fell turned around so that he was also facing Austin. 'Oh dear, that will get you a few years behind bars.'

Rees put his right hand on his chin and thought for a second. 'There is a way out of this for you, Dave. I will only make this offer to you once. If you don't take it, then you will find yourself in a cell at the police station.'

Austin was agitated. He already knew what the deal was going to be. He would have to give up Mickey Chadwell.

'What do you want, Mr Rees?'

'I want to know what has happened to Ben Naylor and I want you to be my eyes and ears inside Mickey Chadwell's operation. Provided you fully cooperate, you will be free to go. This will be our little secret, unless of course you fail to keep to your side of the bargain, in which case Chadwell will get to hear about it and you, my friend, will be a dead man.'

Austin's hands were shaking. Rees had him over a barrel and they both knew it 'Okay, Mr Rees, you have got a deal. Ben Naylor is dead, and he ended up in the car crusher. Mickey didn't kill him. It was two of his boys that did that. Mickey reckoned that Ben was becoming too close to James Murray and was scared that they were going to kill him. You lot arrested Ivor Thomson for killing that boy in Bath. That leaves Stan Perry as the enforcer. I am on my way to meet Mickey now. It looks like I am to replace Thomson. I think it will just be a matter of time before he goes after Murray.'

Patrick Rees lost no time in calling Dan Skelton with the news. The agreement made with Austin was that all he had to do was call Rees when the hit on Murray was to be made.

Chapter Seventy-Four

Skelton and Alexander were walking towards the Saracen's Head. It was early December and the Christmas market was in full swing. Skelton detested this time of year, owing to vast number of visitors to Bath. Of course it was good for the local economy, but it meant that the pubs were very busy and so finding a table for lunch was difficult. Normally, the detectives would leave the station just before 1 pm but today they had left at noon, in the hope they could bag a table.

When they got to the pub, Skelton looked through the window and saw that the pub was relatively empty. He was also delighted to see that his favourite table was vacant. 'Right, Bill, you bag that table and I will get the drinks. Do you fancy fish and chips today?'

Alexander thought for a second and said, 'Yes, fish and chips will go down a treat as will the beer.'

Dale the general manager was behind the bar. 'Hello, Dan, you are early today.'

Skelton placed his hands on the bar and said, 'We wanted to be sure to get a table and luckily my favourite one is free.'

Dale was busy pouring the drinks. 'Dan, you can reserve that table any time. Just give me a call when you know you are coming in. Preferably call before eleven in the morning and tell me what time you are coming in.' Skelton scratched his head and shook it. 'Why the hell did I not think of that?'

Dale laughed. Skelton ordered the food and took the two pints of lager back to the table.

Alexander took a sip of his beer and said, 'So it looks like Chadwell is going to take on James Murray. That will be on our patch and there could be collateral damage. Do you think we should go and warn Murray?'

Skelton picked up his glass and took a long drink. He slowly put the glass down and eyed Alexander. 'You know something, Bill, there is nothing that will give me as much pleasure as seeing that bastard dead. He killed my best friend and got away with it. Patrick Rees has managed to get an informant inside Chadwell's operation, and he will tip us off when the hit is to be made. We need to be ready for it and Bryan Stevens and his firearms unit will be on hand to minimise the collateral. I want you to have the CID team assemble in the incident room tomorrow at ten am along with the firearms unit. We don't yet know when the hit will take place, but we best try and plan for it.'

Dale appeared with the fish and chips and mushy peas. The two cods were enormous!

They were halfway through the meal when about twenty elderly Welsh woman came in the door. They had obviously been to the Christmas market and were now going to have a long boozy lunch. Skelton quickly stood up and caught Dale's eye.

'Two more pints please, Dale.'

It was 10 am the next morning when Skelton entered the incident room. The entire CID team were assembled, as were the firearms officers. Skelton walked up to the lectern and glanced at the wall chart. It contained photographs of the key players, including Murray and Chadwell along with their henchmen. There was also a photograph of Murray's house. Skelton raised his right arm and the room descended into silence. Skelton searched the room and saw Patrick Rees seated in the front row. They exchanged smiles.

'Ladies and gentlemen, I am sure that you are all familiar with James Murray and Mickey Chadwell.' He used a pointer to identify each of them. 'Both are evil killers, especially Murray, who murdered a police officer who was my best friend. Murray got off the charge on a technicality. We have intelligence curtesy of DI Patrick Rees that Chadwell is going to kill Murray, but we don't know where or when. Murray spent time in prison with a close associate of Chadwell called Ben Naylor. They enjoyed a warm friendship, but Chadwell became concerned that Naylor and Murray were going to gang up on him. So, he had Naylor killed and we believe his body went into a car crusher and then into a furnace. We have no evidence to prove that Naylor was murdered, and there certainly won't be any eyewitnesses coming forward.'

Skelton paused for a second in case there were any questions, but there were none. 'Chadwell used to rely on Ben Naylor as his chief enforcer, but with him gone, he now relies on a guy called Stan Perry. He also had another minder called Ivor Thomson, but we arrested him for the murder of Billy Raeburn. We now know that he has brought in an extra pair of hands by the name of Dave Austin. Be under no illusion, Chadwell and Perry are both extremely dangerous men and that is why the firearms unit will be closely involved in this operation. We have, thanks to the ingenuity of DI Rees, an informer on the inside. He will hopefully tip us off when the hit is to be executed.'

Skelton took a sip of water from a glass and continued. 'Here in Bath, James Murray lives in this expensive house.' Skelton pointed to the house and a photograph of Murray. 'He lives there with his girlfriend called Penny. Murray still retains a manor in London which controls drugs and prostitution. He has only lived in Bath a few months and took over the drugs and prostitution from the late Jake Ratten, who we believe he poisoned. Of course, we have no evidence that he killed Ratten, otherwise we would have him behind bars. He inherited from Ratten two minders called Jason Andrews and Jeff Roberts.' Skelton pointed to the photographs of Andrews and Roberts. 'You can consider both of these men to be dangerous and may very well be armed.'

There was complete silence in the incident room as Skelton paused. 'We know that Murray has a lock-up situated on an industrial estate just off the Lower Bristol Road. That's a picture of it there. We believe that Chadwell or his minders will make the hit on Murray at his house. He has no CCTV, nor surprisingly do any of his neighbours. Whilst we think that Chadwell is going to make the hit on Murray, it is quite possible that Murray might go for Chadwell. It is our understanding that the original plan was for Murray and Naylor to form a partnership and take out Chadwell. This would have given Murray control of Bristol.'

Skelton cleared his throat and took the pointer and pointed at the photographs of the scrap yard. 'These are pictures of Chadwell's scrap yard in Bristol. They were taken by a drone yesterday.' He turned and faced Bryan Stevens. 'Bryan, I want you to undertake an evaluation of both Murray's house and the scrap yard. You know what to do, so I won't waste time in telling you. As I said earlier, we have no idea when Chadwell will make his move. We do have the informant on the inside, but we might not know when it's going to happen until shortly before the kick off. Are there any questions?'

Patrick Rees stood up and said, 'I have no idea when this is all going to happen. Hopefully my informant will give us sufficient notice if the hit is to be made on Murray. However, if Murray decides to take out Chadwell, then we will have no way of predicting when that will be. I can only wish you all the very best of luck!'

Chapter Seventy-Five

Chadwell was sitting at his desk and was checking his laptop for emails. It was just after 11 am and he could hear the crane outside in the yard. It was lifting a car up in the air so that a worker could remove the wheels. It was a bitterly cold day and Chadwell got up and put another log in the wood burner. The door opened and in walked Stan Perry along with Dave Austin. They had been out dropping off drugs to the dealers and collecting cash. Perry placed the bag of cash beside Chadwell's computer. 'There you go, Mickey; it all went like clockwork. I haven't counted the cash, but it feels like about twenty grand in there. Do you want some tea?'

Chadwell looked up from the computer screen and said, 'Yes please, a nice hot mug of tea might warm me up. It's bloody freezing out there and it doesn't feel that much warmer in here.'

Dave Austin was busy washing mugs and was waiting for the kettle to boil. Perry had taken a seat next to Chadwell and watched while Chadwell closed down his computer. 'Have you decided when we are going to hit that bastard Murray?'

Austin's ears pricked up. This was the conversation that he had been waiting for. Chadwell folded down the computer screen and sighed. 'I think Murray is carrying on business as usual despite me telling him to go back to London. We need to sort him out and the sooner the better. This is just the sort of weather we need. With these cold winter nights, hardly anyone is out and about. We will do it tomorrow night.'

Perry stood up. Austin brought over two mugs of tea. 'Will you need me for the job, Mickey?'

Chadwell took the hot mug of tea. 'No, Dave, you can have tomorrow night off. Stan and I will sort Murray out. Now leave us alone. I want to brief Stan on what we are going to do.'

Austin left his mug of tea and went out to his car. He drove out of the scrap yard and followed the road to where he could park. He called DI Rees. Rees heard his mobile phone ring and took it out of his pocket. He glanced at the screen and saw that the caller was Dave Austin. His heart missed a beat as he answered the phone.

'Yes Dave, have you any news?'

'Hello, Mr Rees. Mickey and Stan Perry are going to hit James Murray tomorrow night, but I don't know when. They said it would be dark, if that helps?'

Rees got to his feet. 'Are you going to be there?' Rees listened intently.

'No, he has given me the night off. Mickey needs a gun and Stan is going to get him one this afternoon. Stan already has a gun, so they will both be armed.'

Rees ended the call and checked his watch. It was almost noon. He decided to drive to Bath and let Skelton know what was about to take place.

Rees arrived at Manvers Street police station shortly before one. The Christmas shopping traffic had been a nightmare. He raced up the stairs to Skelton's office and knocked on the door and went in. The office was empty, so he made his way to the CID room and saw Ross Turnbull sitting at his desk.

'Ross, is the boss about?'

'Hello, sir. Unfortunately, you missed him by about five minutes. He and Bill Alexander have gone out to lunch. My guess is they are either in Belushi's or the Saracen's Head.'

Rees did not bother to reply. He rushed out the door and headed towards the two bars. Luckily the Christmas market had finished and so there were not so many people about. It was also freezing cold, and he noticed a gritter lorry spreading salt on the road.

He first went to Belushi's and looked inside but there were only a handful of Christmas shoppers tucking into lunch. He crossed the road and looked in the window of the Saracen's Head. He was relieved to see that Skelton and Alexander were seated by the window. He opened the door and went in. Skelton saw him immediately and stood up.

'Patrick, how great see you. What are you drinking and would you like some lunch?'

Rees shook hands with Skelton and Alexander. 'I will have a pint of whatever you guys are drinking and I think I deserve a steak. You once told me that the sirloin steaks are exceptional in this place. So, make it a medium rare for me, please.'

They had to move to another table as the one that they had been using only seated two. Skelton was at the bar and young Dale the general manager was serving him. 'I have made an executive decision, Dale, can we please have three sirloin steaks cooked medium rare, and I need three more pints.'

Dale smiled and said in his soft Welsh accent, 'You and Bill love my steaks, and for that matter all my food. You are certainly becoming good customers.'

Skelton carried the beers to their new table and sat down. 'Well cheers, gentlemen, and here's to a happy Christmas.' They all clinked glasses and sipped their beers. 'Tell me, Patrick, what news do you have for us?'

Rees checked that there was no one in earshot. 'My informant in Bristol tells me that Mickey Chadwell and Stan Perry are coming to Bath tomorrow night to kill James Murray. I don't have a time, but it gets dark here at four. So, I guess you will need to be in position from about three-thirty. The thing is this, I know that both of them are armed. Technically, I should have an armed unit pull them over as soon as they leave the scrap yard. But Murray killed your best friend, who happened to be a cop. So far as I am concerned, he needs to take his chances.'

Skelton thought for a second and took a gulp of beer. 'We have been taking a keen eye on Murray's house. I also speak with his girlfriend Penny once a week on the phone. As you know he has two minders. One is called Jason Andrews and the other is Jeff Roberts. We believe that both of these characters are armed, and they have recently been spending a lot of time at the house. The chances are that one of them will answer the door and all hell will break loose. I personally don't mind that at all, provided there is no collateral damage. I am more than happy if both Murray and Chadwell and one or two of their minders end up dead.'

Dale and his assistant brought over the sirloin steaks. Rees looked at his plate and said, 'My word, that looks good. I think I am going to put in a transfer to Bath!'

They all laughed and chinked glasses.

Chapter Seventy-Six

The following morning at 9 am, the team assembled in the incident room. Inspector Bryan Stevens, the head of the firearms unit, led the briefing. An unmarked police car would be stationed near the scrap yard in Bristol. The lookout would confirm that Chadwell and Perry had left the scrap yard. Stevens and his team would take up position in unmarked cars, close to Murray's house. Skelton confirmed that Murray's girlfriend would not be at the property as she was in London visiting her sister. This would leave Murray and his minders Jason Andrews and Jeff Roberts in the property. When Chadwell and Perry left their car and approached the house, they would be intercepted by the firearms unit and arrested or neutralised. They would take up position at 15.45 and wait.

Skelton went to his office and was followed by Alexander. 'Well, Bill, all we can do now is hope and pray. Bryan and his team are in charge of the operation. It should be a piece of cake for them. The only thing I don't like about this is that Murray is unlikely to come to any harm. The firearms boys and girls will arrest Chadwell and Perry before they can fire a shot. I guess I will have to be patient and get Murray another day. Stick the kettle on, Bill, and I will go to the canteen and get us a couple of sausage sandwiches.'

'Very good, sir.'

The firearms units moved into position at 15.45 in unmarked cars. The windows had tainted glass, so it was virtually impossible to see inside the car. There were three cars, and each contained three officers. The officers were armed with rifles and pistols as well as tasers. By 16.00 it was dark and the road was very quiet. It was another bitterly cold day, so few pedestrians were around. At 18.05 a message came over the radio from the spotter car. Chadwell and Perry had left the scrapyard. They were driving a red Skoda. Bryan Stevens reckoned that they would arrive in about forty minutes. He ordered his officers to stand by.

Chadwell was driving. He had made several trips to the location over the past week. He had decided that he would not actually park the car outside Murray's house. It would be risky taking the car to the house as a neighbour could give the car details to the police. It would be better to park the car a few streets away and walk. It was unlikely that any witnesses would follow them. Chadwell and Perry were both wearing heavy overcoats, and both had a gun in their pocket.

The traffic was slow and it was not until a few minutes before seven that Chadwell parked the car. The road was deserted apart from a few parked cars. It would take them five minutes to walk to Murray's house. Before getting out of the car, both men put on baseball caps, thus making it harder to identify them. Chadwell locked the car and they began walking to the house. They had to turn a corner which was only about twenty metres from the house. Bryan Stevens' team spotted the two men. With it being dark and the men wearing baseball caps, they assumed that they were just a couple of passers by.

Suddenly Murray's front door opened and out walked Jason Andrews, Jeff Roberts and Murray. They were talking amongst themselves and did not appear to have a care in the world. Murray said, 'I am looking forward to this Indian meal, I haven't had one for about two weeks.'

Stevens shouted down the radio. 'It looks like Murray and his mates are going out. Keep your eyes open for that red Skoda, it must be close by now.'

Chadwell spotted Murray and said to Perry, 'Come on, let's go.'

They began running and drew their weapons. Murray was just getting into the driver's seat when Chadwell pulled the trigger. The bullet smashed into his right temple, and he collapsed onto the road, very much dead.

Stevens yelled into his microphone. 'Go go go. Holy shit' Perry shot Andrews in the face and Chadwell shot Roberts in the chest. Both died almost immediately. Bryan Stevens was not for giving them a warning. He used his high-powered rifle and shot Chadwell in the back of the head.

His brains landed on the roof of the car. Perry turned to fire at Stevens. It was his last voluntary movement. Stevens fired and this time the bullet hit Perry in the forehead. He was dead before he hit the ground.

Epilogue

The next morning Skelton was in the kitchen. He had let the boys out into the garden and they were now enjoying a Bonio. He switched the television on and the main news story was the shooting of the five men in Bath. Skelton was smiling. He had at last avenged his best friend's murder. Murray was dead and the icing on the cake was that Chadwell had also been killed. He took two mugs of tea upstairs and gave one to Ken. He stepped into the shower and began singing. He was looking forward to calling Joe Reilly's widow, Sarah, with the good news. He and Ken would take her and her son Daniel out to lunch as soon as possible.

Skelton got dressed and put on a blue overcoat and scarf. He also put on a pair of gloves. He picked up his case and put his iPad inside. He said goodbye to Ken and the dogs and began walking into Bath. It was a cold frosty morning, but he felt on top of the world. There would of course be an independent police investigation into the shootings, but he was confident that that would be a formality. There would be a party in the incident room, but he would take Alexander and Rees to the pub for lunch. It would be Christmas in a few days and his birthday was on Christmas Eve. Skelton called Ken when he got to the office. They would be celebrating Skelton's birthday early in the Saracen's Head!

Skelton would enjoy raising his glass and toasting a rogue no more and to the demise of Murray.

About The Author

Dan Rafferty was born in a small town some 10 miles east of Glasgow. The youngest of four boys, he initially worked in law before moving to London where he enjoyed a highly successful career in finance.

For the past twenty years he has practised as an Independent Expert Witness in the High Court of Justice.

He retired to become an author of crime novels and lives with his partner of forty-one years, and their three black Labradors on the southern slopes of the beautiful Georgian city of Bath.

Coming soon…

Death in Bath

Here is a taster of the next book in the series.

Chapter One

It was Christmas day morning and Detective Chief Inspector Dan Skelton was busy in the kitchen, preparing the turkey for the oven. He had already boiled the potatoes which would go into the oven later to become roast potatoes. It was only eight o'clock and he was still in his dressing gown. His three black labradors consisting of Brenty-boy, Josh and Archie were lying on their beds waiting for Skelton's partner Ken, to take them out for the morning walk. Although it was Christmas, Skelton had to go into work. It would only be a skeleton staff of officers on duty at the police station today. Christmas was usually a very quiet day for the police service, although it sometimes surprised him that hard nosed criminals showed no respect for Christmas day.

Ken came down-stairs and was immediately greeted by the boys who were wagging their tails furiously. Skelton smiled at his partner and said, "I have prepared all the food, and I have written down when the turkey and potatoes need to go into the oven. I should be home by six and we can have dinner at seven. Now I need to go shower and shave. I will drive to the station this morning as Bill has the day off and I might have to go out on a call." Skelton was referring to his deputy Detective Sergeant Bill Alexander, who like Skelton was a Scotsman. Whilst Skelton had grown up just ten miles east of Glasgow and had a refined Scottish accent, Alexander on the other hand had a very broad Glasgow accent. The two men had become very close friends particularly after Alexander had saved Skelton's life in a terrorist attack. Skelton said goodbye to Ken and the boys and went upstairs to shower and shave. Skelton loved taking a shower and had discovered that he did his best thinking whilst under the hot water.

As he got dressed in a bespoke tailored suit, Skelton wondered what sort of day lay ahead of him. Detective Constable Ross Turnbull would be on duty but the rest of the C.I.D team had the day off. Turnbull like Skelton had no children. Skelton thought it only fair, that officers with children should have Christmas day off work, so that they could enjoy this special day with their family. Of course, should a major crime occur, they would have to leave their families and report for duty. Skelton sincerely hoped that his team would enjoy the day without being interrupted by the demands of the job.

Skelton was the head of the Criminal Investigation Department of Avon and Somerset Constabulary based in Manvers Street in the lovely city of Bath. Skelton had attended university in Bath and had fallen in love with this beautiful Roman city and its wonderful Georgian architecture. He had begun his police career in the Metropolitan police in London but had always set his sights on returning to Bath. He had been back in Bath for just less than a year but had already made a name for himself as an outstanding detective. He was lucky to have a small team of detectives who were all very professional. Bath is rightly regarded as a very safe city in which to live. It has a population of ninety thousand, but this is boosted by another sixty thousand students that attend the two universities in the city. Bath University is renowned for its engineering faculty, whilst Bath Spa offers less challenging degrees. Being a world heritage city, it attracts millions of visitors a year and it falls upon Avon and Somerset Constabulary to keep its citizens and visitors safe.

Manvers Street police station is situated right in the heart of the city. It is located close to both the train and bus stations as well as the stunning Bath Abbey, where the first coronation of a king of England took place. The famous Roman Baths are within easy walking distance.

Skelton would usually always walk to work. It was a lovely fifteen-minute walk all downhill. Skelton liked the walk as not only did it keep him fit, but allowed him to plan the day ahead, as best he could. Today however, was different. He would take his beloved 3.2 Jaguar Sovereign to the office. He was mostly dependent on Bill Alexander to drive him to crime scenes, but with Alexander at home enjoying Christmas with his family, he would need his own car for transport to any crime occurring today.

It was just after nine when Skelton parked his car in what was an almost deserted carpark. He recognised Ross Turnbull's car and there were two marked police cars. He got out of the car and made his way to his office. It was a bitterly cold morning, and he was glad that he had pulled on a heavy coat and scarf over his suit. He made his way to his office and removed both the coat and scarf. In his office, he had an electric kettle and a fridge where he kept fat free milk. He put some water in the kettle and went out to the C.I.D room where he found Ross Turnbull busy on his computer. "Merry Christmas Ross" Turnbull jumped out of his chair and held out his hand to greet Skelton. "Good morning, sir, and a very merry Christmas to you. I happen to have a very good bottle of sherry in my desk and perhaps we could have a glass or two at lunch time." Skelton's face broke into a wide smile. "Ross, how could I possibly refuse such a splendid invitation? Provided nothing requires our attention, please feel free to join me at 12.30 in my office. I will fry us up a couple of square sausage sandwiches for lunch and I happen to have a couple of tins of Fosters in my fridge. We need to be careful though, as we are both driving so, I think a glass of sherry and a can of Fosters will keep us under the drink driving limit." Turnbull patted Skelton on his right shoulder and said, "12.30 at your place. Call it a date." The men exchanged smiles and Skelton headed off towards the custody suite.

He was delighted to find the custody sergeant, Dave Roddis on duty. He was in conversation with young PC Luke Meehan. The men stopped talking as Skelton approached. Skelton was smiling broadly and said, "Well I'm glad to see that the uniformed branch have shown up today. Anyone would think it's Christmas! The three officers laughed and exchanged handshakes. Dave Roddis was the best custody sergeant that Skelton had ever met. He had the ability to control prisoners better than he had ever encountered before. A heavy-set man with an enormous beer belly, Roddis could always see the funny side of any situation.

Luke Meehan was in his early twenties. He was a bachelor and lived with his parents in Corsham. He had recently completed his probationary period and was now a fully-fledged cop. He was quite a stocky young man and was well liked by his fellow officers. As he was unmarried and had no kids, he had volunteered to work on Christmas day. Skelton rested his arm on the charge counter and asked Roddis, "How many guests have we got today Dave?" Roddis put his right forefinger on his lips and said, "Now let me think." He frowned for a few seconds and said, "As of now, not a bloody single prisoner. But I have no doubt that young Luke here, will go and spoil that." They all laughed. Skelton touched Meehan on the shoulder and said, "I take it you are single crewed today, Luke. Christmas is usually a quiet day for us but be aware of drunk drivers. A lot of pubs are open for a few hours at lunchtime. If I were you, I would sit up outside one of the pubs not in the city. There are a few pubs in Lansdown, and you need to drive there. Chances are you will nail a drunk driver coming out of one of them." Meehan smiled and said, "Funnily enough sir, I was thinking the same thing. I thought I would head up there around three when the pubs are closing and see if anything catches my eye. But, being Christmas day, I can bet that there will be some domestic disputes in the kitchen." Roddis slapped his hand down on the counter and glowered at Meehan. "If you bring me in a domestic dispute, make sure you arrest the turkey as well. I have my figure to look after, and I am not due my dinner until eight tonight." They all laughed, and Skelton shook hands with his subordinates and headed back to his office.

Skelton made himself a mug of tea and enjoyed a KitKat. He fired up his computer and checked the crime reports from Christmas Eve. There had been a handful arrests for drunk and disorderly and a couple of assaults. Dave Roddis had released the prisoners when he came on duty, hence the empty cells. At eleven o'clock Skelton began phoning his family and friends to wish them a happy Christmas. The last call he made was to Bill Alexander. "Good morning, Bill, and a very merry Christmas to you. Have you started on the Thatchers Gold yet?" Alexander chuckled down the phone. "Merry Christmas to you as well sir. No, I haven't had a drink yet but on the stroke of mid-day, I will be pouring my first. Anything happening at the office?" Skelton leaned back in his chair and yawned. "No, its like a graveyard here Bill. Ross Turnbull has a bottle of sherry in his desk, and I have two cans of Fosters in the fridge. So, at twelve-thirty we will be having a glass of sherry and a couple of square sausage sandwiches." Square sausage sandwiches or Lorne sausages as they are also known, are mostly found in Scotland and the north-east of England. Skelton was brought up on them and absolutely adored them. Since joining Manvers Street, he had converted his colleagues to their delicious taste. Fortunately, Marks and Spencer's in Bath had started selling them and both Skelton and Alexander were big buyers.

Having reviewed numerous witness statements in up-coming trials, Skelton glanced at his watch. It was twelve-fifteen. He got up from his desk and went to his fridge and removed the loaf of bread and took out four square sausages. He went to the kitchen and got out the frying pan and some vegetable oil. He carefully cooked the sausages and buttered four slices of bread. He placed the sausages on the bread and gently seasoned them with a little salt and white pepper. He then added some brown fruity sauce. When he had finished, he placed two sandwiches on two plates and began walking back to his office. He carefully placed the plates on his desk and went through to the C.I.D room. "Come on Ross, get your arse and that bottle of sherry into my office now. We don't want the sausages getting cold." Turnbull got out of his chair and said, "I'm on my way now sir. I've been thinking about those sausage sandwiches all morning. I didn't have any breakfast this morning, so I am more than ready for lunch."

Skelton led the way and Turnbull closely followed with the bottle of sherry in his right hand. In his left hand, he carried two small glasses. "Come on in Ross and grab a chair. I will get the cold Fosters out of the fridge. I'm sorry I haven't got any glasses for the Fosters. We will just have to drink straight from the can." Turnbull placed the two glasses on either side of the desk and dispensed the sherry. "My god these sausage sandwiches smell good. They should see me through the day until I have my dinner this evening." Skelton placed the two cans of Fosters on the desk. He picked up his glass of sherry and said, "Cheers Ross, let's just hope that we have an uneventful afternoon and then we can go home and enjoy a lovely Christmas dinner." They chinked glasses and Turnbull said, "Well I will drink to that. It's been a quiet morning with just two reports of domestic house breaking, which can wait until tomorrow morning when the rest of the team are back." The officers sipped the sherry and then began attacking the sausage sandwiches. Skelton opened his can of Fosters and gulped some of the golden juice down his throat. "You know what, Ross? This is just the perfect Christmas lunch I have ever had!" The men exchanged high fives and leaned back in their chairs, totally content.

Luke Meehan looked at his watch, it was two forty-five. He unlocked the car door with the key fob and got into the driver's seat. It had been a fairly quiet morning, with just a sudden death to take care of. It was an elderly gentleman and there were no suspicious circumstances. He had waited almost an hour for the undertakers to arrive and remove the body. He drove out of Manvers Street police station and headed towards Lansdown. He had decided to drive along the road to Bath racecourse as there were several pubs located in the vicinity. Anyone visiting these pubs would probably need to drive. Meehan was hoping to catch a drink driver. Although he had only been a police officer for two years, he had dealt with numerous fatal collisions involving drunk drivers. His mission today, was to try and prevent another fatal collision. It was bad enough having to tell relatives of a fatality on an ordinary day of the week, but on Christmas day, it would be unthinkable.

Michael Flowers lived in Twerton, one of the less fashionable areas of Bath. He was twenty-six years old and a car mechanic. He was six feet tall with a muscular build but had given up going to the gym nearly two years ago. That had coincided when he first started doing drugs. He had started smoking weed and that had progressed to ecstasy and then cocaine. He lived with his parents in a council flat along with his sister. His father was a builder, and his mother was a teacher's assistant. His sister worked as a hair stylist in a local hair salon. As well as taking drugs, Flowers had also become a part-time dealer to his friends and acquaintances. So far, he had remained undetected by the police as a dealer. He had however three convictions for assault and on the last occasion, had narrowly avoided a prison sentence. He was known to have a short fuse, particularly if he had been doing drugs.

It was mid-day, and Flowers was lying in his bed. He had been out with friends on Christmas Eve and had got drunk. He had staggered home at two in the morning and was now nursing a hangover. His bedroom door opened and his father Tom, pushed his head in. "Are you awake Michael? It's twelve o'clock and me and your mother are going to the pub. Do you want to join us?" Flowers raised his head above the pillow and said, "No thanks dad. I am just going to chill out. What time are we having dinner?" "The turkey will be ready at seven and your grand parents will be here at six. So, make sure you are up and showered before they arrive. I will see you when I get back."

Flowers actually had plans, for this Christmas afternoon. He had arranged to meet his drug supplier from Bristol at a layby just about a quarter of a mile before Bath racecourse. They had met several times at this location, and they had never had a problem with the police. Flowers knew that with it being Christmas, it was highly unlikely that he would see any police today.

Flowers was a violent man and during the two years he had been dealing drugs, he had on occasion had to resort to violence. Some of his customers, simply didn't have the money to pay for the drugs and had ended up owing him money. A few had made the big mistake of not paying the debt when asked. Flowers had shown them no mercy and had savagely beaten them up. One guy had pulled a knife on him which had really scared him. Luckily for Flowers, he was able to wrestle the knife away and he had used it to stab his victim several times in the buttocks. The blade was five inches long with a black handle. He had kept the knife and always carried it when dealing drugs.

At just before two o'clock Flowers got out of bed and went to the bathroom where he showered and shaved. After getting dressed, he snorted a line of coke which made the effects of his hangover vanish. He was now feeling good and was looking forward to having Christmas dinner with his family. He checked his watch, it was time to go and meet his drug supplier. Before heading to his car, he rolled a joint and stuck it in his jacket pocket. He would savour that later in the car. He picked up his phone and rang Ben Scobie, his drug supplier from Bristol and confirmed the usual meeting point in the layby near Bath racecourse.

He owned a black BMW which was two years old and was leased under a finance arrangement. The number plates on the car did not belong to it. Being a car mechanic, he had access to number plates, and he regularly changed plates to beat speeding fines and congestion charges. The cloned plates he was using belonged to a smart car. Flowers was a very confident individual and reckoned that with his salary and the profits from his drug dealing activities, he would be able to pay a deposit to buy a modest flat in Bath within the next six months.

Flowers got into his car and checked his phone. He started the engine and the radio came on. It was the usual Christmas shit but with the coke inside him, he actually started singing along to the songs. He pointed the car towards Lansdown and smiled. He would go and do the deal and then drive home and have a few drinks with his mum and dad and baby sister. He already had half a dozen regular customers lined up to meet tomorrow. Business was good and would get even better leading up to the new year.

The road leading to Bath racecourse was pretty straight, and he was cruising at fifty miles per hour. It was two fifty when he pulled into the layby and switched the engine off. He had at least ten minutes to spare before his supplier turned up, so he took the joint from his pocket and lit it up. Soon he felt on cloud nine and invincible.

Luke Meehan was driving towards Bath racecourse on the lookout for any potential drink drivers or even drug drivers. In recent years the number of drug drivers had increased significantly, and Meehan had the necessary kit to analyse both. He was cruising along at a steady forty miles per hour and the traffic was very light. Most people had already reached their destinations and were enjoying lunch or preparing for dinner. Meehan saw the black BMW parked in the layby and wondered if the driver needed assistance due to a mechanical failure. He made the decision to pull into the layby and see if he could be of any help. Flowers heard the car and looked in his rear-view mirror. He was horrified to see the police car. He had over six hundred pounds in his wallet and some cocaine in the boot. He was also was carrying a blade. With his previous convictions, this could mean some time in prison. He was trying his best not to panic. He checked his mirror again, and was relieved to see that there was only one police officer in the car.

Meehan got out of the car and began to walk towards the BMW. As he got closer, he could smell the cannabis. This could be his first arrest of the day. The driver's window was slightly lowered which was why he had detected the cannabis. He lowered his head and spoke through the lowered window. "Excuse me sir. Could you step out of the vehicle please, I can detect a strong smell of weed out here. Flowers knew he had been caught. The game was up. He would most probably fail a drugs test and all the drugs in the car and the blade he was carrying meant disaster. Flowers opened the door and undid his seat belt. What the fuck could he do?

Meehan watched the suspect as he got out of the car. The guy was bigger than him and he wished that he was not alone on this patrol. "Right sir, I can smell cannabis on you. Have you just had a joint?" Flowers was compliant and said, "Yes officer I just had a smoke whilst waiting for a friend to show up. It is Christmas after all. By the way, happy Christmas to you." He put out his hand to shake the officer's hand and smiled. Meehan instinctively shook the man's hand. "Do you have any identification on you sir?" I need you to take a seat in the back of my police car." Meehan began walking back to his car. Suddenly Flowers had the knife in his hand and viciously stabbed Meehan in the neck. His body armour or stab vest, gave him no protection to his neck. Blood was spouting from the wound and Meehan was unable to press the emergency button on his radio. He was dead in seconds.

Flowers knew that the police car would have a dash camera that would have recorded the murder. The cop also had a camera on his vest jacket which would also have recorded Flowers' every move. He quickly checked the road but not a single car had passed since the cop had pulled in. He had to think very quickly. He opened the driver's door and picked up the lifeless body of Luke Meehan. He manged to get it into the driver's seat and pushed it, so that it lay across the driver and passenger seats. He had blood on his jacket and trousers and there was blood on the ground. He opened the boot of his car and took out the petrol can. He quickly poured about two pints of petrol inside the police car and then lit a match and threw it inside the cop car. The car went up in a massive ball of flames. He closed the driver's door and made his way to his car. Still no cars had passed by the incident. He got into his car and started the engine. He pulled out of the layby and headed towards home. With any amount of luck, the film in both the dash camera and the copper's vest would be destroyed in the inferno. He stopped the car and texted Ben Scobie. The message read, "Police about the meeting is off." He held the phone for a minute and a text message came back from Scobie. "OK".

STUDIES IN ART

OUT OF THE CAGE

THE ART OF ISABEL RAWSTHORNE

The impressions and sense perceptions of man ...
belong in the category of surprises

Paul Valéry

1. Isabel Rawsthorne, Untitled (Dancers), c. 1967; New Art Gallery, Walsall

OUT OF THE CAGE

THE ART OF ISABEL RAWSTHORNE

Carol Jacobi

The Estate of Francis Bacon Publishing,
supported by Francis Bacon MB Art Foundation Monaco,
in association with Thames & Hudson

ACKNOWLEDGEMENTS

My great gratitude goes to those that knew Isabel who have provided so much moral and practical support. First and foremost, her late brother, Warwick Nicholas, his wife, Evelyn, sons and daughters Susan, David, Paul and Nancy, and the wider family, who have so generously shared Isabel's work and their fascinating memories of her. Heartfelt thanks to Biddy Noakes, who has collaborated with the family and cared for Isabel's own artworks with such integrity over twenty-five years, and who has given me an enormous amount of time, energy and inspiration. I have been fortunate in many wonderful conversations with others who knew Isabel, colleagues and friends: of special importance were the Noakes family, Jack, Anna and Mary, and Patricia Lambert and her family who kindly provided access to Pattie's collection and papers pertaining to Isabel. Invaluable insights are owed to John Blake, David Blayney-Brown, Nigel Bonham-Carter, Kim Echlin, Edith Evans, Clifford Frith, Chili Hawes, James Lord, Corinna MacNeice, Monica Mason, Maureen Ramsey, Juliette Ryan, Lady Anya Sainsbury, Veronica Sekules, Elizabeth Stamper, Iris and Nigel Weaver, and Edward and Judith Williams.

This book was made possible by a twelve-month fellowship awarded by the Leverhulme Foundation and the National Portrait Gallery, under the guidance of Peter Funnell, and funded research projects from Brian Clarke and The Estate of Francis Bacon. It is indebted to pioneering research on Isabel by Biddy Noakes, Suzanne Doyle, Martin Harrison and Véronique Wiesinger and to their personal guidance and advice. I am grateful also for the scholarly support of the following individuals and institutions: Aviva Burnstock, Rosie Gleave and the Department of Conservation and Technology at the Courtauld Institute of Art, Paola Carola, Rebecca Daniels, Jo Digger and New Art Gallery Walsall, Helen Draper, Patrick Elliott, Francesca Franci and the Royal Opera House, Philippe Garner, Anaïs Alax Gazeau, Amanda Harrison, Thadée Klossowski de Rola and The Estate of Balthus, Andrew Mayes and the Alan Rawsthorne Society, David Alan Mellor, Jacqueline Munck, Emily Parsons and Liverpool John Moores University, Chika Okeke-Agulu, Lee Richards,

June Rose, Evelyn Silber, Robin Stummer, Martin Thacker, Lisa Tickner, Nicholas Fox Weber, Beth Williamson, Sarah Wilson and Rebecca Winter.

I have benefited especially from the indefatigable critical and editorial help of Martin Harrison and the wisdom and patience of Gillian Malpass, both of whom took the book up and made it a reality. The great generosity of Majid Boustany and the Francis Bacon MB Art Foundation, and the support of the Fondation Giacometti, have made it possible to illustrate Isabel's work in the way it deserves. I must also express my appreciation for the editorial and design assistance of Christina Bradstreet, Caroline Corbeau-Parsons, Marilyn Downes, Brett Harrison, Audrey MacNair, Louis Leatherbarrow, Francesca Pipe and my husband Martin Guy. I owe inexpressible thanks to Martin for the years of travelling, talking and intellectual support, and to my children, Max Jacobi and Bob Guy. Finally, I am grateful to the care of the NHS, which afforded more time to Isabel, myself and several others involved in this book, and made possible Isabel's mature life and art.

Dedicated to the memory of Martin Guy

CONTENTS

Part III

AUTHOR'S NOTE

The monographic form can reinforce the 'difference' accorded to women's artistic careers, so this book takes a more centrifugal structure, investigating the way in which Isabel's art and history were at the centre of – and reconfigured – the art and history of her times. The hitherto unsuspected adventures of her teens and twenties reveal an advanced early career that casts startling light on her peers as well as on her own life and achievements. Although tantalisingly few paintings are known from this period, glimpses are preserved in her memoir and autobiographical notes and her long correspondences with Alberto Giacometti and the photographer Peter Rose Pulham, and her singular vision is corroborated by the work surviving after the 1940s, discussed in later chapters. Rawsthorne's activities, integrity, intellect and incredibly clear perception of modern culture illuminate her own radical painting and new aspects of twentieth-century art.

As much as possible, this book foregrounds Isabel's voice in the form of her works and her writings. The subject of this monograph, now known as Isabel Rawsthorne, worked and exhibited as Isabel Lambert, and over the course of her life she had three other surnames. This text will, therefore, designate her by her forename in its correct spelling, Isabel.

2. John Everard: Isabel Rawsthorne, 1933

3. Isabel Rawsthorne, *Alan and Barbara Rawsthorne* (detail), 1967; Sainsbury Centre for Visual Arts, University of East Anglia

INTRODUCTION

> Isabel doesn't walk she strides; her beautiful *Gauloises* rasping voice would occasionally be modulated to deliver a pronouncement!! This energy is there in abundance throughout her work, they are statements of absolute conviction, terse, staccato and economic.
>
> Clifford Frith[1]

On 6 March 1968, twenty-one paintings stacked in the back of a 1934 Lagonda processed conspicuously along London's Bond Street. They were unloaded at the Marlborough Gallery, without much ceremony, by two tall artists: Clifford Frith, who owned the car, and Isabel Rawsthorne, who had made the works.[2] The effect of the pictures when they were hung on the walls of the gallery was austere in the context of psychedelic 1968. Whole figures and heads were folded into the creases and currents of wide, landscape spaces. A dancer fleetingly identified herself: rotated socket, knotted calf, warped foot caught and carved in painty, gestural *rilievo schiacciato*. In a series of double portraits, old men bantered, their fragile skin churned and divided by the animation of their talk. Between them, empty wine glasses evaporated, like the dancers: one had spilled, and the dark stain resolved itself into the artist's shadow; another held yellow narcissi, spitting like sparklers. The heads in this painting were turning away from each other: an ending – cigarette smoke leaving their mouths like departing souls.

The *vernissage* the following afternoon was busy.[3] The pictures maintained their imperious distance from the gaudy celebrities, philosophers, artists, musicians and a crowd from Soho that included Francis Bacon and George Dyer. Some of the subjects of the paintings were present: ballerinas, composers and poets. Isabel was chic in Left Bank black. Her talk was emphatic and accented, the way the French converse. Their chatter was scintillating, but increasingly tipsy and focused on each other.

Isabel's exhibition debut thirty-five years before, when she was twenty, in the nearby Valenza Gallery, had been a sell-out. Fifteen years later, her second solo show, at the Hanover Gallery in 1949, broke new ground for the School of London and brought eight years of experience in Paris back to her home city. With her colleagues Lucian Freud, Francis Bacon, Peter Lanyon and John Craxton, she was included in David Sylvester's selection of five London painters 'of outstanding talent' who would challenge Paris and New York after the war.[4]

And now, the 1968 exhibition at the Marlborough Gallery unveiled her third, long campaign, the culmination of twenty years of study. During the succeeding two decades, she returned to her studio to develop another set of pictures which she was preparing to display when she died in 1992. In the 1930s, 1940s and 1960s, Isabel was showing revolutionary work at the leading avant-garde galleries of her day. How did she disappear from the history of art?

When Isabel started out as a painter in the 1930s, the art world was a place for relatively privileged people, and to follow her career it was necessary for her to abandon what was expected of someone of her class, as well as of her gender. By the age of nineteen, in 1931, she was fending for herself, would never make a safe marriage and was more exposed than most to the tumultuous events of her century. She was 'authentic' before Jean-Paul Sartre coined the term and, like a latter-day Moll Flanders, invented her life as she went along, through poverty, wars and social struggle, seeking the freedom to paint. Her pictures, dominated by the body, were made in the spirit of research. Her unorthodox lifestyle was an extension of this research, an experiment in existence.

Isabel was a decoy for herself, however. The vivacity with which she pursued the knowledge and independence that would allow her to devote herself to her work created a dazzling persona that eclipsed it. Her astute sense of what was important in art, where the cutting edge lay, led her into friendships with those who would become major names in their century. They loved, painted and sculpted her, and it is the glamour of these images that has taken centre stage. Isabel's beauty, her inquisitive appetite for life and her impatience with convention spun around her a movie-star celebrity that was doomed to imprison her in standard *vanitas* narratives of descent into old age. When Isabel's hair turned grey and both her looks and her social glitter were fading, she was painting her best work.

Isabel was not a reclusive artist, but she kept her work and the art world unusually separate and never embraced the market, rigorous in her disconnection of painting from selling. As well as solo shows, she had many joint ones. She was a collaborator with and confidante to three generations of other artists – Jacob Epstein, Alberto Giacometti and Francis Bacon, also André Derain, Pablo Picasso, Peter Rose Pulham and Roy Noakes. Her knowledge of the art of her century and of most others besides was exceptional, and her intolerance of bullshit precise. She wrote little, however, and only a small part of that was published. The writers James Lord and David Sylvester visited Isabel many times in the course of their research for their respective works on Giacometti and Bacon, but neither of them investigated her studio; and only when Isabel was in her seventies did Veronica Sekules, on behalf of the Sainsbury Centre for Visual Arts in Norwich, conduct interviews with her about her own work. Fortunately, in these last years, Isabel also prepared an autobiography or memoir. Its ironic, laconic style plays with the reader – it is pillow talk, the kind you have when you are at that early stage of exchanging life stories and philosophies, but not all of them. In general, Isabel left her pictures to speak for themselves.

Isabel did not advertise what she was doing after the exhibition of 1968, and few knew she was working. It was sheer good fortune that, on her death and the passing of her personal papers and letters and a large collection of her own artworks to Warwick Nicholas, her brother, the mature masterpieces were saved from her studio. Her early work did not fare so well: her impoverished and itinerant life did not provide a permanent place to make or store pictures until she was forty. Hundreds of drawings and paintings were abandoned in corners of hotel rooms or borrowed studios, misplaced in moves, separations and wars. Within five years of Isabel's death in 1992 (to be followed in a matter of weeks by Bacon's death), the estate, Biddy Noakes and Suzanne Doyle had catalogued her work and, with Karen Southworth at the Mercer Art Gallery in Harrogate and Chili Hawes and Corinna MacNeice at the October Gallery in London, realised Isabel's hope of a retrospective exhibition. With the support of Warwick Nicholas, paintings finally began to enter national collections: the Royal Opera House, the National Portrait Gallery and Tate. After 2000, other curators and art historians independently sought out her pictures, notably Véronique Wiesinger, Martin Harrison and Jo Digger. This book, begun in 2008 with the help of a Leverhulme Fellowship at the National Portrait Gallery, is indebted to their advice, and most especially to the indefatigable labours of Biddy Noakes in researching the paintings. Since the death of Warwick Nicholas in 2010, his estate continues his work and, in collaboration with Biddy Noakes, Evelyn Nicholas has generously placed the main part of Isabel's artistic legacy in public collections, most notably nearly two hundred drawings and paintings of the moving body donated to New Art Gallery, Walsall, in 2012, in memory of Warwick.

This book has had the benefit of extensive access to Isabel's writing and artworks and looks at them in detail, alongside many new French and British sources, and interviews with those who knew Isabel beyond Soho: the Nicholas family, her closest friends and her colleagues. Together, they reveal a nearly unbelievable narrative of art, thought and love enacted through the upheavals of the twentieth century and her relationships with some of its most fascinating figures.

PART I

4. Isabel on the beach, c. 1926; courtesy of Evelyn Nicholas

1 COMING OF AGE IN LIVERPOOL: 1912–1931

A man's life is after all nothing but a series of chance events and the way he, more or less precisely, responds to them.

Paul Valéry[1]

Isabel was with Paul Valéry on biography. She recalled her life in 'vivid, isolated images'. Accordingly, in her last years she composed her autobiography in short factual episodes and statements: 'I was born in London in 1912, daughter of a master mariner, Philip Llewelyn Nicholas of Welsh and Scottish descent, and an English mother, Christine Agnes Warwick. I was christened in Hackney; therefore I hope I am a cockney.'[2] Behind the irony of identifying herself as a Welsh-Scottish-English cockney lies a question about belonging. The 'chance events' that follow trace a life and art experienced as essentially provisional.

The memoir remained incomplete, but we can deduce from it that Isabel did not stay long in Hackney. Lloyd's 'Captains' Registers' record that Philip Nicholas gained his Master's Certificate in 1904, skippered ships for the Harrison Line and worked out of West India Dock in London's East End.[3] As he sailed around the globe, Isabel and her mother moved from port to port, house to house, improvising a life between themselves, but she felt deeply loved by both of her parents.[4] As a toddler, dressed proudly in a sailor suit, she accompanied her mother on trips to meet her father at landfalls around the British Isles and on the Continent. Otherwise, London was Isabel's playground; she was happy sharing Agnes Nicholas's interests and cherished their self-sufficiency.[5] They attended concerts – Handel oratorios, for example – and, from the age of three, Agnes Nicholas took her daughter to sketch in public gardens or at London Zoo.[6] They already thought Isabel would be an artist. Often, they went to museums, and one of Isabel's earliest remembered enthusiasms was the small oil painting hanging in the National Gallery, Jan van Eyck's *Arnolfini Portrait* (1434).[7] That it was a double portrait, man and wife side by side, regarding the viewer with calm recognition, is perhaps significant in light of the importance of the double portrait in her later career.

Isabel was two years old when the First World War began. Philip Nicholas's ship, the SS *Inkosi*, was co-opted to carry troops, while Isabel and her mother waited anxiously for news in a flat in Kew.[8] They were near the botanical gardens, where

Isabel would play and draw the birds. She was sent away to stay for a while with an aunt and two older male cousins in a coastguard's cottage near Winchelsea in Sussex. This she experienced as a 'beautifully free life. I never wore shoes and only ate what I liked ... no cake, only bread and butter; no drink other than water, not even milk.' There, Isabel learned to swim almost as soon as she could walk, while her father plied the more hazardous seas off the Hellespont, the straits swum by the legendary Leander. He spent most of the war in this area, supporting the disastrous Dardanelles campaign against the Ottomans, transferring later to the SS *Inkonka* to transport aeroplanes. An affectionate letter, illustrated with airships and biplanes and full of kisses, written by her father on 18 May 1918, after a period of leave, promised Isabel that, when the war was over, she would take 'a long voyage with Daddy' during which she would see 'many wonderful things'. (According to family history, she and her mother accompanied Philip on a trip to Africa when she was seven or eight.[9]) During the course of the conflict, the Harrison Line lost a third of its fleet: the *Inkosi* was torpedoed and sunk in 1918, but the *Inkonka* was unscathed, and Philip Nicholas returned to civilian duties.

School, when it started for Isabel after the war, was intermittent and, like most children her age, barely noticed. She took lessons in dance, and two of the handful of family photographs from this period show her leaping with pointed toes across the floral carpet of a modest front room, arms sawing the air.[10] Agnes managed to get two sought-after tickets for them to see the world-famous Italian soprano Amelita Galli-Curci on her United Kingdom tour; one wonders what a twelve-year-old Isabel made of the petite, powerful, self-made woman. On the occasions when Agnes went away on trips with Philip, Isabel relished her return to her relatives on the coast, running wild with her cousins, making fires in the open or riding pillion on a motorbike. The British Broadcasting Corporation began in 1922 when she was ten. She was the first generation for whom concerts and plays were available to more than a privileged few, and she would listen avidly on a cat's whisker radio with the older boys.[11] The freedom of movement and imagination that she experienced in Sussex would be necessary to her throughout her life.

Philip Nicholas was an unusual father and encouraged an attitude and outlook that would also shape Isabel's career. He was an amateur naturalist, and his brief and dramatic homecomings were accompanied by an influx of animals that he had collected on his travels. These he left behind to be tended in specially heated and barricaded spare rooms that Agnes set aside in their various homes, until the creatures could be sold or donated to zoos. 'I grew up thinking it was normal to hear scratching, grunts and scraping noises during the night,' Isabel wrote, 'to have alligators in the bath, snakes in bundles of straw. There was one merry occasion when we had a pair of red-handed [?]tamarins and a large rodent called a [?]hooteah in one room, a large, stork like bird in the yard and a rare beetle in a box.[12] The bird was nicknamed "Misery" because of the sad hooting it made at night.' She collected worms and caterpillars to feed a chameleon that Philip bought back for her in 1918, but it did not survive.[13] Amateur studies in zoological gardens, museums and in the countryside were usual among lower-middle-class children like Isabel, but her activities were more than a hobby. Her domestic encounters with wild creatures and their association with an absent father and far-flung adventures were augmented by her avid reading of Philip's books and her own explorations closer to home.[14] Her enthusiasm for natural history underpinned broader interests that chimed with the specifically progressive, scientific spirit that thrived after the war. Both Philip and Agnes came from actively religious families, but Philip became a 'convinced atheist'. Isabel thought this was at least partly in rebellion against his sisters: one an Anglican nun; one, the wife of the Rector of Botley; and one, a governess in a Catholic household in Czechoslovakia. Neither her christening, while Philip was at sea, nor maternal and educational influences prevented Isabel's sharing his materialist views.

What Isabel described as her 'carefree' life ended in 1925, when, at the age of forty-six, Agnes fell pregnant. She expected that she and her daughter would be companions in this as they had been in so much else, but the thirteen-year-old was hardly interested. Her mother reproached her, saying she was 'unnatural', and Isabel's place at her side was soon taken by a baby boy, Warwick Llewellyn Nicholas, born the following spring, on 3 April 1926. In later life, Isabel became closer to her brother; he would prove even more passionate than she about natural history, for example, but she remembered that, at the time, the beginning of his childhood felt like the end of hers: 'the gaiety of childhood had gone forever'.

From this time on, the Nicholases became a relatively conventional family, something alien to Isabel. They settled in Wallasey, near the headquarters of the Harrison Line. Perched on the corner of the Wirral Peninsula facing out to Liverpool Bay to the north and bounded by the River Mersey inlet to the west and south, the town was dominated by docks that echoed the grander ones in Liverpool, across the water. The Nicholases' home at 7 Wallacre Road was a small, semi-detached house on one of the new estates that spread inland between the port and the sea. Isabel was enrolled at Wallasey High School.[15] Lessons took place in the morning so that the domestic duties expected of young women could continue in the afternoon, but she spent most afternoons sketching, roaming barefoot in the dunes and, from May to November, bathing in the sea.

Two years at Wallasey High School advanced Isabel's course without altering it. In 1926, the education of girls beyond twelve was relatively new, and the institution was part of the Girls Public Day School Trust, established late

5. Isabel with fellow students, Wallasey High School, c. 1928; courtesy of Evelyn Nicholas

in the nineteenth century to provide affordable academic, moral and religious education to all classes. Between the lines of Isabel's terse autobiography, we can see that she was not like the other pupils and was ill equipped to be taught formally: she would often avoid classes, staying outside to draw or simply to hide. She participated in art, drama, dance and sport more readily, however, and experienced for the first time having a friend of her own age and sex, Lesley Macdonald. Isabel was impressed that Lesley played the cello; unusually for a girl of her age and class, Isabel herself appears not to have had any music lessons. Her belated attempt to study piano while still at school was unsuccessful, but she was always grateful to have at least learned to read musical notation. It is a measure of Isabel's intelligence (and the determination of her teachers) that, after only two years, she matriculated with her peers in 1928. The school records show that she won the Senior Drawing Prize.[16]

Isabel entered Liverpool School of Art the following autumn.[17] She was sixteen, and her mother made the arrangements, but she was unchaperoned, as free in the city as she had been on coast. The journey from the school to her home in Wallasey was little more than an hour on the Mersey ferry, or by the electric railway through the Mersey Tunnel. Nevertheless, she moved to a flat in Liverpool with two other girl students.[18] Number 12 Hattons Lane, in the garden suburb of Wavertree, was an hour's walk from the School of Art and only a few minutes' stroll from Childwall Woods, a haven for wildlife. Isabel stayed in touch with her family, however, and her brother remembered playing with her in the garden at Wallacre Road after she had moved out.

The School of Art was a successful establishment in an impressive six-storey Victorian building at 68 Hope Street. Its strict principal, George Marples, had studied in Paris and taught at the Royal College of Art in London. His career in Liverpool had been spent preserving the traditions of academic art practice alongside the city's expanding and fluctuating modern design needs.[19] Typically of its time, the school took students from the age of fourteen and concentrated on such vocational trades as furniture making, printing and hairdressing, with only a small number studying fine art. Its records show that Isabel was one of this minority.[20] The more industrial skills were taught in the basement, while the fine-art studios were in the upper rooms, lit by elegant, arched windows. A third of the space was given over to storing Classical casts, which overflowed into the thoroughfares and public spaces.

Despite the rumbustious atmosphere introduced by the influx of soldiers retraining after the war, Liverpool School of Art had hung on to its reputation as a respectable venue for young women. Female students had had access since 1883, and half of Isabel's peers were of her own sex, although more well-to-do than she was. Some viewed their studies as accomplishments on the way to careers as wives and mothers; others may have contemplated teaching. Isabel would have been directed towards the teaching profession by the Girls Public Day School Trust, but, during this period of post-war reintegration and national unemployment, the training and appointment of art teachers was dominated by men.[21] Career manuals for young women, therefore, recommended the exhibition and sale of works as the best hope for securing a role in the fine arts. This indicated an unspoken bias towards those who could afford the risks of an unreliable market, which Isabel could not. It is likely that her motives for becoming an artist were more straightforward: the conviction that she *was* an artist and the momentum of a life already devoted to drawing. This simpler narrative was available to her in biographical or fictional portraits of male artists, and recently, a more progressive, female variation had appeared in literary form in the art student Gudrun Brangwen in D. H. Lawrence's *The Rainbow* and *Woman in Love* (1915 and 1920, but unbanned and available in England only from 1926 and 1921, respectively).[22]

Again, Isabel must have stood out from her fellow students. Her fierce focus and skill were already evident, and she expressed herself in a low, resonant voice with unusual vivacity and directness. Her appearance was also conspicuous: she had grown tall – 1.7 metres – with a characteristic light, slanting, athletic gait, and she retained her expansive gestures.[23] 'She always walked toes out – like a dancer', recalled a friend.[24] Her Celtic colouring, sharp chin and cheekbones and long-lidded eyes gave her an imperious otherness that was belied by her ready expression of surprise and her unfettered laugh. Nonetheless, she finally felt at home: 'I was happy from the beginning, the atmosphere for anyone really interested in working was sympathetic. One could work as much and at what one liked.'

Isabel studied the established subjects formalised by the South Kensington System of art education in the middle of the nineteenth century. These included perspective and drawing and painting from casts, natural forms, landscape, life and memory. The landscape class was run on methods she was used to – observational sketching in parks and museums and from specimens brought back to the studio – and she especially relished the instruction in watercolour.[25] Marples encouraged her pursuit of natural history. He himself studied, drew and photographed birds and published the highly illustrated *Sea Terns or Sea Swallows: Their Habits, Language, Arrival and Departure* in 1934.[26] He had made his name with exquisite etchings that drew on Northern European and Japanese art, both of which would prove foundational to Isabel's painting.[27]

Isabel's preferred teacher was William Penn, Master of the Antique and Still Life. He was a decorated war veteran who had lost a hand at Arras and had trained at the Royal Academy Schools and the Académie Julian in Paris. He was a great raconteur and the first, perhaps, to ignite in Isabel her passion to go to France. She found his Perspective class particularly interesting. It involved huge pieces of paper on which lines were mapped and measured to create a tiny construction in the centre.[28] Penn also taught light and shadow and the architectural orders. Life classes, run by Colin Morris, were equally orientated towards precision. The models held poses for long periods, raised in state on electrically heated thrones.[29] The nude was considered the pre-eminent subject, but life studies at the School were segregated. The models in the women's class were more extensively draped than in the men's.[30] Morris, another alumnus of the Royal Academy, was as tweedy and traditional as Marples – often dressed in a deerstalker – but the students were in awe of his skill with a fine 6H pencil.

Principal Marples was, surprisingly, responsible for the most novel teaching technique at Liverpool. He pioneered the use of photographic slides for instruction and went on to specialise in such lectures in later life. Friday afternoons were set aside for a lantern show of Old Masters, providing Isabel with an unprecedented introduction to the tradition of art. This she supplemented with visits to the city's Walker Art Gallery, as well as with her memories of wandering with her mother through the National Gallery, the British Museum and the Victoria and Albert Museum in London. Marples's projected images were, moreover, seamed with lines that he had superimposed to show geometry and proportion. Isabel came to understand works of art not just as revered objects but as the subject of reproductions that could be activated and turned into working documents. Marples's final flourish before retiring in 1930 was to take the class to London to see the *Exhibition of Italian Art, 1200–1900* at the Royal Academy.[31] This historic show was part of a propaganda offensive by Mussolini's fascist regime in Italy, permitting the appearance in London of a never-to-be-repeated wealth of Renaissance paintings. For Isabel, it was a luxurious encounter with the nude, notably Sandro Botticelli's *Birth of Venus* (c. 1482; Uffizi Gallery, Florence).[32]

Despite the strict teaching structure, Isabel found a flourishing bohemian subculture at the School of Art. A memoir from the period recalls that students rejected the single-sex common rooms and crowded amongst the statues in the corridors.[33] Marples attempted to clamp down on lax behaviour: latecomers, for example, were made to stand on a bench with their hands on their head, but clandestine liberties continued.[34] Isabel described being part of a particularly rebellious 'group of thinkers' frustrated by 'the one view of how things should be done'.[35] Two of the ringleaders were William Stevenson and George McPherson. Marples asked Stevenson to leave, just before he retired, but the young rebel went on to become Principal at the school and McPherson became Head of Sculpture.

The 'thinkers' have, until now, been lost to art history, but their activities were significant. In an interview tape-recorded in 1984, Stevenson recalled one of these. He delighted in subverting the classes in Perspective, challenging fellow students with unusual drawing media – a piece of lead pipe, for example – or constructing objects upside down. His recollection is worth quoting at length:

> I was attempting to understand what it was one was trying to get out of this activity. It was the capacity for feeling, I had to become the element I wished to draw ... I used to say, 'Look, I'm sitting in the third row on seat number so-an-so in the dress circle of the theatre – and I'm going to draw the theatre around me', and I'd go up to the board and do it ... if you have a scale element in one position, then you can project in any direction you want, perspective is to do with the position you are in and the point of view you take. You are part and parcel of the essence of what you are involved in – and in that sense it is a creative process.[36]

Stevenson's reference to theatres evoked the music halls painted by Walter Sickert, and his rejection of conventional perspective in favour of an embodied eye – *in* the world rather than observing from an emotional and physical distance – owed a debt to the older artist. Sickert, moreover, saw embodied perspective as intrinsic to drawing. His account anticipated Stevenson's: 'If you could put on paper by sight the place, that is to say the minute [angle to the viewer] of every line you see, you could draw. Proportion, anatomy, botany, mineralogy, eschatology, skiagraphy, perspective and everything else will follow.'[37] Against many of his contemporaries, Sickert argued that drawing was intrinsic to painting: without it, any work 'is wanting in bite, in bulk in depth, in resonance and in uniqueness'. These two ideas would inform Isabel's vision – and that of the artists with whom she came into contact – for ever.

This student debt to Sickert is unsurprising. His lively letters to *The Times* and writings in *The New Age* and other journals and newspapers (including *The Liverpool Daily Post and Mercury*) grappled with almost every movement and issue of modern art, from Edgar Degas (whom he knew) onwards. His views were non-elitist and appealing to those from ordinary backgrounds, like Isabel. He defended and debated with such radicals as Percy Wyndham Lewis and Jacob Epstein, representatives of the pre-war Vorticist movement, while distaining the more snooty 'Rogerisms', as he called them, of Roger Fry and his Oxbridge-based Bloomsbury set. Crucial to Isabel would be Sickert's elimination of distinctions between so called 'high' and 'low' visual culture, and his pioneering engagement with popular imagery, photography and film.

Isabel described the 'thinkers' (whose name echoed the rebellious 'thinkers' in Fritz Lang's dystopian science-fiction film *Metropolis*, premiered in Britain in 1927[38]), as 'a small group ... which spent nearly all its time drawing from the nude'. Her autobiography reveals that they set up an alternative studio in the first-floor room of an old building in Wood Street, less than a mile from the college. The two boys and three girls defied the segregated life class by posing for each other, the girls naked. Isabel's description of working late into the night with the light from the clock of St Luke's church flooding through the windows (the irony again mischievously unspoken) has an air of Sickert's depictions of nudes in ordinary rented rooms and the dramatic lighting of black-and-white film. Only the ruins of the church exist today, but the studio remains, perched above the shabby yet revered 1950s music venue, the Cabin Club.

A little further down the road from the Wood Street studio was the Sandon Studios Society, run after 1925 by the Bluecoat Society of Arts in an old Blue Coat school. It had hosted Roger Fry's ground-breaking Post-Impressionism shows in 1911 and 1913 and had gone on to become a sanctuary for artists and craftspeople, a venue for exhibitions, campaigns, concerts, readings and debates. Augustus John, probably the most famous English painter of the time, was among its members, and Sickert lectured there in 1924.[39] By 1928, the society was at the centre of Liverpool bohemianism, providing an alternative ethos and atmosphere to the School of Art, and its culture may have encouraged the 'thinkers'.[40] Even by these bohemian standards, however, Isabel's collective studio practice was original. It signalled the first-principles approach and the refusal to conform that would be a constant of her life.

The approach to the nude of the Wood Street ménage addressed that of the dominant nineteenth-century moderns: Degas, Paul Cézanne and the sculptor Auguste Rodin. Rodin and Cézanne had explored the male as well as the female life model, and Isabel especially valued Rodin, 'one of the artists whom I came to love in my early youth ... particularly his drawings'.[41] This focus is significant. The sculptor promoted the sexualised representation of the body as a vehicle for avant-garde ideas, and the embodied eye became synonymous with a one-to-one encounter between artist and model. This privilege was usually the preserve of the financially independent male artist with a private studio. The Wood Street enterprise provided a less elitist alternative, affordable and accessible to male and female students alike. More importantly for twentieth-century art, as shall be seen, the doubling up of artist and model was a new twist on the embodied eye. Its intimacy and equality broke down the artist/model opposition and fulfilled to an even greater degree Stevenson's demand 'to become the element I wished to draw'. In short, the method of the 'thinkers' set aside traditional ideals of the detached observer, the masculine authoritative eye, the classical body and the definitive single contour to place the artist's real person and perception at the centre of representation.

The Wood Street studio addressed the persona of the modern artist as well. The encounter between artist and model, intrinsic to the art of Degas and Rodin, remained central to narratives surrounding living painters such as Walter Sickert and Augustus John and sculptors such as Jacob Epstein. Such narratives were informed by the notion of the artist as 'virile creator', sexually and artistically potent, and of art making 'as a process tantamount to sexualised creation'.[42] Such myths were less available to female colleagues.[43] In fact, in the twentieth century the conventional polarity between protean male artist and passive female sitter increased, against the trends of society as a whole. Isabel's defiant Wood Street arrangement rejected this polarity and retained the initiative for men and women. Their collective practice did not so much reverse gender expectations of the male artist and female model, as go beyond binary genders altogether to something far more interesting, an amalgamation of the artist/model role itself.

Art and life were, for Isabel, it seems, equally experimental, a first-principles process of research, each informing the other. Evidence is growing that, in the interwar period, although some young women were accompanied to college by their mothers, the liberty enjoyed by Isabel was not too unusual.[44] Her teenage independence can be viewed against a broader backdrop of early twentieth-century 'progressive' thought, including the scientific ideas that interested her. In 1928, emancipated and advanced ideals must have seemed singularly viable: the Representation of the People (Equal Franchise) Act, extending the right to vote to all women in the United Kingdom, was passed eight days before Isabel's sixteenth birthday, just as she put her name down for art school. Liverpool was, moreover, like London and Glasgow, a singularly dynamic, multicultural city and an established centre for new thinking and reform on both the Left and the Right. The local campaigner Eleanor Rathbone had set up the first Women Citizens' Association in 1913 and was one of the first six women voted in as Members of Parliament at the 1929 election. The first clinic devoted to educating couples on birth control opened in Liverpool in 1926.[45] The Bluecoat Society of Arts was often at the centre of social debates and acted as a fulcrum between liberal, bohemian and other populations in the city.

Isabel also had access to ideas from further afield. In the late 1920s, newspapers, journals and novels like those by H. G. Wells, D. H. Lawrence and Virginia Woolf circulated new political, social and scientific thought. The attitudes of the breakaway Wood Street studio chimed particularly with the speculations of such writers on open relationships, or of the practical and uninhibited teenage groups described in 1928 in the paperback *Coming of Age in Samoa* by the anthropologist Margaret Mead. Its subtitle was *A Psychological Study of Primitive Youth for Western Civilisation*, and Mead offered an engaging social model in which the naked body and sexuality were directed according to 'suitability and expediency', while marriage was relegated to a mutual convenience, a 'brittle monogamy, often trespassed and more often broken entirely'. Happy partnerships were, Mead asserted, more dependent on the equal material autonomy of the participants than on sexual continence.[46] In 1929, Woolf's essay on female creative life, *A Room of One's Own*, stressed the necessity of material independence to achieve success in the arts.[47] These ideas would prove prophetic for Isabel, and she would never enter a partnership in which she could not participate equally.

Mead's *Coming of Age in Samoa* and Radclyffe Hall's contemporary novel on lesbian love, *The Well of Loneliness*, were discussed extensively in the Liverpool press in the summer of 1929.[48] Further variations on conventional relationships were aired in publications on sexual liberation itself, particularly regarding the redundancy of traditional attitudes to contraception and marriage. A leading voice was that of the pacifist and educationalist Dora Russell. Her book *Hypatia; or, Women and Knowledge* was published in 1925 and was followed in 1929 by that of her partner, Bertrand Russell, *Marriage and Morals*.[49] This coincided with the 1929 World League for Sexual Reform congress, co-organised by Dora, in London. The conference passed progressive resolutions on marriage, divorce, censorship, sex education, birth control, abortion, prostitution and venereal disease.[50] Isabel was an admirer of Bertrand Russell and in later life selected his *History of Western Philosophy* as a twenty-first birthday present for her godchild, Corinna MacNeice.[51]

In May 1931, Isabel's last year at art school, the Bluecoat Society exhibited the most socially provocative artwork of the time, Jacob Epstein's monumental *Genesis* (1931; Whitworth Art Gallery, Manchester).[52] Described by the artist as an 'eternal primeval feminine vision who confronts our enfeebled generation ... with new hope for the future', it had provoked controversy since its unveiling at the Leicester Gallery in London on 7 February.[53] In Liverpool, however, 5,000 visitors viewed it in the month it was there (1,649 on the first day), and it was praised in *The Liverpool Echo* as 'one of the most beautiful sculptures in the world'.[54] The review was alert to Epstein's socially advanced agenda, likening the figure to Lawrence's Lady Chatterley.[55] The powerful, naked, Asiatic woman, defiant in her pregnancy, could have been a Polynesian described by Mead. Isabel must have been one of those to spend six pennies to view the sculpture, but there is no record of her reaction. The physical immediacy of the muscular hands, swollen belly and puckered breasts in mottled Seravezza marble challenged traditional understandings of the classical nude in ways that resonated with her own investigations of the body.

6. Isabel Rawsthorne, ‘Tree Study’, c. 1930s; Fry Art Gallery, Saffron Walden

2 TACTILE EDUCATION: 1929–1933

The total eclipse of the sun that darkened Liverpool on 29 June 1929 may have felt ominous. Soon after, the Wall Street Crash ushered in a worldwide depression. Harrisons laid off a quarter of their ships, and this, and poor health, brought Isabel's father, Philip, permanently to shore.[1] Older children were expected to contribute financially to the household in such circumstances, and Agnes went to the School of Art in July 1930 to ask whether Isabel could take her Drawing Certificate early, in the hope, one has to assume, that her daughter could use the qualification to teach.[2] The new principal, Henry Huggill, had more ambitious plans for Isabel and was not able to permit the request. Although Isabel's 'thinkers' group had been forbidden from exhibiting the drawings made in their Wood Street studio, her work from the School's life class prompted him to recommend her to the Royal Academy in London.

So it was that, in May 1931, Isabel remained in Liverpool, sitting her exams, while the family visited Hove, on the south coast, where her aunt ran a sweetshop. While out walking with Warwick and his sister-in-law, her father, Philip, suffered a heart attack, collapsed and died.[3] Barely a month later, on the strength of eight drawings from the nude, Isabel was awarded a Royal Academy scholarship. This was a significant achievement for her and the School, but an almost insuperable difficulty for her family. Agnes, Isabel wrote, 'was left with no money, a son of five years and a daughter with a scholarship that had no financial aid'. Huggill sought state funding for her, but without success.[4] Somehow, a small amount was scraped together, possibly from Agnes's widow's payment from Harrisons, and she let her daughter go.[5] With no means of support, Agnes and Warwick emigrated to Canada, to live with Thomas Warwick, one of her two elder brothers, both of whom had already emigrated and become successful, 'growing maize and building small towns'.[6] Thomas's wife was an invalid, and Agnes was to help run the house and look after their eight children. Philip's death precipitated Warwick into a childhood even less stable than Isabel's, while his sister set her face to London alone.

On 15 December 1931, an overcast day, Isabel left her Holland Park bedsit for the three-mile walk to the Royal Academy Schools in the city centre.[7] It would be a mere eighteen months before she held a successful one-person exhibition, but on that first morning, crossing a damp and windy Hyde Park, the future must have seemed unclear. The expanse of trees, lawns and paths, the morning pedestrians and horse riders were familiar to her from her early years; the upmarket Georgian townhouses and shuttered shops of Mayfair and the Palladian premises of Burlington House, where the Royal Academy was accommodated, may have felt less friendly. Crates of pictures were being unloaded for the next blockbuster exhibition, *French Art, 1200–1900,* that would occupy the great galleries from January to March.

The Schools were dedicated purely to the fine arts and Isabel enrolled on the course devoted to painting. For first-year students, the emphasis was on drawing from plaster casts and copying from Old Masters, and Isabel must have looked forward to studying the living nude on the encircling benches of the Life Room where William Mallord Turner and the young Pre-Raphaelite Brothers had worked before her. Female students were permitted to draw male models so long as the sitter wore a prescribed arrangement of fabric (several layers) around their loins, and a strap to prevent it slipping.[8] There were fewer women than men students overall, about a third of the total, but the painting course was disproportionately female and popular with wealthy dilettantes. Isabel found the atmosphere 'frivolous' and missed the industrious companionability of her Liverpool friends. The instructors, Academicians, were all male; it would be four more years before a representative of Isabel's own sex, Dame Laura Knight, would be elected to their ranks. The teaching appears to have been complacent and inward-looking compared with that under Marples at the Liverpool School of Art: the President of the Academy, Sir William Llewellyn, was recorded as dismissing the Titian pictures in the *Italian Art* show as inferior works that would not pass the Academy jury.[9]

Isabel was happier sketching elsewhere, and London was a large city through which to roam. The zoological gardens in Regent's Park, accessible for half price (sixpence) on Mondays, offered reminders of her former life: a diving duck that had been donated by her father, and the lugubrious, long-faced old stork, 'Misery'. On her tramps through Hyde Park, she had to divert only a few steps to see Jacob Epstein's controversial relief above its reflecting pool, a memorial to the naturalist and writer W. H. Hudson. It had been erected to hysterical public reaction the year before Isabel had moved north.[10] One description of the figure of *Rima* might aptly describe Isabel herself: '[She] flings her arms out at either side and lets her hair fly in corrugated waves through the air … revels in the proximity of the birds.'[11] In her beloved British Museum and National Gallery, Isabel saw with new eyes pictures she had known as a child: Jan van Eyck's *Arnolfini Portrait* (1434) made a particular impact for its 'unnerving' quality and would always retain a strange importance for her.[12] Her 'most inspiring retreat', however, was to be found in South Kensington in the art and science museums, to which she would continue to return until the end of her life.

Meanwhile, there was a great deal that was new to see in 1932. Sickert's work was at the Beaux Arts Gallery,[13] and many other avant-garde venues could be found in the maze of streets immediately behind the Royal Academy, from affluent Bond Street in the west to rackety Soho in the east. Dividing the two was the generous sweep of Regent's Street, with its Classical facades, the sumptuous gilded premises of the old Goupil Gallery with its Continental shows, and the legendary Café Royal. The street concluded with a flourish at Piccadilly Circus, where a centrifugal array of shops, restaurants, theatres, cinemas and the brand-new electric billboards wheeled around the winged and nude figure of Alfred Gilbert's *Eros* (1892–3), a new aluminium edition of which was unveiled in 1932.[14] Shops and restaurants, plays and concerts were beyond Isabel's pocket. Noël Coward's spectacular *Cavalcade* was a hit at the Theatre Royal, Drury Lane, and at Sadler's Wells a young Ralph Richardson was giving his Henry V, but even the cheaper seats were probably more than she could afford. The exception was the Queen's Hall, where concerts subsidised by Artur Schnabel and the Courtauld family were open to all. Isabel never forgot hearing Schnabel play Beethoven; he was one of the composer's greatest interpreters.[15] Cinemas were an inexpensive and luxurious way of keeping warm during the dark, winter months and as the Hays Code of film censorship had been instituted but not yet enforced, Hollywood films were enjoying a final free-for-all.

Isabel's limited means compounded her alienation from the well-to-do Academy crowd, but she found common cause with one or two other students. She thought Mervyn Peake an 'agile painter', the most obviously talented of her fellows. Like Isabel, he had exotic looks, which he augmented with theatrical clothes, sporting an earring in emulation of the gypsy style favoured by Augustus John, the least conventional Academician. A year ahead of Isabel, he was already exhibiting in nearby cafés and restaurants under the loose heading of the 'Soho Group'.[16] Peake attracted followers, but his fantastical style was not for Isabel. Another whom she put in the category of 'interested in working' was Peter Scott. Although Scott was wealthy, he had, like Isabel, experienced the self-sufficient life of an only child (he was the son of the polar explorer Captain Robert Scott and the sculptor Kathleen Scott). They shared a love of ornithology, and he, having read Natural Sciences at Cambridge and spending most weekends in the country continuing his research, was tremendously knowledgeable.[17]

Isabel's closest friendship was with a second-year student, a sculptor, Frances Bruce, about whom little is known.[18] The Schools' records indicate that

Bruce was a high flyer who had won the Bronze Medal in 1931, the Landseer 2nd Scholarship in Sculpture in 1932 and the prestigious Prix de Rome in 1933. In that year, she was photographed for *The Times*, a woman in spectacles standing sternly beside her winning piece, *Youth* (1933; whereabouts unknown). The sculpture was made up of two figures, a man playing a ukulele and a woman dancing, their head thrown back in song. Although the rhythmic, interwoven composition with instrument and open-mouthed singers referenced traditional art (for example, the cast in the Victoria and Albert Museum of the three choristers in the third panel of Luca della Robbia's Renaissance *Cantoria* (1432–8; Museo dell'Opera del Duomo, Florence), the raised, stylised faces alluded unmistakably to Epstein's notorious *Rima*.[19]

These companions – Peake, Scott and Bruce – had the rebellious independence of Isabel's Liverpool friends. Bruce declared her frustration with the Academy at the Prix de Rome ceremony by flinging her medal at President Llewellyn's feet, and, in 1935, she interrupted her scholarship in Rome to take up employment in Jerusalem. Peake, and Scott abandoned the institution even more prematurely, in 1932. Peake moved to an artist's colony on the island of Sark, where, for a short time, Scott joined him. Both men developed into writers and illustrators: Peake's name is now synonymous with his strange, unfinished *Gormenghast Trilogy* (begun in 1950), while Scott became a pioneer of nature conservation, founding, in 1946, the Severn Wildfowl Trust at Slimbridge in Gloucestershire (now the Wildfowl and Wetlands Trust), and, in 1964, the Society of Wildlife Artists. In the summer of 1932, Isabel ran out of savings and of patience with the institution's stuffy 'finishing school' style, and she, too, left.[20]

Isabel now had no home or income. Her class, youth and gender, as well as her incomplete studies, excluded her from supporting herself by instructing or exhibiting in her area of expertise. She was qualified for elementary teaching, commercial and factory work, or to go into service, but her self-invented, self-reliant life, however, meant that there was little likelihood of her obtaining references or recommendations. For the only time in her career, she sought work as a model. It paid slightly more than the basic wage for manual labour, roughly £100 per year, and it would keep her close to the milieu in which she could paint.[21] She had not reckoned, however, with the traditional demarcation between artist and model. When she approached the Keeper of the Royal Academy for work, 'he was deeply shocked', declaring, 'Oh, you cannot do <u>that</u>', while offering no alternative suggestions. Isabel realised she 'would never be employed at the RA, being an ex-student', and tried another art school, only to be looked over and told that her legs were 'too tapering'. She would need to look outside the Establishment, so Frances Bruce took her to see Jacob Epstein.

As well as being the most notorious artist in Britain at this time, Epstein was the most successful; so it may have taken some courage to walk down the genteel Kensington cul-de-sac of Hyde Park Gate and wait in the porch of his grand, five-storey Victorian home while the bell chimed within.[22] The butler whom Epstein had called 'Jeeves' had been let go, and the artist was in the habit of answering the door himself.[23] Even if Isabel had never met him before, his ample figure was well known from his constant appearances in the newspapers and on the newsreels. She, in turn, must have seemed oddly familiar to Epstein, so close to the figures of his imagination were her determined mouth, long eyes and defiant air.

Despite his fame, Epstein's manner was unassuming, and Isabel was welcomed through to the studio. On the way, she glimpsed busts and heads that he had modelled, as well as Indian, Polynesian and African figures and all sorts of other objects that he and his wife, Margaret, had collected. There was work by Epstein's former protégé Henry Moore, and, in the drawing room, glowing oil nudes and still lifes by Epstein's great friend Matthew Smith, some of which Isabel had probably already seen when they were lent for the painter's recent one-man show.[24] The huge work space, once a ballroom, with elegant ionic columns and large, squared windows, was crowded with figures in plaster and unfinished models in clay wrapped in damp cloths. A visitor of around the same time, the young actor Emlyn Williams, left a vivid record of the studio: 'Mixed up with heaps of wood, piles of clay, stacks of old newspapers and the dust of years [was] every sort of head and limb at every height and angle, from the ruthless stares of statesmen to the writhing thighs of agonized Titians and the swollen hungry lips of giantesses with corrugates wings of hair caught in midstream and ... fierce caverns for eyes.'[25]

Isabel was immediately engaged to sit. She posed on a battered stool, naked to the waist, glad, perhaps, that it was summer. Epstein began by assembling clay around a crossed, wooden armature before becoming immersed in a very fast and decisive sequence of looking, shaping, adding and subtracting. He seems to have chatted more freely with Isabel than he did with Emlyn, who was there for a commissioned piece. They shared their dissatisfaction with the Academy, their fondness for 'realists', Donatello, Andrea del Verrocchio, Michelangelo and Northern European painters, and their preference for museums over galleries.[26] 'After Epstein had been working on my head for a few weeks,' Isabel wrote, 'during which time we had been talking together, he suggested that I come to live in his house, which would make my life much simpler. He was anxious that I should continue working. When not posing I would have much time to do what I wanted.' She stayed for two years.

7. Jacob Epstein, *Sunita*, 1931; New Art Gallery, Walsall

In accepting Epstein's invitation, Isabel turned her back on convention in both life and art. She had allied herself with the artist who, of all those working in London at the time, represented the most extreme point of opposition to tradition. Epstein had twice been rejected by the Academy and was at odds with its president, Llewellyn. A leading radical since the first decades of the century, he had worked with Wyndham Lewis and the Vorticist group and had pioneered the practice of direct carving that the next generation, led by Barbara Hepworth and Henry Moore, were now making synonymous with modernity.[27] Since the war, Epstein had concentrated on modelling figurative portraits, but when he did return to carving, as in *Rima* and *Genesis*, the impact was more disruptive than anything produced by this younger 'Hampstead set'.[28] Whereas they were supported by the aesthetic theorists Herbert Read and Roger Fry, Epstein's apologists were more ad hoc and diluted by popular outcries.[29] In 1932, *The Sculptor Speaks*, a set of interviews compiled by his friend Arnold Haskell after the manner of Auguste Rodin's, *L'Art: Entretiens réunis par Paul Gsell*, proudly reprinted a description by Paul Nash: 'the only artist amongst us who wants to shock. His work is definitely *épatant*.'[30]

In the same year, William Gaunt declared Epstein, 'the scapegoat of the whole modern movement', subject to 'prejudice racial, religious even political.'[31] As an American, a Jew and a conspicuous bohemian, Epstein represented a social 'other'. Furthermore, since 1921, he had divided his time between his wife, Margaret, and the Bloomsbury musician Kathleen Garman, with whom he parented three children. He and his wife also had a long history of accommodating young women in their home as models, friends and lovers. Isabel shared a bedroom with the fourteen-year-old Peggy Jean, the daughter of Epstein and the dancer and actor Dorothy 'Meum' Lindsell-Stewart. Meum had stayed with the couple in the last years of the war, until they encouraged her to return to the stage and allow them to bring up the child.[32] She remained a presence in the house in the form of bronze portraits and a large oil of her wearing a green dress. Peggy Jean, who became Isabel's close friend.[33] Isabel's more recent predecessors had left only months before: Amina Peerbhoy, her son, Enver, and her sister, Miriam Patel, stayed at Hyde Park Gate from 1925 to 1931.[34] They were the daughters of the personal physician of Mahatma Gandhi, but had fled India. Amina, given the name Sunita by Epstein, made a living as a trader at Wembley International Exhibition, as a performer in an underwater circus (she breathed invisibly through a piece of transparent strand of macaroni) and as a model for Matthew Smith.[35] Isabel encountered them only in the copious drawings and sculptures Epstein had made, and she kept one of these, *Sunita* (1931) until her death.[36] (7)

Epstein did not, in the end, engage Isabel as a model; in her own description she was a studio assistant.[37] When interviewed by Epstein's biographer, Stephen Gardiner, she quoted the sculptor's offer verbatim: 'You can come here, you can sit for your portrait, go to school, do your own painting.' This was a reciprocal arrangement close to that which she had pioneered with the 'thinkers'. A studio and materials were the minimum requirement for artists to be able to continue their practice beyond art school, and in London in the 1930s, these cost at least as much again as basic living and accommodation and would have been beyond Isabel's reach. At Epstein's, over the next eighteen months, she produced nearly two hundred paintings and drawings, while Epstein made only a very small number of studies of her: two sculptures and one drawing are known. The latter, *Isabel* (1933; whereabouts unknown), is not a nude shown in a relaxed position, as Epstein's portraits of his models often were, but depicts her in outdoor dress and engaged in intense conversation. Interestingly, it is in watercolour; Epstein was, Isabel remembered, 'greatly interested in what I was doing, which at that time was mostly watercolours'.

Epstein's drawing captured Isabel's investigative, advancing posture and her characteristic wide-eyed surprise. This was replicated in the first sculpture,

Isabel, cast in bronze as a head in 1932 and as a full bust in 1934.[38] (**8**) The overwhelming impression is of ancient eyes in a youthful face. Epstein owned a copy of the bust of Nefertiti (c. 1300 BCE) in the Ägyptisches Museum in Berlin, and the ballet critic Richard Buckle observed that Isabel 'had something of that Nefertiti look which he particularly admired'.[39] Epstein's sculpture, *Isabel*, exploited the impact to be gained from its frontal, symmetrical treatment, the forward lean of Nefertiti's graceful neck and shoulders, and her vector-like chin, nose and gaze. It thus combined general and particular beauty, past art and present life in the manner advised by the French writer Charles Baudelaire: 'Beauty is made up of an eternal, invariable element … and of a relative, circumstantial element … the age, its fashions, its morals, its emotions.'[40]

This adolescent-archaism was a dialogue between Epstein's vision of Isabel and her own. The watercolour shows that Nefertiti's pride and 'forwardness' were a good match for Isabel's demeanour. The sculpture's hair retains the liberated, practical bob of the 1920s, tucked behind the ears and childishly ragged, innocent of the Marcel waves that had already begun to soften and sophisticate hairstyles in the 1930s. Her gaze is level under the abrupt Egyptian fringe and the slight strabismus adds to the sense of intense focus. Her nose is straight, her lips squared off into a pout that is more stubborn than sexy. Her arms are rounded and her neck almost as swan-like as the Egyptian queen's, but the overdeveloped slant between it and the shoulders remind us that she was a sea swimmer. Epstein has rhymed the prominent collarbones with the cheekbones, but, in the manner of Rodin they are not quite symmetrical. The profiles of the breasts are different, as are the movements of the pupil in the eye, and even the dimple in the chin is off-centre.[41] All of these communicate the restless vitality that was intrinsic to Isabel and so important to a sculptor battling to win a living likeness from an inert medium. It was the inquisitive immediacy of Isabel's presence, more than the exoticism of her appearance, that was of value to Epstein, here. It is interesting to compare the bust with that made by Epstein of Albert Einstein (Tate), a portrait of the scientist executed hurriedly and secretly in a cramped cabin on Cromer Beach in 1933, as the scientist fled Nazi Germany.[42] Urgent curiosity is expressed as forward movement in both.

Isabel's works from this period were lost or were sold and are untraced; only reproductions provide clues to her early style. *Giraffes* (c. 1932; formerly Triefus Collection) was included in Arnold Haskell's book on drawing of 1933, *Black and White*, alongside works by Modigliani, Epstein, Moore and others.[43] Isabel was one of only two women and the youngest contributor represented; her free and economical sketch concluded the volume as a nod to the future. *Giraffes* was part of the project that Isabel had outlined to Epstein when he

8. Jacob Epstein, *Isabel*, bronze, 1932, cast 1934; private collection

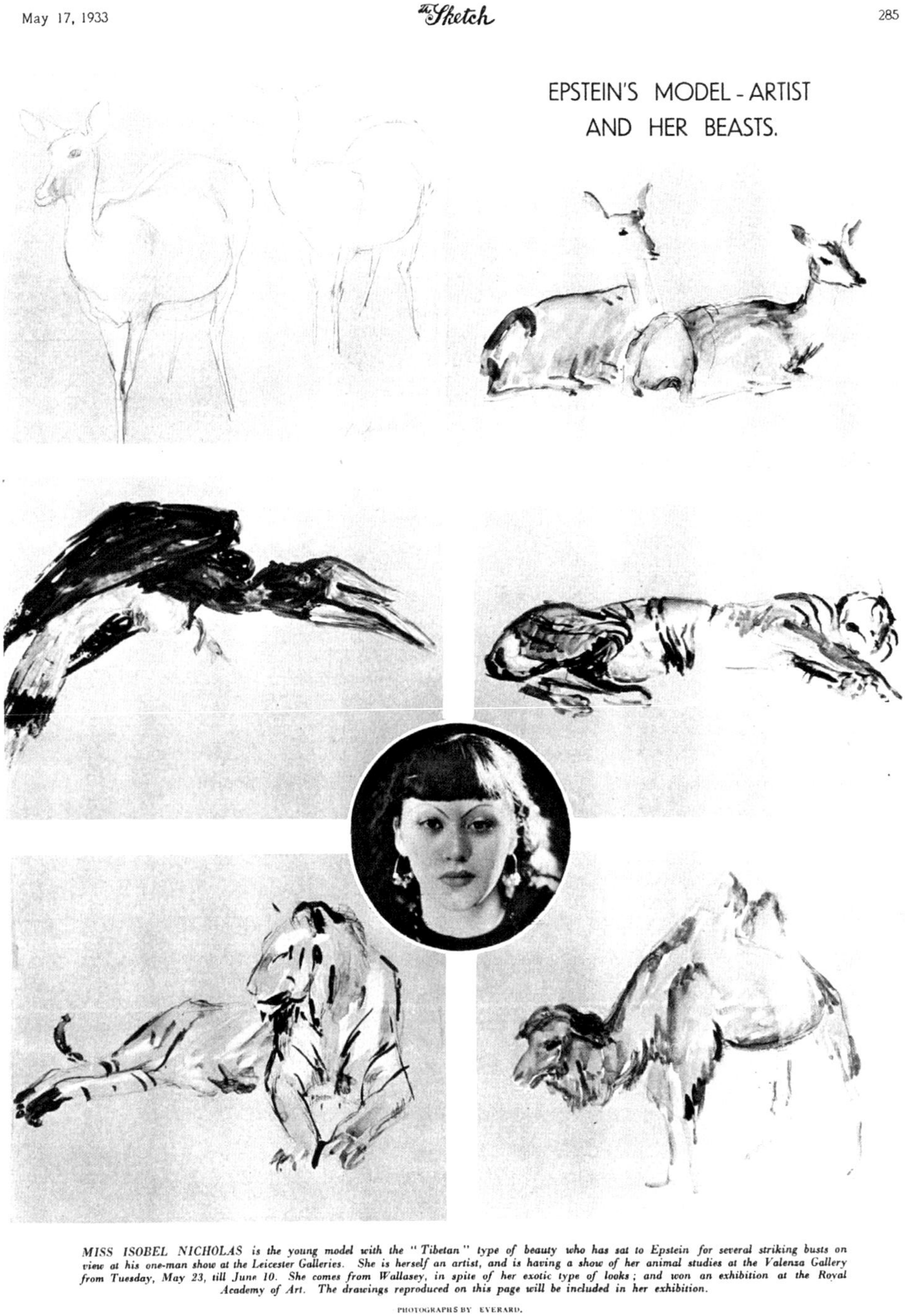

May 17, 1933 The Sketch 285

EPSTEIN'S MODEL - ARTIST AND HER BEASTS.

MISS ISOBEL NICHOLAS is the young model with the "Tibetan" type of beauty who has sat to Epstein for several striking busts on view at his one-man show at the Leicester Galleries. She is herself an artist, and is having a show of her animal studies at the Valenza Gallery from Tuesday, May 23, till June 10. She comes from Wallasey, in spite of her exotic type of looks; and won an exhibition at the Royal Academy of Art. The drawings reproduced on this page will be included in her exhibition.

PHOTOGRAPHS BY EVERARD.

9. 'Epstein's Model Artist and her Beasts', *Sketch*, 17 May 1933

XLIX ISOBEL NICHOLAS *Giraffes*
(Mrs Triefus Collection)

10. Isabel Rawsthorne, *Giraffes,* c.1932, from Arnold Haskell, *Black and White* (1933) invited her to share his studio: a series of drawings and watercolours of animals. We know from her autobiography that she 'spent hours in the London Zoo and made paintings in the Park's landscapes, with swans'. Within a year, she exhibited, at Haskell's Valenza Gallery in London, a body of drawings in an exhibition called *Isobel Nicholas Animal Studies*, which opened on the 23 May 1933. Six of the drawings were reproduced in the *Sketch* in a full-page preview on 17 May.[44]

It was a feat of industry and ability to have a one-person show off Bond Street at only twenty years old. Peter Scott displayed a set of more conventional bird paintings around the corner the following month, and they must have gained satisfaction from the proximity of their successes to their unappreciative *alma mater*, the Royal Academy.[45] Isabel's exhibition was reviewed widely: her work was commended, for example, in an article on notable contemporary paintings in *The Scotsman*, alongside Paul Nash and Stanley Spencer.[46] *The Times* gave it first place among the smaller exhibitions that season, asserting, in a perceptive echo of the Liverpool philosophy, that 'Miss Nicholas feels and not merely observes what she draws'.[47] The reviews lacked the terms usually applied to the work of women artists. They did not mention influence, refinement or, most notably, beauty; Isabel's sense of form was described as 'weighty', her line, full of movement and her colour, 'intense'.[48] All the works were sold.

Some of Isabel's motifs were conventional: tigers and cranes were a favourite of the dynamic Chinese and Japanese ink drawings and prints which she admired in books or in the Victoria and Albert Museum and the British Museum.[49] She also developed a graphic language for such less familiar creatures as reedbucks, bison and vultures. There is a notable absence of the picturesque in these animals, which are more akin to the hunting and sacrificial motifs to be found in Old Master painting, or the archaic and Palaeolithic carvings in the British Museum.[50] This may have been encouraged by the Vitalist drawings of Henri Gaudier-Brzeska. Epstein often spoke about his colleague, who had died in the war, and three of his animated ink representations of an eagle, a vulture and a bison were donated to the British Museum in 1931.[51] The bison had a particular avant-garde currency, associated with the origins of art and man. In 1930, the influential French art journal *Documents* carried illustrations of Palaeolithic reindeer, bison and horses.[52] The widely read book *Art* (1928) by Amédée Ozenfant, published in English in 1931 as *The Foundations of Modern Art*, featured startling juxtapositions of illustrations from the sciences, anthropology and all eras of art, and opened with a pæan to prehistoric wall paintings accompanied by a reproduction of handprints and a bison. A second bison, incised on a stone in Palaeolithic times, was illustrated as an example of 'fundamental humanity'.[53]

Isabel's adventurous approach to line and colour cannot have been unaffected by her relationship with Epstein and his close friend Matthew Smith. Their sympathies lay generally with the painters of the London Group, including Sickert, who were strongly orientated towards the Continent.[54] Isabel's autobiography places the two years at Hyde Park Gate at the beginning of a section she entitled 'The Splendours of Paris', suggesting that she considered it her introduction to the international art world then centred on the French rather than the British capital. Between 1902 and 1905, Epstein had trained, worked and exhibited in Paris with Henri Matisse, André Derain and Pablo Picasso, as well as with the sculptors Constantin Brâncuși and an aged Rodin. He was devoted to Rodin and owned many books about him which Isabel would have devoured. Most important were the precocious insights provided by Epstein's and Smith's admiration of the graphic handling of masters like Rembrandt and Vincent van Gogh, as well as living Fauves and Expressionists: Derain, Matisse, Chaim Soutine and Georges Rouault. Rouault was not generally appreciated in Britain at this date, but he exhibited in London in 1930, and Epstein purchased a *Head of Christ*, declaring him 'the greatest living artist'.[55] Soutine, Derain and Amadeo Modigliani (who had died in 1920), old colleagues of Epstein, had still lifes and landscapes on show at the Cooling Gallery on Bond Street in 1932, and works by Soutine and Modigliani were exhibited alongside Epstein's at the Ben Uri Gallery of Jewish Art in 1933, alongside rich, graphic canvases by another pre-war Vorticist associate, David Bomberg.[56] Epstein's favourite topic, however, was his non-Western artefacts. He had pioneered the collecting of African and Oceanic art in the first decade of the century with Matisse, Derain and Picasso and owned over three hundred artefacts, probably the greatest assembly in private hands in the West at that time.[57] A contemporary described how Epstein loved handling and explaining the pieces as 'a tactile education'.[58]

Epstein returned to Paris regularly, spoke the language and was well informed on French culture. He probably helped to realise Isabel's dream of seeing the city as early as 1932 and certainly took her in April 1933 and February 1934.[59] It was an easy journey by boat, but he tended to travel by plane. Since 1924, Imperial Airways had flown from the London Airport at Croydon, a film-set fantasy of cool, geometric architecture and streamlined silver aircraft. Only a dozen or so passengers travelled on each flight and were entertained with movies and a picnic. Epstein introduced Isabel to the vibrant life of Montparnasse which was centred on the Café du Dôme where he was well known (a seat even bore his name), and amid its cigarette smoke and art deco mirrors she had her first brush with a Parisian avant-garde. Epstein's own generation was accompanied by a younger Surrealist set, led by André Breton. The combative conversations may have sounded to Isabel, with her schoolgirl French, more like music than words, but there were also English-speaking artists, writers and tourists, attracted by the cultural atmosphere and the American Bar. The main purpose of Epstein's trips was to research and purchase artefacts from Africa and Polynesia; Paris was the centre for this trade. His favourite dealer was Ernst Ascher, and his mantra, Isabel recalled, was 'Ascher pas cher'.

Epstein's toing and froing were but one element in an unprecedentedly rich cultural exchange between London and Paris in 1933, dynamised by the exodus that year of left-wing and Jewish artists, writers and dealers from Germany. There were regular displays of established French moderns in London at the French Gallery and elsewhere, but change was in the air. Collectors, critics and dealers, such as the young man-of-means Douglas Cooper, were interested in recent art.[60] In April, Freddie Mayor's new gallery began to exhibit Surrealist and abstract works by Continental artists such as Joan Miró, Max Ernst and Paul Klee, alongside Moore and Paul Nash. Alberto Giacometti's sculpture was shown there in October.[61] Herbert Read's 1933 overview of European modernism, *Art Now,* and the Unit One group, which he set up with Nash, promoted both Surrealist and abstract approaches, including such artists as Moore, Hepworth and her partner, Ben Nicholson. The group held only one show, however, the following year. Isabel remembered that, by 1932, Epstein 'thought nothing of Moore and hated Augustus John, though this, I suspect, was personal. I do not know why.'

Epstein introduced Isabel to an artistic, literary and musical set at the Café Royal on Piccadilly and took her to concerts, theatre and films. Friends and celebrity 'acquaintances', as she wryly called them, including the writer and reformer George Bernard Shaw, came to Hyde Park Gate, and she had warm memories of the occasional 'musical evening when a visiting artist would play'. A note struck from Isabel's autobiography records a particular friend, Florence Lambert, 'Flo', the wife of the famous composer Constant Lambert.[62] Epstein's friend and supporter Arnold Haskell, who, as well as being an art critic and gallery owner was a champion of modern dance, had founded the avant-garde Camargo Society ballet company, superseded by the Vic-Wells Ballet Company in 1931, with Lambert as its musical director.[63] Like Isabel, Flo had been born near the docks in the East End of London, but she had never known her father, a sailor from East Asia, and was brought up in an orphanage. She had a beauty that was similar to Isabel's, and, after working as a maid, she had been 'discovered' by the Bloomsbury crowd.[64] When Isabel met Flo, she was working as a 'mannequin', or fashion model, and living with Lambert in hand-to-mouth fashion in a run-down flat over an Indian restaurant on Percy Street in the Fitzrovia area of London, bordering Bloomsbury

11. Jacob Epstein, *Epping Forest*, c. 1933; Tate

and Soho. The flat had been borrowed from the actors Charles Laughton and Elsa Lanchester (who had gone to Hollywood to film the comedy *The Private Life of Henry VIII*, 1933). Isabel made drawings of Flo, and they enjoyed excursions together, often visiting the zoo with malodorous packets of raw fish to feed the penguins.[65] Isabel was struck by the charisma of Flo's husband and saw him conducting in 1933, probably his eccentric jazz symphony *The Rio Grande* (1929), part Baudelairean crowd scene, part Brazilian carnival, but it would be many years before their lives collided.

In the summers, Isabel and the Epsteins went to Deerhurst, their country retreat, a train ride from London on the edge of Epping Forest. Here, another Victorian house, weather-boarded and less imposing than Hyde Park Gate, looked out onto a wilderness of beech trees, paths and streams. Isabel was in her element. She made landscapes and studies of the flowers from Margaret's garden, and in good weather she, Peggy Jean and sometimes Epstein spent long days in the shady forest, walking, bathing and painting. On a stay in 1933, Epstein intended to work in his studio, direct carving figures, but Isabel recalled that he 'became so interested in my efforts with watercolours that he decided to try some himself. This led to a series of paintings of trees.' Epstein's autobiographical account omitted Isabel's presence, but included an intriguing hint of a love affair behind the work: 'As usual with me, what started as a mere diversion became in the end a passion, and I could think of nothing else but painting. I arose to paint and painted until sundown.'[66] The two artists left Deerhurst at the end of August with hundreds of pictures in gouache on paper.

Although she was much younger, Isabel's relationship with her mentor was a reciprocal one. The Epping Forest episode was an important artistic liberation for Epstein, and watercolour became, in the words of his biographer June Rose, his 'medium of freedom'.[67] Epstein's few watercolours were, up to this point, limited to schematic, red or blue hatching or washes added to his designs. His excursion into oil, the portrait of Meum in 1917, had not been well received.[68] In Epping Forest, with Isabel, his vivacious line finally evolved its chromatic aspect. Initially, red and blue continued to dominate as equivalents for light and dark, carving up nature into sculptural form; but, increasingly, contour loosened into rhythm and hatching gave way to hue. The Tate's *Epping Forest*, 1933, (**11**) with its distribution of blue, red and yellow-green, exemplifies an intermediate stage in this process.

Like a couple contriving a discreet pause between each leaving the site of a tryst, Epstein exhibited thirty-three watercolour landscapes that winter at Tooth and Sons (significantly, Smith's usual gallery), together with the bronze *Albert Einstein* (which was bought for the nation).[69] Two months later, in February 1934, Isabel showed sixteen watercolour flowers in an exhibition called *Watercolours by Paul Nash, Frank Dobson, P. H. Jowett, Adrian Allinson, Isabel Nicholas* at the nearby Redfern Gallery.[70] There is no record of her displaying her landscapes at all. Both exhibitions sold out, but it was Epstein's that garnered most publicity, so surprising was this sudden turn to gaudy nature: 'Mr Epstein in landscape is a new experience and his exhibition of watercolours ... makes the experience a welcome one.'[71] The critic commended their 'savage intensity, in resonant colours – rich red soil, metallic green foliage, and blue or violet reflecting water'.

Isabel's and Epstein's autobiographies each state that they returned to town with a hundred watercolours, not mentioning the other. Such symmetry is odd unless they were working very exactly shoulder to shoulder, each making at least three paintings a day, which is unlikely. Isabel stated that Haskell sold all her pictures, and the Redfern Gallery catalogue lists sixteen flower paintings. There is, however, no sign of Isabel's paintings now, whereas flowers and landscape gouaches by Epstein abound, including subjects – such as *White Roses*, *Sunflowers* and *Dahlias in a Green Jug* – that are identical to those named at the Redfern. They were signed in ink some time after they were painted, and there may be a case for a proper comparative study of these.

Isabel's delayed and diplomatic appearance at the Redfern denied her leadership in the watercolours, but was at least a show at a mainstream venue with modern masters, notably Nash. Jan Gordon of *The Observer* newspaper compared her favourably with her fellow exhibiters, notably Percy Jowett, a war veteran and Head of Chelsea School of Art: 'Contrasts abound this week, none more violent than the inverted one between the flower pieces of Mr Jowett and those of Miss Nicholas. At first sight, one would have attributed the man's work to the woman, and vice versa, so delicate sensitive, almost shy, are those of Mr Jowett; so abounding, bold, and luxuriant those of Miss Nicholas.'[72] Isabel was making a name for herself.

12. Jacob Epstein, *Isobel*, bronze, 1933; Ferens Art Gallery, Hull

3 SAVAGE SOPHISTICATION: 1933

In 1933, Isabel became visible for reasons other than her art. In the press, she was noticed out with Margaret Epstein: 'tall and striking in appearance [she] wears picturesque clothes. No hat ever covers her shoulder length hair.'[1] She accompanied Jacob Epstein to openings and first nights, and a paparazzo snapped them at the premiere of Sergei Eisenstein's *Thunder over Mexico*, a film made in Mexico as a 'moving fresco' inspired by Frida Kahlo and Diego Rivera. (**16**) Just before Isabel's Valenza Gallery show, Epstein held a large exhibition at the nearby Leicester Galleries in which he revealed two bronzes of Isabel, the *Isabel* head and a new half-figure, slightly larger than life-size, which he called by a variation of her name, *Isobel,* 1933.[2] (**12**) Both works sold, and the larger bust, widely celebrated and acclaimed as 'the finest example of the sculptor's art produced in modern times', was lent to the Tate Gallery, where it went on display shortly after.[3] The model for the sculpture became the subject of popular interest, as *The Scotsman* commented: 'Epstein, being the most discussed living Artist in this country, even his models are news.'[4] The *Wallasey News* proudly professed their scoop that Isabel 'was not, as some newspapers declared, a native of Tibet, but a Wallasey young lady', and added that newspapers in all parts of the country 'were engaged in broadcasting the fact of "Isobel's" identity and probably for a time charming Miss Nicholls [*sic*] was the most discussed lady in the universe'.[5]

Epstein's *Isobel* was very different from the earlier *Isabel* and seemed to register the sitter's recent successes. The hair was whisked backwards like that of the figure in *Rima*; the chin, tilted higher; eyes, gazing ahead. The figure displayed more prosperity, being decorated with elaborate, spiral, serpent earrings and bracelets. A silk shawl and chemise cling to and stretch across her arms and rib cage. The fine fabric across the torso pulls at tiny buttons in the manner of Andrea del Verrocchio's marble *Portrait of a Lady* (1475–80; Museo Nazionale del Bargello, Florence). The sensitive fingers and the far-seeing eyes also echo the Renaissance portrait, alluding to its Platonic analysis of the levels of love, from sensual (hands) to spiritual (gaze).

The lofty references to Verrocchio were not noticed by most viewers. Richard Buckle and subsequent commentators have stressed only the sensual

13. Leslie Grimes, '"Genesis" – and Exodus', *The Star*, 5 February 1931

aspect of the work,[6] expressed through an equivalence between sculptural and sexual exploration: 'the sculptor's mastery shows itself in the way that, observing narrowly every minute graduation of plane and outline, he knows by instinct or experience just where to exaggerate the curl of a lip, the length of a neck, the elegance of a waist or wrist, the outward jut of the breast ... her hands with which Epstein has taken more trouble than usual ... a picture of savage sophistication.'[7] This kind of innuendo was common in accounts of modern male sculptors, as David Getsy describes: 'Acts of making ... were mythologised as acts of love, lust, passion, and desire, visible as the sculptor's touch.'[8] A contemporary cartoon showed Epstein 'making' *Genesis*, in a tableau evoking the love of the mythical sculptor Pygmalion for his creation Galatea or legends of the amorous nocturnal visits that stained Praxiteles' Aphrodite of Knidos (fourth century BCE; lost).[9]

The trance-like expression and resolute mouth, given an unhappy downward turn in the cartoon, of the figure of Genesis differ from the glad and open confidence displayed in *Isobel* where the attitude is usually read by commentators as reciprocal carnality, 'premeditated sexuality'.[10] The difference between the earlier *Isabel* and the later *Isobel* constructed a sexual as well as a professional coming of age. The lips are less pouting, more wanton, curving as though towards a kiss. The breasts, exposed above the shawl, are lifted forward, distended, with nipples erect, a tiny cleft pushed into the tip of each, complementing the erotic awareness of the mouth. This sculpture is the first of numberless reinventions of Isabel in terms of sexual power that would follow her through her career.

Isobel was also the first of many representations to link her sexuality to worldly transience. It overlaid the Verrocchio-like exploration of female beauty and desire with the more recent imagery found in Rodin's publication *L'Art*. The half-figure format specifically evoked *Torse de jeune femme* [Torso of a Young Woman] (1909; Musée Rodin) reproduced in front and side view in the book, opposite Rodin's comment on feminine transformation: 'The real youth, the Virgin of puberty where the body in its svelte pride and full of new sap seems to call love and fear it, does not last even a few months ... dissipation, desire and the fever of passion rapidly relax the flesh and release the lines. The girl becomes a woman. This is another beauty, still admirable, but less pure.'[11] Epstein's two sculptures of the nineteen- and twenty-year-old Isabel enact Rodin's image of physical and psychological change from inquisitive adolescent to ardent woman.

This fantasy, to some extent at least, reflected real life: Epstein was by now Isabel's lover. There were many opportunities for intimacy: the trips to Paris and to Deerhurst, and, when Margaret was not around, at Hyde Park Gate itself. Peggy Jean recalled asking her mother why her father's sock was in her bed. Epstein's own bedroom was surveyed by seventy solemn ritual figures, mostly African, and Isabel wondered what it was like for him to wake and find them looking down.[12]

Epstein's Leicester Galleries exhibition presented *Isobel* within a full retrospective of his career, beginning with the little pregnant, stylised *Figure in Flenite* (1912; Tate, London) and concluding with the direct-carved monolith *Primeval Gods* (1933; Tate, London), from which the show took its title. Richard Buckle perceived *Isobel* to be, like the other pieces, 'savage'. The sculpture's allusions to Verrocchio's and Rodin's half-figures were upstaged by references to African and Oceanic art, overt in the surrounding carvings. The hieratic stance and spectacularly full breasts could not fail to remind viewers of *Genesis*. They resembled also Epstein's first African purchase, a damaged figure cut off at the waist, and a new acquisition, a Dogon *Seated Hermaphrodite* in wood (Carlo Monzino Collection).[13] The focused forwardness of the Hermaphrodite's gaze, its torpedo breasts and almost-meeting hands now infused the likeness of Isabel with the 'frank sexuality' that Epstein perceived in these carvings.[14]

Unlike the African prototypes, the *Isobel* was not fully naked. The change of spelling in the name, from Isabel to Isobel, added a foreign flavour, and Buckle detected a touristy, Spanish flamboyance in the clothing (possibly thinking of the topless Spanish women portrayed by the watercolourist William Russell Flint).[15] Epstein's departure from the simple nude represented in *Isabel* and in many of his earlier female portraits, to this contrived exposure of the breasts added a further, culturally specific 'primitive' accent. The dress would have been easily recognisable at the time as a modern take on that of the Cretan Snake Goddess,

14. 'Group above Altar-ledge of Shrine of Snake Goddess as tentatively arranged', from Sir Arthur Evans, *The Palace of Minos at Knossos* (1921)

brought to popular attention at the beginning of the century by the publications of the archaeologist Arthur Evans. Evans believed he had found the ruins of the palace and labyrinth of the mythical King Minos at Knossos on Crete. *Isobel* resembled most closely a set of gold and ivory forgeries published as authentic in 1930, including the so-called *Boston Goddess* (Museum of Fine Arts, Boston), who holds two serpents that spiral up her arms, and the gold-nippled, tightly corseted *Lady of Sports* (Royal Ontario Museum, Toronto).[16] The fringed shawl considered by Buckle to be Spanish was the sacred attribute of these snake goddesses. Furthermore, Evans interpreted and re-presented these artefacts as archetypes of female sovereignty. Epstein's allusions to the Snake Goddess thus developed the *Genesis* fantasy of the eternal, fertile feminine.

In 1933, Minoan references had a special currency. According to the historian Cathy Gere, 'The story of Modernist Knossos began to assume a shape, a sort of call and response between an eccentric array of artists, scientists and assorted visionaries, all trying to make sense of some of the weightiest themes of modernity – the death of god, the woman question, the human appetite for war.'[17] Picasso, André Breton and André Masson adopted the Minotaur, the legendary hybrid of man and bull imprisoned in the Cretan Labyrinth, for the title of their new journal, published first in 1933.[18] Gere links this to the new importance of the nineteenth-century notions of the philosopher Friedrich Nietzsche that the modern era was repeating the history of antiquity (in reverse). In the early 1930s, Mussolini's fascist regime in Italy and the rising Nazi Party in Germany appropriated heroic, militant, Nietzschean visions of Mycenae, informed by Heinrich Schliemann's apparent discovery and excavation of remnants of its triumph over Troy. By contrast, Evans's excavations of the earlier Minoan civilisation tended to be configured into a pacifist, Dionysian alternative; his narratives of matriarchal power and continuity between African and European cultures (Crete being midway between the two continents) were harnessed to left-wing feminist, anti-racist, and anti-colonial positions.[19] In London, the atavistic characteristics of Epstein's public works, as well as his Jewish–Polish heredity, had been the object of anti-Semitic commentary and vandalism for several decades. In 1933, Oswald Mosley's party, the British Union of Fascists, was reaching the peak of its influence. In this context, the Minoan aspect of *Isobel* had precise and timely political significance.

Many of Evans's 'finds' were later restored or even faked and inevitably had a contemporary air, a 'predilection for the covers of *Vogue*', as Evelyn Waugh quipped.[20] The forged Snake Goddess called the *Lady of Sports* was, as Gere says, 'a magnificently perverse bit of 1930s pornography'.[21] 'Minoan modernism' became fashionable and ... gained a purchase on the cultural imagination of the interwar years.'[22] For some, the snake goddesses and the half-human Minotaur were emblems of modern decadence; for others, they were icons of pantheism, a 'natural', free, pacifist utopia. The widely read essay 'The Making of the Goddess' by the feminist academic Jane Harrison cast Knossos as a paradigm for new women of the twentieth century in terms of 'professional, sexual, creative and political equality'.[23] Epstein's superimposition of the characteristics of living and archaic art was part of a broader cultural phenomenon best described by T. S. Eliot in 1923: 'using myth ... manipulating a continuous parallel between contemporaneity and antiquity ... is simply a way of controlling, or ordering or giving shape to the immense panorama of futility and anarchy that is contemporary history ... Psychology, ethnography, and the Golden Bough have concurred to make possible what was impossible even a few years ago. Instead of narrative method, we may now use the mythical method.'[24] *Isobel* was a masterpiece of the 'mythical method'; its archaic appearance delivered *and* authenticated its statement of sexual essentialism and emancipation within the wider social, historical and political narratives of modern times.

Isabel shared Epstein's enthusiasm for the Minoans and styled herself according to archaic models.[25] *The Scotsman* noted her self-fashioning – 'at pains to look and act the part' – and placed her name in inverted commas: '"Isobel" ...

15. Isabel Nicholas arriving for a private viewing of the Royal Academy Summer Show, Burlington House, London, 28 April 1933

16. Isabel Nicholas and Jacob Epstein attending the first night of Eisenstein's *Thunder over Mexico*, Marble Arch Pavilion, 8 January 1934

To say her loveliness is of a most exotic type is putting it mildly.'[26] The variation of her name was, indeed, not Epstein's but her own, adopted at sixteen when she registered at art school.[27] Photographs provide further evidence. A studio portrait (**2**) shows her wearing the spiral earrings, and the paparazzo snap (**15**) reveals tousled, abruptly fringed hair and dramatic make-up that did not conform to the mainstream glamour of the day. It emphasised the apparently Asian aspect of her features, even though she had no Asian heritage. The tinted lips were common in the early 1930s, but the dark kohl eyeliner and extra-white powder was a combination made popular by the Chinese actress Anna May Wong, then at the height of her fame. A comparison between Wong and Marlene Dietrich in *Shanghai Express* (1932; dir. Josef von Sternberg) clarifies the specificity of the look: both women were playing courtesans, but only Wong's eyes were outlined, in conformity with contemporary stereotypes of the 'exotic' Asian. There was a continuity between Epstein's image-making and Isabel's self-fashioning.

Isobel moved beyond the defiantly undressed girl, *Isabel,* to investigate a new kind of portraiture. It was not a single likeness, but a presence haunted by many likenesses – pornographic, Rodin-esque, Renaissance, African and archaic. Each of these brought to the sculpture its own resonances. 'There are no sharp dividing lines in art,' Epstein wrote, 'artists, separated by centuries and continents will enjoy the same experiences and hit on the same truths.'[28] The clutter of his house, the accumulation of Egyptian, African, Pacific, North and South American and modern figures, including the sculptor's own, with masks, vessels, weapons, jewellery, fabrics, often in undifferentiated piles, dramatised this 'fusion of influences'.[29] It expressed an ideal of essentialism, a belief in an 'eternal' and unchangeable human nature, irrespective of race, time or social group, that he shared with contemporaries as different as André Derain and Amédée Ozenfant.[30] Buckle's dubious phrase 'savage sophistication' articulated this fantasy of ancient modernity.

Isabel provided not just the body on to which this philosophy was projected, but a further layer of ideas of her own. Like her contemporary Louise Brooks, she had the capacity to cause 'the work of art to be borne by her ... presence'.[31] Epstein's spectacularly subjective creation was not simply an appropriation and exploitation of Isabel's beauty; it overlapped to a degree with her creation of herself. Her activities in the early 1930s represented a breaking down of the artist/model distinction that continued her Liverpool experiments, and the beginnings of a twentieth-century redefinition of the muse. Epstein's construction and display of a vital, pagan *Isobel* refracted not just her appearance, but aspects of her 'talk', her personality, her profession, the continuation of the search for an alternative femininity that had begun in the Wood Street studio. The feminine roles of Snake Goddess and Hermaphrodite, with their oracular component, reinvented the visionary personae traditionally allocated to male artists and poets. The Minoan allusion evoked her sexual freedom, perhaps already a sexual power. Isabel's 'savage sophistication' manifested the imaginative, antagonistic, protean persona that was the dominant mode of creativity from which women were often excluded.

17. Jacob Epstein, *Jackie with Hedgehog*, 1939, whereabouts unknown, from *Epstein: An Autobiography* (1955)

4 INVISIBLE OBJECT: 1934

In the twentieth century, the pleasures and the responsibilities of progeneration, so central to male creativity myths, had different implications for the reputations and lives of women artists. In the photograph of Epstein and Isabel taken in February 1934 she is, unknown to either party, pregnant. When this came to light, a month later, she moved out of Hyde Park Gate and found herself closer to Flo, in Fitzroy Square (an ironic address under the circumstances, 'Fitzroy' meaning 'king's bastard').[1] On 10 July, a disturbing announcement appeared in *The London Gazette*:

> I, Margaret Epstein, of 21, Fitzroy Square, in the county of London, Spinster, heretofore called and known by the Christian names and surname of Isabel Agnes Nicholas, hereby give notice that on the 2nd day of June, 1934, I renounced and abandoned the use of my said Christian names and surname of Isabel Agnes Nicholas and assumed in lieu thereof the Christian name and surname of Margaret Epstein; and further that such change of names is evidenced by a deed dated 2nd July, 1934, duly executed by me and attested, and enrolled in the Enrolment Department of the Central Office of the Royal Courts of Justice on the 21st day of June, 1934.—Dated the 3rd day of July, 1934.
>
> MARGARET EPSTEIN, late Isabel Agnes (065) Nicholas.

The phrase 'late Isabel Agnes Nicholas' is chilling. The beautiful and celebrated painter, who had just begun to make a name, discarded it. Very few seem to have noticed or known. She disappeared from history, and the *Gazette* announcement is the only certain trace of her until the birth certificate that registers, on 12 September 1934, the birth of her little boy.[2] On it, Isabel legally entered her identity as 'Margaret Epstein'; the father was Jacob Epstein and the child's name was also Jacob Epstein. By October, she was living in Paris and a baby son was announced at Hyde Park Gate.

Sex, conception and reproduction are marginalised events in art history, appropriated by biography, or neglected merely as such. They are particularly problematic when the artist is a woman, often set aside as 'other' to her art making or incorporated into a reduction of that making to self-reflexive illustrations of her life. Sex, conception and reproduction were not, however, isolated or unexamined incidents for women or for men. The events of those obscure months of 1934, personal to Isabel and the Epsteins, interlocked with – and throw light upon – larger social, cultural and artistic affairs.[3]

Isabel's invitation into the Epstein household in 1932 is usually explained in reductive, gendered terms of base needs – his lust, her poverty, and Margaret's alleged failures to provide her husband with either sexual fulfilment or children. Stephen Gardner's objectifying description of Isabel on her arrival at Hyde Park Gate as 'penniless ... young and juicy' may reflect Epstein's perception of her, but the collaboration that followed was more than carnal for all the participants. The ménage and its consequences in 1934 can be understood as an application of the artistic and social ideas that interested Isabel and her circle. Biddy Noakes, a later friend of Isabel, noted her lifelong attraction to people from whom there was something to learn, and observed that part of Isabel's enjoyment of sex was its efficacy in breaking down barriers with someone she wished to know better.[4] Margaret's tolerance of live-in models can similarly be understood as considered. It is usually dismissed as a jealous attempt to distract her husband from his mistress, Kathleen Garman. Although there is evidence for this (Margaret shot and badly wounded Kathleen in 1923 and probably encouraged young models to cooperate with Epstein), she was also consistently committed to the facilitation of Epstein's art, which she saw as a role of huge consequence.[5] The Hyde Park Gate arrangements can be understood, at least in part, as a practical, progressive lifestyle choice.

Isabel described the household as 'rather like living in a well-conducted *pension*', and, after 1923, Epstein's visits to the Garmans (Wednesdays, Saturdays and most evenings between 6 and 7 p.m.) were, like his trips to Paris and his summers in the country, regular and settled.[6] Others in Epstein's circle were exploring such alternative domestic models, not least George Bernard Shaw. Epstein's watercolour of Isabel was purchased by a trailblazer in this area, the artist Amy (Gwen) Wilson, who had lived openly with her husband and lover.[7] Their Smith Square house in Westminster was decorated in the latest art deco style and featured tokens of 'modern', liberal living, most notably a specially commissioned relief by Charles Jagger of an embracing couple surrounded by outraged gossips, entitled *Scandal* (1930; Victoria and Albert Museum, London). Such *ménage à trois* experiments were wittily analysed in 1932 by Noël Coward in his play *Design for Living*. The 1933 film of the same name tactfully moved the action to Paris but located it firmly in the world of writers and artists.

For women, the fresh freedoms of the bohemian circle went hand in hand with fresh insecurities, however.[8] As Elizabeth Wilson has shown, new constraints of gender could be as oppressive as those that had been discarded. Many struggled to maintain identities, careers and status, let alone a living and household, through the vicissitudes of unorthodox lifestyles. Woman artists who were involved with male artists contended with tensions between making their own work and being muse to another's, exacerbated by the demarcation between artist and model which, despite being challenged by Isabel and others, persisted. Isabel's Redfern Gallery show addressed issues of image and income – the £80 that it earned her was approximately the annual wage of an unskilled worker – but her pregnancy and the birth of her son represented a more tragic side of the self-invented life. The child tipped the unconventional Epstein ménage into a new and less benign kind of experiment. There was no question about Epstein's rights as father, and of the two women who had been living at Hyde Park Gate, only one had the status and financial independence to claim and carry out the role of mother. Baby Epstein, called Jackie, was welcomed into a family framework that no longer admitted Isabel. Margaret Epstein appropriated the maternal role, disguising her age (she was sixty) and upholstering herself with a pillow during the summer to appear pregnant.[9] The delight of Margaret and her husband with their belated son, when he appeared, was genuine, and they lavished him with as much love as they had on Peggy Jean.

In the first months of her pregnancy, perhaps Isabel hoped that she and Epstein would bring up the child in Fitzroy Square. The apartment was in his old Fitzrovian stamping ground where many artists lived, not far from the British Museum and her beloved Regent's Park. The elegant Adam townhouse had space where she could continue to work, with large, studio-style windows looking out onto a central garden. There was no question, however, of Isabel and her son being set up as a second Epstein household, a position that was already occupied: Kathleen Garman and her three children by Epstein (Theodore, ten; Kitty, eight; and Esther, five) were barely supported in Chelsea. Epstein's finances were never regular, and Kathleen often needed to support herself, so Epstein may not even have paid completely for Isabel's keep during her confinement, and she may have been semi-dependent on the income from her paintings (selling for the market rate of £16 per piece, less 50 per cent commission).[10] It was around this time that she sent fabric designs to Edinburgh Weavers in the hope of commissions.[11] Nor could Isabel fall back on her own family. She wrote to Agnes, who, although living again in Wallasey with Warwick, was not well placed following the failure of her Canadian venture.[12] There were by now hospitals for unmarried mothers in London, but Epstein's biographer June Rose reports that the baby was born as clandestinely as possible in the quiet suburb of Surbiton.[13]

The freedoms of the flexible, bohemian life were not always in accord; as Isabel's self-determination no longer harmonised with that of the people around her – and was complicated by the new needs of her child – her choices narrowed. If her situation was not unusual, her solution was breathtakingly so, and was characteristically realistic and direct. Isabel set aside her identity to leave that of her child intact. Through the strange device of changing her name, Isabel quite literally became Margaret, and gave birth to a baby that was in every sense possible the Epsteins' son, the sculptor's first and only legitimate male heir. 'Natural' children had no rights to their father's name; Kathleen's son was a Garman.[14] Meum, like countless other separated mothers at the time, had been gradually erased from the life of Peggy Jean; Isabel decisively erased herself. Her existence was hidden from Jackie, as Meum's true relationship was from Peggy Jean, but, unlike Meum, there is no record that Isabel ever went back. She told only her closest intimates, and even in her seventies, with Epstein and Margaret long gone, kept their secret. Jackie was finally informed that Isabel was his mother in 1988, when he was fifty-four, after hints began to appear in the biographies of artists in her circle.[15] There is no evidence that they met again.

Memories of Isabel's presence in the Epstein household persisted in other ways. In 1934, Epstein cast and exhibited the full bust of the first model, *Isabel*, and the plaster can still be seen in the centre of the studio in a photograph taken in the 1940s.[16] He had recently been writing his memoir *Let There be Sculpture,* in which he reproduced the second bust, *Isobel,* renamed *Isabel.*[17] She was, of course, also present in Jackie, seen in the inquisitive gaze and forward-leaning posture of sculptures and drawings of him as a baby, a toddler and a little boy.[18] A sketch of Jackie aged about five and cradling a hedgehog poignantly recalls Isabel's own childhood menageries. **(17)**

In 1955, when Jackie was twenty-one, Epstein returned to the studies of him as a baby in the design of a piece of public sculpture, *Liverpool Resurgent*, intended to go above the main doors of Lewis's department store in Isabel's home town. It comprised three relief panels below a nude male figure standing on the prow of a ship, now a meeting place in the city and immortalised in the song 'In My Liverpool Home': 'We speak with an accent exceedingly rare, / Meet under a statue exceedingly bare.'[19] The triptych of panels showed modern-life scenes representing the renewal of the post-war generation: *Children Fighting, Baby in Pram* and *Children Playing*. In the second of these, Jackie is in a perambulator, attended by a dog with a raised paw. He sits up pertly; his outstretched arms simplify his characteristic reaching posture into a generous/sacrificial pose that partially mirrors the gesture of the mariner above, an echo of his maternal grandfather.

The memory of Isabel is evident also in Epstein's ambitions for his son to be an artist. It must have seemed almost inconceivable that he would not be, given his parentage, but like Peggy Jean, the lad chose his own field of adventure. When

Margaret died in 1947, when Jackie was thirteen, his half-sister, now married and living in America, took over his care. Epstein brought him back to London in 1952, where he chose to study at the Chelsea College of Aeronautical and Automobile Engineering. At nineteen, he borrowed a 2-litre Alta sports car and won the first motor-race to be run on the new British circuit at Brands Hatch. Jackie raced until he was thirty-five and went on to manage the Brands Hatch circuit. As a driver, engineer and manager, he was one of those who transformed the sport into what it is today. He died in 2009, at the age of seventy-four.

Isabel's invisibility between January and September 1934 renders it impossible to know how she experienced these months: how attached she was to the baby when she agreed to the discretion the Epsteins desired, or when, at six months pregnant and with the child moving inside her, she took Margaret's name; or when, finally, she laboured through his birth. We do not know who was with her, how she felt about the experience from which she had shied away when it had happened to her mother, or how long she nursed the child. That the experience was painful can be inferred from Hedli MacNeice's memory of happening upon Isabel in London in September 1934, with two friends; Isabel was tearful and dressed in mourning.[20] The following day, 24 September 1934, Isabel flew to Paris. Fifty years later, her autobiography made no mention of any of the 'events' of the year, simply stating: 'I never saw Epstein again.'

18. Isabel Rawsthorne, *Blois*, sketchbook, c. 1935 or 1945; Tate

5 EXPENSIVE EDUCATION: 1935–1936

Isabel had lost her professional life, her home and her lover, as well as her child. She was once more poor. Someone arranged the flight to Paris and booked her into the Hôtel Delambre, just behind the Café du Dôme. That she felt some kind of bereavement is plain from her autobiographical notes: 'The early days of my life in Paris had a profound effect which is with me today. I felt my actions were inevitable but strange. I felt at home and at the same time alien. The first few weeks were hard and I was longing to go back to England.' The passage reveals a singular aspect of Isabel's character: a tendency to deal with profound emotional crises in private, almost as though they were happening to someone else. The perspective is determinedly practical, the sadness is left literally as a gap in the text and a silence in her life:

> I realised that this feeling, something near to despair, was temporary and necessary as a way of ridding myself of ... [incomplete]. I learned how valuable it is to go to live in a foreign place by oneself. No one has any particular interest in you. You have to make your own decisions and throw yourself open to the surroundings.
>
> My French was very poor. I was shy of speaking. I decided that to read a daily newspaper would help me. I knew that soon I would be forced to speak.

Here begins a strange division in Isabel's persona between her determined gaiety and verve and a clear-eyed melancholy revealed in her art.

The Hôtel Delambre was cheap and clean, but the rooms were too tiny for work. It was only five minutes, however, to the Académie de la Grande Chaumière, an art school where Isabel could pay by the hour for access to a warm studio space and a model. On brighter autumn days, the Jardin du Luxembourg was nearby and the Ménagerie du Jardin des plantes, although the *fin de siècle* air and wrought-iron cages were very different from London's zoo. As dark winter drew in, Isabel's fur coat was a comfort.

The Isabel that comes back into sight in Paris quickly splinters into a constellation of figures. Her secret past left her, to outsiders, strangely without history, without even a name of her own. Over the next six years, reflections and refractions of her presence in the city proliferated: letters, anecdotes in autobiographies and biographies, portraits by Derain, drawings, sculptures and *objets décoratifs* by Giacometti, a handful of photographs and, eventually, in 1940, a series of paintings by Picasso. Isabel's own memoir is, of course, another of these portraits, its episodic structure symptomatic of the full but fragmented life that gave rise to these partial views. Of all the accounts it is the only one to say something about her activity as an artist in pre-war Paris.

Although the memoir is startlingly direct, it took care to protect the sensitivities of others if they were living at the time of writing. As a result, many episodes are omitted and relationships that in reality overlapped were sometimes placed in separate, undefined time frames that cannot always be dated by other means.[1] One of the consequences of this is that no one knows exactly when she met Sefton Delmer, but it was probably late in 1934 or early in 1935. 'Tom' Delmer, as he was known, was a war reporter and foreign correspondent for the *Daily Express* and head of their Paris office. His and Isabel's autobiographies agree that before she left England the *Express* drama critic gave her a letter of introduction to Delmer. Isabel recalled an understandable delay before she felt ready to call, after which Delmer invited her over to the Right Bank, a different world from that of the Left, 'a significant step' as she put it.

Delmer penned a more bravura opening scene, one of his best and most retold tales. His memoir, *Trail Sinister* (1961), describes plucking Isabel fresh on arrival. Its image of her on her first evening in Paris matches Hedli MacNeice's of her last in London – quiet in black, accompanied by two friends – but in one of the paradoxes of Isabel's story, where Hedli remembered her tears, Delmer's anecdote was the first to immortalise her famous laugh. His account omitted the phone call and framed the picture with care:

> Late one evening, at the end of September when I was back in Paris from my travels I had driven up to Montparnasse and was sitting all by myself in the Café du Dome. For me a seat there on the terrace of the Dome or the Coupole with a glass of brandy and a Perrier in front of me was always a pleasure, whether I was alone or had company ... I was glancing through the early morning editions of the Paris dailies that had just come out, checking them over to see whether there was any news I had missed, when my roving eye was caught by three girls who had sat down two tables away from me and were talking, of all improbable languages, in English. One looked like an Arab or a Turk, the second looked like a Russian. The third who had not spoken was wearing a black velvet cape. Her highcheeked face was white,

19. British visitors to UFA film studios, Potsdam-Babelsberg (Sefton Delmer, left), c. 1935

> framed by a stream of russet brown hair that hung down to her shoulders, not quite hiding two spirals of wired gold that hung from each ear. And then as I looked at the slanting eyes and red pouting mouth, first suspicion and then certainty broke in on me. This was she, Isabel, the girl of the bronze. I was so overcome, that as I got up to go over and speak to her I almost overturned the table. 'Please mademoiselle, excuse my intrusion,' I said in my best professional manner. 'I am Sefton Delmer, Paris correspondent of the *Express*. I have been looking at you and I feel certain you must be the famous Isabel, of whom Epstein did that superb bust. Are you?' Isabel gazed at me with wide open friendly eyes and then the bronze that had turned to flesh spoke. Instead of the resonant musicality with which I had endowed her in my dreams came sounds emanating, so it seemed to me, from a larynx made of tin.[2]

Isabel's description of herself at their meeting was shorter and less uncomplicatedly convivial. She was with Doris Ahmed, whose portrait by Epstein had also appeared in the Leicester Galleries show.[3] 'We must have been a strange-looking couple. My Arab friend exotic, with large, black, unsmiling eyes. Myself in a long and tattered dress in black velvet, wearing sandals.'

The truth of Delmer's text is of less interest than its perpetuation of Isabel as a motif. Her transformation into a familiar configuration of male–female desire is augmented by a new slant, male–male competition, sexual and creative. His account set this up by preceding the story with a preamble about encountering Epstein's statue in the Tate. Like Buckle, Delmer constructs her according to racialised categories of the 'exotic' and 'primitive': 'A long necked girl with thick hair falling to her bare shoulders, a pouting almost Negroid mouth, high cheekbones, and those slanting Nefertiti eyes.'[4] Delmer evoked an impassive Egyptian head, something reminiscent of the blank-eyed, bronze femme-fatale *Maschinenmensch* of Fritz Lang's *Metropolis*, to contrast the inert aesthetic vision of the sculptor with his more active, flesh-and-blood gaze: 'My reaction was not at all that of the connoisseur of the arts. It was that of a susceptible bachelor. "You," I said to the bust, "are the girl I am going to marry – if I ever marry at all."' Delmer's verbal description of Isabel borrowed from Epstein's visual one, but added the embellishments of a journalist. Like Pygmalion, his passionate representation 'quickens' the older man's bronze into yellow-lit, russet-haired, metal-voiced, real existence. He mocked and usurped, whether or not he knew it, the cartoon image of a 'post-Pygmalion' Epstein pleasuring himself with his statues.

Delmer was closer to Isabel's age, witty and fascinatingly engaged with the world. His was a dark profession during this troubled period, and off-duty moments were cherished: 'a gay and ebullient companion when he allowed himself to forget his frustration with colleagues who continually refused to realise the real intentions of Hitler's Germany to make war'. Delmer was a talented sybarite and well paid, as the French franc was weak against the English pound. The night of their first meeting they dined and danced till dawn, after which Isabel found herself alone at the Dôme, breakfasting on beer, 'in some confusion' with a 'most remarkable hangover'. Delmer wrote of an impetuous courtship and wedding a few months after Isabel's arrival. In reality, she moved into his Right Bank apartment in 1935, not as his wife, but as his companion, 'secretary', 'assistant', 'colleague', 'a person who helps me with my enquiries', according to whom they were with.

This was another self-invented relationship, conducted on grounds of mutual attraction, affection and benefit. Isabel seems to have reserved for Delmer only charm, cheerfulness and off-hand courage, leaving sadness somewhere else. He perceived her as a glittering celebrity: 'I felt wonderfully glamorous as I walked up and down the platform of the Gare d'Orsay', he wrote, 'with Isabel on one arm and her friend Ahmed on the other.'[5] She assisted him with his work in Paris and elsewhere, and they married on 18 September 1936.[6] Her new passport officially reinstated her name, only slightly changed, Isabel Agnes Delmer; her profession was entered as 'Artist Painter'. Both Isabel's and Delmer's mothers visited Paris shortly after the wedding.

The couple occupied a penthouse in a building on the corner of rue de Castiglione overlooking the grand and exclusive place Vendôme, a few steps to the fashionable boutiques of the rue Saint-Honoré or, in the other direction, the pungent Saint-Honoré market. The apartment had a large balcony, a courtyard with separate accommodation for servants and a studio space for Isabel. The decor was, however, playboy art deco – white walls and white linoleum floor, black oilcloth curtains, black glass and chrome mantelpiece and tables and lamps.[7] For Delmer, it was a tool of his trade, and he called it his 'operating theatre'. A mirrored bar facilitated 'gathering in an ever increasing circle of friends to whom I could appeal for information and help'. Isabel disliked it. She had no experience of 'affluence', as she considered it, and found the luxury vulgar. She was, perhaps, pleased to remember Epstein telling her that Napoleon's celebrated Vendôme Column, which she could see from her windows in the centre of the square, had been toppled by 'Courbet and his mates ... in the revolution of 1870–72'.

Isabel fell in with Delmer's exuberant set, many of them German (Delmer was half German himself). Their two best friends were a princess and a prince, not related to each other. Prince Bernhard of Lippe-Biesterfeld was a businessman and Delmer's fellow bon viveur, a frequent, lively and likeable guest. Princess Mara Scherbatoff, a brilliant linguist, was a White Russian refugee. She worked as Delmer's assistant and lived in the apartment. She and Isabel grew very close: 'I became devoted to her and she to me.' Isabel helped with their entertaining, official and otherwise, running a kind of 'salon'. Delmer recalled that her associates and his made a heady mix:

> Scotland Yard inspectors over in Paris to investigate some Soho murder would find themselves talking to a shockheaded surrealist sculptor or a German diplomat. My Russian secretary, Princess Scherbatoff, would probably be on hand with a couple of Russian aristocrat beauties from the Balenciaga salon, and I would be talking to French politicians or a journalist ... Isabel handled them all beautifully, never appearing to be bothered, apparently letting things run themselves and infecting everyone with her effervescent enthusiasm.[8]

Agnes and Warwick Nicholas, meanwhile, had returned from their failed Canadian venture. While in Canada Warwick had undergone surgery in Toronto for the removal of a tubercular gland in his neck and on arrival in England had been confined for three weeks in the Quarantine Hospital at Tilbury Docks with a misdiagnosis of diphtheria.[9] None of the family would take in Agnes or the boy for fear of contagion, and the nine-year-old was sent to a convalescent home on the south coast at Broadstairs in Kent, while Agnes went back to Wallasey. She moved into a small house in the modest area of Liscard, taking in boarders and looking after an aunt who was suffering from tuberculosis. Isabel visited them both. Warwick was returned to his mother, and even started school, but, after a few months, Agnes suffered a breakdown, and in October 1935, aged nine and a half, he was sent to an orphanage, the Royal Merchant Navy School at Bearwood, near Wokingham in Berkshire. There, he grew even weaker. After Isabel died, Warwick would find many letters from his sister to his mother, pleading with her to find him somewhere better.[10] Eventually, having discovered Warwick in a state of severe malnutrition, Isabel and Delmer intervened. Taking over the costs of his education, they placed him at Colet Court in London, the preparatory boarding school for Delmer's old institution, St Paul's School for Boys.[11] Here he was happier and began to regain strength. Delmer continued to pay for Warwick's keep and education until he was eighteen. In 1939, Warwick continued his education at Dauntsey's, a public school in Wiltshire specialising in science and agriculture, taking his Higher School Certificate in 1944, at a time when most boys were working by fourteen. Agnes Nicholas was able to move south and settle on the coast near her family in New Milton in Hampshire.

True to the Pygmalion tale, or rather to Shaw's fashionable updated version of it, Delmer taught Isabel the secrets of fine living.[12] She called this her 'expensive education'. At the rue de Castiglione he employed an exceptional cook named Anna, the German widow of a French policeman, who lived in a flat in the place du Marché Saint-Honoré. She missed her previous employer, the performer Josephine Baker, who had returned to the United States to star in the Ziegfeld Follies, and talked about her constantly. She made no bones about her disappointment with the quality of Isabel's underwear compared to that of her last mistress, for example, and at Delmer's dinner parties, Anna's speciality, the misnamed 'soufflé surprise', could always be relied upon to reveal a naked miniature of the dancer.[13] Isabel and Anna, nevertheless, became friends, and Isabel began to learn about Continental cooking.

Isabel and Delmer's gastronomic itineraries read like a grand tour of French cuisine. If they went to La Rue or Maxim's, it was 'more for the people than the food', and usually they preferred to escape the social circuit. La Fontaine Gaillon for seafood and Relais de la Belle Aurore for hors d'oeuvre and crêpes were a step away. Over the river there were Lapérouse and La Tour d'Argent. At Les Halles market was the rumbustious La Grille, full of fishermen from the coast. Delmer's favourite was Pharamond, with sawdust on the floor and marble-topped tables on which were served bowls of tripe, bubbling over small braziers. His sports car permitted them to search out places in the suburbs, too, recommended by word of mouth and run by families providing a speciality or wine from farms and vineyards they knew. At weekends, they went to the country, setting out before dawn to speed down empty roads. Their most frequent getaway destination was Blois, but they ventured to nearly every area in France. In Bordeaux, they ate 'more or less continuously' for a weekend at Le Chapon Fin. Here the wine list, including Delmer's beloved Château Ausone, was complete, from before phylloxera days, and Isabel learned to indulge in a *majoration*, the drinking of one wine of successive years.

These interludes were exceptional, however. Delmer worked obsessively and was often away. His memoir makes it clear that he took Isabel's self-sufficiency for granted, and it was intrinsic to their relationship. She saw her time with Delmer as one side only of a 'double life' split between the Right Bank and the Left. Although she had a studio at the rue de Castiglione, she rented a cheap space in Montparnasse by the month: 'The walk between the Right Bank and the Left Bank ... became the foundation of my entire life in Paris as long as I lived there.'

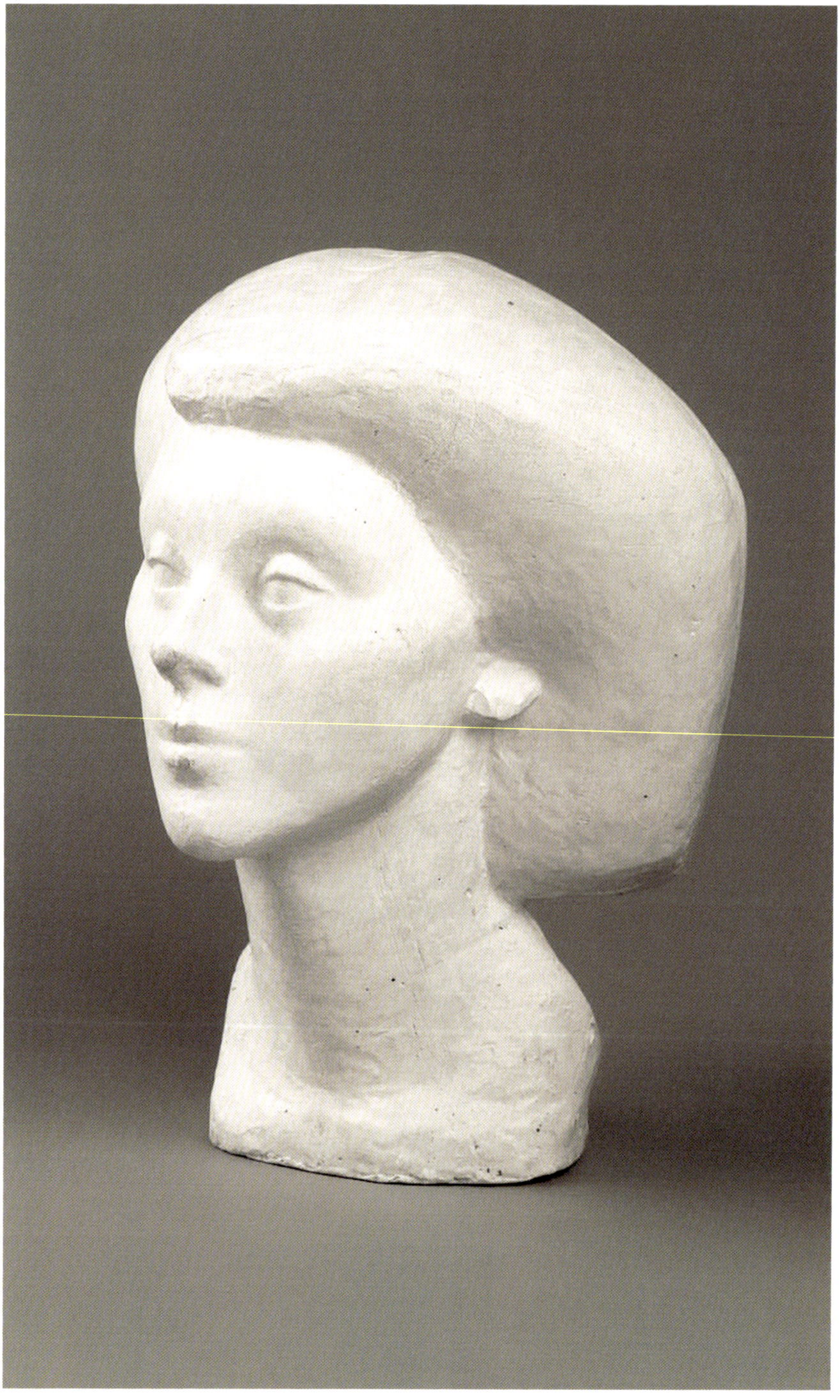

20. Alberto Giacometti, *Tête d'Isabel I* (*L'Egyptienne*), plaster, 1936; Fondation Giacometti, Paris

6 LA PARISIENNE: 1934–1937

The journey from the 1st *arrondissement* to the 14th was about the same distance as that between Holland Park and the Royal Academy, but Isabel felt the difference between London and Paris. Leaving the flat she shared with Delmer in the place Vendôme, she walked down the rue de Castiglione and descended into the Jardin des Tuileries, where the lacy network of straight walks, clipped trees and hedges, and railings had a more confected air than the John Constable look of Hyde Park. The gardens were pale and bright in any weather, illuminated by the pinky-grey grit of the paths and the circular, ornamental lake at its centre. On the far side, Isabel followed the Seine past the half-kilometre of carved stone of the Louvre Palace, finally crossing at the venerable Pont Neuf – its name, meaning 'new', as old as the bridge. The elegant Renaissance arches just touch the Île de la Cité where it divides the river, and continue on to the quai des Grands Augustins on the other side. There, Isabel's route cut into the dense buildings of the Latin Quarter.

Montparnasse was still the confluence of artists, writers, revolutionaries, entertainers, eccentrics and pleasure seekers that it had been in the heady 1920s, but the economic downturn and political upheavals meant that some dealers and many patrons, especially Americans, had left, and artists worked with less hope of exhibitions or sales. Isabel drew from the models at the Académie de la Grande Chaumière, made still lifes in her rented studio or travelled by Métro to sketch in the zoo at Vincennes.[1] She began 'painting in oils for the first time seriously'. Each day, at 5 p.m., artists gathered at Le Dôme café. At first, Isabel went with friends from London: Doris Ahmed; a Scottish poet, Sean Rafferty, who was researching at the Sorbonne; Fiona Garfitt and Denis Clarke Hall, who shared a studio nearby. Garfitt had been a student of Henry Moore; Hall was a Modern Movement architect.

Sometime in 1935, the gallery owner Pierre Colle directed Isabel to the atelier of André Derain in the rue d'Assas, overlooking the Jardin du Luxembourg. The veteran artist was pleased to welcome Epstein's entrancing friend and invited her to sit for him and to use his studio to study from his model. The following day she returned, and Derain began what would become a series of six portraits, with titles such as *La Jeune Anglaise* (c. 1936; private collection).[2] Derain was a great

21. André Derain, postcard of *Portrait de femme aux cheveux bouclés*, 1935–6; Musée des Beaux-Arts de Lyon

22. André Derain, *La Tasse de thé*, 1935; Musée d'art moderne et contemporain de Saint-Étienne Métropole

raconteur, well known in the cafés, and provided Isabel with a swift education in French language and *mores* ...'To me,' she wrote, 'he is all that is French. His looks, his humour (he might have been an actor), his gusto, his intelligence and his reticence. Also his love of continuity.' Derain thought English was hard to use when talking about art; Isabel found this to be true and that French could be 'fluid and yet ... remain precise when discussing artistic notions'. Derain's *La Tasse de thé*, (**22**) depicted Isabel as an English bluestocking in plain, black sweater, leaning thoughtfully on a long, strong hand. The juxtaposition of an ordinary English teapot and French drinking bowl signals a pleasant, plain cross-cultural accord.

Soon, Isabel fell in with the French avant-garde, with the dissident Surrealists, the poets Paul Éluard and Tristan Tzara (the latter the founder of the Dada movement), and, 'fatefully', the sculptor Alberto Giacometti. Giacometti was thirty-two, ten years her senior. Like her, he was a foreigner – Swiss Italian – but he had been in Paris for twelve years. He might have noticed Isabel on one of her prior visits to Paris with Epstein; now he watched her nearly every day, but it was months before they spoke, probably in the autumn of 1935.[3] 'I was aware of a curious sensation when being observed with remarkable intensity by a man with singular features,' she wrote, ' ... one evening, as I rose from the table, he rose at the same time. Advancing he said, "Est-ce qu'on peut parler?"' They seem to have struck up an understanding immediately: 'From then on,' Isabel recalled, 'we met daily, always at five pm.' Giacometti spoke German and Romansh but

23. Béla Bernand: *Terrace, Le Dôme café* (detail), 1936

no English, so they communicated in basic French, and it was weeks before her language improved enough to be 'able to appreciate the force of his conversation'.[4] He shared her left-wing leanings, common among artists of the quarter, but they were misfits, even by Left Bank standards. Their love of fun and their eye for irony were accompanied by a professional isolation and private sadness that were changing the direction of their lives. The disturbing Surrealist objects that Giacometti had exhibited in his one-man show at Pierre Colle's gallery in 1932 had established his name and his international recognition, but, in February 1935, he was expelled from the group, angrily dismissing their entire output as 'masturbation!' He tended towards the more materialist, anthropologically minded, dissident branch of the movement, led by Georges Bataille and had returned to realist methods of working from the model. He had recently suffered the loss of his father and had just returned with Max Ernst from his family's summer home in the Alps where he had carved the tombstone.

A picture snapped in 1936 by the Hungarian photographer Béla Bernand captured Isabel, Giacometti and an unidentified woman, all unaware of the camera, on the terrace of Le Dôme. (**23**) Giacometti has a book in front of him, and, as so often, Isabel leans forward. A slightly later shot allows us to see her smiling. In both photographs, Giacometti gazes across at her. She is wrapped in a dark coat; her hair is crimped with a permanent wave, but not set into any arrangement (it was typical then to have hair set twice a week), and it is difficult to resist the idea that its new, woolly texture is similar to his. Isabel and Giacometti talked in cafés and restaurants and on long strolls through the streets of Paris, especially at night, and eventually she visited his studio. Very different from that of Epstein or Derain, it was in an out-of-the-way street, rue Hippolyte Maindron, a short walk north off the rue d'Alésia. A slatted wooden door opened from the pavement onto a narrow space between two buildings that acted as courtyard, with a communal lavatory and tap. Pale, stained plaster copies of fifteenth-century masters, probably old casts sold off by the Louvre and familiar to Isabel from the Victoria and Albert Museum (Della Robbia's *Cantoria* and Ghiberti's Baptistery doors), haunted the walls.

Giacometti had, for the past nine years, rented part of the top floor of the left-hand building, a room with a roof glazed to one side and accessed by a flight of rickety steps. Isabel was surprised to find it smaller than even her own modest studio, with a bare linoleum floor and un-papered walls lined and scored with diagrams. Giacometti's sculptures crowded at the end, illuminated by the slanting window, either complete or wrapped in damp rags. In the darker part, lit by a suspended bulb, was a low, narrow bed, bookshelf and table; another bed on a mezzanine level served Giacometti's brother, Diego, who was his work partner. It was a single-minded space, excluding anything not to do with the physical necessity of work and rest. It blurred the polarity between artist and model, life and art; there was a strange interchangeableness between tables and trestles, teapot and glue tins, and the bed doubled as a model's couch. Giacometti had spent years creating without any sitter, and sculptural contraptions could at first glance be mistaken for the apparatus that made them. Over the bed, a female form, extruded and tangled into something spider-like, hung as on a thread. In a corner, a woman rose like an enormous spoon. Other not-quite-things asserted an equally human presence. Such a weaving of life and work Isabel found sympathetic.

Like the space, the sculptures evaded the ideals of the heroic, protean artist. The sexualised representation of the body was as important to Giacometti's art as it had been to Epstein's, but his work explored it from a more ambivalent, self-critical perspective. At the Surrealists' exhibition at the Galerie Pierre Colle in June 1933, a life-size plaster torso and legs called *Femme qui marche I* (Walking Woman I) (1932) had been given surreal embellishments with the neck of a cello and flailing arms, evoking the abandoned attitudes and slicked curls of black performers such as Josephine Baker, then so successful on the Left Bank. By the time of Isabel's visit, however, it stood in Giacometti's studio without its accessories, beside a more recent piece, *Personnage féminin* (1934; plaster; Yale University Art Gallery), the artist's return to the full figure. The feminine forms drew on archaic sources with associations of death rather than fertility – stepping, Egyptian tomb figures such

24. Dora Maar: *Personnage féminin* (later *L'Objet invisible, mains tenant le vide),* with *Figure tenant un drapeau, Petit homme,* and *Projet pour une place,* in Alberto Giacometti's studio, c. 1934; Fondation Giacometti, Paris

as the Standing Figure of Nefertiti (Ägyptisches Museum, Berlin). The shoulders and strange hollow under the breasts of *Femme qui marche I* were adapted from a high-contrast photograph of the headless *Kore with Bird from Miletus* (sixth century BCE; Staatliche Museen, Berlin) in *Documents*.[5] Both figures eschewed the generous curves of the older generation's 'eternal' feminine in favour of the modern reserve of the mannequin, an alternative modernity between the wars which, as the cultural historian Mary Roberts has shown, was a 'repudiation of the womb ... a repudiation of breasts'.[6] *Personnage féminin* yearns forward, its thin physique and empty hands reversing the form and concept of the vessel. By 1935, it had been given another title, which, whether intentional or not, was emblematic of Isabel's story: *L'Objet invisible, mains tenant le vide* (*Invisible Object, Hands Holding a Void*).[7]

Moreover, from 1933, Giacometti had begun to publish in periodicals self-consciously post-Freudian fantasies, confessions and jokes. As a result, he became known for overattachment to his mother, sadomasochist fantasies, physical infelicities (sterility, lameness, venereal disease), performance anxiety and an associated preference for prostitutes.[8] They proved a paradoxically potent challenge

25. Alberto Giacometti, *Femme qui marche I*, plaster, 1932 and 1935–6; Fondation Giacometti, Paris

26. Alberto Giacometti, *Femme qui marche II*, plaster, 1935–6; The Peggy Guggenheim Collection, Venice

to the personae of the previous generation of artists, disturbing and displacing their protean sexual and artistic values. These stories were perpetuated beyond Giacometti's death by his sitter and friend from later in his life, James Lord. Lord also believed that the sculptor's meeting with Isabel initiated a decade of sexual and artistic sterility.[9] When Lord put this idea to Isabel in later years, he interpreted her retort that the tales were 'more talk than action' as a confirmation of his conviction that Giacometti was sexually debilitated as a result of the orchitis (inflammation of the testicles) that had afflicted him in his teenage years.[10] The disease is, medically, very unlikely to have caused any kind of sexual difficulty, however, and it is more probable that Isabel's reply saluted the performative aspect of the talk itself.

Lord was of the opinion that Isabel tantalised Giacometti, but kept him at arm's length. Véronique Wiesinger, by contrast, sees signs that they were intimate in each other's company and that Isabel was present and involved when he remodelled *Femme qui marche I* between 1935 and 1936.[11] *Femme qui marche I* (**25**) is robotic – again the mannequin or *Maschinenmensch* comes to mind – whereas *Femme qui marche II*, 1935–6, (**26**) takes on the characteristics of flesh. The hollow in the chest was removed and a more continuous skin-like surface replaced the mannequin joints. The breasts, which had been symmetrical mounds, now fall with perceptible weight, taut down to the nipple and then relaxing into a curve beneath. The cylindrical thighs swell gently to meet the hip, becoming the long 'tapered' legs that disqualified Isabel from art-school modelling. The feet are also less stylised and the figure is buoyant and enlivened by her slanted, dancer's stride.

Like Epstein's *Isobel*, Giacometti's *Femme qui marche II* animated archaic shapes with Isabel's figure and presence, but the persona was different. Giacometti's Isabel is not 'possessed', but dispossessed. The replacement of the bird held to the breast in the photograph of the Kore by a hollow was a reverse of the imagery of Epstein's *Rima*, and ripeness was replaced by reticence. Crucially, the 'quickening effect' is no longer a function of fertility but of mobility. Epstein's investigative, advancing bearing is animated by Giacometti into walking, Isabel's daily journey from Right Bank to Left, her arrivals and departures and the strolls the two artists shared in between.

Giacometti had ample opportunity to view Epstein's first head, *Isabel*, of which Delmer owned a bronze cast, and he confronted the older sculptor *face à face*, with his own *Tête d'Isabel I*.[12] (**20**) Drawings on paper and directly on to his studio walls suggest that it was considered over many months.[13] The Nefertiti forward tilt and the careful differentiation of the eyes of Epstein's bronze inform Giacometti's frontal and profile studies in *Quatre têtes de femme (Isabel)*, c. 1936, (**38**) and he drew reproductions of figures in the Ägyptisches Museum. The studies featured the format and block-like hairstyle of the wooden *Great Royal Wife of Amenhotep II* of the Eighteenth Dynasty, the source, apparently, for Isabel's hair in the photograph taken at Le Dôme.[14] (**23**) These characteristics reappear in *Tête d'Isabel I*, which acquired the alternative title, *L'Égyptienne*. The name had modern associations, also, to Le Sphinx, a famous brothel with a dance bar on the first floor often frequented by Giacometti, Isabel and their friends. This Baudelairean past present was more glancing, paradoxical and unresolved than Epstein's.

Through Isabel, Giacometti got to know and admire Derain, and he, in turn, introduced her to artists of her own age who shared their figurative interests. These included the left-wing painters Francis Gruber and Pierre Tal-Coat.[15] From 1936, Gruber was based at 10 Villa d'Alésia, a stone's throw from Giacometti's workplace.

27. André Derain, *Portrait de Madame Isabel Delmer,* 1936; private collection

Isabel remembered him as 'an overpowering gay blade who talked, drank, and painted at a furious clip'.[16] The sculptor Germaine Richier, whom Giacometti knew both through their Swiss connections and their training with Antoine Bourdelle, had a thriving studio just behind his.[17] Isabel became particular friends with another part-Swiss friend of Giacometti, the painter Baltusz Klossowski de Rola, better known as Balthus. He had only recently settled on the Left Bank, taking a lofty studio in the cour de Rohan, near the Pont Neuf, in 1936. He was a quite different proponent of the figurative approach, however: his paintings set contemporary figures in uneasy sexual and psychological situations in a style inspired by fifteenth-century Italian art. His family – all artists and writers – was part of the French cultural elite, and his patrician pretensions were the cause of great teasing: 'If there had been a monarchy, Balthus would have been a monarchist.' His first exhibition at Pierre Loeb's in 1934 had already made him notorious and won him adulation from the Surrealists.[18]

Isabel was a point of contact for dialogue between artists, herself included. A smaller painting by Derain, *Portrait of Madame Isabel Delmer*, 1936, (**27**) is particularly

28. Isabel in Venice, 1937

29. 'La Parisienne', 1500 BCE; Heraklion Archaeological Museum

interesting. The picture is unusual in identifying Isabel by name and was perhaps a memento of her marriage to Tom Delmer that year.[19] It is painted up-close; pale strokes radiate from the translucent, knowing eyes, recalling a self-portrait by Van Gogh, but their pallor, barely tainted by peach, mauve and viridian, gives the skin a luminous, chalky surface like a Degas pastel. The fair face is framed by a tumble of curls. These and the scarf unmistakably cast Isabel as another ancient character, 'La Parisienne', 1500 BCE, (**29**) a fresco fragment from the palace at Knossos that Arthur Evans named for the bee-stung lips, brisk ringlets and elegant bow of the Minoan priestess (or even goddess) depicted.[20] Like Giacometti, Derain modified Epstein's treatment. The scuffed texture and colour of *Madame Isabel Delmer*, the drape of the goddess's sacred shawl, her kiss curl, the dabs of red at the lips (ears, too) conferred on the sitter a 'Minoan modernism' of a more metropolitan kind than is evident in Epstein's *Isobel*.

A brooch in the shape of a draped female figure, created by Giacometti for the designer and Surrealist Elsa Schiaparelli, c. 1936, (**30**) may also have been made on the occasion of Isabel's marriage, as the style derived from archaic gilded bronze jewellery associated with dowries.[21] The brooch belonged to Isabel until it was mislaid in the 1970s.[22] It is possible that she was also the prior owner of a bracelet

30. Alberto Giacometti, 'Angel of the Annunciation', brooch for Schiaparelli, c. 1936; Sainsbury Centre for Visual Arts, University of East Anglia

bought around 1940 by the German expatriate art dealer Erica Brausen. The bracelet 'Naïad or Chimera', c. 1935, (**31**) is of similar style and date, and Isabel's wide, asymmetric, angled eyes are easy to recognise. Derain's, Giacometti's and Schiaparelli's forms of Minoan modernity exclude all hints of Epstein's fertile, maternal life force. Their chic reinterpretations defuse the tension between 'savage' and 'sophistication', tilting it impeccably towards the latter.

Isabel's archaic roles positioned all those concerned at the centre of the avant-garde, 'call and response' of Minoan ideas, epitomised by Breton's journal *Minotaure* (1933–9), for which Derain designed the third cover. The continuities across images reinforce the sense that they originated, in part, in her own intellectual interests.[23] Just as her appearance in 1936 had an Egyptian air, so a photograph taken in about 1937 reveals 'La Parisienne'-style ringlets. 'Minoan modernism' was one of an array of playfully performed allusions that stressed agency as well as appeal, non-conformism, autonomy and knowledge.

31. Alberto Giacometti, 'Naïad or Chimera', bracelet for Schiaparelli, c. 1935; Musée des arts décoratifs, Paris

The photograph was probably taken on the occasion when Isabel joined Balthus and Antoinette de Watteville, who married that year, on trips to Berne, Verona and Venice.[24] He was a great Anglophile, and they discussed the Shakespearean associations of the cities. Elizabethan literature was fashionable in France during this period, an earthy alternative to the Classical tradition.[25] Isabel's balcony pose recalls the plays, and the masculine jacket and 'English knits', a style based on British sporting clothing, evoke Shakespeare's cross-dressed heroines, such as Julia in *Two Gentlemen of Verona*. Her androgynous clothes echoed a style called *la garçonne*, surveyed by Whitney Chadwick in her study of Parisian women between the wars: an English sporty 'mingling of the masculine and the intensely feminine' made fashionable by Coco Chanel in the mid-1920s.[26] The photograph demonstrates how these clothes overlapped with reassessments of gender roles in avant-garde culture. The *garçonne* style complements the lesbian reputation of the Minoan snake-goddesses and the athletic 'bull-leapers' (in fact boys, but described by Evans as girls), a play on ancient, Elizabethan and Modern cross-dressing.[27]

Isabel tried bisexuality. The trip to Venice was intended, in part, as a sequel to her recent seduction by Balthus's partner, Antoinette. Isabel's autobiography describes their tryst: 'Antoinette ... invited me to dinner. She booked a private room at *Lapérouse*. I put on my most beautiful suit from Creed. It was black, with a short, shaped jacket bound with black braid. With this I wore a white silk blouse with a large cravat, also an extraordinary hat like a black topper bent sideways, swathed with a small, black spotted veil. Antoinette, who loved clothes, was delighted.' Charles Creed was an English designer who specialised in adapting men's tailoring to women's suits, and Isabel's black-and-white outfit was a smoother version of English garb associated with the lesbian androgyne. It had been made famous by Radclyffe Hall and was a trendy look, augmented with monocles and ties, at some Left Bank venues, Le Select for example, not far from Le Dôme. Antoinette, for her part, is characterised in terms of the bronzed bull-leapers themselves: 'We went back to my modest little hotel after dinner. Here, Antoinette made love. She had a slender, muscular body. She was a keen skier and every February went to the mountains. After these skiing holidays she would arrive in Paris with a nut-brown tan all over her body. Crowned with a mass of fuzzy golden hair, blue eyes, she had the appearance of *a remote goddess* [my emphasis].' Isabel does not describe her own nude appearance, but it, too, was carefully styled, her pubic hair removed in the fashion that was understood at this time to be timeless and 'primitive' as well as practical (hygienic).[28] The look was associated with performers such as Kiki de Montparnasse and Josephine Baker, as well as with traditional and archaic art.[29] The drawing by Epstein of Sunita, which Isabel owned, exhibits the same hairless appearance.

The Antoinette affair was conducted, on Isabel's side at least, in the spirit of research and little came of it: 'I do not think I brought her much happiness. When Balthus heard of this incident he was delighted. He hoped we would continue to be lovers. He should have known better.' It is nonetheless refracted by several of Giacometti's biographers as an expansion of their 'man eater' imagery to 'woman eater'.[30] Isabel's androgynous behaviour and garb is more interestingly read as part of a general preference for an unbound life, a 1930s 'hybrid' self-fashioning, which the historian Mary Stewart describes as 'coded allusions to the new, looser styles liberating women's bodies, facilitating mobility and enabling paid labour'.[31] The maker of Isabel's wedding outfit, Edward Molyneux, was, like Creed, an English designer known for streamlined costumes for independent women, the feisty leading ladies of the plays of Noël Coward, for instance. Isabel's dress was typical: corset-free, 'fitted like a swimsuit' and 'perfect for dancing'.

Isabel's preference for black also fits Stewart's definition: both chic and practical. She took it further, wearing it in unsuitable situations to set herself apart, hinting, perhaps, at Baudelaire's view of the colour as a modern mode of mourning: 'We are each of us celebrating some funeral.'[32] If Isabel did not read translations of Baudelaire at art school, she became familiar with him through

Epstein, who considered his poetic masterpiece, *Les Fleurs du mal* (1857), the 'Bible of the modern man … images of revolt, anguish and despair – disgust with the world and self'.[33] Isabel's copy, published in 1929, probably dates from this period. Her library also contained an unusual edition of Baudelaire's essay 'Le Peintre de la vie moderne' (The Painter of Modern Life; 1860), illustrated with reproductions of Constantin Guys's images of Parisian pastimes and fashion, and she embraced Baudelaire's understanding of clothes as art and anthropology.[34] This subject was not one Isabel cared to pursue in paint, but her personal 'style' expressed, enacted and authenticated her invention of self. Her dark sweater in Derain's *La Tasse de thé,* looks forward to the plain, ungendered clothes that she came to prefer after the 1930s and pre-empts the outfit that would become the uniform of the post-war Left Bank intellectual.

The multiple descriptions, pictorial, textual and anecdotal, of imperious self-determination, physical freedom and Dionysian attraction that accumulated around Isabel during the mid-1930s complemented the social, political and cultural positions that she was examining. Her Parisian persona shrugged off conventional expectations in favour of roles of greater flexibility, winning some of the sexual, social and artistic autonomy more often associated with men at this time.

32. Isabel Rawsthorne, *Standing Woman with Folded Arms* (from sketchbook), c. 1935; Tate

7 QUESTIONS OF REALISM: 1935–1937

Isabel described Paris as her 'Mecca', her objective since art school. Her exploratory approach to art and life, historical and scientific perspectives, and the investigative representational processes that went with them found a context on the Left Bank. Most of the portraits, animal studies and still lifes on which she worked before the Second World War were abandoned, lost or destroyed in the conflict, but the handful that survive give a glimpse of her part in an alternative figurative avant-garde.

Isabel's habit of going to Le Dôme after work at 5 p.m. brought her into contact with people from many fields, 'each one curious about the others', and with the debates, petty and profound, that were shaping modern art and ideas. 'Some of the most amusing hours, I spent ... were listening to arguments between Giacometti and Tzara,' she wrote. Surrealism, headed by André Breton, was at its height and Giacometti's Surrealist work had been shown in New York and purchased by the Museum of Modern Art. In the summer of 1936, he participated in the International Surrealist Exhibition in London, which Isabel almost certainly saw. The movement's doctrinaire attitudes and preoccupation with dreams did not interest her, however, and the equivocal role of women within Breton's circle may also have put her off. This chimed with Giacometti's phase of reassessment. He had set aside the aggressive psychosexual themes and combative exclusivity of his Surrealist peers in favour of a wider curiosity about Western and non-Western art and sustained study of the human form.[1] As David Sylvester put it, 'the sculptures of an artist recognised as one of the leading sculptors of the day became the works of a student'.[2] Giacometti had stopped drawing from models in 1926, but he returned to the practice in 1935, working from his brother, Diego, from a professional model, Rita Gueyfier, and from Isabel.

Isabel and Giacometti shared the breadth of their intellectual curiosity – their interest in the techniques of traditional art and popular media, for instance, and in science. 'His conversation was Socratic and his devotion to research absolute,' she wrote, 'It was impossible to spend long in his company and not find yourself questioning yourself.'[3] 'We visited many museums. Sometimes we journeyed to St. Denis and Versailles ... He changed my life definitely, gradually opened my eyes to many, many things.' The exhibition *Les Peintres de la réalité en France au XVIIe*, which opened at the Orangerie shortly after Isabel's arrival in Paris in 1934, was important, and they almost certainly went to the large Cézanne retrospective held there in 1936.[4] Cézanne was an exemplar of commitment to a 'phenomenologically intensified art', as Poul Erik Tøjner has put it, and 'a visual emblem of work, of effort'.[5]

It seems inevitable that Isabel and Giacometti discussed Epstein's commitment to figuration in defiance of modern trends, his successes and his failures, and also his devotion to Baudelaire and to Rodin, which was out of step with avant-garde taste in the 1930s. Rodin's drawings had been a starting point for Giacometti as well as for Isabel, and he no doubt regaled her with a favourite tale of spending his ticket money on a book of reproductions during a journey home from boarding school, and having to stagger back with it through the snowy night on foot.[6] He took her to Rodin's foundry, where he was having his own works cast, and they looked together at the enormous portal, writhing with figures, of *The Gates of Hell* (Musée Rodin, Paris; cast after his death, c. 1916) . 'We would spend a long time in the Louvre together,' Isabel also remembered. At this date, 1935–6, Courbet and Delacroix were prominently hung, the result of the new political mood, and there was a wealth of Old Masters. Giacometti perhaps showed her how the eyeless Cycladic figures, even older than Minoan and smoothed like sea-washed stones, stared more powerfully still.[7] At the Musée de l'Homme, Isabel may have flaunted her 'tactile education' in Epstein's collection of non-Western artefacts. She regretted that there was nowhere equal to London's Natural History Museum in Paris, but Giacometti's favourite haunt, the breathtaking display of skeletons in the Galerie de paléontologie et d'anatomie comparée in the Musée national d'histoire naturelle, was right next to the zoo in the Jardin des plantes.

There was also a lot to be learned in the various studios. Isabel consolidated her relationship with Diego, and he showed her his own sculptures. 'I was lucky to see them. Few people did,' she wrote. With Derain, she saw an experienced 'modern' tackling the problems of technique. She took up his offer of sharing his Italian model once, but 'found it impossible to work'. They saw a great deal of Balthus and were able to observe his fastidious practice.[8] He was 'meticulous with his materials,' Isabel recalled; 'all his canvases were primed professionally, by Italians, with Casa Arti which is considered to be the most permanent ground for oils.' Balthus was old-fashioned, and Isabel recalled that he 'thought the idea of my working was silly'. His chauvinism took a pedagogical form, however, and he talked about the tradition of French art and the methods of past artists: Poussin, Ingres, David, Delacroix, Courbet and Daumier. Isabel, in turn, lent him music. He played her disc of Mozart's *Così fan tutte* so many times while painting his enormous canvas *The Mountain* (or *Summer*, the first of four panels depicting the seasons; 1936–7; Metropolitan Museum of Art, New York) that it wore out. Their visit to Venice was a revelation. Isabel felt 'as though time had been compacted': 'I was lucky to be here with Balthus who knew the city ... We spent the days leisurely, walking about in circles quite often ... in and out of churches and the Academia, laughing a lot. Balthus was a great one for playing jokes on people. We went to Torcello and stared at the Byzantine mosaics.'

As Isabel discovered French art, so Giacometti engaged with British art and artists such as Ben Nicholson. Isabel could talk in French about English publications, ideas and gossip, and perhaps she teased him with the description in *The Times* of one of his Surrealist objects as a 'nut cutlet'.[9] In 1933, Giacometti had begun to learn printmaking in Atelier 17, run by the Englishman Stanley William Hayter at 17 rue Campagne-Première, a street or so away from Le Dôme, exhibiting there in 1935.[10] Picasso and Ernst also developed their printmaking techniques at Hayter's studio. Isabel knew his work from an Atelier 17 exhibition in 1933 at the Leicester Galleries, coincident with hers at the Redfern, and cannot have missed two prints of bison.[11] Hayter's devotion to line as a medium of research akin to the sciences would have been of especial interest to Isabel and Giacometti: 'My approach to art is fundamentally experimental ... Together with disciplines such as physics or mathematics, as with music or poetry, art is an attempt to extend and deepen our knowledge of life and our relations with our world.'[12] She came to admire Hayter intensely; he had the kind of charisma she was drawn to: 'a stretched bow or a coiled spring ... witty, swift, ebullient, sarcastic', as one contemporary described him, and Isabel's correspondence refers to working with him on occasions.[13]

If figuration was unfashionable, it was of the moment. The success of independents working in Surrealist and abstract styles in the 1920s had been propelled by the commercial art market.[14] Its contraction after the Wall Street Crash of 1929 brought into focus the dependence that had grown up between avant-gardes and an upper-middle-class clientele. As a consequence, in the 1930s, many artists and writers were rethinking the nature and value of art. Germaine Richier's commitment to scrupulous work from the model was displayed in her first solo show in 1936.[15] Francis Gruber had made his name with visionary paintings but, like Giacometti, abandoned a successful style in favour of studying models in the studio. Marxist refugees from Germany, such as the writer Walter Benjamin, were changing the intellectual climate, and some with socialist sympathies looked for means of re-engaging with the world. Gruber and Pierre Tal-Coat were part of a new young group rejecting Surrealism and abstraction (except Picasso) called the Forces nouvelles (founded 1934). They collaborated with Marxist organisations such as the Soviet-sponsored Association des écrivains et artistes révolutionnaires (1932–9) and exhibited an accessible, broadly realist style – drawing on traditional art – at the left-wing venue Galerie Billiet-Worms.[16] In 1936, a socialist government, the Front populaire (1936–8), was elected in France, and debates surrounding a Soviet-inspired ideal of Socialist Realism opposed to so-called bourgeois abstract tendencies prompted three public discussions known as La Querelle du réalisme (the problem of realism).[17]

One of the major issues in the Querelle was the relationship between artistic individuality and the needs of the masses. Isabel's and Giacometti's sympathies were left wing, but they resisted the loss of independence involved in commitment to a doctrine or organisation such as Socialist Realism. They confronted the issue in their own way, and, in so doing, redefined artistic practice in a manner that would have far-reaching consequences for the century. Each embarked on workman-like regimes unconnected to any intention to produce, exhibit or sell, uncoupling art from audience and commerce. Isabel saw this as a deliberate decision on Giacometti's part, linked to his rejection of Surrealism. She described his 'astonishing working hours': '10 to 1 or 2pm, small meal, more work until 6 or 7 pm, then descent on cafes and, finally dinner. Home probably midnight, work until 4 or 5 a.m. This was daily, except for the frequent breaks for nights out in the clubs or the Halles or simply talking.' Neither Isabel nor Giacometti exhibited new pieces until after the war, a break of eleven and ten years respectively. A great deal of their work took the form of studies, of which many were destroyed.

Each artist achieved this highly concentrated and self-sufficient approach by a division of their activities between the Left Bank and the bourgeois world on the Right Bank. Just as Isabel's 'double life' took her across the river to paint, so Giacometti crossed the river in the opposite direction to make a living. He and his brother, Diego, derived their income from making decorative objects for interiors designed by Jean-Michel Frank, like a 'renaissance firm', or collective, as Isabel wrote.[18] Their major commissions were coincidently in the place Vendôme, a stone's throw from Isabel's apartment. They supplied fittings and accessories for the *boutique de parfumerie* of Jean-Pierre Guerlain, just opposite the Delmers' front door, as well as, as has been seen, the haute couture salon that Elsa Schiaparelli opened in 1935.

Portraiture was, for most artists, a source of income, especially during the difficult 1930s, but for Giacometti and Isabel it was a field of research. The use of a narrow selection of intimate sitters widened the scope of representation to incorporate knowledge and memory of their appearance, attitudes and presence. This reciprocal looking continued, for Isabel, the approach to drawing that she had pursued in the Wood Street studio in Liverpool. Isabel's autobiography records that Delmer's assistant, Mara Scherbatoff, posed for six drawings and a colour sketch from life in 1936, only one of which survived.[19] It is probably *Head of a Woman*, c. 1936, (**34**) the only large drawing that Isabel kept to the end of her life. The confidential closeness to the picture plane reflects the relationship between the friends. The unusual attention to the active surfaces of the sitter's face reflects the modelling technique employed by Jacob Epstein, who stated in *The Sculptor Speaks*: 'the face is made up of numberless small planes and it is the study of where those planes begin and end, their direction, that makes the individual head'.[20] Those in *Head of a Woman*, however, are more broken by line, the play of contours and the orbits of the curls and the tip of the nose contributing movement as well as form. Comparison with contemporary fashion photographs of Scherbatoff – 'La Nouvelle Coiffure "à l'Ange"' (1935), for example, by Harry Meerson, reveal Isabel's neglect of conventions of idealisation of youth and femininity. The responsive but ambiguous pull and push of muscles around Scherbatoff's mouth, the mischievous pucker at the eye, the folds that tuck the chin down coyly into the neck, all abandon smooth glamour in favour of an impression of individuality and life.

In the Académie de la Grande Chaumière, Isabel finally had the same access to the nude as male colleagues. 'This was a school without teachers ... frequented by people of all ages and races ... In the morning was a three-hour pose, mostly for painters, in the afternoon two poses of half-an-hour each and, throughout the evening, poses of 10 minutes. Everyone there was interested in work and respected other people's activities. If you left a canvas and palette on your seat while you were out of the class, no one would take your place.' A series of these nude studies survives in a sketchbook, now in Tate, London, some figures pinned onto the vertical and diagonal of a corner, like an armature, others marooned on the page, recalling Rodin's drawings.[21] There are interesting differences, however. *Standing Woman with Folded Arms* is typical: it is strikingly unidealised, analytical, almost scientific in style and embraces the immediacy that comes from an unexpected, even ugly contour. (**32**) The model, cut off just below the knees, breasts compressed by the crossed arms, reads like a stern reply to Epstein's *Genesis*. The later studies reinforce a final 'weighty' contour, a statement of confidence or frustration, but, in general, the drawing is elaborated into the form rather than around it. Marks are felt as three-dimensional relationships within the figure, as if the artist is fathoming how the interior can be understood from the exterior.

A last, rare remnant from this period, a seated figure, c. 1936, (**33**) gives us a sense of where Isabel was going with these ideas. The subject is probably the artist herself since she holds a pad on her lap in a format strikingly like Giacometti's *Self-portrait*, c. 1934. (**35**) Both figures are seated on a bed, and although Isabel is further back from the undulating edge, with her legs folded beneath her, the

33. Isabel Rawsthorne, Seated figure (sketchbook), c. 1935; Tate

34. Isabel Rawsthorne, Head of a woman (Mara Scherbatoff), c. 1935; private collection

35. Alberto Giacometti, *Self-portrait*, pencil, c. 1934; Fondation Giacometti, Paris

36. C. van Noorde, 1769, after Jan van Eyck, *St Barbara*, 1437, ex-collection Isabel Rawsthorne

bed appears to be about the same distance from the reflecting surface, and she holds a sheet of paper at the same angle. Giacometti's *Self-portrait* is faceted and Cézannesque, stressing surface contour. Isabel's restless silhouette lacks the definition of her Académie drawings, is lighter, more linear and zigzagged into the figure. The pose and kimono drapery evoke the Japanese ink drawing of which Isabel was so fond, but the central, pyramidal form with its asymmetrical, angular folds and diminished head enhances this reference with another, that of Jan van Eyck's drawing of *St Barbara*, 1437, (**36**) of which Isabel owned a large, printed copy (private collection) . Isabel had seen *St Barbara* in the Royal Museum of Fine Arts during a childhood trip to Antwerp, at a time when St Barbara was an especially significant figure, being the patron saint of soldiers and sailors who dealt with explosives. Isabel's infusing of present portraiture with past art recalls Epstein's past-present method, of course, but it is more playful and paradoxical in her hands.

Isabel was curious about the uncanny presence achieved by Northern Renaissance sculptures and paintings, such as Van Eyck's *Arnolfini Portrait*, which had haunted her since childhood, and she studied them to understand the means by

37. Giacometti's studio with *Tête de Rita*, study for *Tête qui regarde* and *Tète d'Isabel*, 1938; Bibliothèque Kandinsky, Centre Pompidou

which they created this effect.[22] She wrote that she wanted to find a way to equal the 'suspended and unseasable [*sic*] beauty' of the 'the marvellous hands and heads' without the 'insistent pedantry' of Renaissance detail.[23] In 1936, she also copied a reproduction of Dirk Bouts's *Entombment* (1450; National Gallery, London: copy untraced). Her choice of these less well-known works was probably to do with their medium – silverpoint in the case of Van Eyck's *St Barbara* and an unusual greyish, glue-based paint in the case of Bouts's *Entombment*. Grisaille painting interested Isabel because the subdued hues lent a sense of distance and enhanced light-and-shade modelling. *Seated Figure* gives an insight into how she was looking at the works. The placement on the page reproduces the hieratic position within its frame that Van Eyck gave to *St Barbara*. The angular Flemish folds solved some of the problems that she had been struggling with at the Académie: their linear network stands in for an inner architecture, and the body withdraws along the steps of drapery and is placed firmly in space. By borrowing these effects, *Seated Figure* captures the still, distilled presence of the Northern Renaissance figure, achieving a concentration unusual in a sketch.

38. Alberto Giacometti, *Quatre têtes de femme* (Isabel), pencil on letter paper, c. 1935; Fondation Giacometti, Paris

39. Alberto Giacometti, *Trois têtes de femme* (Isabel), pencil on letter paper, c. 1935; Fondation Giacometti, Paris

Several critics have pointed out the limitations of Giacometti's drawing between the wars, and the swiftness of its transformation during these years, posing what the art historian Yves Bonnefoy has called 'the problem of the two periods'.[24] His sketches of Isabel were part of this transformation, an engagement with her technique as well as her appearance. Giacometti admired Isabel's drawings, particularly the nudes, and her understanding of drawing as intrinsic, rather than preliminary, to representation played a role in his renewed interest in line. We can trace these in his drawings of heads. A page of small sketches, *Quatre têtes de femme* (Isabel), (**38**) showing the hairstyle Isabel wore when she arrived in Paris – a longer version of her London fringed bob – can be dated to about 1935 and appears to be an intermediate between the faceted surfaces of his *Self-portrait* or *Deux têtes de femme* (Rita) (1935; Fondation Giacometti, Paris) and the more dynamic, internalised style of *Trois têtes de femme* (Isabel), datable by the ringlets to about 1935. (**39**) Giacometti's marks in the earlier *Quatre têtes* are more vivacious than in his *Self-portrait*, but still stay on the surface of the face. The eyes are separate elements, not yet looped into the bones and hollows of their sockets as they are in *Trois têtes de femme* (Isabel), where the faceting has given way to a more lively line animating the contours and driving into the form like Isabel's drawings.

Thierry Dufrêne sees Giacometti's 'newly honed drawing skills', his breaking and animating of contours and structural interest in drapery, as a marked 'turning point'.[25] These qualities informed the sculpture, too. The subtle irregularity of the ears, hair, brow, nose and chin of *Tête d'Isabel I,* the slight lift of the right lid and compression of the lip, animates the face with suppressed movement. An odd sense of distance is achieved by making the head a little smaller than life size, and the eyes smaller still. In 1937, Giacometti returned to and rethought the sculpture in a second version (Fondation Giacometti, Paris). It acquired a more irregular surface, a move from carving to modelling that would prove decisive. Although the departure brought Giacometti's sculpture superficially closer to Epstein's *Isabel,* it was also an analysis of its limitations. What was in Epstein's hands an expressive addition to the volume of the head, in the manner of Rodin, was for Giacometti a graphic substitute for it. *Tête d'Isabel II* can be understood as an exploration of three-dimensional drawing in form, gesture, light and shadow. It is no accident that in this period Giacometti also returned to painting in a new style that has been called 'linearist', as seen in *La Mère de l'artiste* (1937; private collection) and *Nature morte à la pomme* (1937; Metropolitan Museum of Art, New York). Biddy Noakes summarised the significance of the change from volumetric to optical sculpture: 'When you carve with plaster it's a very, very intellectual process … things with hard edges and shapes and structures … and suddenly he's handling clay, the most sensual material.'[26] Isabel's commitment to breaking down the barriers between art and life, implicating the body of the artist as well as that of the sitter, and her understanding of drawing as the essence of art, a medium for analysing and delving into experience, were vital to Giacometti's phase of reassessment as well as to her own.

Perhaps Isabel's most important contribution was to the rekindling of Giacometti's interest in the full figure. Life classes had not been successful for him at either the École des Beaux-Arts in Geneva (1919–20) or the Académie de la Grande Chaumière (1922–6), and he attended only intermittently. Patrick Elliott has explained that he had found it difficult to grasp the entire nude model: he 'invariably fudges the genital area and misses out the head'.[27] In bringing her ease to Giacometti in his studio, Isabel provided a different kind of opportunity to engage with the body from life. The duplication of the arrangement in the Wood Street studio in Liverpool – the rejection of the artist/model distinction – was an important stimulus to Giacometti to move on to an understanding of the body as portrait and presence in space, the beginning of the intimate practice that would become the foundation of his career. He sketched Isabel full length and unclothed, for example in *Nu allongé les bras derrière la nuque,* c. 1940, (**40**) and drew no other nude until they were parted.[28]

40. Alberto Giacometti, *Nu allongé les bras derrière la nuque (Isabel)*, pencil, 1940; private collection

Later in life, Giacometti told the critic David Sylvester and others that the naked studies of Isabel were made during a failed tryst in June 1940, hours before she was forced to flee the German occupation of Paris. This made a good story, infusing the sketches with intrigue, irony and loss, and shielded the privacy of Isabel and Delmer. It appears not to be true, however. Giacometti was, as Wiesinger has shown, 'not the most punctilious dater of his works: many of them were dated after the fact with a margin of error that was at times considerable.'[29] She has established that Isabel was observed by Giacometti clothed and naked by 1936 and the number and variety of the nudes suggests a greater distribution over time.[30] Although some of the drawings are signed and dated 1940, at least ten are known.[31]

The most immediate precedents for the *nu couché* format at this time were the *odalisques* of Picasso, Matisse and Derain which drew on an array of past art. Most recent was Picasso's superb print series, the *Suite Vollard* created between 1933 and 1937.[32] The pose of Giacometti's *Nu allongé les bras derrière la nuque (Isabel)*, 1940, (**40**) recalls these and Francisco Goya's *The Naked Maja* (1797–1800; Museo Nacional del Prado, Madrid), but the lopsided breasts and bluntly exposed shaved pubis are unidealised, and limbs and sheets create an angled framework, as in Quattrocento drawings. Gruber and Balthus were painting unidealised nudes

41. Francis Gruber, *Étude de nus*, 1938; private collection

by 1938, for example Gruber's *Étude de nus* (**41**) and Balthus's unusually plain *nu couché*, *La Victime I* (1938–46; private collection). All four artists refract, perhaps, an enthusiasm for Sickert, who was famous for his uneasy figures on rumpled beds, and who was exhibiting in Paris as well as London.[33]

Wiesinger presents Isabel and Giacometti's relationship as an equal one of 'mutual influence on each other: he as her guide, she as a muse'.[34] 'We talked a lot', Isabel wrote; 'the atmosphere in this small room was hypnotic and ordinary'. A later sitter described her own encounter with Giacometti which offers some insight to Isabel's experience: 'He enabled me to know myself better, to gain access to my memories and feelings. He gave me back to myself. I was a young woman whom men admired for her looks [but] with no interest in her spiritual or intellectual [life]. He made me look at myself and feel that I was more than able to reflect and think.'[35] Giacometti's drawings of Isabel correspondingly reveal not so much sexual objectification as a simultaneous processing of her person, her ideas and her art. They were reinventing both of these roles. The convergence of artist and model, art and life that Isabel had explored in Liverpool and defended against the odds in London was, with Giacometti, realised as an important redefinition of both.

42.43. Isabel Rawsthorne, *Landscape II* and *Landscape IV*, c. 1937; private collection

8 SENSIBLE EDUCATION: 1936–1938

In 1936, only two decades had passed since the maelstrom of the First World War, yet political upheaval was quickening in Europe again. Many hoped for the best, but Isabel was not naive. She already had painful experience of discord. As a child, she had waited for her father through the conflict, and, as a teenager, she had seen the depression and the workers unrest around the General Strike of May 1926. She and her mother were in Middlesbrough, where her father's ship was probably in port. Angry rioters surrounded their hotel, and their room was commandeered by police as a vantage point from which to address and calm the crowd. The hotel was set on fire, however, and they were forced to escape through the kitchen.[1] As always, Isabel's autobiographic account adds a paradoxical, interrogative twist, concluding her vignette not with the 'red glow' of their blazing building, but with that of the 'furnaces along the skyline', the working conditions suffered by the rioters.

Delmer had no illusions about the new situation. He was a British citizen but had been born and educated in Berlin, and still had German contacts. He had met Hitler, and being on cordial terms with the German hierarchy sharpened his sense of the risk of the non-intervention policy that the regime was securing from Britain and France. Delmer became increasingly frustrated by his inability to do more than report the inevitable deterioration into war. In April 1935, at the Stresa Conference, they looked on in despair as Britain and France shored up the existing treaties with Benito Mussolini's fascist state, only for Italy to invade Abyssinia two months later. In March 1936, Isabel assisted Delmer in Nuremberg, reporting on the remilitarisation of the Rhineland on France's border, and she was in no doubt that his fears were founded: 'It was the first time I saw a torchlight procession, the first time I heard German troops singing. It was an impressive occasion. I sympathised with Tom. I realised that among all the rest of the foreign press he knew more than all of them what it was about.'

Tensions between the ambitions and values of democratic, communist and fascist states were played out in everyday life. In France, the spread of fascism encouraged the election of a socialist government, the Front populaire (1936–8), in May. Sensitivities were heightened in Montparnasse where people of so many nationalities and religions passed through or sought refuge. 'Many people were involved in some way,' Isabel recalled, 'emotions were to be felt among one's friends. Very few people I came across could be described as neutral.' Insecurity strengthened both alliances and intolerances. Isabel did not underestimate the independence of mind and generosity that Delmer brought to their singular partnership. Nonetheless, the accelerating crises that would instigate the Spanish Civil War later in 1936 and the Second World War in 1939 complicated relationships and made the artistic and the self-determined life difficult. It brought obligations for many, including Isabel, to divert their energies towards resistance.

In July, Delmer went to Madrid to see whether Spain was going to become a Marxist state, which he thought would encourage other Marxist popular fronts to create a 'corridor of potential Sovietism on Europe's Atlantic Coast.' A fascist challenge would, on the other hand, provide an ally for Mussolini's Italy and Hitler's Germany. 'Neither prospect pleased me,' he wrote, 'but both sides seemed determined to fight. And I was equally determined to see and report that fight.' To this end, he made arrangements for him and Isabel to drive through Spain in the guise of tourists. When he told her of his plan she 'hopped round the room like a cricket in her enthusiasm'.[2] Delmer rented a villa (from Rudolph Valentino's widow) at their destination, the island of Mallorca, and, on Sunday, 19 July 1936, they set off, as they always did, at 3.30 a.m., to make the most of clear roads.

The couple sped along in Delmer's convertible Ford V-8. Piled in the back was a picnic, Delmer's typewriter, Isabel's easel and paints and, in a wicker basket, her Siamese kitten, Pilbul. Before they even reached the border, however, the war in Spain began. They stayed the night at Perpignan, and Delmer determined to carry on at least as far as Barcelona. Their inoffensive appearance – Delmer 'his most open-air self, obviously a holiday maker' – took them past several roadblocks, but at the fourth, deep in the Pyrenees and long after nightfall, they were stopped. Delmer left a vivid account. The beam of the headlights lit up a group of white-shirted boys who leapt onto the car's running board and held pistols to Delmer's and Isabel's heads. They were fascist rebels. The couple was ordered to stand by the side of the road while the young men searched their belongings, but when they found Pilbul they burst into laughter; they had never seen a Siamese. 'Si Si!' Delmer improvised, 'Un gato muy Anarchista, muy peligroso! Muy Corazon!' – something like, 'a very anarchist cat, very dangerous! Very brave!' The guns were put down to stroke the kitten.

After this, one lad was delegated to navigate Delmer and Isabel to the nearest town in rebel hands, pointing the way gaily with an ornamental duelling pistol, which, alarmingly, he left permanently cocked. When they arrived, the car was requisitioned by a commander, who had taken over from the mayor murdered

44. Isabel, c. 1937

earlier that day. Refugees and tourists were sleeping in the central plaza, but Delmer managed to get a room in a private house. The night was noisy with loudspeakers bellowing revolutionary slogans and music, and distant artillery as the fascists tried to take Barcelona. In the early hours, they saw a lorry full of prisoners being unloaded. The prisoners were taken screaming into the house opposite, where they were subjected to a 'tribunal', and, by dawn, all – in three separate groups – had been shot. When the couple left the house, the street was stained with the blood of a prisoner who had tried to escape. There was no sign of the commander. He had been disposed of, and a new man was in charge.

Reaching Barcelona was out of the question, but the car was returned to them, emblazoned with the initials of the rebel militia. Delmer and Isabel were given instructions to return to France to 'report the glorious struggle'. Two more keen young men escorted them back to the border. Delmer telephoned a report from Perpignan, the first uncensored dispatch from the conflict, and then they dashed hell-for-leather to an airfield in Toulouse to get him on to a flight for Seville. He was to be embedded on Franco's fascist side. Isabel drove back to Paris on her own, a more sober journey than the one on which they had embarked.

Delmer spent six weeks observing the civilian suffering that is the hallmark of civil war. His and Isabel's official marriage took place during his brief return the following month. At this point in Isabel's memoir, her friend Pattie Lambert wrote in the margin: 'What did Giacometti say?' Isabel and Delmer cared for each other, but the marriage was in the spirit of Margaret Mead's 'suitability and expediency' rather than romance, and was prompted by the deteriorating situation. Delmer was 'entirely convinced that his gloomy predictions of the loss of liberty in Europe was growing closer', Isabel wrote, and she, in turn, needed a secure identity (her original name being compromised by her registration as Margaret Epstein). Isabel's notes for her autobiography record Delmer's offer, expressed even more directly than Epstein's: 'if you say "I am his wife" to authority it has some legal force whereas the word friend or employée [*sic*] has none.'[3] Unspoken was the very real possibility that Delmer might be killed on assignment.

Delmer and Isabel had no honeymoon after the wedding: 'The party ended,' Isabel remembered, 'I looked behind the screen in my studio, saw there were no guests.' Within a day or so she was flying out of Le Bourget.[4] The new passport opened the way for her to travel freely. A Polish pass was issued immediately,[5] and a proliferation of visas, stamps and letters reveal that she criss-crossed Europe, apparently alone, for the next four years. These journeys make no appearance in either Isabel's autobiography or Delmer's. Hers mentions vaguely 'travelling outside France sometimes ... I seemed to find myself in Geneva from time to time. I remember we used to eat at a restaurant called the Amphitrion (Amphitryon, a French restaurant popular with foreigners and diplomats)'.[6] If Isabel or Delmer was acting officially as an agent, they may have been bound by an official secrets agreement. If she was acting informally, her activities may have been simply left out of her account, as was so much in Isabel's autobiographical writings, because they were experiences she preferred not to celebrate. She was almost certainly taking letters or copy across borders (since there was considerable sensitivity over censorship during this period), as well as currency or goods, which were regulated. She might also have been maintaining Delmer's contacts; his Europe-wide network was essential to his work, and during the Spanish Civil War he was uncharacteristically confined.

Delmer went back to Madrid, this time reporting from the side of the Republicans. Isabel had trouble explaining to her communist friends that he was with Franco as a reporter not a sympathiser.[7] She wondered if she would see him again, but he emerged at the end of October with only a dislocated shoulder, sustained while leaping a wall under machine-gun fire. She met him at the border, and they went to a sanatorium in Dresden where he could recover and, strangely, take a slimming cure, as stress and toil always filled-out his bulk. Isabel left him there and returned to Paris.[8] In January 1937, they were briefly together at the wedding of their German friend Prince Bernhard, a surprise royal marriage in The Hague, since Bernhard had made a secret love match with Princess (later Queen) Juliana of the Netherlands. 'Holland was en fête,' Isabel recalled, 'there was a magnificent banquet and ball.' She wore black, as usual. With these two exceptions, Delmer was sequestered in Spain for two years, nearly the entire duration of the civil war. When he joined the Republicans, he took his car and teamed up with Ernest Hemingway. They did not like each other, but he could drive and Hemingway had contacts.

When Delmer went to Spain, the *Daily Express* moved the Paris office from the place Vendôme apartment to the offices of the Belgian newspaper *Le Soir*, so Isabel and Mara Scherbatoff had to find somewhere else to live. They moved to the Hôtel St-Romain, a small place on the rue St-Roch, five minutes from the old apartment. Isabel no longer had access to a private phone and relied on Mara to relay Delmer's messages. Her sanctuary was the Café de la Régence, a few minutes away from her hotel and opposite the theatre of the Comédie-Française. It had a radical past going back to the 1789 Revolution and was famous as a historic venue for chess. She kept in touch with their cook, Anna, visiting her little flat in the Marché Saint-Honoré with Balthus: 'Balthus and myself ... sat on the bed and from one iron pot she managed to produce a beautiful meal. She was gay and full of jokes. Her life had been tragic.'

It was around this time that Balthus took Isabel to see Picasso. The veteran artist had taken a new studio at 7, rue des Grands-Augustins, around the corner from Balthus's studio in cour de Rohan, in order to paint the mural for the Pavillon de l'Espagne in the *Exposition internationale* of 1937.[9] Isabel found him welcoming, 'amusing, full of chatter and curiosity' and also met Picasso's partner, the painter and photographer Dora Maar. She visited Maar's nearby studio, 6 rue de Savoie, and was impressed by the 'clarity and balance' of her work, growing to consider her 'a singular person, a mature artist'. Thereafter, she, Giacometti, Picasso and Maar socialised at each other's studios and in the cafés.[10]

In April 1937, the German Luftwaffe bombed the Basque cultural centre of Guernica in support of Franco, an experiment in the demoralising potential of indiscriminate destruction, and Picasso chose it for his subject. His uncompromising representation, *Guernica* (1937; El Centro de Arte Reina Sofía, Madrid), became the definitive image of the war. The Left Bank art world was interwoven with competing Marxist groupings more or less loyal to Moscow. Paul Éluard and Tristan Tzara were, with Louis Aragon, Communist Party members and others, such as Tal-Coat and Gruber, were sympathisers, but Picasso was adopted as the prime artist of the left, despite his predilection for abstraction. Isabel found it 'amusing to observe the wriggling of the French Communist writers ... His painting was hardly "people's art", yet he was their most famous advocate.' She noted with curiosity that, although everyone knew his attitude to the Spanish war, it was never the subject of conversations. Isabel was, with Hayter, one of the few in their circle who had actually seen the conflict. Like Picasso, she and Giacometti kept a degree of political autonomy; all three maintained some friendships outside the Left, with Balthus and Derain, for example, and, despite the newly figurative basis of their art, they rejected the Soviet-inspired Social Realism being pursued by Gruber and others. Giacometti dissociated himself from his earlier collaborations with Aragon.[11] Isabel recalled, 'As the [Spanish] war continued, talk became much more complicated, and the role of the Communist Party was observed quite often with puzzlement. Round the café tables there seemed to be more animation. People lingered.'

Isabel enjoyed a brief interlude of luxury in August with Bernhard and Juliana in the Netherlands, staying at their royal summer residence at Soestdijk: 'I went boar-hunting with Bernhard in the royal park and was given a car and a chauffeur to drive me to Haarlem to see the museum.' Once more she was out of place: 'A second gaffe: Bernhard said kindly, "You shouldn't wear a Parisian hat to go hunting."' In the autumn, Isabel took her trip to Italy with Balthus and his new wife, Antoinette.

Both Isabel and Giacometti returned regularly to their mothers, he for long stays in Majola, she for briefer visits. In 1937, her brother, Warwick, had gained a place at Dauntseys, a public school that specialised in science and agriculture.[12] It was near Salisbury Plain, a safe remove from London if there was to be a war and only an hour or so away from Agnes Nicholas in New Milton, so mother and son were able to enjoy family life on his occasional holidays home. Sometimes this coincided with Isabel's visits, and she and Warwick returned to their old pastime of walking in the woods.[13] Giacometti's family, by contrast, suffered a sudden tragedy. In October, his sister Ottilia died following the birth of a son, Sylvio. Giacometti had listened at her belly during her pregnancy; now he mourned her and cherished his new nephew. Isabel wrote a postcard to him, sending him her mother's address on a reproduction of a fifteenth-century Virgin, Pietro Lorenzetti's *Madonna and Child with St Francis and St John the Evangelist* (1320–25, fresco; Lower Church, San Francesco, Assisi).[14] The attendant male figures were perhaps a consoling reference to Giacometti and Diego as Sylvio's uncles.

The letters Giacometti and Isabel wrote to each other from this date offer a perspective on their deepening working and romantic relationship. It became their habit to exchange pictures of things they had seen, in words, sketches or postcards. The correspondence was, like their conversations, in rudimentary French.[15] The earliest known dated letter, written by Isabel from New Milton on 8 December 1937, is typical. In the foreground is the desire to see each other and the difficulties in the way of this. She says that she will be in England until the New Year, unless she is called to Spain. The dominant topic, however, is art. Isabel writes that, despite the distractions and frustrations of the year, she has made a 'small breakthrough ... I fear you have lost your faith in me. This is understandable, I almost lost it myself. Now, I won't talk about it before I do it.' She also announced the surprising news that she was painting a mastiff dog (whereabouts unknown). Gossip is, as always, minimal, although she mentions that she bumped into a past girlfriend of Giacometti, the American sculptor Flora Mayo, and felt guilty when Flora enquired how well Isabel knew him.[16]

Isabel did not, in fact, stay in England until New Year. Before Christmas, a message came through Mara that, if she went again to the Spanish border Delmer might be able to see her. She travelled alone to St-Jean-Pied-de-Port in the foothills of the French Pyrenees and booked into a hotel to wait. She liked the no-nonsense cheerfulness of the Basque people. The wine was 'nasty' but the food was 'simple and very good: fresh fish, ecrevisses, trout'. She hired a bicycle to explore the foothills and drew the view over the plains. (**43, 44**) In the evenings she got into the habit of riding up to a café on the frontier. Here she enjoyed two glasses of Spanish absinthe, 60 proof and banned in France, before whizzing home downhill in 'what seemed like ten minutes'. Finally, Delmer appeared, and they reunited for a determinedly merry few days. It was difficult, however, to forget their circumstances, and Delmer was pessimistic about the European outlook. Their separation had, moreover, changed their relationship. Sexual fidelity does not seem to have been central to it, but Delmer was sensitive about Isabel's attachment to Giacometti. Her notes for her autobiography stress that she told him only that she was 'sitting' for the sculptor (her emphasis).[17] Nonetheless, some kind of estrangement seems to have resulted. Delmer's memoirs omit the stay at St-Jean-Pied-de-Port and barely mention Isabel from that date on. Parts of Isabel's personal notes for her autobiography concerning this period are removed with scissors, indicating that there were details that she, too, decided to leave out.[18] They remained a couple, but a personal corner had been turned. She accompanied him back to the border , and, on the way, they dined in a restaurant in the coastal town of St-Jean-de-Luz, full of 'the sort of people who gather, as if summoned, to hang on to people engaged in wars'. She left him at the border town of Irun. It, like Guernica not far away, had fallen to the rebels, and she looked at the river, 'where many people ... swam to safety'. Delmer went back to the conflict, and Isabel, to Paris. It was Christmas Eve.[19]

Some people began to accept that German aggression was inevitable, although Parisians still set great store in the defensive deterrent of the Maginot Line. When Delmer moved his base from Madrid to Barcelona, Isabel drove down with supplies. Her passport shows that she crossed the border to the 'Republic Cataluna' on 24 February 1938 and on other occasions.[20] She recalled arriving at

45. Count Muñoz, Isabel Delmer and Prince Bernhard of Lippe-Biesterfeld at Arneguy on the French-Spanish border, 1938; collection of Evelyn Nicholas

the press headquarters, the Hotel Majestic, strikingly presented in a blue Hermès jacket calculated to raise Delmer's spirits, only to find that the dark leather and scarlet trimmings looked like the dark blue and red fascist party uniform and to be told immediately to change. Isabel still succeeded in bringing *joie de vivre* to the residents, and her 'excitable mood', laughter and cargo of provisions precipitated an impromptu party. On this occasion, she stayed for two weeks, and, during the lull in the fighting, she got to know soldiers, medical staff, journalists and others. Surprisingly, she hit it off with the Surrealist poet Benjamin Péret, who, four years before, had aided Breton with Giacometti's expulsion from the group. She met extraordinary women – Marthe Huysmans, the daughter of the Belgian Socialist leader, for example, and the German communist writer and journalist Maria Osten, one of the partners of Mikhail Koltzov, the editor of *Pravda*. Many Republicans had come under the influence of Soviet-style communism and 'advisors' such as Koltzov.

Isabel should have been at home with those who shared her fierce and liberated nature, but she felt as though she was contributing little in comparison to them. Delmer, moreover, was romantically distracted by the intrepid American

46. Isabel Delmer, Spain, 1938; collection of Evelyn Nicholas

journalist Virginia Cowles. Cowles's colleague, the writer and war correspondent Martha Gellhorn, came to Isabel's rescue. As Hemingway's partner (sharing him with his wife), she understood Isabel's predicament and kindly gave her a crash course on 'how to behave at the front': 'what to do when glasses of wine are thrown at you, how to speak Spanish in 24 hours, when to have a party on your own. I was not used to American dash of this kind.' Isabel was appreciative, calling this her 'sensible education', and they became friends.

Delmer gave Isabel his own kind of lesson on how to cope in an air raid. Isabel's visit coincided with the first bombardment of Barcelona, beginning on 16 March 1938. The Luftwaffe attacked at noon, when the streets and cafés were full and Delmer and Isabel were having lunch. He insisted they stroll back to the hotel nonchalantly, where they found 'people standing against the walls and pillars ... crunching noises, and the building shook'. Despite this, Delmer sat down at a table and asked Isabel to fetch him his briefcase from their bedroom on the third floor. 'This he did as an exercise in behaviour, so that I should learn the value of acting naturally. I was grateful a couple of years later.' Two days later, as the tide began to turn against the Republicans, Delmer drove Isabel to Toulouse to catch a flight to Paris. His first-hand stories of the raids spurred the anti-air-raid preparations that were gathering pace across Europe, especially in London.[21]

Four thousand volunteers travelled from England to join the International Brigade and support the Republican cause in Spain, and more came from other countries. Many passed through Paris and the Left Bank haunts. Isabel and Mara were part of a small group who facilitated journeys in and out, looking after refugees, channelling messages and arranging to send supplies, blankets and tins of food or black market pesetas, even though few of these made it to their destination. The publisher and civil rights activist Nancy Cunard was an energetic participant, and Stanley Hayter, who had visited Spain at the invitation of the Ministry of Arts of the Republican government to make a set of prints, sheltered fugitives in his studio. The writer Anaïs Nin, who helped him, recalled, 'The laws were rigid: if one sheltered or fed them there would be a punishment of jail and a fine. These were the fighters, the wounded, the sick. Everybody was afraid to help them.'[22]

To Isabel, it was obvious that, as well as courageous and valuable volunteers, the Republican government was having to deal with 'a lunatic fringe' that was getting in the way. 'On one occasion two girls I knew arrived at the Deux Magots weirdly dressed, with an expensive car. They said they were on their way to drive an ambulance for the International Brigade. This led to a visit to the Halles, much ribaldry and Pernod clouded the glasses and last seen they seemed to be steering to the Porte de Vincennes. Whether they got to Spain I do not know, but I doubt they ever got to the front ... It was not easy to enter Spain'. There were also those whose courage understandably failed. A *Daily Express* diarist, smitten with romantic ideals, arrived in Paris en route to the conflict and stayed with Isabel. When it was time to depart she took him to the station, but as the train began to leave, he panicked, dragging her into the moving carriage, declaring, 'Don't let me go alone. I love you. For ever I love you.'[23]

During the short stretches when Isabel was in Paris, Giacometti was often in Switzerland. It is not surprising, therefore, that, in 1938, with the change in atmosphere, the demanding work and Delmer away, she drew close to a handful of English expatriates of her own age. Peter Rose Pulham was, like Delmer, an avuncular six foot, but handsome with it. (**47**) He was a fashion photographer for *Harper's Bazaar* with a singular, surreal, *brut* style and was regularly surrounded by beautiful women. Although his circle, notably the artists Leonor Fini and Méret Oppenheim, did not overlap with Isabel's, he made a series of photographs of painters in their studios which included Ernst, Picasso, Balthus and Derain.[24] Everything about him was 'measured', his speech, his movements, his tailored suits. Isabel was attracted to his learning. He had the habit of giving his girlfriends classic literature to read – the verse tragedies of Jean Racine and the poems of

47. Peter Rose Pulham, c. 1934; private collection

Edmund Spenser, for example. He was sharp when unsure of himself, however, and his first words on meeting Isabel were: 'Why are you wearing that silly thing?' Like two spies exchanging a code word, she knew he was quoting Heathcliff, or rather Balthus's illustration of the dark hero, 'Why have you that silk frock on, then?'[25] Isabel acknowledged he was right: 'It *was* silly – a black silk suit, not made well.' Rose Pulham was a kind man, however, and witty, with a 'delighted and delightful laugh'.[26] A studio photograph taken in 1934 captures his romantic elegance and a touch of uncertainty beneath.

Rose Pulham's apartment was on the Gothic Île de la Cité where he lived with Anna Maclaren, 'a bewildering beautiful blue-eyed Irish girl', as Delmer described her.[27] She was a mannequin for Elsa Schiaparelli, and a very different character from Rose Pulham – impulsive, unpredictable, her life 'a round of surrealist experiment'. Where he never had any money, she was always generous. The third in their group, Joan Eyres-Monsell, was, like Rose Pulham, a photographer, specialising in architectural views. Isabel recalled with pleasure her beating Tristan Tzara at chess in the Café de la Régence. These friendships, strengthened by the ordeals to come, would last to the end of their lives.

Rose Pulham introduced Isabel to Donald Maclean, who arrived as Third Secretary at the British Embassy in autumn 1938.[28] He was even taller than Rose Pulham, blond, boyishly good-looking and an easy, well-mannered conversationalist. He had profound socialist ideals and enjoyed meeting left-wing friends of Isabel, such as Tzara, although, he was less certain about Giacometti and discreetly asked her whether she thought he was 'on the right side?' Maclean was part of their set for several years, but no one knew he had been recruited to spy for Russia and was passing copies of documents from the Embassy. Communiqués that reflected the laissez-faire tendencies that were frustrating Delmer were of interest to Stalin as he weighed up negotiations with France, Britain and Germany.

Isabel grew closer to Rose Pulham when he gave up photography and settled in Paris to paint in the late 1930s. He continued to wear his classic clothes and to frequent the Café Flore, but as shabbier, thinner bohemian rather than swell. He and Anna Maclaren parted, and he moved to a modest attic on the Left Bank in Hôtel Bisson, 37 quai des Grands Augustins. The flat was adjacent to the Pont Neuf, which was on Isabel's daily route, and a few yards from Picasso's and Balthus's studios. The Irish actress Theodora Rosling (later better known as the writer Theodora FitzGibbon) met Rose Pulham in 1939 and left a description of the room in her autobiography:

> … the patterned wallpaper was peeling and almost the entire floor was covered with bits of screwed up paper. They looked like surrealist children's boats. The bed hadn't been made for some time, was rumpled, crumpled and littered with tubes of paint, more pieces of paper and a beautiful silk dressing gown rolled up in a ball. There were the ashes of a fire in the grate, empty wine bottles, stained glasses, dirty plates, and more tubes of paint on a shelf over the fireplace. An easel stood in the centre of the room and on it was a half-finished painting of a large room empty except a trestle table. The walls and floor of the room were painted in very delicate rainbow colours. The contrast between the painted room and the real one was startling.[29]

Rose Pulham and Isabel shared 'diner intimes [*sic*]', watching the river and beginning a dialogue about art that would sustain them over the most difficult years of their careers.[30] They probably fell in love, but Isabel was often away, had loyalties to Delmer and was deeply involved with Giacometti. Rose Pulham was, for his part, impractical about relationships: 'too indolent to be a sustained lover,' Rosling remarked, 'what energy he had went into his work.'[31]

Isabel's passports show that her travels accelerated as Delmer's frustration at being kept in Spain mounted. The Republican cause was, he could see, lost, and crucial events were unfolding elsewhere. In March 1938, Germany annexed Austria. A chilling eagle-and-swastika stamp in Isabel's passport marks her entrance into the country on 31 May 1938.[32] Hitler's expansionist ambition for the Sudetenland, a largely German-speaking area of Czechoslovakia, on Germany's south-eastern border, was the most urgent concern.[33] Martha Gellhorn was reporting from the Czech side. Isabel entered Germany again at Strasbourg, a crucial element of the Maginot Line, on 14 June 1938 and reached the Czech border at Rozvadov four days later. She was in Germany again on 14 and 31 July and 8 August.[34] Delmer finally extricated himself from Spain in September, but it was too late. He arrived in Berlin in the middle of the month, just as Neville Chamberlain was meeting Hitler. On 30 September, in another ill-judged gesture of pacification, France and England agreed to Germany's annexation of the Sudetenland. Delmer and Isabel immediately went on to Czechoslovakia, travelling through the country with the British journalist Claud Cockburn, Delmer's colleague from Spain and the communist correspondent for the *Daily Worker* and *The Week*.[35] Cockburn was liaising with the *Pravda* editor Koltzov, who was now staying at the Russian Embassy in Prague, because the Russians were poised to activate troops in Czechoslovakia's defence if Britain, France or Czechoslovakia chose to resist. None did.[36] The fate of the Jewish refugees and political radicals who had fled Hitler's regime to Czechoslovakia was sealed, and Delmer and Isabel witnessed the fear as people struggled for permissions and the means to depart. The Munich Agreement that had allowed the annexation also further undermined Republican morale in Spain. Franco launched his final assault and triumphed in April 1939, by which time Germany had taken the rest of Czechoslovakia, too.

48. Émile Savitry: Alberto Giacometti with *Nuit* (1946, plaster; destroyed); courtesy Sophie Malexis

9 UNE PASSANTE: 1937–1940

'To a Passer-by'

Around me thundered the deafening noise of the street,
In mourning apparel, portraying majestic distress,
With queenly fingers, just lifting the hem of her dress,
A stately woman passed by with hurrying feet.

Agile and noble, with limbs of perfect poise.
Ah, how I drank, thrilled through like a Being insane,
In her look, a dark sky, from whence springs forth the hurricane,
There lay but the sweetness that charms, and the joy that destroys.

A flash – then the night ... O loveliness fugitive!
Whose glance has so suddenly caused me again to live,
Shall I not see you again till this life is o'er!

Elsewhere, far away ... too late, perhaps never more,
For I know not whither you fly, nor you, where I go,
O soul that I would have loved, and that you know!

Charles Baudelaire, *Les Fleurs du mal* (2nd edition, 1861)[1]

While Delmer tried to keep up with history, rushing from Czechoslovakia to Palestine, Ukraine, Moscow and Athens, Isabel returned for a while to Paris. It was mid-October 1938. The journalist Claud Cockburn, in Paris as the London correspondent for *Pravda* (a short-lived office), summed up the atmosphere of foreboding with an image of poison gas 'rolling round the Ringstrasse, the Boulevard des Italiens, and Piccadilly Circus'.[2] Isabel knew the outcomes of political upheaval and prejudice: the persecution experienced by Epstein as a Jewish émigré and by herself as a woman artist, an unwed mother, a person without means, all of which had resulted in her exile. Her friend, Mara Scherbatoff, was an exile of a different kind. As a 'White Russian', the granddaughter of a czarina, she had been driven from her home during the 1917 Revolution and was looked on with suspicion by Isabel's left-wing Paris friends. There was, therefore, a political dimension to Isabel's major art project of this period: a full-length oil of Mara walking in a Paris street.

The predicament of the individual amid the forces of history became a major theme for writers and artists undergoing the sweeping technological, political and military changes of the 1930s and 1940s.[3] Their philosophical questions were lived by the many, like Isabel, who sought intellectual and pragmatic solutions to such 'events'. Self-definition and determination, what Georges Bataille called 'sovereignty' and Jean-Paul Sartre, 'authenticity', would be theorised under the heading of Existentialism after the Second World War, but most of their ideas had their origin in the urgent actualities that preceded the war. They condensed around the motif of the walking figure. In an era of mass movement, whether march or flight, Baudelaire's *flâneur* and iterations of the stepping and striding sculptures of archaic art by Rodin and others took on a new significance and character. In 1935, Giacometti made a small plaster of a striding man holding a flag (whereabouts unknown, but visible in the corner of Dora Maar's photograph of his studio.) (**24**) The walking body differed from the dancing body, the avant-garde motif of earlier in the twentieth century in its vectored motion that allowed no turning back. It brought the figure into dimensional relationships with environment (arrival, departure, distance) and time (past, present and future) and animated it not simply with energy, but with individual will.

This updating of Baudelaire's *flâneur* was summed up in the writings of Walter Benjamin, whose edited archive *Passagenwerk* (Arcades Project, 1927–40), on which he was working throughout the decade, placed the nineteenth-century poet at the centre of twentieth-century modernity. Benjamin fled Germany for Paris in 1933, the year before Isabel left London, and frequented the same left-wing cultural circles. He collaborated closely with Georges Bataille as a fellow founder of the Collège de Sociologie (College of Sociology) and publications, such as 'The Return of the Flâneur' (1929), were accessible to German speakers such as Giacometti and Balthus. His most famous essay, 'The Work of Art in the Age of Mechanical Reproduction', was printed in French, translated by Balthus's elder brother, Pierre Klossowski. In 1939, Benjamin returned to the *flâneur* in 'On Some Motifs in Baudelaire', focusing on a Baudelaire sonnet, 'À une passante' (To a Passer-by; see above).[4] The poem concerns a glance exchanged in the street between the poet and a widow, described as a convulsion, a flash, a birth. Benjamin extrapolated this into a model of 1930s subjectivity. For him, consciousness was 'a series of shocks and collisions'; he cited his contemporary, the writer Paul Valéry: 'The impressions and sense perceptions of man ... actually belong in the category of surprises.'[5] This vision was anticipated in Balthus's *La Rue* (1933; Museum of Modern Art, New York), the centrepiece of the artist's breakthrough exhibition in 1934. Each figure in the street is physically and psychologically isolated on his or her course, apart from one violent collision taking the form of an embrace. There is an even closer parallel with Giacometti's funerary *Femme qui marche II* and Isabel's walking figure of Mara, both of which evoke Baudelaire's description of the widow: 'Tall, slender, in dense mourning ... / Agile and noble, with her statue's limbs.' Isabel described Mara in similar language: 'tall, remarkably handsome, and appeared to glide rather than walk, her body leaning slightly forward from the hips'. Benjamin interpreted Baudelaire's widow as a 'figure of shock, indeed of catastrophe'.[6] Mara, for Isabel, and Isabel, for Giacometti, were figures of catastrophe of this kind: they imaged the modern subject as passer-by, displaced and in mourning for a lost moment or thing.

Benjamin went so far as to define modern man as one whose home is the street, and Isabel described the Café de la Régence as her 'second home', in comparable terms. Like Baudelaire's 'Painter of Modern Life', it was necessary for her to be 'away from home and yet to feel at home'.[7] 'Here I wrote all my letters, met my friends, had meals,' she continued, 'they had a special line in oysters, excellent Normandy cider. Large tables lined the walls, equipped with ink.' Benjamin frequented the same café, and her description echoed his evocation of the contingent sensibility of the *flâneur*, written the same year: 'To him the shiny, enamelled signs of business are at least as good a wall ornament as an oil painting is to a bourgeois in his salon. The walls are the desk against which he presses his notebooks; newsstands are his libraries.'[8]

Benjamin's figuring of modern experience reflected wider European events.[9] For refugees, whether from social expectation – women, homosexuals and the politically non-aligned – or from persecution – as the result of war and ethnic and religious oppression – the arbitrary and anonymous encounters of the road and the café replaced family and clan. Benjamin had been dispossessed and displaced by historical events, forced to leave Germany; Mara had lost her father in the Russo-Japanese War and her mother had died during their flight; Isabel had been cast adrift from her family, child and home by more ordinary poverty and prejudice. All replaced the family unit with unconventional, provisional ménages: Benjamin in his shops and cafés; Isabel with Delmer and Mara; and Mara supporting a second household of her governess and her younger sisters.

Artistic work was in, in part, built out of these displacements and the creative process of reinventing lives. The disruptions that prompted artistic projects also left them incomplete, however. Benjamin and Mara as writers, Isabel as a painter, were typical during this period of artists whose reflections on the shocks and discontinuities of modern times were themselves preserved only in provisional and discontinuous forms. Benjamin's and Mara's writings were unfinished: Benjamin did not survive the war, committing suicide in 1940, while evading the Nazis for a second time when they occupied France. The incomplete *Passagenwerk*

49. Alberto Giacometti, *Figurine dans une boîte entre deux boîtes qui sont des maisons*, bronze and glass, 1950; Centre Georges Pompidou

was left with Georges Bataille.[10] Mara stayed during the Occupation to work for the Resistance, but left for a journalism post in New York when the war was over. The long account of her wartime activities that she composed and left in Paris for Isabel was looted. Isabel lost her studios and her work in her flight back to England and never finished her painting of Mara, realising her walking figure only in 1948. Isabel *en passant* became Giacometti's token of the times and initiated a project that would not succeed until 1946.

Crossing the city each day and night, Isabel enacted the central practice of Baudelaire's *flâneur*, the urban stroller observing the sights and sounds of modern life. The Left Bank social scene had shifted to Saint-Germain-des-Prés, closer to the river: 'the Deux Magots and the Café Flore replaced the Dôme as the meeting place'. Late one evening in early 1937, Giacometti saw Isabel in the distance on the boulevard Saint-Michel. It became a 'precious vision', recalled in 1945 in a letter to her and described again in an interview in 1963: 'I saw her standing in the street at a certain distance ... at midnight. I saw the immense black above her and the houses.'[11] The description is remarkably close to Benjamin's of the *flâneur*: 'The street becomes a dwelling for [him]; he is as much at home among the facades of houses as a citizen is in his four walls at home.'[12] From then on, the representation of the memory of a full-length Isabel in the street, standing or moving, became as important to Giacometti as his work on the heads. The new work differed from *Femme qui marche II* in that the body was entire – a complete portrait – and came across as being in the world. As in 'À une passante', Giacometti was after a figure of shock, 'an apparition, the sudden manifestation of a personage in the field of consciousness', as his friend and commentator, the poet Francis Ponge, described the sculptures.[13] He made his figures smaller to appear more distant and placed them on increasingly large plinths to provide a position and setting. Perspective was also created optically, as it had been in the heads; effects of remoteness, indistinctness and relative scale were rendered in light and shadow relief, whittled *into* the form. After the war, *Figurine dans une boîte entre deux boîtes qui sont des maisons* (Figure in a Box between Two Boxes Which are Houses) (**49**) provided the most literal equivalent for Giacometti's Benjaminian vision: the rectangular frame echoes Benjamin's image of the street as 'four walls at home' created by the 'facades of the houses'. An earlier piece, *Nuit*, (**48**) intended for a monument to the French Resistance, is haunted perhaps by the heroism of Mara, but the sawing arm movements, long legs, slanted stance and purposeful gaze are Isabel's. The title reprised the phrase in Baudelaire's 'À une passante': 'puis la nuit! – Fugitive beauté'.

Critics often comment on the masculinity of the artist/*flâneur* figure and the lack of an artist/*flâneuse*, even in the twentieth century.[14] Janet Wolff is emphatic: 'I want to insist that the role of flâneuse remained impossible despite the expansion of women's public activities, and despite the newer activities of shopping and cinema-going. For central to the definition of the flâneur are both the aimlessness of the strolling, and the reflectiveness of the gaze.' However, performance, fashion and consumption – the 'shopping and cinema-going' mentioned by Wolff as a feminine variation of the *flâneur* – were applicable to twentieth-century men, as were strolling and reflectiveness to women. 'Flâneur' was the word Isabel used to describe herself on her nocturnal walks, alone or accompanied.[15] She fits Wolff's definition of the term *par excellence*, as did other women in her circle.

It is, similarly, a commonplace for contemporary and more recent commentators to categorise Giacometti's figures as though the men walk and the women pose, ignoring *Femme qui marche I* and *II*, *Nuit* and its related drawing, *Tight-rope Walker* (1943), and *Figurine dans une boîte*, as well as later works such as *Femme qui marche* (1955, etching; Art Institute of Chicago). The art historian Alex Potts has drawn attention to one of the earliest examples of this peculiarity, Francis Ponge's 'Réflexions sur les statuettes, figures et peintures d'Alberto Giacometti' of 1952. Potts observes that, 'In an attempt to universalise this condition, [Ponge] converted the female figure into a neutralised male "he", echoing an uncertainty expressed by other male contemporaries at the time who tried to

50. Ernst Scheidegger: Alberto Giacometti's studio with *La Femme au chariot*, 1942–3

imagine themselves identifying with the sketchily gendered female ciphers that fascinated them'.[16] David Sylvester's *Looking at Giacometti* of 1994 demonstrated the persistence of this uncertainty. It opened with the statement that Giacometti's male figures were 'active ... walking, pointing. There are busts of a man, but these too are somehow active, the head attentive, watchful. The female is passive, a figure standing motionless, whether with others in a row, parading (as a point of fact) in a brothel, waiting to be chosen, or alone, as if waiting in the street.'[17] Giacometti's purely stationary figures date from after 1950, however, and it was not until 1962 that he acknowledged the universalising distinction: 'It occurred to me that I can never make a woman in any other way than motionless, and a man always striding; when I model a woman, then motionless; a man, always walking. It's the totality of this life that I want to reproduce in everything I do.'[18] Sylvester modified this quite neutral statement to present all women in the street as waiting *racoleuses* (streetwalkers).[19] He neglected the advancing gait and gaze of the wide-eyed Isabels, the watchful busts of the writer Simone de Beauvoir

(1946; Fondation Giacometti, Paris) and others. Even the flexed and sequential knees and feet in the drawing of Isabel (*Femme debout*) which he used to illustrate this page of his text were overlooked.[20]

Twentieth-century commentators usually discuss Baudelaire's and Benjamin's treatments of the *flâneur* according to the same polarised gender convention.[21] Yet, Baudelaire's 'À une passante' describes two walkers and two glances, the man's and woman's gazes meet with a provisional, symbiotic symmetry: 'For I know not where you fled, you know not where I go, / oh you I would have loved (oh you who knew it too)'; Benjamin's *Passagenwerk* draws attention to this, noting the similarity of the line in the poem to one in a love letter by Baudelaire, playing on the word 'too': 'And you know that too, my beauty, whose eyes are too shrewd'.[22] There were, similarly, two artists, Giacometti and Isabel, present in his vision of her on the boulevard Saint-Michel, each defined by the distance between them. Sartre's essay on Giacometti's standing figures, 'La Recherche de l'absolu', written in 1948, four years before Ponge's, states that 'this woman moves ... she appears totally and at once'. He saw that Giacometti's frontal images were not waiting but arriving, appearing with the shock of modern experience.[23]

Ponge's elision of female and male in Giacometti's figures, discussed by Potts, provides an insight into the process of apperception by which gender conventions partially erased Isabel's untraditional presence from the middle of the century onwards. In so doing, he shows us the way contemporaries may have diminished Isabel's image and agency in life, as well. Equally important, however, is Potts's observation of the partial and inconsistent nature of these apperceptions. Sartre's 1948 essay anticipates Ponge's, swerving quite giddily between female personifications such as that quoted above and descriptions of the same figures as male. His intermittent flights into masculinised universals were a product of his idealist commitment to the possibility of universals, of 'absolutes', per se. Giacometti's relative neglect of these was a function of his anti-ideal, materialist approach to existence, shared by Isabel. Human subject positions were explored as a product of contingent circumstance rather than fixed categories, the conditions of the modern city and creative life experienced by both sexes. Far from gendering the figure, Giacometti's practice and his statement of 1962, were, as Wiesinger has pointed out, distinguished by a merging of male and female sitters.[24] This blending is clear in a list made in 1945, at the height of his work on the figures: 'Small D.[iegos] and I.[sabel], that's all. Work on the medium-size I.[sabel]. Work on the tall I.[sabel]. Develop the tall one as much as possible. *From that one make more, D.[iego] and others*' (my emphasis).[25]

We see, therefore, that history has since imposed conventional gender constructions at the expense of quite straightforward evidence of theoretical and actual feminine *flânerie* that were not unacknowledged in their own time. In Isabel's case, the exploratory freedom of movement and techniques of the observer associated with the artist/*flâneur*, and the otherness that went with them, were fundamental to her activity from her teens. In her twenties, displacements and encounters modernised strolling into a more fraught Benjaminian mode. Giacometti's nocturnal walks with the writer Samuel Beckett, initiated in 1937, are often cited as a paradigm of *flânerie*, but his habit of accompanying Isabel through the sleeping city was already established by 1936. She was also wandering Europe, in disguise, sometimes in danger. Isabel's identity and Giacometti's rendering of it were, as Wiesinger says, 'in tune with her tumultuous times' and the redefinitions of the *flâneur* that went with them.[26]

In these restless days of 1938, when Isabel was often away, she and Giacometti had few opportunities to be with each other, and he worked at his statues without the success he desired. As she became more remote and Paris became less secure, the figures were whittled and eroded into more remote, tinier pieces, no more than a few centimetres high. Some, portentously, crumbled altogether. The studio and all who occupied it were shrouded in plaster dust. In the autumn, Isabel and Giacometti had a few days together before it was time for him to leave for his regular visit to Switzerland. On the eve of his departure, 18 October 1938, the couple walked dejectedly across the Pont Royal and through the Jardin des Tuileries. By now, the inevitability of war left them with faltering hope of how or when they could be together, and they knew that there was a possibility that this goodbye might be their last. After leaving Isabel at her hotel, Giacometti was recrossing the place des Pyramides when a car hit him, throwing him to the ground and crushing his foot. He was taken first to hospital and then to recuperate in a clinic in the suburbs, delaying his departure, where Isabel visited him every day. The event engendered a breakthrough in his work that ultimately resulted in his last major interpretation of Isabel, *La Femme au chariot*, 1942–3.[27] (**50**) It is, therefore, worth concluding this chapter with the event and its aftermath.

The non-fatal street stabbing of Samuel Beckett ten months earlier had received considerable publicity and quickly become part of the writer's personal mythology.[28] Giacometti's accident followed a similar pattern. Although the injury healed, it left him with a limp, which took on totemic status for the artist and his commentators. The crash motif was freighted with cultural meaning that had immediate relevance to Giacometti's and Isabel's concerns in 1938.[29] The driverless troop train of Émile Zola's novel *La Bête humaine* (The Human Beast) (1890) initiated a sequence of fictional collisions in literature and film representing the arbitrariness of fate and modern circumstance, and Jean Renoir's film of the book had been filmed in Paris in August and September 1938 (released 23 December).[30]

The accident played an equivalent role in Giacometti's autobiography. In keeping with the violent times, it modified the artist/*flâneur*, the figure in the street, into something more catastrophic and sacrificial.

Giacometti committed the episode to paper early in 1939 and often retold it to friends, but the story first appeared in print in Jean-Paul Sartre's autobiography, *Les Mots*, in 1963. The philosopher interpreted it as Giacometti's Existentialist encounter with the void: 'a kind of joy ... smashed by the stupid violence of chance. "So", he thought, "I wasn't born to be a sculptor or even to live. I was born for nothing." ... I admire this will to embrace everything.'[31] Giacometti objected in furious terms to Sartre's absolutist vision of his heroic recognition of insignificance and vehemently set the record straight the following year in an interview with Gotthard Jedlicka: it wasn't that a 'life he loved more than any other' had been 'upset', as Sartre claimed, but that a life already upset, 'unbearable', had been up-turned *again*.[32] The event was, rather, an ironic, unheroic, liberating revelation of life as 'significant-insignificance, as insignificant-significance' ('so sinwoll-sinnloss, so sinnlos-sinnvoll'). Giacometti's counter-telling executed a virtuoso paradox. He described his tottering relationships with Isabel, circumstances and sculpture in 1938 as a loss of footing: 'je perds absolumment pieds', as he said he told her on the fateful evening. The experience of being flung onto the road and observing his foot 'stood like a part of my body that didn't belong to my body' paradoxically restored his footing and 'clarified' ('geklärt') his romantic relationship.

Giacometti described his perception of the accident to his friend, the Swiss historian of sculpture Carola Giedion-Welcker, using Baudelaire's term 'dédoublement'.[33] His mishap was a paradigm of Benjamin's Baudelairean model of modern consciousness as alienated, distracted, interrupted, a 'technique of the putsch', something that 'hits us between the eyes with things as a car, growing to gigantic proportions, careens at us out of a film screen.'[34] Giacometti's play on foot and footing in the 1964 interview reprised Benjamin's allegorical model of history. He modernised Eliot's mythical method to describe 'allegory' as a provisional moment in the present, briefly transformed through its similarity to a moment in the past, and moments past brought into view through their brief affinity with a moment in the present, 'a dialectical optic that perceives the everyday as impenetrable, the impenetrable as everyday'.[35]. He and Giedion-Welcker were among several theorists who were beginning to write about history in this way, as instant and relational rather than narrative and sequential.[36] Art was not a question of substituting significance for insignificance, but of recognising provisional connections, 'constellations', of significances.[37]

Like Sartre, James Lord invested Giacometti's crash with a heroic reading, but of a different kind. He portrayed it like a nineteenth-century narrative of

Romantic artistic sacrifice. Where Sartre omitted Isabel from the story, Lord foregrounded her as an emasculating muse. Giacometti's solitary journey home was, for him, the result of a tragic failure to gain access to her bed: 'he was unable to make the advances that would have led upstairs to her room'; and his crushed limb was a symptom and sign of this unmanning.[38] Lord accordingly presented Isabel's daily visits to the clinic as poignant meetings between artist/victim and the blithe agent of his fate. He described the news she brought to his bedside, including a new French translation of Daniel Defoe's *The Fortunes and Misfortunes of the Famous Moll Flanders* (1722), as 'gossip'.[39] Moll Flanders was a precursor of Abbé Prévost's *Manon Lescaut (L'Histoire du chevalier des Grieux et de Manon Lescaut*, 1731) retold in *La Dame aux camélias*, and so, to Lord, a type of Isabel.[40] For Isabel, herself, and for Giacometti, the fictional adventuress was more likely to have appeared to be a model of irreverent and itinerant survival. Her absurd eighteenth-century catastrophes were appropriate to twentieth-century circumstances; like Baudelaire's and Giacometti's advancing women, she was a 'figure of shock'.

The introduction of Moll's bawdy tale into the accounts of the accident subverts Sartre's and Lord's interpretations and alerts us to Giacometti's anti-ideal allegorical strategies, his 'dialectical optic'. These would underpin the sculptor's first large figure since *La Femme qui marche II*, *La Femme au chariot*. When Giacometti finally made his delayed journey to Switzerland in 1939 he wrote his account of his experience and painted an image of Isabel on the wall of his studio at Majola.[41] It was nearly life size and was there, like a ghostly occupant of the room, whenever Giacometti returned home. He continued on the small sculptures, but between 1942 and 1945, in the same studio, he enhanced the wall image with plaster and set about recreating it as a free-standing sculpture standing on a cart. Giacometti described the figure as 'a friend whom he loved', and Isabel's slanted silhouette, piled-up hair, slender neck and wide eyes are easily recognisable.[42] Unlike the little pieces, however, the statue asserted a powerful proximity rather than distance. Mario Negri, one of the first people to see it, described it as 'so "present"'. The problems of spatial setting, and movement through it, that Giacometti had been addressing were solved in a new way: the sense of advance was created by wheels. Negri continued: 'like a child's toy, it had four little wooden wheels fixed to a shelf, as if it were on the go, or perhaps as if it had been dragged on a long, faraway journey'.[43]

La Femme au chariot set up a Benjaminian play of anachronism and allegory reflecting Giedion-Welcker's ideas of modern sculpture implicated in historical events.[44] In their substantial catalogue to the exhibition devoted to the work at the Stiftung Wilhelm Lehmbruck Museum in Duisburg, in 2010, Gottlieb Leinz and Véronique Wiesinger connected the wheeled figure to a network of imagery from ancient Egyptian to the modern day. The wheels echo the volutes on the ionic column that elevates the famous Sphinx of Naxos, c. 560 BCE, (**155**) for instance, and the 'chariot' format evokes ancient and modern military advances, marches and funeral processions.[45] Giacometti connected the vehicle both to the marauding car driven by an inebriated American woman, which had injured him, and to a medicine trolley steered by a nurse, who had tended to him, and which he had sketched as he recovered.[46] The actual shape was based on a toy trolley belonging to his nephew Silvio, in itself an ambivalent motif.[47]

A literary transcription that Isabel always carried with her in a sketchbook draws our attention to a particular precedent for *La Femme au chariot*.[48] It was Cassandra's 'Invocation to Apollo' from Aeschylus' *Agamemnon*, the famous climax of the first of three surviving plays of *The Oresteia,* written in the fifth century BCE for the festival of Dionysius. The action takes place outside Agamemnon's palace, to which the victorious Greek commander has returned with the captured Trojan prophetess standing in a chariot or cart.[49] Refusing to step down from the chariot, she turns her prison into a stage to announce Agamemnon's and her own imminent murder within the palace walls at the hands of his wife, Clytemnestra. The story had been of interest to Giacometti for a long time. In 1947, in his account of his work to Paul Matisse, he mentioned that he had read Aeschylus, including 'the Death of Cassandra', as a young man in Rome in 1921–2. Ten years on, in 1932, his sculpture of an *unheimlich* home, *The Palace at 4 a.m.* (**80**) had alluded to the speech that opens the play, the Watchman's description of Agamemnon's palace in the hours before dawn.[50] Ten years on, again, *La Femme au chariot* represented Cassandra.

Cassandra's ability to speak the future had been bestowed by an amorous Apollo, but when she rejected his advances he condemned her to never be understood. The visionary unintelligibility, significant insignificance, of the words of Cassandra's 'Invocation' that became Isabel's talisman were a defiant fusion of art, Apollo's gift and failure. As a result, Cassandra foresees the slaughter that will take place but cannot articulate it clearly enough to prevent it. It was perhaps the dislocated language Aeschylus gave her, vivid but obscure, that made the episode so interesting to Giacometti and Isabel. Cassandra's devastating but indecipherable Invocation at dawn allegorised Giacometti's aesthetic of 'significant insignificance', of triumph in failure in art and life. She was, like Moll Flanders, the American driver, the nurse, Sylvio's mother, a figure of catastrophe, 'caught up' as Gottlieb Leinz puts it, 'between life and death, triumph and death'.[51]

PART II

51. Pablo Picasso, *Le Chapeau à fleurs,* 10 April 1940; Centre Georges Pompidou, Paris, courtesy RMN-Grand Palais and Bertrand Prévost

10 WAR: 1939–1940

What do you think an artist is? An imbecile who has only his eyes if he is a painter, or his ears if he is a musician, or a lyre at every level of his heart if he is a poet, or, if he is merely a boxer, only his muscle? On the contrary, he is at the same time a political being, constantly alert to the heart rending, burning, or happy events in the world, moulding himself in their likeness. How could it be possible to feel no interest in other people, and, because of an ivory-towered indifference, detach yourself from the life they bring with such open full hands?

Pablo Picasso[1]

The year 1939 permitted Isabel a short, unexpected interlude to paint. Balthus was due to be conscripted and Antoinette was staying in the country with Derain, so, for all his disapproval, and to Isabel's delight, he left her the use of his cour de Rohan studio.[2] She lent her hotel room to a friend and moved in. She bought herself some clay and made small sculptures, 'not because I wanted to be a sculptress,' she wrote, 'but I thought it would improve my drawing.' Mara Scherbatoff was too busy to sit for her, and there was no question of models, so she drew bird skeletons based on one purchased at the nearby taxidermist's, Deyrolle, on the rue de Bac (still trading). It can be seen mounted on its perch on a shelf in Giacometti's studio in a photograph taken in 1954.[3] She also painted food, potatoes and anything she had to hand, emulating Balthus's *Still Life* of 1937 (Wadsworth Atheneum of Art, Hartford, Connecticut), a bitter juxtaposition of bread, potato and wine in which the food is pinioned on forks and knives and the carafe is shattered with a hammer.[4]

Paris was emptying. Many artists went south or abroad. Isabel's English friend, Joan Eyres-Monsell had gone to England to marry John Rayner, a colleague of Delmer and a features editor at the *Daily Express*, and had employment photographing buildings vulnerable to bombing. With typical zest, Anna Maclaren was driving with the ambulance corps in Spain and Peter Rose Pulham had persuaded Theodora Rosling to share bohemian semi-starvation in his room in the Hôtel Bisson. Giacometti was around for a while but in May went to Zurich for the Swiss National Exhibition. He demanded a monumental pedestal for one of his tiniest Isabel figures. This was not appreciated by the authorities, and they replaced it with another sculpture on a more conventional scale.

Maria Osten arrived from Barcelona on her way to Moscow to re-join Mikhail Koltsov and their young adopted son. On a recent visit to Russia with fellow journalist Ian Fleming, Delmer had discovered that the *Pravda* editor had fallen victim to Stalin's purges, arrested in December 1939. He was believed to have been killed, although he was not, in fact, executed until 1940. Delmer wrote to Isabel to tell her to warn Maria, and she broke the awful news at a corner table in Les Deux Magots.[5] Maria had been shadowed by Soviet security agents in Barcelona and was clearly also in danger, but, undeterred, stated simply, 'I am going tomorrow.' Loyal to her communist ideals and convinced she could clear her lover's name, she went to Moscow, only to be disowned by both the Establishment and her son, and disappeared herself in 1941.

The poet Benjamin Péret passed through Paris, summoned back from Spain, where he had been fighting for the Republicans, for conscription. Isabel let him lay low at the cour de Rohan and took the opportunity of his company to make portraits, which she gave to him when he left to begin his military service. Neither he nor Balthus served long: the patrician painter was invalided out on health grounds and went south with Antoinette; Péret was expelled for his political activities and jailed, but managed to arrange his release and passage to Mexico in 1941 (as a communist, he was not welcome in the United States).

Soon, Isabel herself was journeying again. The most puzzling excursion was to Germany in July 1939, for which she secured a full year's permit.[6] This coincided with the disastrous breakdown of British and French negotiations with Russia. On 23 August 1939, Stalin changed affiliation to sign a non-aggression agreement with Hitler. One of the contributions to Stalin's decision was intelligence on France's and Britain's reluctance to fight, some of which was being passed by Donald Maclean. Yet, like many communists, Maclean was as horrified by the pact as anyone else and found himself suddenly spying for fascism rather than against it. War was now inevitable and by the date of the pact, Isabel was already on her way to Poland. Having secured a new visa, she arrived in Warsaw on 8 August 1939. She may have travelled alone or met Delmer on the border at Katowice.[7] Again, her presence is not mentioned in either of their autobiographies. The couple stayed at the Hôtel Europejski in Warsaw, and Isabel wrote from there to Giacometti in Switzerland, perhaps to let him know she was safe.[8]

Isabel's letter and Giacometti's reply are fascinating documents. Everything of importance is written between the lines. She gives the impression that she is vacationing, and both adopt a tourist voice – indolent, innocent of politics or any awareness of the devastating events that were unfolding – but the deeper implications of their words are clear. Giacometti tells Isabel of a visit to Venice, whose morbid associations did not need stating. For her part, she describes passing through Berlin and going to the Ägyptisches Museum to look up their old funerary friend the bust of Nefertiti. Her letter 'admired' the autobahns, the means of invasion: 'One can only think of the roads Romans created. As they are placed in the landscape ... they are beautifully made and designed.' Poland was repeatedly compared with the Netherlands, another invasion target: it was 'as flat as Holland (only the sky seems higher and there was more sense of space) and very cultured. All along the route small villages full of horses.' 'Horses and carts. But full,' she added, probably referring to another kind of traffic or to refugees. Of a visit to Gdańsk, a vital strategic port, she wrote, 'It is a lovely city, which reminded me a little of Amsterdam. There is naturally a Dutch influence because of the Hanseatic League: the eighteenth century houses are really beautiful. Inside, there are a lot of English furniture and English porcelain.' This guidebook vision of a Europe connected culturally and technologically is an unusually dark irony. As always, Isabel enthuses about Northern Renaissance painting that she has seen; but her example is, significantly, Hans Memling's *The Last Judgement* (c. 1470; National Museum, Gdańsk).

The letter listed Romania as the next 'sight' on Isabel's itinerary, but this was, in fact, her and Delmer's escape route. Her visa was due to run out, dangerously under the circumstances, on 3 September. Delmer got her on to the last plane leaving on 1 September, so when war was declared on 3 September, she was on a boat in the English Channel.[9] In Geneva, the following morning, Giacometti and his brother Diego reported for Swiss military service. Giacometti wrote to Isabel anxiously from a café across the road from the recruiting office.[10] Only Diego was accepted, as Giacometti was still walking with a stick. Isabel arrived in England exhausted and went to recuperate by the coast with her mother, swimming and cycling. The Germans were bombing Warsaw, but Delmer stayed for four more days before escaping over land.[11]

In the middle of September, Isabel set off to meet Delmer in London and sent Giacometti a postcard, saying that she expected to be back in Paris soon.[12] Instead, and to her frustration, Delmer moved them into an apartment in Lincoln's Inn, near Fleet Street. It was called 9 Stone Buildings. 'In reality the building that we live in is brick,' she wrote in the next letter to Giacometti, only half in jest; 'It is a topic that bothers and grieves me in equal measures.'[13] If the absurdity of war could not be allowed to matter, this could. Delmer had decided to spend the conflict doing something more useful than reporting, and was cultivating contacts to campaign for a serious post. Isabel entertained for him. Anna Maclaren, a favourite of Delmer, was also working in Fleet Street and living in Stone Buildings, and Joan Eyres-Monsell, now Rayner, was close by, in Grey's Inn. In her usual autodidactic fashion, Isabel read André Simon's Wine and Food Society volumes and loitered in Joan's kitchen appropriating her friend's finishing-school skills. This learning she combined with French know-how to produce Continental feasts for Delmer's parties.

'Looking back at this time,' Isabel remembered, 'it was strangely unsatisfactory.' Cut off from her studio and lifestyle and unimpressed by the few pieces of work that had survived her moves, she could not paint. She went to the Zoo, but most of the animals had been removed, and 'Old Misery' was gone. She roamed the nearby City, the business area, when it was deserted at weekends, exploring St Paul's and other Wren churches. Mostly she felt she was just 'sitting on this suspicious island', as she told Giacometti, 'skin wrinkling in the fogs, eyelids drooping, brain clogged.' She followed this complaint with a pictorial code describing some music by Vivaldi; one strongly suspects this was to annoy the censors. Giacometti was also miserable in Geneva. He was smoking less, however, and reading Sophocles, Racine and Shakespeare's comedies – to hear, in his mind, he said, her laugh.[14]

The correspondence indicates that Isabel and Giacometti had decided to be together. In his letters he is unsure about whether to go to Paris, whether she would be there and anxious lest she change her mind. She did not. Against all the odds, she obtained a permit to travel to both Switzerland and France, and crossed the Swiss border on 9 December 1939.[15] The trip might have been related to Delmer's work in some way, or she may have been hoping to find Giacometti. Unfortunately, their letters crossed, and he had returned to Paris a month before, so they were eventually reunited there. Isabel moved back into the Hôtel Saint-Romain. Delmer was in Paris, attached to the French army, but almost immediately he was recalled to England and demanded that Isabel go with him. Before she left, she anxiously sought a guarantee that she would have the right to return and sent a hurried and enigmatic letter to Giacometti, reassuring him of this and ending, 'Carry on with the heads.'[16] It was 23 December: Christmas again.

Letters between Isabel and Giacometti over the following months were full of recollections of their walks though Paris, refracted, of course, through the little figures Giacometti was making. Isabel, by contrast, had no studio. Trapped by the cold, dark evenings, impenetrable fogs, and social rounds, she feared she would become as dreary as she found her companions.[17] As she lost hope of escaping again until the spring, her writing acquired the cadence of mourning: 'I feel exactly as I imagine people feel before they die.' What follows in this letter is a very rare insight into the pressures she felt as a woman artist. After four years of interruptions, she confessed, she had lost sense of progress in her work, or the appetite to continue the battle to prove her intelligence against expectations – perhaps she was merely an ordinary artist; perhaps she had reached her limits? Her confidence in her ability to invent her life also flagged: 'It will be fifty years before I succeed in understanding how I ought to live.'

Giacometti wrote back to this letter immediately and passionately. An unpunctuated torrent of words expressed his distress at the news that she wouldn't be there until spring and at hearing her hopelessness: 'you don't really believe all you say all the time,' he reminded her. She did not have to prove how intelligent she was to him, he added, 'You are! ... you haven't discovered your limits and you are not ordinary ... With you I always feel unbounded directness and honesty, and now because I'm in this café and I wish more than anything that you were here and we might argue a bit I feel as though you are sitting next to me ...' He returned to her work again at the end of the letter: 'above all Isabel do not be disgusted (not the word) or depressed and dissatisfied with yourself, or modest, or anything of that, rather be very proud and superior, and do lots.'[18]

Two earlier letters from Giacometti had crossed with Isabel's. The first was written on a rainy evening in the Café Bonaparte, a communist haunt on the boulevard Saint-Germain. His words were affectionate and tipsy; he had been drinking brandy with Donald Maclean and the spy's new American girlfriend, Melinda Marling. He was worried about not hearing from Isabel.[19] The second, also from the Café Bonaparte, following a bout of flu, apologised for the last, hoping Isabel could read between the lines. He went on: 'I have been writing to you in my mind every day, I often have mental conversations; that's rather vague ... I work hard, get cold, very beautiful winter days ... Do you work, Isabel? What do you do?' [20] Then there followed an extraordinary extended word picture about a dancing skein of dust that he had watched for hours on the ceiling of his room, a disquisition on living line, 'like an animal, an hallucination, a snake and never an animal moved with such beauty.' Friends were only briefly mentioned: Sonia Mosse (Derain's ebullient model), Tristan Tzara, Francis Gruber, Balthus's latest disturbing picture at Pierre Colle's. Then he returned to missing her: 'Every day I wonder how you are, how (not what) you are doing. There is always a space in my mind for you. / Your Giacometti. Write to me Isabel?'

Essentially, Giacometti's letters to Isabel are dominated by their work and their separation. The two were, as the art historian Reinhold Hohl has pointed out, inextricably connected. During this period, Giacometti's effort to realise her presence in clay acquired additional significance. Almost all his time was devoted to a statuette showing her on the boulevard Saint-Germain, 'as he remembered her at a parting' – as Hohl describes it, 'in terms of the way she appeared in the artist's field of vision: as she walked away she slowly shrank to a thin line a tiny spot among the myriad details of the street ... even though he saw progressively less form, shape, and colour and the details dissolved; the tiny "unform" kept its full potency of meaning and undiminished existence for the person seeing it. This was something that had to be expressed in art.'[21]

James Lord suggested that this preoccupation with distance was a dysfunctional one, expressing Isabel's teasing and Giacometti's 'uncertainty'.[22] This was not the case. The letters reveal an intimacy already established. The couple are sensitive to each other's practical and psychological situations and clearly as familiar with the other's work as with their own. There is great tolerance of the fact that, because of their professional circumstances, neither can provide the lifestyle that the other needs. Giacometti may have construed this as a renunciation of his masculine role towards Isabel and, therefore, of what he might expect of her; his letters apologise frequently for being demanding and 'impatient.'[23] Isabel described his predicament as like the doomed and complicated passions of Fabrice in Stendhal's novel *La Chartreuse de Parme* (The Charterhouse of Parma; 1839).[24] Both understood that work came first, however. Their period of transition, the search for 'breakthroughs', was in danger of being overwhelmed by the transitions and upheaval going on in the world. At a time when the value of art and the artist were easily set aside, when many had allied their practice to a political cause, their move away from both their recognised styles and their social 'sets' left them vulnerable. There was indeed 'uncertainty', but it was the uncertainty of their art and their times.

Isabel managed to get back to Paris again in February 1940. She was a welcome face with so many gone, and Giacometti was overjoyed. Isabel was based at the Hôtel Saint-Romain and went to Giacometti when Delmer was away.[25] They stayed in the Hôtel Primavera, not far from his studio, where they could be more comfortable and private.[26] The *drôle de guerre,* or Phony War, was a 'curious, blank time', however. Giacometti worked indefatigably, but progress was elusive, and they were both aware that their freedom was running out. The drawings of Isabel on the bed that Giacometti later dated to 1940 were probably executed during this warm, late spring, as she is naked and on top of the sheets. (**40, 52**)

Picasso had taken the precaution of relocating to Royan on the coast, but he and Dora were often in Paris in these months. The four friends saw each other most days at 5 p.m. in Brasserie Lipp on the boulevard Saint-Germain. Giacometti's prolonged, independent and publicly unproductive phase of reassessment puzzled his colleagues, and, according to Isabel, Picasso 'sometimes would sneak round to la rue Hippolyte Maindron to see what he was up to.' He was aware of Giacometti's artistic crisis, so loaded now with emotional and existential implications too, and Isabel recalled that one evening in Brasserie Lipp, after watching her for a while, Picasso jumped up from his table saying he knew '"how to do it!" Then he dashed back to his studio', she continued, 'and started my portrait right away ... You didn't sit for Picasso, he painted me from memory.' Three bust-length portraits by Picasso, each made over a few hours in the studio on 10, 11 and 14 April 1940, relate to this claim.[27] (**51**) These were not so much likenesses as – as Brigitte Léal has described them – 'composites', variations in Picasso's series of seated figures spanning 1937 and 1941 dominated by the appearance of Dora Maar.[28] Isabel wears one of her

52. Alberto Giacometti, *Woman Reclining*, pencil, c. 1940; Sainsbury Centre for Visual Arts, University of East Anglia,

favourite Robert Piguet hats,[29] and the unusually pale complexion recalls 'the white skinned maidens of Burne-Jones' which Picasso associated with a particular kind of English 'type', a woman 'so different from any he had ever met, who had conquered her own liberty and the hearts of men.'[30] Isabel was certainly this.

Le Chapeau à fleurs (**51**) took on artists who had represented Isabel before. Art historians have identified Picasso's series of *bustes de femme* as an extended conversation with Matisse's Fauve masterpiece *Femme au chapeau* of 1905 (San Francisco Museum of Modern Art).[31] Introducing the likeness of Isabel addressed a second veteran Fauve, André Derain, (**27**) who, as Picasso's biographer, John Richardson, has shown, had been an equally unresolved figure for him since their meeting in 1906.[32] Picasso had also in his younger days known Jacob Epstein, and the two pink curves recall the infamous *Isobel*, reproduced for the first time in Epstein's autobiography earlier in the year.[33] The asymmetry of the head with its fly-away hair recalled Giacometti's most recent *Tête d'Isabel*, 1937–8. Like the sculpture, the painting captured Isabel's vectored demeanour with the *v* of the chin and the gaze intensified by its slight strabismus – but exaggerated both. This dialogue with sculptors can be seen in the context of the debate between painting and sculpture itself, the *paragone*, which had been central to Picasso's career since Cubism.

The sequence was interrupted on 10 May by the German invasion.[34] The BBC Home Service, received in Europe, announced land and sea attacks on the Netherlands, Belgium and France.[35] The Dutch surrendered within days, and by 4 June British and Allied troops in Europe had been evacuated to England from Dunkirk. To Isabel's surprise, the voice of Constant Lambert, the husband of her friend Flo whom she had met when she was living with Epstein, came over the airwaves. He had been in the Netherlands with the Vic-Wells Ballet and witnessed the invasion first hand. His description of bombs, paratroopers and propaganda leaflets descending from the sky, and the company's narrow escape without their belongings, made sober listening in Paris.[36]

The British Embassy prepared to move south to Tours, and Donald Maclean and Melinda scrambled to get married. Rose Pulham and Rosling gratefully accepted Maclean's apartment when he vacated it.[37] Along the Seine, the spring air was smoky from bonfires burning official files and documents. In the Café de Flore, Tzara and others tried to persuade Isabel that it was 'useless' to run to London, which they felt would fall soon after Paris. Diego Giacometti and Francis Gruber were arrested one evening because the police mistook Diego for a German parachutist, thinking the cigarette burns in his overalls were bullet holes. They were released only after a pistol fired through the cloth showed that they were a different kind of mark. Isabel suggested that she and Giacometti should hide their work: 'As his were so small – heads the size of a walnut, or smaller – I decided the best thing would be to make a hole in the floor and put them in there. Some he could take in his pocket.' Isabel's were left at the studio or buried at a farm outside Paris. Typically, both artists were mainly concerned about recent pieces.[38]

As the French government prepared to leave, Delmer managed to get Isabel an air ticket out, which she gave away. She called it her 'bad act ... becoming a nuisance in a grim moment', and Delmer was angry, but she almost certainly passed it to someone whom she felt needed immediate safety even more than she did. It also bought her time with Giacometti. He must have felt keenly the danger of Isabel's being with anyone other than her legal husband at that moment. He had no papers for her or means of protecting her; Delmer, by contrast, capably arranged a second escape for her by car with the journalist George Millar.[39] On 9 June, the eve of Isabel's departure, Delmer took her to a sports shop and bought a leather money belt for her to wear underneath her clothes and a sleeping bag. He insisted on a last meal at Larue, which was not to survive the war; then he left to take Mara Scherbatoff to Poitiers before setting off in search of 'the non-existent front.' Scherbatoff wanted to stay in France with her sisters and governess and was involved in the emerging Resistance. Delmer's last words to Isabel were 'whatever you do, keep going south, not right or left, and wait. Get to Bordeaux, if possible.'

After he had gone, she went to meet Giacometti in Saint-Germain. They had a last drink with Tzara, who, being Jewish, was also about to flee, and afterwards they walked. The Tuileries was deserted and the gardens unkempt, the lawns now knee-high meadows: 'It was a wonderful, clear night. The statues rose from the grass looking graceful. We sat holding hands all that night. I don't think either of us thought we would never see each other again. But we knew that nothing would be quite the same again. A feeling that our age of innocence had passed seems the best way of telling it.' In the five years' separation that followed, the memory of these familiar and moonlit statues, particularly, perhaps, Aimé Millet's *Cassandra seeking the Protection of Pallas* (1877), persisted, possibly, in the conception of *La Femme au chariot*.

Hurried notes written the following day give a vivid sense of the panic of fast-moving events, multiple responsibilities and the sense of seeing loved ones for the last time. Giacometti was at the foundry, fixing what progress he had made by casting little models into bronze so that they could be transported.[40] At the same time, he had been attempting to get an exit visa, but discovered that it could not be done within two weeks, which was as good as never with the Germans being so close. He wrote wondering if Isabel could come to him one more time, if she had changed her plans, even. The 'worst has happened', she replied; she was leaving at 3.30.[41] Touchingly, she fretted that her happiness when they had been together that morning had given the impression that 'I do not take seriously things I take very seriously ... remember it is decided that even if there is a delay of several years ... that I must live with you (to follow my new calling) ... What is terrible in this story is that we will realise the enormity of our decisions only when we are apart without the possibility of communicating. I repeat again that you must have absolute confidence in me. Events may become very bad but we can at least trust in each other.' She was worried he would not leave in time, or be caught with his camera, for which, as a foreigner, he could be arrested as a spy: 'Save your life if you can.' She concluded, 'I can truly say now that I am with you and I love you very much.' Isabel packed three pictures – two drawings given to her by Giacometti and her portrait by Derain – with the merest essentials, and she and George Millar set off.[42] It would be many months before Giacometti knew whether she had reached safety. Most of the population of Paris was on the move. The next morning, 11 June, it was declared an open city; it would not be defended and so, unlike Warsaw or Barcelona, would not be bombed. The sky was stained purple from the smoke of petrol reservoirs set alight by departing French troops; the few bars and cafés that were open were raucous. Speeding south, Isabel and George stayed away from the main route and stopped at farms for food or rest. It took two days to get to Tours, where she posted a card to Giacometti and set off alone by rail for the port of Bordeaux. The lines were congested with trains carrying wounded back from the north, but she reached her destination after 19 hours. About the same time, on 13 June, Giacometti, Diego and Diego's lover, Nelly, finally left Paris. They were on bicycles, but by now the roads were impossibly congested and the Germans were strafing refugees. Two of the many killed were the daughters of the owner of the Hôtel Saint-Romain. Giacometti and Diego were caught fifty kilometres south of Paris, at Étampes, where they witnessed civilians being shelled and shot. It took three more days to reach Moulins, where the Germans overtook them and they turned back. Rose Pulham and Rosling had also left on bicycles, though not together. They just managed to stay ahead of the advancing armies, making do with food and wine bought from farms or stolen from damaged shops.

In Bordeaux, Isabel discovered that the British Embassy had installed itself temporarily in the Château d'Yquem, which she considered 'very clever', since it was one of the best vineyards in France. There she tracked down Maclean. He advised her not to board the Dutch boat in the harbour, as many were doing, because there was no guarantee where it would dock, but to wait until a British ship arrived. Isabel spread this sound advice to others. She sent Giacometti another card. There were no rooms, so she retired to a field with her sleeping bag, but, 'with the kind of enthusiasm that overcomes one at certain times', found herself organising a last meal at the Chapon Fin. That was where Delmer found her. In a scene that looks forward to Ian Fleming's tales of James Bond, he described his entrance, tired and dusty: 'Isabel hailed us with a typical grasshopper leap and shriek of joy. "Here" she cried, brandishing a glass as though this was an evening out in the Left Bank, not our last evening in stricken France, "come and have some of this as an aperitif. It's a Coutet, 1913, specially iced for you."'[43]

On 18 June, Isabel's motley group joined some 1,300 people crammed onto the SS *Madura* (designed for 290), bewildering the paying passengers en route from Bombay. Only one small bag per person was allowed so the quay was lined with abandoned belongings. Some of the refugees were journalists, including Virginia Cowles. Another was Anna Maclaren, to everyone's delight. Delmer managed to secure two deck chairs between the three of them, and they camped in the open air for three days as, to avoid mines, the ship zigzagged 'across the grey, U-boat haunted Atlantic seas'. Fortunately, they were not bombed and docked safely in Falmouth.[44] 'We were met by a wonderful, orderly reception by the WVS [Women's Voluntary Services] who had arranged long trestle tables with tea and plenty of food. I remember taking a walk up a hill. When I reached that fine, short grass I fell on my knees and kissed it. Back home the feeling of order was paramount and the future obscure.'

All possibility of France's continuing the fight had already ceased. Marshal Pétain had taken control of a government prepared to accommodate Hitler's demands. Giacometti, Diego and Nelly were back in Paris. On the day Isabel sailed, the exiled French leader, Charles de Gaulle, broadcast from London his appeal to the French to resist. Earlier that day, Churchill's famous speech had bluntly stated that France's fight was now dependent on Britain: 'the Battle of France is over ... the Battle of Britain is about to begin.'[45] Picasso returned to Paris when the Germans reached Royan, living in his studio on the rue des Grands-Augustins for the remainder of the war. Giacometti subsisted with Diego at rue d'Alésia. They, with the Grubers, the Éluards, the Leirises and the philosophical writers Jean-Paul Sartre and Simone de Beauvoir, whom Giacometti had recently befriended, formed a close circle.[46] Food, fuel and materials were scarce and exhibitions were closely policed, but they worked on as best they could and perceived this as an act of resistance. Derain was in Paris, too; German soldiers had overrun his home in Chambourcy and destroyed many works, and, in 1941, he was pressurised into accepting a cultural invitation to Germany. Sadly, all but Giacometti and Francis Gruber shunned him from then on.

Isabel and Giacometti corresponded throughout the war, but letters had to go via Lisbon to Switzerland to be forwarded to Paris by his sister-in-law, so they took six months. Only one, a note written from London on 25 June 1940, a few days after Isabel got back, has survived. It cannot have arrived much before November, so for many months neither she nor Giacometti would have known whether the other was alive: 'I'm trying everything to send you a letter,' she explained,

> I even wrote to your mother, but without much hope ... I think you must be found in Paris, I wonder how you are, if you are still at the same address, what have you done with the sculptures. Is it is possible to work? I have not lost my confidence in our future even though I need courage sometimes not to, I feel very isolated. You know that the thing that would give me most pleasure is to receive your news, at least know where you are, and that you are not too discouraged, I beg you, do not be too depressed, I must say again that nothing can make me change my decision I took. Nothing. I hope you found the letter that I left you at the hotel. I must wait with as much courage as possible.[47]

Isabel was clearly aware of Giacometti's insecurity as a lover. There is no way of knowing whether he was reassured, or whether he was able to reassure her.[48]

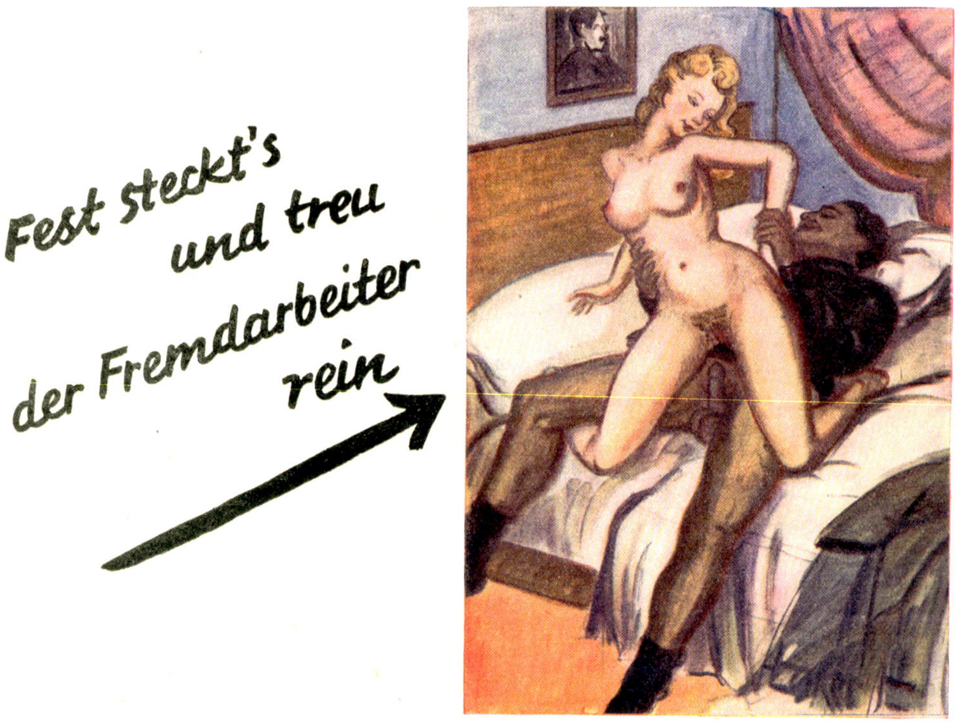

53. Isabel Rawsthorne, 'Watch on the Rhine' greeting card, Italian edition, 1942; courtesy Lee Richards Collection

11 WAR ART: 1940–1944

Isabel did not return to Paris for the duration of the conflict, and war work continued to demand precedence over painting. 'Events' had torn her from the artistic and emotional existence she had created for herself: she had lost her studio, her lover, her colleagues, most of her drawings and paintings and what had become her culture (her French accent would never completely fade). Life was unpredictable, and conventions were set aside. But Isabel was suited to improvised and first-principle endeavours; they focused her talents in unexpected ways and reconfigured her outlook. Art and reality became even more seriously entwined.

In London, Isabel found the atmosphere tense. She went to her mother at the coast to rest, swim, and walk in the woods. Summer had arrived and Warwick was home from Dauntsey's School. He was happy there, was learning to breed trout and had taken charge of the school aquarium. Peter Rose Pulham and Theodora Rosling made it to Bordeaux and regained England a week after Isabel, so when she returned to London, she visited them in their makeshift rooms in Chesil Court, Chelsea. The Macleans were around, too, and she and Donald sunbathed on Peter and Thea's roof.[1] Maclean's career was, paradoxically, prospering, but Theo Rosling was surprised by how low key his married life was, sensing, perhaps, that it was a facade. It was only now that she got to know Isabel. She admired her expressive eyes and 'verve', and her nonconformist, long, straight hair – short locks set in curls declaring patriotic involvement in the war effort had become the accepted style. The linguist Patricia (Pattie) Whitney Smith, whom Isabel would later come to know well, recalled a similarly anti-establishment look when she saw her in 1943 in a BBC lift, where she was struck by both Isabel's beauty and the black, laddered stockings, 'which she carried off with a disdainful air.'[2] This bohemian appearance gave no hint that she had been involved with conflicts in Europe since 1935.

Now, Isabel was impatient for another role. Joan Rayner was working as a volunteer nurse as well as a photographer. The Women's Royal Naval Service – the 'Wrens'– had been re-formed and she decided to join, thinking, perhaps, of her father. Delmer asked her to wait, however, saying that he had other plans. By September 1940, the bombs were falling. Isabel saw the blitzed London docks scorch the sky orange, and the Safe Deposit opposite their flat in Chancery Lane (where Londoners rented strong rooms to safeguard their valuables) took a direct hit and burned to the ground, filling their rooms with smoke and making the glass in the windows too hot to touch. Many people were regularly sleeping in air-raid shelters or had moved into the Underground system, but others, including Isabel and Delmer, made the decision to avoid these. It was an alternative way of coping that Rose Pulham and Rosling adopted also. Such groups ignored the sirens, carrying on with their business or collecting together in pubs, where the conviviality would at least partially drown the fear and noise. Rose Pulham and Rosling's bomb came early, and one night they found themselves clinging to a ledge that was all that remained of their demolished bedroom. What paintings were destroyed no one knows. They eventually relocated to a nearby apartment in Oakley Street, furnished with handouts, where the painter Matthew Smith, likewise forced back to London from France in 1940, was also living.[3]

'Our bomb', as Isabel put it, arrived during a dinner party. She thought it was a clever one, as the guests included Prince Bernhard, who had brought Princess Juliana to safety in England; their Belgian friend from the Spanish Civil War, Marthe Huysmans, with her husband; Delmer's colleague Ian Fleming; the under-secretary at the Ministry of Economic Warfare, Leonard Ingrams, with his wife, Victoria; and Anna Maclaren. Ingrams was handsome and debonair, and Isabel later mentioned a 'whirl' with him.[4] Bernhard was his usual high-spirited self and regaled the table with an exploit of the previous evening, when he had attempted to preserve the blackout by shooting out a light in a distant penthouse with his revolver. As the anecdote reached its climax, Stone Buildings was hit.[5] Isabel's retelling is mischievous: 'After a great jolt and a bang, Tom opened the door and found no staircase ... never have I seen two people move as fast as Ian and Bernhard. How they managed to get past the hole in the stairs, I do not know. They were terrified for their cars outside.' To Isabel's surprise, on discovering their vehicles intact, both men promptly jumped in and drove off! 'Years later,' Isabel wrote, 'when I read the James Bond stories I understood that Bond was Ian's fantasy, skilfully told. Ian thought himself Bond.' With the heroes gone, the rest of the gathering was rescued via the fire-service ladder. Maclaren caused hilarity by admonishing Marthe Huysmans for lighting a cigarette, forgetting that the city was burning as bright as day. Their reduced party trooped to the Savoy Hotel and found a room, returning the following morning to salvage what they could from the flat; Isabel rescued her portrait by Derain but recorded nothing of her more ordinary possessions or of her and Giacometti's work.

Delmer and Isabel stayed for a few weeks in Lansdowne House in Berkeley Square, where she made the most of the indoor swimming pool, until Delmer fell in love with and bought Valley Farm, a remote and beautiful Elizabethan farmhouse in Suffolk. He finally had a war job, something in the Secret Service, and disappeared to Portugal, so Isabel moved their belongings into the farm alone. The nearest town for supplies was a five-mile bike ride away: 'The contrast of my life now, at the Valley Farm by myself, and the clatter I had left behind was grandiose. At first I could not sleep at all. I could hear the distant thump of bombs and really nearly left and went back to London.' Isabel acclimatised, however, to being in the countryside: 'I thought and I still think it is one of the most beautiful places I ever lived in!' The house was on a steep hill with a half-mile drive lined with elms: 'There was an old rosemary hedge, a pond with a moorhen, may trees mounting the field on one side, innumerable rabbit warrens, foxes, the occasional wandering sheep, traps here and there, and the largest mushrooms I can remember seeing; an ancient generator for electricity and the fiercest draughts ever to enter a house ... I found it rewarding to walk out and up and down one of the fields after dark. This was how I got used to various sounds, the scent and the silence and the sounds of the night bewitched me.' The Valley Farm was, as the Paris apartment had been, 'his' home, however, and Isabel never felt she 'really belonged'. It was an idyllic interlude only, and it is surprising and interesting that, in the midst of this peace and beauty, she does not appear to have been able to work.

Delmer came and went. On one visit he left Isabel with a firearms certificate and a 2.2 rifle, 'thinking that I would have a pot-shot at a German if he appeared stumbling downhill'. She occupied a month or two by teaching herself to shoot on the Home Guard's range. One spring day, Delmer rang with mysterious instructions to pack some things and go to London, where she would be met by a car. Isabel had no idea where it was taking her until, to her surprise, she found herself at a pretty house, Larchfield, in the Home Counties village of Aspley Guise.[6] The picturesque setting was, in fact (like something from a Michael Powell and Emeric Pressburger film), one of several top-secret residential units on the Woburn Estate, the seat of the dukes of Bedford, code-named 'LF'. Isabel discovered that she was to be employed there by the Political Warfare Executive, a branch of the Special Operations Executive (SOE) under Leonard Ingrams. It was devoted to broadcasting black propaganda to occupied territories, of which Delmer had been put in charge. The unit collaborated increasingly with the French Resistance, and Isabel was happy to be giving them some kind of support, like Nancy Cunard, who was working as their translator in London, and Mara Scherbatoff, who was conducting operations in far more dangerous circumstances in France itself, helping Allied prisoners to escape.

In August, they moved to larger headquarters in a nearby rectory, The Rookery, code-named 'RAG'. It would be Isabel's home for nearly three years. Initially, the team consisted of three Germans, but it grew to a household of twelve or fourteen, recruited from prisoners of war, refugees and communists. Isabel signed Official Secrets documents, and security was strict. They were not allowed to leave the grounds or visit any shop, pub or even the nearby woods; mail came to a box number, and most went under false names, as did many visitors. There were other houses, Italian and French, and not far away were the now famous code-breaking huts of Bletchley Park, but all were kept secret from each other. Delmer came and went, liaising with other centres and with London, but, apart from a forty-eight hours' release every few months, Isabel had to keep to the village.

To Isabel's dismay, her first duties were domestic: to organise and run the household. Although this was 'hardly attractive' to her, as she wrote, it made use of her experience hosting multinational dinner parties, and she adapted what she had learned in Paris to the reduced resources of wartime rationing. According to her own account, the cook, a local woman named Freda Maddy, was delighted to discover that her mistress had little housekeeping experience and took over her duties. According to others, however, Isabel contributed energy, flare and French expertise, and the food was exceptional.[7] She kept strictly to rations, but Freda's husband had access to fresh game from the Woburn Estate. He also cultivated a cottage garden, although his ambitions to grow prize specimens for the village fete were defeated by Isabel's insistence on eating the vegetables – including his cherished marrows – young, in the Continental fashion. They swapped dried-egg ration coupons for chicken feed, so that they could have fresh eggs, and berries and mushrooms were collected in season. Isabel slipped off to forage in the woods when she could.

As a result of this, the house was fondly remembered as the only one of the units with an ebullient social life. Isabel recalled recreational croquet and target practice in summer and, in winter, chess, reminiscent of the Café de la Régence; some of her opponents were genuine chess champions.[8] There were visits from senior British military personnel: Ian Fleming, now liaison with the Admiralty, Hugh Walmsley, a senior commander in the Royal Air Force, and Joan's husband, John Rayner, were frequently there. Rayner was Delmer's immediate superior at SOE, in charge of 'Rumours'. There were also regular parties. Ellic Howe, who was in charge of Britain's forgery operation during the war, left a description of Delmer holding court at the end of the dining table and orchestrating a cherry-stone spitting competition.[9] Relationships, even engagements, blossomed between residents. Inevitably, this success caused a scandal; the *Sunday Express* sensed a story and, after some research, produced an article headlined '"Fat-of-the-land" Life of German P-O-Ws. Mushrooms cooked in wine!' Luckily, the fact that the unit was not admitted to exist prevented the exposé from being published until after the war. It appeared in February 1946, claiming: 'The German prisoners who did broadcasting and propaganda work for Britain in civilian clothes had a good war here ... The alien propaganda corps, which included women, were lodged in big 10–14 roomed houses standing in their own grounds ... the men all dressed in lounge suits or sports clothes ...'[10]

Isabel still had no studio, but she adapted a spare bedroom, which she used when it was not occupied. When many artists were making landscape their vehicle of expression, Isabel did not paint her beautiful countryside surroundings. She concentrated on still lifes in watercolour. Whenever her room was free, she studied small rodents, birds, reptiles and insects 'in various states of decay.' When it was occupied, 'visitors who stayed the night were surprised when waking in the morning to find their bed surrounded by animal corpses.' These literal *natures mortes*, followed on from the skeletons and humble objects begun before she left Paris. They varied the traditional still lifes, in which creatures jostled in a panorama of foliage and flowers and borrowed, instead, techniques of botanical and scientific recording, presenting just one creature, isolated on a sheet of paper in exact equivalent to the carcass set on the drawing board or table top. The fate of these drawings and paintings is unknown, but Isabel returned to the subject throughout her career, and a glimpse survives in later watercolours executed in the 1970s. (**193**)

It was impossible to access life models or live animals in the zoo, but the intense conservation of motifs throughout Isabel's career, her tendency to select and concentrate her subject matter with the greatest care, suggests that her adoption of these smaller bodies went beyond expediency. In a time of slaughter and threat, she looked at death directly. Not merely looked; the carcasses continued the trend in her art towards representing things familiar to her touch as well as her eyes. These creatures – sought, collected and laid out – were not the allusions to or metaphors of mortality found in official war art, like Moore's figures sleeping in the Underground stations (the Shelter Drawings; c. 1941); they were closer to the bodies that her friends who were wardens in Air Raid Precautions (ARP) were retrieving from bomb sites – simply there, terrible contradictions of presence in the past tense. They were literally a condensation of the problem she and Giacometti had been exploring before the war, the difference between presence and likeness.

Such still-life subjects gained a new significance for artists during the war. In occupied Paris, Picasso had reduced his *vanitas* scenes to blunt carcasses and skulls.[11] Gruber was painting taxidermy specimens and skeletons similar to those Isabel had studied in the cour de Rohan.[12] In London, Rose Pulham moved on from crumpled paper to eggs (precious luxuries) and, in 1941, began to boil rabbits and a horse's head down to pristine skeletons.[13] Birds had special associations with change, fate and forecastings of trouble. Paul Gallico's best-selling novella of 1940, *The Snow Goose: A Story of Dunkirk*, explored the war through the experience of an outcast painter of birds (based partly on Isabel's Royal Academy colleague, Peter Scott).

Life in the Victorian rectory was a far cry from London or Paris. Superficially genteel yet bound by iron rules, its clandestine activities could not have contrasted more with the setting. The conviviality was a necessary relief from a stringent regime that Delmer maintained for his team and himself. It promoted loyalty, however, and he was envied in other branches for the ingenuity, productivity and watertight security of the unit. Everyone's day ran from 8 a.m. until the early hours of the next morning. One visitor gave an evocative description: '[Delmer was] unceasing ... after dinner, from nine until one or two in the morning, discussions of new projects and new themes were broken only by intervals of listening to his own station or even rival ones ... I have seen him squatting on his vast settee ... reading a paragraph of a talk not once or twice but literally dozens of times muttering crossly to himself ... a worried wrinkle would appear on his large brow, and retrieving at least one of his shoes and giving his braceless trousers a heave, he would stump rapidly out of the room to impart a new brilliant idea to one of his writers.'[14]

'Black' propaganda, a term coined by Delmer himself, signified that, unlike 'white', it masqueraded as material produced by the enemy. The unit's first project was a regular German radio programme called *Gustav Siegfried Eins*, scripted, directed and eventually presented by Delmer. It ran from May 1941 and built up the illusion that its presenter, 'Der Chef', was an old-guard patriot broadcasting inside Germany. Subversive and misleading suggestions took the form of loyal rants against inadequacies in Hitler's hierarchy. In order to be convincing, most of the content had to be truthful, and, to this end, Delmer built up an intelligence network through the armed services, the Foreign Office, the Resistance and personal contacts. The success of the broadcast also relied on vulgarity; since black broadcasts were not admitted as anything to do with Britain, usual censorship and standards did not apply. Scandalous, obscene or violent scenarios condemned by Der Chef were the real hook for listeners – what would today be called 'shock radio'. The programme ceased broadcasting in October 1943 with a fake staging of the Gestapo breaking into the studio and shooting 'Der Chef' live on air.

Other radio stations were launched, even an astrological one providing subversive predictions. As the unit's activities diversified, an extraordinary set of people collected in or passed through the rectory. 'One of my favourite contributors to this amazing flood of details', Isabel recalled, 'was the Don whose lifetime passion was taking branch-line trains all over Germany. He knew the timetables so well he got messages to resistance workers to alter the names written on the sides of carriages so they went to the wrong destinations.' In time, Delmer's intelligence became more nuanced and up to date than that collected by mainstream operations, even the Germans themselves. This made 'grey' broadcasts feasible, which German soldiers and sailors knew were British, but would listen to for music (Delmer was a fan of jazz, deemed 'degenerate' in Germany) and for reliable news of home. Cruelly accurate accounts of British bombing of German towns, specifying streets and even buildings, were collated and reported. The terrible twist was that they were broadcast as though they were unfolding live. This must have been heart-rending for the listeners but impossible to switch off for those with friends or family near the targets.

RAG also produced leaflets, pamphlets, manuals and cards to be distributed by the Resistance. It was not long before Isabel's design skills were called upon, and a more 'interesting and useful' life evolved, perhaps Delmer's plan all along. They posed a completely new set of visual and technical problems, which Isabel summarised as follows: 'They were often dropped by air, which meant that size and weight were carefully controlled. Too much printer's ink could lose several thousand at a drop. They must be eye-catching so that people would be curious and pick them up, also quickly legible. Maps were generally distributed by other methods, slipped inside manuals or officials' papers or girly books, especially those designed to be read by submarine crews.' The discussions about the appropriate point or purpose of art which had become increasingly fraught around the tables of Saint-Germain as Europe descended into conflict, were, for a little while, answered. Here was a 'war art' quite different from that being pursued in the outside world by such as Henry Moore. It was small, secret and, therefore, until recently, unsung. It was, however, an extreme art suited to Isabel's first-principles thinking. It distilled the problem of representation down to two phenomenological questions: what was necessary to get someone to look and what was necessary to make them see? Ink was heavy and every mark had to tell.

Isabel worked on one of the most effective projects, the malingering leaflets – manuals with step-by-step instructions on how to fake ailments – created to damage morale and encourage malingering if not outright desertion among the enemy troops. The first of the malingering leaflets (H270) masqueraded as a booklet of sports rules for the German navy (*Sportvorschriften für die Kriegsmarine*) and was distributed in 5,000 copies by the Free French. The first few pages contained legitimate sports hints and then switched to the subversive text about ways of simulating illness which was written by the German expatriate artist René Halkett. Isabel described her work on the leaflet:

> One of the most tricky problems and one of the most enjoyable was my work on a desertion leaflet. A remarkable Canadian doctor [Dr John McCurdy] came to RAG. He persuaded the inmates to make gashes in their arms or legs

> and then bind certain plants to the wound. After some hours the bandages would be removed and hopefully there would be a rash or a swelling that resembled a disabling disease ... I had to make drawings so accurate that there could be no mistake about the plant. This is difficult with wild plants, especially as they had to be not more when reproduced than about two-and-a-half inches long ... As the printing was not unusually good I found the only way to do this was to make drawings that could be reduced by a third. And that these must not be too near together, otherwise they would blur.[15]

In Walter Benjamin's words, 'The work of art reproduced becomes the work of art designed for reproducibility.'[16]

The instructions for malingering went on to be redesigned and camouflaged in many forms, as tiny cigarette papers, matchbooks, hymn books, phrase books and so on.[17] They were highly successful. Isabel's images, previously interrupted, dispersed and destroyed, were suddenly distributed on a scale of many millions. The German authorities even reprinted them to drop on British troops – with Halkett's text translated into English. (**54**)

Isabel learned about typography as well. Delmer's boss, John Rayner, was an expert in this area. In civilian life he had worked with Delmer on the *Daily Express* and been responsible for its redesign, and on his visits to RAG he taught Isabel about type and layout. Rayner also collected antiquarian books and encouraged Isabel to refine her handwriting by copying Elizabethan manuscripts, a change noticed by Giacometti. This came in useful for one of the less serious items made by the PWE, a menu purporting to have been for a party held by Hermann Göring, head of the German air force. Delmer invented outrageously luxurious dishes, and Isabel made a menu card with a typographical border, which, on closer inspection, revealed a chain of people involved 'in sexual experiments'. It never went into production.

In John Rayner, Isabel found a fellow 'enthusiastic wild-life observer, a great walker'. He was a highly cultured and intelligent man, and, like Rose Pulham, his private school and university education had engendered a love of Classics. Isabel, whose own education in this area had been only what she had taught herself by reading translations, was fascinated. They took to going out together for hikes – once thirty-two miles to Dunstable Downs and back – and, at some point, they became lovers. John's wife and Isabel's friend, Joan, was working abroad in the cipher departments of the British embassies in Madrid, Algiers and Cairo, but when she heard of the affair, she wrote to reassure Isabel that it did not affect their relationships. She would herself soon fall for the dashing soldier and writer Patrick Leigh Fermor, with whom she would remain for sixty years. Isabel may or

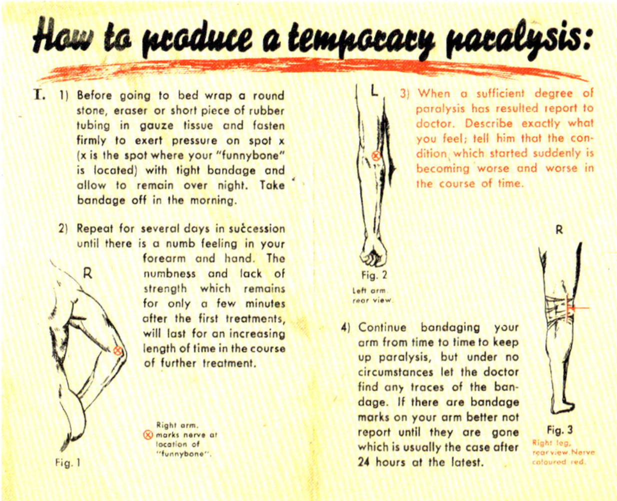

How to produce a temporary paralysis:

I. 1) Before going to bed wrap a round stone, eraser or short piece of rubber tubing in gauze tissue and fasten firmly to exert pressure on spot x (x is the spot where your "funnybone" is located) with tight bandage and allow to remain over night. Take bandage off in the morning.

2) Repeat for several days in succession until there is a numb feeling in your forearm and hand. The numbness and lack of strength which remains for only a few minutes after the first treatments, will last for an increasing length of time in the course of further treatment.

R

Fig. 1

Right arm. ⊗ marks nerve at location of "funnybone".

L

Fig. 2

Left arm rear view

3) When a sufficient degree of paralysis has resulted report to doctor. Describe exactly what you feel; tell him that the condition which started suddenly is becoming worse and worse in the course of time.

4) Continue bandaging your arm from time to time to keep up paralysis, but under no circumstances let the doctor find any traces of the bandage. If there are bandage marks on your arm better not report until they are gone which is usually the case after 24 hours at the latest.

R

Fig. 3

Right leg, rear view. Nerve coloured red.

54. Isabel Rawsthorne with John McCurdy, Malingering Leaflet, 1942, translated from German to English; courtesy Lee Richards Collection

may not have known that, in Geneva, Giacometti, too, had found a companion – an adventurous, twenty-year-old admirer named Annette Arm.

If the relationship brought consolation to Rayner and Isabel during such dark days, it was short lived. It must have been impossible, in their circumstances, to be entirely private, and Delmer and the military hierarchy were less tolerant than Joan. Adultery was considered unpatriotic during the war, undermining morale and the Home Front. Delmer had, moreover, become more important than his superior, so Rayner was sent on operations to Italy.[18] From there he wrote to Isabel constantly – poetic, personal and so-metimes unhappy letters made strange by the necessary discretion and censorship. A page written late in August 1944 was typical: 'Have become very practiced [*sic*] at travelling light, sometimes sleeping under pines, sometimes in shell-shattered palaces, sometimes in HQ bedroom outside which is a baroque Borromini with an owl in it ... As the jeep bounds on I think of the misty hanger and you no doubt think of olive groves and cicadas and the intolerable burden of the midday sun. I believe the brain is said by those who have investigated it to be suspended in the skull by the thinnest film of liquid. In such a bath the whole body passes the day and most of the night.'[19]

When the war was going badly, the inmates of the house came up with an idea that they called 'greeting cards'. These were mass-produced images that had a different kind of use. Instead of instructions and inducements to hurt and damage the body, they were tools of bodily pleasure – pornography. An SOE memo had observed that pornographic images were passed around and kept about the persons of soldiers, and that prisoners of war usually had at least one such picture with them when captured.[20] Isabel was therefore asked to devise 'black leaflets in colour of a highly sexual nature', small enough and erotic enough to be secreted in a pocket or wallet. Hers were very different from those created by Leonard Ingrams's letter-writing unit in 1941 which showed German soldiers coiffing champagne with semi-dressed Parisiennes.[21] The one she felt to be the most effective was 'a picture painstakingly realistic of a foreign worker making love with a bright blonde German girl'. (**53**) The result was described in the SOE memo: 'All the facts portrayed on H316, including the biological ones, are very close to the truth. In order to ensure its automatic circulation, it has been given a definite onanistic value.'

Isabel was aware of the role of erotica and pornography in avant-garde culture, in the work of Balthus, for example, and the writings of D. H. Lawrence, Georges Bataille and Henry Miller. She admired Bataille's surreal story *Histoire de l'œil* (Story of the Eye; 1928) as 'brilliantly original', but did not like Balthus's sexual subjects and dismissed Miller's writing as comically confined by 'Anglo-Saxon attitudes'.[22] The 'greetings card' commissions were an opportunity for her to explore and vary the form. Pornography authored by women was barely known. At the same date, Anaïs Nin was breaking ground in this area, writing with Miller for a private collector in New York, but her stories were not published until the 1970s. In contrast to this, the Resistance distributed thousands of copies of Isabel's images throughout Europe. Joan's lover, Patrick Leigh Fermor, remembered seeing one in Greece and was astonished when he later discovered that Isabel was the artist. Her account of the experience is also interestingly different from Nin's. The writer described her work as unwelcome, a kind of literary prostitution motivated by financial need. Isabel was less oppressed Lucretia and more unashamed Judith. If not exactly the 'patriotic prostitute', as Michel Leiris characterised Judith in *L'Âge d'homme* of 1939, she was philosophical: 'Fancy being employed by the government to create pornography!'[23]

The arrangement of figures in Isabel's 'greeting card', the woman on top of the man, was a standard pornographic pose going back to eighteenth- and nineteenth-century European and Japanese prints. Isabel's use of blue and pink gave her scene a Rococo flavour, reminiscent of Thomas Rowlandson's well-known coloured images (a book of which Isabel owned in later life), such as *Pygmalion and Galatea*, c. 1800.[24] (**55**) H316 employed a similarly dominant placement of the woman above her apparent partner to enhance her accessibility *beneath* the eye of the real partner, who holds the card. The pose provided a view not unlike Jacob Epstein's *Sunita*, which Isabel still owned, or Balthus's *Guitar Lesson* (1934; private collection), which she had observed in his studio in the mid-1930s.

The greetings-card image differed from conventional erotica produced by men for men, however; altered by the artist's female gaze and by the 'black' intent.

55. Thomas Rowlandson, *Pygmalion and Galatea*, c.1800; Victoria and Albert Museum

Isabel varied the conventional orientation by turning the woman's back on her lover. Pornography is characterised by the objectification, separation and framing of individual body parts; for example, it has been remarked that Rowlandson's *Pygmalion and Galatea* gave the male body a wholeness that the superimposed female body lacked – her arms do not join to her shoulders and she has two right hands.[25] Bataille's *Histoire de l'œil* and André Masson's fragmented illustrations for it were extreme examples of this technique, which Isabel knew well. The woman in her image, by contrast, was a continuous form, her body uninterrupted even by a necklace. Instead, it is the man that is reduced to body parts, dramatically dissected by his partner's overlapping shape and the lines of his sweater, socks (a humorous touch?) and the picture's edge. Isabel framed his genitals at the exact centre of the image, separated from the rest of his body, appropriated by the V of the woman's thighs and in the same colours as hers. It is impossible to disconnect the woman's body from her face, her act from her thoughts and will, but his are obscure: his head is turned away.

The 'greetings card' was further modified simultaneously to gratify and undermine. Anyone who found the card would discover its colourful pornographic picture folded within a cover that featured a black-and-white photograph of dead soldiers in a snowy landscape. This bore the first line of a German patriotic song, 'Lieb Vaterland, magst ruhig sein' (Dear fatherland, you may rest assured). Inside, opposite the picture, the song's second line, 'Fest steht und treu die Wacht, die Wacht am Rhein!' (Firm and true stands the watch, the watch on the Rhine!), was parodied, reading instead 'Fest steckt's der Italiano rein' (Firm the Italian sticks it in). A soldier who acquired and wanted to keep the card could have torn off and disposed of the right-hand part bearing these messages, but words on the back of the colour picture, giving statistics on the number of German casualties at the front and numbers of foreign workers in Germany (the implication aimed at race prejudices being that they were taking the soldiers' place) would remain.

The image itself added to the 'black' effect. The enthusiastic and permissive frontality of the woman, her unchallenging sidelong gaze and the overt 'biological details' of her sexual parts, fulfilled the requirement to gratify. They were reinforced by the stereotypical Nordic appearance of the woman favoured and eroticised in racist Nazi art and reminiscent of photographs of Hitler's mistress, Eva Braun.[26] The 'double' character of the picture lay cleverly in its two tonal layers. The woman, bedsheets and whisked-back curtain are 'bright'; but to see the genitals the eye had to decipher a dimmer level executed in browns. There it could not avoid discovering the man's genitals too, the presence of the rival lover, and, off to the side, an equally dark and discomforting male presence, a photograph of Hitler, all in the same hue. The genitals are pointed to by an arrow-shaped shadow running up from the floor, cleverly mimicking the real arrow in the unwelcome caption. The overcoat abandoned in the right-hand corner suggested an opportunistic visit. The absence of an objectifying treatment of the woman's body (Ingrams's greetings cards employed stockings and negligees) and a domestic setting (Ingrams's scenes were set in hotel rooms), made it harder to separate the image of the woman from that of the soldiers' wives and sweethearts.

Isabel made other 'greetings cards', but few details of these have survived. The idea of the postcard itself continued to interest her. It raised issues of the reception of the reproduced image, its repeated 'reactivation', as Benjamin put it, as a portable, physical, personal object. She made a very different, chaste version as a gift to a favourite visitor to House RAG, Father Andraes: 'a tall, willowy Austrian priest who I understood to have been extraordinarily brave. I designed a card for him ... which he took away and said he would make good use of. It was of the Virgin Mary in early Renaissance Style.' This card, a vehicle for prayer, drew on the Madonnas of Van Eyck and Lorenzetti that Isabel loved. Father Andraes was responsible for a religious programme that broadcast to Germans information about the concentration camps. This appalling aspect of the conflict was a vivid motivator at RAG well before the revelations of the Liberation. No one in the house was in any doubt about what was going on, and a shield smuggled out of Germany stating 'Hier sind Juden unerwünscht' hung in the sitting room as a reminder.[27]

In spring 1944, as the day of the Allied invasion of Europe drew nearer, the atmosphere in the intelligence communities grew even more tense. Broadcasting played an important role, and Delmer was one of the very few outside the High

Command and the Cabinet who knew the exact timing of the D-Day landings. Isabel was, like everyone else, in the dark. Four hours' sleep became the norm for all RAG residents, and Delmer himself was woken hourly to authorise the sending-out of information. His memoir characteristically presents this not as the physically punishing ordeal it was (photographs from the time show it took a serious toll on his health), but as a stimulating nightly encounter with his beautiful female courier, who, he said, came to his bedside in motorbike leathers, fresh and damp from the road. In one of his few references to Isabel after 1936, he mentioned that this was when she found herself another bedroom.[28]

During these months, Isabel employed her basic typography skills as the relief editor for *Nachrichten für die Truppe* (News for the Troops), a full-size, daily newspaper produced by RAG from 25 April 1944 to D-Day on 6 June 1944, intended to demoralise and disrupt German troops in advance of the invasion. Like the radio broadcasts, it relied on the fact that most of its content was truer and more up to date than official British or German sources, so that soldiers would read it despite its enemy origin, and some lies could be slipped past. Isabel worked with minimal briefing to an extraordinary split-second schedule. Between 11 p.m. and 3 a.m., she transposed material from RAG's black and grey radio broadcasts into text, edited it and laid it out with photographs and drawn maps, and had it checked and corrected by Delmer. The paper was then printed in editions of up to a million to be distributed at noon by plane and balloon.

The months before D-Day were desperately pressurised. Isabel was, like everyone, mentally and physically exhausted: 'I kept thinking of those airplanes with their engines running, waiting.' It was worse for Delmer. The nature of the duties, dealing with the darkest side of human nature, also took its toll on them both.[29] When there was a lull after the invasion, she and Delmer took forty-eight hours leave to visit the Valley Farm. It was strangely untouched by the war, 'as though we had just gone for a stroll up the hill to fetch some letters.' Isabel's premonition that Delmer's paradise would never be hers was by now evident to them both. She realised she had to remove herself from Delmer and the unit: 'I could not face his way of life for the indefinite future.' Moreover, the Allied landings in Normandy promised peace and the possibility of returning to Giacometti. Isabel went to stay with her mother, who, having had no idea where her daughter had been, was deeply relieved to see her. Her brother, now eighteen, had joined the Fleet Air Arm and was training in Texas. Isabel took a job at the BBC in London. Based at Bush House, her role was the picture editor of *Il Mondo Libero,* a 'white' propaganda magazine supporting the Italian campaign in which Rayner was fighting. She returned to RAG occasionally, but her employment there was over.

56. Isabel Rawsthorne (as picture editor), cover of *Il Mondo Libero*, October 1944

12 IL MONDO LIBERO: 1944–1945

Wartime Isabel – wilful, clever, travelled, with the tastes of a connoisseur, athletic, perfect shot and sexually insouciant – was the kind of woman on whom her colleague Ian Fleming, seven years later, would base the female protagonists of his James Bond books.[1] There were many like her: most were signatories of the Official Secrets Acts and most are now forgotten. Fleming's fictional versions eclipsed them with heroines adapted to post-war codes, ciphers whose sexual and instrumental use to Bond and to Britain was implicit in the later coining of the term 'Bond girl'. They had no plot of their own and were disposed of by the end of the story, if not before.[2] The real world was different. Life went on, and resourceful, unconventional men and women who knew too much were accommodated less easily. Isabel could speak to no one about how she had spent the last three years.

Temporarily, she moved into Rayner's apartment in Palace Gate. He was still in Italy, and she had no intention of sharing her future with him: 'I did not want to marry anyone else at that time. I do not know whether Delmer believed this. I hope so.' Rayner, for his part, was determined to go with SOE to the Far East, where the war was far from over. The reality of being on her own again began to sink in: 'I knew when I left RAG I had also left Delmer. I did not admit this fact to myself immediately ... This did not mean that I forgot the richness and fascination, the gaiety of our life together. As well, there was my gratitude for the way he looked after me and taught me many things.' Isabel was twenty-two when she had thrown in her lot with him, and they had crammed a lifetime's experiences into the decade they had been together. Now she was thirty-two. Her situation must have reawakened memories of her earlier displacement from Hyde Park Gate. The flat was almost in sight of the house, and Jackie, now ten years old, lived there still.

Isabel's autobiographical record of this period reveals behaviour that sounds like depression: 'of these weeks I remember only a weight of misery which nearly crushed me ... I was so desperately unhappy that if it had not been for my gentle work at Bush House I do not know what I would have done'. Her dignity dissolved when she left the office, and she would sit in the bus with tears streaming down her face. Two hard lines appeared on her forehead. She confided in Anna Maclaren, who was also living in Palace Gate, in a 'luxury pad'. Her friend had recently married Rodney Phillips, the publisher of the arts magazine *Polemic*, and was, writing a book about Polish airmen in the RAF.[3] Shocked by the change in Isabel, she advised her to tell someone what was wrong, but this was not Isabel's way of dealing with things. Delmer was unaware of what she was going through; when she bumped into him one day, he quipped, 'You look awful. I don't want to be married to an old woman. A magazine isn't worth it.'

The return to London was also a return to the bombs. During that final year of the war, the raids were shorter and sharper. One visit to Anna's was interrupted by a deafening crack that shook the building. Anna's cry of '"Let's go and have a look!" ... was so characteristic', Isabel wrote, 'that it made me laugh helplessly.' Far more dangerous were the flying bombs: 'These made the most disgusting noise as though a motor-bike were flying through the room you were sitting in ... The trick ... was to know that while the noise was going on you were safe. When it stopped there would be two seconds before it hit. Once I managed to get on the roof and saw one coming over. A curious moment.' Isabel experienced an especially narrow miss at Bush House: the windows were smashed and two people died in the street.

Il Mondo Libero magazine was overseen by Nancy Cunard's cousin Victor, the head of the Italian section of the Information Services, who maintained an atmosphere that was a welcome change from the 'house of exhausted workers' at RAG. Although her duties as picture editor prevented Isabel from painting, she found masking and laying out the photographs an 'enthralling' visual education. The seven issues of *Il Mondo Libero* advertise her ironic eye. Juxtapositions and montages recall the Surrealist journal *Documents* or Amédée Ozenfant's *Art*. They play with allegory and the 'aura' of art, high and low. Bulls, for example, provide a familiar avant-garde motif, simultaneously ancient and modern. They are placed in strangely appropriate juxtapositions with great Italian works of art. (**57**) An anxious, meaty specimen looks over the sacrificial body in Raphael's *Deposition* (1507; Galleria Borghese, Rome), for example, while a pub sign is wafted up on wrought-iron curlicues opposite the same master's *Transfiguration* (1520; Vatican Museum).[4] (**57**)

In her spare time, Isabel walked through a changed city, many buildings open like doll's houses, burned out or ruined. The familiar parks were now cultivated fields and allotments. At least the National Gallery kept up a minimal collection and the shrapnel-pocked Tate Gallery was showing an exhibition of British art, including Pre-Raphaelite canvases with their staring scrutiny of appearance. Isabel drew in the Victoria and Albert Museum, selecting Donatello's *The Ascension with Christ giving the Keys to St Peter* (1428–30).[5] This was a return to the theme of distance and the fifteenth-century saints that she had studied in Paris, but the way Donatello's figures, in the shallowest *relievo schiacciato*, emerge and dissolve

THE BULL

LUNCHEONS & TEAS.

Capolavori della pittura italiana. Raffaello era nel fiore dell'età ed aveva raggiunto la piena maturità artistica quando dipinse la celeberrima "Trasfigurazione" che si può ammirare nella Pinacoteca Vaticana. La fotografia mostra alcuni soldati alleati in ammirazione davanti allo splendido capolavoro. I Musei Vaticani sono stati riaperti al pubblico dopo l'arrivo a Roma delle truppe liberatrici. Essi erano rimasti chiusi per lungo tempo.

24

Osterie e locande in Inghilterra

Clubs and pubs: questi sono i due pilastri della vita sociale in Gran Bretagna. I club sono organizzati con il concetto del riserbo e dell'esclusività: aristocratico o operaio che sia, quando uno va in un club sa già chi incontra o almeno che tipo di gente ci incontra. I «pub» invece rappresentano il principio contrario: si chiamano così, perchè gli inglesi, entusiasti per i monosillabi, abbreviano in tre lettere il nome «public bar», o mescita pubblica. L'italiano che vi entri, memore del modo esuberante con cui osterie toscane o romane s'aprono e si estendono sulla strada, rimane anzitutto colpito da un certo senso di clausura, dovuto alle alte paratie di legno che separano non solamente i bevitori dalla strada, ma anche l'una saletta dall'altra. Una sala è il vero e proprio bar pubblico, un'altra si chiama salone, una terza «privata». In altri tempi, forse, la stratificazione feudale del pubblico rendeva obbligatorio di entrare in una parte o nell'altra, a seconda delle categorie sociali: oggi non c'è nessuno che ti proibisce di andare dove tu voglia. Ciò non toglie però che spontaneamente si finisca dove il modo di vestire, di discorrere e di bere stoni meno con quello di chi sta attorno. La tradizione puritana fa sì che attorno al bere sopravvivano certe formalità, che ne fanno una specie di vizio segreto. Per esempio, nessun inglese si farà mai sorprendere sulla porta chiusa del locale preferito ad aspettare l'ora dell'apertura. Ma quando scocca l'ora in cui il paese cessa di essere proibizionista, paresti signori dignitosi che, facendo le viste di nulla, se ne stavano alla lontana leggendo il giornale, si veggono subitamente marciare con passo spedito alla volta del pub. Un tono tradizionale e pittoresco domina nell'architettura esterna ed interna del pub e specialmente delle locande che si chiamano «inns». Nomi tradizionali come «il toro e il beccaio», «la stemma del Re», «il cigno nero», «la spalla di montone» definiscono ogni osteria. Segretezza e riserbo sono soltanto alla superficie: non c'è posto al mondo dove in verità uno straniero abbia tante possibilità e facilità di concludere amicizie ed affari, quanto sotto le volte di legno o accanto al camino acceso d'una dignitosa e silenziosa osteria di Gran Bretagna.

25

57. Isabel Rawsthorne (as picture editor), 'Pubs of England', *Il Mondo Libero*, November 1944

in touches of shadows caught in the indents of the white marble was reminiscent of the sparing ink strokes of the RAG drawing. The idea of the ascension perhaps appealed as an exploration of the left-behind.

During her forty-eight-hour furloughs from RAG, Isabel had kept some contact with the art world as it survived in London. Rose Pulham and Rosling were still in Chelsea at Chesil Court. He had been serving in the Auxiliary Fire Service based in a barge moored off the Isle of Dogs in East London, but had continued painting and had begun to exhibit.[6] Isabel met his main comrade during the war, the poet Dylan Thomas, who also worked at the BBC. Social life revolved around the insulating warmth, noise and distraction of cinemas and pubs, notably The George near Broadcasting House or gatherings at The Eight Bells by the river, near Rose Pulham's flat. The Eight Bells was the haunt of an aged Augustus John – still holding court and exhibiting a lively eye for Theodora Rosling – and of the travel writer Norman Douglas (one of Nancy Cunard's writing stable), wrapped in his black cape, waspish and waiting impatiently to return to Capri. Dylan Thomas always had paper with him to jot down lines or scribble cartoons, and the companions amused themselves with pictorial games such as *cadavre exquis*, popular with the Surrealists.[7] Some drawings of this kind by Isabel have, remarkably, been preserved.[8] One apparently faraway sun unfolds to reveal

58. Isabel Rawsthorne, comic drawing (Augustus John?) c. 1944; British Library

rotund buttocks.[9] Another opens an egg to release an ecstatic cockerel.[10] The most elaborate emulates Picasso's 'Painter and Model' format, depicting an Augustus John-like figure complete with hat and old-fashioned easel and palette.[11] (**58**) It bears close resemblance to an image of John painting his model in a short, British Pathé film shown in cinemas in 1944 entitled *Picture Personalities: Augustus John*. Isabel changed the model to a more bosomy woman perched on a *chaise longue* and resembling Thomas's wife, Caitlin, whom John had both painted and seduced in her youth. Although executed in only a few lines, the drawing fortifies the artist with a battery of projecting forms – long brushes (stressed in the film), nose, knee and a penis-like foot – while the arms of his anxious target bulge as they press her thighs together.

Isabel, Rose Pulham, Rosling and Dylan and Caitlin Thomas often migrated to Soho to The French House and the decadent Gargoyle Club with its mirrored interior designed by Matisse. Here more artists gathered, and those that had lived on the Continent tended to band together; these included the painters Robert Colquhoun, Robert MacBryde and John Minton and the vivacious Francis Bacon, with whom Rose Pulham had struck up a comradeship.[12] Rosling's memoir of her war years with Rose Pulham, published in 1982, was on Bacon's bookshelf when he died.[13] The critic Cyril Connolly and the wealthy art collector and patron Peter Watson (the sponsor of the London Gallery in Cork Street) had sought to preserve something of the Parisian intellectual climate by setting up an avant-garde literary magazine with a European perspective called *Horizon* (1939–50), no mean feat given the paper shortages and newsprint rationing during the war.[14]

There was also a younger generation, barely in their twenties, including the painters Michael Ayrton, Lucian Freud and John Craxton, the latter two interested in talk of France, which they had not yet experienced. Freud's family had been forced to flee Berlin in 1933. He shared a subject matter with Isabel; encouraged by his teacher, Cedric Morris, he was drawing birds and Soutine's death in Paris on 9 August 1943, while in hiding from the Nazis, may have been the impetus for the first in a series of carcasses, *Dead Bird* (private collection), drawn the same month.[15]

Isabel also knew the poet Louis MacNeice and his new wife, Hedli. Hedli was a stage actor and singer who performed with Dylan Thomas in MacNeice's radio plays. Strangely, she remembered seeing Isabel on her ill-fated last day in London in 1934. Isabel's path had crossed, but not met, MacNeice's in Barcelona during the Spanish Civil War; their outlooks were sympathetic, and she admired his very visual writing. Isabel became godmother to their daughter, Corinna, in 1943.

The relationships made in wartime London, like those in pre-war Paris, would persist throughout the participants' lives. Precariousness and hardship were the substrate for a cultural outlook and heterogeneous set of alliances that were to have spectacular artistic implications in the following years. Yet Isabel's autobiography said nothing of this circle, probably the result of her scrupulous exclusion of anyone still living at the time she was writing, including Bacon and Freud. The coincidence of the ragtag, London-based connections rewards joined-up study.

The artists without an official war position shared a distinct, formative experience. Like Isabel, they were often in covert, harrowing or less recognised occupations. In nearly every case, families, communities and support networks were dispersed. Artworks were destroyed, damaged or lost as a result of explosions, inadequate storage and frequent moves. Materials were impossibly short and studios makeshift compromises, what with the over-demand for intact living accommodation. War work, the difficulties of daily survival and the lack of income eroded time and rendered models a rare luxury. All were cut off from the resources of the Continent and particularly Paris by the Nazi Occupation and the resulting widespread destruction of avant-garde enterprises. These practical difficulties engendered stubbornness and guile. In the mid-1940s, pubs and parties became alternative domestic spaces; a provisional and highly liberal conviviality took the place of disrupted class and family relations. Meagre rations of warmth and food were shared. Rosling remembered 'friendliness, almost a love amongst total strangers ... sexual and social distinctions were swept away'.[16] In the reduced but concentrated cultural sphere, places like The French House and The Swiss pub brought artists together with writers, musicians, servicemen, spies, politicians and racketeers, even the sinister figure of the occultist Aleister Crowley.[17] A network sprang up around the periodicals *Horizon* and *Lilliput* (of which the Austrian-born Mechthild Nawiasky was the picture editor) and the Lefevre Gallery (Robert Colquhoun, Robert MacBryde, Freud and Bacon were launched at the Lefevre between 1943 and 1945).[18] Many, like Isabel, MacNeice and Thomas were connected through the BBC. The George pub in Great Portland Street, 'the glue pot', acted as their unofficial labour exchange. There, clever conversation was leavened and levelled by ironic humour.

Impromptu, often unlikely bonds evolved. In 1942, the writer Peter Quennell passed on an absurdly grand flat in Rossetti House, 72 Flood Street, Chelsea, to Rose Pulham and Rosling, who survived there, with nearly no furniture apart from a bed and easel, by taking in paying tenants.[19] When Rosling left in 1944, Rose Pulham began a relationship with one of his flatmates, Mary Smith, whom he would, to everyone's surprise, marry. Bacon and his childhood nanny, Jessie Lightfoot, made an even stranger family unit in the yet grander bomb-damaged house of the Pre-Raphaelite John Everett Millais at 7 Cromwell Place, South Kensington. They occupied the billiard room and kitchen, where Jessie slept on the table, and augmented the support Bacon gained from his partner, Eric Hall, with illicit gambling parties. Those excluded from the armed forces, such as pacifists, homosexual (sex between men would not be decriminalised until 1967) and foreigners, enriched the artistic scene. Peter Watson supported the partners Colquhoun and MacBryde (the 'two Roberts'), Minton and the Polish painter Jankel Adler in another unorthodox household.[20] A friend from the Ministry of Information, Maitland Pendock, gave Rose Pulham a camera, in the hope he would return to photography. He took nude photographs of Rosling, and in one she sits on a painting by Max Ernst, probably belonging to the writer and collector John Davenport, who later moved into Rossetti House with his second wife, Marjorie (Isabel became a godmother to one of his sons).[21] Mechthild Nawiasky provided Rose Pulham with a small income by publishing the photographs in *Lilliput*, and Pendock repeatedly retrieved the equipment from pawnshops when Rose Pulham exchanged it for money to buy paints.[22] Rose Pulham also took photographs for Bacon of works in his studio that he wanted recorded.[23]

These ad hoc relationships were accelerated by ad hoc intimacies. Confessions, books, rations, rooms and beds were shared with inventive generosity. Friends and acquaintances stayed over with each other rather than brave the blackout. Dylan Thomas was often at Rossetti House, and a profound affection developed between him and 'shabby, humped, elegant Pulham'.[24] Food was more

59. Peter Rose Pulham, *Room with Scaffolding*, 1945; private collection

limited in London than in the country, so communal stews (for which Caitlin Thomas and Robert MacBryde were famous) were concocted and kept going for days, and garlic and herbs were grown on window sills to give their modest, mongrel ingredients a Continental savour.[25] Rosling sewed a set of monk's robes out of blankets which visitors wore to keep warm.[26] Outerwear in turn doubled as bedding: Isabel still had her fur coat, and both Rose Pulham and Dylan Thomas were rarely seen without their trademark outsized overcoats, Thomas's augmented by a pork-pie hat. The bed itself became the not-necessarily-sexual centre of social life, a cosier setting for drinks and chats.[27] Isabel's unorthodox, first-principles life was, for a while, the norm.

As the war drew to a close in 1945, Isabel looked for a way to return to Paris. Patricia (Pattie) Whitney Smith, who had eventually managed to meet the woman who had so fascinated her in the BBC lift two years earlier, secured a Paris posting with the French programme of the BBC, and Isabel followed her lead.[28] She went to see its director, the grand French actor Michel Saint-Denis, and offered to report on French life for the English recovering from the war. Isabel's account of the interview makes a sobering contrast to the anecdotes of chummy recruitments that fill the memoirs of her male contemporaries. Saint-Denis knew of Isabel's familiarity with French culture and language, and of her SOE service, but it was also necessary to convince him that Delmer had no objection to her working. She described the 'immense wave of relief' she felt when she got the job. Immediately, she wrote to Giacometti and Mara Scherbatoff.[29] Pattie Whitney Smith had already left, but her husband, Charles, had to wait on a posting from the Foreign Office, so he and Isabel secured crossings on a boat in May. Isabel and Delmer met and agreed arrangements for a divorce, which could be concluded in two years if she was living in Paris. He offered to provide her with a small income for this period. They both knew she was returning to the artist's life and to Giacometti. In the interim, she took a short holiday in Zennor, on the Cornish coast.[30]

Isabel was able to say goodbye to Rayner in person. The Italian campaign had taken its toll, and his poetic letters to her were descending into Cassandrian incoherence. On reaching Tuscany in February 1945, he sent her a vision of the beautiful Villa I Tatti, lent to him by the art historian Bernard Berenson. The Old Masters there had been removed for safekeeping, but 'a Bonnard, a pilgrimage, and in his studio only one picture other than his own – a Renoir, tiny, naked girl, warming the shivering ancient', adding, 'tell Cyril [Connolly] I went to Auribeau, no food at the Grand Tierre, and the fields still sown with jasmine, strawberries and carnations.'[31] Before he could post the letter, Rayner was wounded and invalided back home, and Isabel visited him in hospital. Like many soldiers, he was anxious about facing her and his old life, calling himself 'the changeling' and the letter took on a lyrical, Cassandrian, incoherence: 'this weary casket-ridden body had had to batter its way ... over shudderingly icy hills, glissade evocative, with hours of introspecting and apprehensions, memories of unkindness to misery, such as to induce an involuntary grinding of the teeth in hateful regret, if the sad always smile at the stupid see you in 3 weeks, of apprehension at whispers, of fateful lunches, of VS2, all mixed with disgust at the changeling, the unavoided selfishness of carapicity wh[ich] honestly has a mental effect, all revolving again in bad dreams in bad strange beds, shivering nights as white as the snow in Nice ... if only a coup foudroyant.'

The couple had a few weeks together before he left for the East. Rayner took her around London introducing her to antiquarian bookshops, and Pattie Whitney Smith recalled seeing her with him in Soho, 'disdainful as ever, very beautiful, very proud'.[32] They visited Tom Driberg, Rayner's fellow journalist at the *Daily Express*, at Bradwell Lodge, his graceful Palladian villa on the Essex coast. On their penultimate evening, Rayner and Isabel went to the ballet. Rayner knew Constant Lambert, who was conducting and who, to Isabel's excitement, invited him for drinks afterwards. Keeping the Vic-Wells Ballet company (renamed the Sadler's Wells Ballet after the war) functioning in wartime had required remorseless endeavour, and the composer was a more jaded celebrity. He was no less energetic and scintillating in his wit, however, and his worsened limp reminded her of Giacometti. She found him 'deeply attractive' and was so nervous that she knocked over a glass. He was not a handsome man, but her susceptibility can be appreciated in the electrifying spectacle of his performing captured on film.[33] Lambert had been separated from his wife, Florence, Isabel's one-time friend, for six years. Flo was enterprisingly making a living as a property developer and was the main carer, with the help of Lambert's mother, for their little boy, Kit, who was eight.[34] Lambert was now lodging with the painter Michael Ayrton in All Souls' Place, next to the BBC's Broadcasting House, and was romantically as well as professionally involved with the prima ballerina Margot Fonteyn – but he told Isabel that he hoped to see her when he went to Paris with the ballet.

Churchill announced Victory in Europe from the balcony of the Ministry of Health in Whitehall on 8 May 1945. Isabel was walking: 'I went to the Mansion House [*sic*] to hear Churchill's declaration. The crowd was quite subdued; the ceremony was quite touching in its simplicity. For one thing, the war in the Far East was still being fought with ferocity. I walked slowly through the parks where there were bonfires burning away and good-humoured crowds circling round. I felt totally alone, desolate. I wandered about for a while.' Isabel's experience is a sobering contradiction to the convention of VE Day as a moment of universal celebration. Unity was not universally felt. Memories of those whose lives had been depleted or lost were sharpened, as were fears for those, like Rayner, who would be fighting on in the East for months to come. The first reports of the concentration camps were emerging. Few relationships had survived the worry, exhaustion, separations and changes of war unaltered. For many, women especially and Isabel certainly, the future was obscure: 'a large hole; once inside what would one find?' Her fond parting from Rayner was painful: 'time to go and time for tears ... I suffered more than he did.' Her recollection of boarding the boat to France a week later expressed her otherness with a new accent, a sense of immense distance and of being without place: 'As the ship drew slowly away from the quay I looked down upon a large eel curving its way beside us. Amazing creature born in the Sargasso Sea, now here.'[35]

60. 61. Isabel Rawsthorne, *La Tour-de-Salvagny I* and *II*, 1946; private collection

13 HOW TO LIVE? 1945–1946

Doctor Foster went to Gloucester,
In a shower of rain.
He stepped in a puddle
Right up to his middle,
And never went there again!

Traditional

After the war, artists' reconstructed lives did not necessarily bring well-being. Work that had been lost could not be replaced, and personalities and perceptions were permanently changed. Within twenty years, a third of Isabel's group would be dead from health and addiction problems – slower, but similar odds, to flying a Second World War bomber. Established artists like Epstein and those, such as Paul Nash, Henry Moore and Graham Sutherland, employed by Kenneth Clark's War Artists Advisory Committee, surfaced with strengthened reputations. Returning servicemen benefited from the standing their time in the forces gave them and also from government schemes for reintegration. A twenty-year-old Eduardo Paolozzi passed from the Air Force into art school in 1943, for instance, and Isabel's brother's service in the Fleet Air Arm provided a funded place to study for a Bachelor of Science majoring in Zoology at the University of Liverpool. Women and those excluded from the forces, because of their sexuality for example, were less likely to have accumulated status or privileges. Many were left with careers filleted of five crucial years; for Isabel, it was ten, a gap she felt ever after.[1] Those who had signed the Official Secrets Act suffered a further apparently blank period in their life. Few knew of Isabel's solitary, courageous work before the war, or her resourceful years at RAG. In its place was the vague impression that she had, as Lord put it, 'whiled away the war'.[2] Having entered the conflict in her twenties, Isabel emerged in her thirties nameless, again.

None of this altered Isabel's focus. She is the first recorded artist not travelling with the forces to get back to Paris, sailing in May 1945, well before others from London, New York and elsewhere began to return the following spring.[3] She took no luggage other than a small bag of clothes. Her few belongings had been left behind in the abandoned studios, the hasty flight from Paris and the German advance, the bombed flat in Lincoln's Inn and her abrupt departures from RAG and the Valley Farm. She had Giacometti's letters, however, carried with her through everything. It was too soon for him to have received the note she had written in February, but he had heard news of her voyage from his brother Diego in Paris, who had spoken to Mara Scherbatoff.[4] He wrote from Geneva of his impatience to see her, but, to his anguish, was unable to leave before he had finished *La Femme au chariot*. Completion evaded him for months.

Scherbatoff, herself, was no longer in Paris either. *Paris Match* had sent her to the United States as a correspondent, and she would soon head its New York office.[5] She had left behind a notebook for her friend, however: 'all during the German occupation she was in Paris and kept a diary dedicated to and for me,' Isabel wrote. The war correspondent Alan Moorehead saw it among Scherbatoff's belongings and read part of it; then it disappeared: 'a great blow to me, but no surprise'. Isabel received an emotional welcome from the proprietor of the Hôtel Saint-Romain and persuaded the French commandant who had requisitioned the hotel for the army to let her have a room there, instead of her BBC accommodation in Montmartre. The proprietor refused to allow her to pay.

Isabel called on Balthus, wondering, perhaps, if his studio was available. He was away, but returned two days later, tracking her down by getting Scherbatoff's telephone number in America from Diego. He wrote to his wife, Antoinette, who had remained in Geneva: 'Friday morning I phoned the St Romain (commandeered by the army like all the hotels). Isabel's voice.'[6] He was clearly moved to hear her after so long. They met immediately, and the letter continues: 'She hasn't changed and the talk starts as sparkling as ever. She connects to everything so naturally, as if we had just left the day before. She works on the radio, in fact her plans are not settled, but she is absolutely determined to stay here. It follows that you'll come too, of course. She is beautiful.'

Sadly, the cour de Rohan studio was occupied; it had been let to Georges Bataille. Although Isabel had nowhere to work, she stayed away from Montparnasse. The Left Bank/Right Bank demarcation retained its significance, and she had the feeling that to cross 'was too dangerous an act, that I would walk out of this job'. She withdrew to her 'tiny eyrie' on the top floor of the hotel and returned to reading and writing at the Café de la Régence. Rationing was still strict, and everything was expensive, so Isabel traded Lucky Strike cigarettes on the black market for necessities. She was warned not to walk out alone after dark, but took no notice, resuming her midnight strolls, using, as a precaution, the skin wallet that Delmer had bought her on the eve of her flight five years before.

Her radio work felt trivial after RAG: 'We were aware that our audience was probably one person in Cornwall, one in N Wales and a mad ham in the Channel.' She enjoyed composing her scripts – some, on French art, were published (untraced) – but she found interviewing difficult. She reviewed films and exhibitions and the new arrangements of pictures rehung in the Louvre, as well as 'couture and French attitudes to the importance of clothes in French life [and] indulged in nasty remarks about the English dress sense'. Early in 1945, Constant Lambert's Vic-Wells Ballet heralded the end of hostilities with ENSA performances of *Miracle in the Gorbals*, *Hamlet* and others at the Théâtre des Champs-Elysées, and Isabel went to see Laurence Olivier's electrifying *Richard III*, brought to the Comédie-Française by the Old Vic, the first foreign company to perform at the theatre, which received a shocked and 'ecstatic welcome'.[7] Michel Carné and Jacques Prévert's masterpiece, *Les Enfants du paradis*, filmed during the Occupation, was on release.[8] Its central character, the glad, godless actress Garance, who imitates a sculpture for a living, could have been based on Isabel. Sad, adrift but 'gay as a lark ... the most alive of us all', she was famous for her laugh, and the film showed her always imperiously walking, arriving and departing, determined to love and live on her own terms.[9] Prévert's theme of the interrelationship between authenticity in art and authenticity in existence quickly took on talismanic significance for Isabel and many others.

Paris was relatively undamaged but run-down and strange without its throngs of foreigners, other than the American soldiers waiting to go home. Artists who had evaded collaboration were being celebrated or rehabilitated. In July, a state funeral was held for Paul Valéry. Resistance fighters were heroised, and Scherbatoff was one of those awarded the Légion d'honneur by Charles de Gaulle, now Prime Minister. But it was also the time of the *épuration*, the purges of collaborators after the Occupation. 'All sorts of tales were told, many were invented for political purposes, I suspect,' Isabel wrote. The newspapers were full of accusations and reprisals. These and the cinemas were a reminder that the war continued. The newsreels broadcast revelations from concentration camps, and, throughout May, survivors of the camps arrived back in France, bringing joy at their return and grief for their ordeals and for the horrifying fates of those who had not survived. In August, the semblance of cooperation between the Allied West and the USSR faltered. A week later, reports arrived of the atomic bombings of Hiroshima and Nagasaki on an incomprehensible scale. For Isabel's generation, born on the cusp of the First World War, this third, 'Cold', war confirmed the modern age as fundamentally aggressive and absurd.[10]

Later in the year, Rose Pulham brought his new wife, Mary, to the Hôtel Bisson.[11] At the radio station, Isabel got to know Pattie Whitney Smith. The younger woman had tearfully come to conclusion that Isabel had seduced her husband, Charles, during their crossing on the same boat, but was assured otherwise, and, by the end of the summer, the couple had joined Isabel at the Hôtel Saint-Romain.[12]

It was through Pattie and Charles that Isabel met the philosopher A. J. Ayer. He, too, had been in the SOE and, with Bertrand Russell, ran the journal *Polemic*, published by Anna Maclaren's husband, Rodney Phillips. Ayer was attached to the British Embassy, living in a swanky borrowed house in the avenue Foch, 'doing a lot of entertaining'.[13] He and Isabel became immediate friends. 'Ayer had a great gift for enjoyment,' she wrote, 'he was fond of food, gregarious and, above all, he loved conversation.' Their discussions must have been singular. Isabel admired the scrupulous materialism of his book *Language, Truth and Logic* (1936); Ayer, for his part, spoke perfect French and had an informed and opinionated love of the arts. He wrote for *Horizon* and had literary connections: Albert Camus and George Orwell attended his parties. He was also an enthusiast for French cinema, and Isabel lent him books on Georges Méliès and dragged him to out-of-the-way showings of films written by Jacques Prévert, such as *Le Crime de Monsieur Lange* (1936).[14] She took her friend further afield, including a culinary and architectural tour of Blois, where she was sad to see the bridge had been destroyed.[15] As Isabel and Ayer matched each other for verve and, by all accounts, sexual charisma, it seems unlikely that they weren't lovers. In July, he took up a Fellowship at Oxford, but often returned in the vacations.

Isabel's instincts about the temptations to leave her secure employment on the Right Bank were correct. One summer afternoon she delivered a script to her radio station ready to be read that evening and went for a drink at Fouquet on the Champs-Elysées. There she heard someone say that Giacometti was expected back and took one of her forthright decisions: 'I crossed the river and never went back to my job again.'[16] Giacometti was not yet, in fact, in Paris, but, once on the Left Bank, she went to see the others that remained of the old circle. Many were still abroad, but Diego Giacometti and Francis Gruber had never left their respective studios off the rue d'Alésia, and Picasso had stayed in the rue des Grands-Augustins. At the height of anti-Semitism in Paris, Gruber had married a Jewess, Georges Bernstein, a courageous act on both their parts, but they had survived the war un-denounced, and he and Paul Éluard had, like Scherbatoff, become prominent figures in the Resistance. Gruber's sober studio figures had received belated praise at the first Salon of the Liberation in October 1944. His triumph was an emaciated, naked *Job* (1944; Tate, London), a poignant anachronism summoning images of the detention camps.[17]

Lack of money, food and intense cold in the winters had taken their toll on Isabel's friends. 'Gradually I began to sense the awful heritage of the Occupation,' she wrote. Gruber had contracted tuberculosis, and his health was deteriorating. Bataille was hard up, and illness had caused him to retire from his archivist post at the Bibliothèque nationale.[18] Balthus was back and relying on the hospitality of a benefactor.[19] Isabel learned that Antoinette had taken a wealthy American lover and remained with their two children in their Villa Diodati in Geneva (once occupied by Lord Byron). Tristan Tzara and Pierre Tal-Coat had returned from the south, where they had managed to avoid deportation. Isabel was sad to see Tzara looking weaker and older: although his prized collection of *objets d'art* and first editions had survived the Occupation, 'he seemed no longer much interested in anything'. Derain was the most altered. Initially, he did not recognise Isabel; when he did, ever the gentleman, he came slowly forward with outstretched hand, but with a dispirited greeting: 'We might never see each other again.' He had been co-opted into a trip to Germany early in the war, but lived in poverty through the Occupation. His Jewish model, Sonia Mosse, had perished in a camp. When the new French government had accused him of collaboration, he had angrily broken contact with the Establishment, and Gruber, Balthus and Isabel made some enemies by continuing their friendship with him.[20] He was painting dark still lifes, such as *Nature morte sur fond noir* (1945; Musée d'art moderne, Troyes), which reduced his trademark glimmering glass into quicksilver notations in black air.

Isabel and Balthus went to tea with Nancy Cunard. Isabel was interested that she, for one, had retained her affluent beauty, 'unique … an allure enhanced by her extraordinary clothes'. They also went together to see Picasso and they found him, as they had in 1937, 'standing nearly naked in a small patch of sunlight coming through the window, with two Spanish friends'.[21] He and Dora had parted. His greeting to Isabel surprised her: '"I have something to show you." He went to the next room and came back with three paintings, turned them round and, fancy, myself.' This was the first Isabel knew that 'He had, indeed, when he made that remark to Giacometti – "I know how to do it" – gone away to prove it'. She was so astonished that, although she knew Picasso would have given her one of the pictures, she did not ask.

Giacometti wrote, but still did not appear; his letters concentrated almost obsessively on reaching Isabel, but in the form of the sculpture more than the person. Cyril Connolly passed through Geneva, bringing news of Isabel when he visited Giacometti to ask him to contribute to *Horizon*.[22] He arrived eventually on 18 September 1945. 'We met in a bar in the evening,' Isabel wrote, 'The bar was dark and we could hardly see each other. I seem to remember we talked with pauses, said little. I think we were both exhausted. I went to the studio the next day. All seemed as usual.' They were reunited, but the distance between them seems to have remained undiminished. Although Isabel's autobiography makes no attempt to conceal her love affair with Giacometti, at this point, when they were finally together, it falls silent, as do the accounts of his biographers. Isabel stated it simply: 'Giacometti continued as he had while in Switzerland.'

Commentators interpret this as an anti-climax of a romantic kind. James Lord suggested that this was because 'the sheen had already gone from her beauty, five years of hard drinking had made her face puffy' – a speculation not borne out by Balthus's record of the impression Isabel made at their reunion – while characterising Giacometti's neglect of his appearance as, in contrast, his 'propensity', resulting in a lined face and a new sexual confidence.[23] Isabel's more terse summary foregrounds work. She and Giacometti met and faced each other that autumn not just as lovers, but as artists, 'exhausted' and with little to show for the five years that had passed. She was thirty-three, he was forty-four; neither had exhibited anything new for a decade or accumulated anything like enough work to remedy this. Despite Giacometti's frantic efforts to complete *La Femme au chariot*, it remained in obscurity in Majola, and the finished pieces he brought back fitted in a few matchboxes. It would be another two and a half years before they confidently placed their discoveries before the public in separate solo shows.

In the following weeks, Giacometti worked with furious focus, making the most of Isabel's and Diego's presence. It was late in the year and cold. The drawing *Nu dans l'atelier*, 1945, (**62**) showed Isabel before the stove, a Cézanne-esque format favoured by Gruber. Her hair is in the style worn by Vivien Leigh in the film *Caesar and Cleopatra* of that year.[24] The image lacks the direct address of the pre-war sculptures, and the stove structure frames the body in a way similar to the trolley of *La Femme au chariot* or the scaffold of *L'Objet invisible* of 1934.[25] Like *La Femme au chariot*, the image interpreted Isabel into allegory. Her habitual attitudes, walking or flung exhausted or inviting on a bed, were replaced by a pose like that of the central figures in Botticelli's *Birth of Venus* (c. 1485; Uffizi, Florence) and *Primavera* (c. 1482; Uffizi, Florence), favourites of both Isabel and Giacometti.[26] The iconography of arrival and marriage of the Renaissance paintings was a peaceful antidote to the sacrificial, military entrance of Cassandra on her chariot, an appropriate celebration of their reunion and also, perhaps, an affectionate reference to the Hôtel Primavera, where the couple now slept. However, Isabel's vivacity was lost in these allusions. Her face is empty, and her limbs curve inwards with no characteristic vectored momentum. When Giacometti looked back at this period, he remembered: 'You start by seeing the person posing for you, but then gradually all the possible sculptures come between you.'[27]

Money was short, and they kept away from Saint-Germain. Most evenings were spent with Diego, Gruber and Tal-Coat at a local restaurant called 'L'Italien', where they ate heaps of cheap pasta and Gruber argued with Tal-Coat about the modernity of Cézanne, while Giacometti and Diego chatted to the waiters in their native Romanche. Giacometti introduced Isabel to others who had endured the Occupation: Georges Bataille and Michel and Louise (Zette) Leiris. Zette still

62. Alberto Giacometti, *Nu dans l'atelier*, pencil, 1945; Centre Georges Pompidou, Paris

ran Kahnweiler's art business and Michel was in charge of the African section of the Musée de l'homme. Isabel thought he 'had a head that looked as though it was made out of wood. I often thought how well it looked among the splendid African sculptures.' She already knew his work in *Documents*, of course, and his autobiographical study *L'Âge d'homme*: 'His style of writing is dense, requires a great deal of attention, is not typically French.' She had found *L'Afrique fantôme*, his account of a journey through Africa in 1931–3, 'enchanting'.

Isabel's need to work was no less urgent than Giacometti's, but he did not encourage her. Their careers and finances were fragile, work permits were hard to come by, and he criticised her for leaving her job at the radio. Balthus had regained the cour de Rohan studio from Bataille, and Diego had kept rue d'Alésia unaltered for Giacometti, but the materials and works Isabel had left in Paris were scattered, and she was still without a space. She went to the nearby Académie de la Grande Chaumière as she had before the war, and looked for studio employment, fabric design or illustration – in which she now had experience – but the market was depressed and nothing was available. Germaine Richier, the Swiss sculptor and acquaintance of Giacometti, and her husband, the sculptor Otto Bänninger, had sustained Richier's practice in Geneva and returned to her Paris rooms after the war. Where their partnership brought Richier a 'release from bourgeois life', as she put it, Isabel was, in her own words, 'being stifled by Giacometti's personality'.[28]

The realization of this faced her with a choice that was unbearably cruel, to give up her long-cherished life with him or to give up art. She prevaricated, escaping into a separate social whirl. The image she used for this unreality was a cinematic one: 'a screen between time now and time in the future'.

During this period, Isabel got into the habit of crossing back to the Right Bank to see Ayer and the Whitney Smiths. At one of Pattie's British Council parties she met the avant-garde composers Elisabeth Lutyens and Humphrey Searle and discovered that they had friends in common: Hedli MacNeice and Constant Lambert. Searle had spent the war teaching the art of killing without weapons, and Isabel was fascinated by the discontinuity between his pre- and post-victory professions. Isabel quickly came to admire Lutyens and her down-to-earth, 'funny and endearing manner'.[29] With them, Isabel also encountered the Polish composer René Leibowitz, a student of Maurice Ravel and Anton Webern, and went to hear his arrangement of Bach's *St Matthew Passion* in the Church of Saint-Sulpice. It had the embodied quality she was after in her painting, 'the absolutely regular tempo throughout seemed to follow the human heart beat'. In opposition to these cultural heights were unpredictable evenings with Pattie and Charles Whitney Smith. When drunk, Charles insisted on going to dives in Les Halles. Pattie was weary of this and, if Ayer was not around to accompany him, Isabel took his place. On one occasion, she found herself locked in a brothel and decided to beat the door: 'A most unpopular act. The management, swearing, let me out and threatened to throw out Charles as well. He managed to catch up with me before I reached the hotel.' Pattie recalled that on their return they would all have a nightcap in her bedroom, 'the occasion being a festive one, which festive atmosphere Isabel always seemed to bring'.[30]

At this point in her life, Isabel wrote something strange in her autobiography: 'By this time I realised that my life was becoming absurd, enjoyable.' This statement was followed by two poems: the nursery rhyme 'Doctor Foster went to Gloucester' and Apollinaire's 'La Carpe' (The Carp).[31] The watery context of both poems evokes an imagery of inundation frequently used after the war. The word *absurde* was, at that time, an Existentialist term for the irrationality of existence, current in the writings of Albert Camus, Jean-Paul Sartre and Simone de Beauvoir. (**63**) Their writings linked 'real choices in the real world' without God or design, 'with all the absurdity of contingent life'.[32] The note of self-criticism in Isabel's sentence most closely echoed Camus. He, like Giacometti, did not accept Sartre's absolute pessimism, understanding absurdity, rather, as a failure of the individual to bring meaning to their world.[33] Camus had encapsulated his ideas in *Le Mythe de Sisyphe: Essai sur l'absurde*, published under Occupation in 1942. The story held a very clear significance for Isabel, and for many others who had experienced

63. Jean-Paul Sartre and Simone de Beauvoir, Paris, c. 1946

the conflict. Sisyphus confronted Death and held him captive, and was punished with an eternity of rolling a rock up a hill, only to have it roll down again. Camus concluded, however, that Sisyphus was happy; that personal meaning could be created out of even absurd endeavour. In this light, the existential point of Isabel's two poems, which reflect the movement's respect for the vernacular 'spoken tongue', is clear. 'Doctor Foster' provided a narrative of inundation and survival; 'The Carp' suggested swimming, sustaining, in the face of death.

The spread of Existentialism into mainstream culture was a symptom of the real need to redefine life and lifestyles after 'History in its most terrible form', as de Beauvoir put it.[34] Isabel's rejection of higher powers and her fierce commitment to the inquisitive, self-invented life were now part of a general ideal, as was her understanding of the interrelatedness of art and life. She and Giacometti were almost certainly squeezed into the audience at Club Maintenant to hear Sartre's historic lecture 'L'Existentialisme est un humanisme' on 29 October 1945 in which he asserted, 'You are nothing else but what you live.'[35] The famous aphorism attributed to Sartre, 'Everything has been figured out except *how to live*' (author's emphasis) reprised Isabel's repeated return to this phrase and this question. 'Man is condemned to be free', he said, 'there is no reality except in action.' 'Authenticity' was lived out through ... ' every creative endeavour not excluding relationships, sexual activity and day-to-day dress and behaviour. Isabel had explored the potential of all of these. The existential paradigm became the writer or artist, engaged with, but not fully compromised by, an imperfect society. Figures such as Vincent van Gogh were adopted as exemplars, but the real heroes were more recent: 'We were never so free as under the German occupation ... ,' wrote Sartre, 'each word became as precious as a declaration of principle.'[36]

Isabel knew Camus through Ayer and was familiar with the writings of Sartre and de Beauvoir. She admired de Beauvoir's work (except for her play, *Les Bouches inutiles*, which Isabel saw at the Théâtre des Bouffes du Nord in October 1945), and they knew each other by sight from the Café de Flore, but when Isabel joined Giacometti and the couple for lunch, the relationship did not blossom: 'I found it quite impossible to talk to her. Not that this mattered as she never ceased talking herself.' Isabel was intrigued by Sartre and de Beauvoir's self-invented relationship, an 'open' arrangement that incorporated other lovers. Given their propensity to talk without listening, she wondered how they managed to communicate: 'Perhaps by letter. It was interesting that they never tutoyed, if such a word can exist, each other in public. Nor did they live in the same house.' Isabel knew better than anyone that the theory of authentic relationships was easier than the practice.

On Christmas Day 1945 – never an auspicious festival for Isabel – she went to a party with Giacometti and left with René Leibowitz, and, shortly afterwards, she and the composer fled to Marseilles.[37] They stayed with a friend of Isabel, Edward Ashcroft, the press attaché at the British Consulate (and the brother of the actress Peggy Ashcroft). They also went to Lyon to stay with Jean Wahl, a professor of philosophy at the Sorbonne.[38] A telegram to Tzara, for whose forthcoming play, *La Fuite* (The Flight), René Leibowitz was composing music, read: 'Ma fuite annule la vôtre' (My flight cancels yours).[39] By February, they had returned to Paris and moved in together to 16 rue Condé, obtained from Georges Bataille, who was relocating to the country.

According to Biddy Noakes, Isabel told her that René Leibowitz was the first and only man with whom she was smitten beyond her control.[40] Yet her autobiography summarises all these events and their life together in a single sentence: 'I became infatuated with an attractive and weak man ... we had little in common except our love of music.' In the margin of the manuscript, Pattie Whitney Smith reminded Isabel of Leibowitz's humour and his love of literature. The couple had little money, but friends loaned furniture and, importantly, the flat was big enough to provide space to paint.[41] Pattie Whitney Smith stayed with them for the first few weeks, as her husband, Charles, had moved to Lyons, and described a merry relationship into which Isabel threw herself completely: 'we always seemed to be laughing ... we sang a little Mozart, read Dylan Thomas'.[42] Isabel admired Leibowitz's intellect. He was at the centre of European left-wing intelligentsia with connections to the Frankfurt School (with which Walter Benjamin had been associated) as well as to the Paris and London avant-gardes. The rue Condé flat was a few doors away from the headquarters of the journal *Les Temps modernes* (named after Charlie Chaplin's film of 1936, *Modern Times*) which Sartre had launched in October 1945. Like *Horizon,* it crossed disciplines, and Leibowitz contributed music essays.[43] He wrote also for Ayer's journal *Polemic*.[44] He was promoting the ideas of Arnold Schoenberg which overthrew the set divisions between notes that had been accepted for centuries; the most promising of his group of students at the time (which Isabel christened 'the queue') was a young Pierre Boulez.[45] Elisabeth Lutyens and Humphrey Searle were pioneering the same ideas in England, and Isabel came to know them better.[46] Some of Isabel's correspondence was on *Les Temps modernes* letter paper, and the telephone number of the journal was in her diary. Given her design and typographical skills she may have had direct as well as indirect involvement.[47]

Leibowitz and Isabel dined with Picasso at the rue des Grands-Augustins or with Sartre's circle at Café de Flore, and Pattie Whitney Smith recalled many intellectual debates. There were also concerts, parties and dancing to jazz or bebop at the Bar Vert or Le Tabou, 'which had Sartrean blessings'.[48] By 1946, Existentialism had caught on internationally (partly as a result of an article in *Life* magazine[49]), and their notoriety was such that the members of the Existential circle could be mischievously caricatured in a contemporary paper: 'The Existentialists ... meet from ten to midnight at the Bar Vert, rue Epstein, where they carve existentialist graffiti in the water closets and telephone booths ... no obscenities, no hearts and arrows, but grave thoughts, which ponder on the void, the tomb, suicide and bikini atoll ... Man – that animal that sings the Marseillaise, if you don't feel too good, get yourself felt by an Other.'[50] Isabel's loose hair and practical black were becoming the Existential 'look', glamorised by the new 'It girl' on the Left Bank scene, with a voice rougher than Isabel's, Juliette Gréco.

In April 1946, Isabel made, with Leibowitz, the first of several visits to Georges Bataille and his current partner, Diane, in the medieval town of Vézelay.[51] Leibowitz borrowed money. The landscape was more to Isabel's liking than the pretty countryside nearer to Paris: 'hilly, enclosed, silent, almost dead – a peculiar kind of rather sinister brooding atmosphere hangs over the hills. / Very hot in summer, often snow in winter. A strong feeling of having once been an important historical place.'[52] They also travelled to see Peter and Mary Rose Pulham, who were living modestly in Conives, deep in the rural interior of France, the Indre. Long into later life, Isabel found herself dreaming of cooking fresh sardines and a duck on a spit in the Rose Pulhams' upstairs kitchen and drinking pre-war burgundy, Pouilly-Fuissé and Gevrey-Chambertin.[53]

More of the London circle came to Paris. Francis Bacon had made his first major sale, *Painting 1946*, to Erica Brausen, still a dealer at the Redfern Gallery in London, and passed through Paris on his way to live off the proceeds in Monte Carlo.[54] Ayer was often about, but he did not like Leibowitz. Years later, a sentence in his memoir made short work of his rival: 'Until I met René Leibowitz, I knew nothing about the theory of atonal music, though I must have listened to a good deal of it without identifying it as such.'[55] Rose Pulham felt similarly.

In June, Leibowitz and Isabel stayed for ten days with Pattie and Charles Whitney Smith at their new home at La Tour-de-Salvagny near Lyons.[56] Pattie recalled cycle rides and drinking Beaujolais nouveau, Leibowitz playing for them or making up ribald songs such as 'Izzie keeps eye on ball'. Isabel sketched expansive landscapes, which she gave to Pattie. It is an indication that all was not well, however, that her recollections were different from her friend's, and were sinister and surreal 'vignettes':

> We had a good evening. René played jazz on the piano. Then he and Pattie went to bed. Charles and myself, having drunk far too much, went wandering about. Charles had a gun and said he would shoot Pattie. I fell asleep in a field. The first thing I saw when I woke up was an approaching tractor. They had a maid who, I think was Polish, who had a funny little boy who kept saying, 'la bébète fout le camps.' In English, I suppose, 'the beastie has fucked off.' It was here that I saw my first plague of locusts. They arrive every three years. On this occasion they stripped completely a plum tree in a couple of hours.

This imagery of violence, plague, displacement and loss of innocence was a reappearance, out of context, of the imagery of war. Similarly, of her life in Paris, Isabel did not recall the dancing at Le Tabou, only the residents of the street emptying buckets of water on the heads of revellers, 'a subject from Hogarth'. Throughout 1946, she felt adrift, always moving from place to place, as in her childhood. Bitterly, she annotated this section of her autobiography '*in media de nostra vita si trovai un nella Oscura*', 'in the middle of my life, I found myself in the dark', a paraphrase of the first lines of Dante Alighieri's *Divine Comedy*.[57]

Contrary to most accounts, Isabel continued to see Giacometti. 'Attraction still apparent', Pattie Whitney Smith later wrote, noting that they continued to meet irrespective of others in their lives.[58] James Lord's story that Giacometti and

Isabel's association ended on Christmas Day 1945 was a sensational narrative that complemented those of the car accident in 1938 and the night of crisis in 1940, but does not accord with the facts. After ten years of shared affections and ambitions they cannot have failed to understand each other's needs and actions. Isabel still appeared in Giacometti's paintings, drawings and sculpture after this date – the emaciated, naked *Standing Figure* (1946; Sainsbury Centre for the Visual Arts, Norwich), for example – and their correspondence continued to his death. To assume that Giacometti returned to making these images exclusively from memory instead of from life, or by the highly productive system of alternating between the two that he had evolved since returning to Paris, is to go against most interpretations of his art during this period as an existential and empirical engagement with the real.

Further evidence that the friendship remained can be found in Giacometti's, Isabel's and Ayer's respective records of visiting the Sphinx brothel together, in anticipation of its imminent closure, one evening in April 1946, only four months after her departure the previous Christmas. The evening was made memorable by a raid, during which Isabel's 'sensible education' proved itself again. 'There was a noise of shouting and banging,' she recalled:

> The door opened and immediately the barmen dropped to the floor behind the counter. The girls disappeared, the few people at the tables got up. Two or three men stood in the doorway, shouting something. Freddie's reaction was immediate. He rose very deliberately from the table and walked towards the men in the door, and very slowly pushed them aside. One of them caught hold of his tie, and wrenched round his neck. He stood there quite still and stared at them. He then called to me, saying 'we'd better go.' So I went to the door, he took my arm and quite slowly we walked out. This air of determination and authority I am sure took the men by surprise. There were many gangs roving around the streets at night, many deserters and black marketeers. As we walked away we heard shouts and car brakes screeching. Freddie was a small man and slim. This night he looked smaller than usual.[59]

A few days later the brothel shut, together with 180 others, outlawed by the communist authorities as bourgeois institutions. Isabel felt it was a mistake to remove 'such a well-conducted, civilised place!'.[60] Giacometti expressed similar regret in an essay published at the end of 1946, 'Le Rêve, le Sphinx et la mort de T'.[61] It was different from the accounts of Isabel and Ayer – a consummate blend of autobiographical experience, dream and invention written across shifting time frames. At least one episode refracted his relationship with Isabel. It described being in bed with a laughing 'amie', who is curious to see the symptom of the venereal disease that the narrator has contracted as a result of the brothel's closure.[62] The girlfriend could have been another, but, in Giacometti's economical prose, the laugh, inquisitiveness and sexual directness encapsulate Isabel exactly. In 1946, the first exhibition of Giacometti's images of Isabel took place. Sculptures and sketches appeared at Pierre Loeb's gallery in May, but the figures were too tiny to make an impact, and it did not improve Giacometti's financial situation (Balthus's show later, in November, his first in Paris since 1934, was even less successful and barely attended).[63] In June, Giacometti joined Gruber at the Galeries Lafayette for the second exhibition of the Salon de Mai, an association of artists opposed to Nazi ideology which had formed in 1943 and had had its first exhibition in 1945. He included an *Isabel couché* (1940; whereabouts unknown).[64] Isabel, meanwhile, was finally able to work in the rue de Condé apartment. She wrote to Peter and Mary Rose Pulham: '[I] know more or less what I want to do. I have been working here on the extremely cursory [landscape] sketches I made, trying to work also from memory (v interesting). Simultaneously I have been struggling with the skeleton of a starling never been in such difficulty or felt so incapable, or made such a mess, but I feel all the same I have for the first time, learned something of what I could do.'[65]

A brief visit from Stanley Hayter brought new stimulation. He had spent most of the war building a successful Atelier 17 in New York and returned in June 1946 to re-establish it in Paris. He found the original space at 17 rue Campagne-Première dilapidated and denuded of plates and equipment, and it is generally assumed he did not revive the workshop until he moved back to France permanently in 1950. However, a letter from Isabel to Rose Pulham, written in July 1946, records that she intended to study etching with Hayter, and it is known that he set up printing facilities for his old teacher and partner Joseph Hecht, who was exhausted by a war spent in hiding as an agricultural labourer. Etchings made by Giacometti during the same period of 1946, the first since he had attended Atelier 17 in the 1930s, suggest that Hayter's presence catalysed activity in this medium for others, too.[66] Lucian Freud made his first two etchings, *Bird* and *Chelsea Bun* (1946), in Paris at this time, while passing through on his way to Greece.

In July, Isabel took Leibowitz to London.[67] She was keen to show him the 'richness' of the fifteenth-century paintings returned to the National Gallery from their wartime refuge in a Welsh mine. They stayed with Anna Phillips (who was divorcing Rodney[68]) and in Rossetti House with John and Marjorie Davenport, where they admired the Picassos and Klees which the couple held on to, despite their poverty. The familiar Chelsea pubs were 'still packed and short of drink'.[69] They went down to New Milton to see her mother and brother, and Isabel picked up a dead nightjar in the woods, which she kept, desiccated, in her bag for many years.[70] Being in London reminded her of the comparative freedom she felt in France, and she and Leibowitz made longer-term plans to move to the country-side outside Paris, 'to work compose / draw landscapes' in more peaceful and economical surroundings.[71] She wrote an optimistic letter to Rose Pulham and Mary, asking if they knew of a place.

As the summer wore on, a new woman arrived in Giacometti's sphere. Annette Arm, his lover from Geneva, joined him in the rue d'Alésia. Balthus scoffed that Giacometti had not gone to the station to meet her, and he, 'always gallant', had done so instead. There was, however, an outing to the Café des Deux Magots and Le Petit Saint-Benoît in Saint-Germain-des-Près to celebrate her arrival.[72] Annette was the same age as Isabel had been when she had first entered the ramshackle studio, and Isabel could not help liking her. She observed that Annette was 'confused' but intoxicated with excitement, devoted to Giacometti and happy to live on nearly fresh air. Not long after this, however, two other new arrivals, a woman and a little girl, appeared at the apartment she shared with Leibowitz on the rue de Condé. They had travelled from Poland, and, to Isabel's shock, Leibowitz introduced them as his wife, Françoise, and their ten-year-old daughter.[73]

Isabel was devastated. She knew this scene. In *Les Enfants du paradis*, Garance, the object of infatuation of so many men, discovers that she can, after all, love one of them. On the brink of being with him, she is approached by his small son, who begs her to leave the family intact, and she departs. The stinging scene between the child and the heroine cannot have failed to remind Isabel of Jackie, and now she was being called upon to abandon her life for a second time for Leibowitz's daughter. In an echo of the conclusion of the film, she removed to a hotel, where René Leibowitz visited her.[74] Then Rose Pulham came to her rescue, offering his and Mary's cottage in the Indre, as they had found a larger apartment nearby. Before leaving Paris, she saw Dora Maar, who commended her courage.[75] They both knew that, for everyone's sake, Isabel was determined to avoid the kind of predicament Dora had found herself in with Picasso's previous lover, Marie-Thérèse Walter, and their daughter, Maya, with whom Picasso continued to remain in contact. They also knew that Isabel was sacrificing, yet again, home and support.

64. Isabel Rawsthorne, *Lizard*, 1946; private collection

14 NATURE MORTE: 1946

'Nature Morte'

(Even so it is not so easy to be dead)
...
Yet even so, no matter how solid and staid we contrive
Our reconstructions, even a still life is alive
And in your Chardin the appalling unrest of the soul
Exudes from the dried fish and the brown jug and the bowl.

Louis MacNeice (1933)

By September, Isabel was alone in Peter and Mary Rose Pulham's two-roomed cottage on a farm near the remote village of Conives. She had let her life in Paris get out of control, 'ignoble and ridiculous'. If the affair with René Leibowitz had been, as she hinted, a way to part with Giacometti, then leaving Leibowitz was to experience two losses at once; a third arrived with a motorbike carrying an official packet, her decree nisi from Delmer. A small diary for 1947, the only one to survive in Isabel's effects, was later relegated to a jotter and its original contents substantially written over, but they can just be deciphered to give us a rare insight into her private thoughts.

Isabel's famous courage had failed, and she could see her future only as 'a terrifying blank'. She struggled with depression: 'Disgust with all arts, above all the folly of ever having endeavoured to try and succeed in them ... no desire for any nameable thing ... Terror of Paris terror of people.'[1] 'All activity seeming absurd,' she wrote, 'only forced into ... actions by the impossibility of the contrary', and added a line from the private journal of Baudelaire: 'le vent de l'aile de l'imbécillité' (the wind of the wing of imbecility). The words described the writer's descent into what he feared might be madness: 'Morally and physically, I always had the sensation of the abyss, the abyss of not only sleep, but the abyss of the action ... I have cultivated my hysteria with joy and terror. Now I am faint and today I had a singular warning, I felt pass over me the wind of the wing of madness.'[2] Isabel's 'abyss of action' had brought her face to face with the subject that opened Camus's *Mythe de Sisyphe*: 'There is but one truly serious philosophical problem, and that is suicide.'[3] If life is absurd and death is inevitable, was life worth living at all?

Camus concluded that even hopeless endeavour had meaning, through endeavour itself, and it was Isabel's belief that she was saved by work. Away from the city, she could manage on the last of Delmer's allowance, and she settled into a routine of roaming and drawing that was reminiscent of her childhood. She read a great deal: the Old Testament – Job and Jeremiah (Job she listed in capitals) – and Classics – Aeschylus and Sophocles.[4] As with Van Gogh, living alone prompted a 'habit of notation' – in her diary, on scraps of paper and in long letters, which are sadly lost or untraced. Van Gogh's description of the Yellow House in Arles, sent to his brother after his own flight from the decadence and distractions of Paris, was fondly echoed in a plan and account of her rooms that she sent to Giacometti.[5] The original is lost, but they were reprised in her autobiography (her notes, like her thoughts, were by now mainly in French):

> The two rooms were part of the farm buildings and approached by a small flight of steps on the outside. They were indeed small. I could have lain in bed and lit the fire in the next room without moving.
>
> The living room had a table, two chairs, a cupboard and an open wood fire. Suspended on a chain was a large iron cocotte on which nearly all the cooking was done. The French for house-warming is *pendre la cocotte*, such is the importance of this utensil. The bedroom had a bed, cupboard, table and towel. Water was fetched from the well. This water, according to legend, was holy. I was told there had once been a chapel on the site of the farm. Hence the name Chapelle de Saint-Marin.

Isabel's life during this period was solitary. Peter and Mary Rose Pulham lived a couple of kilometres away in a modest apartment attached to a château belonging to Jean Charles, comte de Montalembert. Once a week, the Rose Pulhams visited her and, once a week, Isabel cycled over to them. Sometimes she saw her landlady, a Mme Pallancher, who introduced her to local methods of cooking, including a prized recipe for rabbit. She was 'an austere, kind lady living alone and sometimes caring for her nephew'.[6] There was no music or radio, but at night she heard owls, and the cats and rats in the roof reminded her of Left Bank parties. She wrote to Leibowitz, and he visited her briefly: there were things they hadn't had time to say, but the discovery that he was a liar, a 'mithomane' as she put it, had ended the relationship as far as she was concerned. She made a trip to Paris late in the year, probably to attend Balthus's comeback exhibition, *Balthus: Peintures de 1936 à 1946*, at the Galerie Beaux-Arts, and to meet and settle things with Delmer. They had a convivial meal at Fouquet, where he told her he planned to remarry and suggested she do the same. They parted on good terms: 'we had both managed to save that part of our lives we had spent together'. Francis Bacon was staying at the Hôtel Saint-Romain for two weeks, in town for Balthus's show and for

UNESCO's *Exposition internationale d'arte moderne* at the Musée national d'art moderne which included his *Painting 1946* in the British section.[7]

Isabel's six months in the Indre changed her work. She painted landscapes and returned to the still lifes she had made at the cour de Rohan studio and in the RAG bedroom – her subjects were roots, glasses and a pebble, a bluebottle fly, a snail's shell, a small lizard.[8] These were executed in gouache and painted indoors. This was not just to avoid the approaching winter; in the interior environment, objects altered their aspect: 'the immense silence ... made the little room a monastic refuge'. Just as she imagined the rats in the context of Parisian parties, so she viewed the natural forms in the unnatural context of her cottage, estranged like the weirdly gleaming and contrived elements of the artificially lit, symbolically charged still lifes of Chardin and Van Gogh, or Derain, Balthus and Gruber.[9] Her practice also echoed the 'poetic realism' of her cinematic heroes Marcel Carné and Jean Renoir. Although often conflated with documentary and social realism (because of its association with left-wing politics), poetic realism was an enhanced realism that gained tension and intensity from being created in the artificial space of the studio. Isabel's strategy may have been informed by the filmic practice of isolating and lighting objects from the side, sometimes in close-up, sometimes framed or in a mirror, to confer more than ordinary meaning. She exploited the uncanny effect of reflections: 'Sometimes I fixed a small mirror beside the subject to produce a double vision.'

Isabel's approach found sympathy in the poetry of Francis Ponge. His poems were masterclasses in the enhanced observation and representation of everyday objects and may have informed Isabel's still lifes from before the war. Ponge's profile was relatively low in Paris in the 1930s, but he knew Giacometti through his association with the Surrealists and was a close correspondent with Camus.[10] His defiant publication during the Occupation of his collection of thirty-two prose poems, *Le Parti pris des choses*, brought him to the attention of the Left Bank circle.[11] Chardin was an important inspiration for him, and Ponge championed contemporary artists, especially Giacometti, and was often at his studio in 1946.[12] Ponge's title, translated roughly as 'the nature of things', or 'siding with things', draws attention to the way that the poems set aside preconceptions to look at simple objects through an examination of the senses, feelings and intellect. 'The Pebble', for example, ran on for six pages, beginning:

> A pebble is not an easy thing to define.
> If one is satisfied with a simple description,
> one can start out by saying it is a form or
> state of stone between rock and gravel.

But this remark already implies a notion of stone
that has to be justified. On this subject let me not
be reproached for going even farther back than the Flood ... [13]

Ponge set his stone in the originary, but also very contemporary context of the Deluge. This first principles approach, to 'consider all things as unknown, and to ... begin again right from the beginning', as he wrote in 1947, as well as the subjects of his poems – 'The Mollusc', 'The Oyster', 'The Pebble', 'Moss', 'A Piece of Meat' – overlap strikingly with the approach and the subject matter of Isabel's still lifes and suggest that they were informed by his book.[14]

There was a parallel with phenomenological enquiries being pursued by scientists and philosophers, most notably two friends of Isabel: Freddie Ayer and Maurice Merleau-Ponty. In 1945, Merleau-Ponty's *Phenomenology of Perception* proposed a model of knowing, the 'phenomenological reduction', based on a bracketed observation of the object, an *epoché*, excluding pre-judgement, similar to Ponge's approach.[15] His model was the artistic practice of Cézanne, one of the exemplars for Giacometti's and Isabel's studio-based studies.[16] These ideas complemented Isabel's and Giacometti's 'dialectical optic'. Merleau-Ponty and Ponge distinguished between an object and a perceived object, and Ponge gave the second the name 'objeu', *jeu* meaning 'play', which referred to the 'objective play of the mind' upon that object.[17] Merleau-Ponty wrote similarly: 'When I perceive a pebble I am not expressly conscious of knowing it only through my eyes.'[18] Rose Pulham was interested in the poet, and a note on his essay 'Vision and Conception' conjured an *objeu*: 'An egg on a billiard table partakes of the green cloth below and the yellow lamp above and at the same time is a symbol, a hen, an *œuf sur plat*.'[19] Isabel's *Nature Morte* (Two Shells and Feather) of 1946, (**65**) seems to allude to Ponge's poem 'Snails', in which the term *sang froid* provides a scientific and anthropomorphically precise description of the creature and the cool, uncoiling contemplation of the poem itself. It precisely matched the inscrutable white spiral placed at the centre of Isabel's picture.[20]

Isabel was part of a redefinition of still life, after the war. The art historian Jon Wood interprets Giacometti's phenomenological, 'studio-based still life' as a collapsing of two traditional genres – still life and *vue d'atelier* – into what he calls 'vie d'atelier'. For Wood, the choice and grouping of everyday things 'construct multiple meanings and relationships' including 'a personal autobiography or "personalia" ... a situated statement of artistic identity and affiliation'.[21] The arranged appearance of Isabel's objects, the sense of artistic intervention, contributed to their air of significance, relationship and existential narrative in the same way. The unexplained proximity of stone, shells, leaves and feathers in the

65. Isabel Rawsthorne, *Nature Morte* (Two Shells and Feather), 1946; private collection

Nature Morte (Shells, Leaves and Feathers), 1946, (**66**) suggested an offering at an altar, treasures collected by a child, a narrative of the seasons or a *memento mori*.

The autumn of 1946 turned into the famously extreme winter of that year. Wine, water and the world froze, windows were iced; Isabel slept under her fur coat. It was in these bitter conditions that she painted her first masterpiece. The Indre's famous profusion of birds was decimated. The green woodpeckers that in September had filled the fields were particularly vulnerable: the species feeds on the ground, so they were affected by the deep snow, and, on one of her winter walks, Isabel found a dead male.[22] She took it back to the cottage and made a series of studies, including four gouaches, employing artificial lighting to throw a dramatic shadow behind the bird. Like the studies of the snail shell, the versions moved from asymmetry to symmetry, each enhancing significance – *objeu*. At first, Isabel laid the bird on a plain surface, as she had at RAG, but at some point she tied its feet and hung it over the edge of an upright drawing board.[23]

66. Isabel Rawsthorne, *Nature Morte* (Shells, Leaves and Feathers), 1946; private collection

This final format, *Green Woodpecker III,* 1946, (**67**) recalled traditional images of suspended game birds or Chaim Soutine's still lifes of 'hanging' birds, fish and beef carcasses, but the inverted, open-winged shape placed at the exact centre of the image added a hieratic impact, as in Lucian Freud's *Dead Heron* (1945; private collection).[24] The change reflected a concern for the poignancy of the presented object that could be seen in Giacometti exploration of frames and pedestals and in her skeleton purchased at Deyrolle, simultaneously absurd and dignified on its socle. *Green Woodpecker III*, emulated the sacrificial effect of Soutine's powerful, inverted format, but the open wings give a paradoxical sense of life in death, flight in falling. This is underlined by the view of the bird the other way up, *Green Woodpecker II,* on the reverse of the board which gives the effect that it is flapping its wings to escape.

Green Woodpecker III distilled Isabel's careful conservation of motifs. The species had a reputation as an oracle going back to Classical times.[25] It was

67. Isabel Rawsthorne, *Green Woodpecker III*, 1946; Sainsbury Centre for Visual Arts, University of East Anglia

associated with rain ('the wet bird' being a common name) and, like Cassandra, a forecaster of war.[26] Its suspended position in Isabel's study aligned it with the fate of another victim of Apollo, the mythical musician Marsyas, suspended by the god upside down from a tree and flayed.[27] There was also a personal dimension to Isabel's affinity with the woodpecker's fast movements and famous laugh, or 'yaffle'. The noisy bird's silenced state matched her solitude and 'lost ... sense of myself'. The frozen body against the snowy ground expanded her idea of the future as a 'terrifying blank' to a general one, standing for the submergence of Europe under snow that year. The unnaturally extreme winter was experienced by many as a bleak introduction to the Cold War. The woodpecker, predicting nothing, provided a *nature morte* for the uncertain nuclear era.

The essentials of the phenomenological *nature morte*, the rigorous but ultimately elusive realism that gave them their bleak beauty, would remain characteristic of all of Isabel's work. Their matter-of-factness matched her habitual demeanour, but their austerity and reserve make a striking contrast to the open and laughing figure that everyone enjoyed. The private bracket of the studio lay behind the 'screen' of daily life.

68. Isabel Rawsthorne, *Lizard, Leaf and Skeleton*, 1947; British Library

15 PEINTRE CONTRAIRE: 1947

'The Carp'

In your ponds, in your pools,
Carps, how long you live!
Has death forgotten you
Fish of melancholy?

Guillaume Apollinaire[1]

Isabel travelled back to Paris in March 1947. As she left the countryside, the weather finally turned and her diary recorded 'The black crows in gentle browns and greens v fine ... snow sun dark & light luminous skies.'[2] She had survived through to the spring, but there had been no personal transformation; Isabel did not have Romantic illusions that time in the wilderness was anything more than that: 'what have I to show for 5 months of the hardest, most miserable period of my life?', her diary asked; 'a few paintings ... will I be worse? Or am I better?'[3] Her health had recovered but her certainty eluded her. Four times she had created a life that allowed her to paint, and four times events, first death, then birth, then war and finally love, had dismantled it. She must have smiled to find that the Parisian show of the moment was *Van Gogh* – an artist who knew that despair, too.[4]

The tiny 1947 diary, covered in notes and sketches in English and French, stained with coffee and cigarettes, offers a singular glimpse of a decisive shift in Isabel's art and that of her circle. Isabel summarised her condition:

> A new feeling of ease when painting which without other more important qualities is of no value. Alternating confidence and doubt as to my powers. A heaviness of heart, hardly to be born. A new feeling of ease when writing – also leading nowhere unless at the service of remarkable thought ... A horrifying apprehension that 'la vie te ratie' [life is racing me]. / Is there nothing to put on the balance as gain? Work only seems to be gain in future when results will tell. If struggling against despair profits one – but I doubt that it does. Would certainly work better if happier. Less knowledge of myself than before. What will become of me? A certain detached curiosity about this.[5]

Isabel listed the 'material gains' of her exile: '1 dried lizard and mandrake root. Parts of pircot snail shells 1 blu bottle / Added quotations from Agamemnon my own letters.'[6] It is an insight into how little she had to lose that, under the heading 'material losses', she entered only some fillings from her teeth. She set little store by the drawings and paintings in gouache that she had made, seeing them, as usual, as mere trials. She was in a situation little better than fifteen years before, without money, studio or name. She had not exhibited since 1934, had had access to a workspace for barely half of the intervening time and most of her output was scattered, destroyed or lost. She had no income and few belongings of value except her coat and the portrait by Derain, in Delmer's keeping. She arrived at the Hôtel Saint-Romain without a plan other than to work. A note reduced her future to two questions: 'How to keep head above water what do I mean when I say *peintre contraire*?'[7] The following months would be a determined campaign to answer both of these.

Isabel admitted to her diary that her time in the Indre had brought 'the undermining discovery that life all alone is unbearable for long – that is the opposite of liberty and the enemy of repose'.[8] On the other hand, she could not imagine a companion with whom she could exist, and she was still 'tender'.[9] She saw Giacometti. The diary records their 'first night', back at the Hôtel Primavera.[10] She woke with the light at 7.30 a.m. and went into the courtyard garden. Giacometti slept on, and she watched his 'head in bed through window', as she had often done before, with the Baudelairean thought, 'pastpresent'. This vignette lays to rest the myth of Isabel's sexual evasion and affirms the continuity of the relationship with Giacometti – never practical but always necessary. The diary's frequent references to 'keeping my head except between 4 and 6' suggest that that this was when she and Giacometti met.[11] They were discreet, as always; in the 1930s it had been in deference to the dignity of Delmer; now, to that of Annette. Giacometti never pretended fidelity, however, as is demonstrated by his publication in 1946 of the details of how he contracted venereal disease from a sex worker.[12] Pattie Whitney Smith recalled that Isabel always showed Annette 'the greatest friendship and kindness', and Isabel later recalled, 'When I got to know her she was charming, gay, witty and clearly happy. Indeed, she fitted into Giacometti's rhythm with the greatest ease. She has a sharp intelligence of her own. We used to go out together at night ... and often had a funny time together.'[13] The trio met regularly in Les Halles – 'fights, blood, onion soup, snow' – or in Saint-Germain, dining at the inexpensive Petit Saint-Benoît (barely changed today), and sometimes they went away together to the country.[14] Isabel and Annette cemented a friendship that would last all their lives, and, one can only assume, an understanding of their respective, different relationships with Giacometti.

Giacometti and Isabel were eager to show each other the fruits of their five months' work. He was so enthusiastic about what Isabel had done in the Indre that she found it hard to accept his praise – 'curious impression of being taken seriously' – and waited impatiently for the sterner verdict of Balthus, two days later.[15] He was, to her surprise, equally positive, particularly with regard to her landscapes: 'really so beautiful. What progress!'[16] He fancied them to be rather English, like Richard Bonington's watercolours, but the low horizon and zigzag skies were more likely a nod to Balthus himself. The war and the alliance between Britain and France had left Balthus less isolated in his passion for English culture. The idiosyncrasies of Elizabethan literature – 'an abrupt and savage tone of Elizabethan drama as pathetic, passionate and impassioning', as the actor and theatre director Antonin Artaud put it – so different from French classical drama, was a craze in the avant-garde.[17] Balthus encouraged Isabel's new project, a subject from William Shakespeare's *A Midsummer Night's Dream*, which treated the woodland setting from which so much of her imagery originated. Having re-read the play, she now found the most powerful figure to be Bottom, an existential hero, the human animal, embattled and absurd.[18]

Isabel could not afford to stay at the Hôtel Saint-Romain for long and flitted between cheaper lodgings. The spring stayed dull and cold, and she painted in her room in artificial light, observing her starling skeleton and the desiccating carcasses she had brought back from the Indre, as in, for example, *Lizard, Leaf and Skeleton.* (**68**) Like Van Gogh, she made translations of works she liked; probably dating from this time is a copy of a Roman Pompeian mosaic featuring, in the upper register, a cat mauling a bird – which probably reminded her of Picasso's painting of this subject – and, in the lower register, two dead ducks (5 BCE; National Archaeological Museum, Naples).[19] Again, it was difficult to store her works, and only those she gave to Pattie Whitney Smith and Elisabeth Lutyens are known today.

The diary itemises appointments with the dentists and tasks to be undertaken, such as:

> Things to do – mend pen and rings
> Things to avoid – drinks before 7[20]

Hospitality, food, drink and warmth could be found in the cafés and bars, but Isabel chastised herself when she weakened: 'I really should not waste my time now – but it is so cold and so impractical.'[21] Small shopping lists (cotton wool, cigarettes, food) and columns of sums attest to her thrift – she wished her appetite were smaller. One diary entry exclaims simply, 'accounts cunts'.[22] Sleep evaded her. Paraphrasing Aeschylus's *Agamemnon,* she wrote: 'Instead of Sleep there stretches before me an anguish that reminds me of [deleted word] trouble.'[23] She saw this as a sign of weakness, 'faiblesse', and was angry with herself.

One consolation was that Pattie had abandoned Charles Whitney Smith and returned to Paris to a job at the United Nations.[24] Peter Rose Pulham and Freddie Ayer were in Paris from time to time, too. A note about Cyril Connolly reveals her impatience with 'tizzle tazzle': 'Cyril's bantering cynicism ... hedonism, very depressing soppy, snobbish'.[25] She thought carefully about the relationships that mattered to her: 'Other / all / the people that I've known well that I wholeheartedly respect are only 2 T[om] and Alberto. Derain obviously – perhaps his intellect richer but certainly not more original – than that of A[lberto]. G. B[ataille] too. M. L[eiris] ... .'[26] Meals with Michel and Zette Leiris sustained her intellectually and physically, and helped to 'situate' her, as she put it. Isabel wondered what the couple thought of her. This was the first time since 1934 that she had presented herself in Paris as a yet-to-be-recognised artist without the validation of independent means or a name bestowed by being a wife, partner, model or mistress – having, to all external appearances, in fact, actively jettisoned these. She needn't have worried. The Leirises became lifelong friends, and, until his death, Michel sent her a copy of each of his new books. Michel was somewhat smitten with Isabel, but, as she had with Margaret Epstein and Annette Arm, she avoided the tensions that this might have caused, and it did not inhibit her friendship with Zette.[27] In 1953, Picasso gave them his first portrait of Isabel, *Le Chapeau à fleurs*.[28]

If Isabel's personal life was provisional, her art had direction. She had a clear intellectual agenda for her model of the 'peintre contraire', describing it as 'an advance on *le peintre écriture*', the writing painter.[29] By '*écriture*' Isabel meant the graphic element that was fundamental to both her and Giacometti's practice, drawing as an interrogation rather than an 'illustration' of phenomena.[30] As the art historian Patrick Elliott says, Giacometti's 'paintings can be seen as drawings in oil, and many of the sculptures have a graphic, incised element'.[31] This valuation of the mark and the line had found considerable fellow feeling: in 1945, the avant-garde Galerie René Drouin had shown Jean Dubuffet's *brut* outline portraits and Jean Fautrier's harrowing, gestural *Otages* (Hostages) series. In 1946, Stanley Hayter published a pioneering essay on the line of Paul Klee.[32] A revival of printmaking and hitherto, 'lesser' media, such as watercolour, illustration, drawing, doodles and graffiti, were being taken up by the Galerie Drouin and *Les Temps modernes* circles to explore different qualities of mark.[33]

Van Gogh was an important precedent for this post-war understanding of painting as drawing, and drawing as an interrogation of real things. Isabel's 1947 diary featured the artist's name in capitals, underlined three times, and his directional marks are exhibited in the radiating strokes of the wings of *Green Woodpecker III* and in the stern face of one of Giacometti's contemporary portraits, *Isabel* (1947; Fondation Giacometti, Paris).[34] In June 1947, Artaud performed

Van Gogh: le suicidé de la société – his response to the Van Gogh retrospective exhibition at the Musée de l'Orangerie earlier in the year – at an exhibition of his own eccentric drawings at Galerie Pierre.[35] The term '*peintre écriture*' was echoed in his description of Van Gogh's modest subjects executed in a *peinture linéaire*: 'The pure linear painting drove me crazy for a long time when I encountered Van Gogh who painted not lines or shapes, but the things of nature in full convulsion.'[36] Isabel's early encounters, in the circle of Epstein, with the work of Rouault (who was still living) and Soutine (who had died during the war) stood her in good stead as their reputations, and those of their older, gestural predecessors, such as Monet, Delacroix, Turner, Rembrandt and Velázquez, were revitalised as fathers of graphic painting.[37] She and Giacometti looked, too, at the prints and drawings of Dürer, Honoré Daumier, Constantin Guys and, of course, Rodin. The painter and printmaker Pierre Bonnard was another important inspiration, and, in the spring of 1947, the Orangerie mounted an exhibition of his work to coincide with his eightieth birthday (although he had died that January). Isabel wrote in her diary, 'Bonnard – greater and greater'.[38]

Isabel's interest in etching and images based on *A Midsummer Night's Dream* can be seen in this context. She returned to her youthful enthusiasm for Chinese and Japanese brush painting and formed birds and fish from 'calligraphic flourishes'.[39] She revived her wartime studies of calligraphy, typography and illustration, and altered her everyday handwriting to include uppercase letters, arrows and pictograms, while Elizabethan loops and curlicues like those in the credits of *Les Enfants du paradis* appeared around her dates and her signatures. There was nothing decorative about her calligraphic interests; a note stated: 'Japanese idea decoration of a flat surface ie pattern No appeal.'[40]

The pleasure that Isabel and her friends took in ditties, jokes and doodles reflected a general reappraisal of graffiti and scribbles, prehistoric art and the utterances of children and the mentally ill (all so recently dismissed by the Germans as 'degenerate'). Isabel's sketchbook and diary brim with doodles of wine glasses, bottles, flowers and erotica. Substantial Phallaccac fungi known as 'stinkhorns' echo an affectionate name she used occasionally for Giacometti![41] Variations on 'slat', 'slit' and 'slot' extemporise on the suggestiveness of the words as images (the *i* is slit-like, the *o* is open) and sounds ('i' 'o'): 'A slot becomes a slit when it narrows.'[42] An eye, variously an Egyptian 'Eye of Horus' or her own, often stands in for the first-person pronoun *I*, and the first initial of *Isabel*.[43] The calligraphic *I* initial resonated with Giacometti's newly narrow notation for her figure, which Francis Ponge described aptly as 'Struggling with the upward spring the élan of the *I* ... This *I* that cannot contemplate itself, this hazy and meagre apparition'.[44] Was the entry in Isabel's diary – 'today v thin!' – a reaction or a cause?[45]

69. Henri Michaux, 'L'Oiseau qui s'efface', *Apparitions* (1946)

Isabel's term *'peintre écriture'* echoed the early twentieth-century writings of Apollinaire on Chinese pictograms, and throws light on her preoccupation with his four-line poem 'La Carpe', part of a series of poems published in 1911 as *Le Bestiaire ou Cortège d'Orphée* with illustrations by Raoul Dufy. The book opened with a tribute to the drawn line, and each poem was accompanied by a linear woodcut. Its zoological subjects appealed to Isabel, but her repeated transcription of 'La Carpe' into various notebooks suggests that, for her, as for Apollinaire, she was interested in the appearance as well as the sense of the letters. *Le Bestiaire* offered an interesting, dialectical, relationship between image and word; each picture, which strikes the reader more forcefully than the letters, obliterating, rather than illustrating, the verse.[46] In the case of 'La Carpe', the obscurity of the fish brooding in the muddy depths of the poem met the revelation of the fish leaping in the image.

By the 1940s, Henri Michaux was reassessing calligraphy and Apollinaire's ideas about line, and his book of poems *Apparitions*, published in 1946, reproduced

70. Isabel Rawsthorne, *Nature Morte*, 1947; private collection

verses beside images in a similar way to *Le Bestiaire*.[47] It distilled significance down to the individual marks of the pictures and explored the capacity of the lines themselves to create or erase an image in the mind of the viewer. The poem 'L'Oiseau qui s'efface' created an alternating effect of a bird appearing and disappearing which continued in the picture in which the marks are ambiguous: strokes and scuffs that sometimes suggest a bird and sometimes appear to be merely strokes and scuffs.[48] The phenomenological tussle between the way pictures and words generate and 'efface' images in the mind's eye was familiar to Isabel from the very practical problems of devising the multilayered and contradictory experience of reading and viewing the RAG 'greetings cards'.

Apollinaire's carp swimming up to the surface of the muddy water was an analogy for this sudden experience of form in the formless. The abrupt and elusive recognition of a motif in apparently arbitrary marks was, for Michaux, a kind of 'apparition', the title of his book, equating to Ponge's use of the term to describe the effect of Giacometti's sculptures, 'an apparition, the sudden manifestation of a personage in the field of consciousness'.[49] Dubuffet described such recognition as 'convulsive', a 'blow', and all equated to Walter Benjamin's 'shocks and collisions' penetrating the distracted and alienated modern state with a 'decisive, unmistakable experience'.[50] Isabel explored this freer, ambiguously suggestive line. The still lifes done in her room at night, such as *Nature Morte*, (**70**) sport smudges, swivels and curls. A sketch in the diary of Pattie Whitney Smith was almost certainly conjured up, unplanned, at a café table, with the pen she had to hand to write letters.[51] Yet we recognise in the scribbles a precise portrait, the distinctive secretive sparkle of Pattie's eyes in apparently accidental, inky blots and bleeds. They recall Jacques Dupin's vivid descriptions of Giacometti's 'Thousands of dabs and strokes, tossed out, repeated, overlapping, submerged, recur insistently, swift, violent, precise, hallucinatory, and when they are arbitrarily interrupted all they leave behind are the smouldering traces of an approximation.'[52]

These graphic techniques had a Cassandrian capacity to eschew logic and language: 'Respect the impulses, the ancestral spontaneities of the human hand,' Dubuffet advised in his 1945 essay 'La Main parle'.[53] Artaud described his own drawings as 'all sketches, or should I say staggering blows given in all directions of chance, possibility, hazard or destiny'.[54] The art historian Sarah Wilson draws attention to the parallel popularity at this time of Rorschach tests and *decalcomania* – accidental marks made by pressing paint between sheets of paper – pioneered, before the war, by André Breton and Isabel's friend Benjamin Péret. These techniques reversed the conventions of representation: instead of a likeness being consciously imposed on a set of marks, marks ambushed consciousness with a likeness by chance.[55] After the war, Péret and Breton championed the Canadian painter Jean-Paul Riopelle (a friend of Giacometti and Samuel Beckett) as the 'trappeur supérieur' – on account of his ability to 'trap' reality in arbitrary marks in this way.[56]

The post-war strategy of the *Les Temps modernes* circle was different from the chance and automatic techniques employed by the Surrealists in an important way: it was not about accessing the abstract world of the unconscious or dreams, but the physical world of the body. For Michaux, the apparition was a visceral form of communication prior to, and more powerful than, language. Artaud and Becket employed involuntary movements, shouts and silence in their theatrical performances, as James Joyce did in his fiction. Leiris was experimenting with words that communicated body to body by sound rather than conventional meanings.[57] Artists saw line and gesture in a similar way, as registrations of the action of the body of the artist, which would, in turn, affect the body of the viewer. In 'La Main parle', Dubuffet wrote, 'One should feel man and all his weaknesses in all the details of the picture. Likewise the chance events pertaining to the materials used, the hazards of the hand.'[58] Artaud described the brushstrokes of Van Gogh's *Wheatfield with Crows* by means of taste and touch: 'dirty linen twisted with wine and wet blood.'[59] That same year, Gaston Bachelard coined the term 'manual imagination'. Nowhere is this clearer than in Giacometti's *La Main* (1947; private collection), a sculpted hand and forearm, the size and orientation to his own arm and hand outstretched to work, connect the object and the gesture that made it. The embodied art that Isabel had been working towards since Liverpool had found its moment in the post-war Paris. She concentrated increasingly on objects that she had handled. Unlike her early zoo studies, the creatures that she painted from the 1940s were collected, touched, felt, even, in the case of game, skinned, taken apart, cooked and tasted. Her still-life wine glasses, beetles, birds, pebbles and roots appealed to the hand, as had the greetings cards, by being hand-sized, a quality shared with Giacometti's matchbox-sized figures of her.

Despite this progress in sympathy with her peers, or perhaps because of it, by May 1947, Isabel's long 'patience and resistance', as she put it, wavered. During the spring months, she re-experienced the 'despair' that she had confronted the previous year and, extraordinarily, contemplated abandoning art altogether. More than once she wrote in her diary, 'Fit in nowhere'.[60] This seems a strange statement for one so established in Left Bank circles, but her meaning was specific: she was visible, but her art was not. Sometimes she wished she could have accepted this. 'So much better', she wrote, with typical, bitter clarity, 'to have been a "pretty girl".'[61] Although there were many invitations to play the role, she kept to her close circle and avoided what she called 'the Parisian pattern'. In a city where emphasis was on the post-war economic rehabilitation of the male population (women had belatedly won the right to vote in 1944), only an undiluted artistic presence would draw the attention she wanted. Isabel's misery at finding that Gruber, whose profile was now high, had taken up her subjects was expressed in no uncertain terms: 'fuck Gruber with his skeleton'.[62]

Isabel longed for a studio. She needed a refuge and a space to create paintings in oil of exhibitable size, of course, but a studio was also essential to display *herself* as a working artist. The 1947 diary shows a woman whose thoughts and energies were entirely orientated towards this aim. She had written to Giacometti before returning to Paris asking him to retrieve drawings of hers and to keep an eye out for a room.[63] He had no luck with either search, so her next hope was Balthus's studio in the cour de Rohan. The phrase 'C de R' beats through the diary pages: 'And now Balthus and Cour de Rohan? o if i could only have it. All problems take on different aspect.'[64] After seeing more of her work, he promised it for June. 'If I had oils and C de R they'd see something they will,' she wrote to herself, but, heartbreakingly, by May, for some reason, the references stopped and the hope vanished.[65] 'Money and a room of her own' – Virginia Woolf's pronouncement on the necessity for a woman's creative life spoken from the privilege of her Bloomsbury circumstance – mocked Isabel. She wrote in her diary, 'O Independence is' with an arrow back to the 'O'. The unfairness of her predicament is underlined by the proximity on the same page of the superb drawing of Pattie Whitney Smith.[66]

Patronage was not an option. Promising male artists might expect support from a buyer, dealer, publisher, apologist or benefactor. Even established professionals were dependent on these; Balthus had been helped by Princess Caetani when he was hard up after the war, and, in the autumn of 1947, his dealer set up a syndicate of private buyers to guarantee sales. This and an offer of a New York exhibition from the American art dealer Pierre Matisse had put his lifestyle on a secure footing, and while in the south of France with Picasso and Georges Bataille, he began a relationship with Laurence, Georges's daughter by his first wife, Sylvia, so had a new model regularly available.[67] Giacometti's fortunes were also turning. As well as having Annette, Diego and sometimes Isabel as indefatigable sitters, eighteen months of labour had born fruit: at the end of 1946, sixteen pages of photographs in *Cahiers d'art* had shown his small wartime figures to better effect than the Pierre Colle exhibition of the previous year. They included his drawing of Isabel in front of the stove, *Nude in the Studio,* and the new imperious thin sculptures.[68] Like Balthus, his output was encouraged by Pierre Matisse, who was paying for works to be cast for a New York exhibition early in 1948.[69]

For women, by contrast, support was associated with dependence rather than status. Simone de Beauvoir's final chapter of *Le Deuxième Sexe* (The Second Sex, 1949), 'The Independent Woman', equated patronage with the situation of the 'kept woman – wife or mistress'.[70] Her chapter addressed inequalities between the working conditions of women and men and showed how women's choices were restricted to independence or dependent romance. A lover providing pecuniary and practical help or modelling to a male artist, as Eric Hall did for Francis Bacon, was not seen as romantic dependence. Hall's purchase of Bacon's first two paintings in 1945 and donation of them to the Tate Gallery was a turning point in Bacon's career, and the proceeds from *Painting 1946* funded his life in Monte Carlo. By contrast, it was, as de Beauvoir observed, unusual for a female artist to succeed without private means. Even if this 'self-sufficiency' was available, it excluded them from the networks of vested interests that supported male artists.

Isabel rejected dependent romance: her lack of social status and her age, thirty-five, did not deter male admirers. René Leibowitz wanted her to return to rue Condé, an offer Peter Rose Pulham thought she should exploit, since, although he disliked the composer, the apartment was spacious enough for painting. Pattie Whitney Smith introduced Isabel to wealthy men, including a 'svelte, handsome,

71. Isabel Rawsthorne, 'Independence is O' (Pattie Whitney Smith), Diary, Christmas 1947; Tate Archive

Belgian Count', but that path was not for her either. Freddie Ayer suggested that he and Isabel get together in a more unconventional ménage, she in Paris, he in Oxford, and she was amused by the idea of being 'joined with the channel between,' but was not inclined to sacrifice her freedom for this experiment. In March, Constant Lambert kept his promise of visiting her in Paris, but he was travelling with a young Japanese soprano and only passing through on his way to join his former flatmate, Michael Ayrton, to stay with Norman Douglas, who was re-ensconced on Capri. He was still involved with Margot Fonteyn, moreover, and Isabel was still involved with Giacometti.[71]

The 1947 diary is almost entirely concerned with painting and reveals little of Isabel's thoughts on such romantic matters, but an unusual passage hints at her emotional dilemma. It describes an occasion in Les Halles, when Annette had departed, leaving Isabel and Giacometti alone. They said goodbye at the metro, and Isabel set out to stroll home, only to be approached by a young man whom she had noticed gazing at her earlier. They fell into conversation, but Giacometti reappeared, having missed his train. The suitor departed hastily, and Isabel walked with Giacometti to Montparnasse, where they had coffee and 'une petite carresse, / a la main / sur la joue. Premier fois que je fais cela!'[72] She reassured herself that the arrangement with Giacometti had a future – 'Only the C of R – and the rest will work – yes la peinture aussi!' – but the incident had betrayed the relationship's constraints: it was neither one thing nor the other, and preventing her from moving on. Shortly after this, she made a decision:

> 2 things. In order to have some calm to work –
> a) push A to corner...
> b) See what happens with R[73]

The results of these ultimatums went unrecorded but can be guessed at by their coincidence with the decree absolute from Delmer, the cessation of Isabel's hopes for the cour de Rohan studio and a re-entry into the world.

72. Isabel Rawsthorne, Pattie Whitney Smith (detail, inverted, from diary, 1947 – see **71**); Tate Archive

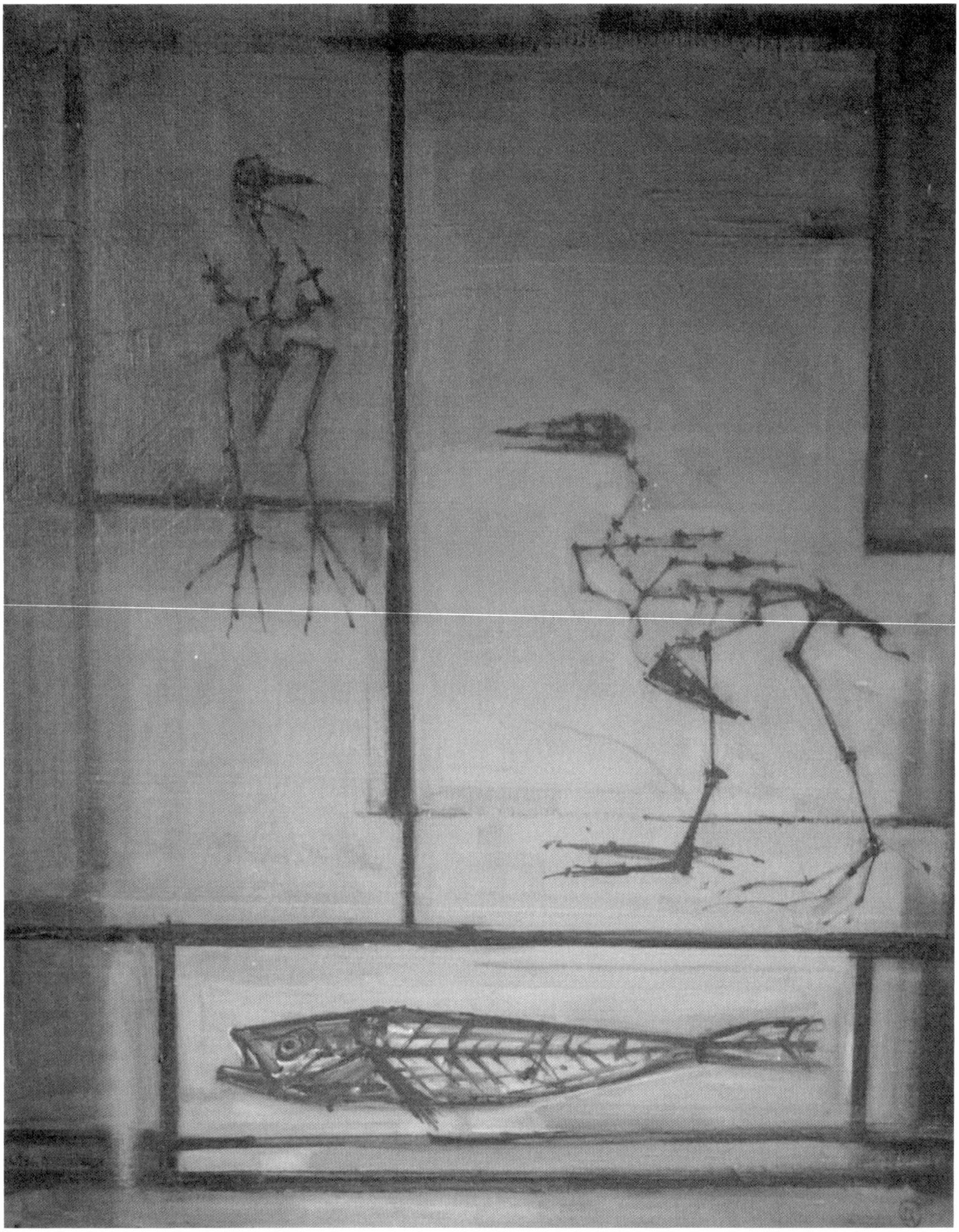

73. Isabel Rawsthorne, *Two Birds and a Fish*, 1947–8; private collection

16 HOMMAGE AU SQUELETTE: 1947–1949

> I believe that Gauguin thought that an artist should seek the symbol, the myth, enlarge the things of life and raise them to that stature of myth. While Van Gogh thought that the myth should be deduced from things themselves, down to earth life.
>
> I think he had it damned right.
>
> Because reality is devastatingly greater than all history, than all fable, than all divinity, than all surreality.
>
> Antonin Artaud[1]

Isabel's commitment to figurative art, distilling the problem of the relation of a person to the world, became, at this time, mainstream. Her neglect of fashionable cliques in favour of those who were pressing these questions of realism had brought her to the heart of the post-war Parisian avant-garde. In the late 1940s, her painting would achieve a new synthesis – agile, finally assured and with equal footing in French and English culture – realised in 1949, in her first exhibition for fifteen years.

It began in May 1947, when Isabel left Paris for a short visit to London. A diary reference to drawings being framed and to the dealer Edouard Mesens, who ran the London Gallery with his fellow Surrealist Roland Penrose suggests that she sold them some work.[2] She caught up with London friends and called on Constant Lambert in his apartment in Thurloe Square. The injection of funds from Mesens would not last long. He had discussed solo exhibitions for herself and for Rose Pulham, some of whose paintings he had also bought. Finding 'calm to work' was now urgent, and London was beginning to look like the only solution.[3] Her days in Paris were numbered.

London had come to life. The Klee retrospective in 1945 and two huge exhibitions in 1946 – *Braque and Rouault* at the reopened Tate Gallery and *Matisse–Picasso* at the Victoria and Albert Museum – had proved exciting catalysts for modern art.[4] 'The young coming up are pretty determined – and people in general have had a good think,' wrote one observer.[5] In 1946, in an astonishing act of idealism, given the utter depletion of the country's coffers, four publicly funded cultural institutions had been created: the BBC Third Programme for the radio; the Sadler's Wells Ballet (evolved from Constant Lambert's Vic-Wells Ballet); the Arts Council; and the British Council, promoting British artists, including several of Isabel's wartime circle, such as Francis Bacon.[6] The following year, the Festival of Britain was announced, a huge national celebration to coincide with the centenary of the Great Exhibition of 1851.

Isabel made contact with a new generation of artists. The Mayor Gallery in London had launched Eduardo Paolozzi, a twenty-three-year-old Scottish sculptor not yet out of art school.[7] Isabel's friend John Davenport had bought his first sculpture (a Picasso-esque bull) and Anna Phillips's ex-husband, Rodney, a large drawing. Paolozzi remembered Anna introducing Isabel to him and he seems to have been a little overawed, recalling, many years later: 'when Isabel Delmer and Anna Phillips entered a restaurant, the diners were transfixed by their beauty and all the raised forks remained suspended in the air until the glamorous pair were seated'.[8] Paolozzi was ebulliently ambitious and impatient to get to Paris – and Isabel liked him. He wrote his address in her diary, and she sent a postcard putting him in contact with Giacometti.[9]

On her return to Paris in June, Isabel and Pattie Whitney Smith moved to the Hôtel de la Cité and a livelier life. The building stood on the quai des Orfèvres on the tip of the Île de la Cité, and Isabel thought the prospect from her first-floor room, encompassing Notre-Dame and the Seine flowing underneath the Pont Neuf, 'one of the most beautiful views in Paris'. On the ground floor, there was a café whose proprietor went fishing every morning at 4 a.m. Opposite was the quai des Grands-Augustins, where Rose Pulham had lived and the Leirises had their apartment. 'Not long to resist a parisian pattern', Isabel decided, '– it was soon time to see one's friends.' The hotel was a stumble away from Le Tabou nightclub and Saint-Germain, and scaffolding on the outside of the building ensured that they could clamber back into their rooms at any hour. As the chilly spring melted into a seethingly hot summer, Isabel worked or sat for Giacometti by day and, before dinner, swam at the Piscine Deligny, an open-air swimming pool in the Seine.[10]

That summer of 1947, Paris filled with visitors from London. In July, the musician Humphrey Searle joined a celebratory evening at Les Deux Magots, followed by dinner at Le Petit Saint-Benoit with Giacometti, Annette, and Pattie Whitney Smith.[11] Paolozzi moved to a nearby room on the Île Saint-Louis borrowed for a while from his fellow British sculptor Raymond Mason. Isabel's brother, Warwick, arrived, and, late in life, he recalled being taken 'by day to Paris museums, the Louvre, Notre Dame, Chartres Cathedral. In the evening we spent time with Isabel's artistic friends. Including Paolozzi and Giacometti.'[12] Pattie Whitney Smith remembered getting drenched by the rain at an outdoor performance of Molière's comedy-ballet *Le Bourgeois gentilhomme*, at Versailles (1670, with music composed by Jean-Baptiste Lully), and also merry gatherings at the Hôtel de la Cité, where the burly Paolozzi belted out Scottish ballads from her *Oxford Book of English Verse*.[13]

Isabel cannot help but have played a role for Paolozzi similar to that fulfilled for her by Derain and Giacometti when she herself had arrived in Paris in her twenties. As well as introducing him at the rue Hippolyte-Maindron, she took him to Deyrolle, where he bought her a skeleton of a bat, and they went to the Musée de l'homme.[14] She shared her enthusiasm for D'Arcy Wentworth Thompson's *On Growth and Form* (1917), a monumental revised edition of which had been published to wide acclaim in 1942.[15] It is not clear whether they were lovers as well as friends. According to William Feaver, Paolozzi was importunate, but on the occasion when Isabel acquiesced it was not a success.[16] Her inclinations were typically towards experienced, knowledgeable men, but she enjoyed his enthusiasm: 'He was a resourceful person and added to his income by getting casual jobs as a porter in places like the Halles.' He pedalled around Paris on a bicycle brought from England. Raymond Mason lent him his old studio, a wooden structure next to a fairground on the avenue Denfert-Rochereau, off the boulevard Montparnasse, in which he also stored Isabel's work.

Isabel was certainly involved, at this date, with Georges Bataille. This was a strange affair, which, like the episode with Antoinette, seems to have arisen out of curiosity. She had studied since the 1930s Bataille's anthropological, philosophical and fictional writings, and his unpredictable intellect, served up in his singularly seductive voice, was perhaps a captivating combination for her.[17] Although they shared the experience of creating pornography, there is no record – because of the Official Secrets Act – of their discussing her wartime work, other than a reference to his annoyance when, while he was reading Henry Miller's latest book for a Parisian publisher, she dismissed Miller 's work as comical. Bataille and his wife, Diane Kotchoubey de Beauharnais, were another couple that conducted their relationship on original terms, pursuing an experimental sex life. Isabel seems to have found ways to avoid the more predictable sessions that might have involved her participation: 'The first time I went home to the flat they proceeded as usual to produce a bottle of home-made vodka. As they never had any money to spare, the method was to buy some pure alcohol from the chemist, add to this red pepper and a little water. What they did not know was that I had a far stronger head than either of them. So I left for home Virgo intacta.' Here, Pattie Whitney Smith annotated the margin of Isabel's autobiography, 'hardly!' Isabel was amused to find the Batailles' country life a contrast to their shoestring hedonism in Paris: 'completely different, quite conventional; Georges working a ten-hour day, Diane cooking and sewing and walking miles'. The visit to the basilica at Vézelay put ideas into their heads, however: 'Georges spoke wistfully of the importance of desecrating the altar and fornication in the crypt ... Diane took me on to the battlements and said it would be fun to push me over.' But, again, Isabel had an escape plan: 'I told her I would introduce her to Antoinette Balthus, which I did, soon after this conversation. It proved to be the greatest success.'

A more serious romantic distraction occurred in the reappearance in Paris of Constant Lambert, on tour with the Sadler's Wells Ballet. Isabel attended their performance of *Job*, inspired by the illustrated edition of the Book of Job by William Blake and with music by Vaughan Williams, which bewildered the audience.[18] This time, Lambert came to Isabel's rooms and 'was enchanted with the place, especially the scaffolding'. Lounging in the café, she recalled, 'it was clear that he was perfectly happy'. When some of the company – Ninette de Valois, Margot Fonteyn and Roland Petit – happened on them one evening, Fonteyn announced, not without ambiguity, 'Enfin, il a trouvé son ambiance.' Lambert stayed on after the ballet had left. Isabel worked during the day, they met for dinner in the evenings, and, to her surprise, despite his lameness he joined her on her latenight walks: 'Paris is even more beautiful at night ... I took Constant to various all-night cafés that I knew. We went to the Halles and along the Bld Sebastopol.'

On Lambert's previous visit, when Isabel had met him and his soprano friend at Les Deux Magots, a man had sold them horoscopes. Now, Lambert confessed that he had found himself switching that of his companion for hers; and that this had 'made an impression which he thought about afterwards' – as though he were already toying with the idea of switching not just horoscopes but partners. He had found in Isabel an intellectual equal, as committed as he to his heroes of French literature – Racine, Baudelaire and Proust, for instance – and they had lots to talk about.[19] However, when Isabel told him that she would soon return to England, the 'information did not seem to be of interest', and she concluded that 'he liked to think of me as living in Paris'. Lambert's desires were always orientated towards younger women of Asiatic appearance. He had spent two years pining for the actress Anna May Wong and writing music for her – without ever meeting her – before marrying Flo, then barely sixteen, and then later falling for the teenaged Fonteyn. Although Isabel had a famously so-called 'oriental' look, she seemed incompatible with Lambert's tastes (as both Flo and Fonteyn had become) in terms of her worldliness and her age. Their affair appeared to be only an interlude.

Nonetheless, shortly after Lambert's departure for London, Isabel was surprised to receive from him a stream of postcards bearing poems, crosswords, musical scraps and quotations from Beachcomber (the nom de plume of the writers of the 'By the Way' column in the *Daily Express*), scribbled in The George pub. Seeing him writing in the bar one day, Elisabeth Lutyens remarked to him, 'I don't think Isabel will marry you because of some postcards – even yours.' She understood Isabel's need for independence: Lutyens herself was married to a conductor, Edward Clark, and supported him, herself and her three children from her previous marriage by composing music for horror films. Her pioneering alternatives to conventional eight-note musical structure were not recognised in England until after Schoenberg's version had been introduced. 'Behind that ebullient, non-stop talking screen', Isabel observed, 'she lived a ... nervous existence, as can be heard in her music in between the dramatic climaxes.'[20]

Ironically, having given up on Paris, Isabel at last secured a place to work there. Paolozzi returned for a while to London and left her his studio.[21] Immediately, she set about painting her skeletons in oils. She lacked human models, but began copies of a large colour reproduction of the Roman Portrait of the Baker Terentius Neo and his Wife (c. 1 BCE, National Archaeological Museum, Naples), a fresco from the atrium of a house in Pompeii.[22] (**82**) It was too little too late, however; she was 'not established as an artist indispensable to either nation', as she put it, and therefore had no permit to work and no prospect of earning a living in France. She confronted her situation with the same level gaze that she and Delmer had adopted in 1936, concluding: 'I would have to make my life more financial.' She prepared to return to London.[23]

Isabel made sad farewell visits to Peter and Mary Rose Pulham and the Batailles.[24] Laurence Bataille was staying with her father and left an intriguing record in a letter to Balthus, noting how sensitive Isabel was when it was suggested that she had a similar 'accent' to Giacometti, and that her famous laugh sounded 'hollow'.[25] On 6 September, behind with her rent, Isabel was turned out of her hotel room and moved herself and her belongings onto Pattie's floor. Next day, they were robbed, probably by the landlord to recoup his losses. The thief selected a length of good cloth and Isabel's fur coat, so her last hours in Paris were spent at the police station. She returned to London on 8 September with only sheets, towels, binoculars, bicycle, sketchbooks, paint box, paints and brushes and books, including her trusty *Larousse gastronomique*.[26] In her bag, she took a pencil, her financial accounts and reading material – William Bedell Stanford's *Aeschylus in His Style: A Study in Language and Personality* (1942), James Thomson's *The Seasons* (1793) and Friedrich von Schiller's *William Tell* (1804). The paintings were probably too difficult to transport and were left behind in Giacometti's, Paolozzi's or Rose Pulham's studio.

London was still in ruins and the autumn, foggy and damp. For the first few days, Isabel took sanctuary with Anna Phillips, who was living in style in one of the Nash terraces overlooking Regent's Park. She was welcomed at The George pub by Anna, Elisabeth Lutyens, Constant Lambert and his close friend Alan Rawsthorne, a fellow composer just out of the army. Rawsthorne was intensely left wing and, with his musical connections in Eastern Europe, may have reminded Isabel of

74. Else Bostelmann, 'Five Lined Constellation Fish', from William Beebe, *Half Mile Down* (1934)

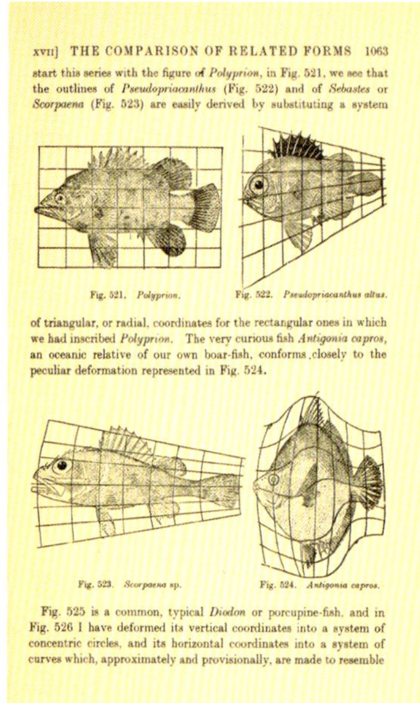

xvii] THE COMPARISON OF RELATED FORMS 1063

start this series with the figure of *Polyprion*, in Fig. 521, we see that the outlines of *Pseudopriacanthus* (Fig. 522) and of *Sebastes* or *Scorpaena* (Fig. 523) are easily derived by substituting a system

Fig. 521. *Polyprion.* Fig. 522. *Pseudopriacanthus altus.*

of triangular, or radial, coordinates for the rectangular ones in which we had inscribed *Polyprion*. The very curious fish *Antigonia capros*, an oceanic relative of our own boar-fish, conforms closely to the peculiar deformation represented in Fig. 524.

Fig. 523. *Scorpaena sp.* Fig. 524. *Antigonia capros.*

Fig. 525 is a common, typical *Diodon* or porcupine-fish, and in Fig. 526 I have deformed its vertical coordinates into a system of concentric circles, and its horizontal coordinates into a system of curves which, approximately and provisionally, are made to resemble

75. 'The Comparison of Related Forms', from D'Arcy Wentworth Thompson, *On Growth and Form* (1942)

Leibowitz. A brief passion sprang up between them – quickly consummated in a one-night stand. However, 'with characteristic dash,' Anna 'asked Constant to dine'. 'Anna and Constant quickly understood each other,' Isabel recalled with affection; 'They were both nature's surrealists.'[27] On 23 September, *The Times* announced Isabel's engagement to Constant Lambert,[28] and, on 7 October 1947, they married at St Pancras Town Hall. Life began as Isabel Lambert, her fourth name, the identity of her professional success.[29]

Rationing was still in place and another cold winter set in: 'continual rain and ... the shortage of cigarettes has become maddening,' Isabel grumbled to Giacometti. She disliked American brands and eventually took to smoking cheroots.[30] By December, she had found Lambert and herself a small apartment in a house at 197 Albany Street, near Regent's Park. They moved in with little furniture apart from two pianos and an easel. Isabel had a studio. She took over a north-facing room and, with barely a break, continued to paint. In later years, she speculated on this unusual newly wed behaviour, but, at the time, it was simply that she and Lambert were 'furiously keen to work ... I did not find this in any way remarkable. It is only now at a long distance that I consider it odd.'[31]

Isabel's great regret about Paris had been that even the Jardin des plantes was no match for the Natural History Museum in London, and it was her first call when she was back in London, 'with memories of the flying bomb days and Rose Pulham'.[32] By the end of 1947, she had also been awarded membership to the Royal Zoological Society, and, as the zoo was steps away from her house, she went there to make 'notations' whenever she liked.[33] In 1948, she planned circular oil panels of 'spiders, beetles, the common house fly',[34] but, in later life, she recalled, 'Mentally I was completely dominated by the same ideas'[35] – the skeletons. At Christmas, she sent Giacometti a postcard toasting their respective work: 'Hommage au sculpteur. Hommage au squelette.'[36] 'I feel completely obsessed', she told him, 'and I have a clear idea what I want to succeed ... Always the same topics. Skeletons of birds, bats, mouse, fish.' She was painting 'the same skeleton in two positions ... but much advanced'.[37]

Her interest in marine life was encouraged by Thompson's *On Growth and Form* and, a new find, William Beebe's *Half Mile Down* (1934) – 'The most beautiful book'. It was full of strange images, particularly the last chapter, 'A Decent into Perpetual Night'. She wrote to Giacometti in barely punctuated excitement, in 1948:

> the learned American who descended in his bathysphere more than three thousand feet below the sea. Unforgettable descriptions of the descent, the glare of an unimaginable blue which appeared to be brilliant but that was too dark to distinguish a blank page from a printed one. Descriptions of fish in waters of deepest black their lights glittering like the stars in motion, and an amazing amount of thousands and thousands of small fragile organisms, large and small. I long to go myself! Astonishing photographs too. If this book is translated into French it is essential reading.[38]

The words 'full fathom' appeared in her sketchbook, referring to Ariel's song in Shakespeare's *The Tempest*, 'Full fathom five thy father lies'.[39]

Further inspiration was available in the growing body of natural-history photography and experiments in cinematography. In Paris, Jean Painlevé, an associate of the Surrealists, pioneered short wildlife films, such as *Le Vampire* (1945), which was about the vampire bat. Painlevé's underwater films, *L'Hippocampe* (The Seahorse; 1945) for instance, revealed scenes comparable to Beebe's. His occasional use of transmitted light provided apparitional, skeletal images that were animated rather than still. It was not until 1953 that Jacques-Yves Cousteau broke onto the scene with his book *The Silent World: A Story of Undersea Discovery and Adventure*, adapted to become the first of his film documentaries; Isabel became a lifelong fan.[40]

In a sustained campaign, working most days morning to evening, Isabel finished sixteen oils and displayed them with eight new gouaches in *Isabel Lambert: Recent Paintings* at the Hanover Gallery from 22 February to 26 March 1949. Isabel and Giacometti thus finally exhibited their new work in solo shows within a year of each other. Isabel's included one portrait, *Copy of Pompeian Painting,* and what she described as twelve 'monochromes ... bird skeletons walking, enclosed in rectangles of varying sizes, in colours of umber, ochres, siennas'. Most of these were in grisaille, but one, *Night* (1948; private collection), depicted 'bats, fish and cat on a blue, grey, umber ground'.[41] Isabel was happiest with *Two Birds and a Fish* (1947–8; private collection) and *Two Birds* (1947–8; untraced), purchased by Sidney Bernstein, the founder of Granada Television.[42]

The catalogue to the exhibition was Isabel's first published statement on art. It was intended to be a text by Michel Leiris, but, in the end, she and Rose Pulham created a montage of quotations.[43] Isabel's Anglo-French vision was declared in the opening sentence, taken from Giacometti's 'À propos de Jacques Callot': 'The greater or lesser plastic quality is no more than the sign of the greater or lesser obsession of the artist with his subject, the form follows the obsession.' Isabel had returned these words to him in her letter written during her preparations for the exhibition: 'I feel completely obsessed'.[44] Her montaged, 'dialectical optic', glancing connections between things, was advertised by an inventory of disparate items in her sketchbook. 'Two drawings of a young nightjar found on the edge of the forest; New Milton; July 25th, 1946; three lizards and a cockchafer; Sir Philip Sydney's "Spondee Sonnet"; there are two pages of precise detail as to how best to cook a rabbit in red wine and brandy; fifteen drawings of a landscape; Cassandra's invocation of Apollo from the Agamemnon; notes on the origin of symbols, and exact indications as to the difference between edible and poisonous fungi.' The familiar juxtaposition of meat and sacrifice, Cassandra's bloody invocation and the rabbit cooked in wine, alerts the reader to allegorical collisions that ricochet through the list as a whole. The phenomenology of objects, Francis Ponge's 'des choses', is reaffirmed by the next quotation in her sketchbook, Artaud's defence of Van Gogh (given in full as the epigraph to this chapter): 'Gauguin ... raise[d] [the things of life] ... to [the] stature of myth. / While Van Gogh thought that the myth should be deduced from things themselves ... / I think he had it damned right.' The final paragraph asserts Isabel's particular, summary vision, citing the dictionary definition of 'quintessence': the search for the 'most essential part'.

The 'Monochromes' were manifestos of Isabel's idea of *peintre écriture.* If the carcasses of the creatures she had been studying earlier in the decade were like their actual-representations, then their bones were their actual-pictograms – an inspired simultaneity of *nature morte* and calligraphy. Her frameworks were not

76. Isabel Rawsthorne, *Two Birds and a Bat*, 1947–8; private collection

77. Germaine Richier, *La Chauve-souris*, bronze, 1946; Tate

literal skeletons, but, to borrow Elizabeth Manchester's description of Germaine Richier's *The Bat*, a 'graphic' analysis of the body.[45] Eleven versions of *The Bat* were cast in 1946 and exhibited in London in 1947 and may have partially inspired Isabel's *Two Birds and a Bat*.[46] (**75**) *Two Fish* recalls Paul Klee's playfully titled *Fish and Line,* which Isabel saw at Klee's first British show at the Mayor Gallery in 1934, but owed more to the material insistence of prehistoric incisings, graffiti, Soutine's 'brushstrokes like flashes', and Japanese and Chinese brush painting.[47] In 1948, Isabel had purchased William Cohn's lavishly illustrated book *Peinture chinoise: 224 Peintures et détails*, but, instead of dashing marks across a white surface, buried her own in shadow.[48] Isabel's figures had the effect of being viewed through glass windows or vitrines. This was enhanced by the way the backgrounds of the monochromes desubstantiated the surface of the canvas, creating a distressed, indistinct depth from which things emerge. The effect was like that of the lithographs of walls covered in graffiti that Dubuffet had produced in 1945, such as *Mur embué* (Misty Wall), or like peering through dusty glass display cases, aquariums, or into the muddy realms of Apollinaire's 'La Carpe'.[49] This imagery of the Natural History Museum and 'faint suggestion of a glass case' was recognised in the review in *The Times*.[50]

The creatures offered an *objeu* of literary, historical and scientific allusions. Unlike the *Green Woodpeckers* of two years before, the skeletal birds were dead/alive and laughing (as their 'yaffle' call alludes to), a literal expression of the life-after-death of her age. Their human demeanour suggested bird-women, Sirens, Harpies or the vengeful winged Erinyes (Furies) of the first two parts of Aeschylus's *Oresteia* – *Agamemnon* and *The Libation Bearers* – which she had been reading. They had recently been modernised in plays such as Eugene O'Neill's *Mourning Becomes Electra* (first staged in London in 1937), T. S. Eliot's *The Family Reunion* (premiered in 1939) and Sartre's *The Flies* (1943), as well as Louis MacNeice's *Agamemnon* (staged in 1945). A variation on the Erinyes, the eponymous subjects of the last play of the trilogy, *The Eumenides*, who delivered justice and watched against future atrocity, became relevant after the war, and Francis Bacon adopted them, rather than the Erinyes, as a basis for the creatures in his *Three Studies for Figures at the Base of a Crucifixion* (1944; Tate, London).[51]

The anatomical, X-ray look of Isabel's skeletons summoned even older associations of dinosaur ancestors. Véronique Wiesinger traces them back to the vertebrae and the pterodactyl suspended within the framework of Giacometti's *The Palace at 4 a.m.*, (**80**) which, in turn, evoked the skeletons in glass cases of the Galerie de paléontologie et d'anatomie comparée in Paris.[52] Giacometti's text accompanying later lithographs of the Galerie de paléontologie in *Paris sans fin* (1957) looked through layers of visual memory in a vitrine aesthetic similar to that seen in the monochromes: 'great windows, scored with their dark armature of bars, shining with the last light of day, still disorientated, lost in the desolation of the room of nameless snakes'.[53] The skeletons in the Galerie were arranged to demonstrate the belief that they revealed continuities between modern to prehistoric creatures, a theme of Thompson's *On Growth and Form*. The monochrome grids recall Thompson's famous calibrated comparative diagrams. Isabel owned an illustration cut from an unidentified book (date unknown; private collection) showing a similarly sequenced row of fish. The link between dinosaurs and modern life was believed to be especially conspicuous in birds, and Isabel's paired skeletons recalled the comparative illustrations in Gerhard Heilmann's 1926 book *The Origin of Birds*, which had done much to popularise the idea.[54]

Isabel maintained close contact with Paris and went there regularly, sometimes borrowing or hiring a studio through Paolozzi or Rose Pulham.[55] In June 1948, she took sketches to show Giacometti, 'because ... your opinion is worth more to me than anything the others might say'. Annette stayed with her in London in October, bringing one of Giacometti's small figures as a gift (untraced).[56] Significantly, a new artistic distance matched Isabel's geographical distance, however. She wrote to Giacometti, 'I know I am communicating ... I'm decided on what to do, I need

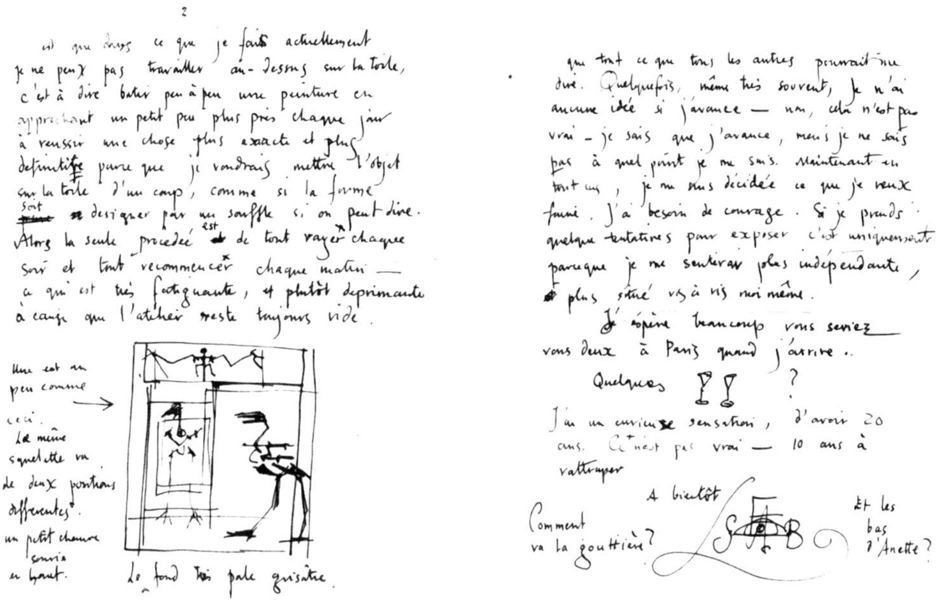
2

ce que dans ce que je fais actuellement
je ne peux pas travailler au-dessus sur la toile,
c'est à dire batir peu à peu une peinture en
approchant un petit peu plus près chaque jour
à reussir une chose plus exacte et plus
definitive parce que je voudrais mettre l'objet
sur la toile d'un coup, comme si la forme
soit désigner par un souffle si on peut dire.
Alors la seule procedé est de tout rayer chaque
soir et tout recommencer chaque matin —
ce qui est très fatiguante, et plutôt deprimante
à cause que l'atelier reste toujours vide.

Une est un peu comme ceci. La même squelette en de deux positions differentes. un petit chauve souris en haut.

Le fond très pale grisatre.

que tout ce que tous les autres pourrait me dire. Quelquefois, même très souvent, je n'ai aucune idée si j'avance — non, cela n'est pas vrai - je sais que j'avance, mais je ne sais pas à quel point je me suis. Maintenant en tout cas, je me suis décidée ce que je veux finir. J'ai besoin de courage. Si je prends quelque tentatives pour exposer c'est uniquement parceque je me sentirai plus independante, plus situé vis à vis moi même.

J'espère beaucoup vous serez vous deux à Paris quand j'arrive.

Quelques ?

J'ai un curieuse sensation, d'avoir 20 ans. Ce n'est pas vrai — 10 ans à rattraper

A bientôt

Comment va la gouttière?

Et les bas d'Anette?

78. Isabel Rawsthorne, letter to Alberto Giacometti, 1948; Tate Archive

courage. If I take a few opportunities to exhibit it is because I feel more independent.'[57] The grisaille hues of Giacometti's and Isabel's work were similar, but his drawings and oils accumulated many modifications one on top of the other, while Isabel wanted something more distilled and apparitional. She and Rose Pulham called it a 'quintessence' and coined the term 'Quintessentialism'.[58] In a letter to Rose Pulham, she quoted the nineteenth-century painter Jean-Baptiste-Camille Corot from a book on his writings, published in 1946: '[we must] submit ourselves to the first imprint. If we have been really touched our emotion will pass to others'. She told Giacometti, 'I cannot work on top of the canvas, ie build paint little by little approaching a little closer every day to succeed in something more accurate and definitive, because I would like the object on the canvas to be sudden, as if the form was designed by a breath if you will. So the only process is to remove every night and begin every morning all over again – which is exhausting and rather depressing.'[59]

What is particularly interesting about Isabel's letter to Giacometti is the possibility that he and Leiris, with whom she was also in touch, drew on its sentiments. Giacometti was alert to the apparitional ambitions of the monochromes when he saw photographs of them in February 1949: 'I really like the bird skeletons in the photographs and the depth as well they stay very light [*très légers*] and they are acutely drawn.'[60] Isabel reported this to Rose Pulham, underlining 'très légers'.[61]

79. Black and white photograph of Isabel Rawsthorne, *Bird and Bat*, 1947; Tate Archive

Leiris's seminal article on Giacometti in *Horizon* in June 1949 identified a new phase in Giacometti's work in similar terms: 'Instead of the patiently elaborated work of art we now have something which rises up suddenly and which is all the more evident for looking as though it has suddenly arrived.'[62]

Isabel reiterated her idea to Rose Pulham in the same month that Leiris's piece appeared: 'I think your idea of working, making a sum of experiments and experiences and putting them into one work is much to be respected, I could never do that, naturally you know.'[63]

80. Man Ray: photograph for *Cahiers d'art* of Alberto Giacometti, *The Palace at 4 A.M*, 1932; MoMA, New York

81. Isabel Rawsthorne, *The Desert*, c. 1948–50; private collection

17 CAT'S CRADLE: 1947–1949

While Isabel and Giacometti shared the theoretical interests, stylistic traits and *brut* finish of their Paris circle, they did not share the visceral aesthetic. They incorporated gestural and *matière* effects into works that retained their enquiring attitude to the observed appearance of the figure. Vital to this was its elusiveness and 'distance' – a single word that appeared in many of Isabel's notebooks.[1] The tenebrism of her monochromes evoked the figure seen far off in shadows, fog or memory that she and Giacometti cherished, but, during the following year, she evolved a more sophisticated approach to space.

Isabel had set out her problem in her 1947 diary: 'search / progressing / in unsolved problem question of "lineal" perspective the depth contained on a flat surface – opposite of Japanese idea – understood by Romans'.[2] Her visual transcriptions of the first-century BCE, Roman Fourth Style, Pompeian couple, Baker Terentius Neo and his Wife, (**82**) which she exhibited at the Hanover Gallery, (**83**) were part of this enquiry. In 1947, when she departed for London, she left behind her trial copies and the reproduction of the Pompeian painting she had been using in Giacometti's studio. Their influence can be seen in his portraits with black, white and red frames like those of Roman Fourth Style paintings. Several examples, including *Isabel* (1947; Fondation Giacometti, Paris), were displayed in a photograph of Giacometti, smiling, taken by Brassaï the same year, and he gave another, *Portrait of Diego in the Studio*, to Isabel herself (1948; whereabouts unknown, known from a photograph).[3] When Elisabeth Lutyens went to Paris in the spring of 1948, Isabel asked her to fetch back with her the 'roman copies'. She worked with them throughout the autumn and on into the following year, with sittings from Irene and Denis ApIvor in her studio, which she decorated in Roman hues: 'deepish grey/white/lighter grey/white walls and white woodwork with brown and Venetian red borders!'[4] The 'double portrait' of the ApIvors (*Copy of Pompeian Painting*) would form her version of The Baker Terentius Neo and his Wife. (**83, 82**)

Isabel placed her reproduction of the Roman double portrait next to her portrait by Derain. 'What I like so much about them', she wrote of the baker and his wife, 'is their unapproachable quality – suspended in a distance. I have my Derain

82. The Baker Terentius Neo and his Wife, c. 1 BCE, photographic print on board; ex-collection of Isabel Rawsthorne

83. Isabel Lambert with *Copy of Pompeian Painting* (Double Portrait), c. 1949; private collection

portrait put up beside one of them and it looks flat, like cardboard by comparison.'[5] It is significant that Roman art pre-dated the adoption of mathematical perspective and achieved *trompe l'œil* effects by other means, such as overlapping, diminishing, orthogonals and framing devices. The Northern Renaissance paintings that Isabel and Giacometti had been copying also pre-dated the systemisation of perspective in that part of the world and provided similar solutions. A more extreme precedent was a Pre-Raphaelite painting, *King Cophetua and the Beggar Maid* (1884; Tate, London), with its exaggerated perspectival boxes within boxes, that Isabel chose for the postcard she sent Giacometti from London in May 1947.[6] (**84**) Isabel's and Giacometti's internal framing devices of the later 1940s, were, like their use of pedestals, a phenomenological bracketing, a response to 'the need to place the figure in an empty space so as to see it better', as Giacometti explained to Pierre Matisse, in 1950.[7] They were a revision of the system of lines with which Isabel had constructed shapes at the centre of large sheets of paper in William Penn's perspective classes at Liverpool.[8] Inner scaffolds such as that explored in the angular drapery of her c. 1935 *Seated Figure* (**33**) knitted with these outer orientating lines. 'Figures were never for me a compact mass,' Giacometti wrote to Pierre Matisse, 'but like a transparent construction.'

The interrogation of linear perspective being made by Giacometti and Isabel was part of a broader theorisation of the framing device in the 1930s and 1940s.[9] In 1928, the Swiss historian Sigfried Giedion (the husband of Giacometti's friend Carola Giedion-Welcker) had published a popular book entitled *Building in France, Building in Iron, Building in Ferro-concrete*, which ascribed an existential significance

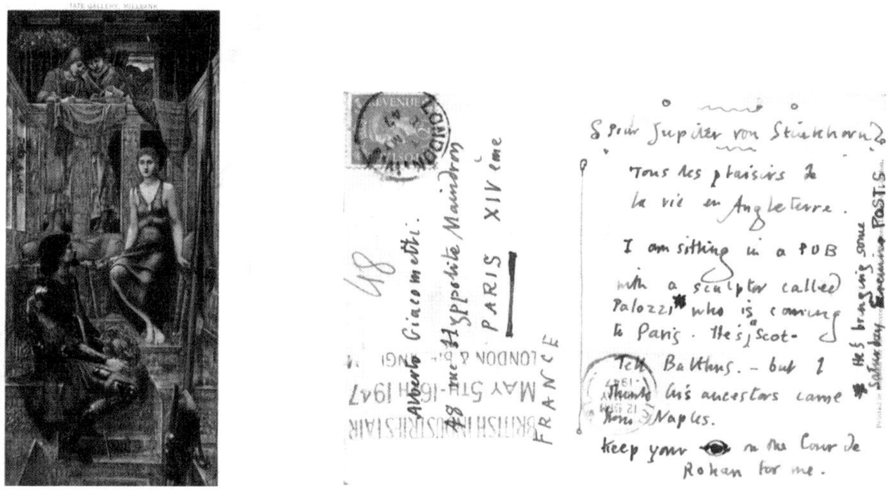

84. Postcard (recto and verso) of Edward Burne-Jones, *King Cophetua and the Beggar Maid*, 1884, with drawn border by Isabel Rawsthorne or Alberto Giacometti, 12 May 1947; Fondation Giacometti, Paris

to transparent iron-and-glass structures. Giedion argued that they represented a fluid, embodied experience of space, different from the geometrically prescribed viewpoint of solid architecture and traditional perspective, an idea later taken up by Walter Benjamin.[10] Giedion admired Giacometti: he saw his sculptures, notably *The Palace at 4 a.m.* (**80**) and *La Place*, 1947–8, (**85**) as a realisation of this sensibility, and he foregrounded the Baudelairean aspects of Giacometti's *City Square* by referring to it as 'Passers-by on a Square'. This understanding of presence in space was, Giedion wrote, ancient and modern, equivalent to the first humans negotiating irregularly shaped and lit caves.[11] Isabel's graffiti-like figures were a counterpart to Giedion's marks in the dark, impacting body to body, nervous system to nervous system, but the monochromes updated Giedion's vision: the grids evoked the scaffolding that rendered the spaces of patched Paris a grim parody of his Modernist ideals – the gloomy glass and metal of the vitrines of Deyrolle or the Galerie de paléontologie et d'anatomie comparée. They drew on Leonor Fini's *brut* sets and costumes for Roland Petit's *Les Demoiselles de la nuit*, which premiered with Margot Fonteyn in 1948 and featured birds and fish against backgrounds of scaffolds and newsprint.[12]

A common source for philosophers in France and Great Britain alike was *An Essay towards a New Theory of Vision* (1709) by the eighteenth-century Irish philosopher George Berkeley. This was a foundation stone for both Freddie Ayer's *Language, Truth and Logic* in 1936 and Maurice Merleau-Ponty's *The Phenomenology of Perception* in 1945.[13] *Language, Truth and Logic* was one of the few books foregrounded from Isabel's range of reading in the notes for her autobiography, and she took Ayer to meet Michel Leiris and Merleau-Ponty in 1945, prompting the first of many animated discussions between the English and French philosophers in which neither would yield: 'Since these arguments tended to become acrimonious,' Ayer remembered, 'we tacitly agreed to drop them and meet on a purely social level, which still left us quite enough to talk about.'[14]

The priority that Berkeley and Merleau-Ponty gave to the perception of distance as a defining component of 'presence' casts light on Isabel's and Giacometti's radical reappraisal of the dimension during this period.[15] Berkeley rejected geometrical models of depth based on a mathematical perspective, arguing that the relatively two-dimensional retina of the eye cannot register three-dimensional phenomena; in other words, we can register space to left or right, up or down, but not near or far.[16] The observation of three-dimensional things in three-dimensional space was, Berkeley believed, generated indirectly, by the accumulation of memories of two-dimensional perceptions and perceptions of other kinds, such as touch. In Isabel's Liverpool days, William Stevenson had described a similar 'capacity for feeling' in perspective: 'you are part and parcel of the essence of what you are involved in'.[17]

These embodied understandings of space participated in wider scientific, phenomenological and philosophical conversations connecting French and British ideas. Leiris's essay on Giacometti of 1929 described a toing and froing of exchanges between subject and object: 'moments ... when the external world opens up so between it and our hearts a sudden communication is established'.[18] This sudden communication reflected the understanding of perception as not so much calculated geometrically as embodied suddenly and convulsively, a blow or apparition. Merleau-Ponty's essay on art, 'Le Doute de Cézanne', published at the same time as *The Phenomenology of Perception*, characterised this as 'l'engrenage', or the entanglement of subject and object.[19] The word equated to the linear look, technique and terminology of both Giacometti's 'transparent construction' and Isabel's monochromes.[20] Rose Pulham translated it as a 'cat's cradle'. Isabel wrote to him in 1949: 'What is so exciting about the art of painting is just what you term the "cat's cradle" to be slung between reality and / the / transformation of it into terms of paint and a flat surface ... For me all the problems are practical and the implications are included in their execution.'[21]

For Merleau-Ponty and others the embodied (rather than perspectival) apprehension of distance was a phenomenological and psychological leap into 'that field into which each perception sets us back, where we are as yet still alone, where other people will appear at a later stage'.[22] They joined Existential writers in making the field, desert, depths and void synonymous with the condition of the individual in an obscure, indifferent universe. Merleau-Ponty's search for presence

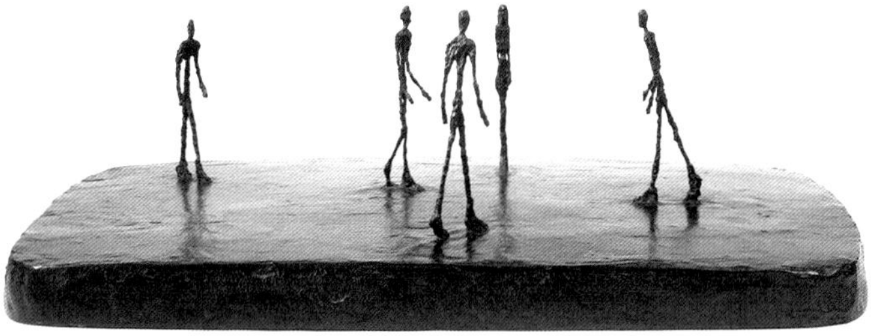

85. Alberto Giacometti, *La Place*, bronze, cast 1949; Solomon R. Guggenheim Foundation Peggy Guggenheim Collection, Venice

in depth echoed Camus's description of Sisyphus: 'He ... begins to advance with some decision only in the middle of that colourless desert where all certainties have become stones'[23] Isabel's figures glimpsed in insubstantial, shadowy backgrounds, and Giacometti's figures adrift on platforms image these ideas.

In 1949, Isabel began a painting called *The Desert*, 1948–50 (**81**) her postponed picture of Mara Scherbatoff walking in the street, which concentrated these ideas into one image. Shortly after marrying Constant Lambert, she watched from her window as he walked along an autumnal street and wrote: 'How revealing it is to see people from a distance.'[24] The title she chose for the picture probably derived from the wet 'desert' in James Thomson's *The Seasons*, which Isabel had been reading again in 1947:

> The desert joys
> Wildly, through all his melancholy bounds.
> Rude ruins glitter; and the briny deep,
> Seen from some pointed promontory's top,
> Far to the blue horizon's utmost verge,
> Restless, reflects a floating gleam.[25]

Isabel described the picture to Giacometti as a variation on his sculpture of her walking along a platform, *La Nuit*, and her blue and umber *Night* (with which she was unhappy): 'a landscape with pigeons, a cat and a character in the distance'.[26]

The painting shows a woman, like Sisyphus, 'advancing into the colourless desert', across an open bombsite opposite Isabel's studio window. It is a *lieu vague*: lamps are unlit, a tree stands as bare as a telegraph pole, a strip of horizon is barred by the spires of churches and a dome, possibly the damaged the National Gallery, dissected by scaffolding. It is 'dark green light at midday', as Isabel described murky London, and the atmosphere exactly fits Paolozzi's contemporary description of the capital: 'moving through the fog all these lost souls somehow ... terribly austere ... that kind of atmosphere of damp astringency'.[27] The thin, branched shape of the lone woman recalls Shakespeare's description in *King Lear* of the 'unaccommodated man', cast out in the rain and wind: 'Thou art the thing itself: unaccommodated man is no more but such a poor bare, forked animal as thou art.' Leiris applied the 'forked animal' to Giacometti's walking figures in his *Horizon* article the following year.[28]

The Desert lacks the assurance of the monochromes, and Isabel was still working on it in the summer of 1949 and again in 1950, but, as research, it is a timely engagement with distance and the 'problem question of "lineal' perspective'. It adapted the Berkeley-like principle of multiple points of view: '3 landscapes in one', as she wrote to Rose Pulham; 'that is to say, to produce effect you really get when walking, your vision being ...' This comment was followed by a diagram expressing perceptions straight-on and to left and right, coinciding.[29] **(86)**

The painting reveals also an early appreciation of another painter who was preoccupied with Berkeley, David Bomberg. Bomberg had exhibited only intermittently since his explosive debut alongside the Vorticist movement before the First World War and, by the 1930s, was almost forgotten in Britain and unheard of on the Continent. His fellow Vorticists, Epstein and Wyndham Lewis, had maintained their admiration for him, however, and Epstein had exhibited with him in a group show at the Ben Uri Gallery when Isabel was living with him in 1933.[30] In 1945, Bomberg took a teaching post at Borough Polytechnic and in March 1947 began to exhibit annually with his students as part of the Borough Group. He published statements about 'a truth and a realism [in nature] which the usual contemporary approach to painting is unable to convey' and taught Berkeley's ideas, stressing his opinion that touch contributed to perceptions of a third dimension.[31] All these are apt for the 'manual imagination' of Giacometti and Isabel and their experiential, rather than calculated perspectival devices.[32] Neither she nor her associates can have missed Wyndham Lewis's review of Bomberg's show at the Arcade Gallery in Bond Street in 1949 which appeared in the same article as his review of Isabel's own show and in which he identified Bomberg as the 'leading spirit' in London.[33]

The Desert drew specifically on Bomberg's war paintings of London shown in a one-man exhibition at the Leger Gallery in 1943 (his first since 1936) and with

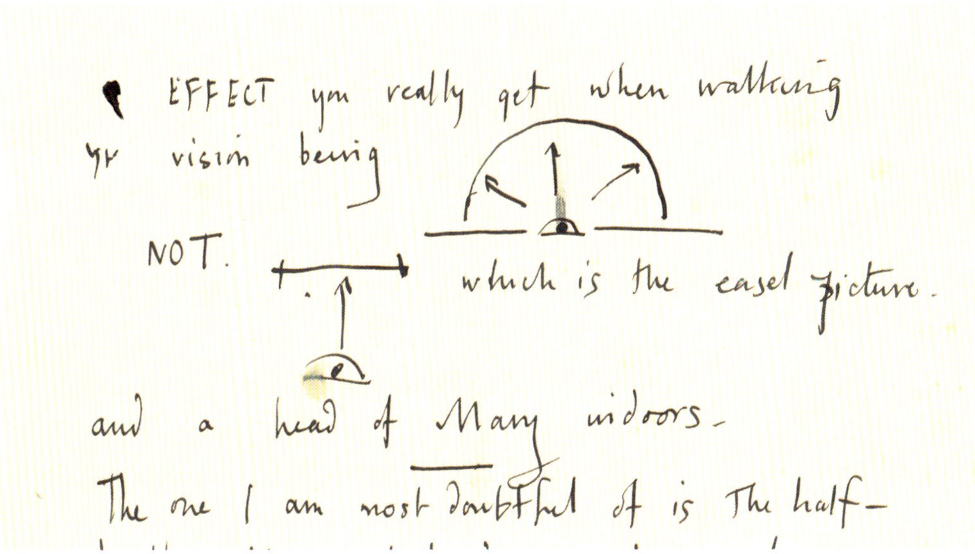

EFFECT you really get when walking
yr vision being
NOT. which is the easel picture.
and a head of Mary indoors.
The one I am most doubtful of is the half-

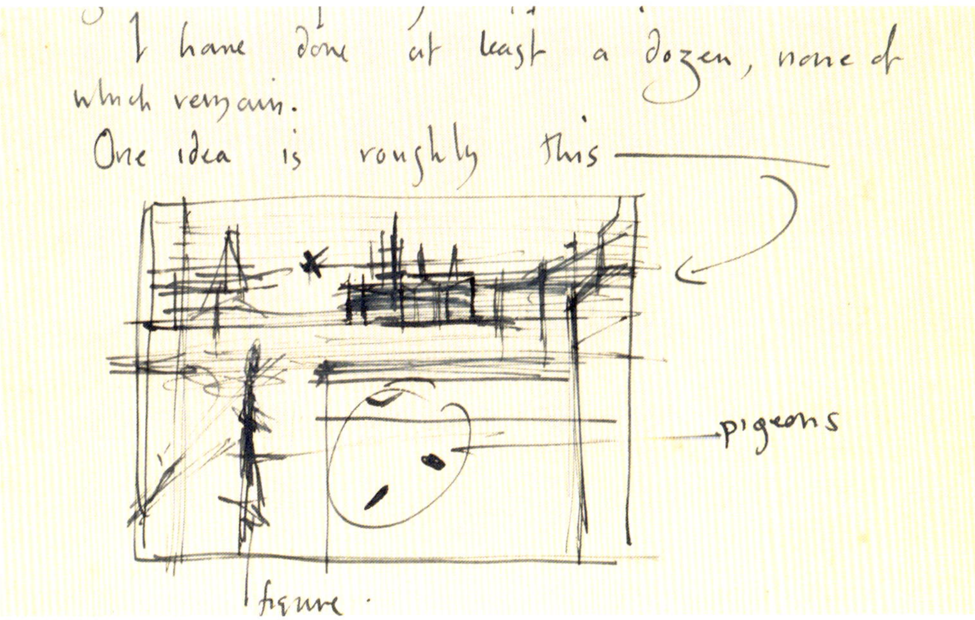

I have done at least a dozen, none of
which remain.
One idea is roughly this —
pigeons
figure.

86. Isabel Rawsthorne, details of letters to Peter Rose Pulham, summer 1949; Tate Archive

87. David Bomberg, *Evening in the City of London*, 1944; Ashmolean Museum, Oxford

the London Group in 1944. *Evening in the City of London,* 1944, (**87**) a view of the battered dome of St Paul's from a bomb site, presents the city as 'a sequence of eerily deserted containers, no more than a skeleton of the metropolis that he knew before'.[34] A more ambitious landscape of the Thames which Isabel planned at the time – 'Dozens of cranes stand up against a gray sky blue – very powerful river, running in a violent curve, dark brown color. And dozens of barges, small boats and vessels from all over the world' – recalled other views by Bomberg, such as *London River* (1946; Government Art Collection).[35]

The painting adopted also Bomberg's way of integrating figure and ground in a dense network of strokes: 'Contours are scored on to the paper with a charcoal sooty enough to have been seized, still smouldering, from the burnt-out wreckage of a bombsite', as Richard Cork described.[36] Isabel created horizontals, orthogonals and repoussoirs with the *hazard* of gesture rather than calculation; brush marks painted through, rather than over, each other with a *matière* paste, take our eye from the tangibly damp and dirty surface of the canvas to the distant dome. Buildings, figure and birds are immersed, like the carp in Apollinaire's poem, in a damp melee of fog, dust and dusk. A splash of water at the figure's feet and glimpses of reflections hint at recent rain and, as with Doctor Foster, to recent tribulation. Swathes of turgid and glossy paint wet the surface. Appropriately, when Isabel had difficulties with the picture, as she often did, she described herself as 'floundering'.[37] Out of this atmosphere swim the three birds, startled by the walking woman, each the merest smear of movement. She, herself, comprises little more; three strokes set her striding, the furthest leg a scratch in the grey pavement, breasts two clots of impasto, barely distinguishable from canvas slubs.

Existentialists employed the phrase 'art autre' to describe artists' self-authenticating action against their environment via their materials: 'marks as an affirmation of essence', to borrow Frances Morris's summary.[38] It equated to Isabel's 'peintre contraire', and her idea of an art conducted authentically in a spirit of research. She rejected the two idealist styles that dominated in Paris in the late 1940s: Gruber's social realism, associated with communism; and formalism promoted, with matching militancy, as its liberal alternative. She was, instead, a pioneer of 'the *informel* ... open representation in free gesture'.[39] The similarity between Bomberg's networks of brushstrokes and work by Isabel and Giacometti in the final years of the decade raises the possibility that she was a conduit for ideas shared across the Channel. Certainly she was a link between Ayer and Merleau-Ponty and their influence on the phenomenological theory and practice of painting-writing. By 1952, the style was variously labelled as *tachisme* or *art informel* and associated with the development in New York of Abstract Expressionism. In 1952, Isabel's phrases peintre 'contraire' and 'cat's cradle' were united in Michel Tapié's seminal definition of this: 'An art of another kind, a new unravelling of the real.'[40]

88. Isabel Rawsthorne, *Three Fish*, 1948; courtesy Nigel Bonham-Carter

18 SCHOOL OF LONDON: 1948–1951

Between 1947 and 1951, Isabel worked and exhibited without break. Her activities were part of a broader revival of the arts in post-war London, culminating in the Festival of Britain. It was her time of convergence; her solitary, artistic path crossing with those of others asking similar questions. As writers and artists of all kinds poured into Paris, and as she then took her place in London, she catalysed connections between them.

During and after the war, Kenneth Clark's stable of 'loyal men and dreamy boys', as Lawrence Alloway called them, were in ascendency in British art.[1] As patron, collector, head of the War Artist Committee and active on many others, Clark had enormous influence and encouraged sculptors and painters with Neo-Romantic tendencies, such as Henry Moore and Graham Sutherland. Artists who had been on the margins during the war, however, were now coalescing into a fast-moving, alternative avant-garde. They connected through the Lefevre Gallery, through Mesens's London Gallery – the home of English Surrealism – and through shared rites of passage in Paris.[2] Mesens's assistant, the jazz musician George Melly, recalled that Rose Pulham, practically forgotten today, was one of the first to challenge the status quo, with *Oil Paintings and Gouaches by Rose Pulham* at the London Gallery in June 1948.[3] Mesens was excited about Isabel's work, calling it '"Noble!!' "dignified" "serious"', but Isabel chose Erica Brausen's new Hanover Gallery.[4] Mesens was loyal to the Surrealists in their increasingly problematic post-war form, while Brausen, who had previously worked in the Redfern Gallery, was associated with dissidents and independents such as Soutine, Giacometti and Bacon.[5] She owned the bracelet that Giacometti had made in 1936 (**31**) and had probably known Isabel in Paris before the war. Isabel's defection was prescient: the London Gallery folded, but two new venues, the Hanover Gallery and the Institute of Contemporary Arts (ICA), became instrumental in introducing the new British art to an international audience.

Isabel's was one of the first exhibitions held at the Hanover Gallery, in February 1949, and the precocious European manifesto set out in the foreword to the catalogue was one of the earliest published statements of its kind. Her show attracted attention from abroad. Leonor Fini visited and thought the paintings ‘the only good things in London’.[6] Offers came in for shows in Paris and Italy.[7] That Isabel saw her work in the context of the fashionable but contentious avant-garde Galerie Drouin – the venue for Tapis, Dubuffet and artists associated with *Les Temps modernes* – is illustrated by the fact that she preferred to wait for that venue, planning a joint venture there with Rose Pulham the following year.[8] Erica Brausen sent pictures to Italy, and, in March 1950, Isabel exhibited in Milan alongside Michael Ayrton.[9]

Brausen was pleased with the display, the sales and reviews in London, but Isabel was not. London was more difficult to conquer than it had been in her twenties. Her long absence, three changes of name and the evolution of her work out of the public eye left little to connect her present pictures to the distinctive line and anthropological eye of the Isabel Nicholas who had exhibited in the next street fifteen years earlier.[10] Wyndham Lewis and Matthew Smith (who bought *Two Fish II*) were amongst the few to recognise the connection.[11] Nor did Isabel do much to exploit publicity. In Paris, her confidants had been more or less restricted to Giacometti, Balthus, Rose Pulham and Paolozzi. In London, only Bacon and Brausen appear to have entered her studio. Extraordinarily, at the opening of the Hanover exhibition, even such friends as Freddie Ayer ‘got quite a shock’ to discover what she had been doing.[12] Bacon complimented her, she reported to Rose Pulham, but ‘no one else responded at all!’ When the reviews came out, she dashed off a note: ‘re an exhibition, monochromes, Tommy Earp Telegraph sympathetic, P[hilip] Toynbee also, WL[Wyndham Lewis], Times, not. Herbert Read “very interesting but we must wait for her next show before exhibiting her in Paris” from BC OK but Mrs Sommerville hated them.’[13] ‘Abroad the only chance,’ she wrote. Astonishingly, within days of her opening, she had left the country with Constant Lambert for Italy.[14] This ill-timed absence was a measure of her impatience with exhibiting, ‘I wish the whole fucking thing were over,’ she had written to Rose Pulham, shortly before; ‘I suppose everybody feels the same.’[15]

The post-war atmosphere in London was less liberal towards art and artists than it had been in the 1930s. *The Times* and *The Observer* had been excited by the challenging nature of Isabel’s drawings of 1933, but assessed the paintings of 1949 with more conventional expectations of gender and style. *The Times* reviewer gave equal attention to the two exhibitions the Hanover was offering, but headlined only one, that of the veteran Fauve painter Raoul Dufy. The writer was disappointed in his or her search for anything that was not ‘fashionable decoration’ by the male artist, or anything that *was* decorative by the woman. Isabel’s ‘strict’ austerity was worse, in this critic’s eyes, for its unfeminine reluctance to please, and the only praise given characterised her work with the catch-all adjectives ubiquitous in reviews of women’s art: ‘her line is always graceful and her colour is laid on with a

89. Isabel Rawsthorne, *Fish, Bird and Figure,* 1947; private collection

delicate touch'.[16] The *Evening Standard*, by contrast, acknowledged the sparseness Isabel prized, but, mindful of the 'rabbit cooked in wine' and the recent exposé of the good times had at RAG, diluted it with cooking metaphors: 'She likes austerity on the canvas but not in the kitchen.'[17] For such an exhibition, February 1949 was also a little too early. British reviewers were not adequately aware of what had been happening in Paris recently to recognise the proto-Tachist, apparitional ambitions of her pictures. Despite the success of *Horizon* in translating and reprinting important French essays – Artaud's on Van Gogh, for instance – only a minority of artists and critics had re-established connections with Continental art.[18] *The Spectator* admired what it called her 'spectres' and understood their anthropological sources: 'Isobel [*sic*] Lambert ... distils something of the silent terrors a museum can inspire. Her barbed and skeletal birds and fishes float in a surreal limbo of the imagination, a hinterland that owes something perhaps to Giacometti.'[19] Most, however, 'did not see the point', as she put it. [20]

After the war, modern European art was, as James Hyman has pointed out, mainly understood through Paul Klee, whose status was catalysed by his death in 1940 and a major exhibition at the National Gallery in 1945.[21] Wyndham Lewis's verdict on Isabel's show in *The Listener* – 'Isabel Lambert stalks Klee successfully with nightjars, lizards, cockchafers, and recipes' – was therefore more of a compliment than she acknowledged.[22] The young writer David Sylvester, who had made for Paris in the summer of 1947, saw Giacometti, similarly, as Klee's successor. By the following year, in the wake of Giacometti's successful New York show and Sartre's eulogy on his standing figures, 'In Search of the Absolute', Sylvester identified him as the 'key figure' of modern art, 'rescuing art from facility and commercialism'.[23] Having gained an introduction to the artist at the Leirises, Sylvester visited the studio in the rue Hippolyte-Maindron and saw figures and drawings not yet exhibited in Europe.[24] Sylvester's time in the city, his friendship with Giacometti and the editorial advice he received from Merleau-Ponty on his first major essay on Klee for *Les Temps modernes* encouraged an appreciation of the phenomenological experiments discussed in the previous chapter.[25] He progressed from his admiration of Klee to recognising an 'embattled minority' at the cutting edge of contemporary art comprising Giacometti and the younger artists who were exhibiting at the Hanover and other advanced galleries.[26] Shortly after Isabel's show, he coined the term 'modernist realism' to distinguish their non-narrative figuration, rooted in post-war experience, from Neo-Romanticism, and he identified them as a kind of School of London (a term purloined and reused in the 1970s).[27]

The Parisian agenda was clarified a month after Isabel's exhibition closed; in June 1949, *Horizon* published Michel Leiris's illustrated article 'Thoughts around Alberto Giacometti'.[28] Later in the year, paintings and sculptures by Giacometti were purchased by the Tate Gallery, and further works by him were exhibited at the Hanover Gallery in a mixed show in 1950.[29] Isabel wrote to him that a 'history of giacometti in england' was under way and that Sylvester was planning a show at the newly established ICA.[30] The exhibition did not happen until 1955, but, in 1952, Sylvester held a debate dedicated to Giacometti, with a panel comprising the sculptors Reg Butler and William Turnbull and the painters Graham Sutherland, Rodrigo Moynihan and Peter Rose Pulham. Herbert Read observed, 'British sculptors have given sculpture what it never had before our time – a linear, cursive quality.'[31]

In 1950, Sylvester paired London artists 'of outstanding talent' with Parisian counterparts in an ambitious exhibition, *London–Paris: New Trends in Paintings and Sculpture*, at the ICA.[32] London was represented by five painters: Isabel, Francis Bacon, Lucian Freud, John Craxton and the St Ives artist Peter Lanyon – and three sculptors – Robert Adams, Reg Butler and Fred McWilliam. Paris sent older artists working in an abstract style, Hans Hartung, Jean Bazaine, André Bloc, Henri-Georges Adam, Jacques Herold, Pierre Pallut and Germaine Richier. The catalogue essay contrived a case for 'modernist realists', Bacon in particular, as a vital British alternative to a Parisian, trans-Atlantic, formalist avant-garde.[33] Each

90. Isabel Rawsthorne, *Two Fish*, 1947; National Galleries of Scotland

artist contributed four works. Isabel showed her best from the Hanover show – *Two Birds* (lent by Sydney and Zoe Bernstein) and *Two Birds and a Fish* – and two new works – *Two Standing Figures* and *Figure* (1950; private collection; discussed in the next chapter). *The Scotsman*, reviewing the show under the misleading heading 'Bad boys run wild', appreciated the 'elusive' nature of many of the works: 'Isabel Lambert seems to have blown her figures off the canvas, leaving only a hint of her presence.'[34]

Isabel liked David Sylvester, although she felt he had a tendency to be 'blown about by every blaze'.[35] The 'School of London' was not a universally accepted title for the group and was usurped by R. B. Kitaj in the 1970s, but it is possible to identify in the artists in whom Sylvester was interested a degree of shared vision. Isabel's Hanover exhibition in February 1949, for example, was preceded at the Hanover in the January by a display of insect-based mobiles by Peter Foldes

91. Eduardo Paolozzi, *Shooting Gallery*, 1947; National Galleries of Scotland

(now better known for his animation), while it was followed at the Mayor Gallery in May by an exhibition of Paolozzi's insect and marine imagery.[36] Sylvester's description of Reg Butler's July/August exhibition that followed Isabel's at the Hanover Gallery, demonstrates their aesthetic continuity: 'you'll think you have run into some hiding place of undiscovered insects, posturing and gesturing in a vain but devastating impersonation of the human race … beings affirming the tragic absurdity of existence.'[37] Marine and zoological imagery became an established token of the London avant-garde and a vehicle for ideas of the scientific, the atavistic and the *informe*. In 1950, Lucian Freud exhibited marine still lifes alongside his portraits at the Hanover.[38] His painstaking style varied from the *brut* tendencies of his peers, but with subtle ingenuity *Still Life with a Sea Urchin* (1949; Harris Art Gallery) presented a literal equivalent of the calligraphic mark – an inky stain leaking from a squid. Paolozzi's joint show with William Turnbull followed Freud's, and Sylvester's foreword for the catalogue noted that its 'principal source is the aquarium' and that to enter the show was as 'to fly like a bird among branches or to swim under water among the inhabitants, mobile or stationary, of the sea'.[39] Turnbull's *Sea Forms* (1949; Tate, London) and the red fish-figures of Robert Adams (untitled, 1949; Tate, London) shared the content and the calligraphic impact of the graphic gouaches Isabel had revealed the previous year, as well as recalling Richier's prints, such as *Insectes*, of 1948–9.

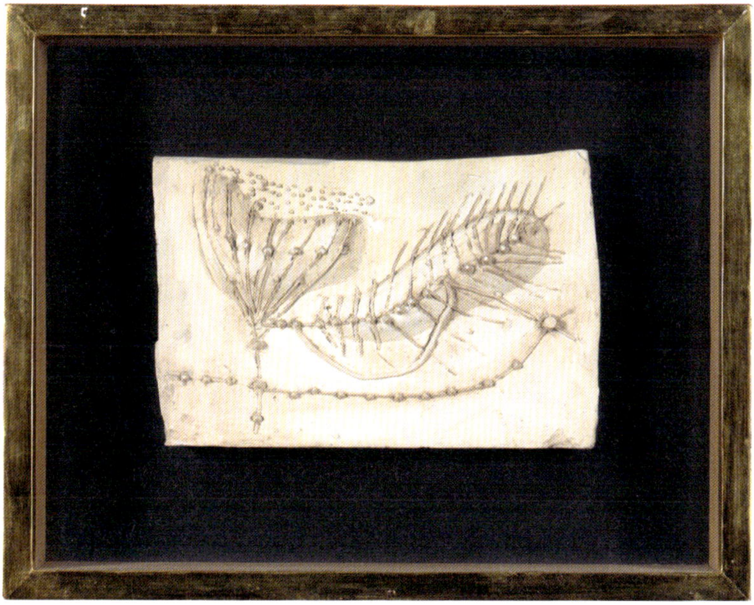

92. Eduardo Paolozzi, *Plaster Relief*, 1948; Tate

Bacon, who had laid low since selling *Painting 1946*, spent more time in London after 1947. He, Isabel, Freud and, when he visited from Paris, Paolozzi were regularly in each other's company and shared ideas, friends and networks.[40] The force of Isabel's radicalism was registered in friction with eminent representatives of Neo-Romanticism, recorded in her memoir and letters. She appears to have been, as Valéry said of Degas, a somewhat 'unbearable guest, spreading wit, terror and gaiety'.[41] At Bacon's studio on 18 December 1948, Isabel met Graham and Kathleen Sutherland and Douglas Cooper.[42] 'Bacon charming as usual', she told Rose Pulham, 'I was rather aggressive I fear. Argued violently with Graham S.' Early in 1950, she railed after a similar spat with Henry Moore.[43] Isabel was even unenthusiastic about Freud's early 'systematic' method, as she described it, 'splitting the face into planes', but she admired his imagery and his success and wrote ruefully to Rose Pulham about his shows selling out.[44] Paolozzi, on the other hand, sold so little that, in 1949, he was forced to return permanently to London and seek a teaching post.

Isabel's pictures were stored in Paolozzi's Paris studio, and her occasional periods there, meant that, between 1947 and 1949, they worked side by side with each other's output. Paolozzi consolidated an aesthetic of 'things' comparable to Ponge's 'choses', and explored the pedestals and frames that were preoccupying Giacometti and Isabel. *Paris Bird* and *Two Forms on a Rod* (both 1948; Tate, London),

93. Harold E. Edgerton, 'A "Splash" of Milk', from D'Arcy Wentworth Thompson, *On Growth and Form* (1942)

94. William Turnbull, *Growth and Form*, poster, 1951; private collection

for instance, combined references to Giacometti's plaster *Table* (1933; then in the collection of vicomte Charles de Noailles) with skeletal forms.[45] He experimented with gridded compositions: *Shooting Gallery*, 1947, (**91**) reminiscent of Giacometti and Isabel's grids, was inspired by the fair next to his studio and suggested 'sudden' representation by characterising a bird as a target, apprehended not so much in a 'blow', as in a rifle shot.

When Paolozzi had exhibited fish and bird sculptures in concrete at his first show at the Mayor Gallery in 1947, he and Nigel Henderson considered themselves the only students at the Slade to prefer museums to art galleries.[46] He found an established practice of this kind of thinking within Isabel's circle, however. Henderson and Turnbull joined Paolozzi in Paris in 1948, and Anna Massey has noted that the experience was a break with Neo-Romanticism for all three young artists, in favour of Giacometti, Galerie Drouin and Sartre. The zoological air of Paolozzi's and Turnbull's eroded, etiolated sculpture suggests that they were looking also at Isabel and Richier.[47]

D'Arcy Wentworth Thompson's *On Growth and Form* was of particular importance. Paolozzi and Turnbull adapted into their work the pronged shape derived from the famous stop-motion illustration 'A "Splash" of Milk' that is the frontispiece.[48] William Beebe's *Half Mile Down* was another shared enthusiasm, and, early in 1949, Isabel asked Rose Pulham, who was living back on the quai des Grands-Augustins, to pass Paolozzi a message that she had ordered a second volume by the author, *The Book of Bays* (1942).[49] Paolozzi made graffiti-like reliefs such as *Growth* and *Fish* (1948; both private collection), suggesting fossilised crustaceans and marine creatures.[50] In London, Isabel designed a series of fish-themed *dessins drôles* (whereabouts unknown), and she and Constant Lambert planned an illustrated article on the nineteenth-century marine biology research centre, the Stazione Zoologica, in Naples (whose aquarium she visited in 1949 and Paolozzi in 1952).[51] By 1951, zoological and marine motifs were, as Martin Harrison has pointed out, mainstream across British art and design.[52] The new ICA was to provide a common venue for science and art, and, in 1951, Nigel Henderson and Richard Hamilton organised there an exhibition entitled *Growth and Form* for the Festival of Britain.[53] Many of the works, such as Hamilton's *Microcosmos: Plant Cycle* (1950; Tate, London), shared the austere, calligraphic air of Isabel's monochromes.

The idea put forward in *On Growth and Form*, of the prehistoric present – resemblances between prehistoric and modern beings – dovetailed into tendencies to conflate the atavistic and futuristic that thrived after the war, epitomised in the title of the second ICA exhibition in 1948, *40,000 years of Modern Art*.[54] This prehistoric vision was not the 'romantic and modish hankering after the barbaric' of early twentieth century 'primitivism', as Carola Giedion-Welcker put it.[55] As we have seen, Giacometti and the School of London artists tended towards atemporal models closer to Benjamin's 'dialectical object', or Ponge's *objeu*.[56] That primordial, embodied idea of presence was given clearest expression when Siegfried Giedion spoke at the ICA in 1950, a talk entitled 'Palaeolithic Art and Modernism'. In Paris, Paolozzi and Turnbull had embraced the more materialist, embodied understanding of the mark being promoted by Dubuffet and the Galerie Drouin circle, Isabel and Giacometti, and Turnbull recalled being struck by Siegfried Giedion's image of man making marks in relation to his own body in the dark of the irregular cave.[57] Such primeval/Parisian notions of chance and *hazard* distinguish Turnbull's technique: 'You moved it [plaster] about until you got what you wanted,' he told Martin Harrison in 2000; 'the ultimate form the work took was a matter of recognition'.[58] French ideas of art as action, impacting body to body, nervous system to nervous system, that were so central to Isabel's practice in the mid-1940s, were a key component for London artists.

Giedion's perception of space that arose from the body rather than from rectilinear logic, unfixed, susceptible to degraded, incomplete, titled, mixed, transparent, even cinematic forms, was relevant to modern experiences of screens and open structures.[59] Modern art was 'governed by man's position – his orientation – in the universe', as Turnbull put it.[60] Henderson's photograph of Turnbull's 1950

Hanover display brings it closer to Isabel's multiple, dissolving frameworks by unfixing the camera. Its movement during exposure skewed, blurred, multiplied structures and rendered them semi-transparent, recalling her 'eyes out of focus'. The effect is similar to the more literally dissolving falls of water of *Fountain*, designed by Paolozzi for the Festival of Britain. David Sylvester christened the tendency, which he observed also in Paolozzi's collages and in the abridged figures in frameworks that Bacon was exhibiting, as 'afocalism'. Isabel's immersive spaces anticipate Sylvester's ideas of 'a picture or sculpture ... devoid of a focal point ... the spectator reads it, not by confronting it as a scene detached from himself, but by entering it and moving about in it'.[61]

Isabel's knowing and independent assimilation of Parisian ideas and her undisguised disdain for even modern establishment figures can only have encouraged her peers. Although on good terms with Herbert Read, for so long the spokesman of mainstream English modernism, her rejection of his idealism pre-empted the principles of the ICA. The eradication of Read's 'obstinate absolutes' would also become the binding tenet of the Independent Group in 1952.[62] Isabel and her circle's enthusiasm for non-fine-art sources laid the foundations for the interdisciplinary democracy of images that would be a principle of both the ICA and the Independent group. Elisabeth Lutyens and Constant Lambert were on the ICA committee and, in May 1950, chaired a discussion on contemporary music and ballet, while Alan Rawsthorne hosted another on music and film.[63]

In July 1952, Sylvester organised a London–Paris exhibition at the ICA, devoted exclusively to 'realism', *Recent Trends in Realist Painting*, although the exhibition failed in its suggestion that figurative art was more vigorous than abstraction, because most of the works appeared to be semi-abstract. Each artist provided two pieces. They included Isabel, Bacon, Freud, Rose Pulham, Sutherland, Minton, William Coldstream and Elinor Bellingham-Smith, along with Giacometti, Balthus, Masson and Grégoire Michonze. Works by Francis Gruber were also present. Younger artists of the new French figurative group L' Homme Témoin (Man as Witness) were exhibited: Bernard Buffet, André Minaux and Paul Rebeyrolle.[64] Isabel's autobiographical notes included Buffet as a significant figure but did not go into detail. His scratched, calligraphic style had striking affinities with her monochromes, and, after his visit to London, he painted several skeletons, such as *Squelette de poisson* (1954; private collection), which strongly recalled Isabel's *Birds and Fish*.[65]

Recent Trends in Realist Painting became an occasion for consolidating positions, primacy and influence. Isabel wrote to Rose Pulham: 'Now everyone going around saying who influenced who or something.'[66] It was not a subject that interested them, and Rose Pulham jokingly claimed to be enclosing an 'early work by Francis Bacon which I executed recently'.[67] Others were less diffident. Paolozzi's later writings and interviews acknowledge he knew Isabel but mention no artistic aspect to their Paris friendship or admit, even, that she was an artist.[68] On the other hand, he presented his exposure to Giacometti in 1947 as decisive.[69] This contradicts Isabel's recollection in her autobiography that in that particular year he 'was no admirer of Giacometti'. It seems likely that, after Giacometti's international resurgence through the Pierre Matisse show and the publication of Leiris's article in *Horizon* in 1949, Paolozzi preferred to claim that the conspicuous effect of the sculptor on his work was direct, rather than via others, including Isabel. Germaine Richier received similar treatment. She was considered a major figure and crucial influence by David Sylvester in 1955, but in an interview with Frank Whitford in 1998, Paolozzi reduced her to 'the Frenchwoman, whose work doesn't really stand up to the ... title [Geometry of Fear]', at which point he is interrupted by Whitford's agreement.[70] This 310-page interview surveying Paolozzi's career paid slightly more attention to Isabel but described her as a model, referring only to her husband's profession, not hers! The neglect of Richier since her premature death in 1959 provides insights into why Isabel's reputation and role failed to be remembered beyond that time, as well. Rose Pulham, by contrast, was happy to tell Isabel, 'I am influenced by Giacometti not directly but via you.'[71] Paolozzi felt a similar need to 'move away' as he put it, from *l'art brut* and liked to say he had refused their offer to exhibit, although in 1949 he contributed to *Les Mains éblouies*, at Galerie Maeght.[72] Rebecca Daniels has noted that Bacon, in a similar way, controlled the public acknowledgement of artists who were said to have influenced him.[73] The following chapters will show that Isabel was the 'artist friend' he mentioned to Sylvester in the 1960s, but without naming her.[74]

These artists were right to distance themselves from traditional models of 'influence' which are wholly inadequate for understanding the richness of relations in London and Paris after the Second World War.[75] The players were individuals rather than masters and disciples. The realities of social mixing and exchanges on the telephone, by letter and in print meant that ideas were circulating within a network, being transformed with each exchange. Artists looked 'with' other artists (present and past) and with an unprecedented plethora of other visual and literary sources. Isabel's long years working on the Left Bank and her particular associates there, not to mention her fluent French, made her by far the most informed and experienced of the School of London group. Her correspondence with Giacometti and Rose Pulham provides valuable glimpses of a far more extensive dialogue carried out mainly in talk, in cafés, restaurants, studios and bedrooms. The most nuanced evidence remaining to us, however, are the works themselves.

95. Isabel Rawsthorne, 'Two Figures', 1950; private collection

19 TWO FIGURES: 1948–1950

> I fight almost with despair amongst the nudes.
> *Les nus couchés, les nus debout, les nus au jardin, les nus à l'intérieur,*
> two together, one alone, sitting by the window – in the colours of earth,
> in the colours of light.[1]

In her Albany Street room, Isabel returned to the figure with a campaign of nudes. They coincided with her professional and personal proximity to Bacon, and they explored the body *in camera* – which Existentialism had made central to post-war art – bringing Anglo-French, proto-Tachist painting to London.[2]

The studio Isabel had made for herself in the apartment at 197 Albany Street finally permitted her the space to employ models. From 1948, she painted nudes in series. Isabel described them as 'The Seasons' and, like *The Desert*, they were informed by Thomson's poem of this title. They nodded to the young women in landscapes, such as *L'Automne* and *Le Printemps* (both private collection), painted by Francis Gruber in 1937, meditations on time, 'sensitive to man, the life of man'.[3] The existential theme gained sharpness from the death of Gruber from tuberculosis in December 1948 at the age of thirty-six, Isabel's age. During his last illness, attended by Alberto and Diego Giacometti, Gruber had returned in his work to the semi-naked figures he had painted before the war.[4]

Isabel paired her figures, as she had in the monochromes. At first, she employed the same grid, calligraphic brushing and 'unimaginable blue' as she had done in the lost monochrome called *Night*. Various versions meant to equate to the season of winter analysed one or two women standing near a window, bisected by Sickert-like gleams and shadows, recalling the silhouetted figures in the shadow theatre she mentioned making around this time.[5] Isabel described the look she was aiming at as something like Marcel Duchamp's painting on glass.[6] She had discussed the phenomenon with Rose Pulham as early as 1946, when she had stayed in his and Mary's cottage in the Indre, recalled by him in a letter to her written in 1956: 'The first idea for it came from looking at the little glass paned window of your shepherds hut ... landscape outside seen through the glass, the room reflected in it, at that moment of dusk when the electric light indoors is equal in strength to the twilight without.'[7] Isabel's 'idea of ambivalence' and 'some enhanced reality' still owed a debt to Marcel Carné's 'poetic realism'. Her *noire* monotones and reflections, and her attention to the lit *mise-en-scène* is revealed in a working note to Rose Pulham: 'artificial light after 4pm (using two models daylight bulb and opaque bulb)'.[8] Nudes for spring and summer varied the vitrine aesthetic and were studied in a greenhouse.[9]

Isabel was at pains to avoid the 'usual kind of engineering in forms' and 'technical habit', that she found unsympathetic in Michael Ayrton's style and Lucian Freud's early detailed approach.[10] This is clarified in her surprisingly partial reaction to the Old Master works she viewed at the exhibition *Art Treasures from Vienna*, organised by the Tate Gallery between 20 May and 3 September 1949. It was a 'disturbing shock ... Never felt the falsity of painting, the overwhelming gap between reality and a picture to such a degree. To start with all human figures seemed too large to look at, many times over life-size ... a shapeless mass of beautiful but totally arbitrary colours ...' In this she included Rubens and Titian: 'there is something about the surface of the paint that is wrong. It is like skin sheet stretched over and flattening the form. It seems to me that when you look at living creatures there is no continuous paintable surface. Rembrandt answered this question but then so did Velasquez and Holbein ... outstanding exceptions.' Isabel's overwhelming impression from *Art Treasures* was of the promise of her own generation: 'Came away much struck with the high quality of modern painting starting from Corot.'[11] She was thinking, by this date, not only of Giacometti and other Parisian pioneers, but also of Bacon.

It is often assumed that Isabel and Bacon's association was solely social and restricted to the Soho scene, but they saw each other, and each other's work, frequently after his return from France in November 1948. He had begun addressing the figure in oils several years before, and at thirty-nine he was a little older than Isabel, but his career had, like hers, been inhibited by the war, personal difficulties and, on occasion, poverty, so they were at a similar stage professionally. Isabel's autobiographical notes record that she met Bacon 'in Paris with Peter'. Bacon had been living in Monte Carlo since June 1946 but was in Paris in November that year, when he stayed at the Hôtel Saint-Romain, saw Balthus's exhibition and searched for a studio.[12] Isabel and Rose Pulham came up from the Indre at the same time, and it was probably on this visit that she and Bacon got to know each other.[13] He was perhaps reflecting the attitude of the Paris avant-garde and his conversations with Rose Pulham and Isabel when, on his return, he wrote to Graham Sutherland rejecting 'the terrible decoration we are all contaminated by'. He included in this Balthus's exhibition and his own *Painting 1946* (1946; Museum of Modern Art, New York) in the British section of the UNESCO show. His conclusion had a Parisian flavour: 'the tenderness which we would all love to get for a change ... can't be done that way it can only come as a technical thing ... I feel more and more that nothing matters or will happen until someone makes a new technical synthesis that can carry over from sensation to our nervous system.'[14] The new departure contributed, perhaps, to Bacon's failure to produce anything exhibitable for many months, but his return to London in 1948 and Brausen's sale of *Painting 1946* to the Museum of Modern Art in New York gave him an impetus at around the same time as Isabel was forging ahead in Albany Street. That they already knew each other is suggested by the fact that Isabel permitted Bacon to visit her studio as early as December 1948 and that they spent Christmas together.[15]

Bacon left no formal record of professional exchanges between himself and Isabel; but their mutual friend, the composer Gerard Schurmann, recalled that he 'thought highly of her talents as a painter'.[16] Her letters record his interest in her work, and she was glad they saw it in the same way, 'something is getting across'.[17] Alert to the spatial ambitions of the monochromes, Bacon even designed for her unusual frames that projected the picture forward. Sutherland arranged to have them constructed by his framer, Alfred Hecht.[18] Elisabeth Lutyens recalled that Bacon and Isabel 'talked shop'.[19] Both were autodidacts, and they discussed each other's progress and were frank about each other's 'weak points'.[20] Isabel wrote to Rose Pulham in February 1949 during her exhibition, 'He says that what I want to do and what he wants to do are not so different – though we approach from opposite ends.'[21] She was not yet sure. After her exhibition closed in March 1949, she visited Bacon's studio at Cromwell Place, where he was preparing for his own in November. His figures still had something of Picasso's, Ernst's and Sutherland's fantastical, distorted and truncated character, and she was put off by 'anamorphic forms on red ground', which she felt were not original. The exception was a 'large landscape with headless figure' (possibly *Figure in a Landscape* of 1945), which she admired.[22] Shortly afterwards Isabel saw a new work, 'man's head stopping above the eyebrows with spectacles' with a 'vaguely ecclesiastical atmosphere' (probably *Head III*, 1949; private collection). This she considered 'very below the belt. I don't like it at all.'[23] At this stage she felt Bacon was, like the painters she had disliked in the *Art Treasures*, too obsessed with surface and 'the photographic delineation of form – wishes as far as I can see, to seize such a quality in paint'.

A rare glimpse of the days they spent together is recorded in a later letter to Rose Pulham.[24] On 30 December 1950, they went to Paolozzi's studio – 'full of amusing and sometimes a little more than that sketches and bric-a-brac' – then returned to Bacon's for lunch, beautifully presented and cooked. Their shared culinary tastes are indicated by a much-thumbed 1897 copy of J.-B. Reboul's *La Cuisinière provençale*, found in Bacon's room on his death.[25] In the evening, they joined Constant Lambert, Paolozzi and friends at the launch of the ICA's new premises at 17–18 Dover Street. They were keen habitués of exhibitions, and if they did not actually keep each other company on visits to galleries and to shows

96. 97. Isabel Rawsthorne, studies for *Interior with Figures I* and *II*, 1949; Tate Archive

such as *Art Treasures*, or *Masterpieces from the Alte Pinakothek at Munich*, held at the National Gallery in 1949, they certainly discussed them.[26]

Isabel joined the sequence of trained artists, following Roy de Maistre, Peter Rose Pulham and Graham Sutherland, from whom Bacon gleaned knowledge.[27] Both artists were broadening their visual sources. They looked at, or 'with' other artists in galleries, fine-art reproductions and photographs, as well as in scientific and printed material of the type discussed in the previous chapter, in the spirit of André Malraux's 'museum without walls'.[28] Bacon's debt to Sickert, is now acknowledged and he also shared Isabel's interest in film, most obviously Eisenstein, but also the 'entrapping spacialities' of French poetic realists.[29] Where Isabel had followed her pre-war treatments of Van Eyck's *St Barbara* with translations of the Roman *The Baker and his Wife*, Bacon had become interested in illustrations of Velázquez's seventeenth-century *Pope Innocent X* (1650; Galleria Doria Pamphilj, Rome). Copying was a standard way for artists to develop expertise, but Isabel and Bacon exploited the freedom that more varied, degraded reproductions, small and inaccurately coloured, allowed, and they exhibited their 'copies' as independent works of art. Just as Isabel showed *Pompeian Couple* at the Hanover Gallery in February 1949, Bacon included a compelling 'head' based on the Velázquez (*Head VI*, 1949, Arts Council) in his November show. It is tempting to see this appropriation as a literal enactment of Carola Giedion-Welcker's description of modern art's triumphant 'dethronement of the "masterpiece" … its anarchistic rejection of all outworn beauties or conventional forms'.[30] Where Isabel's Roman-derived portraits were augmented by their being also likenesses of her neighbours Denis and Irene ApIvor, Bacon's was more aggressively modified by means of further reproductions, photographs of Pius XII and stills of the open-mouthed woman with pince-nez in Eisenstein's *Battleship Potemkin* (both wore round lenses).[31]

Isabel and Bacon were also trying out methods and materials. They examined masters of gesture, for example Velázquez's and Rembrandt's ability to 'hold onto one irrational mark rather than another', as Bacon later put it.[32] These painters were well represented at the *Masterpieces from the Alte Pinakothek* exhibition, and, in 1947–8, their technique was foregrounded as a result of the scandal surrounding *An Exhibition of Cleaned Pictures* at the National Gallery which drew over 600,000 visitors.[33] 'Old Masters became confusingly new,' as one contemporary put it.[34] At the centre of the debate was Rembrandt's *A Woman Bathing in a Stream*, 1654. (**99**) Cleaning had revealed broken and beautiful non-illustrational paint. The woman's hand, in particular, equated to the forces within the body rather than the skin. Another important event for Isabel was the graphic accomplishment on view at the *Hokusai* centenary exhibition at the British Museum: 'most interesting', she wrote to Rose Pulham, '… animals and birds are superb. Really astonishing.'[35]

Bacon moved towards more observational approaches. Rodin became as fundamental to his study of the body as it was to Isabel's.[36] They studied the Impressionist painters revered in Paris for their graphic brushing but considered beyond the pale of modern art in London. In later life, Bacon exhibited his sophisticated appreciation of modern gestural painters – Artaud's, Soutine's and Michaux's 'free marks … true tachism' – , and it became his habit to praise Bonnard, Degas, Cézanne and Van Gogh in terms of the *hazard*, violence and shock in use among Isabel's Paris circle.[37] His famous and apparently eccentric citation of a Monet sunset as an exemplar of his wish to 'trap' the appearance of a mouth was surely a reference to the Monet enthusiast and 'trappeur supérieur' Jean-Paul Riopelle.[38] Another exemplar was the Fauve technique of André Derain and Matthew Smith, Isabel's mentors since the 1930s. Derain was not well represented in London collections, but his *Portrait of Madame Isabel Delmer* (**27**) hung in her home, and, in November 1948, Giacometti sent her a copy he had made of another Derain (whereabouts unknown).[39] Smith exhibited frequently after 1946, culminating in his solo show at the Tate in 1953.[40] He often socialised with Isabel and Bacon.[41] That Bacon became close to the artist is indicated by his catalogue essay for the Tate show.'[42] Bacon's essay stood out from the others in the book in its blunt focus on process, and he complimented Smith on the relationship between accident and recognition in his work, appreciating his 'interlocking of image and paint',

98. Isabel Rawsthorne, 'Three Figures', 1950; The Estate of Francis Bacon

in terms that again recall discussions in Paris: 'the brushstroke creates the form and does not merely fill it in ... every movement of the brush on the canvas alters the shape and implications of the image ... the very substance of the paint, when used in this way, can make such a direct assault on the nervous system.'[43]

Bacon moved towards a more observational approach, and it is this change that was revealed by the paintings exhibited at the Hanover Gallery in November and struck Isabel as being of a completely different quality from those she had viewed in March. Bacon had reduced his compositions to central figures or heads, and she wrote to Rose Pulham that they were in general 'much less peculiar', by which she meant less surreal, 'more austere' – 'a great leap forward'.[44] In so doing she was complimenting Rose Pulham, who had also left behind anamorphic forms in favour of *in camera* subjects, which he had shown to her in Paris in June.[45] Isabel noticed how Bacon's new realism alienated his erstwhile mentor Graham Sutherland: 'I asked Brausen what Graham S said "Nothing" Later he and Bacon dined together. Right at end of evening Graham said "I think the dimensions are interesting."'[46] So impressed was Isabel with one new painting – a 'large male nude walking thro' curtain. Quite unlike anything else' – called *Study for Figure* (later known as *Study from the Human Body)*, 1949, (**100**) that she mentioned

99. Rembrandt, *A Woman bathing in a Stream (Hendrickje Stoffels?)*, c. 1654; National Gallery, London

100. Francis Bacon, *Study for Figure* (later *Study from the Human Body*), 1949; National Gallery of Victoria

it in several letters.[47] The picture was Bacon's first exhibited nude and the title declared a materialist and anthropological engagement with human presence more sympathetic to her and Giacometti's phenomenological approach: 'What I find so incredible about human form, as opposed to all other living forms', she had written a few months before, 'is its complexity which makes it, if one can put it this way, appear over life size, or better to say increases the space around it. This is what is lacking in the vast majority of representations of it.'[48] Wyndham Lewis's rave review of the exhibition expressed a similar appreciation.[49] At the same time, Lewis's vision of Bacon's figures as 'shouting creatures in glass cases' registered an affinity between his and Isabel's vitrine aesthetic, while the critic for *The Observer* linked the pictures to Sartre, to Tennessee Williams's *The Glass Menagerie* and to Duchamp's paintings on glass.[50]

Study from the Human Body reversed any hierarchy in Isabel's artistic relations with Bacon. It was the 'modelling' and the texture and colour of the work that struck her, a form that managed to appear both monumentally present and 'breathed onto glass'. The unusual sculptural physique of the figure in the painting recalled the aged Antoine Nardone (Rodin's model for his *Balzac*), represented in Germaine Richier's *L'Orage* (Storm Man, 1947), which was exhibited at the Anglo-French Art Centre in St John's Wood, London, in 1947 and at Galerie Maeght in Paris in 1948, and reproduced in the catalogues for both shows.[51] The white used against a brownish ground with bravura skill in *Study from the Human Body* responded also to precedents such as Rembrandt's *A Woman bathing in a Stream* (**99**) and Bonnard's *Bathing Woman Seen from the Back* (c. 1919; Tate, London).[52]

Study from the Human Body tackled what Paul Valéry called 'Degas's problem', that the cumulative mark-making over time that went with the investigation of the reality of the figure inhibited the attempt to find an equivalent for the instantaneity of 'presence'. Spontaneity alone was, for Valéry, not enough, and he deprecated modern art's tendency to 'confuse the study with the finished product'. Degas, he felt, in a turn of phrase that validated Bacon's use of photographs, had at least 'dared try to combine the snapshot with the endless labour of the studio' – 'Spontaneity grandly formalised', as Bacon later put it.[53] Bacon's oft-delivered paraphrase of Valéry, the claim to want an instant art that avoided the 'boredom' of pictorial conveyance, was, significantly, not a direct quote; it modified, and thus subtly improved upon, a statement made to Valéry by Degas: 'If there were no tedium there'd be no enjoyment in it.'[54] Valéry's anecdote referred to Degas's copy of a printed reproduction of a work by Andrea Mantegna which achieved in a 'few accents' something much better than Valéry's own copy directly from the work itself – a second precedent for Isabel's and Bacon's use of photographic reproductions. Like Isabel, Bacon was reducing the number of brushstrokes, 'to abbreviate into intensity', as he later expressed it,[55] isolating strong, subtle marks that commanded a calligraphic impact of their own. His Hanover works concentrated the body in moments of materialisation, creating 'that sudden shaking effect of something vital', that Isabel had admired in examples in the Alte Pinakothek exhibition a few months before.[56]

In order to attain this vitality, instead of pursuing Giacometti's archaeological layering of seeing and making, the younger artists embraced a freer play of Existentialist *hasard*.[57] Isabel explained her own negotiation between spontaneity and the 'endless labour of the studio': 'I have 3 canvases covered with succeeding layers of attempts. One layer (now covered) I quite liked, but had to go on and spoil it in order to go further ... the trouble is that all its quality is lost if it is not dashed onto the canvas in incisive, definitive strokes not to be retouched, and this means a practically hopeless vista of time until one has the knowledge and experience also the confidence necessary.'[58] One approach to this problem was to develop images in parallel and series and 'start all over again every night every morning', as Isabel explained. In 1949, Michel Leiris's *Horizon* essay linked the suddenness of Giacometti's sculptures to his practice of sacrificing works that failed to be 'instantaneous'. Isabel and Bacon adapted this cycle of destruction and renewal, abandoning both dead ends and good painting that had been spoiled by too much experimentation; 'just a technical thing,' Bacon said, 'too much

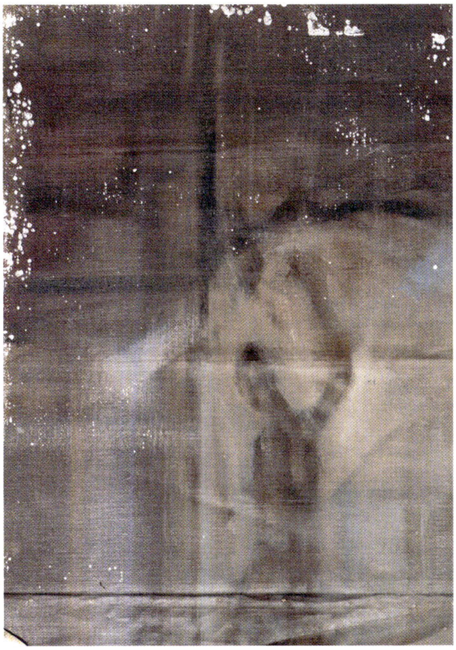

101. Isabel Rawsthorne, *Interior with Figure,* c. 1949; New Art Gallery, Walsall

102. Francis Bacon, *Man at Curtain*, 1950; The Lambrecht-Schadeberg Collection

paint and you can't go on'.[59] In 1948, Isabel sent Rose Pulham a sketch saying, 'I have done at least a dozen none of which remain.'[60] Later in the year, with just a month or so to go to her exhibition, she wrote, 'FB has destroyed all his ... I would certainly like to destroy some of mine but I daren't.'[61] Isabel turned and re-stretched canvases, and most of her oils after 1948 were double-sided and some were turned a second time and painted over again.[62] Many were destroyed in this manner. None of Isabel's nudes survives intact, and only a few can be viewed on scraps of canvas that she saved to reuse.

One fragment, partially painted over, is a rare self-portrait. Isabel is naked except for a skirt and her headscarf, which she wore when she was working. (**115**) Another is *Figure* (August 1949), described in a letter as 'a half torso back view in movement arm stretching out against a very squared background to increase the movement'.[63] Isabel had recently been admiring Renoir in the National Gallery, 'like a breath', and this picture developed a building up of impressionistic marks, 'hints' as she called them. *Figure* was possibly the single nude Bacon admired at her studio in September 1949 (a few weeks later he admired two standing figures). One of his two new paintings exhibited the following year, *Man at Curtain*, (**102**) employed a similar pose set in a shower room [64] When she saw it, Isabel identified

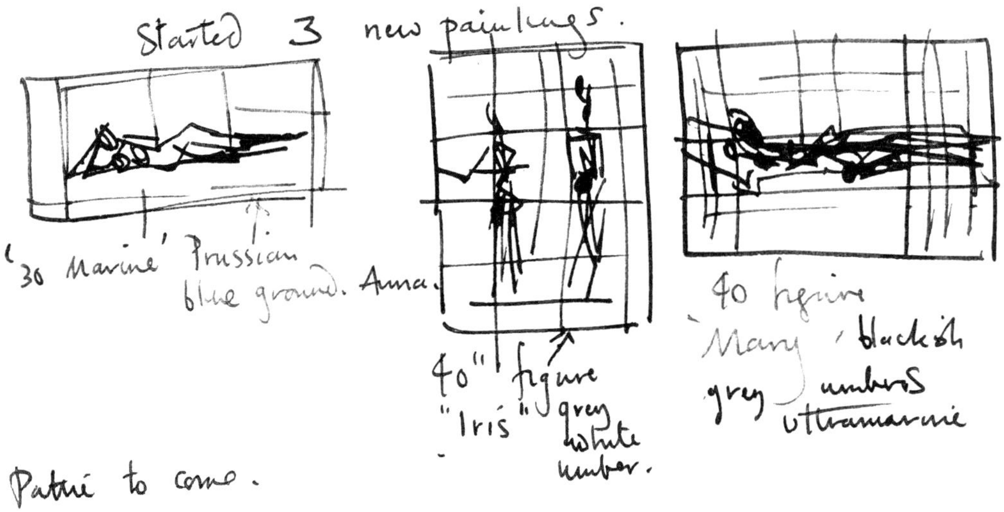

103. Isabel Rawsthorne, letter to Peter Rose Pulham (detail), 7 January 1950; Tate Archive

it as the successor to the *Study for Figure* (*Study from the Human Body*) that she had admired in 1949: 'an arm against a curtain, *scuola di* man thro' curtain (also in show)'.[65] She had reason to appreciate Bacon's achievement, as her own progress was slow. Her determination to seek one 'quintessential' notation multiplied her practical and aesthetic difficulties. 'Bacon understands this,' Isabel wrote to Rose Pulham, 'though wishes to arrive at it by devious means.'[66] She could not share his reliance on printed sources, but her commitment to the phenomenological method resulted in indistinctness.[67] The form of *Figure* is typical in that it barely disturbs its 'envelope' of watery light. Bacon's *Man at Curtain*, by contrast, stands out in the telling contrasts of black-and-white film.

In January 1950, Isabel sent Rose Pulham sketches of '3 new paintings' and wrote that Anna Phillips had sat for '12 quick charcoal sketches and 3 new pictures' (whereabouts unknown). 'She is a good model for me!', she continued, 'somewhat muscular, and fine small head'.[68] (**103**) In May, she managed to secure the services of the artist, poet and very experienced model Iris Tree.[69] Paolozzi was making terracotta shallow reliefs of figures paired similarly to those painted by Isabel, a set of which he gave to Isabel (whereabouts unknown, known from a photograph). He also gave her an old mahogany stretcher, six feet square, on which she painted a large work, *Two Figures* (1950; private collection).[70] This can be seen with a new version of *Pompeian Couple* in a publicity photograph taken in

104. Isabel Lambert, Albany Street, c. 1950

the early 1950s showing Isabel inside the apartment at 197 Albany Street. (**104**) We see a half-length portrait of Mary Rose Pulham on the chair (whereabouts unknown) and Isabel's satchel, brushes and boxes of paint strewn on the table.[71]

The evolution of technique and their destruction of failed works slowed progress for Isabel and Bacon. Isabel declined Erica Brausen's invitation to show at the Hanover Gallery in 1950, and Bacon showed only two new works along with some of the previous year. However, on the recommendation of Bacon and Brausen, Isabel's *Two Standing Figures* and *Figure* were chosen for David Sylvester's *London–Paris: New Trends in Paintings and Sculpture* at the ICA in the spring of 1950. (At the same time, Rose Pulham exhibited single and double nudes at the Hanover Gallery).[72] Isabel was dissatisfied, however, and she wrote to Rose Pulham in March that she found the ICA exhibition unoriginal and her own pictures tedious.[73] *The Times* and Wyndham Lewis echoed her opinion, finding little 'new'.[74] Wyndham Lewis felt that only Bacon was even close to offering the 'New Trends' promised by Sylvester's title. *The Times* made a similar exception of Isabel: the art critic appreciated her graphic skill and recognised the ambition to take up where Impressionism had left off, but did not penetrate to the phenomenological

105. 106. Joan Rayner (Leigh Fermor): Pattie Whitney Smith (later Lambert) and Mary Rose Pulham (later Ryan), Valmondais, 1950; Tate Archive

implications of this and disliked her afocalism – 'effect of getting the eyes out of focus'.[75] Isabel resolved immediately to 'change completely at once' and decided to set her figures in the 'open air'.[76]

In May, she visited Peter and Mary Rose Pulham at their new refuge in Valmondais, a traditional retreat for artists not far from Paris. There she had the luxury of several weeks in a large studio space with Mary as her model. Pattie Whitney Smith joined the party, and she and Mary posed in the orchard and in an upstairs room.[77] Joan Rayner, now divorced from John and settled in Greece with Patrick Leigh Fermor, came to stay and took photographs for Isabel as aide-mémoires.[78] (**105, 106**) Isabel associated the fields around Valmondais with the nearby cornfields of Van Gogh's 'final stay' at Auvers.[79] Although she had been looking at Impressionist and Post-Impressionist work in London, it seems to have been this proximity to where such works were created and the escape from the dreary London light that resulted in the introduction of colour into her work. Unfortunately, none of the Valmondais canvases survived the journey back to England, because they were rolled while too wet, but some were reused, leaving dappled nudes gazing from behind the stretcher bars of later works, such as the final version of *The Desert*.[80] (**81**)

Isabel remade some scenes when she returned to London. The reverse of another canvas shows a luminous open-air interior combining orchard and window 'Three Figures', 1950. (**98**) The figures in it appear to be leaning in, like those in

107. Isabel Rawsthorne, 'Two Figures', 1950, verso of *Flowerpiece* (**139**); private collection

108. Eduardo Paolozzi (attrib.), 'Two Figures', c. 1950

Cézanne's *Bathers* (1898; National Gallery, London). She wrote to Rose Pulham that Bacon was working 'on the same kind of subject' as she was, '(well – I mean nude in open air) and using the brightest colours also. Powdered cerulean etc.'[81] She was surprised, therefore, when the two new works in his September show, *Man at Curtain* and *Fragment of a Crucifixion*, 1950, (**102, 122**) were painted in grisaille, 'a continuation of the others – no great change and no lapis lazuli'.[82] It is likely she was expecting to see *Painting*, 1950, discussed below, in Chapter 20. (**130**)

In December 1950, Isabel was still frustrated with her progress: 'I must say I still notice the same old boring obstacle ... which is a curious reluctance to do whatever comes into my mind, which in my case, would certainly be a good thing I think. I know I am still far too rigid, in youthful corsets – Silly as I know now that I wear them.'[83] Despite the light-hearted reference to her new underwear, the serious aims she set herself would not be resolved for many years and would result in an investigation into the problems of painting the figure that was unique in twentieth-century art.

109. Isabel and Constant Lambert outside St Pancras Register Office after their wedding, 7 October 1947

20 LA MAISON HARPIE: 1947–1951

Two texts for a harpie that is provisionally cosmopolitan:
You profit from all that you take and give back all you get.
A harpy in the hand is hard to hold but a harpy in the home
is a haven from harm.[1]

Whether Isabel and Constant Lambert had deep feelings for each other or not – and the evidence suggests they did – their union was an inventive act offering mutual sanctuary in the shocked aftermath of war. In her new London life, Isabel explored in practical and pictorial forms 'how to live?' The confluence of retrenchment and free-for-all that marked British society after the war, and the vantage point of her unconventional friendships with Lambert and Bacon, focused the question 'how to love?'

When Isabel left France in September 1947, her farewell letter to Rose Pulham and Mary mused, 'A harpy in the hand is hard to hold but a harpy in the home is a haven from harm', and she explained her unexpected flight to London and her betrothal to Lambert in a letter to Giacometti headed 'La Maison Harpie'.[2] She clearly found the second letter difficult to write, and her language mixed the existential with the surreal in an uncharacteristically distanced third person:

London Sensation / A Harpy finds a vampire

... it is with pleasure and regret that I draw your attention to an unexpected event taking place in England and already published in the British press. The news, which has profoundly stirred a select few ('intellectual circles' as they say in English) is the announcement of the wedding, or if you prefer, the amalgamation, of a certain Mr. Constant Lambert (musician, composer, conductor, bon viveur, renowned author of verse-satire questions and humour, a man who loves wine, laughter, the uncommitted life, speed, cats, salamanders, the amenities of life, aquariums, whales, stars, sea, rocks and postcards) – with some lady, who laughs heartily, who loves Paris, and does not intend to forget this city of wonders – Madam Isabel Delmer. This lady, who was never very well disposed towards the idea of marriage, believes that this time she fell on a special case, for reasons of state of mind, nerves, balance, of how to live and many others.

110. Isabel Rawsthorne, *Dead Hare*, 1951; private collection

'An external form of permanence', she told Giacometti, 'will give much more freedom in life than any other solution she could find', and permit both partners to 'work quietly'. There is no record of Giacometti's reaction, but the continuation of notes and visits between them suggests that, if their devotion was battered, it was not broken.[3] The imperatives resulting from their inability to provide for each other must, by now, have been mutually understood.[4]

Isabel received a return blow, however. At lunch one day, during her stay with Rose Pulham and Mary at Valmondais in the summer of 1950, an unnamed visitor (an American girlfriend of Rose Pulham and Sartre) mentioned that Giacometti and Annette had been married for a year. Isabel was stunned. Outwardly, she concealed her feelings and acted as though she knew, but decades afterwards she recalled the 'strange tightness in my chest as though I could not breathe very well'. 'I should not have been surprised', she consoled herself, 'because he had remarked on several occasions that he would ~~his mother want it~~ [*sic*] have to in order to take her home.'[5] Whether it was because Isabel was not Swiss, or simply not conventional, in all the years they had been together, Giacometti had never taken *her* home.

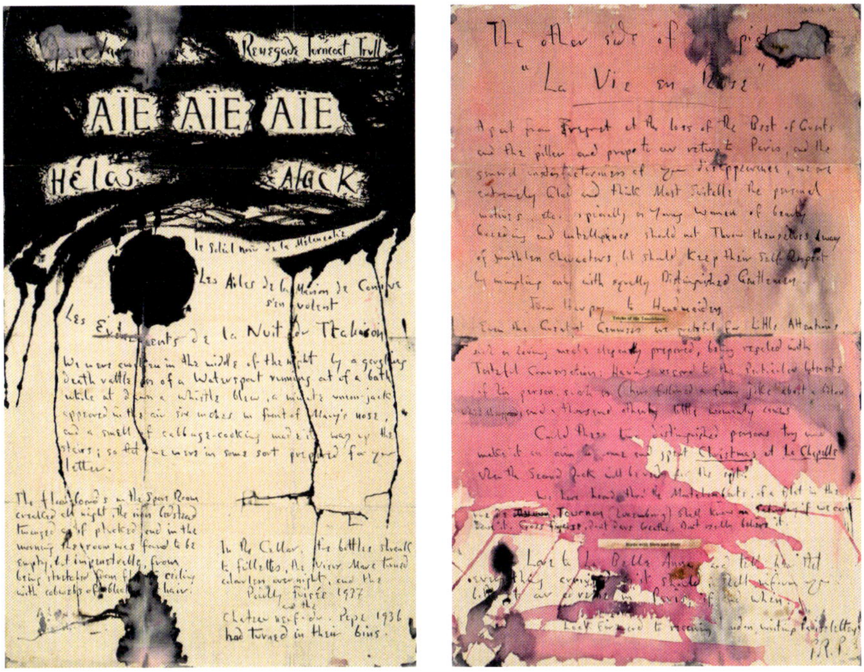

111. Peter Rose Pulham, letter to Isabel Rawsthorne, 1947; Tate Archive

Rose Pulham's response to Isabel's defection from France was more open. His wedding greeting was simply a blank page inscribed with one piece of punctuation, '⸮', the reverse question mark used among some writers to signify an exclamation of irony.[6] A second letter took the form of a calligraphic cry, Artaud-style, headed 'aie aie aie' in brute, gothic black, 1947.[7] (**111**) This fascinating document distilled Isabel's predicament: dark clouds surround an inky disc labelled 'Black sun of Melancholy', a line from Gérard de Nerval's nineteenth-century poem 'El Desdichado' (The Disinherited) in *Les Chimères* (chimeras were also mythical winged animal-women). To this, Rose Pulham added the words, 'The Wings of the Manon of Conives take flight', reinforcing the Siren imagery of the poem. Below is a reference to the eighteenth-century fictional heroine Manon Lescaut, whose true love is unable to save her from penury. It was an unflattering allusion to Isabel's marriage, because Manon left her lover for richer men, but finally returned and died.[8] Rose Pulham created a gothic vision of his and Mary's house in supernatural rebellion at Isabel's departure: 'the floor boards in the spare room creaked all night and the iron bedstead twanged and in the morning the room was found to be empty but impenetrable from being stretched from floor to ceiling with cobwebs of black hair.'

The back of the page was a complete contrast: it celebrated in splashes of pink 'the other side of the picture: La Vie en rose', in reference to Edith Piaf's song of love and longing that was heard everywhere that year.[9] (**111**) Its mock Jane Austen style was sunnier: 'Young women of beauty, breeding and intelligence should not throw themselves away on worthless characters [René Leibowitz? Giacometti? himself?] but should keep their self-respect by mingling only with Distinguished Gentlemen ... Even the greatest geniuses [Constant Lambert] are grateful for little attentions such as loving meals elegantly prepared, being regaled with Tasteful conversation, having regard to the particular interests of the person such as (here followed a joke about a baton suppressed by M [Mary]) and a thousand other little womanly cares.' The pun on Rose Pulham's last name in 'La Vie en rose' taints its reference to Isabel's new life with the old existence. The aphorism, 'From Harpy to Handmaid', makes the juxtaposition explicit.

Attached to the letter were two collaged cuttings, probably snipped from texts about airplanes. They modernise Isabel's avian affinities and extend the Harpy/Chimera/Manon metaphors: the first, reading 'Tricks of the Touchdown', fused suggestions of safe landings and sexual finesse; the second, 'Birds with Slats and Slots', reinforced the double entendre. Both evoke the erotic graffiti and wordplays recorded in Isabel's 1947 Paris diary. They find a parallel in Paolozzi's first contemporary collage, *I was a Rich Man's Plaything* (1947; Tate, London). His idiom is American rather than graffiti/gothic, but the theme is the same, and it, too, juxtaposed a military aeroplane and a femme fatale, a pin-up brunette besieged by a gun and an equally phallic cherry at the end of a slice of pie. (It also introduced the word 'pop', which, six years later, would label the Pop movement.)

Isabel, however, refused to have her wings clipped. She determined to rise above social pretensions, retain her 'savoir vivre, savoir faire, esprit de contraire', as she put it.[10] Lambert was not wealthy, but was well connected. His father and brother were artists, and his family had status in artistic circles. His mother was pleasantly surprised to find that her son had met someone who, although regrettably – to her eyes – 'half welsh', was neither 'coloured' (as she described Flo Lambert) nor a 'dancer' (Margot Fonteyn). Isabel did not appreciate such prejudices, and the two Mrs Lamberts rarely met. Nor did Constant Lambert's long-standing friendship with the Sitwell set and with the composer William Walton diminish Isabel's antipathy for Bloomsbury elitism. Osbert Sitwell reminded her of Derain (she perhaps unwisely told him so), but she found Edith Sitwell 'tedious as person and poet and having airs of being of Plantagenet descent'.[11]

Isabel would have nothing to do with the role of subordinate, supportive wife, disliking Kathleen Sutherland's behaviour for this reason.[12] A photograph of the couple reveals her in unrepentant *garçonne* guise, her usual black sweater augmented only by white collars and cuffs. Fashion plates after the war promoted feminine styles, but Isabel's outfit apes the image of Franklin D. Roosevelt as a young boy that appeared on the cover of *Life* the month of their wedding.[13] She was habitually hatless, and, where other women in her circle wore their hair set in curls, hers was still usually straight.[14] She was never without her satchel containing charcoal and sketchbook, and when Rose Pulham referred to it as a handbag in his foreword to her catalogue, she asked him to remove the word.[15]

It was common for marriage to curtail women's careers, but, as we have seen, painfully aware that ten years had passed without exhibiting, Isabel worked even more energetically than she had done when she was with Delmer.[16] This arrangement solved Lambert's problems, too. In 1947, he was, if anything, in a worse predicament than she, his excessive number of commitments, his ill-health and his heavy drinking having cost him his position as Music Director at Sadler's Wells. 'He was a sad man, and a sick man and a lonely man,' Isabel wrote, 'he had been a public figure since a young man, had acquaintances of all kinds but very few friends.'[17] She stated in her autobiographical notes that she married Lambert to 'to bring him back to life'.[18] Andrew Motion argues in his biographical study, *The Lamberts*, that the partnership was creatively and professionally transformative for them both. Unimpeded by what had been a punishing schedule at Sadler's Wells, Lambert could, for the first time in more than fifteen years, find time to compose again.[19] By the time of their wedding in October of 1947, he was writing a ravishing soundtrack to Julien Duvivier's film *Anna Karenina*, released in January 1948 (Isabel wore an 'experimental' outfit to the premiere, a tight, low-cut dress with red turban).[20] Soon, his recovery brought in requests to conduct with the new BBC Third Programme and the Hallé Orchestra, and even a recall from Sadler's Wells. Unfortunately, in June 1948, they offered him a new artistic directorship, inaugurating a partial return to his self-destructive coping methods. He began to suffer public collapses, which were perceived, unfortunately, as being entirely drink-induced. He flatly refused to see a doctor, having a horror of the medical profession that had developed during a particularly virulent illness in his youth.

Photographs of Isabel and Lambert together in the late 1940s show him, nonetheless, looking unusually well. Isabel encouraged him to rest and to limit 'the dreary round of eating in familiar restaurants'. Her letters reveal the trouble she took to transform their meagre rations into regular meals.[21] Menus with beautiful calligraphy that Isabel made for special occasions are now in the Tate Archive, (**112**) but there are also casual references to everyday French dishes learned in the Indre.[22] The memoir of Elizabeth David, another refugee from Europe (and protégée of Norman Douglas), gives an insight into the pleasure that Isabel, too, must have found in itemising her recipes, '[Writing] words like apricot, olives

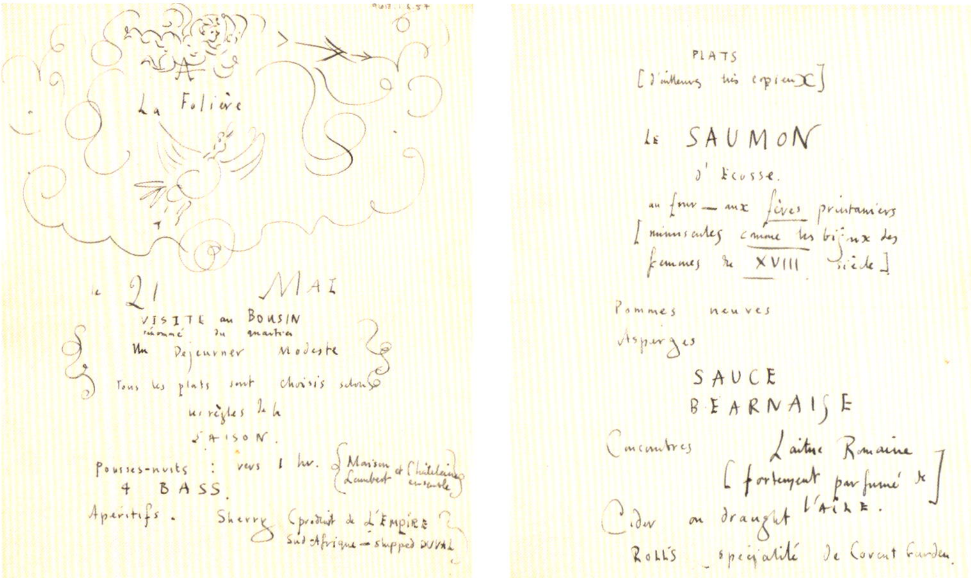
La Folière

le 21 MAI
VISITE au BOUSIN
Un Dejeuner Modeste
Tous les plats sont choisis selon les règles de la SAISON.
Pousses-nuits : vers 1 hr. Maison Lambert et Chatelaine ensemble
4 BASS.
Aperitifs. Sherry (produit de l'EMPIRE Sud Afrique — shipped DUVAL)

PLATS
[d'ailleurs très copieux]
Le SAUMON
d'Ecosse.
au four — aux fèves printaniers
[minuscules comme les bijoux des femmes du XVIII siècle]
Pommes neuves
Asperges
SAUCE
BEARNAISE
Concombres
Laitue Romaine
[fortement parfumé de l'AIL.]
Cider on draught
ROLLS spécialité de Covent Garden.

112. Isabel Rawsthorne, Menu, 21 May 1950; Tate Archive

and butter, rice and lemons, oil and almonds, produced assuagement … . in the England of 1947, those were dirty words that I was putting down.' At this date, olive oil had to be bought at the chemist's and garlic at shops serving Caribbean or Asian communities.[23]

During the war, meat was a significant subject, condensing the daily obsessions and rituals of rationing and simply getting enough to eat, with deeper resonances of death and sacrifice. Bacon's 'butcher's shop painting', *Painting 1946* (1946; Museum of Modern Art, New York) began, so he claimed, as a bird or chimpanzee, only to become a beaming figure surrounded by meat.[24] These animals are usually interpreted as exclusively violent subjects, but the butcher had a multivalent social currency. Butchery also, for example, connoted authenticity: Artaud eulogised Van Gogh's 'butcher's eye'.[25] The family butcher was central to everyone's lives until rationing ended in 1954, and he crossed class conventions. Isabel's butcher in the late 1940s, a 'remarkable man' known always as Mr Dick, was a respected presence in many of her letters.[26] In 1951, he supplied her with a European brown hare, and she painted it before she cooked it. (**110**) The pale palette, leaping pose and outline incised into the paint derived from some of Isabel's favourite objects, the horses in the Assyrian reliefs in the British Museum (Nimrud, 883–859 BCE), but the brushstrokes accumulated phenomenological 'hints', equating to sensing the soft body close at hand.[27] It was meat: 'Whole hare (large brown) costs 4/6! Cheapest thing in England. Friday civet. It's all been marinating,' she wrote; but the treatment emulated Soutine's habit of retaining references to the living creature in the dead one – here, a poignant and paradoxical suggestion of vibrating flanks, defensive eye, its characteristic postures of running and boxing.[28]

Isabel's meals improved Lambert's relationship with, and resistance to, alcohol, all the more so because his difficulties were, unbeknown to anyone at the time, partly due to undiagnosed diabetes. He gave up smoking and drinking spirits, and, for a while, he did not drink at all.[29] Even this reduced regime was more indulgent than Isabel was used to, however. Although a seasoned drinker in French terms, and delighting in parties, her letters to Rose Pulham reveal her frustration when she failed to resist the many temptations to overindulge in drink that London offered.[30]

There was a lot that Isabel and Lambert did not know about each other. 'One of the greatest pleasures I can think of', she remembered of this period, 'is discovering the likes and dislikes of someone you love.'[31] They had much in common. Lambert was a keen habitué of the zoo, for example, and Isabel was no doubt enchanted by his tale of when he and Margot were honoured by having their names bestowed on a male and a female zebra.[32] He had an opinionated relish for culture, but was, like Delmer, different from the Oxbridge-educated crowd. Isabel enjoyed his knowledge and irreverent wit and his endless capacity for fun: 'Whenever I went out with Constant, it might be a small journey to the market, I always felt something extraordinary and exciting would happen. He carried about him the aura of a conjuror.' Lambert was also highly sexed and, by several accounts, an exceptional lover, but Isabel's description of him as having 'great physical beauty' is surprising, given that, by the 1940s, a shambling, rakish ugliness was considered one of his defining characteristics.[33] He was, according to Isabel, 'deeply sensitive', and she found, behind the 'carapace of wit, sharp remarks and great vitality', a hidden loner: 'His life was intolerably rigid. The pattern was one of hard work, which was his nature.'[34] The secret of their unexpected alliance was that they were alike.

Isabel selected their home thoughtfully. Albany Street linked 'the dash of Camden Town' to prim Regent's Park, a 'mixture of raffishness and a certain pale respectability'. The house was a few minutes away from Irene and Denis ApIvor and one of Lambert's oldest friends, the novelist Anthony Powell and his wife, Lady Violet.[35] Rose Pulham remembered it poetically: 'the Dickensian village of fog, quiet, canals, horses and coal fires where the Lamberts live'.[36] One landmark was a shop selling Edwardian-style corsets; Anna Phillips bought one to entertain a lover, and Isabel followed suit.[37] She was 'surprised that Constant did not order one for himself'.[38] Lambert enjoyed pretending to people that they inhabited the disreputable end of the road, immortalised in Sickert's paintings of seedy Camden rooms. He was fond of jazz venues, nightclubs and, like Giacometti, brothels, and his new address allowed him to saunter off to his favourite haunts.[39]

Isabel applied her Left Bank pragmatism to Lambert's romantic routines, both his dalliances and his longer-standing relationships with Laureen Sylvestre, a cigarette seller at the Nest nightclub, and with Margot Fonteyn. He had been intensely involved with Margot for over a decade, since she was seventeen. Even after divorcing Flo, however, he had refused to give up his 'uncommitted life' for the dancer and on one occasion had left her standing at the register office in St Pancras Town Hall. It was a shock to her to hear that he had abruptly wed Isabel at the same place, and an illness that had occurred when Isabel and Constant Lambert first got together returned. She threw herself into her other relationships, particularly that with Roland Petit, a young French choreographer and the co-founder of the Ballets des Champs-Élysées.[40] Yet Fonteyn and Lambert remained friends, and both she and Laureen Sylvestre came often to the house.[41]

Lambert was, in return, disdainful of possessive husbandly postures. Isabel maintained a belatedly chaste but increasingly affectionate relationship with Alan Rawsthorne, who was a companion to them both, and a more intense one with Bacon. There was friction between Lambert and some of her older Paris friends, however, and, intriguingly, he refused to have Paolozzi in the house.[42] The couple lunched with Giacometti and Annette and Michel and Zette Leiris in December 1948, but it was not a success.[43] The Leiris scholar Seán Hand has argued that the ambivalence was mutual, that Leiris's dislike of Lambert's conducting of *Turandot* at Covent Garden in July 1947, as expressed in his notes on opera that were published after his death as *Operratiques*, were a barely concealed expression of his jealousy over Isabel.[44]

The couple's bachelor-like lifestyles continued within the home as well as without. They had few responsibilities. Thirteen-year-old Jackie Epstein had gone to America with his sister, Peggy, and her new husband. Isabel found herself stepmother, instead, to Kit, only a few months younger than Jackie, but Lambert's contact with him was, as it was with Cleo, the two-year-old daughter of Laureen Sylvestre, intermittent.[45] Kit spent most of his time at school or with his mother and grandmother.[46]

Even without children, in the post-war period before the influx of technology, a domestic role was a full-time task, and Isabel was not expected or prepared to undertake this. The couple's lifestyle, perceived as 'slatternly' by some, was a continuation of the Parisian anti-bourgeois model.[47] Isabel put elaborate effort into providing good food and drink, but cleaning or washing up were done only when essential. Rooms were furnished with necessities and strewn with quantities of books and newspaper clippings, similar to Bacon's studio at the time, and shared with Spalding, Lambert's black-and-white cat.[48] Unaware that Lambert's financial advisor was short-changing them, they were usually low on funds, although in 1950, to great excitement, they bought a fridge.[49] Dennis ApIvor recalled the house as 'an absolute shambles', but added, 'we were always dying of laughter'.

Even those who did not approve of Isabel had to admit the couple were happy.[50] Their social life thrived on cultural heterogeneity: 'Took Constant to PAGs [Paganini's restaurant] where Dylan [Thomas] was (very amusing) then with Elizabeth to ML [Michel Leiris], later "The George" – in fact pretty tipsy by the end of the day'[51] was a typical hasty comment to Rose Pulham; 'Today Edith Sitwell, cocktails chez [Roland] Penrose for Max Ernst' was another. These rare snapshots were provided and thus preserved not for their own sake, but for Rose Pulham's interest because of his affection for Thomas and his admiration for Max Ernst.[52] There were often visitors from France: Pattie Whitney Smith and Peter and Mary Rose Pulham in 1948 (Bacon was away and Isabel asked Brausen for the key to his studio so that they could borrow it) and the Batailles early in 1949, for example.[53] Picasso passed through in 1950, his second and last time across the Channel, and stayed with Penrose. Joan Rayner often visited from Greece. Patrick Leigh Fermor had been made Assistant Director of the British Institute in Athens after the war, but had become a travel writer following the successful publication of his first book in 1950, and he and Joan spent most of their time on the move.

Albany Street parties continued the invigorating mixture of Isabel's Paris 'salons' and the wartime avant-garde.[54] She became intimate with the ballet world, too. In August 1950, a performance of Gertrude Stein's *Wedding Bouquet*, spoken by a fully made-up Lambert, was followed by a gathering with Fonteyn, Frederick Ashton and many others; Bacon and Alan Rawsthorne were the last to leave, at 7 a.m.[55] Another memorable evening included Rawsthorne, Elisabeth Lutyens, Anna Phillips, Joan Rayner, Matthew Smith, Anthony and Violet Powell, Margot Fonteyn and ballet friends.[56] Lucian Freud came with Kitty, the daughter of Jacob and Kathleen Epstein whom he had recently married. Bacon was accompanied by Muriel Belcher, patron of the relatively new Soho club, the Colony Room. Cyril Connolly was banned, but gatecrashed anyway. It was a wild affair as a result of the whisky that Fonteyn had brought from New York, mostly consumed by Matthew Smith. A fracas broke out, focused on Lambert's current enthusiasm, who was, as Isabel wrote to Rose Pulham, 'dark v attractive ½ American who got drunk and behaved badly tho' I think she is probably quite a nice character. Had her face slapped by Vera [the Old Vic actress Vera Lyndsey] ... why I don't know.'[57]

The couple spent a lot of time with Tom Driberg, now a Labour politician. He was a fellow Sitwell protégé and long-standing comrade of Lambert. A visit to

Driberg's country house, Bradwell Lodge, or 'Bedwell-on-Sea, Juxta mare', as he liked to call it, at Christmas 1948, began an annual ritual:[58] Christmas Eve dinner in London at Casa Prada followed by a drive to Midnight Mass in the medieval village of Thaxted, where Lambert 'wept copiously', and then on to Bradwell in the early hours. Christmas Day would begin with a bracing walk on the pier. Bacon and Muriel Belcher were usually part of the Bradwell festivities.[59] Initially, Driberg was suspicious of Isabel, as he was besotted with Joan Rayner and not aware of their having come to terms over Isabel's infidelity with her husband. To make matters worse, he was a columnist on the *Daily Express*, where he was politically and personally at odds with Delmer. Isabel and he soon found personal and political sympathies in common, however. Driberg's itinerary across Europe in the run-up to the war had been very similar to her own, including time spent in Spain. A typical summer house party included his fellow Labour politicians Aneurin Bevan and Jennie Lee. Isabel recalled 'fast, pointed conversations on many subjects including Arts, Greek theatre', all set to a sultry soundtrack of Lena Horne.[60] 'I soon fell for the charming Mr Bevan, my welsh blood was sizzling with pleasure.'

Another favourite escape during the early years of their marriage was Faringdon House, the country home, until his death in 1950, of the composer, artist and Surrealist Gerald Tyrwhitt-Wilson, 14th Baron Berners. Again, Bacon was a frequent guest there, although he was closer to Lord Berners's partner, Robert ('Mad Boy') Heber-Percy, who was his and Isabel's age.[61] Faringdon's politely proportioned, eighteenth-century appearance belied the host's irreverent and spectacular style of hospitality. Lord Berners was an enthusiast for birds and kept birds of paradise and doves dyed in rainbow hues; bedchambers with four-poster beds were festooned with flowers, and with open fires on cold days; meals were sumptuously French-style. 'When every sort of luxury has been forever banned in England,' remarked Cyril Connolly, 'Lord Berners will somehow manage to maintain a secret melon house.' He spoke fluent French, knew many of Isabel's Parisian friends, and immediately appreciated her Continental apparel.[62] His house contained an art collection that reflected his catholic tastes: Old Masters, Renoirs, Dalís and so on. Isabel visited Faringdon's folly tower and also nearby Buscot Park, where a whole room was decorated with Burne-Jones's series *The Legend of the Briar Rose*.

Berners's aesthetic of irony and his self-declared war on *ennui* chimed with and perhaps informed Bacon's later public persona. The baron's famously gnomic signs, such as 'Don't throw stones at this notice', can still be seen around Faringdon village. He and Lambert would try outdo each other in composing obscene limericks, assembled in their 'Bishops' Blue Book':

113. Isabel Rawsthorne, *Hillside*, (sketchbook), 1949; Tate Archive

A vice at once strange and unsavoury
Held the Bishop of Oxford in slavery;
Amid screeches and howls
He would bugger young owls
Which he kept in an underground aviary.[63]

Then, when others had retired, they sat up all night listening to records, playing and talking music.

Isabel accompanied Lambert on Continental engagements and within a week of the opening in February 1949 of her Hanover Gallery exhibition they were en route to Italy and Sicily.[64] The long-dreamed-of Greek vacation with Joan Rayner and Paddy Leigh Fermor had been postponed in 1948; now she wrote excitedly, 'I can hardly believe such good fortune will arise. I feel if I can once see Rome, Naples, Etruscan paintings & one Greek temple I shall have had a fill for a long long time to come.'[65] In Sicily, while Lambert conducted concerts in

114. Isabel Rawsthorne, *Temple Ruin* (sketchbook), 1949; Tate Archive

Palermo and Taormina or worked on his new piano duet, Isabel explored.[66] She created Bomberg-esque watercolours and kept a long diary, which she sent to Rose Pulham and Michel Leiris. This detailed her climb up to the antique temple at Segesta, associated with the Trojans Acestes and Aeneas.[67] She sketched the Greek amphitheatre at Taormina, and, on the mainland in Naples, she and Lambert went to the aquarium of the Stazione Zoologica. Returning to London, they both had new projects in mind.

115. Isabel Rawsthorne, Self-portrait, c. 1949; private collection

116. Isabel Rawsthorne, *Interior with Figure*, c. 1950; Fry Art Gallery, Saffron Walden

21 WHAT SONG THE SIRENS SANG: 1950–1951

A sudden blow: the great wings beating still
Above the staggering girl, her thighs caressed
By the dark webs, her nape caught in his bill,
He holds her helpless breast upon his breast.

How can those terrified vague fingers push
The feathered glory from her loosening thighs?
And how can body, laid in that white rush,
But feel the strange heart beating where it lies?

A shudder in the loins engenders there
The broken wall, the burning roof and tower
And Agamemnon dead.
    Being so caught up,
So mastered by the brute blood of the air
Did she put on his knowledge with his power
Before the indifferent beak could let her drop?

William Butler Yeats, 'Leda and the Swan' (1924).[1]

Peter Rose Pulham's draft foreword to the catalogue for Isabel's exhibition at the Hanover Gallery in February 1949 referred to the 'erotic graffiti' that Isabel had begun in Paris. She removed the reference before it was published because she felt it was premature, 'considering the paintings that are there. Much as I want to annoy everyone I want to be on firm ground when I do so.'[2] This firm ground became a focus for her work during the following years. Her exploration of double nudes and double portraits had introduced the factor of relationship and now her exploration of archaic art and literature informed a parallel investigation of sex.

Isabel's alter ego, the harpy, had a rich Classical context. The bird/woman – variously Harpy, Fury, Siren, Chimera (closely related to other hybrids such as Undines, mermaids and Sphinxes) – had been associated with female agency in the nineteenth century and gained a new currency in Surrealist art and literature. Leonor Fini's *Autoritratto con Chimera* (1939; private collection), for example, initiated a series of similar images, and, in 1946, Constant Lambert staged a new ballet called *Les Sirènes*.[3] Isabel's fierce self-determination and forthright voice,

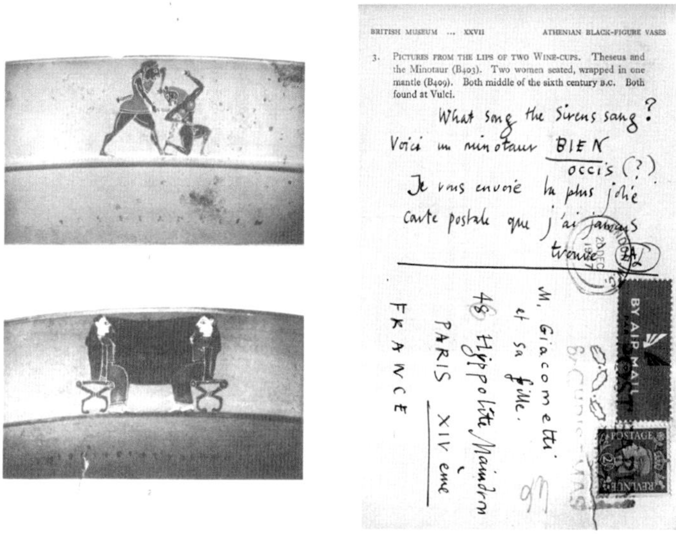

117. Isabel Rawsthorne, postcard to Alberto Giacometti (recto and verso), 20 December 1947; Fondation Giacometti, Paris

her sympathy with the natural world and with birds in particular inevitably drew comparisons with such mythical figures, but the motif seems to have come into particular play as an ambiguous token of independence when she was making commitments to men. Epstein explored the idea of her as chimera or undine in a carving of this title made in Epping Forest at the height of their artistic and romantic relationship in 1933 (private collection). Giacometti represented her as a chimera in the bracelet made the year of her marriage to Delmer, 1936. (**30**) Isabel assumed the persona in the letters to Rose Pulham and to Giacometti in which she explained her flight to London and marriage to Lambert (reciprocated in Rose Pulham's reply; see pp. 249–50). That Christmas of 1947, Isabel sent Giacometti a postcard showing two Greek wine cups in the British Museum, with little images painted where the lips make contact with the rim. One illustrated Theseus slaying the Minotaur; the other, two women sharing a shawl. On the back, Isabel wrote, 'What song the Sirens sang?' and, in French, 'Here is a minotaur well / (?)slain / I send you the most beautiful postcard I have ever found.'[4] Her old friend Diego Giacometti, Alberto's brother, appeared to provide a playful epilogue to the theme on the occasion of his visit to London in 1955 for Giacometti's British Council exhibition: the Harpy figures with which he decorated a wrought-iron table (private collection) for Cecil Beaton combined an allusion to Beaton's designs for *Les Sirènes* and the loose hair, open mouth and exaggerated Minoan-style bust of Epstein's *Isobel*.

The books Isabel brought back to London from Paris in 1947 included an unidentified collection of Greek poetry or philosophy and William Bedell Stanford's

Aeschylus in His Style: A Study in Language and Personality (1942).[5] Tame translations of the Greek originals were available, but Stanford's new account of the raw, illogical and synaesthetic aspects of Aeschylus's language – an 'ambiguity … incoherence, dimness' that he equated to painting – was a revelation to the post-war generation.[6] The postcard that Isabel sent to Giacometti alluded to these Aeschylean themes. The fathomless Sirens' song paralleled Cassandra's obscure Invocation to Apollo, the background to Giacometti's *La Femme au chariot*, both evocations of the stranger in a strange land. The phrase, 'What Song the Sirens sang', was taken from Sir Thomas Browne's *Hydriotaphia, Urn Burial*, a seventeenth-century reflection on Roman ossuaries and existential uncertainty, in which he continued, 'what name Achilles assumed when he hid himself among women, though puzzling questions are not beyond all conjecture.'[7] Isabel may have talked about the work with Giacometti, or thought he would recognise the extract because of its use as the epigraph of Edgar Allen Poe's 'The Murders in the Rue Morgue' (translated into French by Baudelaire).[8]

On her return from Italy in 1949, Isabel made a series of works with Classical Greek, erotic subject matter. An oil copy of a fresco showing an archaic Bacchanalian initiation rite preserved in the first-century BCE Villa of the Mysteries in Pompeii has survived (private collection), but the others may have been lent, lost, destroyed or painted over. However, something of their significance to Isabel and her circle can be reconstructed from her correspondence. A letter to Rose Pulham early in 1950 described rereading *The Oresteia* and books on Athens and Knossos and beginning a set of roundels, which she called 'pornographic medallions'. They were to have a raw Aeschylean rather than a refined Classical accent: 'I expect the first few will be rather arty But hope to progress from them to things more brut.'[9] A few months later, Isabel began 'a copy of Correggio's *Antiope* on upright 30 Marine'.[10] The image of the Classical nymph Antiope lying in an abandoned attitude beneath the gaze of Jupiter/Zeus, disguised as a satyr, in Correggio's *Jupiter and Antiope* (1523; Musée du Louvre, Paris), complemented the *nus couchés* she was currently painting from life. It was Antiope's pose, active rather than passive, teasingly suggesting that her sleep might be feigned, that interested Isabel: 'As for Antiope … the position will be similar only, keeping (I hope, this after all being the point of making the copy) those abrupt fly-away angles.'[11] An open-thighed position, recalling Giacometti's *nus couchés* and Balthus's *La Victime I* (1938–46; private collection), which Isabel had seen in Paris in 1945, distinguished her figures from the convention of relaxed, recumbent nudes.

Small drawings in her letters show that, between 1950 and 1953, Isabel planned and sketched single and double horizontal figures in the tradition of Rembrandt's *Jupiter and Antiope* etching of 1659, or his etching *Couple making Love*

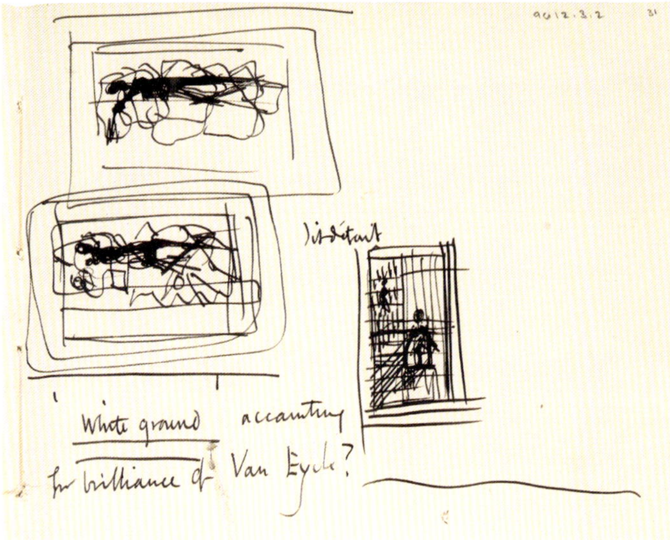

118. Isabel Rawsthorne, *Nus Couchés* (sketchbook), 1953; Tate Archive

(known as *The French Bed*) in the British Museum (1646).[12] She painted over her *Antiope* with *Two Figures*, which was then, itself, abandoned. Early in 1950, Isabel planned a variation, deciding to 'suppress' the cherub and introduce a modern male figure.[13] She tried a 'Bain Turk', after Jean-Auguste-Dominique Ingres's *Le Bain turc* (1862; Musée du Louvre), on the same principle (whereabouts unknown).[14]

The suggestively disturbed sheets that framed the sketches and oils were derived from Delacroix's *Le Lit défait*, 1827.[15] (**119**) Isabel first discussed painting this subject in 1948, when she wrote enthusiastically to Rose Pulham: 'I got a copy of "Arts" the other day with Delacroix's watercolour of a bed undone – wonderful.'[16] The bed equated to a platform and the crumpled sheets created a relief-like architecture of shadows and dents, like the drapery in Northern Renaissance painting. They also hinted at the *vue* or *vie d'atelier* – the bed as location for sleep, sex and art – condensed into modest studios like Giacometti's. Its significance is exemplified by its being the cause of the first argument between Rose Pulham and Thea FitzGibbon, in 1940, which flared when, while he was out, she removed the paints, books and food from his sheets and straightened them. 'I hate made beds,' he shouted, adding with angry irony, 'there is something so squalid about them.'[17] A painting entitled *Un lit défait,* after the Delacroix watercolour, was Rose Pulham's main project during 1949. He lent Isabel his drawings and exhibited the oil at the Hanover Gallery in March 1950 (whereabouts unknown).[18] Isabel's addition, in her own variations on this theme, of two figures on the bed made the sexual activity more explicit. This was emphasised by her insistence on painting naked portraits

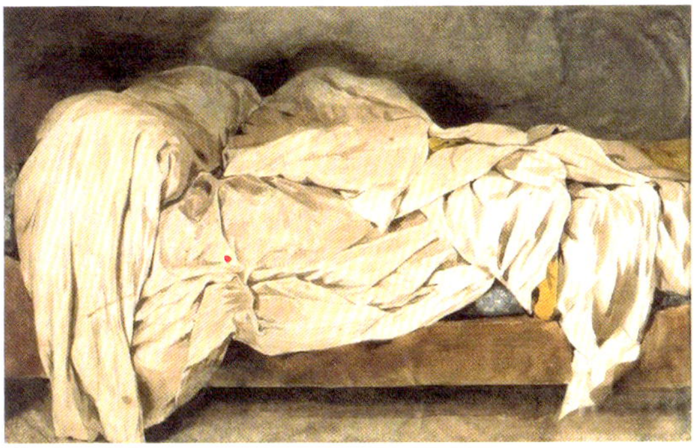

119. Eugène Delacroix, *Le Lit défait*, 1827; Musée du Louvre, Paris

120. Francis Bacon, *Two Figures*, 1953; private collection

rather than nudes: 'Mary drunk', 'Anna, back, lying', as she described one version.[19] In 1953, Bacon entangled two naked men amid Delacroix's folds and cut away Vs of drapery in perhaps his best painting of the decade, *Two Figures* (private collection). He never gave away its source, but in later life quipped, 'I like unmade beds but I like them unmade by love; j'adore les lits défaits, mais défaits par amour.'[20]

The painting about which Isabel was most excited during this period was a 'leda'. Late in 1949 and early in 1950, she made sketches for a 60-inch canvas with a cerulean ground which may relate to a discarded canvas of a nude on a blue background.[21] Like Antiope, Leda was ravished by Zeus, though on this occasion he took the form of a swan rather than a satyr. It was again a subject of one of Correggio's painted metamorphoses, and Isabel was almost certainly familiar with his *Leda and the Swan* (1532; Gemäldegalerie) in Berlin. The nymph's seduction by the god in the form of a bird was a trope of twentieth-century modernism. The violent insemination had become a paradigm for modern subjectivity of the kind theorised by Benjamin and others. It was articulated as a 'sudden blow' in the first line of the most famous of its many modern representations, William Butler Yeats's sonnet 'Leda and the Swan' (1924). Matthew Smith's exactly contemporary series of Leda paintings could be seen in his studio in the 1940s and his beautiful *Leda* screen (1922–5; Corporation of London) was re-exhibited at the National Gallery in 1949.[22] One of Dylan Thomas's comic party pieces was his parodic 'Request to Leda' performed with Nigel Davenport, and, in 1952, he made a thunderous recording of Yeats's poem.[23]

121. Siren Painter, Odysseus and the Sirens, Attic red-figured stamnos, c. BCE 480; British Museum

Unlike the other conquests of Zeus, the story of Leda had prompted Classical sculptors and Old Masters to set aside conventional visual euphemisms and depict directly the sexual act – the *Leda* after Michelangelo (1530) in the National Gallery, London, for example. The convergence of bird and human figured the existential and anthropological ideas that interested Isabel and her circle, at the same time overlapping with Isabel's 'Harpy' persona and her interest in Aeschylean themes. Leda's coupling resulted in the birth of Helen, who was the cause of the Trojan War, and of Clytemnestra, who murdered her husband, Agamemnon, when he returned from it. The explosive syntax of Yeats's poem makes this connection, executing an allegorical conflation of breached hymen and breached city wall, Clytemnestra's conception and her crime: 'A shudder in the loins engenders there / The broken wall, the burning roof and tower / And Agamemnon dead.'

Yeats and Aeschylus were preoccupations Isabel shared at this time with Bacon, for whom Stanford's *Aeschylus in His Style* was also an important text.[24] Bacon was planning to design the sets for the English production of Sartre's adaptation of Aeschylus' *Eumenides*, *Les Mouches*.[25] Moreover, Amanda Harrison has shown the particular importance to Bacon of Yeats and *Leda*.[26] The *Les Mouches* designs did not in the end come to pass, but Isabel's lost Ledas did find a corollary in Bacon's exactly contemporary *Fragment of a Crucifixion*.[27] (**122**) The painting was, with *Man at Curtain*, one of only two new images exhibited with earlier work at his Hanover show in 1950: 'He destroyed the ones inspired by Velasquez pope and the title in the catalogue had to be crossed out,' Isabel wrote. 'The one I prefer is a kind of crucifixion with a street scene in background – ie sketches in charcoal of small motorcars. / on bare canvas. / It is as usual extremely well painted.'[28] The T-cross

122. Francis Bacon, *Fragment of a Crucifixion*, 1950; Stedelijk van Abbemuseum, Eindhoven

was based on Rembrandt's *Deposition* (1633), shown in London in the exhibition of works from the Munich Alte Pinakothek, and the unforgettable detail of traffic passing back and forth behind, indifferent to either suffering or revelation, derived from the setting of Rembrandt's etching of the crucifixion, *The Three Crosses* (1653).[29] Bacon's modern, Monte Carlo equivalent, cars and pedestrians etiolated by distance, adapted the 'forked animals' of Isabel's *The Desert* and Giacometti's *City Square*. The dove of the Holy Spirit that traditionally hovers over the cross was transformed into an image that evoked the Harpy or bird/woman and the 'beating wings' and 'sudden blow' of Yeats's first line. It reverses the genders of the Leda story, exhibiting female labia and an open, lipsticked mouth.

Martin Harrison has drawn attention to a revealing exchange between Bacon and Michel Leiris concerning Aeschylean imagery around the time it reappeared in his work in the 1970s and 1980s: 'I could not paint Agamemnon, Clytemnestra or Cassandra,' Bacon wrote, 'as that would have been merely another kind of historical painting ... Therefore I tried to create an image of the effect it produced inside me.'[30] An inspiration for both the creature and the composition of *Fragment of a Crucifixion* may have been the bird-woman flapping before a man lashed to a wooden mast in one of the most famous representations of harpies, the *Odysseus and the Sirens*, a red-figure stamnos in the British Museum (480 BCE), but Bacon described his bird-woman as 'almost an owl, a sort of owl'.[31] It was based on the plate 'Heraldic attitude of a Barn-Owl in flight' in the photography book *Birds in Action*, published by Eric Hosking and Cyril Newberry in 1949.[32] The dog-like creature over

123. Eric Hosking and Cyril Newberry, 'The cock tawny owl brings a rat to the hen', *Birds of the Night* (1945)

the cross recalls the sacrificial animals that were a feature of Aeschylus's work,[33] and the ghoulish eye juxtaposed with the bird echoes a more recent and literal artistic sacrifice, the loss of an eye to the talons of a tawny owl that had brought the photographer of *Birds in Action*, Eric Hosking, to fame.

Sometime after 1950, Isabel's lost *Leda* found an even simpler successor in the 'beating wings' and 'sudden blow' of Untitled (Owl). (**124**) The large gouache concentrated on the bird's sudden descent on its prey, also based on a Hosking and Newberry book, *Birds of the Night*. The plates in that book that attracted Isabel were those with an apparitional effect of movement captured by strobe or flashlight at night, most notably the left-hand bird, landing with wings and tail splayed, in 'The cock tawny owl brings a rat to the hen'. (**123**) Untitled (Owl) alluded to its intent eye, the intrusive highlight of the claw, the rat swinging from its beak and the blurring of the wing feathers, but Isabel moved the bird to the centre of the image to add a hieratic effect. The 'blow' of its arrival is complemented by a style that brings the image into sight in a correspondingly sudden way. The viewer's eye is at first bewildered by barely differentiated blues and umbers, until it meets the eye of the predator. The instant we recognise this, we apprehend, as though *we* were the prey, the three soft beats of its wings through the sweeping air. The bird does not recognise us in return; its gaze is impersonal, the only fixed point in a night alive with the twists and shudders of the creatures and foliage that it has disturbed. In reducing the composition to just the bird, Untitled (Owl) succeeded in being less 'historical', as Bacon would put it, informed by, but not a representation of the Aeschylean sacrificial imagery of *Leda*.[34] Its style, rather than its subject, is a brilliant equivalent to the paradoxically powerful 'ambiguity ... incoherence, dimness' of Aeschylus's suggestive, synaesthetic, compound terms, which William Stanford equated to painting.

124. Isabel Rawsthorne, Untitled (Owl), c. 1950–60; private collection

125. Isabel Rawsthorne, *Lovers in a Landscape,* c. 1950; Royal Opera House Collections

22 TIRESIAS: 1950–1951

Isabel's Ledas endure only in the reverberations of erotic and Aeschylean themes among her circle, echoes of shared enthusiasms and conversations, but her second venture into existential, archaic and erotic imagery does survive. In 1951, she and Constant Lambert brought Aeschylean themes from the margins to, quite literally, centre stage.

In 1950, Lambert was commissioned by the Sadler's Wells Ballet to write the music for a dance for the Festival of Britain and chose to compose an orchestral piece about the transgendered Tiresias. In the autumn, Isabel wrote excitedly to Giacometti about the project.[1] Frederick Ashton would choreograph and Margot Fonteyn would dance. Leonor Fini – in London collaborating with Sadler's Wells Ballet on another project – suggested Isabel as the designer.[2] Isabel accepted the offer, made by Ashton. Her designs for *Tiresias* would bring the fluid sexual roles that she had negotiated through her persona into her art.

Isabel's letters make it clear that she saw it as an interruption to her painting. She was in good company, however: Picasso's sets for *The Three-Cornered Hat* had recently been revived at Sadler's Wells, and she was interested in the challenge – 'alarm and fascination are about equally balanced'.[3] Financial problems were also mounting. Both Paolozzi and Bacon had taken temporary teaching posts, and Isabel had resigned herself to doing the same. The commission would delay this necessity and bring in £300, a third of which she immediately set aside for her longed-for trip to Greece.[4]

According to a range of Classical sources, Tiresias was a young priest of Apollo who, when he happened upon a pair of snakes mating, hit them with his stick. Hera punished him by transforming him into a woman and making him her priestess for seven years. In some versions he married and had children or gained fame as a prostitute; others provide a different sexual narrative for each year. When Tiresias again came across copulating snakes, he regained his masculine form, but was drawn into an argument between Hera and Zeus about which gender enjoyed most pleasure from intercourse: the man, as Hera claimed; or, as Zeus argued, the woman. Tiresias had no doubt: 'Of ten parts a man enjoys one only.' Hera, insulted once more, blinded him, but Zeus provided compensation, awarding the ability to

126. Roger Wood: Margot Fonteyn as Tiresias and Michael Field as her lover, in Scene 2 of Sadler's Well's Ballet production of *Tiresias*, July 1951; Royal Opera House Collections

predict the future in birdsong. Tiresias was doomed to retain this gift even in Hades. The daring content of the story of Tiresias was central to Lambert's intentions for the ballet. Lutyens recalled that he wished, in Baudelaire's phrase, 'épater la bourgeoisie'.[5] Lambert had been considering Tiresias as a subject for two decades, but even the radical Camargo Society, which had produced ballets in London in the early 1930s, had not been bold enough to take it on. He therefore told Sadler's Wells that the piece was a light satire. Between the wars, Tiresias was, like Leda, a modern trope.[6] The term 'surrealism' had been coined in the Foreword of Apollinaire's play *Les Mamelles de Tirésias* (The Breasts of Tiresias) in 1919, during which a woman became a man by opening her blouse and allowing her breasts, large balloons, to float into the audience. Isabel and Lambert might have seen Francis Poulenc's comic adaptation premiered in Paris during the summer of 1947.[7] Tiresias was a Cassandra-like paradox, a blind seer, who was victim as well as master of his vision. He had been adopted as the main narrator of T. S. Eliot's *The Wasteland* (1922) and featured in Jean Cocteau's play *La Machine infernale* (1934).[8] His ancient voice dissolved certainties, viewing events through a man's and a woman's viewpoint, past and present.

Lambert's daring contribution explored the relativism of identity through focusing on Tiresias' youth rather than his old age, with sex as its core. He wrote, at tremendous speed, an athletic, asymmetrical ballet. The music moved on from his Continental and jazz influences and stressed percussion: it had no strings and

127. *Tiresias*, Scene 1, *Illustrated London News*, 10 July 1951

the first sound was a whiplash. The plot focused on the hero's encounter with the mating snakes (oily clarinet sounds), his transformation from man to woman and back, and the quarrel between Zeus and Hera. The central scene was the lovemaking between the female Tiresias and a male lover, demonstrating her pleasure. Lambert described this to Ashton as a 'grand *pas de deux* starting off slowly and ending up in a state of erotic frenzy. Climax of T's sex life'.[9] Dance and music were configured so that Fonteyn's outer femininity coexisted with an inner masculinity, seen in the angular mirroring of the *pas de deux* and reminiscent of the 'fly away angles' of Isabel's nudes. A bacchanal 'orgy' followed from which Tiresias remained detached until the snakes returned, and she was transformed again. The final act with Zeus and Hera concluded with a diminuendo dying of music until the only sound that remained was the tapping of blind Tiresias's stick, a poignant motif for the lame Lambert, as his biographer, Andrew Motion, notes.[10]

Isabel's many preparatory paintings and drawings for her designs for *Tiresias*, now in the Royal Opera House and the Fry Art Gallery, are the first intact collection of a body of her work to survive. John Craxton was designing Ashton's *Daphnis and Chloë* and initially took Isabel under his wing.[11] Two gouaches, brusque renditions of Craxton-style figures in spatial registers, may be experiments with the 'pornography brut' that she had planned earlier in the year. Lovemaking couples look forward to Bacon's *Two Figures*, while their tomb-like enclosures, conflating sex and death, recall Dylan Thomas's imagery. Isabel determined to distance the ballet from classical clichés of Golden Age Greece and set out to shock. She wrote to Rose Pulham that she was 'sure that the approach must be far more drastic than most people want'.[12] Her final set and costumes moved the action to the, for her, familiar setting of Minoan Crete.

Isabel turned to the Cretan motifs through which she had extended her own sexual persona in the 1930s because, as she wrote to Rose Pulham, 'Cretan dress is very erotic.'[13] Her first efforts were 'too Derain-like ... None are nearly vivid or curious enough.' So she travelled to Oxford to sketch directly from Arthur Evans's archaeological finds from Knossos and reconstructions in the Ashmolean Museum.[14] The male Tiresias of Act 1 was given the minimal skirt and feather headdress of Evans's restored frieze of the so-called Prince of the Lilies (Minoan, fourteenth century BCE; Ashmolean Museum). For the women, Isabel made drawings of the Snake Goddess that had influenced Epstein's *Isobel*. Initially, she considered dressing the dancers in 'false gilt breasts', but thought better of it.'[15] Pauline Claydon, who danced the part of a snake and was one of the chorus, recalled that the bodices were net and nipples rouged.[16] The Virgin, whose role was to bestow upon Tiresias the staff that would strike the snakes, wore gauze over her face on which was painted a displaced eye. Paolozzi produced a series of similar heads around the same time.[17]

To Isabel's surprise, the set builder, Clement Glock, explained that there was no need to adopt the poster-like forms that were usually used for decors; he could imitate whichever medium or texture she supplied.[18] Her *peinture écriture* could be the size of a cinema screen. Isabel set about finding a pictorial force that could survive this transformation. Her instant, emblematic motifs were perfect for this purpose. As the curtain rose at the beginning, the audience saw a front curtain treated like her monochromes: graffiti-like figures, reminiscent of the cover of the journal *Présence africaine*, complemented the references to jazz music in Lambert's score. [19] Her preparatory studies had experimented with combinations of figures, birds, brittle stars and chthonic serpents, the snakes brandished by the Minoan Snake Goddess, appropriate for Tiresias. The final design was dominated by the snake. The 'primordial importance of the sexual element is verified by the capital role of the snake,' Michel Leiris had claimed in *Documents*, 'another phallic symbol in a large number of religions'. [20] Isabel's sketchbooks show her developing its form into a synaesthetic equivalent to the whiplashes in the overture that accompanied the appearance of the front curtain.

Lambert hoped to begin the ballet with young women performing an equivalent of the 'Cretan sport of vaulting in the nude over the horns of a bull', so Isabel's design for Act 1 featured a Minoan bull, '3 times bull size or rather 6 x Spanish bull size – to dominate scene'. The motif was a nod to the bull's erotic currency in writings and drawings, such as Masson's illustrations to Bataille's *Histoire de l'œil*. Isabel based her animal on the famous *Bull Leaping* fresco, from the Palace of Knossos, (Minoan, 14th century BCE; Heraklion Archaeological Museum) and the little Minoan bronze of a bull and acrobat, (fourteenth century BCE) in the British Museum. The *jouissance* of the leapers and the ambiguity that Evans had ascribed to their sexuality were appropriate to the central theme of the ballet. In Act 2, the masculine bull dominating the set was replaced by a feminine 'Dove Goddess' surrounded by birds. It substituted the Classical goddess of love with a more archaic figure reminiscent of Epstein's *Rima*.[21] Rima was, like Tiresias, blind but able to foretell the future through birdsong. The dominating motif of Act 3 was the Minoan *labrys*, or double-headed axe, a symbol of judgement and sacrifice and at the same time an emblem of ambiguity – Clytemnestra's weapon.

The most innovative aspect of Isabel's scheme was colour, an astonishing transformation from the grisaille through which she interpreted real life. During 1950, Isabel had painted 'a series of Minoan subjects' (untraced) for which she made experiments with intense colours with gouache on sized brown paper.[22] Her set designs adapted the colour theories of the painter Franz Marc on music and art and his gendered characterisation of blue, yellow and red: 'Blue is the male principle, astringent and spiritual. Yellow is the female principle, gentle, gay and spiritual. Red is matter, brutal and heavy and always the colour to be opposed.'[23] Each set was dominated by one of these intense hues against which the dance unfolded: for Act 1, 'The most intense blues I can manage'; for Act 2, a 'Landscape in pale viridian'. Isabel toyed with representing the battle of the sexes in Act 3, which takes place in the palace of the gods, by clashes of yellow and blue as seen in one of her preparatory gouaches, but in the end rendered the whole in unprecedented 'glowing amber'.[24] The huge stage of the Royal Opera House at Covent Garden lent tremendous impact to the scheme, and notes in Isabel's sketchbook show that she attended Craxton's lighting rehearsals and that she painted under electric light to understand the colour changes under stage lights.[25]

Isabel enjoyed the 'terrific hazard' of the *Tiresias* project, describing it as 'rather like taking a heady sort of drug'.[26] The Independent Group, the ICA, and associated private galleries with whom Isabel was working had found themselves in tension with a state-sponsored desire for art to incorporate traditional and collective continuities during the Festival of Britain.[27] *Tiresias* was a state commission, but the ballet benefited from presumptions of propriety. Isabel told Rose Pulham that it was permitting a freedom from censorship that they could not have secured in any other way.[28] The premiere at Covent Garden on 9 July 1951 was a gala performance attended by the queen and Princess Elizabeth. Although the programme notes obscured the sexual narrative, referring instead to 'love', the performers did not temper their interpretation and onlookers said that Fonteyn danced with a passion that she never showed in any other role.[29] The shock to the audience must have been immense, and some, including the duchess of Westminster, walked out.[30]

Tiresias survived eight performances. Oxford University Press refused to publish the score, and it was revived only three times over the next four years. The press coyly evaded the ballet's statements about identity and sex and communicated its discomfort by criticising smaller faults. *The Times* acknowledged the daring of

128. Isabel Rawsthorne, costume design for *Tiresias, The Virgin*, c. 1950; Royal Opera House Collections

129. Isabel Rawsthorne, costume design for *Tiresias, Girl Toreador*, c. 1950; Royal Opera House Collections

the ballet's musical style but not its theme; similarly, it recognised the originality of the decor but criticised the 'steely blue, Indian red and glaring primrose yellow' sets for contrasting rather than harmonising with the dancers.[31] The ballet's legendary failure has been exaggerated, however.[32] Many professionals, Marie Rambert, for example, admired the piece, and it was enthusiastically received in the provinces and abroad.[33] Roland Penrose was especially excited by it.[34] When it toured to Paris in 1954, Annette Giacometti sent Isabel a French cutting from *Arts* full of praise.[35] Michel Leiris recognised the Existentialist ambitions and wrote a congratulatory postcard bearing Picasso's *Le Minotaure* (1928; Musée nationale d'art moderne, paris)'.[36] In New York, it was hailed as a work of philosophical and psychological violence, and the design and choreography were seen as 'sharply archaic', combining 'fine research, admirable style and the most carefully considered dramatic connotations'.[37] The opinions of the mainstream British press held sway, however.

Lambert's and Isabel's commitment to the problematic project was in part owing to the fact that the archaic tale staged an existential enquiry being played out for real by homosexual friends – Brausen, Belcher, Bacon and Driberg, for example

130. Francis Bacon, *Painting*, 1950; Leeds Museums and Galleries, City Art Gallery

– as well as colleagues in the ballet. Gender categories were more generally permeable in their circle, and monogamy was rarely taken for granted. Isabel expressed the tensions between this world and habitual English expectations in a rare rant to Rose Pulham: 'We long to put the channel between ourselves and creditors, telephone, beer, BBC, English Newspapers, English Sundays, Cockney speech, housekeeping, other people's worries, and soppy Puritanism of whole place ... Only bright spot ahead – Bradwell for 2 days – next weekend.'[38] The modern relevance of the figure of Tiresias is hinted at by Driberg's adoption of the name, in the 1960s, as his alias.[39] Sexual ambiguity was often explored through codes of this kind, including play-acting and what was called 'eccentricity'. Lord Berners was a conspicuous example: in his privately published novel, *The Girls of Radcliff Hall* (1932), with its punning on the name of the lesbian writer, he re-gendered a group of his friends. Like Isabel, Lambert toyed with gender roles. In 1930, he wrote to Anthony Powell: 'My obsessions are becoming more pronounced I'm afraid but not quite so narrow. I feel rather like Walt Whitman – all races, all colours, all creeds, all sexes.'[40] He famously danced with Dylan Thomas and was renowned for a party piece with the poet Randall Swingler, staging a comical courtship between two snakes: one French, sophisticated and highly sexed (Swingler), the other frigid and English (Lambert).[41]

The name Tiresias was applied also to Bacon, by David Sylvester, who explained: 'The two sexes met in Bacon more than any other human being I have ever encountered. At moments he was one of the most feminine of men, at others one of the most masculine. He could switch between their roles as suddenly and as unpredictably as switching on a light.' [42] Martin Harrison identifies an equivalent 'fusion of figures ... male/female duality' in Bacon's *Painting,* 1950, (**130**) not exhibited until November 1951.[43] Its startlingly sudden departure from grisaille in favour of a red, blue and yellow like Isabel's gendered colour scheme of *Tiresias*, reinforces this suggestion. Both catch the spirit of the abstract American canvases displayed at the ICA that July.[44] The juxtaposition in Bacon's painting of the raised-arm pose, conventionally associated with sexual display, and the bowed shadow lends the figure a further Tiresian duality of life and death, before the curtain and beyond.

Sexual switching had a particular resonance for Isabel and Bacon. Bacon was actively gay, but their relationship during this period became a romantic one. In 1950, they visited Faringdon on their own.[45] Lambert amused them all by beginning a rumour that Isabel had left him for Bacon, and a few weeks later someone told Elisabeth Lutyens, 'Poor Mr Lambert, his wife has left him for a painter!'[46] As a result, the Sutherlands were not the only ones to assume that, after the success of Bacon's solo show in 1949, he and Isabel would marry.[47] Kathleen Sutherland mentioned her presumption to Isabel over a meal. '!', she wrote to Rose Pulham after she'd recounted the mistake; 'Well well – a contrast in 3 husbands.'

Marriage could be a multi-purpose practice in Isabel's circle and regularly involved combinations of heterosexual, homosexual and bisexual partners. Driberg married in 1951, for instance, but this was not for Isabel and Bacon. Their relationship changed, in fact, in this year, when Bacon went travelling with Lord Berners's partner and heir, Robert Heber-Percy: 'gone to N Africa with a group headed by the madboy!!', Isabel told Rose Pulham in January; 'Perhaps Farringdon yet? Two months they are supposed to be away. I wonder. Thebes at the end.'[48] Nothing came of this. Bacon wrote to her, but she could not read his writing.[49] Shortly after he got back, his beloved Nanny Lightfoot died, and he abandoned not only the studio they had shared but, to some extent, London too, spending more time in the country or abroad.

Accounts of a physical dimension to Isabel and Bacon's relationship exist. Reminiscences such as those of the barman at Muriel Belcher's Colony Room may be invented, or may be describing only playful performances of sexual identity such as those discussed above.[50] More reliable are Bacon's own words in his last interview, given to the journalist Frank Maubert for *Paris Match* in 1992:

131. Isabel Rawsthorne, design for *Tiresias,* Scene 1, *In Crete There Lies a Scene*, 1950–1; Royal Opera House Collections

> '*Was it difficult to be gay?*
> On that front, I was an outlaw and remain one. I do not think I am natural. Life is not about that. You know, love is a painful and tiresome disease but it is a necessity.
> *You like bad boys, so they say.*
> And married men. You know, I also made love to Isabel Rawsthorne, a very beautiful woman who was Derain's model and friend to Georges Bataille.'[51]

Bacon's answer evaded categorisation, shifting the emphasis from sex to love, yet making it clear that they 'made love'. The timing of the statement, weeks after Isabel's funeral, was in accord with a code of discretion they shared. She was completely open so long as her frankness did not affect anyone. Hence her memoir spoke about her sex life with Bataille but not with Giacometti, in deference to Annette who was still living; nor about Paolozzi or Bacon. Bacon's interview omits reference to Giacometti and Paolozzi too, but with Isabel gone, he was free to talk about himself. An insight into the affair is provided by Roland Petit, who presented his exactly contemporary 'passionate friendship' with Margot Fonteyn as a template for occasional relationships between women and gay men, which he believed had also ignited between Fonteyn and Rudolf Nureyev. He described an engagement of personalities and interests so intense that it incidentally expressed itself in sex:

'I mean for a moment she has been the greatest woman in my life and I the greatest man in hers. If sex was in the middle somewhere, then she and Nureyev had it. For sure. They had been very close to each other and they loved each other closely. I don't think they have been in bed fucking all night. Probably they had sex a few times ... a sort of caress.'[52] The flaring of a 'passionate friendship,' between Isabel and Bacon after 1949 informs the Leda imagery of *Fragment of a Crucifixion* and the substitution of the traditional male sexual attributes of the bird with explicit female ones.

Behind the risk-taking, play-acting and innuendo of this social group were serious renegotiations of sexuality. Beverly Clark has argued that Lord Berners's *The Girls of Radcliff Hall*, for example, was a response to the female emancipation of the time.[53] During the same period of the 1930s, Isabel's boyish clothes and rejection of female roles were indispensable to her freedom to work and paint.[54] Identities had been further destabilised by the war. The myths and realities of sexual opportunism provided by social disruption, not to mention the blackout, have been well documented.[55] Overall, the liberties, eccentricities and 'esprit de contraire' of the 1940s and 1950s augured the fundamental social changes of the 1960s and 1970s in the U.K., reflected in the decriminalisation of sex between men in 1967 and in the introduction of equal pay for men and women in 1970. In the meantime, however, for many, sexual identity and behaviour were urgent, opportunistic but unresolved questions. Lambert and Isabel's narrative of a man/woman cut to the core of these.

132. Isabel Rawsthorne, design for *Tiresias*, Scene 3, 1950-1; Royal Opera House Collections

133. Isabel Rawsthorne, design for *Tiresias*, Scene 2, *In The Mountains*, 1950-1; Royal Opera House Collections

PART III

134. John Deakin: Isabel Lambert, 1952

23 UNQUIET GRAVE: 1951–1955

> I am beginning to understand what pushes me into painting – the love of seeing and the fact that, as the chosen subject grows in beauty so does it becomes more elusive.
>
> Isabel Lambert[1]

Tiresias past, Isabel spent August 1951 painting nudes for her show at the Hanover Gallery scheduled for November, while Constant Lambert prepared for the Edinburgh Festival. Although she had not wanted to get into the predicament in which Bacon had found himself when his exhibition in 1950 opened at the Hanover with only two new works, she had been fretting that, by postponing the show, she was 'losing the meat for the reflection'[2] Brausen had scheduled works by Pierre Bonnard and Édouard Vuillard for the accompanying display, an interesting juxtaposition for Isabel's figures – and for those of Bacon, who was painting full-length portraits to exhibit immediately after Isabel's show.

The BBC promenade concerts were on, and Lambert conducted his ever-popular *Rio Grande*, but the exertion caused him to collapse.[3] He appeared to have recovered the next day, and Isabel accompanied him to dinner at Edith Sitwell's, where he was on scintillating form. The following morning she left him to sleep in and took an early bus to Anna Phillips's new home in Blackheath, where he would join them for lunch. In later years, she cherished the unsuspecting happiness of the sunny journey on the open deck of the 53 bus, but when Lambert failed to turn up, she rushed back to Albany Street. She found him barely conscious and telephoned Dennis ApIvor, who called an ambulance. Lambert was attempting to speak, but it took a long time to understand that he was begging her not to let them take him away. When the ApIvors arrived he lunged for the window and had to be restrained by Irene and Isabel. On the way to the London Clinic, 'through all the pain and disaster', she could not help thinking, 'but I *have* let them take him away'. As no one was aware of Lambert's diabetes, it was assumed that he would recover, but within hours the hospital called Isabel back to say he was dying. At his bedside, she asked him if he wanted to see anybody else, and his reply was shockingly sharp: 'Yes. We've seen enough of you.'[4] Although she knew that aggression was characteristic of his illness, she never freed herself from the hurt that came from his believing that she had betrayed him. He didn't speak again and died in the early hours of 22 August, two days before his forty-sixth birthday.[5]

Isabel and Kit, who was then fifteen, were dazed by their loss. Questions of how to live and how to love became, for a time, unanswerable. Pattie Whitney Smith, Elisabeth Lutyens and Alan Rawsthorne took over the funeral arrangements, and Isabel fled to Peter and Mary Rose Pulham in France – the Christian service was not for her.[6] She returned to play her part in the memorial, spending the preceding morning, a damp September day, alone in their cold apartment, collecting her courage and answering letters to Delmer and Bacon. To Rose Pulham and Mary, she wrote: 'Everything is as bad as I thought it would be,' adding, 'except for the kindness of friends.'[7] After the service, Frank Otto, the Lambert' financial adviser, told her there was no money. The problems she had experienced in 1946 now returned: she was unwell and her 'memory became a spent jumble of overlapping images'. She withdrew to the country, finding sanctuary first with Delmer at the Valley Farm and later in Zennor in Cornwall, where she had recuperated after the war.[8] Meanwhile, Albany Street was given up. Anna Phillips adopted Isabel's sofa, Elisabeth took in the cat and the contents of her studio went into Frank Otto's garage.[9]

Isabel's passport and private papers reveal that at the end of September 1951, a month after Lambert's death, she and Alan Rawsthorne went to Florence.[10] Careless of convention for herself, Isabel, nevertheless, kept the trip secret to avoid discomforting Lambert's friends and family.[11] Rawsthorne had loved her since their night together five years before, and their profound mutual loss brought them closer. The Florentine streets and churches that Isabel had so often imagined exploring with Giacometti or Lambert were finally walked with him, and he was by her side as she drew the Botticellis in the Uffizi and experienced the 'unexpected silence' of the Donatellos in the Bargello.[12] They talked about painting, Van Eyck, Courbet, Bonnard and the Renaissance masters. Rawsthorne read aloud Virgil and Cennini; Isabel watched him: 'It is so interesting to reflect on the faces of one's friends', but they 'refrained from caresses'. The problem for both of them was Lambert's 'unquiet grave', as Isabel expressed it.[13] Neither was sure how their 'adventure' would continue.[14]

In November, Brausen filled Isabel's Hanover exhibition with *Tiresias* designs.[15] There is no record of Christmas, but in January 1952 she spent a week in France with Pattie.[16] She continued to avoid the London 'racket' and needed to work: 'the obvious thing to do was to go to Paris'.[17] She delayed her departure until 4 March, when the film *The Cruel Sea,* for which Rawsthorne had written his fifth, and best, soundtrack premiered. The edgy composition contributed to the film's success, and it broke all box-office records for the year. On the day before the premiere, John Deakin made a set of portraits of Isabel, one of which was published in *Vogue* magazine the following year.[18] Deakin was part of the Colony Room circle, close fellows with Belcher and Bacon. An exact contemporary of Isabel in age, he had grown up on the Wirral Peninsula and gone to a school a few miles from hers, but they probably met in 1939, when he was a colleague of Rose Pulham in Paris. The *Vogue* text conflated Constant's death with Isabel's designs for the forthcoming production of Richard Strauss's raw variation on the story of Agamemnon and Clytemnestra's daughter, *Elektra*. Deakins's pictures adapted Rose Pulham's technique of photographing through transparent fabrics.[19] Isabel posed like Electra or Baudelaire's '*À une passante*', 'in dense mourning, imperious grief', inscrutable and unusually still, in black gloves beneath a crumpled black veil in a black-draped room.[20] There is a clear echo of the famous press photographs of the strikingly veiled Queen Elizabeth at the funeral of her father, King George VI, two weeks before the photo session, but eyeliner and earrings gave Isabel the air of an older, Aeschylean sovereign.[21]

Isabel reached France on 5 March.[22] She spent a couple of days in Normandy with Joan Rayner and arrived in Paris on 8 March.[23] It would take some time to reinvent her existence again. Her intention and Alan Rawsthorne's hope was that she would go back to London after a year, but neither was sure that she would.[24] This time there was no double Right Bank, Left Bank life. Isabel was poor and in a situation little different than when she had first arrived in 1934. She did not return to the Hôtel Saint-Romain or the Café de la Régence, but went instead to the Left Bank Hôtel de la Louisiane, a cheap, 1920s establishment on the corner of the rue de Buci, just off the boulevard Saint-Germain. For 200 francs a month (about £500 today), the formidable *patronne* was persuaded to rent her an attic with a tiny adjoining studio, 'about ½ the size of yr bedroom', she told Lutyens. One wall was glazed, which provided good light, but it was a chilly spring and there was no heating. The floor was bare and furniture restricted to an iron bed and a gas ring.[25]

La Louisiane was a bohemian residence for artists and writers. It had been the haunt of musicians such as Miles Davis and Juliette Gréco, now a successful chanteuse of the songs of Jacques Prévert and Raymond Queneau. Sartre and de Beauvoir still had rooms there. Peter and Mary Rose Pulham had separated and she was in residence. She had seen Lucian Freud a few times in London.[26] Rose Pulham had his flirtations too, notably with a new young artist and professional model on the London scene, Henrietta Moraes, but he missed Mary.[27] Mary was with her new lover, Desmond Ryan (an Irish Republican writer who was the Paris correspondent for *The Irish Times*). Lucian Freud was also there with Caroline Blackwood, for whom he had abandoned Kitty Garman. Mary eventually married

Desmond and settled outside Paris. Peter remained alone. Valmondais was given up, and he withdrew to his 1946 home in Conives in the Indre.

Isabel worked in her small studio and at the Académie de la Grande Chaumière. Mary Rose Pulham drove her to Valmondais to collect her easels and cookware, and Peter let her take some old canvases he had abandoned. She recommenced work on the *Seasons*.[28] Her phenomenological problem was the same as it had been in 1949: 'one of the most immediate questions to solve / for me/ is how to situate a human figure. So that it partakes of its surroundings (in sculpture this problem does not arise) and yet paint only it.''[29] She reconsidered and discussed her scheme at length in a letter to Lutyens, concluding, 'I'm thinking. I've thought – visually theatrically', and she summarised her plan to Peter Rose Pulham: 'Spring ½ length Mary (sorry, but I must mention her) with hands, in open air (Valmondais) Cool colour. Summer. Nudes in landscape – Autumn figure in town or 2 Nudes lying in salon – Winter (I'd rather not say just yet). But in colour cool earths.'[30] Mary posed until she left the Louisiane, then Isabel set the *Seasons* aside until she could find a way of getting models and a bigger room. She had a reproduction of The Baker Terentius Neo and his Wife and occupied herself with more Pompeiians.[31] She also returned to her humble still lifes, painting mostly eggs (whereabouts unknown). Her main interest, however, about which she wrote frequently, was a view through the attic window.[32] A final version, *Roofs of Paris,* 1952, (**135**) was completed on one of Rose Pulham's used canvases, painted over a figure shown from the back (the model was the textile designer Freda Elliott, who had married Paolozzi in 1951) and later given or sold to Pattie Whitney Smith.[33] She found its red ground interesting to work over. A sketch (*Roofs*, 1952; private collection), survives on the back of an abandoned *Two Figures*. *Roofs* was an unusually close reworking of Picasso's *Toits bleus* (Blue Roofs), which he had painted fifty years before, in May 1901, in similar conditions from his lodgings in Montmartre.[34] Isabel knew the picture well from the Ashmolean, where it had hung since 1939. In her version of the subject, a bird sits on a roof and, as in *The Desert*, another sweeps between the buildings.

Isabel could not shake off her 'blues'. 'Why suddenly this utter depth?', she asked Rose Pulham, 'Worry about the future yes. Where to live – but that is persistent. The past an ever present shadow ... Just a physical reaction to events? no. what? I have detached curiosity about myself which isn't good for me ... There is some worm, maggot, maggot in my head. I wish I knew what it was.'[35] She was mostly on her own. Her tiny allowance, maladministered by Frank Otto, was unreliable, and she subsisted on eggs and vegetables cooked in her room.[36] In the light and warmth of cheaper cafés, she penned letters and read the correspondence of the eighteenth-century traveller Lady Mary Wortley Montagu, eking out

135. Isabel Rawsthorne, *Roofs of Paris*, 1952; private collection, Switzerland

a coffee or a glass of wine.[37] She frequented Le Henri Quatre, Café de Buci and Au Relais Odéon. Occasionally, she went to Les Deux Magots – 'expensive but one can think there' – or even made an excursion to the Café de la Régence. She wrote to Belcher, Bacon – who was again in Africa – Rose Pulham and Lutyens. Only the correspondences with Rose Pulham and with Lutyens have survived, and the latter has been censored (parts of letters have been ripped off). 'I'm slowly getting myself in order,' Isabel told her, 'I miss you all', ending, 'Am better – will I hope – be better still soon – Have the most disturbing dreams. To be expected I assume.'[38]

Paris was different. To Isabel, it seemed as though conviviality had given way to vulgarity. By the 1950s, the familiar cafés were mobbed by moneyed enthusiasts for the Existentialist set. A *famille Sartre* crowded the Café de Flore, and jazz followers and a *bande Prévert* filled the bars and clubs. Isabel told Rose Pulham, 'Never imagined I could live here with so little desire to see any of my

Parisian friends ... Curious. Partly a desire to concentrate.'[39] She steered clear also of Cyril Connolly and the London crowd, walking the boulevard Saint-Germain only between 11 p.m. and 2 a.m., when she could be alone. Wandering through Paris after hours still held its charm: a late-night letter written in her room over a supper of cauliflower and *vin ordinaire* concluded: 'I love the evening in Paris. Voilà quelque chose au manqué outré man[i]ere ... je vais sortir une heure – flâneur, etc.'[40]

Close friends broke her solitude. Joan Rayner and Patrick Leigh Fermor visited sometimes. She breakfasted with Balthus[41] and met up again with Dora Maar, 'looking suddenly a matron and rather distinguished.'[42] But many comrades were absent. Gruber had died, Rose Pulham was writing in Conives, Picasso had settled further south, and Mara had stayed in New York.[43] Derain asked for her, and she went to see him, but he was not well. She was touched to notice that he still kept the half-length portrait of her in his studio.[44] One day, Annette came to the hotel with a gift of cream and ground almonds from Marie-Laure de Noailles, vicomtesse de Noailles (Giacometti's patron). She encouraged Isabel to socialise with them, but there were risks in seeing Giacometti and she was avoiding him especially.[45] However, she attended his party for Michel Leiris at Brasserie Lipp to mark his friend's departure to do field work in the West Indies. (Coincidently, in the same month, March, Warwick, then a PhD student in the Liverpool School of Tropical Medicine sailed to do six months fieldwork in the British Cameroons.) The meal was an extravagant affair. 'Never before eaten two dinners without moving from the table,' Isabel wrote to Rose Pulham, and the following day the grateful owner of the brasserie made Giacometti the gift of a cigarette lighter.[46] After the party, Isabel and Giacometti found themselves together. They renewed their nocturnal walks, and henceforward, met more often, at each other's studios and elsewhere.

A letter to Lutyens provides an insight into the professional and emotional discipline that structured Isabel's spring days: 'Up at 7am, make coffee, work. 10AM cup of Viandox (Bovril), friction with Eau de Cologne & loofah. Wash. Out. shop. 11–12 work. Out – glasses of white Macon in local. Write. 1. Cook lunch (Eggs veg). 2–4 Snooze. 4.30 Coffee Work. 5.30 Out Stroll mutter decide not to go see Giacometti. 6.30 Glass of wine cook dinner, eat – 10.30 Either out coffee beer, or bed – (saying tomorrow I'll go and find Giacometti. His working hours are – 2pm–4pm, 5pm–10pm, 2.30 AM–5 or 6 or 7 AM so it's rather complicated. Seen him a few times. He is charming to me can't understand what's happened. Vraiment de la tendresse dans l'amitié acute [truly the tenderness of a close friendship].'[47] However, she confided in Rose Pulham, 'Seen Giacometti several times. Yesterday at his home. Portraits everywhere. Coffee at the Dome at midnight. He is considerate towards me! ... Our relationship has great charm now – at least it has for me. I hope it has as much for him. I think I must have become a more understanding person lately – my goodness I am fond of him. An hour's conversation is like a long holiday – I mean it has a revivifying effect.'[48] But she added, 'I am very careful not to be around too often for fear of becoming boring.' Her feelings for him had not dimmed; a letter fragment from later in the year reads: 'Tuesday Spent last night till dawn with Giacometti, who was, by chance, and I was, by chance, in the Boulevard at 1am. I am so fond of him – Suddenly – now – at ~~40~~ 39 Odd.'[49] Isabel had not yet seen Deakin's photographs of her, and when, after much badgering, copies arrived, she sent one to Giacometti inscribed 'do you?'[50] The meaning this held for the couple will probably never be accessible, but its inversion of 'I do' somehow suits the figure veiled in black.

Isabel was under no illusions that her relationship with Giacometti could be practical: 'Very worried on account of A. I find my thoughts on this are simple – it could be anything I want if only the execution was possible.'[51] She did not wish to trouble Annette or return to the arrangement she had left in 1947: 'No, I no longer aspire to trapping a whirlwind,' she wrote to Rose Pulham in a reference to the fate of Job. 'I like opposition as you call it to a certain degree. I like being made to use my wits. I like freedom but for me to be free I have to have a frame.'[52] By implication, her frame was Alan Rawsthorne: 'I have a strong feeling that Alan understands my character fairly well, and I am beginning to understand his. I admire his delicacy of behaviour, his discipline, his patience, his sense of purpose, his reserve.'

There were other proposals. Tom Driberg arrived in Paris, a 'cheerful apparition', and offered his 'belvedere' at Bradwell,[53] and Rose Pulham was suggesting cohabitation in Conives, but Isabel knew these would not work.[54] Rawsthorne sent a passionate letter headed 'will you live with me?', declaring that he was sure he could make her as happy as she would make him: 'Your ways may be labyrinthine but in the end the Hound of Heaven has nothing on me.'[55] Finally, Isabel confessed to Rose Pulham that she was 'engaged – *engagé* – as far as you are concerned, as a fellow struggler and as "old friend"'. The familiar wordplay, blurring the very different bourgeois and Existentialist uses of the term 'engaged', tactfully acknowledged the emotional sensitivity of the subject for Rose Pulham. Isabel reassured him that they would remain comrades, and they adopted the habit of calling each other 'cousin'.

Conditions in Isabel's studio room were not ideal, and she still saw her painting, even *Roofs*, as mere research, 'disciplinary, rather than crystallisation'.[56] She avoided Erica Brausen and did not want to exhibit until she had returned to England and could complete the *Seasons* in a larger studio. In March, Peter Watson and David Sylvester had come to Paris in the course of organising *Recent Trends in Realist Painting* for the ICA which would run in London from 2 July to 2 August. Sylvester took it for granted that Isabel would contribute again and offered to take care of her framing, but she was evasive. She introduced him to Balthus, and Watson recruited him and selected some pictures of Rose Pulham's at Pierre Loeb's.[57] In May, Watson returned to Paris for a Michael Ayrton show funded by the British Council and asked again to see Isabel's work. She was discouraged by the 'photographic' understanding of the word realism implied by the promotion of Ayrton, so told Watson, with a sly allusion to the phenomenological challenges of her style, 'nothing seeable yet'.[58] It was Rose Pulham, who had gone back to London for the ICA panel discussion on Giacometti (Giacometti wishing he could heckle from the audience), who extracted one of Isabel's nudes and *The Desert* from Frank Otto's garage and took them to the ICA.[59] Isabel attended the exhibition without enthusiasm, finding it confirmed her conviction that English art, her own included, had a way to go.[60] There is no record of what she thought of seeing her paintings alongside Giacometti's.

Her health was not fully restored, and she went down with measles.[61] She moved into Rawsthorne's small apartment at 106 Baker Street, just down from the fictional address, 221b, of one of his heroes, Sherlock Holmes.[62] After the ICA show closed, she hung Rose Pulham's *Ville Entière* next to *The Desert* in the flat, where they were admired by Paolozzi. She wrote to Rose Pulham with one of her favourite phrases: 'Both you and I seem to have made a good mark *dans les coulisses* [behind the scenes] ... but of course no money.'[63]

Isabel and Alan Rawsthorne were an odd couple, Rawsthorne wry and watchful (he had the rare skill of entering a room silently), Isabel passionately expansive; but he understood her needs as an artist. According to Pattie Whitney Smith, he was the lover who made Isabel happiest.[64] Isabel renewed her acquaintance with her old circle, including Michael Ayrton and his new partner, the cookery writer Elizabeth Balchin. She got to know Clifford Frith, then lecturing at Camberwell School of Art. A student of Victor Pasmore and fellow of Mervyn Peake, Frith was, like Ayrton, one of the favoured generation of British Neo-Romantics. Despite their incompatible philosophies, Frith's lively memories of Isabel are valuable. He recalls the couple affectionately: 'Isabel, over life size, her extraordinary energy ... Alan on the other hand could only move slowly and deliberately. He could take a minute to precisely place the needle on a gramophone record! They were made for each other!'[65]

The young composer Edward Williams, Rawsthorne's protégé and, after the death of Lambert, his closest comrade, described their social stamping ground: 'taking in the George (known as "The Gluepot") and other pubs near the BBC in Portland Place, the restaurants of Soho proper, clubs like the Wine Bar, the

136. Isabel Rawsthorne, design for Strauss's *Elektra*, 1953, *Opera* magazine, 1954

Mandrake and Muriel Belcher's Colony Room, the French pub, the Swiss and many others, to Olwen Vaughan's Petit Club Français off St. James' ... a kind of cultural melting pot, a swirling meeting place of writers, poets, musicians'.[66] Isabel was glad to catch up with her own friends. Bacon was back from Africa, 'forgetting dates' and painting in a borrowed studio in advance of his next Hanover exhibition, just three weeks away. He was deep in a new affair with a handsome and tempestuous fighter pilot turned *demi-mondain,* Peter Lacy. As careers flourished, Soho revelries became freer. Freud threw a champagne party, after which Isabel reported to Rose Pulham that 'Bacon was thrown out of a window 15ft into the area below, by Peter [Lacy], but being drunk survived without damage.'[67]

In 1952, an exhibition of Isabel's paintings would have received a more informed reception than it had in early 1949. Her priority, however, was, understandably, finally to solve the problem of 'how to live'. She had not been able to conclude the *Seasons*; she needed a studio and a living, so she designed the sets and costumes for three productions at Covent Garden: for Richard Strauss's opera *Elektra*; for a ballet by Denis ApIvor based on Lorca's play *Blood Wedding*;

and for *Coppélia*.[68] She also collaborated with Robert Medley's Group Theatre, designing costumes for Pedro Calderón de la Barca's existential allegory, *Life's a Dream* (1635), with sets by Medley augmented with sculptures by Elisabeth Frink, and music by Rawsthorne.[69] The projects established her as a respected designer. *Elektra*, staged at Covent Garden in May 1953, reproduced her apparitional calligraphic technique on a grand scale. The scuffed and scumbled surfaces of the Aeschylean palace wavered into view, and the costumes – the red gown she designed for the Overseer (Joan Sutherland) and the cerise dress of Clytemnestra (1953; Royal Opera House collections), for example – varied from the surroundings in colour but not in tone. The unusual effect was universally praised.[70] For *The Times*, reviewing the production when it was performed again a few years later, the 'monumental set was a match for Strauss's huge orchestra';[71] the 'impressive setting of the palace at Mycenae ... a grey-black courtyard ... enclosed the players like a monstrous cage.'[72] It was still being used and acclaimed twenty-five years later.[73] The unsentimental 'hard lines and violent colours' of Isabel's sets for ApIvor's grim adaptation of Lorca's *Blood Wedding* won praise even from the more conservative reviewers, and critics complained when they were 'prettified' in the late 1960s.[74] In April 1955, her designs for another ballet, *Madame Chrysanthème*, a reversal of the Madam Butterfly story in which it is the sailor who is betrayed, received warm reviews. The music was again composed by Rawsthorne. Her technical innovations were appreciated by *The Stage*: 'A clever use of transparent screens moved by property men in full view.' The effect was like an 'animated Japanese print', translated with Isabel's habitual austerity, 'both beautiful and sordid aspects of the Orient in refined colours with admirable restraint.'[75] In 1963, her design work featured in a major touring Arts Council exhibition, *Three Stage Designers: Leslie Hurry, Isabel Lambert, Sophie Fedorovitch*.

At the same time, Alan Rawsthorne agreed to the plan originally conceived with René Leibowitz, to find an affordable, permanent space in the country. With the help of Tom Driberg's local knowledge, Isabel found Sudbury Cottage, (**140**) a small, seventeenth-century thatched farmer's house in Little Sampford in rural Essex. It was purchased in Alan Rawsthorne's name on 29 October 1952, and they began arrangements to move in and renovate it the following spring. As a result, there would be no show at the Hanover for another year. Brausen obtained a commitment for October 1953.

In the meantime, Isabel found a replacement in London for the life classes at the Académie de la Grande Chaumière. Her contacts at Sadler's Wells gave her access to the dancers' practice rooms in Hammersmith, where she could address the more challenging subject of figures in movement.[76] There was no space for a studio at Baker Street, so she set up at 54 Delancey Street, across Regent's

137. Isabel Rawsthorne, Dylan Thomas, 1952–3; private collection

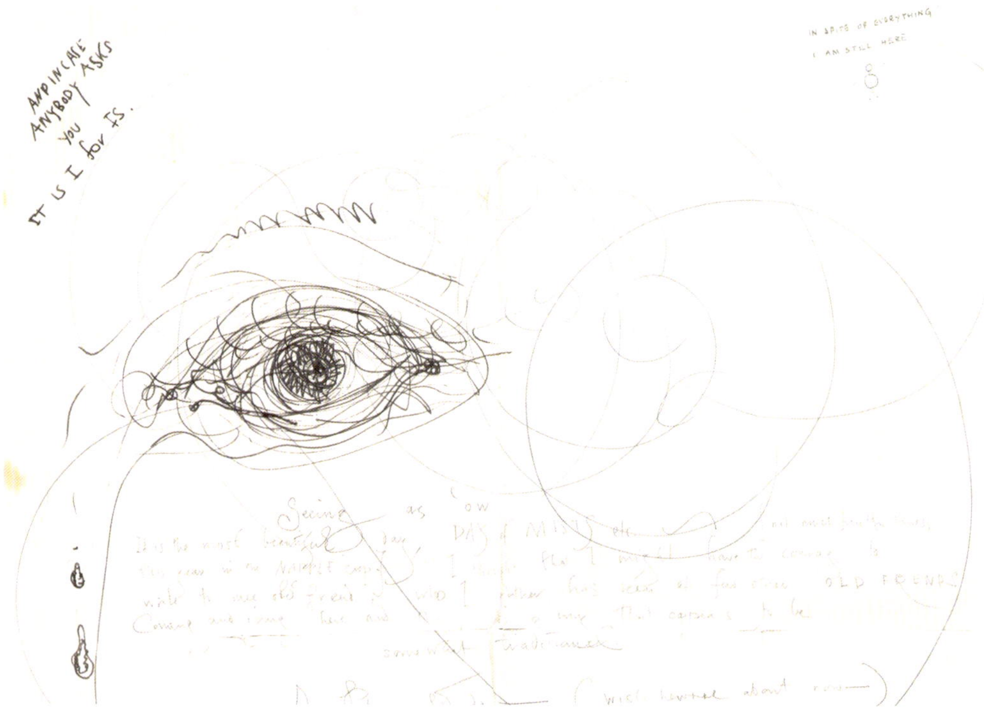

138. Isabel Rawsthorne, letter to Peter Rose Pulham, 1954; Tate Archive

Park, in Camden Town, a house lent to Dylan Thomas by his patron Margaret Taylor. Isabel painted on the first floor, while Thomas completed the play *Under Milk Wood* in a gypsy caravan in the garden. In Paris, Isabel had been struck by Giacometti's 'portraits everywhere'. Now she had Anna Phillips, Irene ApIvor and Muriel Belcher to sit, and when Joan Rayner was in town, she took photographs of them 'to assist' (whereabouts unknown).[77] An undated letter written by Isabel at the Colony Room mentions having no money and leaving a portrait of Muriel there in the hope that someone would buy it for Muriel (1952–3), but its fate and whereabouts are unknown.[78]

The work done in Delancey Street does not appear to have been preserved. The single exception is the small portrait of Dylan Thomas, (**137**) probably kept, like the drawing of Mara Scherbatoff, for emotional rather than artistic reasons. Isabel and Thomas had been friends since the war. An artistic empathy between them is suggested by the zoological imagery of his last poem, 'On his Birthday', which was begun in 1949, shortly after Isabel's first Hanover exhibition.[79] Its central motif, 'birds and fishes pass above and below him on their dying way', as Thomas summarised it to a friend, is startlingly relevant to the monochromes.[80] Isabel and he usually met in the pub, 'telling stories ... he really reminded me of a spider using its threads to entrap its prey', but he must have sat for Isabel during the winter of 1952–3.[81] The painting is a single central figure, in the manner of Giacometti, and a study in distance, or rather, departure. Thomas sits by the first-floor window of her studio, where trains rattle past; the cold north light, reminiscent of Sickert's nearby Camden Town rooms, dissolves his form. He was working and drinking too much and in London for a short interlude between American tours. Rumpled clothing and thinning hair fray the profile into Isabel's characteristic, centrifugal strokes, fanning downwards and outwards, as in her *Seated Figure*, or like his spider's 'threads'. The pale face divides between one eye that is beady and the other that is sad, a restless likeness that refuses to resolve. It is nearly the last known portrait of him: he died in New York the following autumn.[82]

Money continued to be short until the Covent Garden contracts came through, even though Rawsthorne's accountant had extricated Isabel's affairs from the hands of Frank Otto. As another Christmas loomed, she wrote to Rose Pulham that she wished she could have spent it with him in Conives, or at least have 'nipped over to Paris to avoid paper chains in public houses and various peoples parties which I shall be too feeble, no doubt, to avoid owing to the general turgid atmosphere'.[83] She missed Giacometti: 'feeling of being somewhat removed from myself'. Isabel and Alan Rawsthorne finally decamped to Little Sampford in 1953. They were driven down with their belongings by Edward Williams.[84]

Their friends were getting married: Isabel and Alan attended Clifford Frith's wedding to the cellist Vera Murrill at London Zoo in 1953; Pattie Whitney Smith had wed Gerry Lambert, a French architect, and had settled outside Paris in 1954.[85] A year later, on 15 October 1955, Rawsthorne finally realised his wish, and Isabel married him. The reason she gave for agreeing was that the brothers who had previously owned Sudbury Cottage had scandalised the village by living in a *ménage à trois*, and now her own ambiguous presence, variously understood as 'concubine' or 'house keeper', was unsettling local sensitivities once again.[86] She and Alan threw a lively party and friends descended on the cottage. In a surreal moment, one of their neighbours, a maths teacher, Maureen Ramsey, drove past, towing a clanking cement mixer, and the guests hung over the gate toasting her.[87] But Isabel's letter written to Rose Pulham on the occasion of the marriage was, like that written to Giacometti when she married Lambert, ambivalent. The three large sheets began with a defiantly existential claim, 'and if anyone asks you it is i for Is.' Below this the I/eye with which she so often represented herself was scrawled in a tangle of lines three times life size, tipping tears down the side of the page. The last tear was labelled 'guilt', revealing, perhaps, the persistence of Lambert's 'unquiet grave'.[88]

139. Isabel Rawsthorne, *Flowerpiece*, c. 1955–9; private collection

24 ESCAPE TO REALITY: 1953–1959

Isabel arrived at Sudbury Cottage physically and mentally exhausted, 'frozen' as she put it, her health still inexplicably unrestored.[1] There was a great deal to do: the garden was overgrown; the cottage was primitive (its original bread oven was still in the kitchen) and a lot of labour was required to render it habitable. The beams, reputedly salvaged from wrecks, were so seasoned that no nails could be driven into them. A note in her sketchbook paralleled her condition with that of the swallows who shared their roof: 'Must work more systematically now. Days of childish dash coming to a close – Digging nettles out a satisfactory exercise attracts robins etc. As far as I can make out our swallows left late this year end Sept – and what a gale the day they set off. Saw two sitting on top of open / bedroom / window at about 7am – looking / frail / nervous buffeted by gusts; A most touching sight. They were not seen after this.'[2] This image was prescient. Nowhere had ever been home to Isabel for more than a few months or few years. Sudbury Cottage would shelter her for the rest of her life. 'To me', she wrote, 'it was an extraordinary experience to feel a sense of peace ~~and security~~' (the cautious deletion is telling). 'Order came into our lives.'[3]

Isabel's existence had a new kind of duality, split between country and city. She went to London '1 in 10', as she told Rose Pulham, one day in ten, to work at the ballet practice rooms or the Opera House. It was an hour's ride in the private Jennings Bus, which, in the morning, picked locals up along the route, including at her cottage gate, and returned them in the evening.[4] Alan Rawsthorne kept a London *pied à terre*, swapping his Baker Street flat for a place in Brewer Street, which he co-owned with Edward Williams and which was just metres from Muriel Belcher's Colony Room.[5]

In the spring of 1953, Isabel travelled to Italy and then to Germany for a meeting in Munich with the director of the production of *Elektra* that she was designing, and, in the summer of 1954, she finally spent two months with Joan Rayner and Patrick Leigh Fermor in Greece. In general, however, she was increasingly reluctant to interrupt her work.[6] She saw less of her friends: 'Quick lunch Freud, Ann Fleming, Bacon at Etoile ...', she reported to Rose Pulham just before Christmas in 1954.[7] Ian Fleming had married Ann Charteris in 1952, and he was enjoying fame with his first James Bond book, *Casino Royale*, published in April 1953. Freud and Bacon were exhibiting successfully; Bacon was launched in America and was regularly with Peter Lacy in the south of France and Tangiers.[8] The financial freedom and social cachet enjoyed by her circle diluted its appeal for Isabel: 'Been rather infrequently to Muriel's,' she continued in the same letter to Rose Pulham; 'The same only duller. Fewer friends appear.' She bowed out of Ann Fleming's party at the Ritz.[9]

Isabel enjoyed the countryside: 'Here it is lovely and I am more interested in the conversation at the Black Bull than I am in the conversation at Wheelers or in any snob place,' she told Rose Pulham.[10] There was 'hardly any sense of class',[11] and she and Rawsthorne quickly made Essex friends, whom they met in the pub or on the Jennings Bus. Isabel loved to talk science with a local maths teacher, Maureen Ramsey (she of the cement mixer), who had trained as an actress at RADA. The glamorous Catherine Garland, enjoying her release from her fourth marriage to a tyrannical doctor, infected Isabel with her passions for old roses and bridge.[12] Alan Rawsthorne was friends with everyone, the village champion at the local pub pursuit, snookerette, and playing chess regularly with the butcher's boy.[13] He and Isabel shared their cottage with a tabby cat named Maud and, in due course, her kittens: 'A warm lived in home,' as a contemporary described it, 'full of cats and cushions and salivation from kitchen smells. The piano with the hospitable bottles upon its top, the huge logs in the open hearth, the clutter of books and sheet music, and manuscript. And talk, which was rich, effortless and seemingly endless.'[14]

The nearest town was Thaxted, where Lambert had often cried at Mass on Christmas Eve. Sefton Delmer's Valley Farm and Tom Driberg's Bradwell were nearby, and others of Isabel's circle settled in the area: the Swinglers, the Ayrtons and the MacNeices.[15] Bacon was in the habit of staying in Wivenhoe, on the Essex coast, an hour beyond Little Sampford, and bought a cottage there. He often visited Isabel, where he played poker with the redoubtable Catherine Garland and was delighted, one day, Isabel remembered, when she arrived after a bicycle accident with 'a cut knee, with blood flowing down her'.[16] Edward Williams, a frequent visitor, described 'laughter, gaiety, joy and affectionate warmth ... though occasionally, of course, there would be moments of high drama when awesome exclamation and shrieks of incredulous horror – provoked perhaps by some quietly ironic propositions of Alan's – would replace the infectious bursts and shouts of laughter to which Isabel was usually given.'[17] Anna Phillips came from her mansion in Blackheath and eventually moved to near-by Framlingham, where, for a short time, she ran an art gallery. Mary Ryan, Pattie Lambert (formerly Whitney Smith) and Joan Rayner stayed regularly, and Freddie Ayer, 'v funny as usual', occasionally turned up from Oxford.[18] Warwick came when he had time, although he considered his sister's household 'chaos'.[19] Rawsthorne's sister, Barbara, by contrast, was a frequent guest; 'sharp and very witty and kind too', she and Isabel developed a deep fondness for each other.[20]

Isabel took special pleasure in her relationships with young people. Her stepson, Kit, was studying at Oxford before doing his National Service, and turned up sometimes. Two of Isabel's godchildren lived nearby: Corinna MacNeice and the Swinglers' daughter, Judith, would cycle over for tea.[21] She still saw nothing of Jackie, now a young man of twenty, like Kit, and a racing-car driver. Londoners and locals converged on the cottage on summer weekends and played badminton in the garden.[22] The journalist Jeffrey Bernard remembered these visits as 'a treat ... [Isabel] was funny, outrageous and very clever. She was also a brilliant cook of French classic food.' One of his favourite stories was of stargazing with her, one night, and falling in a cesspit. She and Rawsthorne insisted on personally washing him in the bath and donating new clothes. Such was Bernard's affection for Isabel that he gave his daughter the same name. 'She was incredibly abrasive but toned it down with being amazingly soft and kind ... a liberal and tolerant woman who at the same time did not suffer fools gladly ... every time I saw her she made me laugh.'[23]

Warwick graduated with a BSc Hons from the University of Liverpool in 1950 and became a research assistant and doctoral student in the Liverpool School of Tropical Medicine, by which time Agnes had moved to Liverpool to live with him. In 1952, Warwick and fiancée Evelyn Clarkson, a fellow scientist, visited Isabel in Paris and on 8 July 1953 Isabel attended their wedding in Liverpool. The same year Warwick was awarded his PhD and Agnes Nicholas continued to live in Liverpool with the new couple. In 1952 Warwick had visited Isabel in Paris with his fiancée Evelyn and on 8 July 1953 Isabel attended their wedding in Liverpool. The same year Warwick was awarded his PhD and Agnes Nicholas continued to live in Liverpool with the new couple. On one occasion, Isabel and Rawsthorne stayed in a house opposite the Liverpool School of Art and she experienced a 'curious sensation', watching through the window as the professors went in and out. She recognised her old fellows William Stevenson and George McPherson, but did not approach them. She had the intention of sketching the river and docks of Birkenhead, but it is not known whether she did.

As Isabel settled for the first time in a permanent home and Warwick began his family, the cause of her persistent ill-health was finally diagnosed: she needed a hysterectomy. In 1955, at forty-three, Isabel underwent the removal of her womb. As always, she was determined to bounce back. 'The moment I was let out I started walking ...', she wrote to Rose Pulham. She laughed at the doctor's last words: '"I

140. Sudbury Cottage, Little Sampford, Essex, 1953

can assure you it does in no way interfere with your desires". And he more or less said "no you're past as A1 go out and -!"'[24]

The determination to embark on a new phase in her art required courage and energy. Isabel set up a permanent studio in an upstairs room and in a bright, glassed-in area that they attached to the back of the house. Both spaces had a view over fields. One of her first purchases was a gilt mirror.[25] A year after they had moved in, in 1954, at an agricultural show, Alan Rawsthorne spotted a Canadian company selling large wooden pig sheds and, in an inspired act of lateral thinking, ordered one. When it arrived from across the ocean it was erected in their garden. It was strong, built to withstand arctic winters, spacious, with its high-pitched roof, and, crucially, top-lit.[26] A photograph of Isabel at the door shows her looking ill but radiantly happy.[27] This studio provided a literal époché, an enclosed illuminated space, in which she worked for the remainder of her career.

The importance to Isabel of the Sudbury Cottage studio cannot be overestimated. The first twenty-five years of her career, from Wood Street in Liverpool to Delancey Street in London, had been shaped by the temporary rooms and corners, even cafés, in which work was made, and as often mislaid. From 1954,

141. Isabel Rawsthorne, *Flowers by a Window*, c. 1957–8; Fry Art Gallery, Saffron Walden

the last thirty-five years were, by contrast, sustained in her own atelier. She was able to work systematically on any scale she liked and store and accumulate work.

Isabel decided that *Madame Chrysanthème* would be the last theatre design work she would take on. 'Most important, in fact imperative for me to refuse to move from here this house / even for one day for a long period,' she wrote to Annette Giacometti: 'This I am now in the process of achieving – and after all, that is why I wished to come to the country.'[28] The social and financial separation between art and commerce that Isabel had begun in Paris with Giacometti twenty years before, was realised in Essex. She saw her art as unsuited to the market and dismissed her recent work as 'skirmishes', not keeping her appointment at the Hanover Gallery until 1959.[29] She gave some drawings to David Sylvester for *Recent British Drawings* at the Arts Council in 1954, and continued to write to Rose Pulham about showing their *Seasons* together in Paris, but he was progressing slowly and her observations in the ballet practice rooms were taking her in new directions.[30]

Isabel painted with new energy in her spacious shed, working from her drawings of dancers, from friends who would model for 'heads' and from her surroundings. Biddy Noakes recalls the contrast between Rawsthorne composing quietly in his study while Isabel 'banged about in the studio', a radio permanently tuned to a French station.[31] She would often hold loud conversations with herself.[32] She worked standing and was still stretching her own canvases and trying new primings. 'Drawings on casa arte [Balthus's ground medium]' and 'mixture of drawing in chalk and painting in poster colour + ink washes, + oil paint,' she wrote to Rose Pulham just before Christmas 1955, sending him detailed instructions the following March when she had perfected the method.[33]

This zest, as Clifford Frith remarked, appeared in abundance in Isabel's work.[34] The permanence of her new environment did not lessen the impermanence of her themes; if anything, the quality of transience that always sharpened the material immediacy of her images increased. As Isabel wrote in some notes she prepared about herself, in later life, 'I am beginning to understand what pushes me into painting – the love of seeing and the fact that, as the chosen subject grows in beauty so does it become more elusive.'[35] She sketched the landscape and birds and realised the *Seasons* in a new oil series executed between 1956 and 1959.[36] The works were an evolution of the vitrine aesthetic, still lifes that combined interior and exterior, appearing to be set before a window, each containing at least one wine glass. Wine glasses, empty or full, grouped or alone, had embellished the margins of Isabel's diaries and letters since the 1940s to communicate existential nuances: financial want or largesse, excess or morning-after remorse, conviviality or loneliness, but, most frequently, friendship.

In 1953, Isabel had admired the transparent vessels in Pompeian still lifes that she had viewed in Naples, en route to Greece. The following year, André Derain died in a road accident, and Isabel and Giacometti reviewed his work, together, in the memorial exhibition, *Cinquante tableaux importants d'André Derain* at the Galerie Charpentier in Paris in 1955.[37] Where Giacometti had felt that Derain had come up against a wall, he now agreed with her: 'What we want painting to be. Amazing. What has been fashionable to call his inconsistency, his weakness, now appears as a wonder of research. And it is so beautiful – the painting ... no one thinks so – / they will / Even Balthus.'[38] It seems unlikely that Isabel still owned the 'sad still-life' that she had bought from Derain in 1937, but during the 1955 trip to Paris, she recovered a few of her own still lifes from 1946: 'Found some old Indrian gouaches I had forgotten about – glasses on a table with a stone. Not bad.' The glasses had stems, *verres à pied*; they were, like the mounted skeleton, ephemeral yet emphatically staged (the base a kind of socle). Now, a decade on, she adapted them to her rural spring, filling them not with wine or dregs, but with flowers.

In March 1956, Isabel described *Flowerpiece* to Rose Pulham, linking it to the gouaches of 1946: 'from life, a crocus and a snowdrop in a clear glass; right back to the Indre, only in oils this time'.[39] The picture moved on from traditional arrangements and singled the glass out, placing it like a portrait. Giacometti may have been thinking of her when, at the end of his career, he devoted many pages of an interview with David Sylvester to the motif. He was tempted, he said: 'to sacrifice all objects to do a glass ... a glass on a table astounds me much more than before ... in limiting oneself to a single glass, you have much more idea of all other objects than if you wanted to do everything ... '[40] The marks in Isabel's picture that indicate glass and petals have a quality of swimming in and out of view, like those that indicated the birds and figure in *The Desert*, but with a new lightness. The delicate impasto and introduction of yellow recall Derain's late ephemeral style and the last works of J. M. W. Turner. The phenomenological aspects of Turner's late oils and watercolours had come to the notice of modern artists in the 1940s, and, by the 1950s, their painterly quality was receiving serious attention and exhibition.[41] Both would become increasingly central to Isabel's painting.

The two crocuses and two snowdrops in *Flowerpiece* were heralds of new beginnings and, in the language of flowers, brought associations of mutuality. Subsequent still lifes made the same year, while still unusually 'pretty', as Isabel put it, were blotted by blood red roses from Catherine Garland's garden. In *Bowl and Glass of Roses by a Window* (1956–7; private collection), two blooms weighing down frail stems reverse the usual hierarchy of foreground highlight and background shadow. In *Bowl and Glasses of Roses and Window*, the clotted hues of three heavier heads breach the envelope of light like wounds. The appearance of these flowers marks more than the turn from spring to summer. They register a transience of a darker kind, the near simultaneous deaths of Peter Rose Pulham and Mara Scherbatoff.

On the 18 May 1956, impoverished and too proud to reveal the true extent of his difficulties, Rose Pulham had succumbed to malnutrition. He was forty-six, the same age as Constant Lambert had been at his death. His almost daily letters to Isabel and Pattie Lambert from Conives had become streams of consciousness, written in tiny script as he found paper difficult to afford. He was painting a picture for Pattie in anticipation of a forthcoming visit.[42] It may have been accident or design on Rose Pulham's part that, when Pattie arrived, she found him lifeless on his kitchen table. The neighbours would have nothing to do with the body of an atheist and had left him as he was. Alone, Pattie tended to her friend's body and arranged for him to be taken to Paris where he could be cremated with no service, a task that would haunt her for the rest of her life.[43] Isabel went to see Pattie soon after.[44]

Within barely a month, on the 29 June 1956, in America, a car tailing Arthur Miller and Marilyn Monroe, after news of their wedding had broken, misjudged a corner and hit a tree. The journalist in the passenger seat was Mara Scherbatoff. She was thrown through the windscreen and died a few hours later. Isabel's personal reaction to these losses, like her reaction to the sudden death of Constant Lambert, went unrecorded. The stream of scribbled exchanges with Rose Pulham that had refracted parts of her life for ten years fell silent, and her autobiographical notes reveal nothing. They contain the beginning of a sentence about Scherbatoff – 'It made me feel' – but it is incomplete and crossed out twice.[45]

The tone of the still lifes changed, however. The red roses that gash the envelope of light are a clear echo of those with which Rose Pulham alluded to his surname in *Room with Scaffolding*. (**59**) Roses were taken up in the same month by Randall Swingler and Alan Rawsthorne in their collaboration on *A Rose for Lidice*, a song commemorating a rose garden given to the Czech town to celebrate its rebuilding after the war. It was performed by the Purcell Singers, conducted by Imogen Holst, in Thaxted church on 10 June 1956. These tragic roses were, perhaps, behind Bacon's strange phrase: 'the violence of the rose'.[46]

Isabel's last still life, *Flowers in Spring*, of 1957, (**142**) a later version of a 'garden and birds' that she had mentioned in one of her last letters to Rose Pulham, suggested a new restlessness, the format more open and the technique more experimental. The theme is departure; spring is characterised not so much by renewal as by change. A glass was set against a landscape in which dark spiky thorns against a blossoming blackthorn imitated the shapes of a flock of birds disappearing above. These birds derived from Turner's *Angel standing in the Sun*, 1856, (**200**) a contemplation of death painted at the end of the artist's life, a century before. Seasonal narcissi shimmer in the glass. Narcissi were, appropriately, the flower that Persephone was picking when she was abducted by Hades and subsequently condemned to return from the underworld only in the spring. They also evoked the solipsistic pride, suicide and metamorphosis of their namesake, Narcissus, and withdrawal into self-contemplation. In August 1955, Isabel had written to Rose Pulham about reading Robert Graves's *The Greek Myths*, published that year.[47] Graves linked Persephone and Narcissus with an image of the flower springing from earth soaked with the boy's blood.[48] This transformation is dramatised in the coming into being of the image; rising from an extra section of dripped and bare canvas reminiscent of Bacon's paintings or a partly glazed pot. The juxtaposition of raw textile, standing for earth, and apparitional atmosphere and glass distils the elements of Narcissus' fall from the reveries of the river bank into the real watery death beneath his reflection.

In 1959, Isabel finally exhibited four still lifes with eighteen paintings of dancers at the Hanover Gallery; *Flowerpiece*, (**139**) illustrated the cover of the catalogue.[49] She did not use her fifth married name, but remained Isabel Lambert and continued to sign her work, IAL. Her work from the countryside was not what

142. Isabel Rawsthorne, *Flowers in Spring*, c. 1957; private collection

she called 'a town lover's romanticism', for accessorising racy London lives.[50] Her rural existence was an 'escape to reality', as Alan Rawsthorne put it, not an escape from it.[51]

The mourning that Isabel experienced in Paris in 1952, revisited in the succession of deaths that followed, darkened her Baudelairean vision of the fleeting. Alan Rawsthorne had been hospitalised for a month for alcoholism before they had moved to the country, and by 1959 his health was deteriorating once more.[52] Randall Swingler and Louis MacNeice were on a similar trajectory, as was Bacon's partner, Peter Lacy. Lacy would die in 1962 in Tangier, MacNeice, in 1963 and Swingler, in 1967. The still lifes were open-eyed, unsentimental pastorals, which maintained urban and existentialist themes in natural settings, soon to be interrupted by an unexpected personal and professional departure.

143. Isabel Rawsthorne, *Seated Figure, Zaria,* 1961; Ferens Art Gallery, Hull

25 NATURAL SYNTHESIS: 1961

'Isabel wanders in occasionally, waving paper and pencil, wearing black slacks and shrieking with laughter.'[1] So Veronica Leigh, a musician working at Sudbury Cottage in 1958 with Alan Rawsthorne, observed the industrious life he shared with Isabel. There were trips to Paris and London, to the West End with Elisabeth Lutyens to see *West Side Story*, as well as Isabel's Hanover show.[2] Thriving careers took Kit and Warwick abroad. Kit, in Greece, was co-directing the war film *The Guns of Navarone*.[3] In January 1960, Isabel's brother Warwick, with Evelyn and their young family, had arrived in Canberra, where Warwick took up a senior lectureship in the Australian National University. Arrangements had been made for Agnes to stay with Isabel and Alan until the family were settled in Australia, and it was deeply distressing for him to receive the news shortly after arrival that his mother had died on 25 January. Isabel was also badly affected and required medication for some months.[4] Later that year, she accepted a final design commission from the Royal Ballet to raise funds (for *Jabez and the Devil*), and, the following February, in 1961, seven months before the ballet premiered, left for Africa.

Twentieth-century artists had been engaging with African artefacts, but with little knowledge of the traditional cultures from which they believed they came and almost no awareness of contemporary cultures. While some African artists studied or worked with modern artists in Europe, Isabel was one of the first European artists to study with modern artists in Africa. Her experience would revolutionise her work. Rawsthorne, meanwhile, underwent his own 'renewal', as his musical biographer John McCabe put it.[5] The year 1961 inaugurated a productive three years without drink.[6]

Isabel did not go to South Africa, where Bacon often travelled. She chose Nigeria, a country that was in the midst of reinvention, having won independence from British colonial rule in October 1960. She already knew something about the country and the continent: Africa had haunted her imagination since her father's voyages. Her wanderings in the British Museum and her early education in the midst of Epstein's collection of African and Oceanic art at Hyde Park Gate had been reinforced in Paris in the Musée de l'Homme, through her friendship with its director, Michel Leiris, and through reading his *L'Afrique fantôme.* Constant

Lambert had been an enthusiastic promoter of black music, and many Left Bank friends were supportive of the anti-colonial movements that had originated in the 1930s and gathered pace since the war. In the 1950s, the African continent shifted towards decolonisation and cultural autonomy, and there was also an influx of Afro-Caribbeans to Britain. In 1948, Jean-Paul Sartre's essay 'Orphée noir' (Black Orpheus) had introduced the first edition of the journal of the Négritude movement, *Anthologie de la nouvelle poésie nègre etmalgache,* advocating an 'anti-racist racism'.[7] Isabel probably knew Basil Davidson's ground-breaking book on pre-colonial history, *The African Awakening*, published in 1955, since he was a left-wing journalist and old colleague from the Special Operations Executive during the war. She would also have been aware of the French journal *Présence africaine*, which was published in English between 1955 and 1961.[8] Its editor, the Senegalese-born intellectual Alioune Diop, organised the First Congress of Black Writers and Artists in Paris at the Sorbonne in 1956.

Isabel may have met Ben Enwonwu, a pioneering Nigerian artist celebrated in Paris and London. He knew Giacometti and had trained at the Slade School of Fine Art in London and in Oxford from 1944 to 1946, at the same time as Paolozzi. In 1957, the German scholar of Nigerian art, Ulli Beier, adapted Sartre's title, 'Orphée noir', for his famous vehicle for modern Nigerian authors, the magazine *Black Orpheus*, while, in 1958, the Nigerian author Chinua Achebe published the milestone novel *Things Fall Apart*.[9] In 1960, Ulli Beier published *Art in Nigeria 1960*, a book that celebrated traditional and contemporary African painting and sculpture.[10] The concluding chapter announced a new generation of modern artists about to emerge from two institutions, the Yaba Technical College in the south and the Nigerian College of Arts, Science and Technology in Zaria in the north.[11] In 1959, Clifford Frith had been appointed Head of the College in Zaria.[12] Isabel accepted his and Vera's invitation to visit.[13]

Isabel sailed in January 1961, one of a handful of passengers on the SS *Winnebar*, a 1930s cargo steamer owned by the Elder Dempster Lines. It took several weeks to thread its way south from Tilbury Docks, through the Bay of Biscay to Majorca, Madeira, Sierra Leone, Ghana and, finally, Nigeria. She missed Rawsthorne and wrote regular and generous letters. Three closely written sheaves of A3 sketchbook sheets survive and allow us a brief restoration of insight into her life and thoughts. On the boat, Isabel got up at dawn for a saltwater bath and solitude on deck, drawing or watching the birds and fish, porpoises and Portuguese man o' war (whereabouts unknown), sightings of which reduced and increased as they moved away or towards land.[14] She had no difficulty with seasickness and relished the gusty skies and tumultuous waves, enjoying the irony of 'divine services' being cancelled when the weather was at its worst. Other passengers weren't so happy:

'blew hard during the night ... crashing crockery everywhere, larks from silent film days in dining room, soup getting into others laps.'

Isabel was lonely at first, however, and unsure of what she was going to achieve. The passengers seemed dauntingly middle class, but she found common ground. They were, like her, professionals: a woman radiographer, a woman student of linguistics, missionaries, a civil servant, a railway man. She made friends with the crew – the Irish radio operator was a fellow artist and Spanish Civil War veteran. Most were returning to Africa, and Isabel was keen to learn from their experience. She soon settled, noting that 'what might be called one's Somerset Maugham defense mechanism is by now established', and even kept her things neat, out of consideration for her cabin-mate.[15] Although most of her fellow passengers were teetotal, they were eager gamblers, so in the evening they dined and danced and played games. In a few cases, they talked about books; Isabel as always travelled with several. She enjoyed and passed round Laurie Lee's relatively new *Cider with Rosie* (1959). Nabokov's *Real Life of Sebastian Knight* struck her, on the other hand, as 'pretentious emptiness', and she turned gratefully to her reference books, a *History of Astronomy* and an unidentified book about the Gulf Stream. As usual, Michel Leiris had sent her his latest, probably his dream diary *Nuits sans nuit et quelques jours sans jour*, which was 'delightful and very funny'.[16]

The boat arrived at Nigeria on 12 February 1961, and the passengers disembarked outside the capital, Lagos.[17] Isabel was disappointed to be told she could not swim in the sea and made do with the hotel pool. In a surreal moment, she entered the bar to hear the television broadcasting Constant Lambert's familiar *Horoscope Suite* (1937) accompanying a pair of conjurers.[18] The air conditioning in her room prevented her from sleeping, and she was relieved to escape the following morning to catch her flight north to Kaduna. From the aeroplane window, she watched the repetitive expanse of unfamiliarly shaped hills in misty light. Clifford and Vera were waiting to meet her and whisked her into their car and off to Zaria. Isabel tried to catch glimpses of villages along the road, the Muslim Hausa people, decorated mud architecture and long-horned cattle. Zaria town, itself, was a mix of traditional and newer buildings, and the Nigerian College of Arts, Science and Technology was set on its own in the countryside a mile or so further on.

Clifford and Vera had a large house with a terrace and even larger garden, beautifully kept by the previous principal's wife, but since left to revert to dry wilderness. 'I arrive in the middle of the Hamadan [Harmattan],' Isabel told Alan, 'a kind of sirocco or mistral, blowing from the Sahara, quite a cold wind full of fine dust that upsets people.'[19] Although Vera was delighted to see her friend, she was disturbed by the weather, in delicate health and often resting. Isabel, by contrast, enjoyed the climate. She was given a large room with a balcony, which she used

144. Nok sculpture of a seated man, c. 500, Musée du Louvre, Paris

145. Isabel Rawsthorne, *Study of Heads, Zaria*, 1961; private collection

to paint, and she spent a good deal of time in the college. She was excited by the facilities there: a new printing press, typesetting and photographic equipment, and 'an excellent library with reference books, ornithology, botany, etc'. Isabel attended the college life classes, and Clifford Frith gives an insight into her habitual industry: 'We were in the studio at seven until nine. Back to work until twelve thirty break for drinks, then on until two, lunch and siesta then paint until dinner at eight. It was a long day but we got a lot of work done, and Isabel was working hard the entire time she was with us so as usual our time together was given over to that other important preoccupation, whiskies and sodas and a great deal of laughing!'[20]

In Africa, Isabel was able to make a concentrated study of portraiture, painting a little boy and girl and a young professional nude model from the sculpture school.[21] The resulting drawings and gouaches lack the decorative and generic effects often lent to African sitters by Western painters. *Reclining Figure, Zaria* (1961; private collection) energises Giacometti's un-idealised *nus couchés* with the ebullient, efficient line that Isabel was developing with her dancer drawings. The breasts are not only lopsided, but one is flattened completely under the weight of the body. Both the seated and reclining figures emphasise heads and faces, hands and feet, with confident graphic notations. Isabel was on the way to achieving her aim of equalling 'the marvellous hands and heads – suspended and unseasable [*sic*] beauty' that she had for so long admired in Van Eyck, but without his 'pedantry'.[22]

Isabel drew the monkey that lived in the garden and, like Clifford, sketched local people, street scenes and landscapes. Poised women with baskets on their heads recall paintings of this subject by Frith and Yusuf Grillo, a final-year Zaria student.[23] Many, such as *Landscape, Zaria* (1961; private collection), depict the flat savannah beyond the town. Colour suddenly returned to her painting, perhaps partly due to the equatorial light. 'The Harmattan wind reduced the normally intense light and colour down a few tones,' Frith recalls, 'it certainly influenced my work and I'm sure it did with hers.'[24]

Isabel noticed that the college students were not local, and the diploma qualification was based on the National Diploma of Design in the United Kingdom. The college had therefore begun in geographical and ideological opposition to the efforts of Beier and Wenger to promote art 'arising from the people and not as subjects taught and introduced from outside', as Leary puts it. Beier followed Ben Enwonwu in feeling that modern Nigerian art might embrace traditional, indigenous and foreign forms. In 1950, Enwonwu had argued in *Présence africaine* that 'European artists like Picasso ... were influenced by African art [but], they expect the African to stick to their traditional forms even if he bends down to copying them.'[25] This was the reason he was not influenced by Giacometti, he said, because Giacometti was influenced by Africans. Clifford Frith was sympathetic to this position, and the art historian Chika Okeke-Agulu has described how he changed the profile of the college.[26] Frith took advantage of Independence to introduce a degree rather than a diploma, moderated by Goldsmiths College, University of London, and the college gained university status in Frith's last year, 1962. He put an end to the narrowly English syllabus of 'dull and conventional realistic' styles that dominated mainstream art teaching in the country – 'Euston Road ditherings',[27] as he called it: 'I felt a wider approach was needed ... One of the first things to do was ... to examine world art rather than just the European tradition. None of the students had ever seen a good original painting! I got the museum at Jos to loan us a whole series of pieces [notably ancient local Nok sculpture]and put them in glass cases, and I learned a great deal from my students!'[28]

The students had taken things into their own hands before Frith took over, and, in October 1958, they had founded a Zaria Arts Society. Alan Leary remembers that there were 'a number ... notably Demas Nwoko and Bruce Onobrakpeya, who while fulfilling the requirements of the course, established their personal styles to a great extent by working independently in their hostel rooms.'[29] By the time Isabel arrived in 1961, Uchefuna (Uche) Okeke, Bruce Onobrakpeya, Demas Nwoko, and other final-year students had developed a Zaria Arts Society style.[30] She described it as 'fascinating – just as high a standard I imagine as a school in London only different, quite definitely something different, not only in subject matter'.[31] That same spring, the Zaria Arts Society made their first appearance alongside Southern Oshgobo sculptors in an exhibition called *Contemporary Nigerian Art* in Lagos. Beier's review of the show heralded the group as 'essentially modern' and autonomous in their

146. Isabel Rawsthorne, *Landscape, Morning*, 1961; private collection

synthesis of 'traditional forms and Western techniques'.[32] Zaria came to be seen as the jumping-off point for modern African art. By luck or judgement, Isabel was again with artists who were doing the most serious, innovative work in their field. Isabel socialised with the students and attended their parties.[33] There is no record of whether they were the so-called 'Zaria Rebels', and she does not appear in Uche Okeke's diaries, but it seems probable, given her own art-school career and that they were the senior students at this date preparing for their first major exhibitions.[34] Some of them gave her 'lessons' in 'High Life' music and took her to local places. It is tempting to imagine Isabel talking to them about Picasso, Giacometti and Bacon, or her reservations about Sartre.

The Rebel style was a development of Enwonwu's demand that modern African artists have all artistic ideas at their disposal, theorised and named by Uche Okeke 'Natural Synthesis'. Ideas about the 'fusion' of literature, music and the arts characterised Nigerian modernism as a whole at this date.[35] The students drew on indigenous art and European influences according to principles similar to Existentialist personal 'authenticity': 'The Contemporary Nigerian artist must accept those influences that are vital to him.'[36] Yusuf Grillo explained, 'It does not matter whether these are drawn from Yoruba sculpture or Picasso paintings, both of which, incidentally, I find exciting.'[37] The eclectic intellectual nature of the method was very much in sympathy with Isabel's 'Quintessentialism': 'a very systematic approach to image-making', as Chika Okeke-Agulu writes, 'that implied

147. Isabel Rawsthorne, *Figure of a Woman*, 1961; Ferens Art Gallery, Hull considerable intellection and conscious decision-making in terms of what artistic traditions to explore and what specific elements from these traditions to subject to formal experimentation'.[38]

The Zaria Rebels' principle of personal synthesis could act in both directions. Isabel's savannah landscapes reworked her 1949 experiment *The Desert* in a Zaria idiom. Where European preconceptions of inland Africa might expect a desert of a more literal kind than bomb-scarred London, Isabel painted the landscape as a vivacious, populated place, the skies animated with clouds, birds and foliage. The figures were not the 'exotic ladies carrying picturesque waterpots', as Beier described Frith's figures;[39] they imitated Giacometti's 'branched' walking stance with a longer gait, arms elegantly articulated before and behind. The distinctive shape of Kufena Hill punctuates every horizon like Cézanne's Mont Sainte-Victoire. Isabel reconsidered, too, the graphic brushing of *The Desert*. This, combined with the new bright hues, are reminiscent of Derain and of Bacon's suddenly colourful series of representations of Van Gogh's walking figure in the lost work *Painter on the Road to Tarascon* (1888), which was exhibited at the Hanover Gallery in 1957.[40]

While Frith advanced a technique based on his training with Victor Pasmore, Isabel tried out Zarian methods. Okeke's fantastical experiments with colour, space and form were not for her, and her Nigerian work is closest to the more figurative approaches of Demas Nwoko and their non-Zaria Society friend Jimoh Akolo.[41] Her graphic portraits transformed into vivid and forceful gouaches. Rough brushed figures advanced forward against the picture plane like the compressed compositions of Akolo. Isabel's *Figure of a Woman*, 1961, (**147**) used the narrow format of his *Talking Drum*, one of the works exhibited at *Contemporary Nigerian Art* in 1961 (Michael Crowder collection), to intensify an unusually static frontal figure reminiscent of Giacometti's *Tête d'Isabel*.[42] (**20**) Like Akolo's picture, it is executed in dominant colours of red and ochre.

The most important experiments that Isabel made during this brief period were with form. The abstract appropriations from traditional African sculpture explored by Epstein, Giacometti and many other peers had not seemed valid to her before. Now they had a real context. Epstein's idea that the apparent distortions of African sculpture were, in fact, ways of bringing it closer to reality could be tested, as the artefacts in the art-school vitrines were informed by Nigerian life and by the knowledge and ideas of the Rebels. Gouache studies executed by Isabel, such as *Study of Heads, Zaria*, (**145**) *Head of a Woman, Zaria* and *Two Figures,* 1961, (**150**) exhibit the extruded, directional orientation and stern gaze of Nok terracotta sculptures. Heftier, banded strokes relate to the coils of clay from which the sculptures were built. The most pronounced technical effect, however, came not from traditional sculpture but, again, from contemporary painters. This is clearest

148. Isabel Rawsthorne, *Three Figures*, 1961; New Hall Art Collection, Murray Edwards College, Cambridge

149. Demas Nwoko, *Praise Singer*, 1961; private collection

in Isabel's *Three Heads* (1961; private collection): all hint of the picturesque is gone; a suggestion of a plain stair and rail signals the college perhaps. Two men and a woman are authoritative. They wear a mixture of Nigerian dress including the white robes and cap of the Hausa and the colourful clothes and jewellery of other ethnic groups. The tight composition and brusque bushing are again close to Akolo. Isabel's new interlocking of shapes recalls his *Four Female Figures* (1961; private collection) and the three central heads in Nwoko's *Praise Singer*, 1961,[43] (**149**) at the same time as they acknowledge Georges Rouault's *The Three Judges* (1936; Tate, London) or a Northern Renaissance *Ecce Homo*.[44] The internal discontinuity, the way each character exhibits its own stylisation in terms of costume, colour and painterly execution, is similarly reminiscent of the more daring and difficult distortions of Nwoko's *Praise Singer*.

Isabel flew home from Kano on 31 March and reached Essex and an overjoyed Alan Rawsthorne the next day.[45] He was much improved. In her absence, he had received an honour, the Commander of the Most Excellent Order of the British Empire, and Isabel no doubt teased him, given his extreme-left leanings; 'pip-squeak socialist' was her favourite, fond phrase.[46] Her contact with Nigerian art did not necessarily end with her return to England, however. In March 1961, Basil Davidson had given a lecture at the ICA, and talks and displays on African culture continued throughout the year. Over the following decade, 'Natural Synthesis' came to characterise Nigerian and African modernism, and transnational exchanges gathered pace. In 1962, Demas Nwoko arrived in Paris to study theatre design, and Jimoh Akolo came to London the following year, holding an exhibition in 1964.[47] *Contemporary Art from Africa* was staged at the ICA in 1967. No Zaria Society work entered national collections, however.[48]

150. Isabel Rawsthorne, *Two Figures*, 1961; private collection

151. Jimoh Alolo, *Talking Drum*, 1960,*Nigeria Magazine*, 68, 1961

Some of Isabel's work was left behind, but she brought back dozens of drawings and gouaches. Her work had changed for good, and she carried on with figures and heads. Away from Africa, they became even more synthetic motifs, incorporating other imagery and ideas. Her 'Quintessentialism' distilled this complexity into simpler, apparitional images. *Three Figures, Zaria* and the savannah scenes evolved into *Three Figures*, c. 1961, (**148**) and *Two Figures*, c. 1961. (**150**) The cloaked torsos against a hill and landscape recall Nwoko's *Ogboni Chief*, but they are faded, as though in memory, adapted to a greyer, European vision and more subdued northern light. Kufena Hill wavers behind a more desert-like terrain. *Two Figures* admits only the subtlest colour difference between the background and the foreground drapery. As a result, the serried, skeletal men process like the birds in the post-war monochromes. The limbs have been reduced to a single, central hand and forearm pressed against the picture plane, at once a reinterpretation of Epstein's *Rock Drill Torso*, with its mask-like head and single arm, of Palaeolithic handprints, of Giacometti's *La Main* and of the hand of the artist. *Two Figures* is more broken in its brushing, giving the effect that a hand has actually been pressed against the canvas. The new motif of the hand would reappear many times.

A last series of vertical canvases, *Head I–V* (all private collections), as were executed in the mid-1960s. They adopted the narrow shape of Akolo's *Talking Drum*, but faded the men further into more minimal, apparitional presences. They still occupy the very front of the image, but the tall format opens above their heads to suggest simultaneously immense distance and submergence, as though the figures might be buried. *Head I* and *Head II* (**152, 153**) enhanced this effect by introducing sand into the paint, giving it the texture as well as the colour of earth. In some places, conglomerations create a low relief, recalling the dimpled and modelled surfaces of Nok sculpture and Hausa buildings as well as a stony desert terrain. A relief technique also evolved in the work of Zaria artists such as Bruce Onobrakpeya.

Although reduced to torsos, Isabel's figures still give the impression of walking through the landscape. The textured, gestural brushing and the directional emphasis of the anatomical distortions lend them movement, and the cut-off creates a sense that they are crossing an aperture of time. The layers of landscape in these pictures recalled geological strata. Isabel cannot have been unaware, given her long-standing interest in archaeology, of the discoveries of Mary Leakey, her contemporary in age and spirit, who, in 1961, had taken over excavations of stone-age settlements in Olduvai Gorge in Tanzania.[49] The African Heads resembled widely publicised photographs of the famous fragments of *Homo habilis* that Louis and Mary Leakey had unearthed that year. Their composition matches, for example, contemporary descriptions of this 'first man' surveying the savannah, published in a *Life* magazine article in November 1961. Isabel's emphasis on head, hands and landscape distilled the three characteristics that were widely discussed in the case of *Homo habilis* to mark man out as man: so-called cranial capacity, manipulation of tools and upright walking habit.

The synthesis of modern and ancient associations in *Head I–V* was not a regression to nostalgic atavism or essentialist ideals of the 'universal nature of man'. It applied Existential notions of the prehistoric present to enquire what it is to be human at all. African imagery had not entered Isabel's work until it had, for her, a modern context. Natural synthesis informed her attempts to build a visual technology for the difficult task of representing presence. The African Heads were interchangeable in this period with a series of heads of Alan Rawsthorne. Isabel's work over the remainder of the decade was a development of Zarian principles beyond the context of Zaria.

152. 153. Isabel Rawsthorne, *Head I* and *Head II*, 1961; private collection

154. Isabel Rawsthorne, *Figure in a Landscape* (Alan Rawsthorne), c. 1965; private collection

26 LE VISAGE HUMAIN: 1953–1968

> The human face is an empty face, a field of death …
> It is precisely up to the painter to save this face by restoring its personal features.
>
> Antonin Artaud[1]

Sudbury Cottage allowed Isabel systematically to research and reinvent the figure *in camera*. In certain interesting ways her campaigns interwove with those of Giacometti and Bacon, with the difference that, as they moved into the limelight, she neglected it. After the war, Existentialism gave figuration in general and portraiture in particular, a new currency. Giacometti's figures, busts and heads gained international success. He stayed in his studios at Majola and rue Hippolyte-Maindron, however, still working with a handful of sitters, usually Diego or Annette. Isabel, Bacon and others, notably Lucian Freud, took portraiture in other directions during this period. Their habit of returning again and again to a small circle of intimates continued the practice of Giacometti as they took on the problem of representing a head, a presence, that he had made the defining challenge of his career, but they went their own way. For Isabel, portraiture was her last salute to Giacometti and her statement of liberation.

Isabel's top-lit studio provided an *epoché*, or illuminated enclosure, and Bacon adopted a similar environment in 1961 when he settled in a top-lit permanent studio, also his last, at 7 Reece Mews. While Isabel's peers were exploring mainly single figures, she was especially interested in the double portrait that she had continued to study since depicting Denis and Irene ApIvor in the format of The Baker Terentius Neo and his Wife in 1948. Painting in pairs multiplied the difficulties of securing models but remained Isabel's priority for her nude, moving figure and conventional portraits. Two Northern Renaissance double portraits in the National Gallery, Van Eyck's *Arnolfini Portrait*, 'the painting that obsessed me for years', and Hans Holbein's *The Ambassadors*, 1533, (**156**) were talismanic images.[2]

In the years before Isabel's trip to Nigeria, her progress with portraiture had been slow. In Italy in 1953, she finally saw the Pompeian frescoes, including The Baker Terentius Neo and his Wife – a 'tremendous shock … The Reality being so different from anything I had seen in reproduction,' she wrote to Rose Pulham: '– they must be the paintings / the / most different from their photographs. Astonished by the wonderful luminous colour – (a titian would look clumsy and sooty beside

155. Sphinx of Naxos, c. 560 BCE, Delphi Archaeological Museum, Greece

156. Hans Holbein, *The Ambassadors*, 1533; The National Gallery, London

one) – the excellent state of preservation and the daring in composition.'[3] This experience had a critical effect. A powerful dissatisfaction with her technique ensued, and Isabel determined to originate another. On her return, she discarded recent pictures, including a new portrait of Muriel Belcher which she had made from memory: 'The only person who saw this painting was Bacon when he came on a visit to see where we now lived I think he liked it. Was disappointed with it and so destroyed it.'[4] Bacon and Brausen visited the cottage to view paintings for her exhibition, but Isabel postponed, and when Brausen offered her an American show in 1956, she sent no reply, telling Rose Pulham, 'I'm not ready yet.'[5] The disruption to her work was perhaps one of the reasons that, when Bacon went to Rome later, in 1954, he famously did not go to see the painting that he had reworked from a reproduction so many times, Velázquez's *Innocent X*.

Isabel threw herself into technical experiments beginning with a series of small heads (15 by 20 centimetres) on Venetian red or sepia ground (whereabouts unknown).[6] Her handling of paint benefited from her engagement with Old Masters, especially Delacroix. The exhibition *Eugène Delacroix, 1798–1863*, at the Wildenstein Gallery in London in June–July 1952, provided an interesting comparison with the contemporaneous *Recent Trends in Realist Painting*. Isabel reread Delacroix's journal shortly after, transcribing a beautiful passage into her sketchbook:[7] 'Veronese lays on flat the ½ tint of the flesh and that of the shadow

157. Isabel Rawsthorne, *Portrait (Muriel Belcher)*, c. 1953–5; private collection

[I have noticed from my own experience that by this procedure alone one gets an astonishing amount of illusion] He finds it sufficient to blend the two together with a greyer tone– / A very beautiful violet for flesh: the tint made of lake and vermillion mixed (not too well blended) with the tone of delicate viridian terra verte and white. / a very thick impasto ... in a v warm- v. ref tint. On this a glaze of terra verte with a little white – half tone iridescent opal grey.'[8]

Isabel regretted destroying *Muriel* and made more. Two versions, painted on the back of old canvases of the *Seasons*, survive, one very faint (c. 1953–5; private collection) and another more finished, *Portrait (Muriel Belcher)*, c. 1953–5. (**157**) In *Portrait (Muriel Belcher)*, Muriel faces the viewer *contre-jour*, as in the portrait of Dylan Thomas, (**137**) but is accompanied by her profile reflected beside her. Isabel probably used the gilded mirror that she had bought when she moved in to Sudbury Cottage. She was searching for short cuts to presence, and *Portrait (Muriel Belcher)* developed her system of likeness-within-likeness, augmenting Muriel's appearance with a reference to an archaic sculpture, the 'Sphinx of Naxos'. (**155**) Giacometti had drawn on the sculpture for *The Chariot* during the war, and, in 1954, Isabel encountered the statue itself in the Archaeological Museum at Delphi. Delphi was the very setting of Aeschylus's *Eumenides*, written when the twice life-size winged woman watched over the site on a column ten metres high.[9] The nearby Siphnian Treasury, which Isabel thought contained 'the most stunning sculpture' she had ever seen, was topped by similar winged female figures.[10] The head and shoulders of these provided an uncanny equivalent for Muriel's severe hairband, prominent cheeks, ironic smile and hollow-eyed gaze. Isabel's doubling of the sitter with the sculpture and redoubling with the mirror deepened her investigation of likeness and the relative nature of identity.

Like Bacon's enthroned popes and film close-ups, the sphinx gave Muriel a performative aspect. This theatrical component of identity was something both artists and, as Frank Mort has written, Muriel herself, understood first hand.[11] The Sphinx was, like the Harpy, a trope for feminine games and guises, but the Sphinx–Muriel was almost certainly, like the sphinx in Leonor Fini's *autoportraits*, self-fashioned by the sitter. Isabel's picture reflects Muriel's practice of presenting herself at her club, the Colony Room, on her stool, like a sculpture on its stand or the tripod of the Delphic Oracle, her features strictly framed by her hair and delineated in powder and pigment, as she guarded the threshold with profane and gnomic wit.

Isabel's move to the country did not inhibit her dialogues with Bacon. An earlier version of Muriel reflected in a mirror, incorporating Bacon-style vertical shuttering, accompanies the Delacroix transcription and variations on the *nus couchés*, in her sketchbook.[12] The choice of the Sphinx of Naxos was perhaps informed by Bacon's paintings of the Great Sphinx of Giza of 1953 and 1954, albeit his was the Egyptian rather than the Greek version of the figure and was inspired in part by his visit to that country. Bacon, in turn, augmented an early foray into painting from the model, *Sketch for a Portrait of Lisa* (1955; Sainsbury Centre for Visual Arts, University of East Anglia) with an equivalent archaic sculpture, the bust of Queen Nefertiti, the famous features of which had informed Giacometti's *Tête d'Isabel* and Epstein's first *Isabel*.[13] *Epstein: An Autobiography*, published in the same year, reproduced both *Isabel* and the bust of Nefertiti.[14] Bacon made a painting of Muriel, *Miss Muriel Belcher* (private collection) in 1959 and *Sphinx – Portrait of Muriel Belcher* in 1979, the year she died (Museum of Modern Art, Tokyo).

Isabel's *Portrait (Muriel Belcher)* cut off the figure at the shoulders and placed her on a table in such a way as to take on the object-like quality, as well as the appearance, of a sculpture, a conceit used by Bacon in *Head of Woman* (1960; private collection). The effect was enhanced by strong modelling and a scatter of highlights down one side, recalling Cézanne's paintings of plaster figures and Artaud's eulogy to him in 'Le Visage humain', in which he stated that 'he painted a head as if it were an object'. Francis Ponge attributed the impact of Giacometti's sculpture, an 'apparition, the sudden manifestation of a personage', to a similar quality of 'thing-ness'.[15] The representation of Muriel in the form of a bust, sought a similar impact, creating the shock of the familiar in the unfamiliar and the animate in the inanimate. Isabel reinforced the uncanny tension between the two by adopting a scumbled way of painting flesh like the 'double vision' that she had admired in Bacon's work since seeing his first pope figure, *Head VI*: 'a beautiful texture ... quite extraordinarily (hell!) brilliant. A most beautiful pearly colour and like Velázquez ... "dissolving" is Bacon's own expression, for this kind of double vision.'[16] Where he created a tender rawness, however, Isabel's surfaces retain a more ambiguous distance between vivacity and cool marble or glass (bust or mirror).

From 1953, Isabel was able to see again Picasso's portrait of her, *Le Chapeau à fleurs* (*Buste de femme*) (**51**) after he gave it to Zette and Michel Leiris, and, in 1955, she encountered again, at the posthumous exhibition of Derain's work, the large portrait of her that he had kept in his studio: 'The last he did of me. I wish I had it.'[17] Giacometti's London exhibition that year also changed her perspective. She felt ready to challenge him: 'Of course I admire and appreciate more / now / his work, but, great though he is, his judgement is very particular – very coloured. I think almost all artists of quality tend to see younger followers exclusively as pupils – imitators. I no longer am fascinated by every word / I understand much more, certain aspects of his achievement, and see, at the same time, his limitations.'[18] As in 1949, Isabel sought to free herself from the accumulation of marks over extended periods of observation. Regular sketching, especially the study of moving dancers, was resulting in the evolution of marks and lines of vivacity and economy. This is evident in the 'few sketches of Alan f f [full face] and profile', of which Isabel remarked in 1956: 'Rather pleased with this.'

Despite this, her visit to Zaria caused her to reject her earlier portraits again, and the majority, including *Portrait (Muriel Belcher)*, appear to have been discarded, taken off their stretchers to be turned and reused for other paintings.[19] An unusually large, life-size oil portrait of Alan Rawsthorne in bright colours was abandoned, the head and part of the lower body violently scratched out. The next portrait of Rawsthorne interpreted the aged composer very differently, in almost exactly the format of the African *Head V*. The features and setting of *Figure in a Landscape (Alan Rawsthorne)*, c. 1965, (**154**) zigzag into each other in the manner of Nwoko or the heavy strokes of Bomberg.[20] The sad creases of Rawsthorne's eyes were made in paint channelled like terracotta clay or furrowed earth. At the same time, *Alan in a Landscape* found a synthesis with other traditions of art, adapting the African format to something closer to the head and broad shoulders of Giacometti's male portraits. Isabel had admired 'a very large (over life size) flat portrait of

Diego in bronze', in 1955.[21] She also introduced the stern 'presence' that she and Giacometti liked in Northern Renaissance art; the earth-coloured cloak against the red lower register is like that of Giovanni Arnolfini in Jan van Eyck's *Arnolfini Portrait*. Movement was even more dramatised than it had been in Nigeria. The overall sweep to the right exaggerated the effect of Edvard Munch's well-known painting *The Scream* (1893; National Museum, Oslo), encouraged perhaps by the Arts Council's exhibition *The Graphic Work of Edvard Munch, 1963–1944*, held at the Burlington Galleries in 1964.[22] The sidelong look and raised hand common to both Giovanni Arnolfini and the woman with a stylus in the Pompeian *Baker and his Wife* were adapted slightly, captured as though Rawsthorne is conducting music, smoking a cigarette or emphasising a point. Isabel used the movement as an existential signature, a characteristic of an individual body and state. 'Man is … the sum of his actions', as Sartre said, and 'draws his own portrait'.[23]

Building on the *brut* brushing of *The Desert* and the Zaria paintings rather than the 'hints' of *Dylan Thomas* and *Muriel*, *Portrait of Alan in a Landscape* evolved more varied applications of paint. The importance of the Zaria oils was that they explored the idea, condemned as 'inconsistency' in the work of Derain but praised in the work of Chika Okeke and Demas Nwoko, that style itself could be synthetic, could vary between and within canvases according to what was being painted and what seemed, in Yusuf Grillo's word, 'vital'.[24] Thus the diversity of sources central to each of Isabel's images since the 1940s was, by the mid-1960s, complemented by a diversity of technique. *Portrait of Alan in a Landscape* combined the bumpy and gritty surface of the African Heads with painterly areas of impasto.

Bacon was also exploring heads and figures, often in white, black, brown and terracotta, and exhibiting them at his new gallery, Marlborough Fine Art. Isabel may have been encouraged by the increasingly plastic swipes and smudges with which he was building up his forms. She appears to have been the subject of at least one of these, *Head of a Woman*, in 1961 (destroyed by fire in 1966).[25]

Isabel's seriousness about heads in the mid-1960s was catalysed by Giacometti's gift to her in 1963 of bronzes of *Tête d'Isabel I* (cast 1961; Fitzwilliam Museum, Cambridge) and *Tête d'Isabel II* (cast 1963; Sainsbury Centre for the Visual Arts, Norwich) and by his major retrospective at the Tate Gallery in 1965.[26] Although Giacometti still painted or sculpted most days, he was tying up loose ends. In 1962, he had finally exhibited the first *La Femme au chariot* at the Venice Biennale, where he won the Grand Prix for sculpture, and he was selecting pieces from across his career to cast. After a visit to his studio in Paris in the summer of 1963, Isabel wrote to Annette, 'what remains in the head was an impression of a great burst of energy', and said that she considered his Tate show 'the best exhibition of his lifetime'.[27] There she, Bacon and others had the benefit of reviewing an uncompromising fifty-year enquiry into problems of 'presence', concluding, as it had begun, with studies of Diego, and with a new series of paintings of Yvonne Poiraudeau ('Caroline'). Isabel saw a good deal of Annette and Giacometti in the run up to and aftermath of the exhibition, in Paris and also in London, with which Giacometti 'fell in love'.[28] After a trip to London in September 1964, Annette stayed on for a while at the cottage, and, in 1965, Giacometti visited her there, too: 'after the show just for fun', as Isabel told Elisabeth Lutyens, 'characteristically he drove down one night in a London Taxi'.[29]

It was during this period that Bacon finally came to know Giacometti, probably in 1963, although James Lord reported Isabel's telling him that they had encountered each other briefly in a café in Paris in 1960.[30] He also told a tale of them all enjoying a meal in London at which Bacon, when it was concluded, gleefully overturned the table, complete with dishes and glasses.[31] Bacon also made the acquaintance of Michel and Zette Leiris, probably in 1964.[32] This relationship, encouraged by their shared friendships with Isabel and with Sonia Orwell, would flourish.[33] These new encounters altered Bacon's approach to portraiture and catalysed a sustained engagement with the likeness of Isabel. He abandoned any work from life and began a series of heads and figures of himself and his close circle of friends: his new partner, George Dyer, Muriel Belcher, Henrietta Moraes, Lucian Freud and Isabel.

Isabel was fifty-two, Bacon was fifty-five, and they had known each other for two decades. Painting her was, as it had been for the previous generation, an opportunity for him to analyse and advance on particular predecessors, not only Giacometti and Derain, whose familiar portraits of her were in her cottage, but also Picasso, whose *Le Chapeau à fleurs* (*Buste de femme*) hung in the Leirises' apartment.[34] (**51**) Bacon used Alan Rawsthorne's rather than Isabel's professional surname, Lambert, for his titles, calling the first *Study for a Portrait (Isabel Rawsthorne)* (1964; private collection). *Study for a Portrait* recalled the white, black, brown and terracotta palette and format of Giacometti's 1949 *Isabel in the Studio,* marooning her on a chair within a geometric space, knees protruding from her skirt. Dynamic brushstrokes animate the face, however, in a manner singular to Bacon. The art writer Michael Peppiatt, who met Bacon and Isabel in 1964, suggested that they shared an 'animal exuberance', and that her 'magnetism and a mobility of expression ... captivated Bacon. Her face would assume a look of extreme indignation, followed by one of raucous good humour, and then a glance of seduction, all dropped like masks and as rapidly replaced.'[35]

Bacon's smaller heads appear to have taken ideas from Derain's *Portrait of Madam Isabel Delmer* and from reproductions of Epstein's *Isobel.* Bacon's *Study of Isabel Rawsthorne* (1966; Centre Pompidou, Paris) imported the sweeping

158. Isabel Rawsthorne, *Head with Rose*, 1965; private collection highlights that circle the eyes and the end of the nose seen in photographs of Epstein's sculpture. It adapted Derain's luminous white, turquoise, pink and red touches in the skin and created Isabel's slight strabismus by exploiting the sideways glance and borrowing Derain's arresting effect of the mismatch of the bright brown and shadowed iris. Perhaps the most beautiful orchestration of the Fauve colour scheme, however, was *Studies of George Dyer and Isabel Rawsthorne* (1970; private collection). Bacon gave these to Isabel, where they hung near the Derain.[36] He gave *Study of Isabel Rawsthorne* and *Self-Portrait* (1971, Centre Pompidou; Paris) to Michel and Zette Leiris, who hung them near the Picasso.[37] Bacon displayed six portraits of Isabel at his 1967 exhibition at the Marlborough Gallery and made twenty-seven between 1964 and 1971.[38]

Throughout the 1960s, Isabel painted portraits and double portraits of Rawsthorne paired with his sister, Barbara, or a friend or a reflection. Like the still lifes of the 1950s, they often incorporated a wine glass. She and Bacon made more serious use of photographs as surrogate studies. He commissioned John Deakin to take several sets.[39] Studio images of a seated George Dyer reprise Giacometti's *in camera* format, and Henrietta Moraes is captured naked on a rumpled bed, a *nu couché*. Isabel is, typically, photographed in the street, *debout,* as Giacometti so often represented her, shot close-up and full length.[40] The location is Soho, opposite The French House. Dean Street Records, specialising in film soundtracks (referencing, perhaps, Rawsthorne's profession), is in the background. The photograph is undated, but the vinyl records on display suggest early 1965. In the same year, Isabel commissioned a large set of photos from the photographer John Blake (private collection). Some were of Rawsthorne in his study or in the fields – hints for *Figure in a Landscape (Alan Rawsthorne)* – but others were double portraits of her and Alan together, in the cottage and the studio. (**163**) Several record Rawsthorne's smoking/speaking gesture seen in *Figure in a Landscape (Alan Rawsthorne)*. (**154**)

In 1965, Isabel addressed her own likeness. She had tried twice before, in her 1935 *Seated Figure* and her 1950 *Reflected Nude*. *Head with Rose* was the first she would exhibit. (**158**) It was based on a John Blake photograph of her in blurred profile *contre-jour*. Her hair is pushed into peaks by the working headscarf that she has taken off and dropped on the table in the foreground. The rose in an almost invisible *verre à pied* derives from the still lifes, white rather than red, for memory. Self-portraiture was a special challenge. Isabel's image had already been adapted, appropriated and placed before the public by the most authoritative artists of her century: Epstein, Derain, and Picasso. She had met twelve versions of herself in Giacometti's Tate exhibition alone. His *Têtes d'Isabel I* and *II* stood in her studio, Derain's *Madame Isabel Delmer* hung in her cottage. Deakin's shots of her were littering Bacon's floor as he worked up portraits of her more recent self. *Head* *with a Rose* is a statement of Isabel's stubborn independence from what others saw and made of her. The sexual mystique that had infused every representation of her since the first paparazzi snap with Epstein in 1933 was firmly set aside. The title was surely a spirited riposte to Picasso's rose-decked *Chapeau à fleurs*; the references to fashion in the Isabels of Derain and Picasso are replaced by her working scarf extending the head in the manner of Nok sculpture. The familiar black, high-neck sweater, so chic in Derain's *La Tasse de thé,* is monolithic, more like that in Giacometti's *Buste de Diego*. What was shapely is here convulsive, undulating forward to present the head. Formal and feminine beauty is rejected with bravery beyond even contemporary self-portraits by Bacon, closer to the aesthetic refusal of the portraits by Antonin Artaud which she had seen in Paris in 1947.[41] A line, a smear and a thumbprint bring into view, into touch, the advancing nose. A sliced impasto catching the shadow along its longest edge simultaneously accomplishes the flat of the forehead and adds the famous troubled crease that arrived in 1944. The likeness darkens Baudelaire's beauty with a harsher transience, matching Artaud's eulogy to Van Gogh's heads: 'explosive smoke from the beating of a bursting heart'.[42]

In 1965, the publisher Thames and Hudson commissioned a book of Isabel's drawings and requested that Giacometti write the foreword. He had seen some of her work, and she planned to take more recent drawings to Paris to show him at the end of the year, but Giacometti was taken into hospital with bronchitis. Isabel was optimistic, relieved he was getting medical treatment and rest, and postponed her visit.[43] After Christmas, she offered to go to him in Switzerland, but early in the morning of 11 January, she heard on the radio that her friend had died. Her flowers were the first to arrive.[44] A faltering letter to Elisabeth Lutyens recorded some of her feelings: it was a 'catastrophe'. 'He was one of the very few people who followed this "Geish" against all odds,' she added. At the end of the letter she wrote, 'I am' [and left a blank], '—Time the scythe.'[45]

Giacometti's death marked a sea-change for the younger painters. In 1967, Bacon reprised Giacometti's images of Isabel in the street in *Portrait of Isabel Rawsthorne Standing in a Street in Soho.* (**159**) This street-walking figure within a cube related closely to the sculptor's *Figure Contained in a Box between Two Boxes which are Houses.* (**49**) The car/bull in the background was perhaps an allusion to the notorious climax of their love story, when Giacometti was hit by a car on the way home from her hotel, or a recollection of the bull and the blue that dominated Scene I of *Tiresias,* evoking Bataillian links between bulls, sexuality and the sexual themes of her first ballet design. Isabel took on Giacometti's project of how to make a likeness of a head with a new bravura rhythm, executing between 1966 and 1968 twenty portraits of Alan Rawsthorne, twelve of which she exhibited at

159. Francis Bacon, *Portrait of Isabel Rawsthorne Standing in a Street in Soho*, 1967; Staatliche Museen zu Berlin

160. Roy Noakes, *Alan Rawsthorne*, plaster, 1965; private collection

161. Isabel Rawsthorne, sketch of Alan Rawsthorne, c. 1966; Fry Art Gallery, Saffron Walden

the Marlborough Gallery in 1968.[46] Where Bacon set off his impasto heads with smooth background planes of colour, Isabel created softly brushed spaces that evolved her 1940s vitrine aesthetic. In 1961, Merleau-Ponty published his last phenomenological essay, *L'Œil et l'esprit* (The Eye and the Mind). Concentrating on painting, it developed a non-definitive, immersive model of perception by which the body simultaneously experiences itself and others in the world, a good analogy for Isabel's doubles and underwater effects.[47]

The sculptural double was introduced in a new way. In 1964, Isabel had befriended two young sculptors who had moved to Little Sampford, Roy and Biddy Noakes. Roy, good-looking and charmingly misanthropic, had also been born in the East End and pursued his career with fierce refusal to compromise.[48] His devotion to modelling in the Italian tradition of Donatello, Medardo Rosso and Giacomo Manzu was in sympathy with Giacometti's understanding of sculptural surface as relief, but Noakes believed figurative form could be freed from its outer contour and emerge from within. These ideas won him few friends in British sculpture, where modernism was thought of as clean-edged, abstract or constructivist, but they interested Isabel.[49] She commissioned Noakes to model a head of Rawsthorne, *Alan Rawsthorne*, 1965, (**162**) and incorporated its sculptural quality into her portraits. She did away with the perimeter of the head and configured the

162. Isabel Rawsthorne, *Alan Rawsthorne*, 1966; National Portrait Gallery, London

features in a paste of paint and sand. In her portrait of Rawsthorne reflected in a mirror, (**162**) we feel as well as see the crepey fold of a lid, the bruised concavity around the inner eye, the indents of the jowl and the smooth, spreading flush of a pinkish cheek. The colour does not so much represent flesh, as turn paint into its tactile peach-and-grey equivalent. It has the earthy quality of the African figures, Rembrandt's umbers, a graffitied wall.

The painter Amédée Ozenfant bluntly stated in his *Foundations of Modern Art* (1931): 'To imitate something is to stuff it', and Giacometti had spent his life searching for a way, as Sartre put it, to 'mould a man in stone without petrifying him'.[50] The head distilled this problem; how to avoid the horror of a cadaver, as Giacometti asked, 'miserable debris to be thrown away'.[51] He reiterated the idea in an interview with David Sylvester in 1964, describing a head without vivacity as 'a dead object ... an extremely unpleasant sort of object'.[52] The encrusted surfaces of Isabel's *Alan Rawsthorne* render the face as just such 'debris', animated by ephemeral likeness; presence registered as action; momentary equivalents for form and shocks of familiar texture. A photograph of the painting shows us just a scatter of shadows, but standing in front of it we perceive varied forms and movements with our eyes and our skin. *Alan Rawsthorne* thus achieved the embodied art that Isabel had been researching since Liverpool. Bacon, too, was configuring strokes

163. Isabel Rawsthorne, *View through a Window I*, 1967; Sainsbury Centre for Visual Arts, University of East Anglia

and whirls in increasingly three-dimensional layerings.[53] 'There is an area of the nervous system', he explained to David Sylvester, 'to which the texture of paint communicates more violently than anything else.'[54]

The smeared skull-like effect of the portraits of Rawsthorne linked them back to the skeletal birds and fish and to the anamorphic skull stretched across the foreground of Holbein's inscrutable *Ambassadors*. This is most overt in *Alan and Barbara Rawsthorne,* (**164**) in which the necklace of the second head echoes the medallion worn by the left-hand figure in Holbein's painting, Jean de Dinteville. (**156**) Between the two figures, spreading like spilled wine, is an equivalent for the anamorphic skull itself. The face is probably the artist's own. Holbein's shape had been significant for Giacometti from his Surrealist days and informed his later elongated figures.[55] In 1964, the psychoanalyst Jacques Lacan published his famous discussion of *The Ambassadors* in his *Seminar IX*, collected in 1966 in his *Écrits*.[56] Lacan was connected to Isabel's Paris circle, and a student of his, Paola Carola, had become Giacometti's model in 1958.[57] Developing the ideas of Bataille and Merleau-Ponty, he suggested that the discontinuity of the anamorphic form exemplified the discontinuity of vision itself, representing the real not in the illusion, but in a disruption of illusion, the *informe*.[58] Isabel's face in the double portrait fits Lacan's description of the experience of this rupture of the gaze as a gaze returned, 'the eye which flies in the foreground of *The Ambassadors*', invading the field of vision like a stain, 'pulsatile, dazzling and spread out'.

164. Isabel Rawsthorne, *Alan and Barbara Rawsthorne*, 1967; Sainsbury Centre for Visual Arts, University of East Anglia

In 1967, Isabel reintroduced landscape into the portraits and changed their shape from vertical to horizontal. This increased the distance between the figures and gave greater emphasis to exquisite *verres à pied*. The first of these canvases depicted Alan and Barbara Rawsthorne, but the largest and last of the series, nearly two square metres, mirrored her husband with another self-portrait. *View through a Window II* (1967; Tate) shows the couple facing each other, as in the other portraits. In its pair, *View through a Window I*, 1967, (**163**) their backs are turned. Isabel's vectored profile, reminiscent of Giacometti's *Tête d'Isabel II*, is subtly present in sweeping strokes. Alan Rawsthorne's face is literally double, simultaneously in profile and turned towards us. It is a luminous painting in which forms dissolve in pale greys laced with rainbow hues. The setting is the glass room at Sudbury Cottage that overlooked the fields, so the entire scene is *contre-jour*. The air of distance and departure and the presence of narcissi recall *Flowers in Spring*. (**142**) The wine glasses between the couple suggest both friendship and their fatal addiction. In the sky, what at first appears to be a single bird is, on closer inspection, an impasto Concorde (images of which had begun to circulate in 1967, two years before its maiden flight). Like the wine glasses, it was a motif both of accord – 'concord' – and of leaving, emphasised by the concentric rings of the sonic boom. The smoke from a burning house in the distance echoes the cigarette smoke that leaves the figures' mouths. Proximity and remoteness, recognition and strangeness stand in for proximities and distances of a psychological kind.

The portraits of Alan Rawsthorne revisited and reversed the relation Isabel had assumed with Giacometti: Rawsthorne was her intimate, lover and fellow artist, and elusive in his own way; frail health lent a sense of temporariness. Isabel was fifty-nine when she lost him; he died from an alcohol-related illness on 24 July 1971. He was sixty-six, the same age as Giacometti. At her request, Roy Noakes went to the hospital and made a death mask (National Portrait Gallery, London), which she drew upon in making her last head, Untitled (Death Mask of Alan), 1971. (**165**) This small canvas is at the same time unsentimental and very tender. It has the greatest embodied presence of any of Isabel's works and is far more about touch than about vision. The rectangle is filled with a head just less than life-size, as it appears when you look down on it from a few feet above. With an unbelievably moving poetry, the face, the shade of the white pillow behind, is visible only in the shadows created by its scarified texture, the actions in the paint. It is subtly anamorphic, looking wrong upright; shadows and point of view resolve only when the picture is *held* flat in the hands.

Isabel's portraits were a phenomenological enquiry into likeness as a means of knowing others. They accumulated clues and ideas from an extraordinary array of art past and present and theoretical developments in the field, and expanded the category of 'representation', from relatively conventional phenomena such as reflection, sculpture, photography, memory, symbol or attribute to the more unexpected – a sibling, a voice or the scented gesture of a cigarette. Yet Isabel's last contemplation of Rawsthorne was consistent with the handled bird and animal carcass studies of thirty years before. She looked for the presence that Bataille found most powerfully, paradoxically, in its absence: 'The body never ceases to be haunted … so much so that if death reduces it to the level of a thing, the spirit is more present than ever. The corpse is the most complete affirmation of the spirit.'[59]

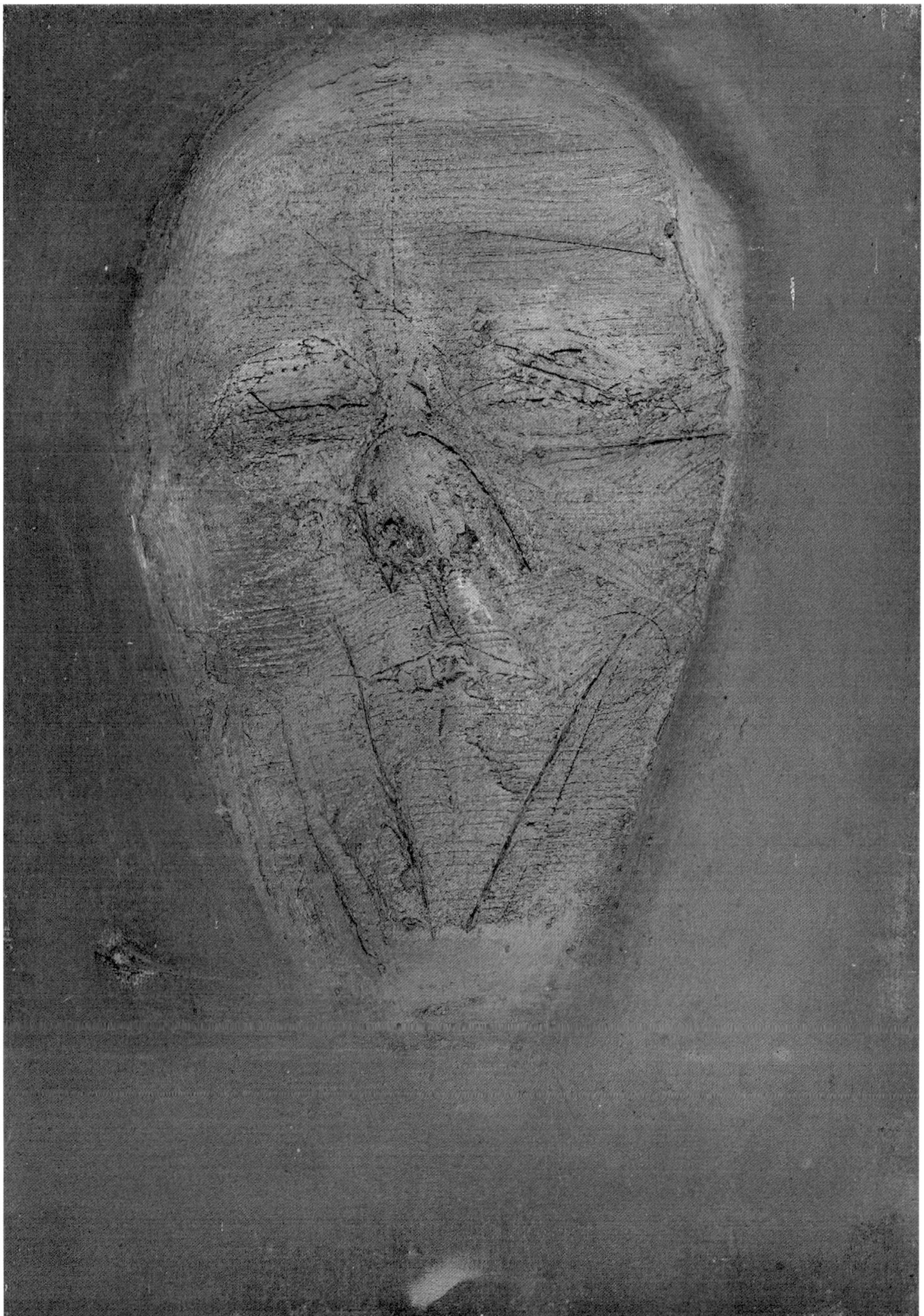

165. Isabel Rawsthorne, Untitled (Death Mask of Alan), 1971; Sainsbury Centre for Visual Arts, University of East Anglia

166. Isabel Rawsthorne, *Dancers (dans les coulisses)*, c. 1966–9; New Art Gallery, Walsall

27 MOVING BODIES: 1952–1968

There is no arguing among the muses, they work all day,
very much on their own. In the evening, work unfinished,
they do not talk, they gather and dance.

Paul Valéry[1]

When Degas was asked by Gustave Moreau, known for his elaborately decorated art, 'Are you really proposing to revive painting by means of the dancer?', he gave a curt reply: 'And you, are you proposing to restore it with jewellery?'[2] The dancer was Isabel's primary pursuit between 1952 and 1969. To her, the bodies in action that she was able to study at the Royal Ballet practice rooms were an advance on the traditional still model.[3] They were a special case of the *in camera* figure and a continuation of her rethinking of her *Seasons*, 'visually, theatrically'. The difficulty and novelty of this challenge forced Isabel to start almost from scratch. The result, over two decades, was an evolution in the depiction of the dancer that challenged her predecessors. At the end of her life, Isabel told her friends Iris and Nigel Weaver, who collected her paintings for the Fry Art Gallery, that she felt that in this specific problem she had advanced on Degas.[4]

Isabel's first observations appear to have been of Frederick Ashton's *Symphonic Variations*.[5] She wrote to Rose Pulham in 1955: 'Making chalk and ink drawings with bits of gouache when required. 3 lay-out pads full of action drawings as basic material made at Hammersmith rehearsal rooms and a sheet of card with signs on it made on the stage during a performance (never again! Frightened of the scenery) and a role of wallpaper with bits of Margot in "Sleeping B[eauty]".'[6] For twenty years, she concentrated on a handful of steps from a small number of pieces, notably two Diaghilev ballets – *Daphnis et Chloé* (1912) and *Les Biches* (1924) – and *Kingdom of the Shades* (1963). Texts Isabel wrote for catalogues insisted that her paintings were not generic dancers but 'moving portraits' that continued her phenomenological enquiry, the search for presence.[7] She concentrated on performers she knew, whose appearance and attitudes became familiar. Margot Fonteyn was a central focus, sometimes with her partners Michael Somes and Rudolf Nureyev, but Isabel also returned again and again to see Antoinette Sibley, Svetlana Beriosova and others.[8]

The images were, therefore, not so much depictions of the stage as stagings of the body. The work of choreographers offered another, different equivalent to

167. Isabel Rawsthorne, 'pastiche' of ten figure drawings, c. 1950–55; New Art Gallery, Walsall

168. Isabel Rawsthorne, *Study of a Ballet Dancer*, c. 1960; Fry Art Gallery, Saffron Walden

her ideas about framing the body. Frederick Ashton talked to her about the way in which the stage contained and, as a result, contributed to the physical impact of the dancer's movements: 'It is essential', she would later write, '... that it should be enacted in a confined space. The limits of the studio or stage put the spectator at a certain distance in a framework that helps to define the transient quality of the spectacle and keep him [the viewer] in a state of suspension.'[9] One is reminded of Isabel's decision in Paris on how to live: 'to be free I have to have a frame'.[10]

The stage or practice rooms were a theatrical enhancement of the *in camera* studio setting, 'a world apart', as Isabel put it. They had gridded floors and mirrored surfaces that developed Isabel's vitrine aesthetic; 'places of great beauty with walls of glass. Places of space and light, where the individual body can be seen at any distance, seemingly endless combinations of pattern are to be seen here, in a very special setting created entirely for the use of those that experiment with the body.'[11] Isabel's understanding of theatrical illumination led her to treat it as another tangible, three-dimensional structure. In her studies of dancers, geometric slabs of light and shadow interpenetrated the figure, creating a medium in which to suspend and measure it. The gouache and charcoal *Dancer* (1950s; Walsall New Art Gallery, Walsall) is an example: it tallies with the impression the artist John Craxton had of Fonteyn, when watching her from the wings: 'the figure of a swimmer'.[12] In 1959, Isabel exhibited four still lifes and eighteen dancers at her third Hanover show to good reviews. *The Observer* placed it second in the running order of the Gallery Guide and was alert to the spatial implications of the works exhibited and their dialogue with Bacon: 'studies of charred, emaciated ballerinas practising a dance macabre in a mist grey-brown classroom. A hint of Francis Bacon's nightmare no-man's land.'[13]

In 1956, Isabel wrote to Rose Pulham: 'I am trying to be methodical: and to make my pictures easier to see. If, o if, I could make them seeable.'[14] One approach to making the dancer seeable was to 'situate a human figure. So that it partakes of its surroundings ... yet paint only it.'[15] Isabel addressed this by incorporating the space-frame inside the body, an equivalent of Giacometti's idea of a 'sculpture which creates space around it' or Alan Rawsthorne's idea of music that left sound behind it.[16] The dancers were, as she said, 'signs', like musical notes on their bars/ *barres*; internal and exterior armatures acted as the 'cat's cradle' that 'put the spectator at a certain distance to define the transient quality of the spectacle'. Isabel's drawings clarified what Giacometti found elusive when working from the model: 'I lacked what I felt for the entirety, a structure ... a kind of skeleton in space.'[17]

The practice-room studies provided Isabel with an exceptional test and an opportunity: to extend her phenomenological method to 'define the excitement of watching a living body in movement'.[18] Crucially, by the 1950s, Giacometti had set this problem aside. In the early 1930s, his Surrealist constructions had pioneered real kinetic effects with components that swung or rolled, an idea he later adapted in the wheeled *Femme au chariot*. Throughout the 1940s, he experimented with a disturbed balance in the walking figures and *Falling Man* (1947–50; Kunsthaus Zürich), but, in 1946, he jotted in a notebook, 'cave drawings, caves, caves ... there and only there, movement has succeeded. Look to see why, to find the possibilities, but I doubt it. And this goes for sculpture, painting and reliefs.'[19] By the 1950s, he had stilled his sculptures. Annette was almost always depicted standing or sitting, for example, as was Isabel in his last painting of her. In 1962, he told David Sylvester that 'tension takes place of movement'.[20]

Isabel's dancers exhibited this tense effect, but she was not prepared to neglect movement per se. Giacometti believed a frozen gesture was unsatisfactory; 'he was', Isabel said, 'of the opinion that it was impossible to make a portrait in motion, that memory lasted one second ... I do imagine Rodin would have agreed.

169. Isabel Rawsthorne, *Dancers (Nureyev and Fonteyn)*, c. 1961; private collection

Certainly Bacon does not agree.'[21] Her choice of words linked Giacometti's point of view to Rodin's famous statement in *L'Art* about walking figures: 'the painter or the sculptor ... represents the transition from one pose to another – he indicates how insensibly the first glides into the second. In his work we still see a part of what was and we discover a part of what is to be.'[22] Isabel pre-empted the suggestion of her friend Merleau-Ponty in *L'Œil et l'esprit* in 1961 that Rodin's idea could be improved upon.[23] She said Rodin was uppermost in her mind when she first went to the rehearsal studios of the Royal Ballet.[24] Her dancers interrogated his model and Giacometti's. Her ambition to transcend the one-second memory and 'make a portrait in motion' paraphrased an alternative theory advanced in Paul Valéry's discussion of Degas's ballerinas in his book *Degas, Danse, Dessin*, published in 1936. Unlike Giacometti, Valéry was convinced of the 'durability of the instantaneous element of memory'.[25] His argument focused on Degas's use of Eadweard Muybridge's stop-motion photographs of horses which he described as stepping 'like a première danseuse'. Isabel reversed Valéry's anthropomorphic view, likening dancers to animals: 'Dancers, like animals, can move with speed or stealth, leap with concentrated force or collapse immediately; can balance, can remain completely still.'[26] Muybridge's sequences of photographs were, of course, part of what Sam Hunter called, in 1952, Bacon's 'whole literature of the mechanics of motion',[27] and Harrison notes that his development of 'more mobile postures', later in the decade 'entangled' Muybridge with Rodin.[28] Isabel's scrutiny of real figures in repetitive routines, repeated in turn in various angles in the rehearsal-room mirrors, and her registering of indications from bodies that were actually moving, were like Muybridge's multiple exposures, *in life*, non-stop motion.

John Craxton described Fonteyn in the following terms: 'I suddenly had a revelation. I realised what form in space was. It was like looking at a statue. A lot of statues are not good all the way round – they have a back and a front, but she had sides to her. There was a wonderful seamless beauty.'[29] Isabel represented this spectacle with a variation on the Cubist/Futurist/photographic multiple exposure, collecting memories of different positions and 'sides' into drawings and then synthesising these drawings into paintings in the studio. Her work space was littered with prior and preparatory sketches, and she would sometimes collage a selection for easier reference. Some of these so-called *pastiches* were framed and exhibited, and a set of sixteen drawings made in Covent Garden in 1960 was bound together and published in Paris in 1991 by the poet, painter and photographer Philippe Clere in an elegant special edition of his photojournal *Akte*.[30] (**167**)

The outcome can be appreciated in Isabel's large gouache *Dancers (Nureyev and Fonteyn)*, 1961. (**169**) It addressed Rodin's prototype of movement, *L'Homme qui marche* (1899–1900; Musée Rodin, Paris) and Giacometti's last moving figure

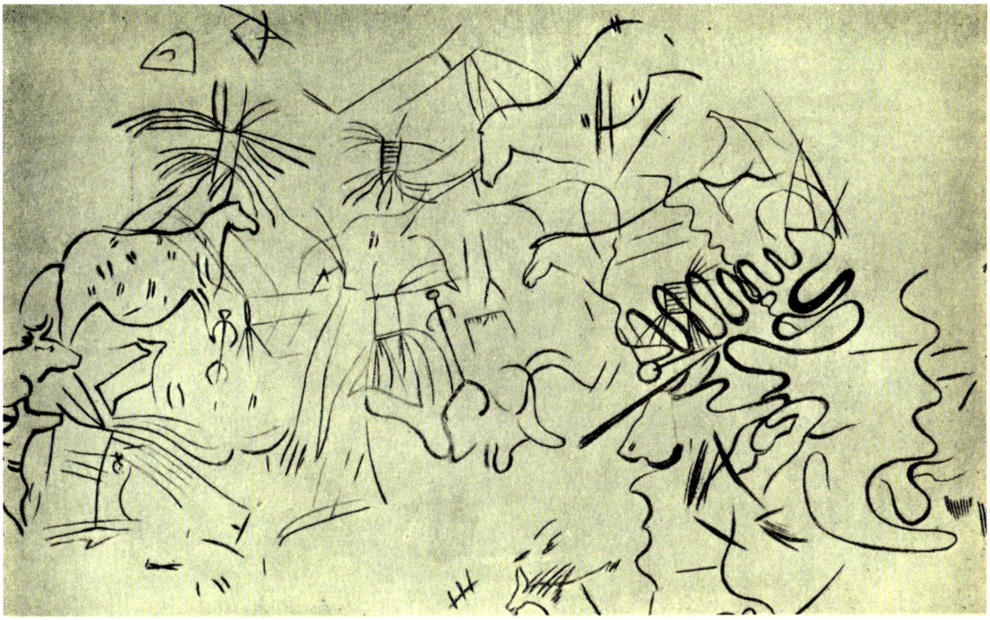

170. Drawing of a Cueva de la Pileta painting, from Amédée Ozenfant, *Foundations of Modern Art* (1931)

of the same name (1949), six of which he cast in 1961. These walking figures suggested movement in the Egyptian manner with both feet on the ground – 'a part of what was and ... a part of what is to be', as Rodin put it. The right leg of Isabel's walking figure, by contrast, reads as being both on and off the floor, and the hips and head simultaneously suggest a profile and a turning-away, while the leading arm elongates into future space. These optical paradoxes exploit the alternative model that Valéry called '*creative* seeing' or 'willed seeing'.[31] This was the difference, for him, between Muybridge's stop-motion photographs and the work of art – the latter augmented the intermittent shots with an understanding that filled gaps in sense perception.

Around this time, Bacon's figures also became more flexed and their limbs rendered in richer strokes, evoking something like an analysis of the bone, muscle and sinew that bring the compression or extension about, while hands dissolve at the extremity – as seen in *Lying Figure* (1959; Kunstsammlung Nordrhein-Westfalen, Düsseldorf), for example, which is comparable to Isabel's roughly contemporaneous *Dancer* (private collection). Working with the model, without the short cut of photographs, Isabel stripped the body down more slowly than Bacon was doing, however, and 'quintessence' or 'crystallisation' arrived only with time.

By the mid-1960s, unnecessary anatomy had been eliminated and spontaneity achieved in sinuous, scintillating hints. An insight into the kind of selections

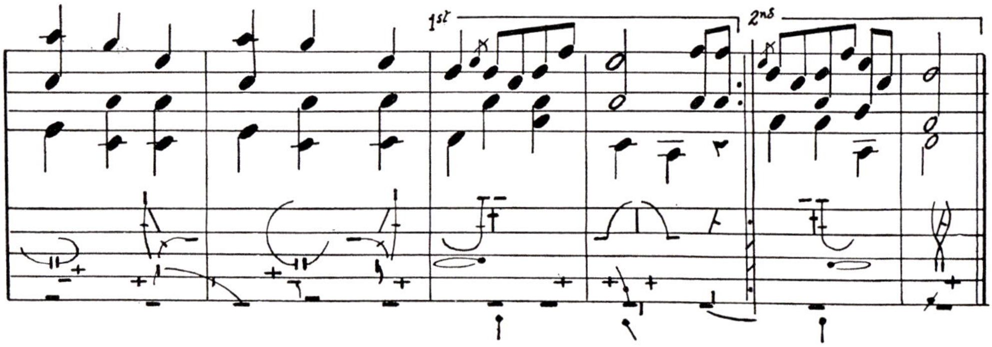

171. Benesh notation, from Rudolf and Joan Benesh, *An Introduction to Benesh Dance Notation* (1956)

172. Isabel Rawsthorne, Study of dancers, c. 1967; New Art Gallery, Walsall

Isabel was making in front of her motif and back in the studio is indicated by the elimination of the heads in favour of necks. Where her nudes somehow look right with larger heads, her dancers' heads diminish in relation to the limbs, like Giacometti's figures. This is because, in the context of the dance, the head merely marks the outer limit of the body while the neck is the culmination of the spine, which articulates the movement: 'Ballet enhances certain aspects of the body for its own special purposes. It isolates the body's workings ... pinpoints the attention on the spine, the pelvis, the legs.'[32] Images of Beriosova, for example, identify her through her singular neck – a tense, surging curve configures the elongated muscular frame, sloping shoulders and scull extruded into a small, turned-up nose. When Isabel said that she was making 'moving portraits', she was not thinking of the dancers as celebrities but as beings: 'they are people and so have emotional implications of a different order. I try to understand as much as possible about their individual shapes and gestures.'

The enriched understanding of the moving body went hand in hand with an enriched understanding of the moving line. Hundreds of drawings, most of which survive in the collection of the New Art Gallery, Walsall, advanced Isabel's mark making. This can be seen by comparing drawings of leaping dancers from the early and mid-1960s. Although Bacon used found printed images for his preparatory work, Matthew Gale and Martin Harrison agree that the transitional period of 1959 to 1962 also involved limited drawing on his part.[33] This took place almost exclusively on the canvas and is rarely visible (hence his claim that he didn't sketch, 'just starts right out painting'), but it can be seen on unfinished works such as those in Dublin City Gallery The Hugh Lane.[34] A page from Bacon's 1959 copy of *The Drawings of Michelangelo* shows a brief linear conversation with the master.[35] Bacon's rare purchase of a picture by Henri Michaux also dates to the early 1960s, and no doubt Rawsthorne shared his admiration of the way Michaux's 'free marks' remade the human image 'moving and falling and so on'.[36]

Neither Isabel's nor Bacon's engagement with line was a regression to traditional preparatory methods of establishing shape, detail, arrangement or even pose. Isabel shared Bacon's waspish disdain for Michael Ayrton's assertion that Bacon couldn't/didn't draw: 'Is drawing what you do? I wouldn't want to do that!'[37] They set aside the age-old debate between drawing and painting, line and colour to build on the post-war 'advance on *peintre écriture*', expanding the role of the graphic mark. Both artists learned from Degas's 'X-ray' perception: his directional pastel marks that drew into the body – what Bacon described to David Sylvester in 1966 as the 'grip and twist', 'the spine almost coming out of the skin altogether'.[38] 'Few sights seem to be more mysterious and beautiful than the curve of the spine, running from the base of the skull to the arch of the foot,' Isabel wrote.[39] Their open treatment of the body rejected the traditional surface 'skin sheet stretched over and flattening the form', which Isabel disliked.[40] She explored the way a line or accident of the medium could equate to the extension or compression of a muscle, the turn of a joint, twist, torque and vector. Every mark became a motion: a flick of the pencil or a loop of ball-point pen, a surge of charcoal charging across the paper, a scratch, rip, a smear or splash of paint, registered physically on the body of the viewer as they were pushed, pulled and turned by the body of the artist.

In both Isabel's and Bacon's work, line became extraordinarily agile in the ways it could be suggestive. The artists drew on everything from the simultaneously volumetric and dynamic nuance of an Honoré Daumier contour to the diagrammatic bluntness of an arrow. One is reminded of the lines in Ozenfant's pictorial analyses of 'sensations and elements in form' and Bacon's youthful dalliance with shorthand.[41] The lines in these new drawings were distinctive in being complexly superimposed. This superseded the Cubist/Futurist multiple view that Bacon and Isabel considered 'mechanistic' and lacking in 'implications'.[42] It had more in common with embodied overlayerings of the prehistoric painting they admired, for example those in Cueva de la Pileta, reproduced (in black and white) in Ozenfant's *Foundations of Modern Art*.[43] (**170**)

The notation of movement was a vivid issue within the ballet context during this period. It is amazing to realise that, until the 1950s, there was no way to record dance in written form. The first code was created by the Sadler's Wells ballerina Joan Benesh and her mathematician husband, Rudolf, and was adopted at Covent Garden in 1955.[44] They described it as a kind of 'dancer script'. Its bars, pertaining to different levels of the body between the head and the floor, recall Bacon's and Isabel's horizontal scaffolding. A similar blending of the body, graphic line and musical notes had been explored in Jean Painlevé's film *Écriture de la danse* in 1948. Like Painlevé's, the Benesh approach was sympathetic to Isabel's anthropological perception of movement as 'body language'. It was perceived as a tool for 'the aesthetic and scientific study of all forms of human movement' and was quickly adapted, for example, to record Aboriginal dance.[45]

Rudolf Arnheim's essay 'Concerning Dance' of 1946, republished in 1966 in *Towards a Psychology of Art*, argued for dance as an embodied art form: 'A dancer's body must not only allow us to understand ... but make us experience it by movements whose visible dynamic quality correspond.'[46] Arnheim characterised the curviness of movement: 'having to rely essentially on the curved and gradually changing movements that fit organic muscle'. Isabel understood this: 'Ballet isolates the body's workings, fitting it into a series of circles', and, during the 1960s, her strokes became more concave.[47] The circles that appear at the left ankle and the right knee of Bacon's *Lying Figure* were also characteristic in his work by this time.

173. Isabel Rawsthorne, *Fonteyn as Chloe II*, 1968; Royal Opera House Collections

It is significant that, in 1967, Bacon addressed the walking figure in the shape of a full-length image of Isabel, *Portrait of Isabel Rawsthorne Standing in a Street in Soho*. The non-aligned legs and swinging skirt reinforce the sense that it is a response to the walking image of her that so obsessed Giacometti; particularly, perhaps, to the photographs reproduced in *Cahiers d'art* in 1946 of a nearly life-size sculpture in the street (an early variation of *Femme debout*, or *Leoni* (c. 1948), on the pavement outside 46 rue Hippolyte-Maindron).[48] Bacon folded one of John Deakin's photographs – a three-quarter view of Isabel in Dean Street – and held it together with a piece of paper to introduce three-dimensional distortions, creases and rips. He wrote on the back 'Rouault', connecting the image to this artist's bold streetwalkers.[49] The splash at Isabel's feet recalls her Doctor Foster rhyme and replicates the Tachist spray at the heels of the figure in her own *The Desert*. (**81**) A small portion of underpainting left uncovered near the right hand of the figure unmistakably alludes to her drawing practice as well as his.

Bacon was evolving his figures into large canvases with bright grounds and was exhibiting regularly. By contrast, Isabel, as always, envisaged most of the many hundreds of drawings and even some gouaches and oils she made between 1953 and the mid-1960s as merely a means of learning, and five years passed between the exhibition of her first dancers in 1959 and the progress she revealed in the thirty drawings curated by Roland Penrose and shown at the ICA.[50] Further paintings appeared in *Dancers of the Royal Ballet: An Exhibition of Drawings and Gouaches by Isabel Lambert*, at the Mermaid Theatre in September 1966 and the Arts Council Gallery, Cambridge, in 1967. The fact that these were quickly followed by the 1968 exhibition at the Marlborough Gallery, the leading avant-garde venue in London at that time, indicates that, in the mid-1960s, Isabel knew that something had been accomplished.[51]

Over a decade of seeing and drawing gave Isabel the ability that Paul Valéry ascribed to Degas, of 'conjuring from the whole complex of what is seen the one pencil stroke that is right'.[52] She was able to put down fewer, more continuous marks that satisfied several criteria at once, a dynamic armature that also summoned up outer contour and interior structure, gesture and direction, force and obstruction. 'Human beings do not have a simple architecture like animals,' Merleau-Ponty wrote in *L'Œil et l'esprit*, 'and it is not even possible to say where they begin ... [but we] discover in each object the particular way in which a certain flexuous line which is, so to speak, its generating axis is directed through its whole extent.'[53] This paraphrases Valéry's summary of Degas's 'life's quest' [to] 'discover even in rapid movement, the one and only linear pattern which while defining a momentary pose of the body'.[54] Isabel's 'flexuous' line could transport the body through several moments with an almost magical effect of duration: 'A choice has to be made when attempting to record the movements of any living creature,' she wrote, 'and it is the necessity of choosing from a continuously changing vision that is the reason for the intense satisfaction I find in doing it.'[55] Her success was summed up by a contemporary critic, Oswell Blakeston, when he described the dancers as 'an after image of expectancy'.[56]

The Marlborough exhibition represented an artist at the peak of assurance. In 1967, Isabel 'crystallised' her ideas into three pairs of large oils, including two pairs of horizontal double-squares nearly two metres wide which, with *View through a Window I* and *II*, dominated the show. They were titled *Movement from the Ballet La Bayadère I* and *II* (**179**) and *Sibley Rehearsing I* and *II* (1967; private collection). A third, large rectangular oil, *Fonteyn as Chloe* (1967; Royal Opera House), was exhibited without its pair (1967; private collection).

Impasto elements of the oils achieved Giacometti's ambition to have the real immediacy of the sculptural object without its unreal bulk and weight.[57] Just as Isabel discarded the traditional polarisations between drawing and painting, line and hue, she cast away the age-old *paragone*, the stand-off between painting and sculpture. Like the portraits, the dancers blurred the boundaries between the two, the sense of seeing something and of being in its physical presence. Her skill was to lay intricate shapes down in a gesture; a virtuoso impasto, *rilievo schiacciato*, applied or removed in a breath-taking array of incisions and swipes. Giacometti's etiolated models dematerialised form by the movement of the eye and hand as it dictated myriad adjustments; Isabel's dancers dematerialised through the movement of the model itself. The taut belly of the left-hand *La Bayadère* dancer is also already a hip bone, for example; the skeletal fingers of Fonteyn as the collapsed Chloe *in Chloe II* become the long withdrawing trail of her nails across the stage. Keith Roberts, in *The Burlington Magazine*, described the effect: 'Against a background of thin almost transparent swathes of paint, coagulations of pigment have been allowed to accumulate, like sand blown into drifts. The backgrounds shimmer and the spidery ridges take on the character of arms and legs glimpsed in motion, never still, as discernible and yet as intangible, as the dagger in *Macbeth*.'[58]

The large oils also realised Isabel's ambition of the 1940s to present figures in relationships of twos and threes. Bacon often discussed the technical challenge of this, telling David Sylvester in his last interview that he 'always hoped to make a great number of figures without a narrative'.[59] His exemplar in this conversation was Cézanne's *Bathers* (see p. 244), and he appreciated, perhaps, *La Bayadère*'s emulation of its flying buttress structure, implementing what Valéry described as Cézanne's 'balancing of opposing, compensating forces'.[60] Isabel's 'moving portraits' also challenged her friend's opinion that portraiture could not be achieved without the face. Bacon may not have felt she succeeded; around 1986,

174. Isabel Rawsthorne, Margot Fonteyn, 1968; private collection

175. Isabel Rawsthorne, Svetlana Beriosova, 1968; private collection

176. Isabel Rawsthorne, *Svetlana Beriosova*, 1968; private collection

177. Auguste Rodin, *Three Shades*, plaster, 1886 (part of *The Gates of Hell)*; Musée Rodin, Paris.

178. Alberto Giacometti, *Three Men Walking (Small Square)*, bronze, 1948; Metropolitan Musem of Art, New York

he was uncertain 'whether it would be possible to do a portrait of somebody just by making a gesture of them',[61] but he was no doubt aware of the ambition of the intention, and he purchased *La Bayadère II.*[62] Bacon's friend Robert Medley recalled: 'He bought one or two examples of work by people that he admired, and rather unexpected people. I can't remember their names now.'[63]

Movement from the Ballet La Bayadère I and II was based on 'The Kingdom of the Shades', Act III of the original 1877 Russian ballet *La Bayadère* and reintroduced from beyond the Iron Curtain by the Kirov Ballet in 1961.[64] The new version was the vehicle for Nureyev's debut when he joined the Royal Ballet after his defection from the Soviet Union.[65] He played the warrior hero Solor, and Fonteyn, the lover, Nikiya, a temple dancer. The setting of the story was the ancient palace beloved by Isabel's circle in which Nikiya is sacrificed for the sake of Solor's state marriage.[66] 'The Kingdom of the Shades' is the act in which he meets her in a dream of Nirvana, high in the Himalayas. Isabel painted the *pas de trois* of three Shades in converging arabesques. The trio evokes the love triangle at the ballet's heart. This variation of the triangle, a person haunted and inspired by not a living lover but a dead one, must have recalled Constant Lambert's 'unquiet grave', an experience that, by 1968, she shared with Bacon, who had lost Peter Lacy in 1962.

Although the bodies of the Shades are not shown in their entirety in the painting, the dancer and choreographer David Nixon has noted that the angle between heel and knee is apparent and correctly identical for all three.[67] A still from a later performance shows that the synchronisation is an overall effect that does not exist on a momentary basis. The particular steps of the *pas de trois* never actually coincide from one angle of vision. Isabel answered Rodin's objection to the frozen moment by painting the condensed sensation of symmetry experienced by the eye and mind and effected by the shared musical beat and concentration in the centre of the stage – Valéry's 'creative seeing'.

The painting does not depict the Shades' costumes, but the chiffon scarves/shrouds are present in translucent swathes of white and grey, evoking Renaissance precedents: the three converging dancers on the left hand panel of Donatello's *Cantoria* and the Three Graces in Botticelli's *Primavera,* both of which Isabel had copied (an exhilarated linear memory of *The Birth of Venus* explodes into a tangle of dancer drawings in one of her last sketchbooks[68]). The trio were, of course, first and foremost, an answer to Rodin's group of Shades surmounting *The Gates of Hell*, 1899, (**177**) and to Giacometti's reworking of it in *Three Men Walking,* 1948. (**178**) Isabel's broken, flickering forms and yellow smears fit Dante's description in the *Inferno* of the wounds inflicted upon three shades by burning stones and tongues of fire. The figures of both Rodin's *The Three Shades* and Giacometti's *Three Men Walking* point downwards; Isabel's are orientated upwards as well, towards an alternative oblivion, *jouissance.* The effect was captured in the haunting description of Isabel's studio by the writer Kim Echlin: 'a room full of women's bodies, charcoal drawings were tacked up the length of the walls, study after study of ballet dancers, hands and toes lifted to the sky, pointing to the grave'.[69]

The Marlborough oils were nearly a final statement, a distillation of research into the human body, especially the animated body, initiated in 1948. Isabel saw her twenty-year study of dancers, augmented by mid-century theories of art, philosophy and perception, as moving on from her forebears. If the *Birds and Fish* shown at the Hanover Gallery in 1949 were a manifesto of *peinture écriture,* the Marlborough show could be understood as a manifesto for *peinture sculpturale.* Isabel gave the public and the critics no opportunity to appreciate or come to terms with this, however. Although the dancers were collected together again in 1986 for a large and successful exhibition at the October Gallery, astonishingly, by the 1970s, when she was approaching sixty, she was already absorbed by a new artistic venture.[70]

179. Isabel Rawsthorne, *Movement from the Ballet La Bayadère II*, 1967; The Estate of Francis Bacon

180. Isabel Rawsthorne, *Migration I*, c. 1970; private collection

28 SILENT SPRING: 1955–1971

The more science prolongs its sight,
the wider do dreams extend their wings and flight.

Amédée Ozenfant[1]

It is hard to find a description of Isabel that does not adopt animal terms to describe her exotic looks, dancer's stride, wary self-sufficiency and sexual charisma. Wildlife metaphors were commonly used to describe and usually denigrate women at this time, but were especially frequent in Isabel's case and for once reflect a real identification with animal life. Her affinity with the laughing woodpecker cannot have been far from her mind when she painted its frozen body during her desolate months in the rural French Indre, or resurrected it to laugh again during the desperate mix of survival and hedonism in post-war Paris and London. Even in her fifties, she was described by Biddy Noakes as 'an extraordinary beauty, also very very intelligent, also a will of her own, almost like people were trying to tame her all the time, tossing her head, almost like a horse'.[2] Such identifications were neither indulgent nor anthropomorphic, but based on her curiosity about physical and psychological continuities between living beings.

The convergence of the human and non-human was a general interest among the avant-garde after the war. It was expressed, for example, in 1945 in the intercutting of animal and human in Painlevé's films: the seahorse ballerinas in *L'Hippocampe*, or, in *Le Vampire*, the juxtaposition of footage of a vampire bat lapping blood from a wound with a clip from F. W. Murnau's 1922 vampire film *Nosferatu*. The concept is bluntly overt in the coupling of bird and woman in Isabel's *Leda* and Bacon's Leda-like *Fragment of the Crucifixion*, as well as his contemporary, ape-like *Heads I–V* and *Man with Monkey* (1951; private collection), in part responses to the research carried out into the behaviour of humans and chimpanzees in the 1920s by the American psychologist Robert Yerkes.[3] Both artists continued with these interests in the 1950s and 1960s. In 1956, Bacon painted *Two Owls* (1956; private collection) – a pair of long-eared owls from *Birds of the Night* on a blue background.[4] Matthew Gale sees them as an iteration of *Fragment of a Crucifixion*. The female body and owl are more subtly fused, the stance and coiffure of the bird uncannily like Giacometti's exaggeration of

181. Isabel Rawsthorne, *Baboon and Child*, c. 1962; Tate

182. Isabel Rawsthorne, *Baboon*, c. 1962; Tate

Isabel's imperious crest in *Femme debout*, featured in *Cahiers d'art* (1946) and exhibited in London in 1955.[5] Isabel, meanwhile, adapted her blue monochromes into a series of monkeys.

In 1952, Konrad Lorenz's book *He Talked with Beasts, Birds and Fish* was published in English as *King Solomon's Ring* by Mechthild Nawiasky, a friend of Isabel and Bacon. Of interest was Lorenz's identification of a 'language' of action and gesture.[6] Lorenz's description of birds and animals confined in cages (citing Yerkes) suggested an alternative *in camera* subject. His book stressed the cruelty of the practice, especially for monkeys and apes. Isabel adapted 'notations' of caged monkeys made in London Zoo in Regent's Park and the sketches of the so-called 'Blue Monkey' Minoan fresco reconstructed by Arthur Evans (fourteenth century BCE) that she had made in the Ashmolean in Oxford in 1951 (Tate, London).[7] Two finished oil versions, known from photographs, were stolen from her studio in 1993, but two gouache and charcoal studies, *Two Baboons I* and *II*, survive (c. 1962; private collection).[8] At first glance, it is difficult to distinguish the animals in their fathomless blue-and-umber shuttered settings from the dark dancers that she was painting at the same time. The calligraphic shapes hang like musical notes on a bar.

Two remaining oils, *Baboon and Child* and *Baboon* (**181, 182**), are outstanding works and, very unusually, hung in Isabel's home from at least 1965 until the end of her life.[9] They addressed a long, linked art history, from archaic sculpture – depictions of the Egyptian baboon deity Thoth which Isabel knew well from her visits to the British Museum, for example – to the 'primitive' figures of twentieth-century Moderns, with whom she associated, such as Derain's *Figure accroupie* (1907; Museum Moderner Kunst, Vienna). The diptych constituted a defiant reply to the carvings Epstein had made during their last year together: *Baboon* answered his squat *Elemental*, while the womb-like embrace of *Baboon and Child* surely confronted, with a restrained but terrible poignancy, *Primeval Gods*.[10]

Baboon and *Baboon and Child* rejected the 'primitivism' of the older generation in favour of a more modern material directness. Again, they were based on living animals observed in London Zoo in Regent's Park and in Zaria, Nigeria. We experience them as solitary and up-close, dark against light, in the case of the male, and light against dark, in the case of the female. *Baboon* sits in the traditional pose of thought and melancholy, most famous in the form of Rodin's Dante, *The Thinker* (1880; Musée Rodin, Paris). It recalls the dynamic drawing of Picasso's *Baboon* print (1936, printed 1942; Museum of Modern Art, New York) but the debonair air in the Picasso is replaced by an introverted demeanour. *Baboon and Child* echoes Picasso's sculpture *Baboon and Young* (March 1951; Museum of Modern Art, New York) and Demas Nwoko's *Mother and Child* (1961; private collection[11]), but in Isabel's work, the baby's back is turned on the parent, creating a more embattled pairing as both look out in the same direction. The two paintings are studies in confinement, communicated not by the cage itself but by the way it registers in the containment of the bodies. Each is animated only by will, expressed in the intent gazes and pulses of dark and light over compressed limbs. The echoing shapes of *Baboon and Child* distil the serial pairs of Isabel's skeleton monochromes of the 1940s and the double portraits. The idea of the prehistoric present that underlay the earlier paintings is suggested in the ambiguous distinction between skeleton, foetus and baby. Both pictures seem to visualise Artaud's Existentialist vision: 'We are not yet born, we are not yet in the world, there is not yet a world, things have not yet been made, the reason for being has not yet been found.'[12]

The technique of the Baboon paintings developed this idea. They negotiate a borderland between form and *informe*, representation and its lack, a sophisticated manifestation of Merleau-Ponty's 'field into which each perception sets us back, where we are as yet still alone'.[13] The three animals materialise in marks that synthesise their gestures with the artist's. There is sand in the paint, and each brushstroke differs in consistency, colour and direction, articulating the thrust, weight and texture of a component of the figure. In *Baboon*, a heavy brown arc

183. Isabel Rawsthorne, *Migration VI*, c. 1970s; private collection bows the back and withdraws the arm, folding at a dry, crumbling elbow. Quick swishes turn the head towards us to reveal incised, incisive eyes. The greatest simultaneity occurs in the furrows that trail long fingers over the knees. This notation was suggested, perhaps by the non-descriptive gestures that bring into view the hand in Rembrandt's *A Woman Bathing*. *Baboon and Child* comprises intermittent smears of white on a russet ground like the drapery in Rembrandt's picture. The spine imitates the peristaltic press of Japanese cherry blossom or Bacon's *Study of a Human Body*. The word 'baboon' is scratched like graffiti in the detritus at the bottom of the cage.

The accomplished *matière* that Isabel achieved in the Baboon paintings suggests that they date to after the visit to Zaria in 1961 and informed the development of the dancers and the portraits during that decade. Although those projects took up most of Isabel's time, she was planning new wildlife subjects. On 27 October 1961, she wrote to Annette Giacometti, 'Beautiful scenery everywhere. I'm doing another ballet decor, and then I'll renounce the theatrical work, otherwise I would never paint my three beautiful cats, birds flying over the fields, flowering shrubs, or anything. Too bad for the money, but our needs are different in the country!'[14] The absence of evidence of exhibition of the Baboons may be explained by circumstances surrounding the founding in 1964, by Peter Scott and others, of the Society of Wildlife Artists. In its first years, it operated with very little fanfare at the Art Federation Galleries just off Trafalgar Square, and the records of these early displays have not survived in the society's archives.[15]

At the end of the 1960s, after the Marlborough exhibition, Isabel set aside figures and portraits and returned to wildlife. An extraordinary series of paintings of flamingos date from about this time. It is possible that she had glimpsed the birds on the coast of Nigeria, but more likely her interest was sparked by Peter Scott's pioneering flamingo collection at the Wildfowl and Wetlands Trust at Slimbridge in Gloucestershire, which he had founded in 1946 and which she visited at least once in 1973. The ornithologist Leslie Brown had also published the first ground-breaking study of the species in his beautifully illustrated *The Mystery of the Flamingos* (1959).[16] In 1968, Bacon included a loping flamingo in the left panel of *Two Figures lying on a Bed with Attendants* (Museum of Contemporary Art, Tehran). Isabel turned the long-legged, nomadic birds into another 'forked animal', placed in twos and threes to suggest distance. Their fragile, pink calligraphy and watery setting recalled one of Isabel's last dancer canvases, the beautiful *Two Dancers en rose* (1968; New Art Gallery, Walsall).

In the spring of 1969, as the days lengthened and the weather warmed, Isabel returned to paint the landscape around her cottage, considered a decade before in her still lifes. On 24 May, she wrote to Annette Giacometti: 'the landscape

184. Isabel Rawsthorne, *Migration III*, c. 1970s; private collection

185. Carol Jacobi: View from Sudbury Cottage, 2008

is amazingly beautiful. I have not worked until a few weeks ago, I've started three fairly large paintings in yellow.'[17] She went straight into oils in the same dimensions as *View through a Window* and *Movement from La Bayadère*. Upright, the canvases had the presence of standing stones. Seven survive from the series, since titled *Migration I–VII*. They were dominated, in *Migration I*, by blue, yellow and terracotta, and by blue, yellow and grey in the others. The stained fields of colour look like a reaction to Bacon's bright backgrounds and the Pop era, but they have a closer kinship to the work of Craigie Aitchison, whose first exhibition at the Marlborough Gallery in 1968 had coincided with Isabel's.[18] Where Bacon preferred the matt, flat field created by house paint, Isabel and Aitchison built up planes of colour in oil, retaining an unfathomable dissolving quality. Aitchison's paintings at this stage were small and the influence was perhaps two-way.[19]

Isabel's turn to luminous yellow and blue also registered an event in the Essex countryside: the sudden appearance at the end of the 1960s of yellow fields of flowering canola (oilseed rape). These were the most recent and most visible symptom of the industrial, sometimes dysfunctional, farming practices that followed the shortages of the war. After moving to Little Sampford in 1953, Isabel had become very concerned with the effect of these practices on rural wildlife populations.[20] In 1962, Rachel Carson's international bestseller *Silent Spring*, an account of the countryside poisoned by pesticides, raised the profile of the environmental movement.[21] Isabel wrote for *Oryx*, journal of the Fauna and Flora Preservation Society and was a voice in the campaign that ultimately succeeded in regulating dangerous pesticides in 1985 and, in 1992, banning the wasteful burning of stubble. In the Migration pictures we find the mistle thrushes, hawkweed, cranesbill and wild roses of the local hedgerows, departing swallows and hawks at prey. We see also nature depleted and displaced: a dead crow, for instance; land gulls and swallows held in the hand while they are ringed for research. (**180, 183, 184, 187, 188**) Continuity and extinction are referenced in skeletal pterosaur forms scratched into the yellow paint in *Migration I*, *II* and *VI*, like fossils.

Isabel observed the birds in the wild and in the hand, and acquaintances or her cats brought carcasses that she could study. Decomposing bodies littered the studio as they had in the 1940s. Isabel adapted her now consummate technique to the character of each creature. Little dead goldfinches were depicted beak up, chests a tiny burst of feathers, as though still singing. Whether mere flicks of disappearance in the distance, or captured between curled fingers, arrows flying, flattened cadavers, or fragments of buried bone, the birds were animated by a newly vivacious draughtsmanship, by the sense of transience created by the uncertainty of the viewer's eye, unable quite to catch what it sees.

The Migration paintings set these particular lives and deaths in a broader drama inspired by discussions with Peter Rose Pulham and Isabel's reading on Greek religions, especially Robert Graves's *The White Goddess*.[22] The book described a pre-Homeric, matriarchal period divided into three seasons rather than four. Isabel found Graves's ideas of a literary and mythical scheme connected to natural conditions sympathetic, of course, and enjoyed his 'special pleading', as she put it, for feminine nature. She questioned his accuracy, wondering, for example, whether the importance he gave to leaf-fall as a seasonal marker took into account the density of deciduous trees existing in Greece in ancient times, but connected his model to her observations of local farming. She decided on: '3 Seasons corresponding to 3 phases of the Mother goddess, nymph, woman, crone, which also correspond to the 3 phases of the moon, waxing, full, waning, and to the 3 Fates (Erinyes). This idea appeals to me. I suspect autumn of being redundant, a town lover's romanticism. In the country there really are only 3 Spring (sowing) Summer (reaping) Winter (ploughing).' The three colours of the Migration paintings may derive from these seasons.

The arcs and circles in the paintings evoke the mounds for burning charcoal and the *omphalos*, or navel-boss, described by Graves and others as sacred to the matriarchal religion. The *omphalos* stone was thought of as a means to communicate with the gods, its hollow interior a source of vapours breathed by the Oracle. In 1954, Isabel had seen the most famous *omphalos* at Delphi, associated with Python, the chthonic serpent that had guarded it, and with Apollo, who had slain Python to take control of the *omphalos*.[23] In 1955, she described it in her last letters to Rose Pulham and included one in her set for the ballet *Elektra*.[24] The dark arcs of *Migration V* and *VI* recall their shape, and the shadowy birds almost hidden in these dark areas may be references to the chthonic deities, the Erinyes or Eumenides, 'daughters of Earth', 'daughters of the night'.[25]

The swathes of yellow divided from the blue suggest night and day, sea and sky, sea and land, and mythical cycles of creation and loss, light and dark, life and death. The colours were, as in Aitchison's pictures, indebted to the passages of lapis or azurite and gold in Early Renaissance altarpieces and manuscripts, and give the birds an air of those that act as symbols in these paintings. They recall especially the illuminations of the months in the Limbourg brothers' *Les Très Riches Heures* (1410), which Rose Pulham had proposed to Isabel as an antecedent for the notion of reducing the seasons from four to three (spring: March–May; summer: June–November; winter: December–March).[26] The circles and relief roundels in *Migration IV* (**187**) echo the sun, moon and planets at the top of these illuminations.

Rose Pulham had complained to Isabel that her division of the year into three seasons was 'a purely agricultural one taking no account of the Solar System … you as a pagan cannot object to giving the son his due, quite apart from filial respect'.[27] 'Filial respect' was one of Rose Pulham's familiar wordplays on the son/sun/Apollo, deity of creation, vision and art. The golden disc that features in a rare watercolour by Isabel, *Hand and Swallow,* belonging to her old friend Mary Rose Pulham (now Mary Ryan) (no date; private collection) and appears most strongly in *Migration V*, is an unmistakable allusion to this idea. It returns us to Cassandra's Invocation to Apollo, while its form, a swallow held against the glowing disc, recalls the winged figure in Turner's *Angel in the Sun*. The soaring bird caught temporarily in the hand set within the yellow round is an exquisite example of Isabel's 'crystallisation'. For all its poetic play – *objeu* – it is a literal representation of both the bird and the conditions under which she fleetingly observed birds held, quivering, in the hand for ringing, an extemporisation of 'manual imagination', a manual *epoché*. At the same time, their beaks and orientation have something of the appearance of a pen, piece of charcoal or brush held above the picture as it was made. More than a metaphor for inspiration, it is an actual capturing of life. Touch is traced in the extraordinarily vivacious smears and pricks, scratches and dabs.

The astonishingly vital summaries of flower and bird forms in the Migration paintings are all the more impressive when we realise that Isabel was, by the time she was working on them, losing her sight. Yet, the evidence of her letters, of the memories of her by her friends and of her work output does not indicate any lessening of activity.

The photographer Edward Morgan made a merry portrait of Isabel in about 1970 for his planned book on East Anglian artists.[28] In 1969, she and Rawsthorne went to Scotland and the Isles of Scilly as well as to Liverpool and Belfast, where he received honorary doctorates.[29] Isabel was in Paris for the opening of Giacometti's posthumous retrospective at the Orangerie in October 1969, and again, on a trip with Bacon, in April 1970.[30] On 12 March 1970, James Lord made his first visit to Sudbury Cottage to research his biography of Giacometti. Lord did not recall the sculptor talking to him about Isabel beyond one off-hand comment: 'A real devourer of men ... A tigress. No. More like a panther.'[31] This sounds like a tease on Giacometti's part, poking fun at Lord's old-fashioned idea of artists' models as femmes fatales, a prejudice exposed in the camellia plant he brought to Isabel as a gift, alluding, surely, to Alexandre Dumas's notorious heroine in *La Dame aux camélias* (1848).[32] He was disappointed when she met him at the station in her habitual understated garb – 'all grey' – and he viewed with distaste her hands – 'heavy, coarse, cracked, and dirty ... in contrast to the remaining finesse of her features' – not connecting their appearance to her work. He was equally disconcerted by her 'lithe and easy' stride and the readiness of her throaty laugh. 'The strength of her personality was immediately definite, sharp as a dagger,' he later wrote, 'but also a performance, something one could stand away from and consider for one's safety, perhaps? ... yet a rare, singular state of being. It filled up time and space like a natural element, water or air.'[33] Lord's writings give a strangely ungenerous view of Isabel's hospitality, taking no account of the fact that his visits, made between 1970 and 1973, coincided with the private difficulty of her husband's last illness and his death in July 1971.

Alan Rawsthorne was, as Lord observed, slowing down. He composed a piece for voice and piano entitled *Two Fish* and began an elegy for guitar for the classical guitarist Julian Bream, on which he was still working when he died. Bream finished the elegy and honoured Rawsthorne by performing it at his funeral at Thaxted parish church. Afterwards, mourners dropped flowers one by one into the grave; Isabel flung hers in angrily.[34]

186. Edward Morgan: *Isabel Lambert*, c. 1970

187. Isabel Rawsthorne, *Migration IV*, c. 1970s; private collection

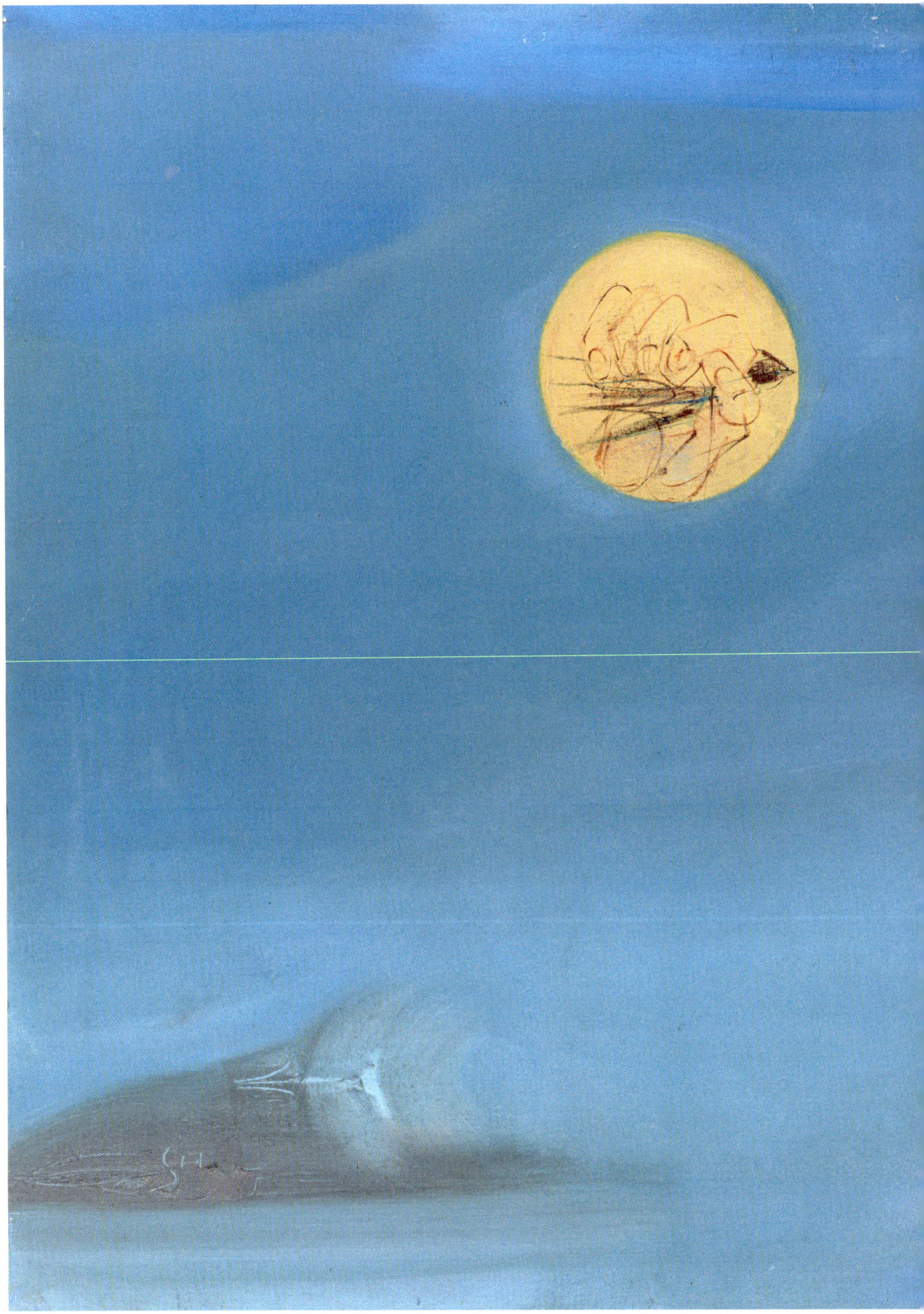

188. Isabel Rawsthorne, *Migration V*, c. 1970s; private collection

189. André Morain: Michel Leiris and Isabel Rawsthorne at Le Train Bleu, Paris, October 1971

29 HEMLOCK: 1971–1992

Isabel was alone. To make matters worse, her neighbours and friends the Noakes family moved to Cambridge to be closer to schools for their children and to Biddy's art-teaching post. Occasionally, Isabel went to London, or over to France, and in October 1971 she was again Bacon's guest in Paris, this time at the elegant seventeenth-century Hôtel des Saints-Pères, for the *vernissage* of his retrospective exhibition at the Grand Palais.[1] It was a triumphant achievement for a living British artist, and, to celebrate, he threw a sumptuous dinner at Le Train Bleu. Despite the gilded Belle Époque splendour, a photograph of Isabel and Michel Leiris shows her clad in plain black, hair dyed dark again but tousled and her famous cow-lick untamed. (**189**) They are in conversation. The glittering event was sadly overshadowed. Two days before the picture was taken, George Dyer, semi-estranged from Bacon and in difficulties with alcohol and drugs, had died in his room at the Hôtel des Saints-Pères.

Christmas was difficult, but Isabel had visitors, and Bacon sent her John Russell's new monograph on him, inscribed, 'To Isabel with deep affection.'[2] The following year, Isabel returned to the Hôtel des Saints-Pères for the occasion of the seventieth birthday of Diego Giacometti.[3] In the spring of 1973, she saw her doctor and began a healthier regime, relinquishing spirits and taking only wine and, on some days, apple juice.[4] She began a diary – as she had in her period of recovery in 1947 – which shines a brief light on her everyday life. There were several trips to London – in June to see Corinna MacNeice and Joan, who had married Patrick Leigh Fermor in 1968 – and visits to exhibitions such as *Pioneers of Modern Sculpture* at the Hayward Gallery in September – 'nothing useful'.[5] In June, she also entertained at home. James Lord, returning for the third time, had dinner there with Warwick Nicholas and Jeffrey Bernard – a strange mix.[6] Warwick was in England to research his book *The Biology of Free-Living Nematodes* (1975), and stayed with his sister before moving to Cambridge to be nearer the university. Bruce Bernard also stayed for a few days.[7]

There were a surprising number of concerts to attend and a week at the Cheltenham Music Festival, where Alan Rawsthorne's music was performed. Isabel enjoyed a day at the Wildfowl and Wetlands Trust at Slimbridge, but she found the West Country too 'overcrowded, stuffy, ordered, rich' for her liking.[8] She met up with Elisabeth Lutyens and Judith and Edward Williams, and Roy and Biddy Noakes came at the end of the week and drove her back. She was glad to get home to work. Just before she left, one of her cats, Henrietta (named for Henrietta Moraes), had brought her a weasel, and she had left it desiccating in the studio. 'Never had a weasel before!' The remainder of the diary is dominated by observations of the mice, swallows and other wildlife around the cottage or seen on walks. She still thought nothing of walking ten miles or more in a day.[9] Warwick described her as 'a dedicated naturalist and conservationist' and she must have enjoyed their conversations during his stay.[10]

Isabel's abandonment of stage-set design and her failure to make an effort to exhibit her work left her with slim means. Julian Bream recalled that 'her financial position ... was pretty precarious', and he completed Alan Rawsthorne's unfinished elegy for guitar partly because he was anxious for her to receive Rawsthorne's fee.[11] But she refused any direct practical or financial help and the composer Gerald Schurmann, who continued to visit, recalled that she was 'too proud or too stubborn to accept ministrations from friends', even Bacon.[12] Only Roy and Biddy Noakes's daughter, Mary, always welcome at the cottage, was permitted occasionally to tidy or clean. When the thatch needed repair, Isabel decided to move. With Bacon's blessing, she sold back to the Marlborough Gallery the portraits he had given her, and she sold Giacometti's *Tête d'Isabel* to David and Lisa Sainsbury. With the proceeds, she re-thatched Sudbury Cottage and purchased a small terraced house in Cambridge on Ferry Path, just across the River Cam from Jesus Green.[13] Warwick stayed in the house until his return to Australia in October. Isabel then let the cottage to a young geologist completing his doctorate and his wife and returned to Cambridge.

Her diary ceases at this point, but her letters reveal that she met Paris, Soho and Essex friends as usual. James Lord and David Sylvester visited her to enquire after her correspondence with Giacometti. She enjoyed studying in the university's Museum of Zoology and the Fitzwilliam Museum, and drank with Roy at the *Locomotive* pub on Mill Road, a haunt for musicians and students from the nearby polytechnic. A regular at the pub was the Australian Jack Lindsay, a prolific writer in many fields, who had published biographies of Blake, Turner and Courbet.[14] Lindsay was a fan of Noakes, and his socialism and independence of mainstream definitions of modern painting chimed with Isabel's views.[15] He believed Turner had anticipated the Moderns, including Bacon.[16] With the livelier social life came temptations to drink, however. Sometimes Isabel kept to wine, but when she took spirits, she became loud, argumentative – 'nasty happy', as Biddy Noakes put it.[17] She also missed the country, and, in 1975, returned to Sudbury Cottage.

190. Isabel Rawsthorne, *Possums in Moonlight*, c. 1977; private collection

In 1974, Anna Phillips curated a small exhibition of Isabel's work at her Framlingham gallery, but few knew she was still working.[18] In fact, despite her fading eyesight and alcohol consumption, she was thinking and painting a good deal. This is illustrated by her output in 1977. In January, Isabel flew to Australia and stayed for two months with Warwick and his family in Canberra and at a holiday house that they took on the south coast of New South Wales.[19] It was an opportunity to get to know her nephews and nieces. They visited art galleries, explored the surroundings by car and Isabel loved swimming in the local pool and the sea. She found the new terrain and wildlife fascinating and sketched a good deal. At night at the coast, she sat outside in the dark drawing the possums as they ate watermelons put out for them. In one of the drawings, the animal seems to have paused as the artist's outstretched hand, a trace of her chalky fingers, extend towards it.

On Isabel's return to England, these sketches were combined with watercolours of Australian vegetation to become two limpid gouaches, *Possums in Moonlight I* and *II*. (**190**) The days at the coast and Warwick's academic research

191. Isabel Rawsthorne, *Seashore*, c. 1977; private collection

on nematodes and marine ecosystems may have suggested two new, radiantly yellow beach pictures (c. 1977, private collection).[20] The writer of *Silent Spring*, Rachel Carson, was also a marine biologist, and earlier bestsellers, such as *The Edge of the Sea* (1955), may have been a source for these works and for the shells at the edge of *Migration VII* .

The paintings of this period reveal a new approach to setting. The blue, umber and occasionally rose grounds developed into something closer to Turner's 'colour beginnings' – broad and delicately tinted areas swept in before the application of lively drawn or painted lines. This may have been catalysed by conversation with Jack Lindsay; his biography of Turner connected his non-illustrational washes to Cézanne and Picasso.[21] In addition, some of Turner's most beautiful 'colour beginnings' were displayed in the exhibition *Turner in the British Museum: Drawings and Watercolours* from May 1975 to February 1976.[22]

In the summer of the same year, Isabel embarked on another journey, overland to Greece with Mary Ryan and Mary's teenage daughter, Juliet. She recorded their road trip in a lively illustrated journal, now in the Tate Archive, London. The three women drove south from Paris and through Italy, reaching

192. Isabel Rawsthorne, *Chess Players*, c. 1977; private collection

Florence in August and going on to Rome and Naples, cities where Isabel found memories of lovers, as well as favourite works of art.[23] She was fascinated by the progression of landscapes and the movements of land and sea, forests and lakes that had brought them about. Her perspective echoed D'Arcy Wentworth Thompson's *On Growth and Form*: 'The facts of geographical distribution or even of the migration of birds lead on and on to speculations regarding lost continents, sunken islands.'[24] At the tip of Italy, Isabel sketched bathers on the beach at Bari, intrigued by their 'Italian shapes', and swam while they waited for the ferry at Brindisi.[25] This took her to Patmos, from where she travelled on alone to stay with Joan and Patrick Leigh Fermor at their beautiful house in Kardamyli, on the southern coast of the Peloponnese, overlooking the Ionian Sea. She rested and drew portraits and landscapes of the surrounding olive groves. She left behind pictures for Joan of her cats and of Joan and Paddy playing chess on the terrace.[26] (**192**) The latter composition reprised Burne-Jones's lovers in his beautiful chalk drawing *The Backgammon Players* (1861), which Isabel knew well from her visits to the Fitzwilliam Museum in Cambridge.

Isabel explored the islands alone, camping in the open and watching shoot ing stars.[27] She visited the windblown site of Agamemnon's palace at Mycenae where Cassandra had stood. The Lion Gate reminded her of making sketches for *Tiresias* in the Ashmolean Museum in Oxford.[28] Wasps, like little furies, tormented her at Epidavros. There she made her bed on the beach and gazed up at the moon and Orion. In the morning, she was greeted by 'kingfishers, swallows, crows, flock of small brownish birds, lizards, a pale blue jellyfish, starfish'.[29] All the while, thinking of her three seasons, she continued to wonder 'what it was like' in the distant past, 'what kind of trees, where was the sea'.[30] Eventually, she made her way back via Ravenna and then Venice, where there were even older

193. Isabel Rawsthorne, *Death of a Gull II*, c. 1982–3; Sainsbury Centre for Visual Arts, University of East Anglia

memories of Giacometti and Balthus before the war.[31] At home, Isabel developed the lovely drawings of Joan Leigh Fermor into particularly ephemeral oils (c. 1972; private collection).

As Isabel approached seventy years old, her glaucoma became too advanced for her to make journeys alone, even to Paris and London.[32] There were fewer parties or friends to call; she still saw Bacon, but rarely, at the Colony Room. Her drinking was systematic and at its worse on social occasions. She may also have been harder of hearing. A concert given in 1980 by Biddy Noakes's daughter Anna, who became a professional flautist, was accompanied by unquenchable conversation from Isabel in the audience.[33] There was a reprieve in 1979. Professor John Scott, head of the Vitreoretinal Service at Addenbrooke's Hospital in Cambridge, operated on Isabel's eyes and was partially successful. Although she was left almost blind in one, she regained her sight in the other. Isabel was ecstatic to have some independence and to be able to look and work again. It was around this time that she and Biddy Noakes went to see a production of Peter Shaffer's psychosexual drama *Equus* (1973) at Cambridge Arts Theatre.

194. Isabel Rawsthorne, *Hemlock, Mouse and Shell*, c. 1985; Fry Art Gallery, Saffron Walden

The widening of Isabel's focus brought about by the operation may account for her new compositions. Discrete areas of detail were no longer isolated on bright grounds, and she returned to the greys of her earlier, observed phenomenological studies. She wrote to Roy and Biddy saying that she had acquired corpses of an 'Iceland Gull, pygmy shrew and pregnant Stoat' and realised them in a series of outstanding gouaches and oils.[34] Shrews, stoats and birds materialised within frameworks of water, land and light from miraculously minimal arrangements of inky, non-illustrational marks, while remnants of her grids manifested as precisely ruled lines. (**202**) For Biddy Noakes, this bravura handling represented Isabel's defiant display of her restored vision, and she gave one of the finished works, *Death of a Gull II*, c. 1982–3, (**193**) to her surgeon.[35]

These late paintings epitomised Isabel's ethos of beauty in transience by deepening the themes of Carson's *Silent Spring*. In sketches such as *Two Gulls* (1979; private collection), she developed the graceful rounded head and draped wings that identified the species in *Migration V* and *VI* into a more dynamic, diagonal notation, conveying the Bataillian sense of life in death. In this and *Death of a*

195. Isabel Rawsthorne, *Hemlock*, c. 1985; private collection

Gull I, II and *III* (c. 1982–3; private collections), she returned to and rethought the central format of *Green Woodpecker III*. (**67**) Cold settings with stalks of water hemlock carved in Giacometti-like grisaille updated the winter freeze of 1946 to Carson's chemical winter. Poisoned gulls were not uncommon in the fields around Isabel's home.[36] In 1960, the painter and plantsman Cedric Morris, who lived in Suffolk, not far from Isabel, had painted a landscape littered with bird corpses as 'homage' to pesticide manufacturers; it was exhibited as *Landscape of Shame* (Tate, London) in London in 1981.[37] Isabel's imagery is closer to the famously dystopian introduction to Carson's book, 'A Fable for Tomorrow', which describes teaming winter roadsides falling under the 'shadow of death', 'lined with brown and withered vegetation ... silent and still'.[38]

The Hemlock series distilled the central achievement of Isabel's landscape still lifes from 1955: their rejection of sentiment and the Ruskinian oppositions

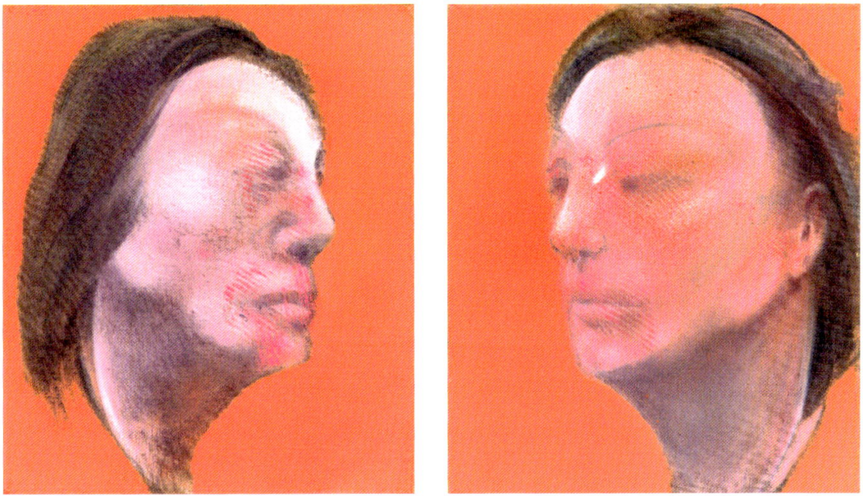

196. Francis Bacon, *Studies of Isabel Rawsthorne*, 1983; private collection

between industry and nature, present and past that persisted in British twentieth-century art. Unlike Morris's or Carson's 'silent spring', her nature was poisonous too. Hemlock is an ancient and highly toxic species, and, because Isabel had drawn poisonous plants for the black propaganda leaflets during the war, she knew that winter was the time of year when its roots are most fatal. It recalls, too, the nuclear winter that haunted her woodpecker; her brother had told her that, if there were a nuclear war, nettles and hemlock would inherit the planet.[39] Man and nature, past and future were in bleak accord.

As always, Isabel's natural motifs resonated with Classical allusion. The title *Death of a Gull* alluded to the death of Socrates, and hemlock was Socrates' poison of choice. Thoughts of this solution to 'how to live' – suicide – were frequent companions, especially when her eyesight deteriorated again. Colour beginnings for oils in the Hemlock series lay down landscape layers in skilfully applied trickles and drips, but the detail of plants and animals were barely begun .

Two last portraits of her made around this time capture the persistence of Isabel's charisma into old age. After a gap of twelve years, Bacon painted a last tender diptych, *Studies of Isabel Rawsthorne*, 1983. (**196**) Working from memory and photographs (the photograph of her with Michel Leiris seems to have been a source, (**189**) he blended old and young. The skin is still opalescent, the hair swept back from a haughty brow is brown rather than grey, and the background is orange with energy. There is none of the wild brushwork of the 1960s images, however. Isabel's mouth is closed; the 'talk' and 'shriek' are absent. *Studies of Isabel Rawsthorne* is sober, having, as Martin Harrison notes, the devotional

197. Roy Noakes, *Portrait of Isabel Rawsthorne*, bronze, 1985; New Art Gallery, Walsall

dignity of a Northern Renaissance portrait. He also notes, however, the smudged right eye and scatter of red that allude to Isabel's operation and to Bacon's fears for his own vision.[40]

The last portrait ever made of Isabel was the only one she commissioned herself. Biddy and Roy Noakes and their three children had left Cambridge for a stone farmhouse in Yorkshire where Roy might work with fewer distractions. In 1984, Isabel asked him to visit and make another head. He stayed at Sudbury Cottage for two weeks and created a dialogue with Isabel's remaining *Tête d'Isabel I*, which sat a few yards away from where he worked. The result was very different from the undulating portraits of her and Rawsthorne that he had made in the 1970s. On his return to Yorkshire, Roy sketched a quick profile on his kitchen wall (there to this day) and continued to refine the head, casting it in 1985. (**197**) The result, neither 'look-like-look' – Roy's word for representational portraits – nor abstract, was one of his finest works. *Isabel* is enigmatic, again closed mouthed, and undeniably old. With minimal modelling, the bronze reflects back a suggestion of thinning hair, fallen brow, folded lids over dim eyes. Yet, like Bacon's *Studies of Isabel Rawsthorne,* the shining surfaces and a neat parallelogram of chin, cheek and crest of hair have the pert and luminous beauty of a girl.

In 1985, Isabel was admitted in a state of alcoholic breakdown to Fulbourn Psychiatric Hospital. She remained there for only a few days, discharging herself almost as soon as she came round, but the short stay was to have far-reaching consequences for her legacy. Fulbourn, one of the first purpose-built Victorian County Pauper Lunatic Asylums and latterly a bleak prison, had recently been transformed by the progressive psychiatrist David Clark. By 1985, it was world renowned as a research centre for the treatment of psychiatric illnesses and alcohol and substance abuse.[41] Clark promoted non-drug based 'social therapy', administered by a 'therapeutic community' of psychiatric nurses. In the 1970s, geriatric nurses at Fulbourn pioneered liaison with social workers in the community to identify and encourage patients' capacity to live independently, and Isabel was able to go back to her cottage.[42] A psychiatric nurse often visited, and friends rallied round.[43] A local couple, Joe and his wife, were engaged to attend, as far as Isabel would let them, to her needs. Biddy Noakes remembers their bringing homemade apple pies. Isabel was happy to return to her garden, her cats and her work. A photograph of her at this time in her kitchen, where she loved to cook, shows her close to her radio, usually tuned to a French station. Sometimes, Isabel kept to the regime of drinking only wine that her doctors encouraged; at others, she returned to spirits. Alarmingly, her photographer friend, John Blake, gave her a gun – a First World War air pistol – to protect herself from burglars who might be tempted by her collection of art. Isabel was, of course, very capable of using it.

One of Clark's treatment methods was 'reality orientation' and through extreme good fortune Isabel's nurse suggested that she begin to write – something she had not done since her time with RAG and her radio days in post-war Paris – and suggested she make a record of her life.[44] An added impetus may have been the eventual appearance of Lord's *Giacometti: A Biography*. He had ceased to have contact with Isabel after 1973 and was alienated from Annette Giacometti, as well. When the book appeared, the two women were horrified, Isabel mainly on behalf of the Giacomettis.[45] The book was criticised generally for not penetrating Giacometti as an artist, and many agreed with Isabel that Lord had 'got into water he doesn't understand'.[46]

Finally, something of Isabel's extraordinary past and character were committed to paper in four notebooks. Many pages vanished, snipped out with scissors, probably because they pertained to people still living, notably Bacon. Isabel also solicited short texts from friends, such as Pattie Lambert. By the time the first chapters were typed, she had distilled them to curt prose, understated but never insignificant. The manuscript was proofed by Pattie Lambert and another friend, the journalist Alix Coleman, and sent to the publishing house John Murray; it went no further, but fortunately a version survives in the Tate Archive.

Other distractions came in the form of exhibitions. *Dancers in Action*, a display of thirty-three of Isabel's dancer drawings and two oils was curated by

198. Isabel Rawsthorne, *Geese*, c. 1988; private collection

Corinna MacNeice and Chili Hawes at the October Gallery in London in 1986. They had opened the gallery in 1979 to show world art, and it was a particularly appropriate venue for Isabel's synthetic style. Her new writing habit extended to the catalogue, and, unusually, she contributed an extended account of the thinking behind her moving portraits. The exhibition was a success. Everyone gathered again in Thaxted the following year for a seventy-fifth birthday party at the Town Hall. During 1988, Isabel was approached by Veronica Sekules, a curator at the Sainsbury Centre for Visual Arts, about the possibility of the first retrospective exhibition of her work. The Sainsbury Centre was a new kind of gallery supported by David and Lisa Sainsbury and had opened only a decade before in a Modernist, Norman Foster building on the campus of the University of East Anglia in Norwich.[47] It housed the Sainsburys' works by Giacometti and Bacon and an extensive collection of non-Western art, the perfect setting for Isabel. The exhibition would be a stunning revelation of her early career, which, in her immersion in the moment, she rarely mentioned, and of her revolutionary late work. At this date, the new Migration or Hemlock series, and the Greek and Australian paintings were not only unseen but unsuspected. In London, it was said that she had not worked for decades.

Isabel painted on. Her last pieces, made when she was nearly blind, drawing in near darkness like Sigfried Giedion's man in a cave, were an extraordinary culmination of her embodied method and 'manual imagination'. A gossipy note from Anna Phillips, written in 1988, mentions posting to her the skeletons

199. Isabel Rawsthorne, Study of geese, c. 1988; Tate

of four baby tits and apologises for not thinking to send the nest as well. Isabel also had new living models.[48] She had exchanged her gun for geese to act as her guards – Schurmann remembered her fending them off with a dustbin lid when she fed them.[49] She named them after Joe (who had brought them to her), Juliet (Ryan) and Mary (Noakes). They became companions in emulation of Konrad Lorenz's famous experiments of living with the socially astute greylag geese, and just as they shared her cottage, so she was not averse to sleeping on the straw in their pen.[50] Isabel took up her 1940s sketchbooks and filled the empty pages with the fabulously looping, living, ebullient forms of her geese. The confidence and economy of the multivalent lines conveying shape, movement and relationship all at once underlines her achievement since the concentrated encounters with little corpses in the bedroom of House RAG. Intent only on her current project, as always, Isabel cut up and re-stretched Migration canvases to make four large oil studies of the geese (c. 1988; private collection). Two were unfinished; the two others betray her deteriorating vision in their reduction of detail and return to colour, but their presence and movement is vivid. A fifth work made at this time bears an imperceptible, folded nude, and looks back to the Baboon paintings.

Corinna MacNeice took her godmother away for a weekend. Just before leaving, Isabel retrieved a freshly laid goose egg, wrapped it in a cloth and popped it in her bag. There it stayed until they returned, when, like a toast to Rose Pulham's disquisition on the egg, it was retrieved and turned into an omelette for their supper.[51] The egg appeared in spectral form in several paintings. These look, at first glance, like unfinished 'colour beginnings', with ovals waiting to be filled; but they were, in fact, images of a small pool Isabel had asked Joe to make in her garden, shaped precisely to present a perfect ellipse.[52] It was a variation on her mirror, or on the reflective bodies of water in Monet's garden, or even on the glassy pools painted by Burne-Jones. Corinna recalled: 'She was so pleased about it and so I think it was something she had dreamed of for a while. It was a fair size I remember, on a level with the ground and reflecting only sky. So you might see blue with puffy clouds or you might catch reflections on a grey day like an Isabel painting, all oyster shell greys.'

One of our last glimpses of Isabel comes from the writer Kim Echlin, who called on her in the spring of 1989. Echlin was researching a book on the writer Elizabeth Smart, whom Isabel had known well in her Soho days. Echlin found the cottage with rails fixed to the walls and Isabel moving 'along the edges of the room like a shadow', a spectre of her dancers at the *barre*.[53] They talked in the glass room, looking out at the fields, and when they had finished, Isabel offered the key to her studio. It was too early in the year for her to have reopened it, but Echlin saw the charcoal dancers, back, perhaps, from the October Gallery. Encouraged by her reaction, Isabel directed her to her current workplace, a recapitulation of the bedroom in House RAG: 'At the top of the narrow, worn, dipping staircase was a plain light-filled room with a bare wooden table.' A dead thing. a little grey mouse with a long tail, lay arranged on some dry leaves and grasses on the table. There was a half-finished canvas standing to the side and the dead mouse was lightly sketched in, the ghostly beginnings of a *nature morte*.[54]

Some barely decipherable notes, written during a return to hospital, give us almost unbearable access to the mind of someone facing death, unflinching, curious, wryly amused. On a scrap of paper Isabel wrote: 'for Euthanasia / Could this be read as a plea? / I write in a dangerous place! / You should be at home.'[55] On another scrap: 'some people I have known were suicides but I do not know their motives / One Michel [Leiris], tried twice but failed / Pills beside his wife.'[56] On another: 'One of Alan's favourite words is now mine "fancy" his love for "humble" / ~~This~~ word Fancy fancy has no answer [...] no sickness / I last night I was thinking of how and where I should manage to lie me down.' Then, as though literally turning over her thoughts, on the back she scrawled, 'As an op could be [...] to hang I could not would fail and the horror for the finder I know so little I have hardly any choice maybe what I write.'[57] A third scrap contemplated time: 'Was curious and not unpleasant to think I would find my own measurable future.' Then she drew a triangle. And on the other side: 'this was gentle feeling. Perhaps the writing of my memoirs was and truly marks as it kept in sequence the amazing contrasts which I had faced.'[58] The last scrap reads: 'I suppose the experience of a hospital an old people's home, a [indecipherable], is a usual setting for love of life and so a love of the characters of the people I loved touch me with their hands, what I did not know about them does not harm me'. Another triangle, and on the other side, perhaps tired, her language, becomes Cassandrian, at once incoherent and compellingly vivid: 'have now no longer with a form in my ditch or running in the field, no swallow in the stack sign me to leap while I a new austerity is will stop your life.'[59]

Isabel was filling her sketchbooks with names – 'the people I loved' – listed, in a shaky hand, over and over like incantations. By now, the books contained a record of nearly seventy years of seeing: ungainly nudes, scrutinised beetles, birds, shells, gestural landscapes, Minoan antiquities, unravelled geese and tremulous letters intermingled on the same pages. In January 1991, Veronica Sekules wrote to Isabel with the news that, at the last minute, her exhibition had been cancelled.[60] This was a tremendous disappointment to Sekules and must have been a deep blow to Isabel. Later in the year, Nigel and Iris Weaver helped her arrange her paintings around her studio for a Japanese visitor, but it was nearly the last sight anyone had of her, or her work.

In the depth of the following winter, on 27 January 1992, Isabel dropped to her death from her top stair. She was buried in the Thaxted churchyard, and her friends held a memorial service at which Edward Williams read a eulogy.[61] A few weeks later, Bacon died in Spain. Her will bequeathed one or two pictures and the remaining Giacomettis – *Tête d'Isabel I* and *Diego in the Studio* – to friends, and the house and contents and the residuary of her estate to her brother, including sketchbooks, diaries, letters, four volumes of handwritten autobiographical notes, an unfinished autobiography in typescript and other personal papers.[62] Biddy Noakes gave the geese a home in Yorkshire and in cooperation with Isabel's brother, began working to promote Isabel's artistic legacy.

When the studio was opened up, the desiccating body of a sparrowhawk was discovered on a table. It had been there since the previous summer perhaps longer. Nearby were five sparrowhawk paintings. The largest of these, a gouache painted on the back of a *Dancer,* still stood on the easel (*Sparrowhawk*, c. 1990).(**200**) Like the paintings of woodpecker, owl and gull, the Sparrowhawk series opened the wings of the bird. This enhanced the characteristic curved profile that permits this species to penetrate small openings between branches and undergrowth and appear without warning above its prey. Because sparrowhawks feed on other birds, they are especially susceptible to poisoning. The most aggressive pesticides had been banned by 1985, but hawks continued to be affected, and Isabel's carcass may have been a casualty.[63]

200. J. M. W. Turner, *Angel Standing in the Sun*, 1846; Tate

The hawk was a bird of death in several senses. Giacometti had employed the motif for tombs, thinking of the Egyptian god Horus. The hovering perspective with the light behind its wings was characteristic of the way it was seen by its prey just before it swooped. Death has a contradictory presence, however. We view the bird both from below, as the victim, and from above, contemplating a corpse. The outstretched wings are also those of the inert specimen on the table, prostrate as well as predatory. The gaze is cold and oblique because it is dead, as well as deadly. The Bataillian life in death paradox of *Green Woodpecker* is reversed.

The rainbow effect of the light behind the primary feathers, most noticeable in *Sparrowhawk*, (**201**) recalls once more Turner's *Angel Standing in the Sun*, (**200**) referenced thirty-five years before in *Flowers in Spring*, (**142**) on the death of Rose Pulham, and again in the Migration series. Isabel would have known that Turner's picture, painted late in his life, was a reflection on mortality. Jack Lindsay had devoted a chapter to the painting in his second book on Turner, quoting the words with which the picture was exhibited: 'The morning march that flashes to the sun; The feast of vultures when the day is done'.[64] Isabel substituted Turner's angel with the birds, as always replacing metaphor with fact. The sword is replaced by the skeletal tail. The arc is created by the wings, an ellipse evoking the egg and the pool. An oil *Sparrowhawk* in green (stolen in 1993), blended bird and egg completely.

201. Isabel Rawsthorne, *Sparrowhawk*, c. 1990; private collection

Below Turner's angel are representations of the vicissitudes of love: Delilah cuts Samson's hair; Adam and Eve discover the body of their son Abel; Judith lifts the head of Holofernes; and a skeleton cries with a baby at its feet. Below the sparrowhawk, we discover the purpose of the last lists in Isabel's sketchbooks. The same names are incised into and under the paint; some are so faded that they cannot be read, but Tzara, Derain, René and Louis can be deciphered. The clearest is Alberto. They, too, represent the vicissitudes of love: 'the characters of the people I loved touch me with their hands', as Isabel described them in Fulbourn. To complete this idea, as so often, she includes her own hand. The shadowy side of the arc indicates her fingers, registered and represented in trembling traces of charcoal barely dusting the surface. It flutters like a bird, a gesture of farewell and at the same time the 'touch' that was making the image.

Turner's Angel and Isabel's hawk equate phenomenological limits to the limits of life, but where Turner explored vision Isabel included touch as well, adapting Turner's Apollonian angel to Cassandra's Aeschylean 'ambiguity ... incoherence, dimness'. Turner's painting preserved its Romantic subject matter, while the unfinished state of Isabel's Sparrowhawk series is somehow true to a career spent exploring existential apperception.

202. Isabel Rawsthorne, *Stoats and Moon*, c. 1985; private collection

203. Isabel Rawsthorne in her studio, c. 1961

AFTERWORD: 'AND IF ANYONE ASKS YOU IT IS I FOR IS'

> Man is nothing else but what he purposes ...
> nothing else but the sum of his actions.
>
> Jean-Paul Sartre[1]

> I was trying to describe a certain gesture and sound of Isabel's (impossible anyway over the phone) like an extended 'phiewww' accompanied by an elegant arm gesture in full extension sideways as in dance ... I took it to be an illustration of simultaneous timelessness and speed in the transient.
>
> Corinna MacNeice[2]

We do not ask how Degas, Picasso, Giacometti or Bacon found themselves daily at liberty in a space of their own. Even artists famed for their privations, such as Van Gogh, or for taking their practice into the field, Van Gogh again, cannot be thought of without their studio. The social constraints against which successful Moderns rebelled tended to be comfortable enough to furnish the security and contacts that made their rebellions possible. After the war, the armed forces offered this security too, as, eventually, did the welfare state. This was not the case for Isabel; how to paint was how to live, courageously improvised through the events of her century. Her Royal Academy scholarship coincided with the loss of home and family, and her first professional success at twenty-two was left behind with her lover and her child. Fifteen years later, when Constant Lambert died, everything had to be rebuilt again. On each of these occasions, and through most of the decade dominated by the war, Isabel was without liberty or workspace. That within less than eighteen months of having the Albany Street studio she produced a ground-breaking solo exhibition for the Hanover Gallery was remarkable.

The lack of a studio was a nearly insurmountable impediment not only to making and keeping art, but also to identifying as an artist. The sixteen years between Isabel's solo appearances at the Redfern Gallery in 1933 and at the Hanover Gallery in 1949 were matched both by Bacon's fallow period between the solo exhibition at his self-created Transition Gallery in 1934 and the exhibition at the Hanover in 1949, and by Giacometti's delay in exhibiting new work between 1932 and 1946. Yet, Bacon's and Giacometti's *vie d'atelier* perpetuated their visibility as well as their activity as artists and, by the 1950s, were an intrinsic part of their public personae. Isabel's itinerant existence meant her artistic identity was far more fragile. Her improvised workspaces were, moreover, for many years clandestine: the illicit Wood Street studio in Liverpool that secured her access to the nude; the atelier of Epstein occupied under cover of being his assistant/model; the covert double life of the 1930s; and, of course, the secret room in House RAG. Four years at Albany Street and a few months at Delancey Street gave her practice only a brief London presence before, forced to begin again at forty, she sacrificed it for the removed permanence of Sudbury Cottage in Essex.

For Isabel, the studio was, moreover, a private space other to her extrovert public persona, visible only to those who came to the country and whom she chose to admit. There was a contrast between the public energies of her life and the private energies of her work. For all Isabel's love of conviviality and conversation – the chance to talk 'to tatters', as she sometimes put it – she let her art speak for itself and took little interest in building a following or clientele.[3] She did not network for status or money and had no patience for deference where she did not see it was due. Neither did she promote her name through her likeness. It was a successful strategy for her peers: Picasso, Giacometti and Bacon became as well known as their work, as did Leonor Fini. But Fini observed that, in her case, and that of other women artists, reputations were sexualised and infantilised: 'woman child ... muses rather than artists'.[4] Isabel was perhaps discouraged by press coverage of this kind that she had received in 1933; there are remarkably few photographs of her after this date, she rarely made herself the subject of her own art and did little to exploit her spectacular presence in the work of others.

Isabel did not market herself or her work and compounded the delays brought about by her exile from London and the war by exhibiting only when she felt she had done something new. An even greater wariness intervened in her later years. When, in 1972, James Lord asked when she planned to show next, 'she shrieked with laughter and said, "Don't you ever dream that you're walking stark naked through Piccadilly Circus?"'[5] During the last two decades of her life, when she was making her most ambitious and accomplished paintings, Isabel cooperated only with those she trusted: Anna Phillips, Corinna MacNeice, Nigel and Iris Weaver and Veronica Sekules. The cancellation of Sekules's Sainsbury Centre show was a major misfortune.

The turning point was the event that began this book: the exhibition 'Isabel Lambert' at the Marlborough Gallery in 1968. The unveiling of Isabel's largest and most original body of work to date at the leading gallery in London should have secured her reputation, but its timing brought Isabel's career into a collision course with Bacon's. David Mellor argues that 1966 marked the moment when the

204. Francis Bacon and George Dyer at the private view of the *Isabel Lambert*, exhibition at Marlborough Gallery, 1968

Marlborough was building Bacon's fame.[6] A photograph, taken at Isabel's *vernissage,* shows Bacon and George Dyer threading through the crowd, Bacon holding the catalogue featuring *Alan and Barbara Rawsthorne III* (1967; whereabouts unknown) on the cover.[7] (**204**) Unusually, however, the booklet opened to show reproductions not by Isabel, but *of* her – a detail of the head of Bacon's *Portrait of Isabel Rawsthorne Standing in a Street in Soho* and of Giacometti's *Tête d'Isabel I* (photographed by John Blake). Bacon's conspicuous presence at the opening of the exhibition and the catalogue reminds us that *Isabel Lambert* was his stage, too.

John Russell described the period between 1966 – the year of Giacometti's death and Bacon's exhibition at his gallery, the Galerie Maeght – and 1971 – the year in which he was writing and of Bacon's retrospective at the Grand Palais – as the time when the artist proved himself in the context he considered the supreme test: Paris.[8] The two images published in Isabel's catalogue in 1968 were, correspondingly, presented with contrived symmetry. Giacometti's *Tête d'Isabel* was titled *Head of Isabel Lambert* (as given to it by David Sylvester in the catalogue of Giacometti's Tate exhibition), while Bacon's *Portrait of Isabel Rawsthorne Standing in a Street in Soho* was cropped to a detail that matched the head, neck and hair of the sculpture and given an almost identical description, 'Detail from a portrait of Isabel Lambert'. (**205**) The restless highlights, directional planes, leading chin and rotating sockets shared by the two images draw attention to a stylistic commerce so close that we are forced to ask whether Giacometti's bronze, which Bacon had

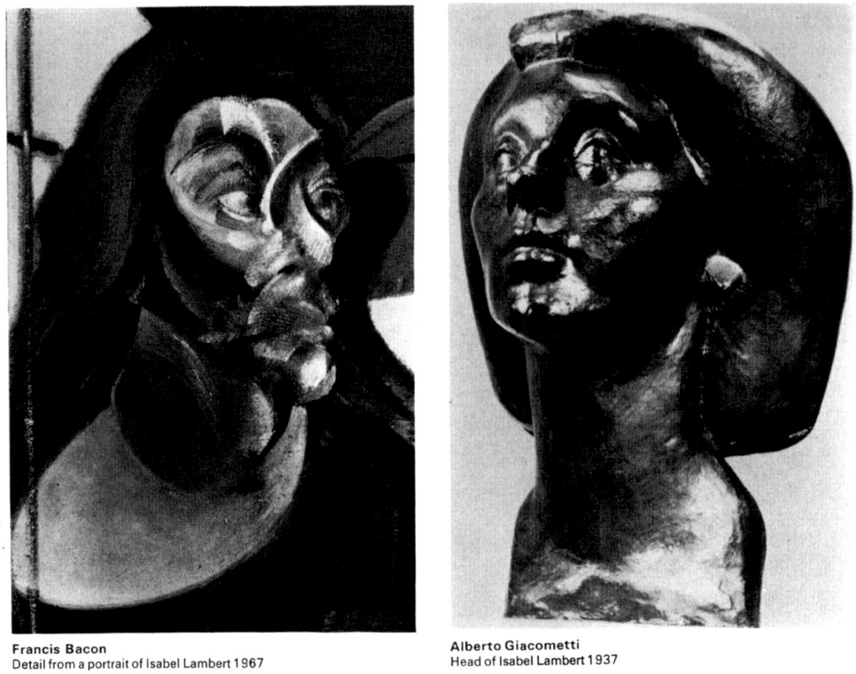

205. Illustration in *Isabel Lambert* catalogue, Marlborough Gallery, 1968

encountered at the Tate Gallery and many times at Isabel's cottage, was a direct source (if not Blake's photograph itself). Thus, the catalogue aligned Bacon with the established, deceased and mythologised older artist, while Isabel, the actual collaborator with both, became only their shared subject matter.

The reproductions of the two portraits might have been a statement of solidarity, something like the reproduction of Bacon's handwritten testimony in the catalogue *Alberto Giacometti: dessins* for the Galerie Claude Bernard, eight years later.[9] The exhibition was, after all, a crystallisation of debates among the three artists. It was read, however, as an equation of the two men as more experienced mentors. Despite the similarity in Isabel's and Bacon's ages compared with that of Giacometti, it was from this date that she was described as their follower: 'Isabel Lambert's paintings reflect the influence of Giacometti and Bacon whose portraits of her appear at the front of her catalogue,' stated *The Times* the day after the exhibition opened (in a review that was, incidentally, headed 'Aitchison's New Paintings', referring only to the concurrent display by Craigie Aitchison).[10] One can imagine Isabel's famous expletives as she read this, or Keith Roberts's even more iniquitous conclusion in *The Burlington Magazine*, that her style was reminiscent of '*Ayrton* and Bacon's' (author's emphasis).[11]

In the London of the late 1960s, excited by everything American, the austere, philosophical, French flavour of Isabel's art (made mainstream now in the work of artists such as Gerhard Richter), was a challenge, but the Marlborough Gallery's archives record many enthusiastic notices for the exhibition, especially from those who had followed Isabel's career since the war – Oswell Blakeston's appreciative article 'Isabel Lambert – Craigie Aitchison', for instance.[12] Yet the Marlborough's director, Harry Fischer, ignored these and her name and her achievements when he wrote to the fifty-six-year-old painter as though she was a novice, commiserating on a 'not very encouraging show' and complimenting her on her 'tenacity' to succeed in the end![13]

More decisive than Isabel's loss of equality, at this time, was the loss of her name. The exhibition was advertised in the press not under the name of the artist, but under the title of Bacon's paintings of her: 'Craigie Aitchison: Recent Paintings and Isabel Rawsthorne: Recent Paintings and Drawings, March 9–April 3'.[14] Just as she had given up Isabel Nicholas in 1934 for Margaret Epstein, so, thirty years later, Isabel Lambert, associated with two decades of work exhibited at the Hanover, ICA and elsewhere, not to mention her reputation for design, was replaced by Isabel Rawsthorne, subject. This designation, perpetuated by the fame of Bacon's paintings, transformed her in the public imagination from artist to model, a profession she had at no time, in fact, embraced. After her failed approach to the Royal Academy at nineteen, she never sought to model for a living. All of Bacon's portraits of her (with the possible exception of one), all of Picasso's portraits and many of Giacometti's were made from memory. Isabel Lambert was, in Martin Harrison's words, 'the model who wasn't there'.[15]

When the Tate Gallery accessioned Bacon's *Isabel Rawsthorne* in 1966, the sitter was described as 'a well-known painter and designer', but the ascending status of Giacometti and Bacon during these decades replaced her professional identity with a mythologised one that represented her exclusively as muse.[16] This was compounded by her colleagues' habit of referring to her without mention of her profession. A description of an interview given by Bacon at his Tate retrospective in 1985 is typical: 'he glances down at *Isabel Rawsthorne*: "In a deformed way it is quite like her. She was a great friend of Giacometti's. A lot of the very early things Giacometti did are about her. Somebody with fantastic vitality."'[17] Even when revealing their affair, after her death, in his last interview to *Paris Match* in 1992, he spoke of her as 'Isabel Rawsthorne, a very beautiful woman who was Derain's model and Georges Bataille's girlfriend.'[18] By the time Isabel died, many obituarists understandably wrote her up as a model, 'one of the most profoundly scrutinised human subjects in western art'.[19] If her work was mentioned, she was 'also' a designer and painter, or just a designer, the pictures barely described and never named, and, astonishingly, this continued in reviews of posthumous exhibitions.[20] Eduardo Paolozzi's introduction to the catalogue to the exhibition *Isabel Rawsthorne: Painting the Ballet* at the Michael Parkin Gallery in July 1998 celebrated her solely as a beauty, and *The Times* notice characterised her as 'the former muse of Picasso and Giacometti'.[21] A display of her wildlife paintings at Oxford University's Museum of Natural History followed the pattern: 'Isabel Rawsthorne, former muse, reveals her concern for ecology.'[22]

Daniel Farson's 1993 book, *The Gilded Gutter Life of Francis Bacon*, and its 1998 off-shoot, the film *Love is the Devil,* fixed in the mind of the public the laughing, shrieking, imbibing Isabel, and the image continued to circulate in most accounts – for example, Henrietta Moraes's 'The Curse of the Drinking Classes' in *The Independent* in 1996.[23] Isabel was fifty-two when Bacon first painted her, but signs of physical maturity were habitually conflated with signs of dissipation and constantly compared with her youth: 'a life of uninhibited exuberance until the onslaught of old age'.[24] In the 1990s, Isabel became, with John Deakin, Henrietta Moraes, Peter Lacy and George Dyer, a Baconian *vanitas*, an exemplar of the always-open mouth, and, sadly, for both artists, Bacon's superbly tender paintings of her came to be perceived as merely illustrations of this.

Even more influential was Lord's bible-sized bestseller, *Giacometti: A Biography,* which, from 1985, was the main account of both Giacometti and Isabel.[25] His interviews with her garnered little more than a titillating and troubling sense of her physical presence, 'threatening but at the same time captivating'.[26] He did not study Isabel's work or have access to her autobiography or the research of recent scholars such as Véronique Wiesinger, who published Isabel and Giacometti's full correspondence in 2007. Relying mainly on gossip, his Isabel was a condensation of sexual myths orientated around the trope of the femme fatale: 'a spectacular beauty. Something exotic, suggesting obscure origins was visible in her full mouth, high cheekbones, and heavy lidded, slanting eyes from which shone forth a gaze of exceptional though remote intensity.' Fantasies of her eastern origin were animated with Giacometti's tigress imagery: 'Tall, lithe, superbly proportioned, she moved with the agility of a feline predator ... a prodigal exuberance, a fierce animal confidence, in her right to do as she pleased.' The famous laugh was amplified into a Siren song: metallic, almost strident ... like music from a strange country played on an unfamiliar instrument, and her laughter was a kind of wild indomitable shriek'. Most damagingly, Lord imagined Isabel's life devoted to selfish pleasure, merely toying with serious (masculine) art: 'Though not herself a true artist, Isabel instinctively understood a great deal about *men* who were' (author's emphasis).[27] Stereotypes of primitivism constructed a creature of instinct rather than intellect that would dominate her reputation for many years.[28]

The perpetuation of reductive ideas about artists' relationship with their human subjects that Isabel and her colleagues did so much to overturn devalues her work and that of all of her peers. Her artistic persona – modern Minoan, *flâneur* (as she styled herself), Cassandra or Harpy – her open-eyed materialist vision and her unparalleled *peinture écriture* were intrinsic to the images she inspired as well as those she made. We are far enough now from the twentieth century to see that the adventures of the figurative avant-garde had the same momentum as abstraction and Surrealism, and, from her late twenties, despite these two trends then holding sway, Isabel was a driving force. Her search for an embodied art and her belief that representation itself was a challenge, not a copy but a meeting with the real, articulated progressive artistic and scientific thought. Isabel's understanding of the art of her time and of the past, especially her years at the heart of dissident Surrealist and Existentialist circles and her studies in Zaria, lent her images exceptional resonance. The unwavering necessity to paint and her prescient instinct for the cutting edge impelled fifty years of innovation. Isabel's role in the careers of two of the figures who most successfully challenged the claim of Surrealism and of abstraction to be the art of modernity – Giacometti and Bacon – was critical. The strength and – with the exception of Jacob Epstein – length of her reciprocal working friendships with these and other great artists, composers and writers of her day were unmatched. To represent her was to represent an artist, and therefore to think about art and how it related to life. It was, with Giacometti especially, part of a broader interrogation of traditional distinctions between artist and subject. She was the subject that looked, and spoke, back, that would dominate his late work.

Thus a broader picture emerges. Since the nineteenth century, individualism has been prized in art, and painters and sculptors have been fastidious in setting themselves apart from all but the most unimpeachable influences, almost always deceased and, without exception, men. Critical and art-historical commentary followed the lead of artists in celebrating singularity. As a result, women artists appear unconnected, they are linked to fathers, teachers and lovers, while their colleagues, disciples and rivals are invisible, or misrepresented as fathers, teachers and lovers. Illustrious careers seem strangely without issue or impact, even, somehow, self-indulgent. Far more important than the effect of this on our understanding of the art of women, however, is the effect on our understanding of the art of the twentieth century as a whole. The erasure of connections has left our picture of twentieth-century culture shockingly incomplete, missing rich, art-historical narratives of men and women, obscure and eminent alike. Isabel's career is a missing link that brings to life some of the most exhilarating international dialogues in twentieth-century art.

ENDNOTES

Where not otherwise indicated, all direct quotations from Isabel Rawsthorne in the main text are from her (unpublished) autobiography; Tate Archive; TGA 9612.2.

INTRODUCTION

1 Email communication with the author, 4 July 2010. I am grateful for the trouble taken by Clifford Frith to recall Isabel; in 1968, Frith was Head of Fine Art at Croydon College of Art.
2 Ibid.
3 *Isabel Lambert*, London: Marlborough Gallery, 8 March–3 April 1968.
4 Notes, undated minutes, ICA Committee for *London–Paris: New Trends in Painting and Sculpture*, 7 March–4 April 1950, cited in James Hyman, *The Battle for Realism: Figurative Art in Britain During the Cold War, 1945–1960*,London and New Haven: Yale University Press, 2001, p. 36.

1 COMING OF AGE IN LIVERPOOL: 1912–1931

1 *Collected Works of Paul Valéry*, 15 vols, Princeton, NJ: Princeton University Press, 1956, vol. 12: *Degas. Manet. Morisot*, trans. D. Paul, p. 6; Valéry's book *Degas, Danse, Dessin*, from which this quotation is taken, was initially published in 1936.
2 Isabel Rawsthorne, 'Unpublished Autobiography', TGA 9612.2, p. 1. Isabel made a strange error, for her father's name was in fact Philip Owen Nicholas; he was born in London 4 October 1879 and died 5 May 1931, and Agnes Christine Nicholas was born in London 1 January 1880 and died in January 1960.
3 Master's Certificate, London 1904, 035361, in 'Index to the Captains' Registers of Lloyd's of London', Guildhall Library, MS 18567, vol. 83, 1904–11.
4 Isabel Rawsthorne, letter to Peter Rose Pulham, [spring] 1952, TGA 9612.1.3.80.
5 Patricia Lambert, 'What I remember about Isabel', notebook, February 1986, private collection, p. 1v.
6 Rawsthorne, 'Autobiographical Notes', TGA 9612.2.4.4.
7 Isabel Rawsthorne, letter to Peter Rose Pulham, 3 July 1949, TGA 9612.1.3.27.
8 Lloyd's 'Captain's Register', London Metropolitan Archives: City of London, CLC/B/148/B/025/MS18569/029, records that Philip Owen Nicholas served as First Mate on the SS *Inkosi*, Official No. 115582, on 09/04/1913 Cape colonies, Ascension, St. Helena, Natal, Algoa Bay, 24/10/1913, 23/04/1914 and 31/07/1914; and the SS *Inkonka*, Official No. 109650, on 24/02/1915, 04/12/1915 and 08/04/1916. My thanks to Bridget Howlett, Senior Archivist, Guildhall Library.
9 Susan Pulvers, in conversation with the author, 27 November 2018; Philip Nicholas, letter to Isabel Nicholas, 18 May 1918, private collection, with thanks to Evelyn Nicholas.
10 Lambert, 'What I remember about Isabel', p. 2.
11 The cousins were Marmaduke and Nevil Lance; one later became an assistant to the pioneer of television, John Logie Baird.
12 Tamarin monkeys are found in Central and South America and the 'hooteah' rodent was probably a hutia, found in the Caribbean.
13 Philip Nicholas, letter to Isabel Nicholas, 18 May 1918, private collection.
14 Evelyn Nicholas, in conversation with Biddy Noakes, 18 August 2011.
15 Now Weatherhead High School, a Media Arts College.
16 Wallasey High School Year Books, 1830/7/12. My thanks to William Meredith Archivist, Wirral Archives Service.
17 Later renamed Liverpool College of Art and now part of Liverpool John Moores University.
18 Warwick Nicholas, correspondence with the author, 15 May 2009.
19 Colin Morris, 'History of Liverpool Regional College of Art, 1825–1970', MPhil. dissertation, Liverpool Polytechnic, 1985, p. 114.
20 Admissions Records, Liverpool School of Art, Special Collections and Archives, Liverpool John Moores University. My thanks to Emily Parsons.
21 Katy Deepwell, *Women Artists Between the Wars: 'A fair field and no favour'*, Manchester: Manchester University Press, 2010, p. 64.
22 D. H. Lawrence, *The Rainbow*, London: Methuen and Co., 1915, and London: Martin Secker, 1926; *Women in Love*, New York: Thomas Seltzer,

1920, and London: Martin Secker, 1921.
23 Her height is confirmed in her passport when she was Isabel Delmer (passport 31765, TGA 9612.2.12).
24 Biddy Noakes, in conversation with the author, November 2007.
25 Morris, 'History of Liverpool College', p. 129.
26 George Marples and Anne Marples, *Sea Terns or Sea Swallows: Their Habits, Language, Arrival and Departure,* London: Country Life, 1934.
27 'George Marples', obituary, *The Times*, Saturday, 23 December 1939, p. 8.
28 Morris, 'History of Liverpool College', p. 126.
29 Ibid., p. 117.
30 Typical up to the Second World War; see Deepwell, *Women Artists Between the Wars*, p. 50. At Liverpool, they remained segregated until 1939 (Morris, 'History of Liverpool College', p. 124, n. 4).
31 Morris, 'History of Liverpool College', p. 131.
32 James Fenton, *School of Genius: A History of the Royal Academy of Arts*, London: Royal Academy of Arts, 2006, p. 256.
33 N. Harrison, 'These Hallowed Halls or what would matron say!', *Maze* (Liverpool College of Art Journal), June 1951.
34 John Keates, interview with Colin Morris, in 'History of Liverpool College', p. 124.
35 William Stevenson, interview with Colin Morris, in 'History of Liverpool College, p. 126.
36 Ibid., pp. 129–30.
37 Walter Sickert, 'Stone Ginger', *The New Age*, 19 March 1914; reproduced *Walter Sickert: The Complete Writings on Art*, ed. Anna Gruetzner Robins, Oxford: Oxford University Press, 2000, p. 345.
38 *Metropolis* (1927) was on general release after its London premiere at the Marble Arch Pavilion, 21 March 1927.
39 Sandon Studios, Executive Committee Minutes, 22 September 1924, Liverpool Record Office, MS 367 SAN 1.4.7.
40 See Roderick Bisson, *The Sandon Studios Society and the Arts*, Liverpool: Parry Books, 1965; Peter Richmond, *Marketing Modernisms: The Architecture and Influence of Charles Reilly*, Liverpool: Liverpool University Press, 2001, p. 73.
41 *Isabel Lambert*, London: Marlborough Gallery, 8 March–3 April 1968, n.p.
42 David Getsy, *Rodin: Sex and the Making of Modern Sculpture*, New Haven and London: Yale University Press, 2011, p. 180.
43 See Carol Duncan, 'Virility and Male Domination in Early Twentieth-Century Vanguard Art', in *Feminism and Art History*, ed. Norma Broude and Mary Garrard, New York: Harper and Row, 1982, pp. 293–313; this idea is developed in detail in Lynda Nead, *The Female Nude: Art, Obscenity and Sexuality*, London: Routledge, 1992.
44 Elizabeth Wilson, *Bohemians: The Glamorous Outcasts,* London: I. B. Tauris and Co., 2000, pp. 100–3.
45 Emily Jones, 'The Establishment of Voluntary Family Planning Clinics in Liverpool and Bradford, 1926–1960: A Comparative Study', *Social History of Medicine*, vol. 13, August 2010.
46 Margaret Mead, *Coming of Age in Samoa: A Psychological Study of Primitive Youth for Western Civilisation*, London: William Morrow and Company, 1928, pp. 106, 109.
47 Virginia Woolf, *A Room of One's Own*, London: Hogarth Press, 1929.
48 See, for example, H. G. Wells's tale of a woman student, *Anne Veronica*, London: T. Fisher Unwin, 1909; Radclyffe Hall, *Well of Loneliness*, London: Jonathan Cape, 1928.
49 Dora Russell, *Hypatia: or, Women and Knowledge,* London: Kegan Paul, Trench, Trubner and Co. Ltd., 1925; Bertrand Russell, *Marriage and Morals*, New York: Horace Liveright, 1929, published in England the following year, London: George Allen and Unwin. 1930. In 1924, Dora Russell set up the Workers' Birth Control Group with Katharine Glasier, Susan Lawrence, Margaret Bonfield, Dorothy Jewson and H. G. Wells.
50 Norman Haire, ed., *Sexual Reform Congress, London 8–14. IX. 1929, WLSR World League for Sexual Reform: Proceedings of the Third Congress*, London: Kegan Paul, 1930.
51 Corinna MacNeice, in conversation with the author, 10 April 2011; Bertrand Russell, *A History of Western Philosophy and Its Connection with Political and Social Circumstances from the Earliest Times to the Present Day*, New York: Simon and Schuster, 1945.
52 Henry Moore Archive, Perry Green, 1997.52.
53 Jacob Epstein, *Epstein: An Autobiography*, 2nd edition, with an introduction by Richard Buckle, London: Art Treasures Book Club, 1963, p. 139.
54 'Jacob Epstein's Genesis', *Liverpool Echo*, 20 May 1931; Bisson, *The Sandon Studios Society*, p. 174.
55 D. H. Lawrence, *Lady 'Chatterley's Lover,* Florence: Tipografia Giuntina, 1928. The novel was banned in the United Kingdom until 1960, but available in a private edition (London: Mandrake Press, 1929).

2 TACTILE EDUCATION: 1929–1933

1 Warwick Nicholas, in correspondence with the author, 15 May 2009; Dawn Littler and Sarah Starkey, 'T. and J. Harrison Ltd', Liverpool: National Museums of Liverpool, 2006, MMM.2005.59.
2 Principal, Liverpool College of Art [probably Henry Huggill], letter to Agnes Nicholas, 10 July 1930, Book 6, January 1930, Special Collections and Archives, Liverpool John Moores University, p. 12.
3 Warwick Nicholas, in correspondence with the author, 15 May 2009.
4 Principal, Liverpool College of Art, Henry Huggill, letter to Agnes Nicholas, 7 July 1931, Book 12, January 1931–20 January 1932, Special Collections and Archives, Liverpool John Moores University, p. 487.
5 My thanks to John Winrow, Assistant Curator, National Museums Liverpool, for this information from the Harrison Archive.
6 Warwick Nicholas, in correspondence with the author, 15 May 2009.
7 Attendance Records, Royal Academy Library; my thanks to Elizabeth King, Research Assistant.
8 H. Cliff Morgan, 'The Schools of the Royal Academy', *British Journal of Educational Studies*, vol. 21, no. 1, February 1973, p. 100.

9 James Fenton, *School of Genius: A History of the Royal Academy of Arts*, London: Royal Academy of Arts, 2006, p. 258.
10 Terry Friedman, '*The Hyde Park Atrocity*'. *Epstein's Rima: Creation and Controversy*, Leeds: The Henry Moore Centre and Leeds City Art Galleries, 1988.
11 Richard Cork, 'Image from Stone: Epstein as Carver', in *Jacob Epstein: Sculpture and Drawings*, ed. Evelyn Silber and Terry Friedman, Leeds: Henry Moore Foundation, Leeds City Art Gallery and Whitechapel Art Gallery, 1987, p. 28.
12 Rawsthorne, 'Autobiographical Notes', TGA 9612.2.4.8–9.
13 *Paintings by Richard Sickert*, London: Beaux Arts Gallery, April–May 1932.
14 Alfred Gilbert, *The Angel of Christian Charity* (1892–3), known as 'Eros', was the statue at the top of the Shaftsbury Memorial Fountain (1885–93).
15 Rawsthorne, 'Autobiographical Notes', TGA 9612.2.4.8–9.
16 Mervyn Peake (1911–1968) exhibited at the Chat Noir, Old Compton Street, in 1931, the Regal Restaurant, December 1931–January 1932, and Wertheim Gallery, 3–23 January 1932, as the 'Twenties Group'.
17 Sir Peter Markham Scott (1909–1989); see Peter Scott, *The Eye of the Wind* (1961), revised edition, London: Brockhampton Press, 1964, pp. 73–6.
18 Royal Academy Library; my thanks to Elizabeth King, Research Assistant.
19 'Frances Margaret Bruce', *The Times*, 28 January 1933, p. 14.
20 Attendance Records, Royal Academy Library; my thanks to Elizabeth King, Research Assistant.
21 Martin Postle, 'Naked Civil Servants: The Professional Life Model in British Art and Society', in *Model and Supermodel: The Artist's Model in British Art and Culture*, ed. Jane Desmarais, Martin Postle and William Vaughan, Manchester: Manchester University Press, 2006, pp. 19–20.
22 There are several reminiscences of this event, for example, Stephen Gardiner, *Epstein: Artist against the Establishment*, London: Flamingo, 1993, p. 325.
23 Gardiner, *Epstein*, p. 316.
24 *Recent Paintings by Matthew Smith*, London: Arthur Tooth and Sons, April 1932; 'Mr Matthew Smith Art Exhibition', *The Times*, Friday, 8 April 1932, p. 19.
25 Emlyn Williams sat for Epstein in 1932, around the time Isabel arrived: *Emlyn: An Early Autobiography, 1927–1935*, Harmondsworth: Penguin, 1976, p. 263.
26 Henry Moore, 'Jacob Epstein', *Sunday Times*, 25 August 1959, quoted in *Henry Moore: Writings and Conversations*, Berkeley: University of California Press, 2002, pp. 149–50. Moore came into Epstein's sphere of influence in the 1920s. For Epstein on Donatello's realism, see Jacob Epstein and Arnold L. Haskell, *The Sculptor Speaks: Jacob Epstein to Arnold L. Haskell, a Series of Conversations on Art*, London: Heinemann, 1931, p. 124.
27 Penelope Curtis, 'How Direct Carving Stole the Idea of Modern British Sculpture', in *Sculpture and the Pursuit of a Modern Ideal in Britain, c.1880–1930*, ed. David Getsy, London: Ashgate, 2004, p. 302.
28 Charles Harrison, *English Art and Modernism*, 1981, New Haven and London: Yale University Press, 1994, pp. 207–11.
29 For an analysis of the social focus of criticism, see Anne Wagner, *Mother Stone: The Vitality of Modern British Sculpture*, New Haven and London: Yale University Press, 2005, pp. 221–30.
30 Paul Nash, *Weekend Review*, 18 April 1931, quoted in Epstein and Haskell, *The Sculptor Speaks*, p. xii; Auguste Rodin, *L'Art: Entretiens réunis par Paul Gsell*, Paris: Bernard Grasset, 1911.
31 William Gaunt, 'Jacob Epstein and the Old Testament', *The Studio*, 1932, vol. 103, pp. 290–1.
32 Gardiner, *Epstein*, pp. 152–4; Jo Digger, New Art Gallery, Walsall, conversation with Jackie Epstein reported to the author July 2010.
33 Silber and Friedman, *Jacob Epstein*, p. 181.
34 Roshan McClenahan, the niece of Amina Peerbhoy, in conversation with the author, July 2011.
35 Gardiner, *Epstein*, pp. 261–3; Cressida Connolly, *The Rare and the Beautiful: The Lives of the Beautiful*, London: Harper Perrenial, 2004, p. 91.
36 Sunita continued to model for Smith until 1933, before returning to her family in India. Shortly afterward she died (Alice Keene, *The Two Mr Smiths: The Life and Work of Matthew Smith*, London: Lund Humphries, 1995, p. 53).
37 June Rose, *Demons and Angels: A Life of Jacob Epstein*, London: Carroll and Graf, 2002, p. 186.
38 Jacob Epstein, *Let There be Sculpture: An Autobiography*, London: Michael Joseph Ltd., 1940, p. 376; Evelyn Silber, *The Sculpture of Jacob Epstein, with a Complete Catalogue*, Oxford: Oxford University Press, 1986, no. 221.
39 Richard Buckle, *Jacob Epstein: Sculptor*, London: Faber and Faber, 1963, p. 194; the Nefertiti 'mask' is discussed in detail in Jacob Epstein, *Epstein: An Autobiography*, 1955, London: Beaverbrook Newspapers, 1963, pp. 192–3.
40 Charles Baudelaire, 'Le Peintre de la vie moderne' (The Painter of Modern Life), *Le Figaro*, November–December, 1863.
41 An acknowledged shared trait between Rodin and Epstein; see, for example, 'Leicester Galleries: Recent Sculpture by Jacob Epstein', *Burlington Magazine*, March 1920, no. 204, vol. 36, p. 146.
42 Epstein, *Let There be Sculpture*, pp. 77–8.
43 Mrs Triefus might be Fanny Ettlinger, of the French jewellery family, Ettlinger and Triefus, who married Edward Triefus
44 *Isobel Nicholas: Animal Studies*, London: Valenza Gallery, 23 May–10 June 1933; according to Isabel, the gallery was run by Arnold Haskell; 'Epstein's Model-Artist and her Beasts', *Sketch*, 17 May 1933.
45 *Wild Fowl by Peter Scott*, London: Ackerman Galleries, July 1933.
46 'London Notes, Contemporary Paintings, Some Notable Works', *Scotsman*, 29 May 1933, p. 15.
47 'Animal Studies from the Zoo', *The Times*, 24 May 1933, p. 14.
48 Deepwell, *Women Artists between the Wars*, pp. 263–4; comments on Eileen Agar, Katherine Hale and

Doris Chapman in 'Bloomsbury Gallery', *The Times*, Wednesday, 12 April 1933, p. 10, are an exactly contemporary example.

49 Rawsthorne, Sketchbook 3, TGA 1 9612.3.3.12v.

50 Also, the bison incised on a pebble, Palaeolithic, British Museum, AN183516001.

51 For example, Gaudier-Brzeska, *Bison*, c. 1913, British Museum 1931,0214.50; a collection of his animal sketches entered the Tate Gallery in 1930.

52 Georges Bataille, 'L'Art primitif', *Documents*, vol. 2, no. 7, 1930, p. 394.

53 Amédée Ozenfant, *Art*, Paris: Budry, 1928; *The Foundations of Modern Art*, trans. John Rodker (1928), New York: Brewer, Warren and Putnam, 1931, pp. xiii–xv, 185–6.

54 Epstein's list is interesting as a formative influence on Isabel: 'Walter Sickert, Matthew Smith, Gertler, Meninsky, Ginner, Gore, Gilman, Wyndham Lewis, Roberts, Karlowska, and Bevan; also Gaudier and myself as sculptors' (*Let There be Sculpture*, p. 217).

55 Epstein purchased this work at the St Georges Gallery in 1930; *The Times*, 27 June 1930, p. 12.

56 *Paintings by Renoir, Derain, Modigliani, Utrillo, Laurencin, Soutine*, London: Cooling Gallery, February 1932; Soutine's work could also be viewed in black and white in Waldemar George, *Soutine*, Paris: Éditions Le Triangle, 1928.

57 Bassani and McLoad, 'The Passionate Collector', p. 12.

58 L. B. Powell, unpublished reminiscence, March 1983, in Silber and Friedman, *Jacob Epstein*, p. 2.

59 Gardiner, *Epstein*, p. 325; Isabel's passport records that she travelled on 6 February 1934 under her maiden name, Nicholas (passport 188547, TGA 9612.2.12.5).

60 *Picasso, Renoir, Manet, Cézanne, Matisse etc*, London: French Gallery, March–April 1933; also, *French Paintings: Ingres to Cézanne*, London: Alex Reid and Lefevre Gallery, July 1933.

61 'The Mayor Gallery', *The Times*, 13 October 1933, p. 12.

62 Née Florence Chuter (Andrew Motion, *The Lamberts: George Constant Lambert and Kit*, London: Faber and Faber, 1986, p. 187).

63 Constant Lambert's father, George Lambert, was a Russian-Australian painter and Associate of the Royal Academy, London; his brother, Maurice Lambert, was a sculptor. Lambert's biographer, Richard Shead confirms that Isabel met Lambert in 1932, 'when she was 20' (Shead, *Constant Lambert*, London: Simon, 1973, p. 151). Neither Epstein's nor Lambert's biographies mention the other by name except in relation to Isabel. However, the two men almost certainly met each other in 1926, when Epstein was involved in Lambert's musical circle (Epstein, *An Autobiography*, p. 116). According to Shead, they came together through the Sitwell family, who were living on Glebe Place (*Constant Lambert*, p. 43). The strongest connection between the two men in the early 1930s was Arnold Haskell, a close collaborator with Epstein, as both dealer and biographer, and with Lambert through the Carmargo Society ballet company (Motion, *The Lamberts*, pp. 182–3).

64 According to Ninette de Valois, quoted in Shead, *Constant Lambert*, p. 9.

65 Rawsthorne, 'Autobiographical Notes', TGA 9612.2.4.13.

66 Epstein, *Let There be Sculpture*, p. 142.

67 Rose, *Demons and Angels*, p. 188.

68 Epstein's *Portrait of Meum* (1917) was criticised when it was exhibited at the Grosvenor Gallery (*The Times*, 18 April 1917, p. 11).

69 Epstein records that there were fifty in his memoir, *Let There be Sculpture*, p. 376.

70 See also 'The Mayor Gallery', *The Times*, 13 February 1934, p. 10.

71 'Art Exhibition: Mr Jacob Epstein', *The Times*, 8 December 1933, p. 12.

72 'Art and Artists: A Study in Contrasts', *Observer*, 4 February 1934, p. 12.

3 SAVAGE SOPHISTICATION: 1933

1 *Daily Mirror*, 8 May 1933, p. 9.

2 *Jacob Epstein: 'Primeval Gods' and Other New Carvings and Bronzes*, London: Leicester Galleries, opened 27 April 1933.

3 Evelyn Silber, *The Sculpture of Jacob Epstein, with a Complete Catalogue*, Oxford: Oxford University Press, 1986, no. 232; 'Isobel' by Jacob Epstein bought by J. W. Freshfield, Wyndham Club, St James' Square, see *Mapping the Practice and Profession of Sculpture in Britain and Ireland 1851–1951*, University of Glasgow History of Art and HATII, online database 2011 [http://sculpture.gla.ac.uk/view/object.php?id=msib6_1207663611, accessed 18 Jul 2019].

4 'London Notes, Contemporary Paintings, Some Notable Works', *Scotsman*, 29 May 1933, p. 15.

5 'Isobel –Wallasey Girl who sat to Epstein', *Wallasey News*, n.d., 1933, clipping, private collection.

6 Lynda Nead surveys the conflation of artistic and sexual practice in attitudes to life studies in *The Female Nude: Art, Obscenity and Sexuality*, London: Routledge, 1992, pp. 50–52; Anne Wagner analyses this with special attention to Epstein's *Genesis* in *Mother Stone: The Vitality of Modern British Sculpture*, New Haven and London: Yale University Press, 2005, pp. 224–5.

7 Richard Buckle, *Jacob Epstein: Sculptor*, London: Faber and Faber, 1963, p. 209; for an overt example, see James Lord's comment on Epstein in *Giacometti: A Biography*, New York: Farrar, Straus and Giroux, 1986, p. 209: 'care for tactile attributes sometimes led the sculptor's hand to stray from the model's effigy to her person'.

8 David Getsy, *Rodin: Sex and the Making of Modern Sculpture*, New Haven and London: Yale University Press, 2011, p. 12.

9 'At daybreak this sign of his amorous embraces was discovered, a sign which ever since has marked the goddess', Pseudo-Lucian, *Erōtes*, trans. Austin Harmon, in *Lucian: Dialogues of the Dead; Dialogues of the Sea-Gods; Dialogues of the Gods; Dialogues of the Courtesans*. Loeb Classical Library

No. 431, Cambridge, MA: Harvard University Press, 1921, vol. 3, 1921, verses 15–16. The pairing of 'Genesis' and 'Exodus' suggests an ironic reference is being made to Epstein's Jewish background.
10 And 'aggressively sexual' (Evelyn Silber and Terry Friedman, eds, *Jacob Epstein: Sculpture and Drawings*, Leeds: Henry Moore Foundation, Leeds City Art Gallery and Whitechapel Art Gallery, 1987, pp. 247, 252); see also Lord, *Giacometti*, p. 162: 'a feline predator … a fierce animal confidence'.
11 Auguste Rodin, *L'Art: Entretiens réunis par Paul Gsell*, Paris: Bernard Grasset, 1911, p. 149, photograph by Eugène Druet; translation by author.
12 June Rose, *Demons and Angels: A Life of Jacob Epstein*, London: Carroll and Graf, 2002, p. 190.
13 Ezio Bassani and Malcolm McLeod, *Jacob Epstein: Collector,* Milan: Associazione Poro, 1987, p. 267; Ezio Bassani and Malcolm D. McLeod, 'The Passionate Collector', in Silber and Friedman, *Jacob Epstein*, p. 13.
14 Epstein, *Let There be Sculpture*, London: Michael Joseph Ltd., 1940, p. 191
15 Buckle, *Jacob Epstein*, p. 209.
16 Reproduced in Arthur Evans, *The Palace of Minos: A Comparative Account of the Successive Stages of the Early Cretan Civilization as illustrated by the Discoveries at Knossos*, London: MacMillan and Co., 5 vols, 1921–36, vol. 3 (1930), pp. 125–9, figs 305, 318.
17 Cathy Gere, *Knossos and the Prophets of Modernism*, Chicago: University of Chicago Press, 2009, pp. 125–32; Evelyn Waugh, *Labels: A Mediterranean Journal,* London: Duckworth, 1930, p. 228.
18 *Minotaure*, ed. André Breton and Pierre Mabille, Geneva: Albert Skira, 1933–9.
19 Gere, *Knossos and the Prophets of Modernism*, pp. 125–32; Waugh, *Labels*, pp. 143.
20 Gere, *Knossos and the Prophets of Modernism*, pp. 125–32; Waugh, *Labels*, p. 137.
21 Evans, *The Palace of Minos,* vol. 3, pp. 117–18, plate. 17.
22 Gere, *Knossos and the Prophets of Modernism*, p. 202.
23 Ibid., pp. 86–7; Jane Harrison, 'The Making of the Goddess', in *Prolegomena to the Study of Greek Religion*, Cambridge: Cambridge University Press, 1903, revised 1922.
24 T. S. Eliot, 'Ulysses, Order, and Myth', *The Dial*, November 1923, reprinted in *Selected Prose of T. S. Eliot*, London: Faber and Faber, 1975, pp. 177–8.
25 Rawsthorne, 'Autobiographical Notes', TGA 9612.2.4.34.
26 'London Notes, Contemporary Paintings, Some Notable Works', *Scotsman*, 29 May 1933, p. 15.
27 Admissions Records, Liverpool School of Art, Special Collections and Archives, Liverpool John Moores University; my thanks to Emily Parsons.
28 Jacob Epstein and Arnold L. Haskell, *The Sculptor Speaks: Jacob Epstein to Arnold L. Haskell, a Series of Conversations on Art*, London: Heinemann, 1931, pp. 94–6.
29 Richard Cork, 'Image from Stone: Epstein as Carver', in Silber and Friedman, *Jacob Epstein*, p. 30.
30 André Derain, quoted in Gaston Diehl, *Peintres d'aujourd'hui: Les Maîtres*, Paris: Charpentier 1943, pp. 9–10: 'Art is, and will always be, the memory of generations'.
31 Lotte H. Eisner, *L'Écran démoniaque: Les Influences de Max Reinhardt et de l'expressionnisme,* Paris: André Bonne, 1952, p. 300.

4 INVISIBLE OBJECT: 1934

1 June Rose, *Demons and Angels: A Life of Jacob Epstein*, London: Carroll and Graf, 2002, p. 190.
2 Patricia Lambert, 'What I remember about Isabel', notebook, February 1986, private collection, p. 2 facing.
3 Anne Wagner, *Mother Stone: The Vitality of Modern British Sculpture*, New Haven and London: Yale University Press, 2005, p. 6.
4 Biddy Noakes, in conversation with the author, November 2007; see also Lambert, 'What I remember about Isabel', p. iv.
5 Cressida Connolly, *The Rare and the Beautiful: The Lives of the Beautiful*, London: Harper Perrenial, 2004, pp. 43–4.
6 Margaret Epstein employed male butler/cook/house-parlourmen, *The Times*, 17 January 1933, p. 4; Connolly *The Rare and the Beautiful*, pp. 90, 108.
7 Purchased, Redfern Gallery, London, 1957.
8 Elizabeth Wilson, *Bohemians: The Glamorous Outcasts,* London: I. B. Tauris and Co., 2000, pp. 85–6.
9 According to Peggy Jean Epstein, quoted in Rose, *Demons and Angels*, p. 190.
10 Jacob Epstein, letter to Kathleen Garman, October 1927, quoted in Connolly, *The Rare and the Beautiful,* pp. 95–7. See the account books of the Redfern Gallery for the prices paid to Isabel.
11 Edinburgh Weavers, founded 1929, with Alastair Morton as its director, pioneered avant-garde, artist-designed textiles; Paul Nash was one of their designers.
12 Warwick Nicholas, in correspondence with the author, 15 May 2009.
13 Rose, *Demons and Angels*, pp. 190–91.
14 Connolly, *The Rare and the Beautiful*, p. 45.
15 Jo Digger reports that Jackie Epstein was informed about Isabel in 1988; this was a few years after James Lord published gossip from Isabel's circle in *Giacometti: A Biography*, New York: Farrar, Straus and Giroux, 1986, pp. 162–3.
16 Felix Man (Hans Baumann), *Hewlett Johnson; Sir Jacob Epstein*, bromide print, c. 1940, National Portrait Gallery, London, NPG P15.
17 Epstein, *Let There be Sculpture*, p. 103.
18 Two of the many examples are *A Babe* (1935) and *First Portrait of Jackie: Bust with Arms* (1935), see Evelyn Silber, *The Sculpture of Jacob Epstein, with a Complete Catalogue*, Oxford: Oxford University Press, 1986, nos. 260, 261.
19 *In My Liverpool Home* (1962), written by Peter McGovern and recorded by The Spinners (*Quayside Songs Old and New*, 1963).
20 Recalled by her daughter, Corinna MacNeice, in conversation with the author, 10 April 2011.

5 EXPENSIVE EDUCATION: 1935–1936

1 Carol Jacobi, 'Muse und Malerin: Isabel Lambert 1912–1992', in *Alberto Giacometti: 'Die Frau auf dem Wagen' Triumph und Tod*, ed. Véronique Wiesinger and Gottlieb Leinz (Wilhelm Lehmbruck Museum, Duisberg, and Fondation Alberto et Annette Giacometti, Paris), Munich: Hirmer Verlag, 2010, p. 140.
2 Sefton Delmer, *Trail Sinister: An Autobiography*, vol. 1, London: Secker and Warburg, 1961, p. 242.
3 National Museums of Northern Ireland Online Collection notes, for Jacob Epstein, *Ahmed* (1932), Ulster Museum, BELUM-U966; the prophet-like bust *Ahmed* is very different from his images of Isabel – a long serious face, muscular neck and body swathed in folds. It was exhibited with both busts of Isabel at the Leicester Galleries in 1933.
4 Delmer, *Trail Sinister*, p. 241.
5 Ibid., p. 243
6 Isabel Delmer, passport, TGA 9612.2.12.1.
7 Delmer, *Trail Sinister*, p. 251.
8 Ibid,, p. 243. The 'Soho Murder' of an international smuggler, Max Kassel ('Red Max'), was perpetrated on 24 January 1936 by ex-convict Charles Lacroix, alias Robert Vernon, accompanied by Suzanne Bertron, alias Mrs Naylor. They were tried in Paris in April 1936.
9 Warwick Nicholas, in correspondence with the author, 15 May 2009.
10 Isabel Rawsthorne, three letters to Agnes Nicholas, Paris, undated (1937–8), private collection.
11 Chris Bryant, 'Warwick Llewellyn Nicholas, 3 April 1926–5 May 2010', *Newsletter of the Australian Society for Parasitology*, vol. 21, no. 3, August 2010, p. 3; also Colet Court Archives (my thanks to the archivist, Valérie Nolk).
12 George Bernard Shaw's *Pygmalion: A Romance in Five Acts* (1912) was inspired by a previous generation of artists' cultivation of working-class models.
13 Delmer, *Trail Sinister*, p. 243.

6 LA PARISIENNE: 1934–1937

1 Rawsthorne, 'Autobiographical Notes', TGA 9612.2.1.48
2 Patricia Lambert, 'What I remember about Isabel', notebook, February 1986, private collection, p. 2. Six images of Isabel, all signed but not dated, appear in Michel Kellermann, *André Derain: Catalogue raisonné de l'œuvre peint (1935–1954)*, Paris: Édition Galerie Schmit, 1992, vol. 3: no. 1930, *Portrait de femme*, 1935–6, oil on canvas, 38.7 × 32 cm, Musée des Beaux-Arts de Lyon; no. 1707 (titled *Portrait of Madam Isabel Daimler*), *Portrait de Madame Isabel Delmer*, 1936, oil on canvas, 33 × 24.2 cm, private collection; no. 1823, *Isabel Lambert*, 1936, oil on canvas, 77 × 74 cm, North Carolina Museum of Art; no. 1824, *La Tasse de thé*, 1934–9, oil on canvas, 92 × 74 cm, Musée national d'art moderne, Centre Georges Pompidou; no. 1826, *La Jeune Anglaise*, 1934–9, oil on canvas, 84 × 73cm, private collection; no. 1822, *Isabel Rawsthorne assise dans l'atelier de l'artiste*, 1935–6, oil on canvas, 46.5 × 51 cm, Musée d'art moderne, Troyes, donation Pierre et Denise Lévy. A large red crayon drawing, *Portrait de Femme Isobel Lambert?*, 60 × 43 cm, was advertised for sale in *The Times* in 1976; the advert also mentions 'others', but gives only a telephone number – 01 946 0706 ('Saturday Bazaar', *The Times*, 15 May 1976, p. 13).
3 According to Patricia (Pattie) Lambert, Isabel's closest friend, Giacometti watched Isabel for a year (Lambert, 'What I remember about Isabel', p. 2v).
4 Isabel Rawsthorne, Autobiographical Note, c. 1970, private collection, p. 1; this note has only recently come to light and was possibly prepared for James Lord, who visited Isabel at about this time, but kept because it had sketches on the back. It contributes to the evidence put forward by Véronique Wiesinger that Isabel began speaking to Giacometti much sooner after her arrival in September 1934 than has hitherto been assumed – spring or autumn 1935 (as Giacometti summered in Switzerland) (Véronique Wiesinger, 'Introduction', in *Alberto Giacometti, Isabel Nicholas: Correspondances*, Paris: Fage Éditions, 2006, p. 31). Pattie Lambert stated that Giacometti watched Isabel for about a year (see note 3 above), which would date the meeting to autumn 1935).
5 *Documents* 6, 1930; Giacometti had a full set in his studio (Rosalind Krauss, *The Originality of the Avant-Garde and Other Modernist Myths*, Cambridge, MA: MIT Press, 1985, p. 60, n. 39).
6 Roger Boutet de Monvel, 'De l'influence des modes sur le mœurs', *Vogue*, 1 April 1922, quoted in Mary Roberts, 'Samson and Delilah Revisited: The Politics of Fashion in 1920s France', in *The Modern Woman Revisited: Paris between the Wars*, ed. Whitney Chadwick and Tirza True Latimer, New Brunswick, NJ: Rutgers University Press, 2003, p. 75.
7 Laurie Wilson, *Albert Giacometti: Myth, Magic, and the Man*, New Haven and London: Yale University Press, 2003, p. 154.
8 Giacometti published and talked about his unheroic sex life: for example, 'Rideau Brun' and 'Hier, sables mouvants', *Le Surréalisme au service de la Révolution*, May 1933, no. 5, pp. 15, 44–5; 'Le Rêve, le Sphinx et la mort de T', *Labyrinthe*, 15 December 1946, no. 22/23, p. 12. According to James Lord, 'He felt constrained to explain repeatedly in public and in private why whores made the most satisfactory mistresses'(*Giacometti: A Biography*, New York: Farrar, Straus and Giroux, 1985, p. 47).
9 Lord, *Giacometti*, p. 194. Lord surveyed many of Giacometti's relationships, as well as his regular engagement of prostitutes (pp. 47–8) and attended again to Giacometti's orchiditis, impotence and homosexual inclinations in the slim volume *Mythic Giacometti*, New York: Farrar, Strauss and Giroux, 2004. In fact, it is almost unknown for orchiditis to cause impotence or sterility (Alfred Evans and Richard Kaslow, *Viral Infections of Humans: Epidemiology and Control*, New York: Springer, 1997, p. 540).
10 James Lord, 'Sudbury Cottage', in *A Gift for Admiration: Further Memoirs*, New York: Farrar, Straus and Giroux, 1998, p. 55.
11 Véronique Wiesinger, 'Isabel and Other Intimate Strangers', in Martin Harrison and Véronique Wiesinger,

Alberto Giacometti, Francis Bacon: Isabel and Other Intimate Strangers, New York: Gagosian Gallery, 2008, pp. 218–19.
12 The descendants of Sefton Delmer sold a bronze described as 'Jacob Epstein *First Portrait of Isobel*, modelled and cast in 1932' at Christies Sale 9242, Twentieth Century British Art, South Kensington, London, 2 November 2001. As there is no mention of this cast in Silber's catalogue, it seems most likely that it is a version related to that exhibited at the Leicester Galleries in 1933, given to Isabel or purchased by Delmer at an early date.
13 Wiesinger, *Correspondances*, p. 31.
14 Véronique Wiesinger ('Isabel and Other Intimate Strangers', in *Alberto Giacometti, Francis Bacon*, p. 218) cites as a source a photograph of Queen Tiyi in Hedwig Fecheimer, *Die Plastik der Ägypter* , Berlin: Bruno Cassirer, 1920.
15 Tal-Coat's real name was Pierre Louis Epstein.
16 Ian Chilvers and John Glaves-Smith, 'Francis Gruber', in *A Dictionary of Modern and Contemporary Art Oxford Reference Online*, Oxford University Press, accessed 25 May 2011.
17 *Germaine Richier*, Paris: Galerie Max Kaganovitch, 1936.
18 *Balthus* at Pierre Loeb's Galerie Pierre, 13–28 April 1934.
19 Kellermann, *André Derain*, vol. 3, no. 1707, where the title is misprinted as *Portrait of Madam Isabel Daimler*; it relates closely to no. 1930.
20 The fresco and Evans's reconstruction were widely reproduced from 1901 onwards; see, for example, Arthur Evans, *The Palace of Minos: A Comparative Account of the Successive Stages of the Early Cretan Civilization as illustrated by the Discoveries at Knossos*, London: MacMillan and Co., 5 vols, 1921–36, vol. 4 (1935), pt. 2, p. 335, fig. 319, pl. XXXIB.
21 The bracelet has been identified as a Chimera or a Naiad; a Naiad or Undine-like figure would seem appropriate given the wave-like form and Isabel's affinity for swimming. Undine's tale of being abandoned by her husband after having his child is also apposite.
22 Biddy Noakes, in conversation with the author, November 2007.
23 Gere, *Knossos and the Prophets of Modernism*, p. 228; *Minotaure*, ed. André Breton and Pierre Mabille, 1933–9; the journal was replaced after the war by *Labyrinth* (1944–6), in reference to the Minotaur's domain. See Theodore Ziolkowski, *Minos and the Moderns: Cretan Myth in Twentieth-Century, Literature and Art*, Oxford: Oxford University press, 2008.
24 The date of this visit was probably the journey recorded in her passport as 12 March–16 April 1937 (TGA 9612.2.12.7).
25 Sarah Wilson, 'Artaud, homo sacer', in *Artaud*, Madrid: La Casa Encendida, 2009, pp. 4–5.
26 Whitney Chadwick and Tirza True Latimer, 'Gender and Sexual Identity after World War I', in *The Modern Woman Revisited*, p. 66; the term became fashionable as a result of Victor Margueritte's best-selling novel, *La Garçonne* (Paris: E. Flammarion, 1922); Cecil Beaton, *The Glass of Fashion*, London: Weidenfeld and Nicholson, 1951, p. 165; Mary Stewart, *Dressing Modern Frenchwomen: Marketing Haute Couture, 1919–1939*, Baltimore: Johns Hopkins University Press, 2008, p. 188.
27 Gere, *Knossos and the Prophets of Modernism*, p. 122; Balthus made sketches of the Minotaur (e.g., *Minotaur and Young Girl*, 1934, private collection).
28 See Alberto Giacometti, *Isabel Reclining*, signed and dated 1940, FAAG.
29 See, for example, Jean-Gabriel Domergue *The Black Venus Portrait of Josephine Baker* (1928), sold Sotheby's Impressionist and Modern Art, New York, 29 September 2007; in the 1930s, the removal of pubic hair was also a standard practice during childbirth (V. Basevi and T. Lavender, 'Routine Perineal Shaving on Admission in Labour', *Cochrane Database of Systematic Reviews*, 2014, issue no. 11).
30 James Lord, quoting Peter Watson, in *Some Remarkable Men*: *Further Memoirs* New York: Farrar, Straus and Giroux, 1996, p. 195. Michael Peppiatt extemporises on the innuendo of Isabel's 'omnivorous sexuality' (*In Giacometti's Studio*, New Haven and London: Yale University Press, 2010, pp. 91, 108).
31 Stewart, *Dressing Modern Frenchwomen*, p. xii.
32 Charles Baudelaire, *The Painter of Modern Life and Other Essays*, trans. Jonathan Mayne, London: Phaidon, 1995, p. 127.
33 Jacob Epstein, 'Introduction' to the catalogue for *An Exhibition of Drawings by Jacob Epstein for 'Les Fleurs du Mal' of Charles Baudelaire*, London: Arthur Tooth and Sons, 1938, n.p.
34 See Peter Wollen, 'The Concept of Fashion in The Arcades Project', *Boundary 2*, Spring 2003, vo.l 30, no. 1, pp. 131–42; Gustave Geffroy, *Constantin Guys: Historian of the Second Empire*, London: The Studio, 1935 (trans. from *Constantin Guys: L'Historien du Second Empire*, Paris: G. Crès, 1920), now in the library of Biddy Noakes.

7 QUESTIONS OF REALISM: 1935–1937

1 Robin Spencer, 'Giacometti's Break with Surrealism: Abstraction, Hegelianism and the Communicating Vase', in *Giacometti: Critical Essays*, ed. Peter Read and Julia Kelly, Aldershot: Ashgate, 2009, pp. 65–6.
2 David Sylvester, *Looking at Giacometti*, London: Chatto and Windus, 1994, p. 140.
3 Reinhold Hohl, *Alberto Giacometti*, Stuttgart: Gerd Hatje, 1971, trans. as *Giacometti: Sculpture, Painting, Drawing*, London: Thames and Hudson, 1972, p. 79.
4 *Les Peintres de la réalité en France au XVIIe siècle*, Paris: Orangerie des Tuileries, November 1934–February 1935; *Cézanne*, Paris: Orangerie des Tuileries, May–October 1936.
5 Poul Erik Tøjner, *Cézanne and Giacometti: Paths of Doubt*, Ostfildern : Hatje Cantz, 2008, pp. 31–2; see, for example, Georges Rivière, *Cézanne: Le Peintre solitaire*, Paris: Librairie Floury, 1933.
6 James Lord, *Giacometti: A Biography*, New York: Farrar, Straus and Giroux, 1986, pp. 26–7.
7 See, for example, Charles Seltman, 'Sculptures archaïques des Cyclades', *Documents*, vol. 1, no. 4, 1929, pp. 188–90.

8 See Carol Jacobi, 'Isabel', in *Derain, Balthus, Giacometti: Une amitié artistique*, ed. Jacqueline Munck, Paris: Musée d'art moderne de la Ville de Paris, 2017, pp. 166–173.
9 Véronique Wiesinger, *Alberto Giacometti, Isabel Nicholas: Correspondances*, Paris: Fage Éditions, 2006, p. 30; Spencer, 'Giacometti's Break with Surrealism'; *The Times*, 13 October 1933, p. 12, for Giacometti's *Sculpture en bois* (1932), exhibited in London at the Mayor Gallery.
10 *Groupe de l'Atelier 17*, Paris: Galerie Pierre Loeb, 13–27 May 1935; Peter Michael Stephan Hacker and Stanley William Hayter, *The Renaissance of Gravure: The Art of S. W. Hayter*, Oxford: Clarendon Press 1988, pp. 99–100.
11 'Art Exhibitions Leicester Galleries', *The Times*, 2 February 1934, p. 10.
12 Stanley Hayter, *New Ways of Gravure*, preface by Herbert Read, London: Routledge and Kegan Paul, 1949, p. 18.
13 Anaïs Nin, *The Diary of Anaïs Nin*, vol. 3: *1939–1944*, ed. Gunther Stuhlmann, New York: Swallow Press, 1969, p. 125; Isabel Rawsthorne, letter to Peter Rose Pulham, 14 July 1946, TGA 9612.1.3.3, and 11 August 1955, TGA 9612.1.3.88.
14 Natalie Adamson and Toby Norris, eds, *Academics, Pompiers, Official Artists and the Arrière-garde: Defining Modern and Traditional in France, 1900–1960* Newcastle: Cambridge Scholars, 2009, p. 8.
15 Toby Norris, 'The Querelle du réalisme and the Politicization of French Artists during the Great Depression', *PART: Journal of Art History at the CUNY Graduate Center*, March 2007, p. 1.
16 Catherine Bernard-Gruber and Armelle Vanazzi, *Francis Gruber*, Paris: Ides et Calendes, 1989, pp. 163–5; see Sarah Wilson, 'Francis Gruber: Espace politique, espace eschatologique', in *Francis Gruber, l'œil à vif*, Nancy: Musée des Beaux-Arts, 2009.
17 'La Querelle du réalisme' debates were held from 16 May to 30 June 1936 at the Maison de la Culture, a communist sponsored cultural organisation led by Louis Aragon.
18 Patricia Lambert, 'What I remember about Isabel', notebook, February 1986, private collection, p. 4; Rawsthorne, 'Autobiography', private collection, p. 3, c. 1970.
19 Isabel Rawsthorne, *Princess Mara Scherbatoff*, Sketchbook 1, TGA 9612.3.1.37, also 9612.2.1.scrap 1A. My thanks to Jacqueline Munck and Anaïs Alax Gazeau for sharing photographs of Scherbatoff: Harry Meerson's 'Princesse Sherbatoff: Hairstyle to the Angel' (1935) and, by an unknown photographer, '"Heure intime": Princesse Scherbatoff' (Vigny Perfumes, 1938), from the collection of the Musée d'art moderne de la Ville de Paris.
20 Jacob Epstein and Arnold L. Haskell, *The Sculptor Speaks: Jacob Epstein to Arnold L. Haskell, a Series of Conversations on Art*, London: Heinemann, 1931, p. 78.
21 Rawsthorne, Sketchbook, TGA 9612.3.3, p. 10.
22 Rawsthorne, 'Autobiographical Notes', TGA 9612.2.4.9.
23 Isabel Rawsthorne, letter to Rose Pulham, 3 July 1949, TGA 9612.1.3.27.
24 Yves Bonnefoy, 'Giacometti: Le Problème des deux époques', *Connaissance des arts*, December 1991, no. 478, pp. 34–5.
25 For example, Giacometti's *D'après Konrad Witz: Saint Barthélemy retable du miroir du salut* (1942' FAAG); Thierry Dufrêne, 'Giacometti's Geneva Period 1941–1945; The Birth of a New Sculpture', in *Giacometti: Critical Essays*, p. 116.
26 Biddy Noakes, in conversation with the author, January 2010.
27 Patrick Elliott, 'Drawings by Alberto Giacometti. Paris', *Burlington Magazine*, May 2001, vol. 143, no. 1178, p. 315.
28 I am grateful to the Fondation Giacometti for drawing to my attention the number and range of Giacometti's drawings of Isabel from life.
29 Véronique Wiesinger, 'Femme au Chariot / Frau auf dem Wagen: Epos und Mythos zugleich', in *Alberto Giacometti: 'Die Frau auf dem Wagen', Triumph und Tod*, ed. Véronique Wiesinger and Gottlieb Leinz (Wilhelm Lehmbruck Museum, Duisberg, and Fondation Alberto et Annette Giacometti, Paris), Munich: Hirmer Verlag, 2010, p. 50.
30 Ibid., p. 54.
31 Laurence de Buzon-Vallet, *Alberto Giacometti: La Collection du Centre Georges Pompidou, Musée national d'art moderne: Saint-Étienne, Musée d'art moderne*, Paris: Centre Pompidou, 1999, p. 122.
32 For example, Pablo Picasso, *Two Women at Rest* (1931), in *Suite Vollard* (1933–7), Paris: Lacourière, 1939.
33 Sickert often exhibited in Paris, for example, in *Trois peintres anglais: R. Walter Sickert, Matthew Smith, Christopher Wood*, Paris: Galerie Bing, 16 June–7 July 1939.
34 Wiesinger, 'Die Frau auf dem Wagen / Frau dem Wagen: Epos und Mythos zugleich', p. 54.
35 Paola Carola, interview with Cristina Carrillo De Albornoz, 'Giacometti Enabled Me to Know Myself Better', *Art Newspaper*, April 2010, no. 223; see also Paola Carola, *Monsieur Giacometti, je voudrais vous commander mon buste*, Paris: Éditions Léo Scheer, 2008.

8 SENSIBLE EDUCATION: 1936–1938

1 The short-lived, government-sponsored *British Gazette* (ed. Winston Churchill, 3–13 May 1926), published when print union strikes had depleted most other newspapers, described riots in Middlesbrough from 4 to 6 May. This accords with Isabel's description of the blast furnaces, which were still burning in the early days of the strike.
2 Sefton Delmer, *Trail Sinister: An Autobiography*, vol. 1, London: Secker and Warburg, 1961, pp. 263–8.
3 Ibid., TGA 9612.2.1.scrap 1A
4 Isabel Delmer, passport, TGA 9612.2.12: stamped for Le Bourget, 24 September 1936.
5 Isabel Delmert passport, TGA 9612.2.12: 19 September 1936.
6 Isabel crossed the Swiss border on 14 September 1937 (Isabel Delmer, passport, TGA 9612.2.12.9-8: stamped for Geneva).
7 Rawsthorne, 'Autobiographical Notes', TGA 9612.2.4, inside front cover.
8 Delmer, *Trail Sinister*, pp. 278–9; Isabel Delmer, passport, TGA 9612.2.12: stamped for Dresden 23 October 1936,

and withdrawals of money are recorded for 26 and 30 October in Dresden: '500 rm 30 October 1936'.

9 Pavillon de l'Espagne, *Exposition internationale des arts et techniques dans la vie moderne*, 25 May–25 November 1937.

10 Confirmed by Reinhold Hohl, *Giacometti: A Biography in Pictures*, Stuttgart: Hatje Cantz, 1998, p. 89; *Balthus: Works and Interviews*, ed. C. Costanzini and M. Bal, Barcelona, 2008, pp. 148–9.

11 Alberto Giacometti, response to the survey 'Ou va la peinture?', *Commune*, no. 22, June 1935, p. 1135; an account of Giacometti's collaborations with Louis Aragon in *La Lutte* in 1932 is given in Leslie Rubin, 'The Lost Years: Alberto Giacometti's Return to Figuration 1932–1937', MA thesis, Courtauld Institute of Art, University of London, 1990.

12 Chris Bryant, 'Warwick Llewellyn Nicholas, 3 April 1926–5 May 2010', *Newsletter of the Australian Society for Parasitology*, vol. 21, no. 3, August 2010, p. 1

13 Warwick Nicholas, email correspondence with the author, 15 May 2009.

14 Isabel Rawsthorne, postcard to Giacometti, n.d. (probably autumn 1937), in Véronique Wiesinger, *Alberto Giacometti, Isabel Nicholas: Correspondances*, Paris: Fage Éditions, 2006, p. 54

15 Published in full by the Fondation Giacometti. Quotations are given here in the author's English translation, and the idiosyncratic style, grammar and vocabulary are not corrected.

16 Isabel Rawsthorne, letter to Giacometti, 8 December (?)1937, in Wiesinger, *Correspondances*, pp. 54–5.

17 Rawsthorne 'Autobiographical Notes', TGA 9612.2.1.55.

18 Ibid., TGA 9612.2.1.34.49.

19 Isabel Delmer, passport, TGA 9612.2.12.14: visa for Spain, 24 December 1937.

20 Isabel Delmer, passport, TGA 9612.2.12.14,18–19: stamped for Barcelona and records of crossing the Aduana de la Junquera, 4 February 1938, 24 February 1938 and 18 March 1938.

21 Delmer, *Trail Sinister*, p. 347.

22 Anaïs Nin, *The Diary of Anaïs Nin*, vol. 2: *1934–1939*, ed. Gunther Stuhlmann, San Diego, New York and London: Harcourt Brace & Company, 1967, p. 125.

23 Delmer, *Trail Sinister*, pp. 337–8.

24 For a survey of Rose Pulham's associates at the end of the 1930s, see Theodora FitzGibbon, *With Love*, London: Century Publishing, 1982, pp. 16–17; also Peter Rose Pulham. 'Living in Paris', *Harper's Bazaar*, 26 July 1939. p. 52.

25 'Why have you that silk frock on, then?' (1933; private collection), illustration for chapter 8 of Emily Brontë's *Wuthering Heights*, published in *Minotaure*, vol. 2, no. 7, 1935, pp. 60–61.This particular work was very well known, since Balthus had remade it as a full painting, *Cathy Dressing* (1933; Pompidou Centre, Paris) and exhibited it at the notorious exhibition *Balthus* at Pierre Loeb's Galerie Pierre, 13–28 April 1934.

26 FitzGibbon, *With Love*, p. 22.

27 Sefton Delmer, *Black Boomerang*, London: Secker and Warburg, 1962, p. 1; Peter Webb, *Sphinx: The Life and Art of Leonor Fini*, New York: Vendome Press, 2009, pp. 58, 161.

28 On the rue Bellechasse; FitzGibbon, *With Love*, p. 69.

29 Ibid., p. 11.

30 Fondly recollected in a letter from Isabel to Rose Pulham, 4 June 1949, TGA 9612.1.3.25.

31 FitzGibbon, *With Love*, p. 141.

32 Isabel Delmer, passport, TGA 9612.2.12.21.

33 Delmer, *Trial Sinister*, pp. 361–2.

34 'eingetraten 13 Juni 1938, commissariat special 15 Juin 1938', written again in red, 8 Oct 1938, Isabel Delmer, passport, TGA 9612.2.12.19–20

35 Delmer, *Trial Sinister*, pp. 361–2.

36 Rawsthorne, 'Autobiographical Notes', TGA 9612.2.4.2; Claud Cockburn, *I, Claud ... The Autobiography of Claud Cockburn* (1956), Harmondsworth: Penguin, 1967, pp. 170–71. It is interesting to note that despite the evidence of Isabel's papers and passports, neither Delmer nor Cockburn mention her presence with them in Czechoslovakia, or acknowledge each other in any part of their autobiographies.

9 UNE PASSANTE: 1937–1940

1 Charles Baudelaire, *The Flowers of Evil*, trans. Cyril Scott, London: Elkin Mathews, 1909, p. 58.

2 Claud Cockburn, *I, Claud ... The Autobiography of Claud Cockburn* (1956), Harmondsworth: Penguin, 1967, p. 173.

3 Jacob Golomb, *In Search of Authenticity: From Kierkegaard to Camus*, London: Routledge, 1995, p. 3. Golomb provides an analysis of the development of these issues.

4 Walter Benjamin, *The Arcades Project* (1955), ed. Rolf Tiedemann, trans. Howard Eiland and Kevin McLaughlin, Cambridge, MA: Belknap Press, 1999, J19, 1; J 22, 1; J21a, 4; J26a, 3; J87a, 6; J90a, 5.

5 Paul Valéry, *Analecta*, Paris: Gallimard, 1935, p. 264, quoted Walter Benjamin, 'Über einige Motive bei Baudelaire', in Walter Benjamin, *Illuminations* (1968), ed. Hannah Arendt, London: Pimlico, 1999, pp. 158; see also Walter Benjamin, *Charles Baudelaire: A Lyric Poet in the Era of High Capitalism*, trans. Harry Zohn, London: New Left Books, 1973, p. 116.

6 Benjamin, 'Über einige Motive bei Baudelaire', pp. 171, 166.

7 Charles Baudelaire, 'The Painter of Modern Life' (1860), in *The Painter of Modern Lifae and Other Essays*, trans. Jonathan Mayne, London: Phaidon, 1995, p. 9.

8 Walter Benjamin, 'Das Paris des Second Empire bei Baudelaire' (1938), in *Charles Baudelaire: A Lyric Poet*, p. 37; for Benjamin's descriptions of the Café de la Régence, see Benjamin, *The Arcades Project*, D2a, 9, D3, 6.

9 Gershom Scholem, 'Walter Benjamin and His Angel', in *On Jews and Judaism in Crisis*, New York: Schocken, 1976, pp. 231–5.

10 Walter Benjamin: *Schriften*, ed. Theodor Adorno and Gretel Adorno, Frankfurt am Main: Suhrkamp, 1955.

11 Alberto Giacometti, interview Pierre Dumayet, *Le Nouveau Candide*, 110, 6–13 June, reprinted in Alberto Giacometti, *Écrits*, Paris: Éditions Hermann, 1990, p. 284; Giacometti, letter to Isabel, 30 July 1945, in Véronique Wiesinger, *Alberto Giacometti, Isabel Nicholas: Correspondances*, Paris: Fage Éditions, 2006, p. 84.

12 Benjamin, 'Das Paris des Second Empire bei Baudelaire', p. 37.
13 Francis Ponge, 'Réflexions sur les statuettes, figures et peintures d'Alberto Giacometti', *Cahier d'arts*, 1952, reprinted in Francis Ponge, *L'Atelier contemporain*, Paris: Gallimard, 1977, p. 177.
14 Janet Wolff, 'Gender and the Haunting of Cities; Or, the Retirement of the Flâneur', in *The Invisible Flâneuse?: Gender, Public Space and Visual Culture in Nineteenth-century Paris*, ed. Aruna D'Souza and Delmer McDonough, Manchester: Manchester University Press, 2006, p. 21; Wolffs's essay refines and updates her seminal publication 'The Invisible Flâneuse: Women and the Literature of Modernity', *Theory, Culture and Society*, 1985, vol. 2, pp. 37–46. Although definitions of the *flâneur* vary and overlap with figures such as the artist, the dandy etc, other voices tend to concur: Griselda Pollock, for example, considers the *flâneur* as 'an exclusively masculine type' ('Modernity and the Spaces of Femininity', in *Vision and Difference: Femininity, Feminism and Histories of Art*, London: Routledge, 1988, p. 67); also Anthony Vidler, 'Bodies in Space/ Subjects in the City: Psychopathologies of Modern Urbanism', *Differences: A Journal of Feminist Cultural Studies*, 1993, vol. 5, no. 3, pp. 31–53. For a summary of the application of the model of the *flâneuse* to practices of performance, fashion and consumption, see Whitney Chadwick, 'Introduction', in *The Modern Woman Revisited: Paris between the Wars*, ed. Whitney Chadwick and Tirza True Latimer, New Brunswick: Rutgers University Press, 2003, p. xix,
15 Isabel Rawsthorne, letter to Rose Pulham, 11 p.m., [March] 1952, TGA 9612.1.3.76.
16 Alex Potts, 'Giacometti and the Basis of Sculpture', in *Giacometti: Critical Essays*, ed. Peter Read and Julia Kelly, Aldershot: Ashgate, 2009, p. 145; Ponge, 'Réflexions sur les statuettes, figures et peintures d'Alberto Giacometti', p. 168; also Jean-Paul Sartre, 'La Recherche de l'absolu', in *Alberto Giacometti: Exhibition of Sculptures, Paintings, Drawings*, New York: Pierre Matisse Gallery, 1948, p. 4 (also published in French in *Les Temps modernes*, 28 January 1948, pp. 1153–63).
17 David Sylvester, *Looking at Giacometti*, London: Chatto and Windus, 1994, pp. 10–11.
18 Alberto Giacometti, quoted in P. Schneider, 'Au Louvre avec Alberto Giacometti', *Preuves*, September 1962, 139, pp. 23–30.
19 Sylvester, *Looking at Giacometti*, p. 100.
20 Alberto Giacometti, *Femme debout* (recto); *Groupe de personnages* (verso), 1946, signed lower right, 'Pour Max Ernst trés affectueusement Alberto Giacometti', graphite and charcoal on paper, 62.7 × 48 cm, sold at Christie's 'Post War and Contemporary' sale, 9 May 2006.
21 Crescenzo, 'Giacometti and the Kauffmann Tomb', p. 101.
22 Benjamin, *The Arcades Project*, J19, 1.
23 Sartre, 'La Recherche de l'absolu', p. 1153.
24 Véronique Wiesinger, *Alberto Giacometti: Una retrospectiva*, Barcelona: Ediciones Poligrafa, 2012, p. 18.
25 Alberto Giacometti, Notebook, summer 1945, FAAG, inv. 2000-0111, I am indebted to Véronique Wiesinger for her analysis of the synthetic nature of Giacometti's figures.
26 Wiesinger, *Correspondances*, p. 34.
27 Véronique Wiesinger, 'Giacometti's *Woman with a Chariot*: Between Epic and Myth', in *Alberto Giacometti: 'Die Frau auf dem Wagen', Triumph und Tod*, ed. Véronique Wiesinger and Gottlieb Leinz (Wilhelm Lehmbruck Museum, Duisberg, and Fondation Alberto et Annette Giacometti, Paris), Munich: Hirmer Verlag, 2010, p. 41. Rawsthorne omitted this story from her autobiography but told it to her friend and editor, Pattie Lambert (Patricia Lambert, 'What I remember about Isabel', notebook, February 1986, private collection, p. 2v).
28 Samuel Beckett was stabbed in the chest by Robert-Jules Prudent, described as a French pimp, while walking home through Paris with friends on the night of 6 January 1938. This was publicised in *Le Figaro* and elsewhere (James Knowlson, *Damned to Fame: The Life of Samuel Beckett*, New York: Grove Press, 1997, pp. 261–2).
29 Car and train crashes were a staple of films from the silent era onwards, for example, Louis Feuillade's *Un accident d'auto* (1907) or Charlie Chaplin's *Sunnyside* (1919); they also made potent plot devices in literature, for example, in E. M. Forster, *Howards End* (London: Edward Arnold, 1910), discussed in Andrew Thacker, 'E. M. Forster and the Motor Car', *Literature and History*, vol. 9, no. 2, Autumn 2000, pp. 37–52; and in F. Scott Fitzgerald, *The Great Gatsby* (New York: Charles Scribner's Sons, 1925).
30 Émile Zola, *La Bête humaine*, Paris: Charpentier, 1890.
31 Jean-Paul Sartre, *Les Mots*, Paris: George Braziller, 1963, pp. 144–5
32 Alberto Giacometti in conversation with Gotthard Jedlicka, 20 March 1964, 'Begegnung mit Giacometti', *Neue Zürcher Zeitung*, 16 January 1966: 'Im übrigen hatte es wieder einmal das Leben übernommen, einen Zustand, der für mich unerträglich geworden war, ohne mein Dazutun in Ordnung zu bringen.'
33 Alberto Giacometti in conversation with Carola Giedion, 19 August 1955, quoted in Reinhold Hohl, *Giacometti: A Biography in Pictures*, Stuttgart: Hatje Cantz, 1998, p. 94.
34 Benjamin, 'Das Paris des Second Empire bei Baudelaire', p. 100; Walter Benjamin, 'These Spaces for Rent', in *Einbahnstraße* (One-Way Street), 1930, reprinted in *One Way Street and Other Writings*, trans. J. Underwood, Harmondsworth: Penguin, 2009, pp. 97–8.
35 Walter Benjamin, 'Der Surrealismus; die letzte Momentaufnahme des europäisches Intelligenz (Surrealism: The Last Snapshot of the European Intelligentsia)', in *Die literarische Welt* (World Literature), vol. 5, nos. 5–7, January–February 1929, reprinted *in One Way Street and Other Writings*, p. 157.
36 Carola Giedion-Welcker, *Moderne Plastik: Elemente der Wirklichkeit; Masse und Auflockerung*, Zürich: H. Girsberger, 1937, p. 18.
37 Benjamin, *The Arcades Project*, H 16; 'Über den Begriff der Geschichte' (On the Concept of History (1940)), *Neue Rundschau*, vol. 61, no. 3, 1950, reprinted in Walter Benjamin, *Illuminations* (1973), ed. Hannah

Arendt, London: Pimlico, 1999, p. 255.
38 James Lord, *Giacometti: A Biography*, New York: Farrar, Straus and Giroux, 1986, pp. 194–5.
39 Probably Daniel Defoe, *Moll Flanders*, trans. Marcel Schwob, Paris: Gallimard, 1934.
40 Abbé Prévost, *Manon Lescaut: L'Histoire du chevalier des Grieux et de Manon Lescaut*, 1731.
41 Alberto Giacometti, in conversation with Gotthard Jedlicka, 20 March 1964, 'Begegnung mit Giacometti,' *Neue Zürcher Zeitung*, 16 January 1966. The account was 29 pages long.
42 Wiesinger confirms that *The Chariot* was an image of Isabel (*Correspondances*, p. 42).
43 Mario Negri, 'Frammenti per Alberto Giacometti', *Domus*, July 1956, reprinted as 'All'ombra della scultura', *Narratori*, no. 78, Milan, 1985, p. 71.
44 Carola Giedion-Welcker, *Modern Plastic Art*, p. 8.
45 Reproduced in, for example, Pierre de La Coste-Messelière, *Delphi*, Paris: ed. du Chêne, École française d'Athènes, 1943.
46 Alberto Giacometti, letter to Pierre Matisse, 29 December 1950–5 January 1951, in *Écrits*, p. 96; see also Gottlieb Leinz, 'Das Bein von Alberto Giacometti: Erinnerungen an den Tod', *Pantheon*, no. 55, 1997.
47 Véronique Wiesinger, 'Die Technik Femme au chariot / Frau auf dem Wagen: Epos und Mythos zugleich', in Wiesinger and Leinz, *Alberto Giacometti: 'Die Frau auf dem Wagen', Triumph und Tod*, ed. Wiesinger and Leinz, p. 41.
48 Peter Rose Pulham, 'Isabel Lambert', in *Isabel Lambert*, London: Hanover Gallery, 1949.
49 Leinz's argument that Giacometti's sculpture was informed by both Classical and Celtic chariots from societies orientated towards female worship suggests that Giacometti was juxtaposing Greek and non-Greek references.
50 Alberto Giacometti, letter to Paul Matisse, in *Alberto Giacometti: Sculptures, Paintings, Drawings*, New York: Pierre Matisse Gallery, 19 January–14 February 1948, p. 2; Alberto Giacometti, 'Le Palais à 4 heures', *Minotaure*, no. 3/4, 1933, p. 46.
51 Gottlieb Leinz, 'Die Frau auf dem Wagen: Vom "Heuwagen" zum "Grossen Glück"', in Wiesinger and Leinz, *Alberto Giacometti: 'Die Frau auf dem Wagen', Triumph und Tod*, p. 108.

10 WAR: 1939–1940

1 Pablo Picasso, interview with Simone Téry, 'Picasso n'est pas officier dans l'armée francaise', *Les Lettres françaises*, 24 March 1945, p. 6, translated in Alfred H. Barr, *Picasso: Fifty Years of His Art*, New York: Museum of Modern Art, 1946, pp. 247–8.
2 Balthus was not conscripted until 2 September 1939, but he must have left the cour de Rohan studio to Isabel earlier than this, as she left for Germany in July 1939; Balthus, in conversation with Nicholas Fox Weber, in Nicholas Fox Weber, *Balthus: A Biography*, New York: Knopf, 1999, p. 405.
3 Ernst Scheidegger, *Sketches for 'La Femme au chariot' on the Wall of Giacometti's Studio, Paris*, 1954, Foundation Ernst Scheidegger Archive.
4 Sefton Delmer, *Trail Sinister: An Autobiography*, vol. 1, London: Secker and Warburg, 1961, p. 399; Rawsthorne, nude and skeleton, Sketchbook 1, TGA 9612.3.24-25, potato, 16.
5 Delmer, *Trial Sinister*, p. 387.
6 Isabel entered Germany on 30 July/1 August 1939 on a stamp issued to last from 27 July 1939 to 27 July 1940; Isabel Delmer, passport, TGA 9612.2.12, p. 27.
7 Delmer, *Trial Sinister*, p. 392; Isabel Delmer, passport, TGA 9612.2.12, stamped 'Hotel Europejski Warsaw 8 sierp 1939' on 8 August 1939, p. 25, and a Polish visa is dated August 1939 to 3 September 1939, p. 22.
8 Isabel Rawsthorne, letter to Giacometti, Tuesday, August 1939, in Véronique Wiesinger, *Alberto Giacometti, Isabel Nicholas: Correspondances*, Paris: Fage Éditions, 2006, pp. 60–61; Giacometti, letter to Isabel Rawsthorne, August 1939 (TGA 9612.1.2.7), in ibid., pp. 62–3.
9 Rawsthorne, Notebook, TGA 9612.2.10.14; water-damaged Sketchbook, TGA 9612.2.10.14.
10 Giacometti, letter to Isabel Rawsthorne, 2 September 1939 (TGA 9612.1.2.1), in Wiesinger, *Correspondances*, p. 64.
11 Delmer, *Trial Sinister*, pp. 395–7.
12 Rawsthorne, letter to Giacometti, 14 September 1939, in Wiesinger, *Correspondances*, p. 65.
13 Isabel Rawsthorne, letter to Giacometti, October 1939, in Wiesinger, *Correspondances*, p. 66.
14 Giacometti, letter to Rawsthorne, 19 October 1939 (TGA 9612.1.2.2), in ibid., p. 68.
15 Geneva 17–11 December 1939, Isabel Delmer, passport, TGA 9612.2.12, pp. 26–31.
16 Isabel Rawsthorne, letter to Giacometti, 23 December 1939, in Wiesinger, *Correspondances*, p. 70.
17 Isabel Rawsthorne, letter to Giacometti, 8 January 1940, in ibid., p. 71.
18 Giacometti, letter to Isabel Rawsthorne, 18 January 1940 (TGA 9612.1.2.3), in ibid., pp. 73–4.
19 Giacometti, letter to Isabel Rawsthorne, Thursday, January 1940, in ibid., p. 56.
20 Giacometti, letter to Isabel Rawsthorne, Thursday, January 1940 (TGA 9612.1.2.9), in ibid., pp. 57–8; the letters are undated, but Giacometti's mention of Melinda Marling, as well as the cold dark evenings, places them definitively in early 1940 (Maclean met Marling in January 1940).
21 Reinhold Hohl, *Giacometti: Sculpture, Painting, Drawing*, London: Thames and Hudson, 1972, p. 133; see Giacometti quoted in Jean Clay, 'Alberto Giacometti: Le Dialogue avec la mort d'un trés grand sculpteur de notre temps', *Réalités*, no. 215, December 1963, 215, pp. 135–45.
22 James Lord, *Giacometti: A Biography*, New York: Farrar, Straus and Giroux, 1986, p. 18.
23 'Is it terribly bad to say it?' (Giacometti, letter to Isabel Rawsthorne, 18 January 1940 (TGA 9612.1.2.3), in Wiesinger, *Correspondances*, pp. 73–4).
24 Patricia Lambert, 'What I remember about Isabel', notebook, February 1986, private collection, p. 2v.
25 Isabel Rawsthorne, 'Autobiographical Notes', Tate Gallery Archive, TGA, 9612.2.2.1.5.
26 The Hôtel Primavera was often used by Giacometti. It may be what is now the Hôtel Les Jardins d'Alésia, 34 rue d'Alésia, adjacent to the Alésia Métro station and one kilometre from the

studio; it is distinguished by a central garden with rooms off.

27 Carol Jacobi, '"I have something to show you": Pablo Picasso's Portraits of Isabel Rawsthorne', *Burlington Magazine*, vol. 159, no. 1374, September 2017, pp. 220–27.

28 Brigitte Léal, *Collection art moderne: La Collection du Centre Pompidou, Musée national d'art moderne*, Paris: Centre Pompidou, 2006, p. 132.

29 Alix Coleman, 'More than Muse Material', *Guardian*, 30 January 1992, p. 69.

30 Roland Penrose, *Picasso: His Life and Work*, London: Victor Gollancz, 1958, pp. 33, 62.

31 Yve-Alain Bois, *Matisse and Picasso*, Paris: Flammarion, 1999, p. 161.

32 John Richardson, *A Life of Picasso*, vol. 3: *The Triumphant Years, 1917–1932*, New York: Alfred A. Knopf, 2007, p. 77.

33 Jacob Epstein and Arnold L. Haskell, *The Sculptor Speaks: Jacob Epstein to Arnold L. Haskell, a Series of Conversations on Art*, London: Heinemann, 1931, p. 103.

34 Pablo Picasso, *Buste de femme*, 10 April 1940, *Buste de femme*, 11 April 1940, *Buste de femme*, 14 April 1940; see Christian Zervos, *Pablo Picasso*, Paris: Cahiers d'art, 1932–78, vol. 10 (1959), nos. 383, 384, 385.

35 10.30 a.m., 10 May 1940, BBC Home Service.

36 Constant Lambert, 20 May 1940, BBC Home Service.

37 The apartment was on the rue Bellechasse; see Theodora FitzGibbon, *With Love: An Autobiography, 1938–1946*, London: Century Publishing, 1982, p. 69.

38 Lord, *Giacometti*, p. 213.

39 Delmer, *Trial Sinister*, p. 399.

40 Giacometti, letter to Isabel Rawsthorne, 10 June 1940 (TGA 9612.1.2.3), in Wiesinger, *Correspondances*, p. 76.

41 Isabel Rawsthorne, letter to Giacometti, 10 June 1940, in ibid., p. 77.

42 It is not known which drawings Isabel packed, but a possibility is *Portrait de Isabel Rawsthorne,* in Giacometti's mid-1930s style, sold at 'Impressionist and Modern Art', Sotheby's, London, 24 March 1999, lot 00261, previously in Isabel's collection.

43 Delmer, *Trial Sinister,* p. 404.

44 Sefton Delmer, *Black Boomerang: An Autobiography*, vol. 2, London: Secker and Warburg, 1962, p. 1.

45 Charles de Gaulle, BBC Home Service, 18 June 1940; Winston Churchill, speech in the House of Commons, *Hansard*, HC Deb 18 June 1940, vol. 362, cc51–64.

46 Simone de Beauvoir, *Force de l'âge*, Paris: Gallimard, 1960, p. 288.

47 Isabel Rawsthorne, letter to Giacometti, 25 June 1940, in Wiesinger, *Correspondances*, p. 81.

48 Giacometti had the impression that Isabel did not receive all of his letters (Giacometti, letter to Rawsthorne, 30 July 1945 (TGA 9612.1.2.5), in ibid., p. 82).

11 WAR ART: 1940–1944

1 Theodora FitzGibbon, *With Love: An Autobiography, 1938–1946*, London: Century Publishing, 1982, p. 69. The Macleans lived in King's Mansions, Lawrence Street.

2 Patricia Lambert (formerly Whitney Smith), 'What I remember about Isabel', notebook, February 1986, private collection, p. 1.

3 FitzGibbon, *With Love*, p. 96.

4 Isabel Rawsthorne, letter to Rose Pulham, 21 October 1953, TGA 9612.1.3.7.

5 Sefton Delmer, *Black Boomerang: An Autobiography*, vol. 2, London: Secker and Warburg, 1962, p. 4; Isabel included the anecdote in a letter to her mother (letter to Agnes Nicholas, 1940, private collection).

6 Ellic Howe stated that the Delmers had arrived by 12 May 1941 (Ellic Howe, *The Black Game: British Subversive Operations against the Germans during the Second World War,* London: Queen Anne Press, 1982, p. 102).

7 Ibid., p. 135.

8 Delmer, *Black Boomerang*, pp. 149–50.

9 Howe, *The Black Game*, p. 135.

10 John Gordon, '"Fat-of-the-land": Life of German P-O-Ws. Mushrooms Cooked in Wine', *Sunday Express*, 17 February 1946.

11 Stephen Nash, ed., *Picasso and the War Years: 1937–1945*, London: Thames and Hudson, 1999, p. 31.

12 For example, a bird on a stand features in *Nature morte à l'oiseau et au vase renversé* (1944, private collection.

13 FitzGibbon, *With Love*, pp. 98–9; the first of these was probably *Skull of Horse* (1941, private collection).

14 Hugh Walmsley, 'Mr Walmsley's Sketch of Tom', in David Garnett, *The Secret History of PWE: The Political Warfare Executive, 1939–1945*, London: St Ermin's Press, 2002, pp. 46–7.

15 Lee Richards, *The Black Art: British Clandestine Psychological Warfare against the Third Reich*, Peacehaven: Psywar, 2010, p. 132.

16 Walter Benjamin, 'The Work of Art in the Age of Mechanical Reproduction' in Benjamin, *Illuminations* (1968), ed. Hannah Arendt, London: Pimlico, 1999, p. 218.

17 Howe, *The Black Game*, pp. 222–4.

18 My thanks to Lee Richards for providing this information.

19 John Rayner, letter to Isabel Rawsthorne, 2 September 1944, TGA 9612 .1.1.12.

20 Anonymous, Memorandum, no date, Special Operations Executive Archive, TNA HS 6/694.

21 Richards, *The Black Art*, p. 219.

22 Georges Bataille, *Histoire de l'œil, par Lord Auch*, Paris: Pascal Pia et René Bonnel 1928; Henry Miller, *Tropic of Cancer*, Paris: Obelisk Press, 1934, and *Tropic of Capricorn*, Paris: Obelisk Press, 1939. Isabel is quoting Lewis Carroll, *Through the Looking-Glass* (1871), but the phrase probably came from nearer to home (see Angus Wilson's excavation of English sexual mores in his novel *Anglo-Saxon Attitudes,* London: Secker and Warburg, 1956, set among archaeologists and anthropologists in Isabel's part of the world, Suffolk).

23 For Lucretia and Judith, see Michel Leiris, *L'Âge d'homme*, Paris: Gallimard, 1939, quoted in *Manhood: A Journey from Childhood into the Fierce Order of Virility*, trans. Richard Howard, Chicago: University of Chicago Press, 1984, pp. 93–5. Both Nin and Rawsthorne made these comments in retrospect at the end of their life, Rawsthorne in 1985, Nin in 1979 (Anaïs Nin, preface, *Little Birds*, London: W. H. Allen, 1979, p. viii).

24 Biddy Noakes, in conversation with the author, November 2007: she lent them to a fellow artist, Roy Noakes, in the 1970s.

25 Adam Komisaruk, 'Pygmalion's

"Wanton Kind of Chace": Hogarth, Rowlandson and the "Line of Beauty"', *Studies in Eighteenth-Century Culture*, vol. 33, 2004, p. 383.
26 Eric Michaud, *The Cult of Art in Nazi Germany*, trans. Janet Lloyd, Stanford: Stanford University Press, 2004, pp. 156–9.
27 Walmsley, 'Mr Walmsley's Sketch of Tom', p. 48.
28 Delmer, *Black Boomerang*, p. 153.
29 The reverse psychological effect on Delmer and its influence on the end of his relationship with his wife is the subject of the TV documentary *Secret History: Sex Bomb*, Channel 4, 28 June 2004.

12 IL MONDO LIBERO: 1944–1945

1 Donald McCormick, *The Life of Ian Fleming*, London: Peter Owen, 1993, p. 151. For example, Vesper Lind was partly based on SOE agent Christine Granville (Ian Fleming, *Casino Royale*, London: Jonathan Cape, 1952).
2 A great deal has been written on this subject, for example Michael Denning, 'Licence to Look: James Bond and the Heroism of Consumption', in *The James Bond Phenomenon: A Critical Reader*, ed. Christoph Lindner, Manchester: Manchester University Press, 2003, pp. 56–75; for the specific masculinity of some Bond girls, see Jaime Hovey, 'Lesbian Bondage, or Why Dykes Like 007', in *Ian Fleming and James Bond: The Cultural Politics of 007*, ed. Edward Comentale, Stephen Watt and Skip Willman, Indiana: Indiana University Press, 2005, pp. 42–54.
3 Anna Maclaren, *Poland at Arms*, London: John Murray, 1942.
4 *Il Mondo Libero*, September 1944, p. 18, and November 1844, p. 25. My thanks to Martin Harrison for providing access to the copies in his collection.
5 Isabel Rawsthorne, 'Autobiographical Notes', Tate Gallery Archive, TGA 9612.2.4.47, Isabel's drawing of 1944 is untraced, but she kept John Pope-Hennessy's book *Donatello's Relief of the Ascension with Christ Giving the Keys to St. Peter* (London: Victoria and Albert Museum, 1949) in her studio until the end of her life (now, private collection).
6 *Fire Service Exhibition*, Burlington House, 1943.
7 Theodora FitzGibbon, *With Love: An Autobiography, 1938-1946*, London: Century Publishing, 1982, p. 119.
8 Elisabeth Lutyens, Correspondence, British Library, Music MSS RBMRR: 64463–64773.
9 Lutyens, Correspondence, BL MSS RBMRR: 64470
10 Ibid., BL MSS. RBMRR: 64469
11 Ibid., BL MSS RBMRR: 64466; in 1944, John was a familiar figure and sitting to Matthew Smith.
12 Patricia Lambert recorded that Isabel and Francis Bacon first came across each other during the war (Patricia Lambert, 'What I remember about Isabel', notebook, February 1986, private collection, p. 3v). Rose Pulham knew Bacon well during the war (*Too Short a Summer: The Photographs of Peter Rose Pulham, 1910–1956*, ed. Val Williams, York: Impressions Gallery of Photography, 1979, p. 10), and George Melly remembered them as friends and fellow painters in and after the war (George Melly, *Don't Tell Sybil: An Intimate Memoir of E.L.T. Mesens*, London: Heinemann, 1997, p. 91).
13 FitzGibbon, *With Love*, included in Bacon's Books Donation 1, Dublin City Gallery The Hugh Lane.
14 Rose Pulham had known Cyril Connolly since at least 1934 (Cyril Connolly, Journal, 15 April 1934, quoted in Cyril Connolly and David Pryce-Jones, 'Journals, 1928–34', *Grand Street*, vol. 2, no. 3, Spring 1983, p. 84).
15 Richard Calvocoressi, *Early Works: Lucian Freud*, Edinburgh: Scottish National Gallery of Modern Art, 1997 p. 16; see also *Chicken in a Bucket* (1944, private collection).
16 FitzGibbon, *With Love*, p. 79.
17 Ibid., p. 100.
18 Mechthild Nawiasky met Peter Rose Pulham and hence Isabel through Theodora FitzGibbon in 1939 in Chesil Court; their affectionate nickname for her was 'no more whisky'; FitzGibbon, *With Love*, p. 35.
19 Ibid., p. 120.
20 At 77 Bedford Gardens.
21 Isabel Rawsthorne, letter to Peter and Mary Rose Pulham, July 1946, TGA 9612.1.3.3.
22 Peter Rose Pulham, 'Surrealist Artists', *Lilliput*, 1943, vol. 13, nos. 1–6.
23 John Rothenstein and Ronald Alley, *Francis Bacon: Catalogue Raisonné and Documentation*, London: Thames and Hudson, 1964, Appendix A.
24 Dylan Thomas, letter to John Davenport, 8 January 1941, in *Dylan Thomas: The Collected Letters*, ed. Paul Ferris, London: Weidenfeld and Nicolson, 2000, p. 533; FitzGibbon, *With Love*, p. 117.
25 Barbara Skelton, *'Tears before Bedtime' and 'Weep No More'*, London: Faber, 2008, p. 31; FitzGibbon, *With Love*, pp. 108–9.
26 FitzGibbon, *With Love*, pp. 53, 66.
27 Ibid., p. 134; Skelton, *'Tears before Bedtime' and 'Weep No More'*, p. 31.
28 Lambert, 'What I remember about Isabel', p. 1.
29 Giacometti, letter to Isabel Rawsthorne, 14 May 1945 (TGA 9612.1.2.4), in Véronique Wiesinger, *Alberto Giacometti, Isabel Nicholas: Correspondances*, Paris: Fage Éditions, 2006, p. 81.
30 At the Berriman, Boswednack, Zennor, Cornwall.
31 John Rayner, letter to Isabel Rawsthorne, 9 February 1945, TGA 9612 .1.1.16.
32 Lambert, 'What I remember about Isabel', p. 1.
33 *Workshop: In Search of Constant Lambert: A Portrait of Constant Lambert and His Music by His Friends and Colleagues*, dir. Barrie Gavin, BBC, 1965; BFI National Archive tx 26.7.1965.
34 Lambert lived with Ayrton from February 1944 to May 1946, according to Richard Shead, *Constant Lambert*, London: Thames Publishing, 1973 pp. 132, 151.
35 Jean Rhys, *The Wide Sargasso Sea*, London: André Deutsch, 1966.

13 HOW TO LIVE? 1945–1946

1 Isabel Rawsthorne, letter to Giacometti, 1948, in Véronique Wiesinger, *Alberto Giacometti, Isabel Nicholas: Correspondances*, Paris: Fage Éditions, 2006, p. 97.
2 James Lord, *Giacometti: A Biography*, New York: Farrar, Straus and Giroux, 1986, p. 248.

3 Patricia Lambert, 'What I remember about Isabel', notebook, February 1986, private collection, p. 2v.
4 Giacometti, letter to Isabel Rawsthorne, 14 May 1945, TGA 9612.1.2.4.
5 Isabel's autobiography adds: 'The history of the Scherbatoff family seems to illuminate our time. The sister called Zenia, a great beauty, married just before the fall of Paris a young count, half German, who had a factory in France and became a collaborator. The other two remained single. Immediately after the war ended he took his wife and the two sisters to the Argentine where no doubt he had a cache of money.'
6 Balthus, letter to Antoinette Klossowski de Rola, June 1945, private collection (my thanks to Thadée Klossowski de Rola).
7 Ninette de Valois, speech to the Vic-Wells Association, Morley College, 16 June 1945, quoted in Katharine Walker, 'Robert Helpmann: Dancer and Choreographer. Part Two', *Dance Chronicle*, vol. 21, no. 2, 1998, p. 242.
8 *Les Enfants du paradis*, dir. Michel Ćarne, premiered at the Palais du Chaillot on 9 March 1945.
9 Jacques Prévert, *Les Enfants du paradis*, trans. Dinah Brooke, London: Faber and Faber, 1968, pp. 88–9.
10 The term 'Cold War' was coined by George Orwell in 1945, in 'You and the Atomic Bomb', *Tribune*, 19 October 1945; see Carol Jacobi, 'A Kind of Cold War Feeling', in *British Art in the Nuclear Age*, ed. Catherine Jolivette, Farnham: Ashgate, 2014, pp. 19–50.
11 David Mellor, 'Introduction', in *Too Short a Summer: The Photographs of Peter Rose Pulham, 1910–1956*, ed. Val Williams, York: Impressions Gallery of Photography, 1979, p. 23.
12 Lambert 'What I remember about Isabel', p. 1.
13 A. J. Ayer, *Part of My Life*, London: Collins, 1977, p. 281
14 *Le Crime de Monsieur Lange*, 1936, dir. Jean Renoir, screenplay Jacques Prévert, a film with socialist sympathies about a publishing cooperative; Ayer, *Part of my Life*, p. 285.
15 Ayer, *Part of My Life*, pp. 288–9.
16 Pattie Lambert remembered her resignation coinciding with an escape to Blois with A. J. Ayer (Lambert, 'What I remember about Isabel', p. 1), who dates this weekend to before July (Ayer, *Part of My Life*, p. 289).
17 Sarah Wilson, 'Francis Gruber: espace politique, espace eschatologique', in *Francis Gruber: L'œil à vif*, ed. Claire Stoullig, Nancy: Musée des Beaux-Arts, 2009.
18 Michel Surya, *Georges Bataille: An Intellectual Biography*, 1992, trans. Krzysztof Fijalkowski and Michael Richardson, New York: Verso, 2010, p. 350.
19 This was Princess Caetani, née Margarite Chapi, an editor and benefactor of hundreds of writers; she paid also for Dylan Thomas's teeth to be fixed and supported the writing of *Under Milk Wood*, spring 1952.
20 Balthus, in conversation with Nicholas Fox Weber, in Nicholas Fox Weber, *Balthus: A Biography*, New York: Knopf, 1999, p. 345. For example, Jean Oberlé, the painter and Free French broadcaster for the BBC during the war, chastised Isabel for meeting collaborators (77).
21 See also John Pudney, 'Picasso: A Glimpse in Sunlight', *New Statesman and Nation*, 28, no. 708, 16 September 1944, pp. 182–3.
22 Giacometti, letter to Isabel Rawsthorne, 30 July 1945 (TGA 9612.1.2.5), in Wiesinger, *Correspondances*, p. 82.
23 James Lord, *Giacometti: A Biography*, New York: Farrar, Straus and Giroux, 1986, p. 248.
24 *Caesar and Cleopatra*, 1945, dir. Gabriel Pascal, adapted from the play *Caesar and Cleopatra* (1901) by George Bernard Shaw.
25 See Thierry Dufrêne, 'Giacometti's Geneva Period (1941–45): The Birth of New Sculpture', in *Giacometti: Critical Essays*, ed. Peter Read and Julia Kelly, Oxford: Ashgate Publishing, 2009, p. 121.
26 Laurence de Buzon-Vallet relates *Nude in the Studio* to a copy of the Venus next to a reproduction of Botticelli, *Birth of Venus*, in a book in Giacometti's library (*Alberto Giacometti: La Collection du Centre Georges Pompidou, Musée national d'art moderne*, Paris: Centre Pompidou, 1999, p. 124).
27 Alberto Giacometti, interview with André Parinaud, 'Entretiens avec Giacometti – Pourquoi je suis sculpteur', *Arts*, 13–19 June 1962, p. 873, reprinted in Alberto Giacometti, *Écrits*, Paris: Éditions Hermann, 1990, pp. 236–48.
28 Germaine Richier in conversation with Hermann Hubacher, *Germaine Richier*, ed. Valérie Da Costa, Zurich: Kunsthaus Zürich, 1963, no. 71, p. 150; Richier returned in April 1946; Lambert, 'What I remember about Isabel', p. 2v; Isabel Rawsthorne, letter to Rose Pulham, 7 August 1955, TGA 9612.1.3.93.
29 Isabel Rawsthorne, 'Autobiographical Notes', Tate Gallery Archive, spare sheet 96 12.2.2.1 8/9.
30 Lambert, 'What I remember about Isabel', p. 1; their outings usually merely took in a local café.
31 Guillaume Apollinaire, 'Le Carpe', in Guillaume Apollinaire and Raoul Dufy, *Le Bestiaire ou cortège d'Orphée*, Paris: Deplanche, Éditeur d'Art, 1911.
32 Simon Wilson, 'Paris Post War: In Search of the Absolute', in *Paris Post War: Art and Existentialism 1945–55*, ed. Frances Morris, London: Tate Publishing, 1993, p. 25.
33 Albert Camus, *Le Mythe de Sisyphe: Essai sur l'absurde*, Paris: Gallimard, 1942; *The Myth of Sisyphus*, trans. Justin O'Brian 1955, Harmondsworth: Penguin, 2000, p. 11.
34 Simone de Beauvoir, *La Force des choses 1944–51*, 1963, *Force of Circumstance*, trans. Richard Howard, Harmondsworth: Penguin, 1968, p. 47.
35 Published as *L'Existentialisme est un humanisme*, Paris: Éditions Nagel, 1946; Michel Leiris, *Journal: 1922–1989*, Paris: Gallimard, 1992, p. 422, 4 November 1945.
36 Jean-Paul Sartre, 'La République du silence', *Les Lettres françaises*, 9 September 1944.
37 Isabel Rawsthorne, postcard to Patricia Whitney Smith, 11 January 1946, private collection.
38 Lambert, 'What I remember about Isabel', p. 6. Jean Wahl was a member of Georges Bataille's secret society Acéphale from 1936 to 1939 and contributed to his journal of the same name (Allan Stoekl, 'Introduction', in Georges Bataille, *Visions of Excess:*

Selected Writings, 1927–1939, ed. Allan Stoekl, Manchester: Manchester University Press, 1986, p. xix.
39 Tristan Tzara, *La Fuite: Poème dramatique en quatre actes et un é pilogue*, Paris: Gallimard, 1947.
40 Biddy Noakes, in conversation with the author, November 2008.
41 Isabel Rawsthorne, letter to Peter and Mary Rose Pulham, June 1946, TGA 9612.1.3.2.
42 Lambert 'What I remember about Isabel', p. 6.
43 René Leibowitz, 'Le Musicien engagé', *Les Temps modernes*, vol. 4, no. 40, February 1949, pp. 322–39.
44 Sabine Meine, 'Leibowitz, René', *The New Grove Dictionary of Music and Musicians*, London: Macmillan, 2001, 14, p. 501.
45 Lambert recalled René's pupils at the time as 'Andris Casanova, Miggs, Boulez etc' ('What I remember about Isabel', p. 6).
46 Elisabeth Lutyens, *A Goldfish Bowl*, London: Cassell, 1972, p. 164.
47 Isabel Rawsthorne, letter to Peter and Mary Rose Pulham, June 1946, TGA 9612.1.3.2.
48 Lambert 'What I remember about Isabel', p. 6
49 Bernard Frizell, 'Existentialism', *Life*, 17 June 1946, pp. 59–67, p. 67.
50 *Samedi Soir*, 3 May 1947, p. 1, trans. by the author
51 TGA 9612.2.2.1.47.
52 Rawsthorne, recollected in a letter to Rose Pulham, 14 June 1949, TGA 9612.1.3.26.
53 Rose Pulham, letter to Rawsthorne, 21 August 1955, TGA 9612.1.123.
54 Bacon stayed in Monte Carlo from July 1946 to November 1948.
55 Ayer, *Part of My Life*, p. 288.
56 Isabel Rawsthorne, letter to Peter and Mary Rose Pulham, July 1946, TGA 9612.1.3.3.
57 Dante Alighieri, *Comedia* (1304–21): 'Midway on the journey of our life / I found myself within a forest dark, / For the clear path had been lost'.
58 Lambert, 'What I remember about Isabel', p. 2v.
59 Ayer, *Part of My Life*, p. 289.
60 Loi de Marthe Richard, 13 April 1946.
61 Alberto Giacometti, 'Le Rêve, le Sphinx et la mort de T', *Labyrinthe*, no. 22/23, 15 December 1946, p. 12.
62 The suggestion is, perhaps, that it was the unavailability of the Sphinx and its familiar girls that led the narrator to a less tried-and-tested liaison.
63 Galerie Pierre Loeb, 22 May to 6 June 1946.
64 *2ème Salon de Mai*, Galeries Lafayette, June–July 1946, Paris: Galeries Lafayette, 1946, unpaginated. I am grateful to the FAAG for drawing this to my attention.
65 Isabel Rawsthorne, letter to Peter and Mary Rose Pulham, June 1946, TGA 9612.1.3.2.
66 Alberto Giacometti, *Sculptures in the Studio* (recto) / *Chair in the Studio* (verso), 1946, FAAG; printing was a major Resistance activity and print-making facilities were available to artists such as Picasso at Roger Lacourière's print workshop, for example (Laurence Dorléac, *L'Art de la défaite,* Paris: Éditions du Seuil, 1993, pp. 279–85).
67 Lambert 'What I remember about Isabel', p. 2.
68 Rodney Phillips later married the dancer and actress Marika Rivera, the daughter of the artists Diego Rivera and Marie Vorobieff (Marevna).
69 Barbara Skelton, *'Tears before Bedtime' and 'Weep No More'*, London: Faber, 2008, pp. 75–6.
70 25 July 1946; see Peter Rose Pulham, 'Isabel Lambert', in *Isabel Lambert*, London: Hanover Gallery, 1949, n.p.
71 Isabel Rawsthorne, letter to Peter and Mary Rose Pulham, July 1946, TGA 9612.1.3.3.
72 Isabel Rawsthorne, 'Autobiographical Notes', TGA 9612.2.2.1.79.
73 Lambert, 'What I remember about Isabel', p. 2. Lambert added that René felt his absence was affecting his daughter's health.
74 Pattie Lambert, letter to Biddy Noakes, 11 November 1997, private collection, p. 3.
75 Lambert 'What I remember about Isabel', p. 1.

14 NATURE MORTE: 1946

1 Rawsthorne, Diary, 1947, TGA 9612.2.7, written on the pages for February.
2 Rawsthorne, Diary, 1947, TGA 9612.2.7, written on the pages for January; Charles Baudelaire, *Journaux intimes: Mon cœur mis à nu* (published posthumously, 1909), in *Intimate Diaries*, trans. Christopher Isherwood, introduction by T. S. Eliot, London: Blackamore Press, 1930, 23 January 1862.
3 Albert Camus, *Le Mythe de Sisyphe: Essai sur l'absurde*, Paris: Gallimard, 1942, *The Myth of Sisyphus*, trans. Justin O'Brian (1955), Harmondsworth: Penguin, 2000, p. 11.
4 Rawsthorne, Diary, 1947, TGA 9612.2.7, written on the pages for March.
5 Isabel Rawsthorne, letter to Giacometti, untraced but referred to in Giacometti's letter to Isabel, late 1946 (TGA 9612.1.2.10 and 9612.1.2.11), in Véronique Wiesinger, *Alberto Giacometti, Isabel Nicholas: Correspondances*, Paris: Fage Éditions, 2006, p. 87; Vincent Van Gogh, letter to Theo van Gogh. Arles, Friday, 21 September 1888, in *Vincent van Gogh: The Letters*, ed. Leo Jansen, Hans Luijten, Nienke Bakker, Amsterdam and The Hague: Van Gogh Museum and Huygens ING, 2009, http://vangoghletters.org, Letter 685, accessed 24 August 2019.
6 Patricia Lambert, 'What I remember about Isabel', notebook, February 1986, private collection, p. 3.
7 Francis Bacon, letter to Graham Sutherland, 19 October 1946, quoted in Martin Hammer, *Bacon and Sutherland: Patterns of Infinity in British Culture of the 1940s*, New Haven and London: Yale University Press, 2005, p. 237.
8 Rawsthorne, Sketchbook 4, TGA 9612.3.4: lizard (p. 37), beetles (p. 38), view and beetles (p. 41); 'glasses on a table with a stone', although currently untraced, was recovered and described in 1955 in a letter to Rose Pulham, TGA 9612.1.3.101.
9 Frances Morris, 'Francis Gruber', in *Paris Post War: Art and Existentialism 1945–55*, ed. Frances Morris, London: Tate Publishing, 1993, p. 129.
10 Peter Read, 'From Spectre to

Sceptre: Giacometti's Sculpture in the writing of Francis Ponge', in *Giacometti: Critical Essays*, ed. Peter Read and Julia Kelly, Aldershot: Ashgate, 2009, p. 174; Lois Dahlin, 'Entretien avec Francis Ponge, ses rapports avec Camus, Sartre et des autres', *The French Review*, , vol. 54, no. 2, December 1980, pp. 271–81.

11 Francis Ponge, *Le Parti pris des choses*, Paris: Gallimard, 1942 (written between 1924 and 1939), reprinted in Francis Ponge, *The Nature of Things*, trans. Lee Fahnestock, New York: Red Dust.

12 Francis Ponge, *De la nature morte et de Chardin*, Paris: Hermann, 1963; see John Stout, 'The Text as Object: Francis Ponge's Verbal Still Lifes', *Symposium*, vol. 47, no. 1, 1993, p. 50.

13 Ponge, *Le Parti pris des choses*, p. 46.

14 Francis Ponge, 'Concerning the Pebble', *Essays on Language and Literature*, ed. J. L. Hevesi, London: Allan Wingate Publishers Ltd, 1947, p.129.

15 Rawsthorne, *Still Life - Briars and Shells*, 1947, oil on board, 50 x 70 cm, sold by Geoff Woods at Morgan O'Driscoll Online Irish Art Sale, 2 July 2012, lot 3.

16 Charles Palermo, 'Tactile Translucence: Miró, Leiris, Einstein', *October*, 97, Summer 2001, pp. 31–50.

17 Lee Fahnestock, 'Introduction', in Ponge, *The Nature of Things*, pp. 8–9.

18 Maurice Merleau-Ponty, *La Phénoménologie de la perception*, Paris: Gallimard, 1945, *The Phenomenology of Perception*, trans. Colin Smith, London: Routledge, 2006, pp. 297–8.

19 Peter Rose Pulham, notes, private collection; my thanks to Philippe Garner for the transcription.

20 Francis Ponge, 'Snails', Paris, 21 March 1936, in *Le Parti pris des choses*, p. 22.

21 Jon Wood, 'From "vue d'atelier" to "vie d'atelier": 46 rue Hippolyte-Maindron and the Beginnings of Giacometti', in *Giacometti: Critical Essays*, ed. Peter Read and Julia Kelly, Aldershot: Ashgate, 2009, p. 27.

22 Antony Clare Lees, *The Cult of the Green Bird: The Mythology of the Green Woodpecker*, Lancaster: Scotforth, 2002, p. 9.

23 Camus, *Le Mythe de Sisyphe*, p. 107.

24 For example, Frans Cuyk Van Myerop's *Still Life with Fowl*, c. 1670, Groeninge Museum, with its startling shadows flung on the surface behind, and André Derain's *Still Life with Dead Game*, 1938, Metropolitan Museum of Art, New York. William Feaver states that Giacometti mentioned *Dead Heron*, seen in *La Jeune Peinture en Grande Bretagne* at the Galerie René Drouin in 1948, to Lucian Freud over dinner in 1949; William Feaver, *The Lives of Lucian Freud: Youth*, London Bloomsbury, 2019, p. 312.

25 Lees, *The Cult of the Green Bird*, pp. 1–2; Robert Graves, *The Greek Myths*, vol. 1, Harmondsworth: Penguin, 1955, p. 193.

26 Lees, *The Cult of the Green Bird*, p. 9; Graves, *The Greek Myths*, p. 231.

27 Titian's late *Flaying of Marsyas*, 1575, in Kroměříž Archbishop's Palace in the then Czechoslovakia was the best known.

15 PEINTRE CONTRAIRE: 1947

1 'La Carpe', in Guillaume Apollinaire and Raoul Dufy, *Le Bestiaire ou Cortège d'Orphée*, Paris: Deplanche, Éditeur d'Art, 1911, author's translation; written several times in Rawsthorne's papers and autobiography.

2 Rawsthorne, Diary, 1947, TGA 9612.2.7, written over 24 November 1947.

3 Ibid., facing 14 March.

4 *Van Gogh*, Le Musée de l'Orangerie, Paris, 24 January–15 March 1947.

5 Rawsthorne, Diary, 1947, facing 3 March.

6 Ibid., facing 14 March.

7 Ibid., facing 4 March.

8 Ibid., facing 3 March.

9 Ibid., facing 22 March.

10 Ibid., facing 7 April.

11 Ibid., facing 1 April.

12 Alberto Giacometti, 'Le Rêve, le Sphinx et la mort de T', *Labyrinthe*, 15 December 1946, no. 22/23, p. 12.

13 Patricia Lambert, 'What I remember about Isabel', notebook, February 1986, private collection, p. 4.

14 Rawsthorne, Diary, March 1947; According to Pattie Whitney Smith, the Swiss artist Roger Montandon joined them on the country retreat and many dinners (Lambert, 'What I remember about Isabel', pp. 3–6).

15 Rawsthorne, Diary, 1947, facing 7 and 14 April.

16 Ibid., facing 19 and 20 April.

17 Antonin Artaud, *Van Gogh: Le Suicidé de la société*, Paris: K éditeur, 1947, p. 27.

18 Rawsthorne, Diary, 1947, facing 12 April.

19 Rawsthorne, *Copy of a Roman Mosaic*, Sketchbook 4, TGA 9612.3.4, p. 18.

20 Rawsthorne, Diary, 1947, inventory, n.p.

21 Ibid., facing 26 April.

22 Ibid., Notes.

23 Ibid., last pages: the quotation from Aeschylus, *Agamemnon*, 178–9, is quoted in William Stanford's *Aeschylus in His Style: A Study in Language and Personality* (Oxford: Blackwell, 1942, p. 130), which Isabel owned by 1947.

24 Lambert, 'What I remember about Isabel', p. 4.

25 Rawsthorne, Diary, 1947, facing 27 February.

26 Ibid., facing 3–4 April.

27 Seán Hand, *Alter Ego: The Critical Writings of Michel Leiris*, Leeds: Legenda, 2004, pp. 60–62.

28 Isabelle Monod-Fontaine, *Donation Louise et Michel Leiris: Collection Kahnweiler-Leiris* Paris: Éditions du Centre Pompidou, 1984, p. 178.

29 Rawsthorne, Diary, 1947, facing 20 February.

30 Ibid., discussion of *A Midsummer Night's Dream* series written over and facing 12 April.

31 Patrick Elliott, 'Drawings by Alberto Giacometti. Paris', *Burlington Magazine*, vol. 143, no. 1178, May 2001, p. 315.

32 Stanley William Hayter, 'The Apostle of Empathy: Paul Klee', *Magazine of Art*, April 1946, p. 39.

33 Georges Bataille and Alberto Giacometti, *Histoire des Rats (Journal de Dianus)*, Paris: Minuit, 1947; Georges Bataille and Jean Fautrier, *Alleluia: The Catechism of Dianus*, Paris: Auguste Blaizot, 1947; Jean Dubuffet and Eugène Guillevic, *Les Murs*, Paris, Édition Fernand Mourlot, 1945; also Jean Dubuffet and Francis Ponge, *Matière et mémoire ou Les Lithographes à l'école*, Paris, Éditions Fernand Mourlot, 1945.

34 Rawsthorne, Diary, 1947, facing 20

February and facing 3 March 1947.
35 *Portraits et dessins par Antonin Artaud*, Galerie Pierre, June 1947.
36 Artaud, *Van Gogh: Le Suicidé de la société*, p. 23.
37 Isabel's diary mentions Alfred Werner, who went on to write about Jewish artists: *Modigliani, Utrillo, Soutine*, New York, Tudor Pub. Co., 1969 (Rawsthorne, Diary, 9 May 1977).
38 Rawsthorne, Diary, 1947, written over 20 February. Balthus placed Bonnard at the origin of his aesthetic (James Thrall Soby, 'Balthus', *Bulletin of the Museum of Modern Art*, vol. 24, no. 3, 1956–7, p. 3).
39 Isabel is likely to have known the Hokusais in the Victoria and Albert Museum from her student days in London; Rawsthorne, Sketchbook 1, TGA 9612.3.3, 12v; Rawsthorne, Diary, 1947, written over 20 February.
40 Rawsthorne, Diary, 1947, written over 20 February.
41 Ibid., Notes. Isabel addressed Giacometti as 'Jupiter von Stinkhorn', perhaps a joke referring to his generous endowment or his sexually transmitted infection (Rawsthorne, postcard to Giacometti, 8 May 1947, in Véronique Wiesinger, *Alberto Giacometti, Isabel Nicholas: Correspondances*, Paris: Fage Éditions, 2006, p. 89.
42 Rawsthorne, Diary, 1947, last pages; similar to the capitalised wordplays in Artaud, *Van Gogh: Le Suicidé de la société*.
43 See, for one of many examples, Isabel Rawsthorne, letter to Rose Pulham, 15 November 1948, TGA 9612.1.3.10.
44 Francis Ponge, 'Joca Seria: Notes sur les sculptures d'Alberto Giacometti' (1951), reprinted in *L'Atelier contemporain*, Paris: Gallimard, 1977, pp. 168, 187.
45 Rawsthorne, Diary, 1947, written over 3 March.
46 Willard Bohn, 'Contemplating Apollinaire's "Bestiaire"', *Modern Language Review*, vol. 99, no. 1, January 2004, p. 45.
47 Henri Michaux, *Apparitions*, Paris: Le Calligraphe, 1946; Cordell Yee, 'Reading within the Lines: Henri Michaux and the Chinese Art of Writing', *Review of Literatures of the European Union,* December 2008, p. 8.
48 Margaret Rigaud-Drayton, *Henri Michaux: Poetry, Painting and the Universal Sign*, Oxford: Clarendon Press, 2005, pp. 130–31.
49 Francis Ponge 'Joca Seria', pp. 168, 187; Francis Ponge, 'Réflexions sur les statuettes, figures et peintures d'Alberto Giacometti', *Cahiers d'art*, 1952, reprinted in Francis Ponge, *L'Atelier contemporain*, Paris: Gallimard, 1977, p. 177.
50 Jean Dubuffet, 'La Main parle', in *Notes pour les fins-lettrés*, 1945, quoted in Maurice Tapies, preface to *Mirobulos, macadam & Cie: Hautepates de J. Dubuffet*, Paris: Galerie René Drouin, 1946, n.p.; Walter Benjamin, 'Über einige Motive bei Baudelaire', in Walter Benjamin, *Illuminations* (1968), ed. Hannah Arendt, London: Pimlico, 1999, p. 158.
51 Rawsthorne, Diary, 1947, facing 21–28 December.
52 Author's translation; Jacques Dupin, 'Une écriture sans fin', preface to Alberto Giacometti, *Écrits*, ed. Michel Leiris and Jacques Dupin, Paris: Herman, 1990, p. xiv.
53 Dubuffet, 'La Main parle', n.p.
54 Antonin Artaud, 'Le Visage Humain', in *Portraits et dessins par Antonin Artaud*.
55 André Breton, Benjamin Péret and Oscar Dominguez, 'D'une décalcomanie sans objet preconcu', *Minotaure*, 8, 1936, pp. 18–23; Dr Hermann Rorschach, *Psychodiagnostic*, Paris: Presses universitaires de France, 1947; Émile Malaspine, 'La Peinture intégral', *Cahiers d'art*, no. 22, 1947, pp. 288–92.
56 Elisa Breton, André Breton and Benjamin Péret, preface to *Exposition Riopelle*, Paris: Galerie Nina Dausset, 1949.
57 Michel Leiris, 'Glossaire j'y serre mes gloses', in *Le Revolution surrealiste*, 15 April 1925, 3, p. 7; see also Michel Leiris, *Aurora*, Paris: Gallimard, 1946.
58 Jean Dubuffet, 'La Main parle', n.p.
59 Vincent van Gogh, *Wheatfield with Crows*, 1890, Van Gogh Museum, Amsterdam; Artaud, *Van Gogh: Le Suicidé de la société*, p. 26.
60 Rawsthorne, Diary, 1947, written over 31 March, and 'I don't fit in' facing 13 April.
61 Ibid., facing 18 April.
62 Ibid., facing 14 April.
63 Giacometti, letter to Isabel Rawsthorne, late 1946 (TGA 9612.1.2.10 and 9612.1.2.11), in Wiesinger, *Correspondances*, p. 87.
64 Rawsthorne, Diary, 1947, facing 11 April.
65 Ibid., facing 14 April.
66 Ibid., facing 21–28 December.
67 Nicholas Fox Weber, *Balthus: A Biography*, New York: Knopf, 1999, p. 416.
68 'Alberto Giacometti: Sculptures et dessins recents', *Cahiers d'art*, 1946, pp. 253–68.
69 *Alberto Giacometti: Exhibition of Sculptures, Paintings, Drawings*, Pierre Matisse Gallery, New York, 19 January–14 February 1948.
70 Simone de Beauvoir, *The Second Sex*, trans. Constance Borde and Shiela Malovany-Chevallier, London: Vintage, 2011, pp. 737–8.
71 Isabel identifies the singer's name as Aki, and Richard Shead says she was a Japanese soprano (Richard Shead, *Constant Lambert*, 1973, London: Thames Publishing, p. 147). No other information about her has been traced.
72 Rawsthorne, Diary, 1947, written over 21–25 April.
73 Ibid., facing 5 and 6 May.

16 HOMMAGE AU SQUELETTE: 1947–1949

1 *Van Gogh: Le Suicidé de la société*, February 1947, cited in the catalogue to 'Isabel Lambert', Hanover Gallery, London, 22 February–26 March 1949.
2 Isabel Rawsthorne, Diary, 1947, TGA 9612.2.7, last pages, n.p.
3 Ibid., facing 5 May.
4 *Matisse–Picasso*, Victoria and Albert Museum, London, 5 December 1945–15 January 1946; *Braque and Rouault*, Tate Gallery, London, 11 April–22 May 1946.
5 Humphrey Jennings, letter to Cicely Jennings, 1945, quoted in *Pandaemonium: Coming of the Machine as Seen by Contemporary Observers, 1660–1886*, London: André Deutsch, 1985, p. 146; Jennings was a filmmaker, also an associate of the Surrealist set and the founder of the GPO Film Unit and Mass Observation.
6 *Exposition internationale d'art moderne*, Musée national d'art

moderne, Paris, 18 November–28 December 1946.
7 *Drawings and Sculptures by Eduardo Paolozzi*, Mayor Gallery, 14 January–1 February 1947.
8 Eduardo Paolozzi, interview with Frank Whitford, National Life Story Collection: Artists' Lives, British Library, C466/17, pp. 42–3; Eduardo Paolozzi, *Isabel Rawsthorne Painting the Ballet*, London: Michael Parkin Gallery, 1998, n.p.
9 'E Paolozzi 28 Cartwright Gardens W.C nr Kings Cross', in Paolozzi's hand, Rawsthorne, Diary, 1947, last pages, n.p.; Rawsthorne, postcard to Giacometti, 8 May 1947, in Véronique Wiesinger, *Alberto Giacometti, Isabel Nicholas: Correspondances*, Paris: Fage Éditions, 2006, pp. 88–9.
10 Patricia Lambert, 'What I remember about Isabel', notebook, February 1986, private collection, p. 4; see, for example, Alberto Giacometti's drawing, *Tête d'Isabel*, 1947, private collection, sold at the 'Art impressioniste et moderne' sale, Christie's, Paris, 20 May 2011, lot 92.
11 Isabel Rawsthorne, 'Autobiographical Notes', Tate Gallery Archive, TGA 9612.2.79, facing.
12 Warwick Nicholas, email correspondence with the author, 15 May 2009.
13 Lambert, 'What I remember about Isabel', p. 4.
14 Paolozzi, *Rawsthorne Painting the Ballet*, n.p.; Lambert 'What I remember about Isabel', p. 6.
15 Eduardo Paolozzi encountered *On Growth and Form* in Paris (Nigel Henderson, *Nigel Henderson: Paintings, Collages and Photographs*, London: Anthony d'Offay Gallery, 1977, n.p.).
16 William Feaver, *The Lives of Lucian Freud: Youth*, 2019, p. 339.
17 Isabel Rawsthorne, postcard to Rose Pulham, Vézelay, undated, TGA 9612. 1.3.8.
18 *Job: A Masque for Dancing*, 1931; choreography by Ninette de Valois, music by Ralph Vaughan Williams. Fonteyn's biographer dates Isabel's involvement with Constant Lambert from early 1945, and places the episode at the Hôtel de la Cité two years earlier: Meredith Daneman, *Margot Fonteyn*, London: Viking, 2004, p. 187. Constant Lambert and the ballet were in Paris early in 1945, but Isabel's date is confirmed by Patricia Lambert, living in the same hotel in 1947.
19 Daneman, *Margot Fonteyn*, p. 187.
20 Rawsthorne, 'Autobiographical Notes', TGA 9612.2.4.2.
21 Lambert, 'What I remember about Isabel', p. 4.
22 1947–9, known only from a photograph (private collection).
23 Rawsthorne, 'Autobiographical Notes', TGA 9612.2.2.58.
24 Isabel Rawsthorne, letter to Peter and Mary Rose Pulham, spring 1947, TGA 9612.1.3.4.
25 Louise Bataille, letter to Balthus, Vézelay, early September 1947, collection Thadée Klossowski de Rola.
26 Rawsthorne, Diary, 1947, TGA 9612.2.7, written on the pages for March; Prosper Montagné maître cuisinier, avec la collaboration du docteur Gottschalk, *Larousse gastronomique*, Paris, Éditions Larousse, 1938; first English edition 1961
27 Rawsthorne, 'Autobiographical Notes', TGA 9612.2.2.1.79.
28 *The Times*, Tuesday, 23 September 1947, p. 7.
29 Isabel Rawsthorne, letter Giacometti, October 1947, in Wiesinger, *Correspondances*, p. 90.
30 Isabel Rawsthorne, letter to Giacometti, early 1948, in ibid., p. 97; Isabel Rawsthorne, letter to Rose Pulham, 10 January 1951, TGA 9612.1.3.49.
31 Rawsthorne, 'Autobiographical Notes', TGA 9612.2.4.9.
32 Ibid., TGA 9612.2.4.27.
33 Ibid., TGA 9612.2.4.28-29: 'felt quite happy with myself'.
34 Isabel Rawsthorne, letter to Rose Pulham, late 1948, TGA 9612.1.3.13.
35 Rawsthorne, 'Autobiographical Notes', 9612.2.4.9.
36 Isabel Rawsthorne, postcard to Giacometti, 19 December 1947, in Wiesinger, *Correspondances*, p. 90.
37 Isabel Rawsthorne, letter to Giacometti, late 1947/early 1948, in ibid., p. 97.
38 Isabel Rawsthorne letter to Giacometti, 1948, in ibid., p. 99; William Beebe, *Half Mile Down*, New York: Harcourt, Brace and Company, 1934, pp. 162–6.
39 Rawsthorne, Sketchbook 4, TGA 9612.3.4, p. 25.
40 Biddy Noakes, in conversation with the author, November 2007; Jacques-Yves Cousteau and Frédéric Dumas, *The Silent World: A Story of Undersea Discovery and Adventure, by the first men to swim at record depths with the freedom of fish*, New York: Harper and Brothers, 1953; *Le Monde du silence*, 1956, dir. Jacques-Yves Cousteau and Louis Malle.
41 Isabel Rawsthorne, letter to Rose Pulham, late 1948, TGA 9612.1.3.13.
42 Isabel Rawsthorne, letter to Rose Pulham, n.d., TGA 9612.1.3.20; Rawsthorne, 'Autobiographical Notes', TGA 9612.2.4.31; *Two Birds*, Hanover Gallery Ledger, 22 February 1949, TGA 863.1.2.
43 Isabel Rawsthorne, letter to Rose Pulham, late 1948, TGA 9612.1.3.12.
44 Alberto Giacometti, 'À propos de Jacques Callot', *Labyrinthe*, no. 17, 15 April 1945, p. 3.
45 Elizabeth Manchester, 'La Chauve-souris', https://www.tate.org.uk/art/artworks/richier-the-bat-l02176, accessed 30 August 2019.
46 *Germaine Richier: Rétrospective*, Paris: Fondation Maeght, 1996, p. 70; *Sculptures of Germaine Richier / Engravings: Studio of Roger Lacourière*, London: Anglo-French Art Centre, 1947.
47 'London Gallery', *The Times*, 17 January 1934, p. 17; Edith Hoffmann, 'Soutine in Paris', *Burlington Magazine*, vol. 115, no. 844, July 1973, pp. 484–6. There were many opportunities for Isabel to view Soutine's fish – for example, *Still Life Salmon* was shown at Adams Gallery, March–April 1939. *Two Fish* also recalls Braque's design for René Char, *Le Soleil des eaux*, Paris: J. Matarasso, 1949; Isabel was a fan of Char's writings (Rawsthorne, Diary, 1947, TGA 9612.2.7, written over 13 March).
48 William Cohn's *Peinture chinoise: 224 peintures et détails*, Paris: Phaidon, 1948, given to the artist Roy Noakes in the 1970s (now, private collection).
49 Jean Dubuffet, *Mur embué*, reproduced in Jean Dubuffet and Eugène Guillevic, *Les Murs*, Paris: Édition Fernand Mourlot, 1945.
50 *The Times*, 8 March 1949, p. 7.
51 David Sylvester suggested that Francis Bacon's *Three Studies for Figures at the Base of the Crucifixion* represented the Eumenides, and, in 1959, Bacon concurred (letter to Tate Gallery,

9 January 1959,TG cataloguing files).
52 Elizabeth Cowling, 'Elective Affinities: Giacometti in the Palace of Bones', *Apollo*, October 2003, pp. 34–42.
53 Alberto Giacometti, *Paris sans fin, 1957–65*, Paris: Éditions Verve, 1969, plates 80–84, quoted (and translated) in Cowling, 'Elective Affinities', p. 37.
54 Gerhard Heilmann, *The Origin of Birds*, London: H. F. and G. Witherby, 1926. The theory received impetus in 1942, from William Beebe's 'Evolution of a Lizard into a Bird', *Proceedings of the Eighth American Scientific Congress*, no. 3, 1942, p. 296, but Isabel does not seem to have discovered Beebe until 1948, after conceiving the skeleton paintings.
55 Isabel discusses an 'attick, rue Boissonade' and Peter's studio, 25 rue Daguerre (Isabel Rawsthorne, letter to Rose Pulham, [summer 1949], TGA 9612.1.3.67).
56 Isabel was in Paris in the summer of 1948 (Rawsthorne, letter to Rose Pulham, 7 August , TGA 9612.1.3.9; Isabel Rawsthorne, letter to Giacometti, 30 October 1948, in Wiesinger, *Correspondances*, p. 95.
57 Rawsthorne, letter to Giacometti 1948, in Wiesinger, *Correspondances*, p. 99.
58 Giacometti spoke at length about seeing grey ('the colour I feel, that I see, that I want to reproduce') to Gotthard Jedlicka 1958, quoted in Reinhold Hohl, *Giacometti: A Biography in Pictures*, Stuttgart: Hatje Cantz, 1998, p. 160; 'Quintessentialism' referred to by Rose Pulham in a letter to Isabel, 31 November 1948, TGA 9612.1.1.17.
59 *Corot raconté par lui-même et par ses amis*, vol. 1: *Pensées et écrits du peintre*, ed. Pierre Courthion, Geneva: Pierre Cailler, 1946, p. 89; Isabel Rawsthorne, letter to Rose Pulham, n.d., TGA 9612.1.3.72A; Isabel Rawsthorne, letter to Giacometti, 1948, in Wiesinger, *Correspondances*, p. 97.
60 Giacometti, letter to Isabel Rawsthorne, February 1949, in Wiesinger, *Correspondances*, p. 96.
61 Giacometti, quoted in a letter from Isabel to Rose Pulham, February 1949, TGA 9612.1.3.20.
62 Michel Leiris, 'Thoughts around Alberto Giacometti', trans. Douglas Cooper, *Horizon*, 114, June 1949, p. 416.
63 Isabel Rawsthorne, letter to Rose Pulham, 14 June 1949, TGA, 9612.1.3.26.

17 CAT'S CRADLE: 1947–1949

1 See, for example, a water-damaged sketchbook, TGA 9612.2.10.83.
2 Rawsthorne, Diary, 1947, TGA 9612.2.7, last pages, n.p.
3 Véronique Wiesinger, *Alberto Giacometti, Isabel Nicholas: Correspondances*, Paris: Fage Éditions, 2006, p. 45; Isabel Rawsthorne, letter to Giacometti, 27 April 1948, in Wiesinger, *Correspondances*, p. 94; Giacometti's *Portrait of Diego in the Studio* (1948; private collection, Switzerland) was seen in Isabel's cottage by James Lord on 12 March 1970 (James Lord, 'Sudbury Cottage', in *A Gift for Admiration: Further Memoirs*, New York: Farrar, Straus and Giroux, 1998, p. 49), and it was bequeathed to Pattie Lambert, who sold it before her death in 2010.
4 Isabel Rawsthorne, letter to Rose Pulham, 1 December 1948, TGA 9612.1.3.29.
5 Isabel Rawsthorne, letter to Rose Pulham, [1948], TGA 9612.1.3.14 2/2.
6 Isabel Rawsthorne, postcard to Giacometti, 8 May 1947, in Wiesinger, *Correspondances*, p. 89.
7 Giacometti, letter to Pierre Matisse, 1950, in Alberto Giacometti, *Écrits*, Paris: Éditions Hermann, 1990, p. 96: 'D'avoir la figure dans le vide pour mieux la voir'.
8 Colin Morris, 'History of Liverpool College of Art, 1825–1970', M.Phil. dissertation, Liverpool Polytechnic, 1985, p. 126.
9 Giacometti, letter to Pierre Matisse, 1947, published in English in *Alberto Giacometti*, New York: Pierre Matisse Gallery, 1948.
10 Siegfried Giedion, *Building in France: Building in Iron, Building in Ferro-concrete* (1928), trans. J. Duncan Berry, Santa Monica: The Getty Center for the Study of Art and the Humanities, 1995, p. 167; Tyrus Miller, '"Glass before its time, premature iron": Architecture, Temporality, and Dream in Benjamin's Passagenwerk', in *Walter Benjamin and the Arcades Project*, ed. Beatrice Hanssen, London: Continuum International Publishing Group, 2006, pp. 240–41; Detlef Mertins, 'The Enticing and Threatening Face of Prehistory: Walter Benjamin and the Utopia of Glass', *Assemblage*, no. 29, April 1996, p. 11.
11 Later written up in Siegfried Giedion, 'Space Conception in Prehistoric Art', in *Explorations in Communication*, ed. Edward Carpenter and Marshall McLuhan, Boston: Beacon Press, 1960, and in Siegfried Giedion, *The Eternal Present: The Beginnings of Art*, New York: Pantheon Books, 1962.
12 *Les Demoiselle de la nuit*, 21 May 1948, Théâtre Marigny, music by Jean Françaix, choreography by Roland Petit, decor by Leonor Fini (Peter Webb, *Sphinx: The Life and Art of Leonor Fini*, New York: Vendome Press, 2009, pp. 138–9).
13 A. J. Ayer, *Language, Truth and Logic* (1936), Harmondsworth: Penguin, 2001, pp. 38–9; Maurice Merleau-Ponty, *La Phénoménologie de la perception*, Paris: Gallimard, 1945, *The Phenomenology of Perception,* trans. Colin Smith, London: Routledge, 2006, pp. 297–8.
14 A. J. Ayer, *Part of My Life,* London: Collins, 1977, p. 285. For an analysis of the debates between Ayer, Bataille and Merleau-Ponty, see Nick Trackakis, 'Meta-Philosophy of Religion: The Analytic-Continental Divide in Philosophy of Religion', *Ars Disputandi*, 2007, p. 7.
15 See James Hyman, *The Battle for Realism: Figurative Art in Britain during the Cold War, 1945–1960*, New Haven and London: Yale University Press, 2001, p. 21, for the importance of A. J. Ayer in post-war art.
16 George Berkeley, *An Essay towards a New Theory of Vision*, Dublin: Jeremy Pepyat, 1709.
17 William Stevenson, taped interview with Colin Morris, transcribed in 'History of Liverpool College of Art', pp. 129–30.
18 Michel Leiris, 'Alberto Giacometti', *Documents*, vol. 4, September 1929, p. 129.
19 Maurice Merleau-Ponty, 'Le Doute de Cézanne', *Fontaine*, vol. 8, no. 47, December 1945, p. 90.
20 Giacometti, letter to Pierre Matisse,

published in English in the Pierre Matisse Gallery's *Alberto Giacometti*.

21 Isabel Rawsthorne, letter to Rose Pulham, 3 July 1949, TGA 9612.1.3.27.

22 Merleau-Ponty, *Phenomenology of Perception*, p. 298.

23 Albert Camus, *Le Mythe de Sisyphe: Essai sur l'absurde*, Paris: Gallimard, 1942, *The Myth of Sisyphus*, trans. Justin O'Brian (1955), Harmondsworth: Penguin, 2000, pp. 27, 30.

24 Isabel Rawsthorne, 'Autobiographical Notes', Tate Gallery Archive, TGA 9612.2.4.9.

25 Isabel Rawsthorne, letter to Rose Pulham, late 1948, TGA 9612.1.3.13.

26 Isabel Rawsthorne, letter to Giacometti, August 1948, in Wiesinger, *Correspondances*, p. 97; letter to Giacometti, early 1949, TGA 9612.1.3.14: 'I hate my painting called night'; letter to Giacometti, 2 March 1949, TGA 9612.1.3.56.

27 Paolozzi, interview with Frank Whitford, National Life Story Collection: Artists' Lives, British Library, C466/17, p. 49.

28 William Shakespeare, *King Lear*, Act III, Scene 4; Michel Leiris, 'Thoughts around Alberto Giacometti', trans. Douglas Cooper, *Horizon*, 114, June 1949, p. 411.

29 Isabel Rawsthorne, letter to Rose Pulham, 29 August 1950, TGA 9612.1.3.28.

30 During the Second World War, Bomberg lived near the Epsteins at 41 Queen's Gate Mews, a few steps away from Isabel's home between 1944 and 1945, and when she and Leibowitz visited England in the summer of 1946, Bomberg was exhibiting at the Arcade Gallery with her fellow Royal Academy student Mervyn Peake.

31 David Bomberg, 'Approach to Painting', in *First Borough Group Exhibition*, London: Archer Gallery, 1947.

32 See, for example, the way the brushstrokes both describe and equate to the act of touching the lower body in Bomberg's *Nude*, 1943, Tate, London.

33 *Third Annual Exhibition of the Borough Group*, Arcade Gallery, Bond Street, March 1949; Wyndham Lewis, 'Round the London Galleries', *The Listener*, vol. 41, no. 1050, 10 March 1949, p. 408.

34 Richard Cork, *David Bomberg*, New Haven and London: Yale University Press, 1987, p. 255.

35 Isabel Rawsthorne, letter to Giacometti, autumn 1950, in Wiesinger, *Correspondances*, p. 102. Wiesinger's provisional date of 1954 for this letter can now be revised to autumn 1950.

36 Cork, *David Bomberg*, p. 255.

37 Isabel Rawsthorne, letter to Rose Pulham, 14 June 1949, TGA 9612.1.3.26.

38 Frances Morris, Introduction, in *Paris Post War: Art and Existentialism 1945–55*, ed. Frances Morris, London: Tate Publishing, 1993, p. 22.

39 Genevieve Bonnefoi, *Les Années fertiles, 1940–1960*, Paris, 1988, p. 23, quoted in Sarah Wilson, 'Humanism and Terror', in *Paris Post War*, p. 30.

40 Michel Tapié, *Un art autre où il s'agit de nouveaux dévidages du réel*, Paris: Gabriel-Giraud et fils, 1952.

18 SCHOOL OF LONDON: 1948–1951

1 Lawrence Alloway, *Nine Abstract Artists: Their Work and Theory*, London: Tiranti, 1954, p. 2.

2 Martin Harrison, *Transition: The London Art Scene in the Fifties*, London: Merrell, 2002, pp. 13–14.

3 George Melly, *Don't Tell Sybil: An Intimate Memoir of ELT Mesens*, London: Henemann, 1997, p. 91.

4 Isabel Rawsthorne, letter to Rose Pulham, 15 November 1948, TGA 9612.1.3.10. Mesens purchased three gouaches for £60 in 1948 (Rawsthorne, letter to Rose Pulham, 1948, TGA 9612.1.3.12).

5 Isabel Rawsthorne, letters to Rose Pulham, 17 November 1948, TGA 9612.1.3.11, and late 1948, TGA 9612.1.3.12.

6 Isabel Rawsthorne, letter to Rose Pulham, 9612.2.4.32; Fini was 'emballée', carried away, with them (Rawsthorne, letter to Rose Pulham, 5 September 1950, TGA 9612.1.3.40).

7 Isabel Rawsthorne, letter to Rose Pulham, 24 February 1949, TGA 9612.1.3.19.

8 Isabel Rawsthorne, letters to Rose Pulham, TGA 9612.1.3.19, and 12 April 1950, TGA 9612.1.3.36.

9 Isabel Rawsthorne, letters to Rose Pulham, March/April 1949, TGA 9612.1.3.23.1v, 4 June 1949, TGA 9612.1.3.25, and 1 August 1949, TGA 9612.1.3.32; Michel Leiris, letter to Isabel, 1 April 1949, TGA 9612.1.1.3; Isabel also mentions packing pictures in September 1950 (letter to Rose Pulham, 5 September 1950, TGA 9612.1.3.40).

10 The Hanover Gallery at 32a St George Street was metres away from the Valenza Gallery.

11 Hanover Gallery Ledger, TGA 863.1.2, 22 February 1949.

12 Isabel Rawsthorne, 'Autobiographical Notes', Tate Gallery Archive, TGA 9612.2.4.32.

13 Isabel Rawsthorne, letter to Rose Pulham, February 1949, TGA 9612.1.3.20.

14 Richard Shead, *Constant Lambert*, 1973, London: Thames Publishing, pp. 155–6; a long account can be found in Isabel Rawsthorne, letter to Rose Pulham, March/April 1949, TGA 9612.3.3.23; Isabel asked Rose Pulham to pass the letter on to Michel Leiris.

15 Isabel Rawsthorne, letter to Rose Pulham, early 1949, TGA 9612.1.3.65.

16 'Hanover Gallery: Raoul Dufy's Paintings', *The Times*, 8 March 1949, p. 7. See, for another example of a typical review of women's art, 'Fame and Promise', *The Times*, 13 August 1940, p. 6: '*In the Greenhouse* is a good example of Miss Alison Debenham's tenuous and delicately luxurious handling', a review of *Artists of Fame and Promise*, Leicester Galleries.

17 Isabel Rawsthorne, letter to Rose Pulham, 2 March 1949, TGA 9612.1.3.56.

18 Antonin Artaud, 'Van Gogh: The Suicide Provoked by Society', trans. Peter Watson, *Horizon*, January 1948.

19 *Spectator*, 1949, vol. 182, p. 287.

20 Rawsthorne, 'Autobiographical Notes', TGA 9612.2.4.32.

21 James Hyman, *The Battle for Realism: Figurative Art in Britain during the Cold War, 1945–1960*, New Haven and London: Yale University Press, 2001, p. 21.

22 Wyndham Lewis, 'Round the London Galleries', *Listener*, vol. 41, no. 1050, 10 March 1949, p. 408.

23 David Sylvester, 'Curriculum Vitae', in *About Modern Art: Critical Essays 1948–2000*, London: Chatto and Windus, 1996, p. 15.

24 David Sylvester, oral testimony, 1988, cited in Laurence de Buzon-Vallet, *Alberto Giacometti: La Collection du Centre Georges Pompidou, Musée national d'art moderne: Saint-Étienne, Musée d'art moderne*, Paris: Centre Pompidou, 1999, p. 124.
25 David Sylvester, 'Paul Klee: La Période de Berne', *Les Temps modernes*, January 1951 (worked on 1949–50); reprinted in Sylvester, *About Modern Art*, pp. 38–47.
26 Hyman, *The Battle for Realism*, p. 2.
27 David Sylvester, '"Auguries of Experience". The Ides of Art: Six Opinions on What is Sublime in Art', *The Tiger's Eye: On Arts and Letters*, vol. 1, no. 6, 15 December 1948: pp. 50, 57; Sylvester, 'The Problems of Painting: Paris–London 1947', *L'Âge nouveau*, October 1948, pp. 107–10.
28 Michel Leiris, 'Thoughts around Alberto Giacometti', *Horizon*, vol. 19, no. 114 (1949), p. 416; for its influence see, for example, Eduardo Paolozzi, letter to Nigel Henderson, quoted in *Eduardo Paolozzi: Writings and Interviews*, ed. Robin Spencer, Oxford: Oxford University Press, 2000, p. 64.
29 See Martin Hammer, *Bacon and Sutherland*, New Haven and London: Yale Univeristy Press, 2005, p. 219: the three works purchased by the Tate Gallery from Giacometti were the sculpture *Man Pointing* (1947) and the paintings *Seated Man* (1949) and *Interior* (1949); *Oeuvres Choisis* was at the Hanover Gallery from 4 July to 11 August 1950.
30 Isabel Rawsthorne, letter to Giacometti, autumn 1950, in Véronique Wiesinger, *Alberto Giacometti, Isabel Nicholas: Correspondances*, Paris: Fage Éditions, 2006, p. 102.
31 '*Alberto Giacometti' in the 'Points of View'* series (starting January 1952), Institute of Contemporary Arts, 13 May 1952; Isabel Rawsthorne, letter to Giacometti, May 1952, *Correspondances*, p. 100; Herbert Read, Introduction, in *New Aspects of British Sculpture* (26 Biennale, Venice), London: British Council / Westminster Press, 1952.
32 *London-Paris: New Trends in Painting and Sculpture. An Exhibition of the Work of 16 Artists*, Institute of Contemporary Arts, New Burlington Galleries, 7 March–4 April 1950; Isabel Rawsthorne, letter to Giacometti, October 1947, in Wiesinger, *Correspondances*, p. 90.
33 Léon Degand and Benedict Read, forewords, in *London-Paris: New Trends in Painting and Sculpture.*
34 'Bad boys run wild', *Scotsman*, 9 March 1950, p. 8.
35 Isabel Rawsthorne, letter to Rose Pulham, [?spring 1952], TGA 9612.1.3.70.
36 *Eduardo Paolozzi: Drawings and Bas-Reliefs*, Mayor Gallery, 10–31 May 1949.
37 David Sylvester, 'Microcosmos of a Sculptor', in *Reg Butler Sculptures*, London: Hanover Gallery 1949, n.p.
38 *Recent Paintings and Drawings by John Craxton and Lucian Freud*, London Gallery, October–November 1947.
39 David Sylvester, 'Paolozzi and Turnbull's Sculptures', in *Kenneth King, Eduardo Paolozzi, William Turnbull*, London: Hanover Gallery, 21 February–18 March 1850, n.p.
40 Isabel Rawsthorne, letter to Rose Pulham, Christmas 1948, TGA 9612.1.3.16: 'Several evenings of drink and conversation with Bacon and Eduardo. I like his last things very much. Small bas reliefs with figures.'
41 Paul Valéry, *Collected Works of Paul Valéry*, ed. D. Paul, vol 12, p. 10.
42 Isabel Rawsthorne, letter to Rose Pulham, December 1948, TGA 9612.1.3.14½. A 'Lord A' was also there.
43 Isabel Rawsthorne, letter to Rose Pulham, early 1950, TGA 9612.1.3.63.
44 Isabel Rawsthorne, letters to Rose Pulham, 12 April [1950], TGA 9612.1.3.36, and 17 November 1948, TGA 9612.1.3.11.
45 Diane Kirkpatrick, *Eduardo Paolozzi*, London: Studio Vista, 1970, pp. 11–18.
46 Paolozzi described drawing in the Pitt Rivers Museum in Oxford, and his fellow students' lack of interest in doing this (interview with Frank Whitford, National Life Story Collection: Artists' Lives, British Library, C466/17, p. 39, also p. 42).
47 Anne Massey, *The Independent Group: Modernism and Mass Culture in Britain, 1949–59*, Manchester: Manchester University Press, 1995, p. 36.
48 D'Arcy Wentworth Thompson, *On Growth and Form*, facing title page; Turnbull's new theorisation of the independence of size and scale might also owe something to Thompson, p. 24.
49 Isabel Rawsthorne, letter to Rose Pulham, early 1949, TGA 9612.1.3.65.
50 Reproduced and discussed in Alex Kitnick, 'The Brutalism of Life and Art', *October*, no. 136, Spring 136, p. 64.
51 Isabel Rawsthorne, letter to Giacometti, October 1947, in Wiesinger, *Correspondances*, p. 90.
52 Harrison, *Transition*, p. 97.
53 *Growth and Form*, Institute of Contemporary Arts, London, 3 July–1 September 1951.
54 *40,000 Years of Modern Art: A Comparison of Primitive and Modern*, Institute of Contemporary Arts, London, 20 December 1948–29 January 1949, curated by Roland Penrose.
55 Carola Giedion-Welcker, *Modern Plastic Art*, p. 17.
56 Ibid., p. 11.
57 John-Paul Stonard, 'Used Future: The Early Sculptures of Eduardo Paolozzi', in *Eduardo Paolozzi: Archaeology of a Used Future. Sculpture 1946–1959*, ed. Peter Selz and John-Paul Stonard, London: Jonathan Clark Fine Art / The Paolozzi Foundation, 2011, p. 21; see also Harrison, *Transition*, pp. 104–5, for the influence of Jean Dubuffet; later written up in Siegfried Giedion, 'Space Conception in Prehistoric Art', in *Explorations in Communication*, ed. Edward Carpenter and Marshall McLuhan, Boston: Beacon Press, 1960, and Siegfried Giedion *The Eternal Present: The Beginnings of Art*, New York: Pantheon Books, 1962.
58 William Turnbull, interview with Martin Harrison, in Harrison, *Transition*, p. 112.
59 Edward Wachtel, 'The First Picture Show: Cinematic Aspects of Cave Art', *Leonardo*, vol. 26, no. 2, 1993, pp. 135–40.
60 William Turnbull, interview with Harrison, in Harrison, *Transition*, pp. 111–12.
61 David Sylvester, *About Modern Art: Critical Essays 1948–96*, London: Chatto and Windus, 1996, p. 13.
62 Anne Massey, *The Independent Group: Modernism and Mass Culture in Britain, 1949–59*, Manchester: Manchester University Press, 1995, pp. 44–5.

63 'Three Discussions on Contemporary Music', Institute of Contemporary Arts, May 1950: 'Music and Ballet', chair, Constant Lambert; 'Music and Opera', chair, the Earl of Harewood; 'Music and Film', chair, Alan Rawsthorne.
64 *Recent Trends in Realist Painting*, Institute of Contemporary Arts, 2 July–2 August 1952.
65 Bernard Buffet, *Squelette de poisson*, 1954, private collection, sold at Sotheby's 'Impressionist and Modern Art' sale, 20 October 2004, lot W04714; see also *Squelette d'oiseau*, 1964, engraving, private collection.
66 Isabel Rawsthorne, letter to Rose Pulham, 11 August 1952, TGA 9612.1.3.81.
67 Peter Rose Pulham, letter to Isabel, 26 [?18] August 1952, TGA 9612.1.1.20.
68 Eduardo Paolozzi, *Isabel Rawsthorne Painting the Ballet*, London: Michael Parkin Gallery, 1998.
69 Paolozzi, interview with Frank Whitford, p. 6.
70 David Sylvester, *Germaine Richier*, London: Hanover Gallery, 1955; see Sarah Wilson, 'Germaine Richier: Disquieting Matriarch', *Sculpture Journal*, December 2005, 14, pp. 51–70; Paolozzi, interview with Frank Whitford, p. 101.
71 Peter Rose Pulham, letter to Isabel, 26 [?18] August 1952, TGA 9612.1.1.20.
72 Paolozzi, interview with Frank Whitford, p. 61.
73 Rebecca Daniels, 'Francis Bacon and Walter Sickert: Images Which Unlock Other Images', in *Francis Bacon: New Studies. Centenary Essays*, ed. Martin Harrison, Göttingen: Stedl, 2010, pp. 71–4; see Michael Peppiatt, *Bacon: Anatomy of an Enigma* (1996), London: Constable, 2008, pp. 351–2; Daniel Farson, *The Gilded Gutter Life of Francis Bacon*, London: Century, 1993, pp. 34, 98–100.
74 See David Sylvester, *Interviews with Francis Bacon*, London: Thames and Hudson, 2008, p. 67.
75 Carol Jacobi, 'Cat's Cradle: Francis Bacon and the Art of "Isabel Rawsthorne"', *Visual Culture in Britain*, vol. 10, no. 3, 2009, p. 311.

19 TWO FIGURES: 1948–1950

1 Isabel Rawsthorne, letter to Giacometti, autumn 1950, in Véronique Wiesinger, *Alberto Giacometti, Isabel Nicholas: Correspondances*, Paris: Fage Éditions, 2007, p. 102.
2 Isabel Rawsthorne, 'Autobiographical Notes', Tate Gallery Archive, TGA 9612.2.4.30.
3 Francis Gruber, interview with Madeleine Riffaud, in 'Interviews et Opinions: Francis Gruber', *Arts de France*, 5 April 1945, p. 29.
4 Boris Taslitzky, 'Mon ami Francis Gruber', *L'Humanité*, 3 November 1949, p. 3.
5 Isabel Rawsthorne, letter to Rose Pulham, 4 June 1949, TGA 9612.1.3.25.
6 Isabel Rawsthorne, letter to Rose Pulham, 14 June 1949, TGA 9612.1.3.26.
7 Rose Pulham, letter to Isabel, 12 February 1956, TGA 9612.1.1.28.
8 Isabel Rawsthorne, letter to Rose Pulham, 19 November 1950, T GA 9612.1.3.41.
9 Isabel Rawsthorne, letter to Rose Pulham, 4 June 1949, 9612.1.3.25.
10 Isabel Rawsthorne, letter to Rose Pulham, 17 November 1848, TGA 9612.1.3.11.
11 Isabel Rawsthorne, letter to Rose Pulham, May 1949, TGA 9612.1.3.24.
12 *Balthus: Peintures de 1936 à 1946*, Galerie Beaux-Arts, 25 November–10 December 1946; *Exposition internationale d'arte moderne*, Musée national d'art moderne, 18 November–28 December 1946
13 Rawsthorne, 'Autobiographical Notes', TGA 9612.2.4.33.
14 Francis Bacon, letter to Graham Sutherland, 30 December 1946, quoted in Martin Hammer, *Bacon and Sutherland*, New Haven and London: Yale University Press, 2005, pp. 237–8.
15 Isabel Rawsthorne, letter to Rose Pulham, Christmas 1948, TGA 9612.1.3.15; see also TGA 9612.1.3.16.
16 Gerard Schurmann, 'Still Further Recollections', *The Sprat*, Newsletter of the Alan Rawsthorne Trust and The Friends of Alan Rawsthorne, no. 55, October 2008, p. 5.
17 For example, Isabel's letter to Rose Pulham, 31 December 1948, TGA 9612.1.3.17.
18 Isabel Rawsthorne, letters to Rose Pulham, 31 December 1948, TGA 9612.1.3.17, and 24 February 1949, TGA 9612.1.3.19.
19 Elisabeth Lutyens, *A Goldfish Bowl*, London: Cassell, 1972, p. 200.
20 Isabel Rawsthorne, letter to Rose Pulham, 31 December 1948, TGA 9612.1.3.17.
21 Isabel Rawsthorne, letter to Rose Pulham, 'Feb to March 2' 1949, TGA 9612.1.3.56.
22 Isabel Rawsthorne, letter to Rose Pulham, 21 March 1949, TGA, 9612.1.3.21. *Figure in a Landscape* (1945), did not enter the Tate Gallery until 1950, or it could have been a lost related image, perhaps a precursor of the *Figure in a Landscape* (1950), now in the Phillips Collection, Washington, DC
23 Isabel Rawsthorne, letter to Rose Pulham, spring 1949, TGA 9612.1.3.23.
24 Isabel Rawsthorne, letter to Rose Pulham, 30 December 1950, TGA 9612.1.3.43.
25 J.-B. Reboul, *La Cuisinière provençale* (1897), Marseille: P. Tacussel, date unknown, included in Bacon's Books Donation 1, Dublin City Gallery The Hugh Lane.
26 Isabel Rawsthorne, letter to Rose Pulham, 2 March 1949, TGA 9612.1.3.56; *Masterpieces from the Alte Pinakothek at Munich*, The National Gallery, London, 26 April–7 August 1949, (letter to Rose Pulham, [1949], TGA 9612.1.3.32); also *Landscape in French Art 1550–1900*, Royal Academy of Arts, 10 December 1949–5 March 1950 (letter to Rose Pulham, 2 January 1950, TGA 9612.1.3.64).
27 Isabel Rawsthorne, letter to Rose Pulham, late 1948, TGA 9612.1.3.13; continuation of same letter, 9612.1.3.14 2/2.
28 André Malraux, *Psychologie de l'art: Le Musée imaginaire*, Paris: Skira, 1947.
29 Martin Harrison, 'Bacon's Paintings', in *Francis Bacon*, ed. Matthew Gale and Chris Stephens, London: Tate Publishing, 2008, p. 54. An image of Jean Gabin in Marcel Carné's *Le Jour se lève* (1939), torn from Nicole Vedrès, *Images du cinéma français* (Paris: Éditions du Chêne, 1945), remained in Bacon's studio at his death (Martin Harrison and Rebecca Daniels, *Incunabula*, London: Thames and Hudson, 2008, fig. 103); Rebecca

Daniels, 'Francis Bacon and Walter Sickert: Images Which Unlock other Images', in *Francis Bacon: New Studies. Centenary Essays*, ed. Martin Harrison, Göttingen: Steidl, 2010, pp. 78–81.
30 Carola Giedion-Welcker *Modern Plastic Art*, p. 10. See also Giacomo Manzù's 'Cardinals' series begun in the late 1930s – for example *Cardinal* (1947–8), purchased by the Tate Gallery in 1948 and exhibited in *Modern Italian Art* at the gallery, June–July 1950.
31 *Life*, vol. 19, no. 18, 29 October 1945, pp. 37–8.
32 David Sylvester, *Interviews with Francis Bacon*, London: Thames and Hudson, 2008, p. 59; Isabel separates Rembrandt and Velàzquez again as exceptional (Isabel Rawsthorne, letter to Rose Pulham , 3 July 1949, TGA 9612.1.3.27).
33 See H. Ruhemann, *The Cleaning of Paintings: Problems and Potentialities* (1968), New York: Hacker, 1982, p. 79.
34 Alan Jenkins, *The Forties*, London: Heinemann, 1977, p. 170.
35 Isabel Rawsthorne, letter to Rose Pulham, 2 March 1948, TGA 9612.1.3.56.
36 See Martin Harrison, *Movement and Gravity: Bacon and Rodin in Dialogue*, London: Ordovas Gallery, 2013.
37 A copy of Monroe Wheeler's *Soutine* (1950; Museum of Modern Art, New York) was in Bacon's studio at his death and was included in Bacon's Books Donation 1, Dublin City Gallery The Hugh Lane; Francis Bacon interview with Hugh Davies, 'Interviewing Bacon, 1973', in *Francis Bacon: New Studies*, pp. 96, 100; Martin Harrison, *In Camera – Francis Bacon: Photography, Film and the Practice of Painting*, London: Thames and Hudson, 2006, p. 154. Harrison also notes Bacon's admiration of Daumier ('Bacon's Paintings', in *Francis Bacon*, ed. Gale and Stephens, p. 48); Bacon, c. 1960s, quoted, Sylvester, *Interviews with Francis Bacon*, pp. 63–4; a copy of *Bonnard*, a special issue of *Le Point: Revue artistique et littéraire*, Lanzac: Le Point, 1943, was included in Bacon's Books Donation 1, Dublin City Gallery The Hugh Lane; David Sylvester noted that Bonnard was pre-eminent for Bacon (*Francis Bacon: The Human Body*, London: Hayward Gallery, 1998, p. 22).
38 Jean-Paul Riopelle and his work were featured in the colour article 'Old Master's Modern Heirs: The Scorned Work of Monet's Later Years Inspires a Present Generation', *Life*, 2 December 1957, pp. 98–9; his work is juxtaposed with the 'summer blaze' of one of Monet's extraordinary late versions of the *Japanese Bridge* (c. 1920), for an example of Bacon's discussions of 'trapping appearance', 1966, quoted in Sylvester, *Interviews with Francis Bacon*, p. 50.
39 Isabel Rawsthorne, letter to Rose Pulham, 15 November 1948, TGA 9612.1.3.10.
40 John Gedhill, *Matthew Smith: Catalogue Raisonné of the Oil Paintings*, London: Lund Humphries, 2009, p. 229.
41 Isabel Rawsthorne, letters to Rose Pulham, Christmas 1948, TGA 9612.1.3.16, and early 1951, TGA, 9612.1.3.50.
42 Francis Bacon, 'Matthew Smith: A Painter's Tribute', in *Matthew Smith: Paintings from 1909 to 1952*, London: Tate Gallery, 1953, p. 12.
43 Ibid.
44 Isabel Rawsthorne, letter to Rose Pulham, 30 December [?1949], TGA, 9612.1.3.43. 'Austere' was a compliment paid to Isabel's own paintings at this time.
45 Isabel Rawsthorne, letter to Rose Pulham, probably 4 June 1949, TGA 9612.1.3.25.
46 Isabel Rawsthorne, letter to Rose Pulham, 25 November [1949], TGA, 9612.1.3.33.
47 Isabel Rawsthorne, letters to Rose Pulham, 25 November [1949], TGA, 9612.1.3.33, and again 30 December [?1949/50], TGA 9612.1.3.43.
48 Isabel Rawsthorne, letter to Rose Pulham, 1 August 1949, TGA 9612.1.3.32.
49 Percy Wyndham Lewis, 'Round the London Art Galleries', *Listener*, vol. 62, no. 1086, 17 November 1949, p. 860.
50 Wallis Neville, 'Nightmare', *Observer*, 20 November 1949, p. 6.
51 *Sculpture of Germaine Richier*, Anglo-French Art Centre, London, 8–30 September 1947; *Germaine Richier*, Galerie Maeght, 22 October–10 November 1948, catalogue texts by Francis Ponge, Georges Limbour. Giacometti's drawings of Rodin's sculpture *Homage to Balzac* (1946) was purchased by Robert and Lisa Sainsbury in 1952.
52 David Sylvester, 'The Paintings of Francis Bacon', *Listener*, 3 January 1952, pp. 23–4.
53 Paul Valéry, *Degas, Manet, Morisot*, trans. D. Paul, Princeton: Princeton University Press, 1960, pp. xxxiii, 25, 30; Hugh M. Davies, 'Interviewing Bacon, 1973', in *Francis Bacon: New Studies*, p. 108; Daniel Farson, *Soho in the Fifties*, London: Pimlico, 1987, p. 117.
54 Valéry, *Degas, Manet, Morisot*, pp. 50, 94.
55 Sylvester, *Interviews with Francis Bacon*, p. 176.
56 Isabel Rawsthorne, letter to Rose Pulham, 1 August 1949, TGA 9612.1.3.32.
57 Isabel Rawsthorne, letter to Rose Pulham, 15 April 1951, TGA 9612.1.3.51.
58 Isabel Rawsthorne, letter to Rose Pulham, 7 August 1948, TGA 9612.1.3.9.
59 Sylvester, *Interviews with Francis Bacon*, p. 18.
60 Isabel Rawsthorne, letter to Rose Pulham, summer 1948, TGA 9612.1.3.67; also Isabel Rawsthorne, letter to Giacometti, August 1948, in Wiesinger, *Correspondances*, p. 97.
61 Isabel Rawsthorne, letter to Rose Pulham, 14 December, TGA, 1948 9612.1.3.14½.
62 Bacon's and Rawsthorne's techniques have been the subject of research projects by Joanna Shepherd at Dublin City Gallery The Hugh Lane, by Joanna Russell and Elke Cwiertnia at Northumbria University, and by Rosie Gleave at the Courtauld Institute of Art, London.
63 Isabel Rawsthorne, letter to Rose Pulham, 1 August 1949, TGA 9612.1.3.32.
64 Isabel Rawsthorne, letter to Rose Pulham, August/September? 1949, TGA 9612.1.3.39. The letter includes a sketch of the picture.
65 Isabel Rawsthorne, letter to Rose Pulham, 21 September 1950, TGA 9612.1.3.68.
66 Isabel Rawsthorne, letter to Rose Pulham, 1 August 1949, TGA 9612.1.3.32.

67 Isabel Rawsthorne, letters to Rose Pulham, 7 January 1950, TGA 9612.1.3.44, and 2 January 1950, TGA 9612.1.3.64.
68 Isabel Rawsthorne, letter to Rose Pulham, 7 January 1950, TGA 9612.1.3.44.
69 Isabel Rawsthorne, letter to Rose Pulham, 2 May [1950], TGA 9612.1.3.37.
70 Isabel Rawsthorne, letter to Rose Pulham, 19 November 1950, TGA 9612.1.3.41.
71 Unknown photographer, Isabel Lambert, Albany Street, TGA 9612.4.1.4 H.
72 *Two Girls*, *Reclining Nude* and *Figure in a Room*, Hanover Gallery Ledger, TGA 863.1.2; *P. Rose Pulham / E.Q. Nicholson / Keith Vaughan*, Hanover Gallery, London, 21 March–15 April 1950; Rawsthorne, letter to Rose Pulham, 4 June 1949, TGA 9612.1.3.25.
73 Isabel Rawsthorne, letter to Rose Pulham, 3 March 1950, TGA 9612.1.3.34
74 Percy Wyndham Lewis, 'Round the London Galleries', *Listener*, vol. 43, no. 1104, 23 March 1950, p. 522.
75 'French and English Art: New Trends in Painting and Sculpture', *The Times*, 14 March 1950, p. 9.
76 Isabel Rawsthorne, letter to Rose Pulham, 14 June 1949, TGA 9612.1.3.26.
77 Isabel Rawsthorne, letter to Rose Pulham, 7 January 1950, TGA 9612.1.3.44, also 'Autobiographical Notes', TGA 9612.2.4.37–38; Patricia Lambert, 'What I remember about Isabel', notebook, February 1986, private collection, p. 7v.
78 Isabel Rawsthorne, letter to Rose Pulham, March [?] 1952, TGA 9612.1.3. 76.
79 Rawsthorne, 'Autobiographical Notes', TGA 9612.2.4.37.
80 Isabel Rawsthorne, letter to Giacometti, autumn 1950, in Wiesinger, *Correspondances*, p. 102.
81 Isabel Rawsthorne, letter to Rose Pulham, 29 August 1950, TGA 9612.1.3.28.
82 Isabel Rawsthorne, letter to Rose Pulham, 21 September 1950, TGA 9612.1.3.68.
83 Isabel Rawsthorne, letter to Rose Pulham, 30 December 1950, TGA 9612.1.3.43.

20 LA MAISON HARPIE: 1947–1951

1 Isabel Rawsthorne, letter to Peter and Mary Rose Pulham, spring 1947, TGA 9612.1.3.4.
2 Isabel Rawsthorne, letter to Peter and Mary Rose Pulham, autumn 1947, TGA 9612.1.3.4; Isabel Rawsthorne, letter to Giacometti, October 1947, in Véronique Wiesinger, *Alberto Giacometti, Isabel Nicholas: Correspondances*, Paris: Fage Éditions, 2006, p. 90; Isabel described their previous home, Constant Lambert's flat at Thurloe Square, as 'vampire towers' (letter to Peter and Mary Rose Pulham, 15 November 1939, TGA 9612.1.3.7).
3 A new passport was secured in Isabel's married name on 19 May 1948, and she and Constant Lambert travelled to France on 31 May, returning 14 June; they went again on 9 September, returning in October 1948 (Isabel Lambert, passport 905237, TGA 9612.2.13.6).
4 Patricia Lambert, 'What I remember about Isabel', notebook, February 1986, private collection, p. 3v.
5 Isabel Rawsthorne, 'Autobiographical Notes', Tate Gallery Archive, TGA 9612.2.4.38; Annette Arm married Alberto Giacometti on 19 July 1949.
6 Rawsthorne, 'Autobiographical Notes', TGA 9612.2.4.13; the *point d'ironie* or reverse question mark was promoted by Alcanter de Brahm (*L'Ostensoir des ironies: Essai de métacritique*, Paris: Bibliothèque d'art de 'la Critique', 1899).
7 Peter Rose Pulham, graphic letter to Isabel, 1947, TGA 9612.1.1.36.
8 Abbé Prévost, *Manon Lescaut: L'Histoire du chevalier des Grieux et de Manon Lescaut*, 1731.
9 Edith Piaf, 'La Vie en rose' (Life in Pink), 1946, tune by Louis Guglielmi.
10 Isabel Rawsthorne, letter to Rose Pulham, undated fragment [?1948], TGA, 9612.1.3.30.
11 Rawsthorne, 'Autobiographical Notes', TGA 9612.2.4.20.
12 Isabel Rawsthorne, letter to Rose Pulham, December 1948, TGA 9612.1.3.14½.
13 'F. D. R. at 13', *Life* 6 October 1947.
14 This can be seen in photographs of Isabel; Enid Evans, in conversation with the author in 2008, recalls Isabel standing out at Warwick's wedding in 1953 with her hair worn long and straight.
15 Isabel Rawsthorne, letter to Rose Pulham, early 1949, TGA 9612.1.3.65.
16 Isabel Rawsthorne, letter to Rose Pulham, 8 August 1948, TGA 9612.1.3.58.
17 Andrew Motion, *The Lamberts: Geroge, Constant and Kit*, London: Chatto and Windus, 1986, p. 240.
18 Rawsthorne, 'Autobiographical Notes', TGA 9612.2.4.7.
19 Motion, *The Lamberts*, pp. 240–42.
20 Rawsthorne, 'Autobiographical Notes', TGA 9612.2.4.26; she thought Vivien Leigh 'fragile in the role of Anna'.
21 Isabel Rawsthorne, letter to Rose Pulham, 10 January 1951, TGA 9612.1.3.49.
22 Isabel Rawsthorne, enclosure in letter to Rose Pulham, 21 May [?1950], TGA 9612.1.3.57; one of these menus is four sides long (enclosure in letter to Rose Pulham, n.d., TGA 9612.1.3.54).
23 Elizabeth David, quoted in David Kynaston, *Austerity Britain: 1945–1951*, London: Bloomsbury, 2008, p. 200.
24 See David Sylvester, *Interviews with Francis Bacon*, London: Thames and Hudson, 2008, p. 11.
25 Antonin Artaud, *Van Gogh: Le Suicidé de la société*, Paris: K éditeur, 1947, p. 35.
26 See, for example, Rawsthorne, 'Autobiographical Notes', TGA 9612.2.4.12; Isabel Rawsthorne, letters to Rose Pulham, autumn 1947, TGA 9612.1.3.611947; autumn 1947, TGA 9612.1.3.12, late 1948, TGA 9612.1.3.14 2/2, 26 August 1950, TGA 9612.1.3.40 and 15 April 1951, 9612.1.3.51.
27 Isabel frequently discussed the Assyrian reliefs in the British Museum and the Fitzwilliam Museum, Cambridge (Biddy Noakes, in conversation with the author, November 2008).
28 Isabel Rawsthorne, letter to Rose Pulham, 10 January 1951, TGA 9612.1.3.49.
29 Anthony Powell, *To Keep the Ball Rolling: The Memoirs of Anthony Powell*, vol. 3: *Faces in My Time*, London: Heinemann, 1980, p. 221; Richard Shead, *Constant Lambert*,

London: Simon, 1973, p. 151; Meredith Daneman, *Margot Fonteyn*, Harmondsworth: Penguin, 2005, p. 205.
30 See, for example, her letter to Rose Pulham, late 1948, TGA 9612.1.3.13: after binging with Constant Lambert and Alan Rawsthorne, she wrote, 'I have alcoholic depression.'
31 Rawsthorne, 'Autobiographical Notes', TGA 9612.2.4.8–9.
32 In July 1943, Constant Lambert had had to step in when Fonteyn's dancing partner, Robert Helpmann, had refused his zebra and insisted on giving his name to a llama (Gerald Iles, Superintendent, Belle Vue Zoological Gardens, Manchester 1954, quoted in Shead, *Constant Lambert*, p. 129).
33 Motion, *The Lamberts*, p. 188; Roland Petit, *J'ai Dance sur les flots*, Paris: Bernard Grasset, 1993, p. 298.
34 Motion, *The Lamberts*, p. 240.
35 1 Chester Gate was ten minutes' walk away (Powell, *To Keep the Ball Rolling*, p. 221).
36 Peter Rose Pulham, letter to Ruth Shedaski, 3 October 1948; my thanks to Philip Garner for kindly providing this reference.
37 Isabel Rawsthorne, letter to Rose Pulham, 30 December 1950, TGA 9612.1.3.42.
38 Rawsthorne, 'Autobiographical Notes', TGA 9612.2.4.11.
39 Ibid., TGA 9612.2.4.20.
40 Fonteyn fell ill on 27 February 1947 (Daneman, *Margot Fonteyn*, p. 207).
41 Ibid., p. 210.
42 Isabel Rawsthorne, letter to Rose Pulham, 21 March 1949, TGA, 9612.1.3.21.
43 Rawsthorne, 'Autobiographical Notes', TGA 9612.2.4.33.
44 Seán Hand, *Alter Ego: The Critical Writings of Michel Leiris*, Leeds: Legenda, 2004, pp. 60–62.
45 Motion, *The Lamberts*, p. 178; Isabel's letters suggest that Kit was at Albany Street on occasions.
46 See Motion, *The Lamberts*, p. 255.
47 Ibid., p. 241.
48 Sam Hunter, 'Francis Bacon: The Anatomy of Horror', *Magazine of Art*, January 1952, vol. 45, p. 12 (TGA, 9612.2.4.31). Martin Harrison has pointed out that, although Hunter's photographs are often thought of as early evidence of the famous chaos of Bacon's studio, this was not yet established; in his text, Hunter described it as like a laboratory.
49 Constant Lambert's financial advisor was Frank Otto. His financial incompetence came to light only when it was too late, in 1951 (Rawsthorne, 'Autobiographical Notes', TGA 9612.2.4.6).
50 For example, Dennis ApIvor, the dancer William Chappell and Frederick Ashton, quoted in Motion, *The Lamberts*, p. 241.
51 Isabel Rawsthorne, letter to Rose Pulham, 1948, TGA 9612.1.3.13.
52 Isabel Rawsthorne, letter to Rose Pulham, 12 April 1950, TGA 9612.1.3.36.
53 Isabel Rawsthorne, letter to Rose Pulham, early 1949, TGA 9612.1.3.66.
54 Rawsthorne, 'Autobiographical Notes', TGA 9612.2.4.20.
55 Isabel Rawsthorne, letter to Rose Pulham, 5 September 1950, TGA 9612.1.3.40; Isabel Rawsthorne, letter to Rose Pulham, 30 December 1950, TGA 9612.1.3.43.
56 Isabel Rawsthorne, letter to Rose Pulham, early 1951, TGA, 9612.1.3.50.
57 Isabel Rawsthorne, letter to Rose Pulham, early 1951, TGA, 9612.1.3.50.
58 Isabel Rawsthorne, letter to Rose Pulham, Christmas 1948, TGA 9612.1.3.16.
59 Isabel Rawsthorne, letter to Rose Pulham, Christmas 1950, TGA 9612.1.3.42.
60 Isabel Rawsthorne, letter to Rose Pulham, June (?)1949, TGA 9612.1.3.31.
61 See Mark Amory, *Lord Berners: The Last Eccentric*, London: Chatto and Windus, 1998.
62 Isabel's outfit was by Maggie Rouse for Anna Lovre ('Autobiographical Notes', TGA 9612.2.4.18).
63 Recalled by Humphrey Searle, 'Quadrille with a Raven: Memoirs by Humphrey Searle', 1985, unpublished, Music Web International, Chapter 11.
64 Shead, *Constant Lambert*, pp. 155–6; a full account can be found in Isabel's letter to Rose Pulham and Michel Leiris, March/April 1949, TGA 9612.3.3.23.
65 Isabel Rawsthorne, letter to Rose Pulham, 2 March 1949, TGA 9612.1.3.56.
66 *Trois pièces nègres, pour les touches blanches*, premiered by the BBC in 1949.
67 Isabel Rawsthorne, letter to Rose Pulham and Michel Leiris, March 1949, TGA 9612.1.3.23.

21 WHAT SONG THE SIRENS SANG: 1950–1951

1 William Butler Yeats, 'Leda and the Swan', *The Dial*, vol. 76, June 1924, p. 493.
2 Isabel Rawsthorne, letter to Rose Pulham, early 1949, TGA 9612.1.3.65.
3 Also Leonor Fini, *La Bergère des Sphinx* (1941; La Galerie Minsky) and *Sphinx Philagrial* (1945; La Galerie Minsky), which include skulls and a prostrate lizard; *Les Sirènes* was premiered on 12 November 1946 by Sadler's Wells Ballet, with music by Gerald Berners, choreography by Frederick Ashton and sets by Cecil Beaton.
4 Isabel Rawsthorne, postcard to Alberto Giacometti, 20 December 1947, in Véronique Wiesinger, *Alberto Giacometti, Isabel Nicholas: Correspondances*, Paris: Fage Éditions, 2007, p. 93.
5 Rawsthorne, Diary, 1947, TGA 9612.2.7, written on the pages for March.
6 William Stanford, *Aeschylus in his Style: A Study in Language and Personality*, Oxford: Blackwell, 1942, pp. 128–9, 63–6.
7 Thomas Browne, *Hydriotaphia, Urn Burial, or, a Discourse of the Sepulchral Urns lately found in Norfolk* (1658), London: The Chiswick Press, 1820, Chapter 5, p. 73.
8 Edgar Allen Poe, 'The Murders in the Rue Morgue', *Graham's Magazine*, April 1841; trans. Charles Baudelaire as 'Double assassinat dans la rue Morgue', *Le Pays*, 25 February–7 March 1855.
9 Isabel Rawsthorne, letter to Rose Pulham, 2 May [1950], TGA 9612.1.3.37.
10 Isabel Rawsthorne, letter to Rose Pulham, 4 June 1949, TGA 9612.1.3.25, see Alberto Giacometti, *Médaillon*

décoratif (c. 1936, FAAG); Isabel Rawsthorne, letter to Rose Pulham, 1 December 1949, TGA 9612.1.3.29.
11 Isabel Rawsthorne, letters to Rose Pulham, 7 January 1950, TGA 9612.1.3.44, and 2 January 1950, TGA 9612.1.3.64.
12 Isabel Rawsthorne, letter to Rose Pulham, 2 May 1950, TGA 9612.1.3.37.
13 Isabel Rawsthorne, letters to Rose Pulham, 7 January 1950, TGA 9612.1.3.44, and 2 January 1950, TGA 9612.1.3.64.
14 Isabel Rawsthorne, letter to Rose Pulham, 19 November 1950, TGA 9612.1.3.41.
15 Isabel Rawsthorne, letter to Rose Pulham, 7 January 1950, TGA 9612.1.3.44.
16 Isabel Rawsthorne, letter to Rose Pulham, late 1948, TGA 9612.1.3.13.
17 Rose Pulham, quoted in Theodora FitzGibbon, *With Love: An Autobiography, 1938–1946*, London: Century Publishing, 1982, pp. 18–19.
18 Sold 13 April 1950, Hanover Gallery Ledger, TGA 863.1.2; *P. Rose Pulham / E. Q. Nicholson / Keith Vaughan*, Hanover Gallery, 21 March–15 April 1950; Isabel Rawsthorne, letter to Rose Pulham, 4 June 1949, TGA 9612.1.3.25.
19 Isabel Rawsthorne, letter to Rose Pulham, 24 January 1950, TGA 9612.1.3.45.
20 Comment made in conversation with Michael Peppiatt, quoted in Peppiatt, *Francis Bacon: Anatomy of an Enigma* (1996), London: Constable, 2008, p. 270.
21 Isabel Rawsthorne, letter to Rose Pulham, early 1959, TGA 9612.1.3.63.
22 John Gledhill, *Matthew Smith: Catalogue Raisonné of the Oil Paintings*, London: Lund Humphries, 2009, pp. 99–100.
23 Dylan Thomas, 'Request to Leda – Homage to William Empson, a collaboration with Nigel Davenport', *Horizon Magazine*, vol. 6, , July 1942 p. 6; *Dylan Thomas Reads the Poetry of Yeats*, Caedmon Records, 1952.
24 Hugh Davies, *Francis Bacon: The Early and Middle Years, 1928–1958*, New York: Garland, 1978, pp. 51–3.
25 Bacon had abandoned the idea by January 1951, 'because producer is a silly amateur' (Isabel Rawsthorne, letter to Rose Pulham, 21 January 1951, TGA 9612.1.3.49); the production was never realised. Michael Peppiatt, in his biography of Bacon, called his chapter dealing with the early 1950s 'Hounded by Furies' (Peppiatt, *Francis Bacon: Anatomy of an Enigma*).
26 Amanda Harrison, 'Un coup soudain', *Francis Bacon: La France et Monaco*, Paris: Albin Michel, 2016, pp. 96–112.
27 Isabel Rawsthorne, letter to Rose Pulham, early 1950, TGA 9612.1.3.63.
28 Isabel Rawsthorne, letter to Rose Pulham, on big piece of sketchbook, 21 September 1950, TGA 9612.1.3.68.
29 Robert Melville called it a 'beginning of a Deposition' (Robert Melville, 'The Iconoclasm of Francis Bacon', *World Review*, January 1951, p. 64); Martin Harrison ('Francis Bacon: Extreme Points of Realism', in *Francis Bacon: The Violence of the Real*, ed. Armin Zweite, London: Thames and Hudson, 2006, pp. 45–6) also notes the allusion to Henri Michaux; Rembrandt's *Deposition* (1633) was also illustrated in black and white in *Masterpieces from the Alte Pinakothek at Munich: Illustrated Supplement to the Exhibition Catalogue*, London: Arts Council / The National Gallery, plate 40.
30 Francis Bacon, letter to Michel Leiris, n.d. [?1980–83], MS, La Bibliothèque littéraire Jacques Doucet, Paris, quoted in Harrison, 'Francis Bacon: Extreme Points of Realism', pp. 38–9.
31 David Boxer, 'The Early Work of Francis Bacon', PhD thesis, Johns Hopkins University, 1975, pp. 156–9.
32 Eric Hosking and Cyril Newberry, *Birds in Action*, London: Collins, 1949, plate 76; Boxer, 'The Early Work of Francis Bacon', pp. 156–9.
33 William Stanford discusses dog imagery extensively, especially the watch dog, and lists each incidence of the motif (*Aeschylus in His Style: A Study in Language and Personality*, Oxford: Blackwell, 1942, p. 124).
34 Francis Bacon, letter to Michel Leiris, n.d. [?1980–83], La bibliothèque littéraire Jacques Doucet, quoted in Harrison, 'Francis Bacon: Extreme Points of Realism', pp. 38–9.

22 TIRESIAS: 1950–1951

1 Isabel Rawsthorne, letter to Giacometti, autumn 1950, in Véronique Wiesinger, *Alberto Giacometti, Isabel Nicholas: Correspondances*, Paris: Fage Éditions, 2006, p. 102.
2 Isabel Rawsthorne, letter to Rose Pulham, 5 September 1950, TGA 9612.1.3.40; Peter Webb, *Sphinx: The Life and Art of Leonor Fini*, New York: Vendome Press, 2009, p. 147.
3 Isabel Rawsthorne, letter to Rose Pulham, 10 January 1951, TGA 9612.1.3.49.
4 Isabel Rawsthorne, letters to Rose Pulham, 30 December 1950, TGA 9612.1.3.43, 19 November 1950, TGA 9612.1.3.41 and 10 January 1951, TGA 9612.1.3.49.
5 See Andrew Motion, *The Lamberts: George, Constant and Kit*, London: Chatto and Windus, 1986, p. 251.
6 Mikhail Iamposlki, *The Memory of Tiresias: Intertextuality and Film*, Berkeley, Los Angeles, London: University of California Press, 1998, p. 3.
7 Poulenc's *Les Mamelles de Tirésias* premiered at the Opéra-Comique in Paris on 3 June 1947; Guillaume Apollinaire, *Les Mamelles de Tirésias*, 1917.
8 T. S. Eliot, 'The Wasteland', *Criterion*, October 1922; Cocteau's *La Machine infernale* premiered on 10 April 1934 at the Comédie des Champs-Élysées.
9 Constant Lambert, draft synopsis for Frederick Ashton, 195, Royal Opera House Archive.
10 Motion, *The Lamberts*, p. 252.
11 Isabel Rawsthorne, letter to Rose Pulham, 19 November 1950, TGA 9612.1.3.41; *Daphnis and Chloë*, music by Maurice Ravel, choreography by Frederick Ashton, sets by John Craxton, premiered on 5 April 1951 at Sadler's Wells.
12 Isabel Rawsthorne, letter to Rose Pulham, 30 December 1950, TGA 9612.1.3.43.
13 Isabel Rawsthorne, letter to Rose Pulham, 10 January 1951, TGA 9612.1.3.49.
14 Isabel Rawsthorne, letter to Rose Pulham, 1950, TGA 9612.1.3.48.
15 Isabel Rawsthorne, letter to Rose Pulham, [?autumn] 1950, TGA 9612.13.3.48.

16 Pauline Claydon, unpublished letter to Rebecca Winter, spring 2007, private collection.
17 Beth Williamson, 'Collaborations in Theory and Practice: The Early Work of Eduardo Paolozzi and Anton Ehrenzweig', paper delivered at the conference 'New Approaches to British Art, 1939–1969', Courtauld Institute of Art / University of York, 4–5 June 2009.
18 Isabel Rawsthorne, letter to Rose Pulham, [?autumn] 1950, TGA 9612.1.3.48.
19 Alioune Diop, ed., *Présence africaine*, first published in November 1947 was the leading journal in the Négritude movement, with some articles in English; see also Isabel's gouaches, for example *Fish, Bird and Figure* (1947; private collection).
20 Michel Leiris, 'Á propos du "Musée des Sorciers"', *Documents*, vol. 2, May 1929, pp. 109–16.
21 Jo Digger, Curator New Art Gallery, Walsall, in conversation with the author; the details of the sets were derived from Theodore Fyfe's water-colour 'Imaginary Restored Facade of the Central Tripartite Shrine' from the West Wing of the Central Court at Knossos (Ashmolean Museum. Oxford), reproduced in Arthur Evans, *The Palace of Minos*, London: Macmillan, 1921–36, vol. 2, fig. 527.
22 Isabel Rawsthorne, letter to Rose Pulham, 2 May 1950, TGA 9612.1.3.37.
23 Webb, *Sphynx*, pp. 139–40; Franz Marc, letter to Auguste Macke, 9 December 1910, in Franz Marc, *Briefe, Aufzeichnungen und Aphorismen*, Berlin: P. Cassirer, 1920. This collection of Marc's writings was read in Isabel's circle in the 1930s, in Derain's and Epstein's generation, and was read later for his proto-phenomenology (see, for example, Samuel Beckett's ruminations, diary, 19 November 1936 (Mark Nixon, *Samuel Beckett's German Diaries 1936–1937*, London: Continuum International Publishing Group, 2011, pp. 164–5)).
24 Isabel Rawsthorne, letter to Rose Pulham, [?autumn] 1950, TGA 9612.1.3.48.
25 Isabel Rawsthorne, letter to Rose Pulham, Sunday, 15 April [1951], TGA 9612.1.3.51.
26 Isabel Rawsthorne, letter to Rose Pulham, Sunday, 15 April [1951], TGA 9612.1.3.51.
27 Anne Massey, *The Independent Group: Modernism and Mass Culture in Britain, 1949–59*, Manchester: Manchester University Press, 1995, pp. 14–16.
28 Isabel Rawsthorne, letter to Rose Pulham, 10 January 1951, TGA 9612.1.3.49.
29 Mary Clark, *The Sadler's Wells Ballet: A History and an Appreciation*, London: A. & C. Black, 1955, p. 264.
30 Isabel Rawsthorne, 'Autobiographical Notes', Tate Gallery Archive, TGA 9612.2.4.45.
31 'Sadler's Wells Ballet Gala Performance', *The Times*, 10 July 1951, p. 6.
32 *Yorkshire Post and Leeds Intelligence*, 10 July 1951, p. 2.
33 Isabel Rawsthorne, letter to Rose Pulham, September 1951, TGA 9612.1.3.52
34 Peter Rose Pulham, letter to Isabel, 1952, TGA 9612.1.1.18.
35 *Tiresias*, Sadler's Wells Ballet, Opéra Garnier, 4 October 1954, discussed in Isabel's postcard to Alberto and Annette Giacometti, 30 September 1954, FAAG, in Wiesinger, *Correspondances*, p. 105; 'Tiresias' clipping from *Arts*, 1954, private collection.
36 Pablo Picasso, *Le Minotaure* (1928; Musée d'art moderne, Paris); Michel Leiris, postcard to Isabel, 23 October 1954, TGA 9612.1.1.4.
37 John Martin, 'Tiresias', *New York Times*, 25 September 1955.
38 Isabel Rawsthorne, letter to Rose Pulham, 12 April 1950, TGA 9612.1.3.36.
39 Appended to his crosswords for *Private Eye* during the 1960s, collected in *Private Eye Crosswords*, London: Hutchinson, 1983.
40 Constant Lambert, letter to Anthony Powell, 1 May 1930, quoted in Richard Shead, *Constant Lambert*, London: Simon, 1973, p. 79; Powell also recalled Constant Lambert's bisexual interests in pornography (*To Keep the Ball Rolling: The Memoirs of Anthony Powell*, vol. 2, London: Heinemann, 1980, pp. 172–3).
41 Motion, *The Lamberts*, p. 160; Shead, *Constant Lambert*, p. 163.
42 David Sylvester, *Francis Bacon: The Human Body*, Berkeley, Los Angeles and London: University of California Press, 1998, pp. 38–9.
43 Harrison, 'Francis Bacon: Extreme Points of Realism', p. 41; the ambiguity of the sponge/chignon held at the back of the head derives from Degas's *The Tub* (1886; Musée d'Orsay, Paris, then in the Louvre).
44 *Symbolic Realism in American Painting, 1940–1950*, Institute of Contemporary Arts, London, 18 July–18 August 1950.
45 Probably autumn 1950; Isabel Rawsthorne, letter to Rose Pulham, 19 November [1950], TGA 9612.1.3.41.
46 Elisabeth Lutyens, *A Goldfish Bowl*, London: Cassell, 1972, p. 200.
47 Isabel Rawsthorne, letter to Rose Pulham, 25 November [?1949], TGA 9612.1.3.33.
48 Isabel Rawsthorne, letter to Rose Pulham, 10 January 1951, TGA 9612.1.3.49.
49 Isabel Rawsthorne, letter to Rose Pulham, Sunday, 15 April [1951], TGA 9612.1.3.51.
50 Ian Board was the barman; quoted in Daniel Farson, *The Gilded Gutter Life of Bacon*, London: Century, 1994, p. 167.
51 Francis Bacon, interview with Frank Maubert, spring 1992, in 'Bacon L'Écorché solitaire', *Paris Match*, 14 May 1992, p. 93.
52 Roland Petit, *J'ai dansé sur les flots*, Paris: Bernard Grasset, 1993, p. 298.
53 Adela Quebec (Lord Berners), *The Girls of Radcliff Hall*, privately printed, 1932; Beverly Lyon Clark, *Regendering the School Story: Sassy Sissies and Tattling Tomboys*, London: Routledge, 1996, pp. 245–7.
54 Isabel Rawsthorne, letter to Rose Pulham, undated fragment [?1949], TGA 9612.1.3.30.
55 Gail Braybon, for example, puts both sides in *Evidence, History, and the Great War: Historians and the Impact of 1914–18*, New York: Berghahn Books, 2005, pp. 93–8.

23 UNQUIET GRAVE: 1951–1955

1 Quoted in the catalogue for *Isabel Lambert*, Hanover Gallery, London, 1949, n.p.
2 Isabel Rawsthorne, letter to Peter Rose Pulham, 30 December 1950, TGA 9612.1.3.43.
3 Prom 16, Wednesday, 15 August 1951, Royal Albert Hall: *Rio Grande* and Ravel's *La Valse*.
4 Isabel Rawsthorne, 'Autobiographical Notes', Tate Gallery Archive, TGA 9612.2.4.54.
5 See Andrew Motion, *The Lamberts: George, Constant and Kit*, London: Chatto and Windus, 1986, p. 257.
6 Isabel Lambert, passport 905237, TGA 9612.2.13.7–8: '25 Août 1951 entrée', '3 September 1951 sortie'. Isabel stayed at Valmondais with Peter and Mary Rose Pulham.
7 Isabel Rawsthorne, letter to Peter and Mary Rose Pulham, 7–8 September 1951, TGA 9612.1.3.52.
8 Rawsthorne, 'Autobiographical Notes', TGA 9612.2.4.56.
9 Isabel Rawsthorne, letter to Rose Pulham, 27 [March] 1952, TGA 9612.1.3.75; the garage was located at 56 Perham Road, London, W14.
10 Isabel Lambert, passport 905237, TGA 9612.2.13.9 and 30: 'polizia frontiera 25 Set 1951', 'entrata ott 1951 uscita', '17 Oct 1951 sortie'.
11 Rawsthorne, 'Autobiographical Notes', TGA 9612.2.4.56.
12 Rawsthorne, 'Autobiographical Notes', TGA 9612.2.4.56–60.
13 'The Unquiet Grave' was a traditional folksong, with associations with classical myth, such as that concerning Tiresias, but the idea was current in twentieth-century culture, for example, Cyril Connolly, *The Unquiet Grave*, London: Curwen, 1944.
14 Rawsthorne, 'Autobiographical Notes', TGA 9612.2.4.62 (1952).
15 *Designs for 'Tiresias' by Isabel Lambert*, Hanover Gallery, 6 November–8 December 1951 (Hanover Gallery Ledger, 7 November 1951, TGA 863.1.2). Edith Sitwell bought the gouache of the front drop.
16 Isabel Lambert, passport 905237, TGA 9612.2.13.8: '16 Jan 1952 sortie ' [2]5 Jan 1952 entre'.
17 Rawsthorne, 'Autobiographical Notes', TGA 9612.2.4.56.
18 John Deakin, *Isabel Lambert*, Rathbone Street Studios, 3 March 1952, published in 'People are talking about ...', *Vogue*, May 1953, p. 119.
19 See, for example, Peter Rose Pulham, *Photograph,* fashion study, c. 1933–6, Victoria and Albert Museum, London.
20 Deakin used the same costume and setting for a series of photographs of Elizabeth Smart.
21 Associated Press, 'Funeral of King George VI', 15 February 1952.
22 Isabel Lambert, passport 905237, TGA 9612.2.13.7: '5 March 1952 entrée'.
23 Isabel Rawsthorne, letter to Rose Pulham, [March 1952], TGA 9612.1.3.69.
24 Isabel Rawsthorne, letter to Rose Pulham, [1952], TGA 9612.1.3.70.
25 Isabel Rawsthorne, letter to Elisabeth Lutyens, 15 April 1952, Elisabeth Lutyens, Correspondence, British Library, Music MSS RBMRR: 64456; Isabel Rawsthorne, letter to Rose Pulham, [1952] TGA 9612.1.3.69.
26 Constant Lambert introduced Mary Rose Pulham to Lucian Freud at a dinner during a visit to London in August 1950 (Isabel Rawsthorne, letter to Rose Pulham, 29 August [1950], TGA 9612.1.3.28; Peter Rose Pulham, letter to Isabel, 1952, 9612.1.1.18. Mary had also been seeing Michael Middleton, the art critic of *The Spectator*.
27 Peter Rose Pulham, letter to Isabel, winter [1952], TGA 9612.1.1.18.
28 Isabel Rawsthorne, letter to Rose Pulham, [March 1952] TGA 9612.1.3.69.
29 Isabel Rawsthorne, letter to Rose Pulham, 3 July 1949, TGA 9612.1.3.27.
30 Isabel Rawsthorne, letter to Rose Pulham [March 1952], TGA 9612.1.3.76
31 Ibid.
32 Isabel Rawsthorne, letter to Rose Pulham [spring] 1952, TGA, 9612.1.3.80.
33 Peter Rose Pulham, letter to Isabel, 21 August 1955, TGA 9612.1.1.23).
34 Pablo Picasso, *Blue Roofs, Paris,* May–June 1901, accessioned to the Ashmolean Museum, 1939. The view looks out of his lodgings at 130, boulevard de Clichy.
35 Isabel Rawsthorne, letter to Rose Pulham, spring 1952, TGA 9612.1.3.70.
36 Isabel Rawsthorne, fragment of letter to Rose Pulham, [summer] 1952, TGA, enclosed with TGA 9612.1.3.77.
37 Isabel Rawsthorne, letter to Rose Pulham, spring 1952, TGA 9612.1.3.70.
38 Isabel Rawsthorne, letter to Lutyens, spring 1952, Lutyens, Correspondence, BL MSS RBMRR: 64455.
39 Isabel Rawsthorne, letter to Rose Pulham [spring] 1952, TGA, 9612.1.3.80.
40 Isabel Rawsthorne, letter to Rose Pulham, 11 p.m., [March] 1952, TGA 9612.1.3.76.
41 Isabel Rawsthorne, letter to Rose Pulham, spring 1952, TGA 9612.1.3.70.
42 Isabel Rawsthorne, letter to Rose Pulham, spring 1952, TGA 9612.1.3.78.
43 Peter Rose Pulham 'The Camera and the Artist', *The Listener*, 24 January 1952; also broadcast on the BBC Third Programme.
44 Isabel Rawsthorne, letter to Rose Pulham, [March] 1952, TGA 9612.1.3.76.
45 Isabel Rawsthorne, letter to Rose Pulham, spring 1952, TGA 9612.2.4.62.
46 Isabel Rawsthorne, letter to Rose Pulham, [March] 1952, TGA 9612.1.3.76.
47 Isabel Rawsthorne, letter to Elisabeth Lutyens, spring 1952, Lutyens, Correspondence, BL MSS RBMRR: 64457.
48 Isabel Rawsthorne, letter to Rose Pulham March 1952, TGA 9612.1.3.76.
49 Isabel Rawsthorne, fragment of letter to Rose Pulham [summer] 1952, TGA, enclosed with 9612.1.3.77.
50 John Deakin, *Isabel Lambert*, March 1952, inscribed on the back by the sitter, FAAG (Véronique Wiesinger, *Alberto Giacometti, Isabel Nicholas: Correspondances*, Paris: Fage Éditions, 2007, p. 102). In a letter to Rose Pulham, Isabel wrote, 'tell that tiresome Mr Deakin that he must send those photographs he took tell Muriel not to give him anymore drinks until he has. Love to FB' ([spring 1952], TGA 9612.1.3.69); she mentions their arrival shortly after ([spring] 1952, TGA, 9612.1.3.80).
51 Isabel Rawsthorne, letter to Rose Pulham, spring 1952, TGA 9612.1.3.69.
52 Isabel Rawsthorne, letter to Rose Pulham, spring 1952, TGA 9612.1.3.86.
53 'Cheerful apparition that he was ...

but don't think that would do' (Isabel Rawsthorne, letter to Rose Pulham spring 1952, TGA 9612.1.3.70).
54 Isabel Rawsthorne, letter to Rose Pulham, spring 1952, TGA 9612.1.3.86.
55 Alan Rawsthorne, letter to Isabel, 1952, MS Royal Northern College of Music Archive, GB 1179 AR.
56 Isabel Rawsthorne, letter to Rose Pulham, Au Relais Odéon, 9 p.m., March 1952, TGA 9612.1.3.76.
57 Isabel Rawsthorne, letters to Rose Pulham, spring 1952, TGA 9612.1.3.86, and March 1952, TGA 9612.1.3.75.
58 *Michael Ayrton Paintings and Drawings*, 20 May–6 June 1952, Galerie Galanis-Hentschel; Isabel Rawsthorne, letter to Rose Pulham, late May 1952, TGA 9612.1.3.77.
59 Ibid.
60 Isabel Rawsthorne, letter to Rose Pulham, 11 August 1952, TGA 9612.1.3.81.
61 Isabel Rawsthorne, letter to Rose Pulham, 7 August 1955, TGA 9612.1.3.93.
62 Edward and Judith Williams, in conversation with the author, May 2009.
63 Isabel Rawsthorne, letter to Rose Pulham, late 1952, TGA 9612.1.3.74.
64 Patricia Lambert, in conversation with the author, November 2008.
65 Clifford Frith, email correspondence with the author, 4 July 2010.
66 Edward Williams, 'Isabel Rawsthorne, 1912–1992', transcript of a tribute delivered at Thaxted church at the memorial service held in honour of Isabel on 27 February 1992 (private collection, n.p.).
67 Isabel Rawsthorne, letter to Rose Pulham, 30 November 1952, TGA 9612.1.3.73.
68 *Elektra* opened at the Royal Opera House, London, on 13 May 1953; *Blood Wedding* (music by Denis ApIvor and choreography by Alfred Rodrigues) opened at the Royal Opera House on 5 June 1953; *Coppélia* opened at the Royal Opera House on 2 March 1954; Isabel's designs for it (TGA 894.17.3.2.1–14) do not seem to have been used, and Osbert Lancaster is credited.
69 Isabel Rawsthorne, seventeen consume designs for *Life's a Dream*, Group Theatre, 1953–4, TGA 894.17.3.1–18.
70 'Music', *Spectator*, May 1953, vol. 190, p. 672; *New Statesman and Nation*, 1963, vol. 86, p. 661.
71 'A Fine Electra at Covent Garden', *The Times*, 18 November 1957, p. 3.
72 'Electra', *The Times*, 1 May 1954, p. 3; 'Electra', *The Times*, 14 May 1953, p. 2, quoted in Alan Jefferson, *The Operas of Richard Strauss in Britain, 1910–1963*, London: Society for Theatre Research / Putnam, 1963, p. 31. The production was successfully revived in May 1954, November 1957, June 1968 and October 1973.
73 Stanley Sadie, 'Electra', *The Times*, 29 October 1973, p. 12; William Mann, 'Elektra', *The Times*, 7 May 1977, p. 9.
74 'The Sadler's Wells Ballet, Blood Wedding', *The Times*, 6 June 1953, p. 8; Clive Barnes, 'Pretty Deaths', *Spectator*, 28 August 1953, vol. 203, p. 252; John Percival, 'Histrionic Revival', *The Times*, 10 May 1968, p. 9. The sets for *Blood Wedding* were equally praised: 'Music', *Spectator*, June 1953, vol. 203, p. 252; the backcloth was exhibited in *The Dancer in Literature and Photography*, Manchester Central Library August–September 1953, and mentioned in the review of the exhibtion, 'An Exhibition on Dancing', *Manchester Guardian*, 20 August 1953, p. 10.
75 'Madame Chrysanthème', *The Stage*, 7 April 1955, p. 18; *Sketch*, 20 April 1955, p. 29.
76 Isabel Rawsthorne, quoted in *Isabel Lambert: Recent Paintings*, n.p.
77 Isabel Rawsthorne, letter to Rose Pulham, 30 November 1952, TGA 9612.1.3.73; Rawsthorne, 'Autobiographical Notes', TGA 9612.2.4.38.
78 Isabel Rawsthorne, letter to Rose Pulham, undated fragment, TGA 9612.1.3.92.
79 Dylan Thomas, 'Poem on his Birthday', in *Collected Poems, 1934–1953*, London: J. M. Dent and Sons, 1953.
80 Dylan Thomas, summarising 'Poem for his Birthday' in a letter to Bill Read in July 1951, quoted in Paul Ferris, *Dylan Thomas: The Biography* (1989), London: Y Lolfa, 2006, p. 272. The poem's other focus, the wound, also chimes interestingly with Aeschylean concerns discussed in Chapter 21. The lines 'The rippled seals streak down / To kill and their own tide daubing blood / Slides good in the sleek mouth', concluding verse 3, echo Aeschylus's synaesthetic conceit, 'the reek of human blood smiles out at me' (*Eumenides*, 253, quoted in William Stanford, *Aeschylus in His Style: A Study in Language and Personality*, Oxford: Blackwell, 1942, p. 109), which was a talisman for Francis Bacon (see Dawn Ades, 'Web of Images', in *Francis Bacon*, London: Tate Gallery, London 1985, p. 19).
81 Rawsthorne, 'Autobiographical Notes', TGA 9612.2.4.66v.
82 *Portrait of Dylan Thomas* was never exhibited. The Canadian painter Gordon Stuart (b. 1924), made the last known painting of Dylan Thomas, painted over three afternoons in September 1953 in Thomas's writing shed in Laugharne in Wales, just before the poet's final departure for America, and left a description of the poet sitting. Gordon Stuart, interview with Margaret Keenan, BBC Wales, broadcast 16 June 2010.
83 Isabel Rawsthorne, letter to Rose Pulham 30 November 1952 TGA 9612.1.3.73.
84 Edward Williams, in conversation with the author, 18 May 2009.
85 Frith, email correspondence with the author, 4 July 2010; Isabel Rawsthorne to Rose Pulham, 1953, TGA 9612.1.3.92.
86 Rawsthorne, 'Autobiographical Notes', TGA 9612.2.4.7.
87 Maureen Ramsey, 'A Snapper up of Unconsidered Trifles', *The Sprat*, Newsletter of the Alan Rawsthorne Trust and the Friends of Alan Rawsthorne, no. 62, October 2008, p. 24.
88 Isabel Rawsthorne, letter to Rose Pulham, autumn 1954, TGA 9612.1.3.91.

24 ESCAPE TO REALITY: 1953–1959

1 Isabel Rawsthorne, 'Autobiographical Notes', Tate Gallery Archive, TGA 9612.2.4.3.
2 Rawsthorne, Sketchbook, Saturday, 3 October 1953, TGA 9612.2.2.32.
3 Rawsthorne, 'Autobiographical

Notes', TGA 9612.2.4.9.
4 Ibid., TGA 9612.2.4.7 and 67; David Blayney Brown, in conversation with the author, 12 September 2012.
5 John McCabe, *Alan Rawsthorne: Portrait of a Composer*, Oxford: Oxford University Press, 1999, p. 146.
6 Isabel Rawsthorne, letter to Annette Giacometti, 27 October 1954, in Véronique Wiesinger, *Alberto Giacometti, Isabel Nicholas: Correspondances*, Paris: Fage Éditions, 2006, p. 105.
7 Isabel Rawsthorne, letter to Rose Pulham, 9 December 1954, TGA 9612.1.3.99.
8 *Francis Bacon*, Durlacher Brothers, New York, 20 October–14 November 1953.
9 Peter Rose Pulham, letter to Isabel, 21 August 1955, TGA 9612.1.1.23; Isabel Rawsthorne, letter to Rose Pulham, 9 December 1954, 9612.1.3.99.
10 Isabel Rawsthorne, letter to Rose Pulham 21 October [1953], TGA 9612.1.3.97.
11 Rawsthorne, 'Autobiographical Notes', TGA 9612.2.4.14.
12 Ibid., TGA 9612.2.4.15–16.
13 Isabel Rawsthorne, letter to Rose Pulham, summer 1953, TGA 9612.1.3.95.
14 Obituary of Alan Rawsthorne, *Cambridge Evening News*, 28 July 1971, p. 3.
15 Isabel Rawsthorne, letter to Rose Pulham, autumn 1954, TGA 9612.1.3.91.
16 Rawsthorne, 'Autobiographical Notes', TGA 9612.2.4.18.
17 Edward Williams, 'Isabel Rawsthorne, 1912–1992', transcript of a tribute delivered at Thaxted church at the memorial service held in honour of Isabel on 27 February 1992 (private collection, n.p.).
18 Isabel Rawsthorne, letter to Rose Pulham, July 1955, TGA 9612.1.3.101.
19 Enid Evans, in conversation with the author, June 2009.
20 Isabel Rawsthorne, letter to Rose Pulham, 7 August 1955, TGA 9612.1.3.93.
21 Edward and Judith Williams, in conversation with the author, May 2009.
22 Biddy Noakes, in conversation with the author, January 2009.
23 Jeffrey Bernard, 'Isabel Rawsthorne', *Independent*, 4 February 1992.
24 Isabel Rawsthorne to Rose Pulham, (?)1954, TGA 9612.1.3.92; Isabel also suffered bronchitis during this period (Isabel Rawsthorne, letter to Rose Pulham, 7 August 1955, TGA 9612.1.3.93).
25 Rawsthorne, 'Autobiographical Notes', TGA 9612.2.4.2.
26 Biddy Noakes, in conversation with the author, November 2007.
27 Photographer unknown, 'Isabel at her Studio, Sudbury Cottage', c. 1954, private collection.
28 Isabel Rawsthorne, letter to Rose Pulham, 9 December 1954, TGA 9612.1.3.99; also Isabel Rawsthorne, letter to Annette Giacometti, 27 October 1954, in Wiesinger, *Correspondances*, p. 105.
29 Isabel Rawsthorne, letter to Rose Pulham, 17 November 1948, TGA 9612.1.3.11.
30 *Recent British Drawings*, an anthology curated by David Sylvester, Institute of Contemporary Arts, London, 10 February–27 March 1954; other exhibitors included Robert Adams, Kenneth Armitage, Elinor Bellingham-Smith, William Coldstream, Diana Cumming, Lucian Freud, Martin Froy, A. H. Gerrard, Peter Lanyon, Isabel McWhirter, Robert Medley, Henry Moore, Eduardo Paolozzi, Victor Pasmore, Matthew Smith, Graham Sutherland and Denis Wirth Miller.
31 Peter Rose Pulham, letter to Isabel, 21 August 1955, TGA 9612.1.1.23; Biddy Noakes, interview with Jo Digger, recorded New Art Gallery, Walsall, 14 June 2012.
32 This is according to Alan Rawsthorne, quoted in James Lord, 'Sudbury Cottage', in *A Gift for Admiration: Further Memoirs*, New York: Farrar, Straus and Giroux, 1998, pp. 51–2.
33 Isabel Rawsthorne, letter to Rose Pulham, 17 December 1955, TGA 9612.1.3.98.
34 Clifford Frith, email correspondence with the author, 4 July 2010.
35 Isabel, quoted in *Isabel Lambert: Recent Paintings*, Hanover Gallery, 1949, n.p.
36 Isabel Rawsthorne, letter to Rose Pulham, March 1956, TGA 9612.1.3.102.
37 *Cinquante tableaux importants d'André Derain*, Galerie Charpentier, June 1955.
38 Isabel Rawsthorne, letters to Rose Pulham, March 1952, TGA 9612.1.3.69, and July 1955, TGA 9612.1.3.101.
39 Isabel Rawsthorne, letter to Rose Pulham, March 1956, TGA 9612.1.3.102; also *2 Glasses and an Oyster*, 1946, untraced.
40 Giacometti in1964, quoted in David Sylvester, *Giacometti: Sculptures, Paintings Drawings, 1913–1965*, London: Tate Gallery, 1965, p. 8.
41 *The Turner Collection from Petworth House* was at the Tate Gallery from 17 May to 15 June 1951, but most pertinent was *J. M. W. Turner, R.A: 1775–1851: A Selection of Twenty-four Oil Paintings from the Tate Gallery*, Arts Council of Great Britain, May 1952–May 1953, complemented by *Le Paysage anglais de Gainsborough à Turner* at the Musée de l'Orangerie, Paris, February–April 1953; Sam Smiles provides a detailed analysis of these phases of discussion of Turner's late work in *J. M. W. Turner: The Making of a Modern Artist*, Manchester: Manchester University Press, 2007, p. 185.
42 Peter Rose Pulham, letter to Isabel, 12 February 1956, TGA 9612.1.1.28.
43 Patricia Lambert, in conversation with the author, November 2008.
44 Isabel Lambert, passport 430118, TGA 9612 .2.14.9: 21 June 1956.
45 Rawsthorne, 'Autobiographical Notes', TGA 9612.2.1.44.
46 Francis Bacon, conversation with Daniel Farson, recorded in Farson, *The Gilded Gutter Life of Francis Bacon*, London: Century, 1993, p. 10.
47 Isabel Rawsthorne, letter to Rose Pulham, 7 August 1955, TGA 9612.1.3.93.
48 Robert Graves, *The Greek Myths*, Harmondsworth, Penguin, 1955, vol. 1, chapter 85.
49 *Isabel Lambert: Recent Paintings*, Hanover Gallery, London, 17 February–13 March 1959.
50 Isabel Rawsthorne, letter to Rose Pulham, Sunday, 7 August [1955], TGA 9612.1.3.93.
51 Alan Rawsthorne, quoted by John McCabe from personal recollection, *Oxford Dictionary of National Biography*.
52 McCabe, *Alan Rawsthorne*, p. 202.

25 NATURAL SYNTHESIS: 1961

1 Veronica Leigh, diary, May 1958, quoted in John McCabe, *Alan Rawsthorne: Portrait of a Composer*, Oxford: Oxford University Press, 1999, p. 146.
2 Isabel Rawsthorne, 'Autobiographical Notes', Tate Gallery Archive, TGA 9612.2.4.12.
3 *The Guns of Navarone*, dir. John Lee Thompson, Columbia Pictures, 2 2 June 1961.
4 Isabel Rawsthorne, letter to Giacometti, August 1960, in Véronique Wiesinger, *Alberto Giacometti, Isabel Nicholas: Correspondances*, Paris: Fage Éditions, 2007, pp. 106–7.
5 McCabe *Alan Rawsthorne*, p. 202.
6 Edward and Judith Williams, in conversation with the author, May 2009.
7 Jean-Paul Sartre, 'Orphée noir', introduction *to Anthologie de la nouvelle poésie nègre et malgache*, ed. Léopold Senghor, Paris: Presses universitaires de France, 1948, p. xiv.
8 Basil Davidson, *The African Awakening*, London: Jonathan Cape, 1955.
9 *Black Orpheus*, ed. Ulli Beier and Janheinz Jahn, Lagos: Nigerian Ministry of Education, September 1957; the magazine ran until 1975. Chinua Achebe, *Things Fall Apart*, London: Heinemann, 1958.
10 Ulli Beier, *Art in Nigeria 1960*, Cambridge: Cambridge University Press, 1960, pp. 9–13, 23.
11 Ibid., p. 24.
12 Frith took over from Patrick George, who was a Slade fellow (Clifford Frith, email communication with the author, 4 April 2010).
13 I am grateful to Alan Leary for this background information (email correspondence with the author, 13 December 2011). He notes that the institutions were 'under the aegis of the Council for Overseas Colleges of Arts, Science and Technology, COCAST and in Nigeria there were three Colleges of AST in each of the regions of the Federation – Enugu in the Eastern Region, Ibadan in the Western Region and Zaria in the north, each headed by a vice-principal. They were intended to offer graduate-level qualifications but awarded diplomas rather than degrees ... Students were selected by interview on the basis of their interests and secondary school examination results.'
14 Isabel Rawsthorne, letter to Alan Rawsthorne, February 1961, Royal Northern College of Music Archives, GB 1179 AR.15.
16 Isabel Rawsthorne, letter to Rose Pulham, 26 September 1955, TGA 9612.1.3.96. Leiris's *Nuits sans nuit et quelques jours sans jour* (Paris: Gallimard) was published in 1961; other books published at this time were his *Race and Culture* (Paris: UNESCO, 1961), and *Vivantes cendres, innommées* (Paris: Gallimard, 1961), but they were not portable. Leiris sent Isabel his *Fourbis* (Paris: Gallimard, 1955) on its publication in September 1955.
17 Isabel Rawsthorne, passport, TGA 9612.2.14.8.
18 Isabel Rawsthorne, letter to Alan Rawsthorne, February 1961, Royal Northern College of Music Archives, GB 1179 AR.
19 Isabel Rawsthorne, letter to Alan Rawsthorne, 20 February 1961, Royal Northern College of Music Archives, GB 1179 AR.
20 Frith, email communication with the author, 4 April 2010; Isabel Rawsthorne, letter to Alan Rawsthorne, March 1961, Royal Northern College of Music Archives, GB 1179 AR.
21 Isabel Rawsthorne, letter to Alan Rawsthorne, March 1961, Royal Northern College of Music Archives, GB 1179 AR.
22 Isabel Rawsthorne, letter to Rose Pulham, 3 July 1949, TGA 9612.1.3.27.
23 Grillo's style was the most idealised of the group, a kind of Orphist treatment of statuesque figures, such as *Two Yoruba Women*, 1960, exhibited in *Contemporary Nigerian Art*, 1961.
24 Frith, email communication with the author, 4 April 2010.
25 Ben Enwonwu, 'Problems of the African Artist Today', *Présence africaine*, June–November 1956, pp. 8–10.
26 Chika Okeke-Agulu, email correspondence with the author, 4 April 2011. I am grateful to Professor Okeke-Agulu for the information about the college that follows; see: Chika Okeke-Agulu, *Postcolonial Modernisim, Art and Decolonisation in Twentieth-Century Nigeria,* Durham, NC: Duke University Press, 2015, p. 82.
27 Frith, email correspondence with the author, 4 April 2010; Beier, *Art in Nigeria, 1960*, p. 24.
28 Jos Museum, Jos, then the National Museum of Nigeria, with artefacts from 500 BCE onwards.
29 See Uche Okeke, diary, quoted in *The Arts Society: A New Consciousness*, ed. Chika Deke and Pat Oyelola, Lagos: National Gallery of Art, 1998, pp. 270–89; Uche Okeke, Demas Nwoko and Bruce Onobrakpeya first discussed the society on 6 October 1958.
30 Chika Okeke-Agulu, 'Nationalism and the Rhetoric of Modernism in Nigeria: The Art of Uche Okeke and Demas Nwoko, 1960–1968', *African Arts*, vol. 39, Spring 2006, pp. 27–37, 92–3.
31 Isabel Rawsthorne, letter to Alan Rawsthorne, February 1961, Royal Northern College of Music Archives, GB 1179 AR; see *Zaria Art School 1955–1990: Catalogue of an Exhibition by Students and Lecturers of the Department of Fine Art and Industrial Design, Ahmadu Bello University, Zaria*, National Commission for Museums and Monuments, Nigeria, 1990 (the exhibition ran from May to June 1990).
32 Ulli Beier, 'Contemporary Nigerian Art', *Nigeria Magazine*, vol. 68, March 1961, p. 31; also Ulli Beier, *Demas Nwoko, Uche Okeke Chika,* Legos, Mbari, 1961; Okeke-Agulu, email correspondence with the author, 4 April 2010.
33 Isabel Rawsthorne, letter to Alan Rawsthorne, 11 March 1961, Royal Northern College of Music Archives, GB 1179 AR.
34 Chika Okeke-Agulu, email correspondence with the author, 4 April 2011.
35 Later in 1961, the influential Mbari Artists and Writers Club was set up in Ibadan by the artists Demas Nwoko, Uche Okeke, Bruce Onobrakpeya and Ulli Beier, with the authors Wole Soyinka, John Pepper Clark, Ezekiel Mphahlele (a South African) and Cyprian Ekwensi, and the composer Akin Euba. They exhibited an international variety of modern art, including Malangatana Ngwenya (Mozambique), Ibrahim el-Salahi (Sudan), Vincent Kofi (Ghana), Skunder Boghossian (Ethiopia), Jacob Lawrence (USA) and Susanne Wenger (Austria).

36 Chika Okeke-Agulu, 'Nationalism and the Rhetoric of Modernism in Nigeria', p. 30.
37 Marshall Mount, *African Art: The Years since 1920*, Indiana: Indiana University Press: 1973, p. 133.
38 Okeke-Agulu, 'Nationalism and the Rhetoric of Modernism in Nigeria', p. 28.
39 Ulli Beier in conversation with Chika Okeke-Agulu in 2011, quoted in Chika Okeke-Agulu's email communication with the author, 4 April 2011.
40 An inspiration to both Isabel and Bacon's new painterliness during the late 1950s and early 1960s may have been Jean-Paul Riopelle's work as featured in the colour article on Monet, 'Old Master's Modern Heirs: The Scorned Work of Monet's Later Years Inspires a Present Generation', *Life*, 2 December 1957, pp. 98–9.
41 For example, Uche Okeke, *Ana Mmuo*, 1961, National Museum of African Art, Smithsonian Institution, Washington, DC
42 Jimoh Akolo, *Talking Drum*, 1960, Michael Crowder Collection; reproduced in Beier, 'Contemporary Nigerian Art'.
43 Demas Nwoko, *The Praise Singer*, 1961, sold, Modern and Contemporary Art Auction, Art House Contemporary Limited, Lagos, 8 May 2012.
44 Jimoh Akolo, *Four Female Figures*, 1961, private collection; sold Bonhams, New York, 10 March 2010, lot 27; Georges Rouault's *Three Judges* was acquired by the Tate Gallery in 1940 and exhibited in *Braque and Rouault*, Tate Gallery, April–May 1946, and *Rouault*, Tate Gallery, October–November 1966. Francis Bacon was preoccupied with the presentational Ecce Homo format; see Kent L. Brintnall, *Ecce Homo: The Male-Body-in-Pain as Redemptive Figure*, Chicago, University of Chicago Press, 2012.
45 Isabel Rawsthorne, letter to Alan Rawsthorne, March 1961, Royal Northern College of Music Archives, GB 1179 AR; Isabel Rawsthorne, passport, TGA 9612.2.14.8: departed Kanu, 31 March 1961.
46 Biddy Noakes, in conversation with the author, November 2007.
47 *Jimoh Akolo*, Commonwealth Institute Art Gallery, 1964; also *Yusuf Grillo, Jimo Akolo: Two Nigerian Artists*, Piccadilly Gallery, 1965.
48 *Contemporary Art from Africa*, Institute of Contemporary Arts, London, 17 March–15 April 1967, extended to 22 April 1967. Works currently in public collections in the UK are Uche Okeke, *Fantasy and Masks*, c .1960, University of Birmingham, and Jimo Akolo's *Hausa Drummer*, 1961, *Hausa Procession*, 1963, and *Northern Horseman*, 1963, at the University of Sussex.
49 Kenneth MacLeish, 'In Deepest Africa: A Startling Link to Man', *Life*, 24 November 1961, pp. 84–93.

26 LE VISAGE HUMAIN: 1953–1968

1 'Le Visage humain', in *Portraits et dessins par Antonin Artaud*, Paris: Galerie Pierre, n.p.
2 Isabel Rawsthorne, 'Autobiographical Notes', Tate Gallery Archive, TGA 9612.2.4.13.
3 Isabel Rawsthorne, letter to Peter Rose Pulham, summer 1953, TGA 9612.1.3.100.
4 Rawsthorne, 'Autobiographical Notes', TGA 9612.2.4.10.
5 Isabel Rawsthorne, letter to Peter Rose Pulham, March 1956, 9612.1.3.102.
6 Isabel Rawsthorne, letter to Peter Rose Pulham, summer 1953, TGA 9612.1.3.100.
7 Walter Friedlander's classic text, *David bis Delacroix* (Bielefeld: Velhagen and Klasing, 1932), appeared in English the same year (trans. as *David to Delacroix*, Cambridge, MA: Harvard University Press, 1952).
8 Eugène Delacroix, *Journal de Eugène Delacroix*, Paris: Plon, 1932, vol. 2, p. 41; Rawsthorne, Sketchbook, TGA 9612.3.3.30v.
9 Isabel perhaps flew to Rome and travelled overland, since she entered Rome on 3 April 1954 and Greece on 29 June 1954, leaving on 10 August (Isabel Lambert, passport 90523, TGA 9612.2.13). The sculpture was widely reproduced.
10 Rawsthorne, Sketchbook, TGA 9612.3.3.9v; Rawsthorne, 'Autobiographical Notes', TGA 9612.2.4.1.61v.
11 Frank Mort discusses Muriel Belcher's self-fashioning in *Cultures of Consumption: Masculinities and Social Space in Late Twentieth-Century Britain*, London: Routledge, 1996, p. 154.
12 Isabel Rawsthorne, Sketchbook, TGA 9612.31.
13 Martin Harrison, *In Camera – Francis Bacon: Photography, Film and the Practice of Painting*, London: Thames and Hudson, 2006, p. 160.
14 Jacob Epstein, *Epstein: An Autobiography*, London: Hulton Press, 1955, pp. 130, 188.
15 Francis Ponge, 'Réflexions sur les statuettes, figures et peintures d'Alberto Giacometti', *Cahiers d'art*, 1952, reprinted in Francis Ponge, *L'Atelier contemporain*, Paris: Gallimard, 1977, p. 160.
16 Isabel Rawsthorne, letter to Rose Pulham, 30 December 1949, TGA 9612.1.3.43.
17 Isabel Rawsthorne, letter to Rose Pulham, July 1955, TGA 9612.1.3.101.
18 Isabel Rawsthorne, letter to Rose Pulham, 1955/6, TGA, 9612.1.3.45.4, 5.
19 Isabel Rawsthorne, letter to Rose Pulham, March 1956, 9612.1.3.102.
20 See, for example, David Bomberg *Self-portrait*, 1937 Arts Council Collection.
21 Isabel Rawsthorne, letter to Rose Pulham, July 1955, TGA 9612.1.3.101.
22 Isabel may also have seen *Paintings, Etchings and Lithographs by Edvard Munch*, Tate Gallery, London, 31 October –1 December 1951.
23 Jean-Paul Sartre, 'L'Existentialisme est un humanisme', delivered at Club Maintenant, 29 October 1945, published as *L'Existentialisme est un humanisme*, Paris: Éditions Nagel, 1946, p. 57.
24 Rawsthorne, letter to Peter Rose Pulham, 1955, TGA 9612.1.3.101; Chika Okeke-Agulu, 'Nationalism and the Rhetoric of Modernism in Nigeria: The Art of Uche Okeke and Demas Nwoko, 1960–1968', *African Arts*, vol. 39, Spring 2006, p. 30.
25 Martin Harrison and Rebecca Daniels, *Francis Bacon: Catalogue Raisonné*, London: EFB Publishing, 2016 cat. no. 61-18D; two further portraits, cat. nos. 61-25 and 61-26, might also represent Isabel.
26 *Alberto Giacometti: Sculpture Paintings Drawings, 1913–65*, Tate Gallery, July–August 1965.

27 Isabel Rawsthorne, letter to Alberto and Annette Giacometti (although addressed within the letter to Annette), 3 September 1963, in Véronique Wiesinger, *Alberto Giacometti, Isabel Nicholas, Correspondances*, Paris: Fage Éditions, 2007, p. 108; Isabel Rawsthorne, letter to Lutyens, [early 1966], Elisabeth Lutyens, Correspondence, British Library, Music MSS RBMRR: 64460–60v.
28 Isabel Rawsthorne, letter to Alberto and Annette Giacometti, 3 September 1963, in Wiesinger, *Correspondances*, p. 108.
29 James Lord, 'Sudbury Cottage', in *A Gift for Admiration: Further Memoirs*, New York: Farrar, Straus and Giroux, 1998, p. 43; Isabel Rawsthorne, letter to Lutyens, [early 1966], Lutyens, Correspondence, BL MSS RBMRR: 64460–60v.
30 Isabel Rawsthorne, letter to Alberto and Annette Giacometti, 3 September 1963, in Wiesinger, *Correspondances*, p. 108; Lord, 'Sudbury Cottage', p. 56.
31 Lord, 'Sudbury Cottage', p. 73.
32 Bacon's meeting with Leiris is usually stated as having taken place in the mid-1960s. Bacon owned books by Leiris dated 1964 and after, including a new edition *of L'Âge de l'homme* (Paris: Gallimard, 1964), originally published in 1946.
33 Michael Peppiatt, *Bacon: Anatomy of an Enigma* (1996), London: Constable, 2008, p. 204.
34 Bacon had many books on Giacometti in his studio, the earliest being first editions of Jean Genet, 'L'Atelier d'Alberto Giacometti', in *Derrière le miroir*, no. 98, *Alberto Giacometti* (Paris: Maeght, June 1957), also Jacques Dupin, *Alberto Giacometti* (Paris: Maeght, 1962), and others, included in Bacon's Books Donations 1 and 2, Dublin City Gallery The Hugh Lane.
35 Peppiatt, *Bacon: Anatomy of an Enigma*, p. 251.
36 James Lord saw the paintings contained in a single gilded frame hanging in Sudbury Cottage on 12 March 1970 (Lord, 'Sudbury Cottage', p. 50).
37 Isabelle Monod-Fontaine, *Donation Louise et Michel Leiris: Collection Kahnweiler-Leiris*, Paris: Centre Georges Pompidou, 1984, p. 178.
38 *Francis Bacon: Recent Paintings*, Marlborough Fine Art, London, March–April 1967.
39 Henrietta Moraes, *Henrietta*, Harmondsworth: Penguin, 1995, p. 71.
40 The weather in the photographs suggests wintertime and *Camelot*, released on the Allegro label in 1964, can be seen in the window.
41 *Portraits et dessins par Antonin Artaud*, Galerie Pierre, Paris, 4–20 July 1947.
42 Artaud, 'Le Visage humain', n.p.
43 Isabel Rawsthorne, letter to Giacometti, December 1965, in Wiesinger, *Correspondances*, p. 111
44 This account may not be accurate as it was reported by Lord, 'Sudbury Cottage', p. 69.
45 Isabel Rawsthorne, letter to Lutyens, [early 1966], Lutyens Correspondence, BL MSS RBMRR: 64460–60v.
46 *Isabel Lambert*, 8 March–3 April 1968, Marlborough Gallery, London.
47 Maurice Merleau-Ponty, *L'Œil et l'esprit* (1961), trans. as 'The Eye and the Mind', by Carleton Dallery, in Maurice Merleau-Ponty, *The Primacy of Perception: And Other Essays ...*, ed. James M. Edie, Evanston: Northwestern University Press, 1964, p. 164.
48 David Thomson, *Roy Noakes Sculpture*, October Gallery, 1989, unpaginated.
49 Martin Harrison, 'Roy Noakes' (2003), in *Roy Noakes Sculpture and Paper Works*, London: Arts Council, 2009.
50 Jean-Paul Sartre, 'The Search for the Absolute', in *Alberto Giacometti: Exhibition of Sculptures, Paintings, and Drawings*, New York: Pierre Matisse Gallery, 1948, p. 4.
51 Alberto Giacometti, 'À propos de Jacques Callot', *Labyrinthe*, no. 7, 15 April 1945, p. 3.
52 David Sylvester, *Giacometti: Sculptures, Paintings, Drawings, 1913–1965*, London: Tate Gallery, pp. 5–6.
53 Joanna Shepard, 'A Game of Chance: The Media and Techniques of Francis Bacon', in *Francis Bacon: A Terrible Beauty*, p. 169.
54 John Russell, *Francis Bacon*, London: Thames and Hudson, 1993, p. 21.
55 Angel Gonzalez, *Alberto Giacometti: Works, Writings, Interviews*, Barcelona: Polygrapha, 2006, pp. 53–6.
56 Jaques Lacan, *Seminar XI, Le séminaire, Livre XI: Les Quatre Concepts fondamentaux de la psychanalyse* (1964), texte établi par Jacques-Alain Miller, in *Écrits*, Paris: Éditions du Seuil, 1966 (*The Four Fundamental Concepts of Psychoanalysis*, trans. Alan Sheridan, ed. Jacques-Alain Miller, London, Hogarth Press, 1977, pp. 86–9).
57 Paola Carola, *Monsieur Giacometti, je voudrais vous commander mon buste*, Éditions Léo Scheer, 2008.
58 Lacan's *Écrits* is visible on Bacon's bookshelf in photographs taken of his studio after his death and reconstructed at Dublin City Gallery The Hugh Lane.
59 Georges Bataille, *Theory of Religion* (1948), trans. Robert Hurley, New York: Zone Books, 1989, p. 40.

27 MOVING BODIES: 1952–1968

1 Paul Valéry 'Degas', in *Degas, Manet, Morisot*, trans. D. Paul, Princeton: Princeton University Press, 1960, p. 7.
2 Valéry, 'Asides', in *Degas, Manet, Morisot*, p. 33.
3 *Isabel Lambert*, Marlborough Gallery, London, 1968, n.p.
4 Iris Weaver, in conversation with the author, August 2008.
5 Isabel Rawsthorne, 'Autobiographical Notes', Tate Gallery Archive, TGA 9612.2.4.40, *Symphonic Variations* premiered April 1946.
6 Isabel Rawsthorne, letter to Rose Pulham, 11 August 1955, TGA 9612.1.3.88; Fonteyn first danced *Sleeping Beauty* with the Vic-Wells ballet company on 2 February 1939.
7 *Isabel Lambert: Recent Paintings*, n.p.
8 *Kingdom of the Shades* premiered with Fonteyn and Nureyev in the lead roles on 27 November 1963.
9 Isabel Rawsthorne, 'The World of Movement', in *Isabel Lambert: Dancers in Action. Drawings, Paintings, Stage Designs*, London: October Gallery, 1986, n.p.
10 Isabel Rawsthorne, letter to Rose Pulham, spring 1952, TGA 9612.1.3.86.
11 Rawsthorne, 'The World of Movement', n.p.
12 John Craxton quoted in Meredith Daneman, *Margot Fonteyn*, London: Viking, 2004, p. 271.

13 *Observer*, 22 February 1959, p. 18.
14 Isabel Rawsthorne, letter to Rose Pulham, 30 March 1956, TGA 9612.1.3.102.
15 Isabel Rawsthorne, letter to Rose Pulham, 3 July (?)1949, TGA 9612.1.3.27.
16 Isabel on Alan Rawsthorne's *Sonata for Violin and Piano dedicated to Szrgeti* ('Autobiographical Notes', TGA 9612.2.4.69v).
17 Alberto Giacometti, 'Letter to Pierre Matisse', 1947, published in English in *Alberto Giacometti*, New York: Pierre Matisse Gallery, 1948; this provides a technical perspective on Giles Deleuze's characterisations of Bacon's figures as 'like a trapeze apparatus upon which the flesh is the acrobat' (*Francis Bacon: The Logic of Sensation*, 1981, London: Continuum, 2008, p. 17).
18 Rawsthorne, 'The World of Movement', n.p.
19 Alberto Giacometti, notebook for 1946, quoted in Laurie Wilson, *Alberto Giacometti: Myth, Magic, and the Man*, London: Yale University Press, 2003, p. 242.
20 David Sylvester, *Giacometti: Sculptures, Paintings, Drawings, 1913–1965*, London: Tate Gallery , pp. 5–6.
21 Alberto Giacometti, notebook for 1947, in *Écrits*, Pris: Hermann/FAAG, 2007, p. 531; Rawsthorne, 'Autobiographical Notes', TGA 9612.2.4.1.
22 Auguste Rodin, *L'Art: Entretiens réunis par Paul Gsell*, Paris: Bernard Grasset, 1911, pp. 84–6.
23 Maurice Merleau-Ponty, *L'Œil et l'esprit*, Paris: Gallimard, 1961 ('The Eye and The Mind', trans. Carleton Dallery, in Maurice Merleau-Ponty, *The Primacy of Perception: and Other Essays ...* , ed. James M. Edie Evanston, Northwestern University Press, 1964, p. 183).
24 *Isabel Lambert*, Marlborough Gallery, London, 1968, n.p.
25 Valéry, 'Work and Beware', in *Degas, Manet, Morisot*, p. 38.
26 Rawsthorne, 'The World of Movement', n.p.
27 Sam Hunter, 'Francis Bacon: The Anatomy of Horror', *Magazine of Art*, January 1952, p. 13.
28 See Martin Harrison's discussion on the contemporary reworking of *Study from the Human Body, Man Turning on the Light* (ex-Royal College of Art collection), in the lot notes for the sale 'Post War and Contemporary Art', Christie's, 14 October 2007.
29 John Craxton quoted in Daneman, *Margot Fonteyn*, p. 271.
30 *Isabel Lambert: Dancers, Covent Garden 1960*, special issue of *Akte*, no. 6, December 1991.
31 Paul Valéry, 'Horse, Dancer, Photograph', in *Degas, Manet, Morisot*, pp. 40–41; 'Seeing and Copying', in ibid., p. 36.
32 Rawsthorne, 'The World of Movement', n.p.
33 Matthew Gale, *Francis Bacon: Working on Paper*, London: Tate Publishing, 1999; Martin Harrison, 'Francis Bacon: Extreme Points of Realism', in *The Violence of the Real*, ed. Armin Zweite, London: Thames and Hudson, 2006, p. 52. Bacon's quip about liking Giacometti's drawing, sometimes taken as a veiled belittlement of his modelling, or his sculpture in general, is a perfectly transparent compliment, reiterating Sylvester's appraisal of Giacometti's drawing as 'perhaps the most perfect aspect of his art'. It indicates precise understanding of Giacometti's graphic painting and sculpture (David Sylvester, 'Perpetuating the Transient', in *Giacometti,* London: Arts Council, 1955, as reproduced and revised in Sylvester, *About Modern Art: Critical Essays, 1948–2000*, London: Pimlico, 2000, p. 55; Francis Bacon et al., *Alberto Giacometti: Dessins*, Paris: Galerie Claude Bernard, 1975; Jacques Dupin, interview with Michael Peppiatt, quoted in Peppiatt, *Francis Bacon: Anatomy of an Enigma* (1996), London: Constable, 2008, p. 349; James Lord, *Giacometti: A Biography*, New York: Farrar, Straus and Giroux, 1985, p. 430.
34 Hugh Davies, 'Interviewing Bacon, 1973', in *Francis Bacon: New Studies. Centenary Essays*, ed. Martin Harrison, Göttingen: Steidl, 2010, p. 99.
35 Marked page (torn from L. Duissler, *Die Zeichnungen des Michelangelo*, Berlin: Gebr. Mann, 1959), Dublin City Gallery The Hugh Lane.
36 Davies, 'Interviewing Bacon, 1973', p. 96. According to Robert Medley, the purchase was made in the 'late 1950s' (transcript of an interview with Andrew Lambirth, 4 May 1994, in *Artists' Lives*, National Life Story Collection, British Library, transcript, p. 3). Sylvester is vague about dates – he reproduces a work of 1962 'formerly in the collection of Francis Bacon', but does not identify it; he dates the purchase and subsequent disposal of the picture to 'not long ago' in an interview conducted in 1966 (David Sylvester, *Interviews with Francis Bacon,* London: Thames and Hudson, 2008, p. 61).
37 Peppiatt, *Francis Bacon: Anatomy of an Enigma*, p. 278.
38 Sylvester, *Interviews with Francis Bacon*, pp. 46–7; Bacon included Degas's *After the Bath, Woman Drying Herself* (1890–5; The National Gallery, London) in *The Artist's Eye: Francis Bacon. An Exhibition of The National Gallery Paintings selected by the Artist*, National Gallery, London, 23 October–15 December 1985.
39 Rawsthorne, 'The World of Movement', n.p.
40 Sylvester, *Interviews with Francis Bacon*, pp. 46–7.
41 Amédée Ozenfant, *The Foundations of Modern Art*, trans. John Rodker (1928), New York: Brewer, Warren and Putnam, 1931, pp. 261–3; Sylvester, *Interviews with Francis Bacon*, p. 188.
42 Davies, 'Interviewing Bacon, 1973', p. 102.
43 Ozenfant, *Foundations of Modern Art*, p. 47.
44 Fernau Hall, 'Ballet', in *The Cambridge Guide to the Arts in Britain Since the Second World War*, ed. Boris Ford, vol. 9, Cambridge: Cambridge University Press, 1988, p. 89.
45 Rudolf and Joan Benesh, *An Introduction to Benesh Dance Notation*, foreword by Arnold Haskell, London: A. and C. Black, 1956, p. 102.
46 Rudolf Arnheim, 'Concerning Dance', *Dance Magazine*, 1946, reprinted in Arnhem, *Toward a Psychology of Art: Collected Essays*, Berkeley and Los Angeles: University of California Press, 1966, p. 262.
47 Rawsthorne, 'The World of Movement', n.p.
48 Michel Leiris, 'Thoughts around Alberto Giacometti', trans. Douglas Cooper, *Horizon*, no. 114, June 1949, facing p. 412; see also Christian

Zervos, 'Alberto Giacometti: Sculptures et dessins recents', *Cahiers d'art*, 1945–6, pp. 253–68, featuring a new sculpture of Isabel, p. 260.
49 Francis Bacon working document composed of John Deakin's *Three-quarter View of Isabel in Dean Street* (1965), Dublin City Gallery The Hugh Lane, RM98F11:2 1212.
50 *Isabel Lambert: Drawings*, Institute of Contemporary Arts, London, November 1965–January 1966, described by Isabel in a letter to Alberto Giacometti, December 1965, in Véronique Wiesinger, *Alberto Giacometti, Isabel Nicholas: Correspondances*, Paris: Fage Éditions, 2006, p. 111.
51 *Isabel Lambert*, 8 March–3 April 1968, Marlborough Gallery, London.
52 Valéry, 'Digression', in *Degas, Manet, Morisot*, p. 57.
53 Merleau-Ponty, *L'Œil et l'esprit*, p. 183.
54 Valéry, 'The Nude', in *Degas, Manet, Morisot*, p. 49.
55 Rawsthorne, 'The World of Movement', n.p.
56 Oswell Blakeston, 'Isabel Lambert – Craigie Aitcheson', *Arts Review*, 30 March 1968, p. 163.
57 Sylvester, *Giacometti: Sculptures, Paintings, Drawings*, p. 6.
58 Keith Roberts, 'Current and Forthcoming Exhibitions', *Burlington Magazine*, vol. 110, no. 781, April 1968, p. 231.
59 Sylvester, *Interviews with Francis Bacon*, pp. 63–4.
60 Valéry, 'Degas the Soneteer', in *Degas, Manet, Morisot*, p. 63.
61 Sylvester, *Interviews with Francis Bacon*, p. 175.
62 Liz Beatty, email communication with the author, 15 June 2010.
63 Medley, transcript of interview for *Artists' Lives*, p. 3. Bacon 'got tired of it in the end and sold it or gave it away' (Sylvester, *Interviews with Francis Bacon*, p. 61).
64 *La Bayadère* (The Temple Dancer), music by Ludwig Minkus, choreography by Marius Petipa, premiered by the Imperial Bolshoi Ballet in St. Petersburg in 1877; revived by the Kirov Ballet at the Palais Garnier on 19 May 1961.
65 'The Kingdom of the Shades' from *La Bayadère*, premiered by the Royal Ballet at Covent Garden on 27 November 1963. The Royal Ballet version featured only one of the seven sections of the original ballet.
66 Rawsthorne was presented as a Cassandra by herself and Giacometti (Carol Jacobi, 'Muse und Malerin: Isabel Lambert und Alberto Giacometti', in *Alberto Giacometti: "Die Frau auf dem Wagen". Triumph und Tod*, ed. G. Leinz, Duisberg: Wilhelm Lehmbruck Museum, p. 152), and, Michael Peppiatt suggests, by Bacon, too (Peppiatt, *Francis Bacon: Anatomy of an Enigma*, p. 262).
67 David Nixon, in conversation with Biddy Noakes, 18 September 2010.
68 Rawsthorne, Sketchbook 3, TGA 9162.3.3.
69 Kim Echlin, *Elizabeth Smart: A Fugue Essay on Women and Creativity*, Toronto: Women's Press, 2004, p. 220.
70 *Isabel Lambert: Dancers in Action. Drawings, Paintings, Stage Designs*, October Gallery, London, May–June 1986.

28 SILENT SPRING: 1955–1971

1 *The Foundations of Modern Art*, trans. John Rodker (1928), New York: Brewer, Warren and Putnam, 1931, p. vii.
2 Biddy Noakes, in conversation with the author, April 2010.
3 Biddy Noakes has noted Isabel's enthusiasm for Robert Yerkes and Konrad Lorenz, in conversation with the author, November 2007; Martin Harrison, 'Francis Bacon. Extreme Points of Realism', in *The Violence of the Real*, ed. Armin Zweite, Thames and Hudson 2006, p. 54, n. 27; a paint-splattered copy of Robert M. Yerkes and Ada W. Yerkes's *The Great Apes: A Study of Anthropoid Life* (1929) New Haven: Yale University Press, 1945) was in Bacon's studio at his death (Bacon's Books Donation 1, Dublin City Gallery The Hugh Lane). Bacon was later a fan of J. Z. Young's *Introduction to the Study of Man* (Oxford: Oxford University Press, 1971), which he showed to Hugh Davies (see Davies, 'Interviewing Bacon, 1973', in *Francis Bacon: New Studies. Centenary Essays*, ed. Martin Harrison, Göttingen: Steidl, 2010, p. 111.
4 Eric Hosking and Chris Newberry, *Birds of the Night, with a Chapter on the Eyes and Ears of Owls*, London: Collins, 1945, p. 71, pl. 48: 'Newly fledged long-eared owls'.
5 Matthew Gale, 'Points of Departure', in *Francis Bacon: Working on Paper*, London: Tate Publishing, 1999, p. 24; Christian Zervos, 'Alberto Giacometti: Sculptures et dessins récents', *Cahiers d'art*, 1946, vols 20–21, p. 260; Michel Leiris, 'Thoughts around Alberto Giacometti', trans. Douglas Cooper, *Horizon*, 114, June 1949, p. 412, facing.
6 Konrad Lorenz, *King Solomon's Ring*, trans. Mechthild Nawiasky, London: Crowell, 1952, pp. 185–6.
7 Rawsthorne, 'Sketches of monkey from Minoan fresco', Sketchbook, TGA 9612.3.2.40; see *Monkey and Papyrus, Monkey in Landscape, Palace of Knossos* (Minoan, fourteenth century BCE, Ashmolean Museum, Oxford); both Minoan pieces are reproduced in Arthur Evans, *The Palace of Minos*, London: Macmillan, 1921–36, vol. 2, fig. 264 and colour plate X.
8 *Baboon I* and *II*, c. 1962, oil on canvas, photograph, private collection; *Two Baboons I and II*, c. 1962, private collection, gouache on card; verso *Fonteyn and Nureyev* and *Fonteyn Stepping*, respectively.
9 *Baboon and Child* can be seen in John Blake's photographs of Isabel and Alan Rawsthorne in 1965 (private collection).
10 Judith Collins, 'Early Carvings', in Evelyn Silber and Terry F. Friedman, *Jacob Epstein: Sculpture and Drawings*, Henry Moore Sculpture Trust, 1987, p. 139.
11 Nwoko's *Mother and Child* is reproduced in Ulli Beier, *Contemporary African Art*, London: Pall Mall Press, 1968, p. 42.
12 Antonin Artaud, *84*, no. 8/9, 1948 p. 282.
13 Maurice Merleau-Ponty, *The Phenomenology of Perception*, trans. Colin Smith, London: Routledge, 2006, p. 256
14 Isabel Rawsthorne, letter to Annette Giacometti, 27 October 1961, in Véronique Wiesinger, *Alberto Giacometti, Isabel Nicholas: Correspondances*, Paris: Fage Éditions, 2006, p. 105.
15 September–October 1964; 3 August–3 September, 1965; 1–30

September 1966, Society of Wildlife Artists, Art Federation Galleries, 6 1/2 Suffolk Street, London, WC2 (my thanks to Joseph Leppard for supplying this information).
16 Leslie Brown, *The Mystery of the Flamingos*, London: Country Life, 1959.
17 Isabel Rawsthorne, letter to Annette Giacometti, 24 May 1969, in Wiesinger, *Correspondances*, p. 114.
18 G. Brett, 'Aitchison's New Paintings', *The Times*, 25 March 1968, p. 6; *Craigie Aitchison*, Marlborough Fine Art, 3 March–4 April 1968.
19 See, for example, the intermittent birds, rectangular shapes and colours of Craigie Aitchison's screenprint *Africa* (1969; Tate, London).
20 Biddy Noakes, in conversation with the author, November 2007. Copies of *Oryx* can be seen on the table in John Blake's photographs of Isabel and Alan taken in 1965.
21 Rachel Carson, 'Silent Spring', *New Yorker*, vol. t16, 23 and 30 June 1962; published as *Silent Spring*, New York: Houghton Mifflin, 1962.
22 Robert Graves, *The White Goddess: A Historical Grammar of Poetic Myth*, London: Faber and Faber, 1948. Isabel was also reading Walter Otto, *The Homeric Gods: The Spiritual Significance of Greek Religion,* London: Pantheon, 1954 (Isabel, letter to Rose Pulham, summer 1953, TGA 9612.1.3.95).
23 Robert Graves, *The Greek Myths*, Harmondsworth, Penguin, 1955, vol. 1, p. 82.
24 Isabel Rawsthorne, letter to Rose Pulham, 14 August 1955, TGA 9612.1.3.87.
25 These standard descriptions derive from Hesiod's *Theogony*, 185, and Aeschylus's *Eumenides*, 307; Isabel Rawsthorne, letter to Rose Pulham, 7 August 1955, TGA 9612.1.3.93.
26 Peter Rose Pulham, letter to Isabel, 11 August 1955, TGA 9612.1.1.22.
27 Ibid.
28 The book was not published, but the photographs were exhibited in *Artists in Camera*, Minories Gallery, Colchester, 1972.
29 Isabel Rawsthorne, letters to Annette Giacometti, 24 May 1969 and October 1969, in Wiesinger, *Correspondances*, pp. 114–15, 117.
30 *Alberto Giacometti,* Orangerie des Tuileries, Paris, 24 October 1969–12 January 1970; see James Lord, 'Sudbury Cottage', in *A Gift for Admiration: Further Memoirs*, New York: Farrar, Straus and Giroux, 1998, p. 57, and Patricia Lambert, 'What I remember about Isabel', notebook, February 1986, private collection, p. 4.
31 Lord, 'Sudbury Cottage', p. 69.
32 James Lord, *Giacometti: A Biography*, New York: Farrar, Straus and Giroux, 1986, p. 175; Lord, 'Sudbury Cottage', p. 47. Dates in Lord's text do not match with contemporary correspondence in Isabel's archive. For example, he provided the picturesque setting of Friday, 13 September 1970 for the handover of photocopies of seven of Giacometti's letters, whereas Isabel wrote to Annette Giacometti on 3 October saying she had given them to Giacometti two days before (Lord, 'Sudbury Cottage', p. 63; Isabel Rawsthorne, letter to Annette Giacometti, 3 October 1970, in Wiesinger, *Correspondances*, p. 119).
33 Lord, 'Sudbury Cottage', pp. 46, 48, 51, 61.
34 McCabe, *Alan Rawsthorne*, p. 285.

29 HEMLOCK: 1971–1992

1 *Francis Bacon*, Galeries nationales du Grand Palais, 26 October 1971–10 January 1972.
2 John Russell, *Francis Bacon*, London: Thames and Hudson, 1971. Isabel's inscribed copy is now in a private collection.
3 James Lord, 'Sudbury Cottage', in *A Gift for Admiration: Further Memoirs*, New York: Farrar, Straus and Giroux, 1998, pp. 70–71.
4 Rawsthorne, Diary, 19 July 1973, TGA 9612.2.8
5 *Pioneers of Modern Sculpture*, Hayward Gallery London 20 July–23 September 1973; 2 September 1973, TGA 9612.2.8
6 Lord provides the date of 7 June 1973, 'Sudbury Cottage', p. 73; Isabel's diary records Lord's visiting on 29 June 1973 (TGA 9612.2.8); Warwick arrived 2 May 1973 and left in October, Lambert 'What I remember about Isabel', p. 1.
7 Rawsthorne, Diary, 14–15 August 1973, TGA 9612.2.8.
8 Rawsthorne, Diary, 19 July 1973, TGA 9612.2.8
9 Rawsthorne, Diary, 14 August 1973, TGA 9612.2.8; in August, Rawsthorne took part in a sponsored walk of fourteen miles.
10 Warwick Nicholas, email communication with the author, 15 May 2009.
11 Julian Bream, letter to John McCabe, 4 October 1997, quoted in John McCabe, *Alan Rawsthorne: Portrait of a Composer*, Oxford: Oxford University Press, 1999, p. 281.
12 Gerard Schurmann, 'Still Further Recollections', *The Sprat*, Newsletter of the Alan Rawsthorne Trust and The Friends of Alan Rawsthorne, no. 55, October 2008, p. 5.
13 Biddy Noakes, in conversation with the author, September 2010; the house on Ferry Path in Cambridge was purchased for £8,500 in 1972/73; Rawsthorne, Diary, 28 June 1973, TGA 9612.2.8.
14 Jack Lindsay, *William Blake: Creative Will and the Poetic Image,* London: Fanfrolico Press, 1927; *J. M. W. Turner: His Life and Work. A Critical Biography*, London: Harper and Row, 1966; *Gustave Courbet: His Life and Art,* London: Harper and Row, 1973.
15 Jack Lindsay, *Roy Noakes*, The Archer Gallery, 1975.
16 Jack Lindsay, 'Turner's Life: A New Perspective', *Studio International*, May 1966, vol. 171, no. 878, p. 264.
17 Biddy Noakes, in conversation with the author, 8 March 2013.
18 *Isabel Lambert: Exhibition of Work*, Framlingham Art Gallery, Suffolk, 1974.
19 Isabel Rawsthorne, passport, 9612.2.15.8,9: 3 January–3 March 1977.
20 Warwick Nicholas, *The Biology of Free-living Nematodes*, Oxford: Clarendon Press, 1984.
21 Lindsay, *J. M. W. Turner*, p. 201.
22 For example, *The Roman Campagna with the River Tiber and Ponte Molle in the Distance* (1819; Tate, London), *The Moon behind Clouds: ?Study for 'Shields Lighthouse'* (1823–6; Tate, London).
23 Rawsthorne, Diary, 1977, TGA 9612.2.9.11–13, 18–20; see also Isabel Rawsthorne, postcard to Roy Noakes, 25 August 1977, private collection.

24 D'Arcy Wentworth Thompson, *On Growth and Form* (1917), revised edition (Cambridge: Cambridge University Press, 1942, p. 3.
25 Rawsthorne, Diary, 1977, TGA 9612.2.9.25, 32.
26 Ibid., TGA 9612.2.9.62, 56–7.
27 Ibid., TGA 9612.2.9.60.
28 Ibid., TGA 9612.2.9.21, 44.
29 Ibid., TGA 9612.2.9.68–71.
30 Ibid., TGA 9612.2.9.21, 44.
31 Ibid., TGA 9612.2.9.81–3.
32 Anna Phillips, letter to Isabel, 17 August 1988, TGA 9612.1.1.37.
33 Biddy Noakes, in conversation with the author, November 2007.
34 Isabel Rawsthorne, letter to Roy and Biddy Noakes, n.d., TGA 9612.1.3.1 8.
35 Biddy Noakes, in conversation with the author, March 2010; sold to Betty Stamper, on John Scott's death by Scott's widow.
36 Rachel Carson, *Silent Spring*, New York: Houghton Mifflin, 1962, p. 102.
37 See *Tate Gallery: Illustrated Catalogue of Acquisitions 1986–88*, London: Tate Publishing, 1996, p. 446; *Sir Cedric Morris: A Retrospective Exhibition,* Blond Fine Art, London, 9 April–9 May 1981.
38 Carson, *Silent Spring*, pp. 21–2.
39 Biddy Noakes, in conversation with the author, November 2007.
40 Martin Harrison, 'Francis Bacon: The Pulsations of a Person', in Valentina Castellani, Martin Harrison and Véronique Wiesinger, *Isabel and Other Intimate Strangers: Portraits by Alberto Giacometti and Francis Bacon*, New York: Gagosian Gallery, 2008, p. 211.
41 David Clark, *The Story of a Mental Hospital: Fulbourn 1858–1983*, London: Process Press, 1996, p. 193.
42 Linda Powell-Proctor, Nancy Chege and Brian Savage, 'Creating and Working with Small Groups in a Psychogeriatric Hospital', *Nursing Times*, 23 September 1981, pp. 1639–82.
43 Biddy Noakes, in conversation with the author, November 2007.
44 Biddy Noakes, in conversation with the author November 2007; J. Adams, 'Challenge and Change in a Cinderella Service: A History of Fulbourn Hospital, Cambridgeshire, 1953–1995', PhD thesis, The Open University, Faculty of Health and Social Care, 2009, p. 151.
45 Nicholas Shakespeare, 'Masterpiece or Travesty?', *The Times*, 28 June 1986, p. 10.
46 Ibid.
47 Veronica Sekules, in conversation with the author, May 2009.
48 Anna Phillips, letter to Isabel, 17 August 1988, TGA 9612.1.1.37.
49 Gerard Schurmann, 'Still Further Recollections', *The Sprat*, Newsletter of the Alan Rawsthorne Trust and The Friends of Alan Rawsthorne, no. 55, October 2008, p. 5.
50 Biddy Noakes, in conversation with the author, November 2007.
51 Corinna MacNeice, in conversation with the author, 10 April 2011.
52 Corinna MacNeice, email communication with the author, 15 April 2011, and in conversation with the author, 10 April 2011.
53 Kim Echlin, *Elizabeth Smart: A Fugue Essay on Women and Creativity*, Toronto: Woman's Press, 2004, p. 219.
54 Ibid.
55 Rawsthorne, insert in 'Autobiographical Notes', TGA 9612.2.2.1 4/9.
56 Ibid., TGA 9612.2.2.1 2/9.
57 Ibid., TGA 9612.2.2.1 3/9.
58 Ibid., TGA 9612.2.2.1 5/9.
59 Ibid., TGA 9612.2.2.1 6/9; there is an echo here of Aristotle's well-known axiom, the basis of science and natural philosophy: 'Natura non facit saltus' – nature does not leap.
60 Veronica Sekules, letter to Isabel, 8 January 1991, TGA 9612.1.1.43.
61 Edward Williams, 'Isabel Rawsthorne 1912–1992', transcript of a eulogy delivered at Thaxted church at the funeral of Isabel Rawsthorne, January 1992, private collection, n.p.
62 The Last Will and Testament of Isabel Agnes Rawsthorne, 6 December 1986, District Probate Registry, Winchester.
63 Control of Pesticides Regulations, introduced in 1986; Simon Wood, *Birds of Essex,* London: A. and C. Black, 2009, p. 199.
64 Jack Lindsay, *Turner: The Man and his Art*, London: Grafton, 1985, p. 154; also *J. M. W. Turner: His Life and Work*, p. 213.

AFTERWORD

1 'L'Existentialisme est un humanisme', delivered at Club Maintenant, 29 October 1945, published as *L'Existentialisme est un humanisme*, Paris: Editions Nagel, 1946, p. 57.
2 Email communication to the author, 15 April 2011.
3 James Lord, 'Sudbury Cottage', in *A Gift for Admiration: Further Memoirs*, New York: Farrar, Straus and Giroux, 1998, p. 47.
4 Peter Webb, *Sphinx: The Life and Art of Leonor Fini*, New York: Vendome Press, 2009, p. 69.
5 James Lord, 'Sudbury Cottage', p. 69
6 David Mellor, 'Framing Bacon: Reception and Representation from Little Magazine to TV Screen, 1945–1966', *Visual Culture in Britain*, vol. 10, no. 3, p. 233.
7 TGA, 9612.4.1.22H.
8 John Russell, *Francis Bacon*, London: Thames and Hudson, 1971, p. 168.
9 Francis Bacon et al., *Alberto Giacometti: dessins*, catalogue, Paris: Galerie Claude Bernard, 1975.
10 G. Brett, 'Aitchison's New Paintings', *The Times*, 25 March 1968; p. 6.
11 Keith Roberts, 'Current and Forthcoming Exhibitions', *Burlington Magazine*, April 1968, vol. 110, no. 781, p. 231.
12 Oswell Blakeston, 'Isabel Lambert – Craigie Aitchison, *Arts Review*, 30 March 1968, p. 163.
13 Harold Fischer, letter to Isabel, 17 April 1968, TGA 9612.1.1.40. Positive reviews of the exhibition included: 'Gallery Guide', *Observer*, 17 March 1968; Max Chapman, 'Around some of the new shows with Max Chapman', *What's On in London*, 22 March 1968; Oswell Blakeston, 'Isabel Lambert – Craigie Aitcheson, *Arts Review*, 30 March 1968, p. 163.
14 *The Times*, Monday, 4 March 1968, p. 13.
15 Martin Harrison, in conversation with the author, October 2009.
16 *Tate Gallery Report 1966–67*, London: HMSO, 1967, p. 18.
17 Jane Withers and Anthony Fawcett, 'Carcasses and Crucifixes', *The Times*, 20 May 1985, p. 10.
18 Francis Bacon, interview with Frank Maubert, spring 1992, in 'Bacon

L'Écorché solitaire', *Paris Match*, 14 May 1992, p. 93.

19 'Isabel Rawsthorne', *The Times*, 13 February 1992, p. 15; an exception was Martin Gayford, 'More than a Face to Remember', *Daily Telegraph*, 25 July 1998.

20 See *Daily Telegraph*, 29 January 1992, *Evening Standard*, 14 January 1998, *The Times*, 2 February 1998.

21 Eduardo Paolozzi, 'Introduction', in *Isabel Rawsthorne: Painting the Ballet*, London: Michael Parkin Gallery, 1998; *The Times*, 12 September 1998, p. 32.

22 'Exhibitions', *The Times*, 21 November 1998, p. 42.

23 Henrietta Moraes, 'The Curse of the Drinking Classes', *Independent*, 6 April 1996.

24 Farson, *The Gilded Gutter Life of Bacon*, p. 165, circulated in most accounts of her, for example, her obituary in the *Daily Telegraph*, 29 January 1992, and Nicholas Ahad, 'The Woman Who was a Walking Work of Art, Isabel Rawsthorne', *Yorkshire Post*, 15 August February 2008.

25 James Lord, *Giacometti: A Biography*, London: Faber and Faber, 1986. Lord's preface introduces himself as, first, a model and friend to Giacometti and, secondarily, his biographer. It is possible that his personal aspirations affected his view of longer-standing models and friends; both Isabel and Giacometti's wife, Annette, felt his published account was inaccurate (Biddy Noakes, in conversation with the author, November 2007).

26 Lord, 'Sudbury Cottage', pp. 57–69.

27 Akihiko Takeda's essay on a later friend and sitter of Giacometti, the academic Isaku Yanaihara, notes a reductive characterisation by Lord ('An Unknown Country: Isaku Yanaihara's Giacometti Diaries', in *Giacometti: Critical Essays*, ed. Peter Read and Julia Kelly, Farnham: Ashgate, 2009, p. 205, n. 12). Amina Peerbhoy (Epstein's 'Sunita') suffered similarly in biographies of Epstein: in the absence of research, it was assumed she was without education or culture, although Richard Buckle gives some account of her spirited career (Buckle, *Jacob Epstein: Sculptor*, London: Faber and Faber, 1963, p .146).

28 Lord, *Giacometti: A Biography*, p. 161; Michael Peppiatt described her as a 'force of nature' in *In Giacometti's Studio*, New Haven and London: Yale University Press, 2010, p. 31, and repeatedly as a 'man-eater' – for example, 'the man-eater who went on to gobble up a couple of mild-mannered if alcoholic English composers' (p. 111, also pp. 29, 107, 88); like Lord, Peppiatt implies an 'exotic' genealogy, suggesting that she was conceived on one of her father's voyages rather than with her mother (*In Giacometti's Studio*, p. 111); Isabel's genealogical record provides no evidence for this theory (my thanks to Martin Harrison for his definitive research on this matter).

206. John Blake: Isabel Rawsthorne, c. 1990

INDEX

Surnames in parentheses indicate other names under which the person has entries.

*Numbers in **bold** type relate to illustrations.*

PICTURE CREDITS

cover, 2. © John Everard Estate; Courtesy of Bruce Warwick
7. © Estate of Sir Jacob Epstein
8. © Estate of Sir Jacob Epstein
11. © Estate of Sir Jacob Epstein
12. © Estate of Sir Jacob Epstein
17. © Estate of Sir Jacob Epstein
19. © Ullsteinbild / TopFoto
22. © ADAGP, Paris and DACS, London 2020
23. © Estate of Béla Bernand; photo credit © TopFoto
24. © Dora Maar Estate/ ARS, © ADAGP/Fondation Giacometti
36. © Wellcome Collection
41. © Estate of Francis Gruber ADAGP, Paris
48. © Estate of Émile Savitry; Photo: Émile Savitry courtesy Sophie Malexis
50. Photo: 2020 Stiftung Ernst Scheidegger-Archiv, Zurich
51. © Succession Picasso / DACS, London 2017
55. © Victoria and Albert Museum, London: Given by Michael Sadleir
59. © Estate of Peter Rose Pulham
63. © TopFoto
72. © Tate
77. © Estate of Germaine Richier
80. © Man Ray 2015 Trust / DACS, London 2020
87. © Estate of David Bomberg
91. © The Paolozzi Foundation, Licensed by DACS 2020
92. © The Paolozzi Foundation, Licensed by DACS 2020
94. © Estate of William Turnbull. All rights reserved, DACS 2020
99. © The National Gallery, London
102. © TopFoto
105. © Estate of Joan Leigh Fermor
106. © Estate of Joan Leigh Fermor
109. © TopFoto
111. © Warwick Llewellyn Nicholas Estate. All rights reserved, DACS 2020
119. Photo (C) RMN-Grand Palais (musée du Louvre) / Michel Urtado
126. © Roger Wood/Royal Opera House/ArenaPAL
134. © John Deakin Archive
149. © Demas Nwoko
151. © Jimoh Akolo
154. © Estate of Roy Noakes, photo credit © John Blake
155. © Alamy Stock Photo / photo: Chris Hellier
156. © The National Gallery, London
185 © Carol Jacobi
186. © Edward Morgan
189. © André Morain
197. © Estate of Roy Noakes
200. © Tate, London
203. © Tate, London
204. © Tate, London
206. © John Blake

We gratefully acknowledge the support of the Fondation Giacometti, Paris, in the making of this book.

FONDATION-
GIACOMETTI

First published in the United Kingdom in 2021
by EFB Publishing and Thames & Hudson Ltd,
181A High Holborn, London WC1V 7QX

www.francis-bacon.com

www.thamesandhudson.com

British Library Cataloguing-in-Publication Data
A catalogue record for this book is available from the British Library

ISBN: 9780500971055

Printed by PUSH, London
Bound in Belgium by Brepols

Design and production: Brett Harrison
Editor: Gillian Malpass
Picture researcher: Francesca Pipe
Index: Jenny Knight – for First Edition Translations Ltd, Cambridge, UK.
Proofreading: Robert Tuesley Anderson – for First Edition Translations Ltd, Cambridge, UK.

As Series Editor of *Studies in Art*, I wish to join with Carol Jacobi in recognising the invaluable support of the Francis Bacon MB Art Foundation. My warm thanks are due to Biddy Noakes, for her unstinting, long-term efforts to facilitate the appreciation of Isabel Rawsthorne's work, and to Gillian Malpass for her sensitive treatment of a lengthy and complex project.

Martin Harrison